PRAISE FOR THE VAMPIRE ROMANCES OF
LINDA LAEL M

Time Withou

"Linda Lael Miller keeps getting better
to treasure, savor, and remember." —*Affaire de Coeur*

"Heart-wrenching scenes . . . engrossing historical characters and
period atmosphere." —*Publishers Weekly*

"Mesmerizing . . . Ms. Miller comes up trumps in this intricate tale
featuring the sexy, arrogant vampire destined to become an all-time
favorite with romance readers of every persuasion. Long live Valerian!"
—*Romantic Times*

"Ms. Miller takes us from past to present with ease, giving the reader a
look at how it all started and leaves us hoping for more . . . Valerian
and Daisy are powered with such intensity that the sparks between
them leap at the reader." —*Rendezvous*

Forever and the Night

"Bravo! What a tale. I was hooked from page one."
—Jill Marie Landis,
bestselling author of *After All* and *Until Tomorrow*

"Move over, Anne Rice! *New York Times* bestselling author Linda Lael
Miller has created a sensually luscious supernatural romance . . .
thrilling . . . chilling . . . This novel provides such a powerful emphatic
link between readers and the unforgettable characters that the audience will feel their joy, rage, fear, and hope . . . Ms. Miller's first supernatural romance is so good that readers will consider *Forever and the
Night* an immortal classic." —*Affaire de Coeur*

"Ms. Miller takes the reader into the world of the damned . . . dark
and mystical . . . hot and sensuous . . . a not-to-be-missed story!"
—*Heartland Critiques*

"Aidan and Neely are a very special pair. Readers will root for them
through every suspenseful twist and moving love scene right to the
bittersweet ending." —*Gothic Journal*

continued . . .

Into the Night

Linda Lael Miller

BERKLEY BOOKS, NEW YORK

A Berkley Book
Published by The Berkley Publishing Group
A division of Penguin Putnam Inc.
375 Hudson Street
New York, New York 10014

Copyright © 2002 by Linda Lael Miller.
Time Without End by Linda Lael Miller copyright © 1995 by Linda Lael Miller.
Tonight and Always by Linda Lael Miller copyright © 1996 by Linda Lael Miller.
Cover art by Franco Accornero.
Text design by Kristin del Rosario.

PRINTING HISTORY
Berkley trade paperback edition / October 2002

Visit our website at
www.penguinputnam.com

Library of Congress Cataloging-in-Publication Data

Miller, Linda Lael.
    [Time without end]
    Into the night / Linda Lael Miller.
        p.   cm.
    Contents: Time without end—Tonight and always.
    ISBN 0-425-18615-6
    1. Valerian (Fictitious character)—Fiction.   2. Occult fiction, American.   3. Love
stories, American.   4. Vampires—Fiction.   I. Miller, Linda Lael. Tonight and always.
II. Title: Tonight and always.   III. Title.

PS3563.I41373 T56 2002
813'.54—dc21

                                                                        2002074444

PRINTED IN THE UNITED STATES OF AMERICA

10   9   8   7   6   5   4   3   2   1

TIME WITHOUT END

For Doreen Drago,
Valerian's good friend and mine.
Heartfelt thanks from both of us.

TONIGHT AND ALWAYS

For Judith Stern Palais,
the consummate pro and a loyal friend,
with love, appreciation, and
great admiration.
Thank you.

Time Without End

Prologue

A hush fell over the audience as the full-sized glass coach rolled onto the stage, drawn by six perfect white horses with golden manes and tails. Dense fog tumbled and spun along the floor, rising slowly, encompassing the silent, gilded wheels of the carriage, swirling around the black iron pillars of the old-fashioned streetlamps lining the wings.

Daisy Chandler had been on a stakeout until half an hour before, and she'd arrived in the theater of the new Venetian Hotel just in time for the finale. Even though she'd lived in Las Vegas all her life, and knew more than a little about trickery and sham, she held her breath as the carriage door opened.

The magician stepped out of the coach onto the stage.

Tall and very broad in the shoulders, he stood just behind the fog-dimmed footlights, regarding the audience in imperious silence for a few moments, as though deciding whether or not these particular people were worthy of his presence, let alone his performance. He wore a plain tuxedo, exquisitely tailored, beneath a flowing black velvet cape embroidered with glimmering threads of every conceivable color, and his chestnut hair was thick, slightly too long over his collar, and faintly shaggy. His features were patrician, his complexion pale with a pearlescent glow to it.

Although Daisy could not see his eyes in the darkness, she would have sworn his gaze touched her, passed by, and then returned to cast some subtle spell.

Daisy felt an immediate wrench of sorrow and joy deep within herself, a recollection of great love and even greater tragedy. A fury of faded pastel images fluttered in her mind, like antique valentines . . .

Memories.

Daisy tried to shake off the fanciful impression. She was a cop, and an especially pragmatic one at that. She didn't believe in magic, or in memories of things that had never happened to her in the first place. She'd been having spooky dreams, on and off, ever since she was eight years old, but that fell into another category entirely.

She shifted in her seat, wondering why she'd come to see a magic show instead of going home to her apartment for a Lean Cuisine, a hot bath, and some badly needed sleep. Hell, she'd even laid out the seventy-five bucks for a ticket . . .

Daisy bit her lower lip. She'd heard about the magician, who billed himself simply as Valerian—with no Greats or Magnificents or Incomparables tacked on for purposes of pizzazz—from her friends. They said his tricks were impossible, that other sleight-of-hand specialists were flying in from the world over, hoping to figure out how he did it all, and Daisy had wanted to see the act for herself.

It was as simple as that. Wasn't it?

She realized she was holding her breath, and ordered herself to take in air, but her hand trembled as she reached for her glass of diet cola. Her gaze never left the commanding figure dominating center stage.

Daisy was enthralled, like all the other spectators, as Valerian raised his arms high in the air, turned his back to the audience, and faced the team and carriage. The metallic threads in his cape seemed to ripple and undulate under the stage lights, and Daisy shook her head, overwhelmed by another flood of footloose, whimsical remembrance.

The magician lifted his hands slowly, gracefully, from his sides, palms up, and as he did so, the fairy-tale coach and all the horses rose a few inches off the floor, then a foot, then several feet.

The silence in the room was explosive, absolute. No one spoke, or coughed, or cleared a throat. The horses seemed unconcerned with the fact that their hooves weren't touching the floor; they moved in place, as though they were trotting on top of a cloud, and the carriage wheels spun accordingly.

Valerian turned, in a swirl of shimmering color, and glared fiercely at the audience, seeming to challenge them to question the trick. Then the fog dissipated, and Cinderella's coach-and-six were still jostling along in mid-air, supported by nothing at all.

Daisy scooted to the edge of her chair, frowning, her practical cop's mind racing even as her emotions wrestled with the lingering sense of poignant recognition. She knew razzle-dazzle when she saw it. No matter how polished the magician, no matter how sophisticated the trick, illusions were illusions. There could be no question that her eyes were fooling her, but she was more than mystified by what she was witnessing—she was unnerved.

The wizard gestured, and a half dozen of the requisite dancing girls pranced onto the stage, three on one side, three on the other. At another silent command from Valerian, a trio of the skimpily clad women moved to sit cross-legged under the suspended coach. One of the three seated beneath the horses glanced upward with a thoughtful expression, then produced an umbrella.

A twitter of nervous laughter rose from the crowd, but that feeling of collective breath-holding remained.

Having proven, ostensibly, that there were no wires supporting the coach-and-six—an idea Daisy had already dismissed as preposterous anyway—the dancing girls scrambled out from under it.

Valerian raised an arm, and the coach door opened again. A glittering gold ladder stretched with soundless grace to the stage floor, and the girls ascended, one by one, into the carriage. The door closed behind them.

There was a sort of psychic drumroll, something felt rather than heard. Then the great deceiver raised his arms again, and the onlookers cried out in wonder, Daisy included, when the team began to move, still suspended, pulling the coach out over all their heads, making a grand and glorious sweep before returning to the stage.

Daisy's mouth dropped open. She closed her eyes, then opened them again.

The coach-and-six settled gracefully back to the floor of the stage, then rolled out of sight.

The audience soared to its feet, clapping and cheering wildly. The magician bowed deeply, a small, ironic smile lifting just a corner of his mouth, then vanished in the proverbial cloud of smoke.

Daisy sank back into her chair, still in shock. The horde of tourists straggled out, murmuring among themselves, speculating. Soon, the theater was empty, except for a few waiters, and the stage, with its tiered curtain of ivory silk, was dark.

Daisy remained, her heart in her throat, inexplicable tears burning in her eyes, obeying some unspoken command because she could not find the strength to defy it. Waiting.

For Daisy, the show was far from over.

1

Dunnett's Head, Cornwall
September 1348

"YOU'VE ruined both of those lads," Noah Lazarus groused from his position next to the table, mallet in hand. His wife, Seraphina, stood gazing out of the shop window, looking for those scoundrel sons of hers. He spat in an effort to gain her notice, knowing beforehand that he would fail. "The names you gave them, Sera—Krispin, Valerian—names fit for the sons of princes and kings. And me naught but a bootmaker!"

Seraphina turned those extraordinary violet eyes on him at last, and even though they flashed with contempt, Noah was glad of her notice. He knew he was pathetic, but in such moments he couldn't make himself care.

"They are fine lads," she said acidly. The late afternoon sun came through the thick, bubbled glass of the window, playing in her rich chestnut hair. Noah marveled that such a creature had bound herself to the likes of him, under the laws of God and man, that she'd lain with him, borne the children he sired.

Just then, Noah caught a glimpse of the boys, returning from the keep overlooking the small seaside village and the wild Irish Sea. Valerian, the elder, was seventeen, tall and straight as a ship's mast, with powerful shoulders and his mother's dramatic coloring. He had strong bones, unblemished skin, and straight white teeth, Valerian did, and he was so physically perfect that Noah could hardly believe he was the get of his own loins. It was as though the boy had willfully taken all the best of his parents for himself, leaving little or none for the children who followed.

Krispin, smaller than his brother, fair-haired and as delicate as a girl, came next. He'd managed to survive, at least—that was more than could be said for the others.

Poor little Royal had been born three years after Krispin, only to have his mother confer that embarrassment of a name upon him. He'd been a blue and spindly twig of an infant; hadn't even survived a fortnight. As for the two girls, well, *those* wretched creatures, twins they'd been, had both given up the ghost before they could be christened.

The door of the shop swept open, and Valerian strode in. He wore the plain garb of a tradesman's son, leggings and a tunic of the cheapest wool, and yet he looked out of place, as he always did. More like a dandy down from London Town than the pauper he was. He kissed his besotted mother on the forehead, and she glowed as if she'd just been blessed by John the Baptist, or one of the lesser saints.

Valerian's eyes met Noah's, and the old knowledge passed between them; they had always despised each other. That day the whelp carried an unbelievably rare and precious item—carelessly, of course—in the curve of one arm. It was a book, bound in leather, and Noah knew without looking that its parchment pages would have been painstakingly inscribed by one monk or a succession of them, and exquisitely illustrated with vivid colors and fragile brush strokes.

Noah's heart clenched, and he felt a thin sheen of perspiration dampen his forehead and upper lip. "Where did you get that?" he demanded in a hoarse whisper. Jesus, Joseph, and Mary, the manuscript was worth more than the shop and all its contents—more, probably, than the whole village of Dunnett's Head. If such a treasure were to be damaged, or lost, there would be hell to pay.

And it would be Noah who paid, not his son. It was always Noah.

Valerian—God, how he hated that pretentious name, hated even more that it fit the young rogue so well, in its innate elegance—smiled in that way that made his father want to box his ears. Noah had done exactly that often enough, as it happened, and relished every blow, but Seraphina invariably coddled the rotter afterward and made the rest of them suffer.

"It belongs to the baron," Valerian said, following a short silence. It was as close as he'd ever come to explaining anything he said or did; he seemed to have some personal rule against giving reasons.

Krispin, that nimble shadow of a boy, spoke at last, in a quavering and earnest voice. "Our tutor told us we could take it," he burbled. "Just until we go back for our lessons. . . ."

Noah felt the blood pounding under his right temple. Lessons. Books. That had been the start of it, Seraphina's foolish insistence that her sons be taught to read, to yearn after poetry and art.

The older man fixed his gaze on Valerian. "Take it back to the keep," he commanded in a tone of coldness and thunder. "Now."

Valerian's look, indeed his whole manner, was one of purest insolence. "I will not," he replied very quietly.

Noah closed one fist—he was a big man, and stronger than his son, and he wanted with all his soul to strike the impudent pup over and over, to force him to his knees, to make him bleed and whimper—but Seraphina was beside her husband in a trice. She gripped Noah's hard arm in her small hands, their tiny bones fragile as a bird's skeleton beneath her silken flesh, and looked up at him with both a plea and a warning in her strange purple eyes.

He could bear no more of it, her choosing this whelp over him, her own mate. It was an abomination! "This is still my house, my shop," Noah said evenly. "And I, God help me, am still your father. I am the master here, and you will do as I tell you or take a hiding the likes of which you've never imagined."

"Noah!" Seraphina whispered, horrified, clutching at him again.

"Enough!" he rasped at her, wrenching his arm free and nearly over-setting her in the process, glowering all the while into Valerian's mag-nificent, hateful young face. After a few deep and tremulous breaths, he managed to speak more calmly. "Now. What shall it be?"

Valerian spat onto the rush-covered floor.

His behavior was beyond enduring; Noah wrenched the precious manuscript from the lad's grasp, shoved it into Seraphina's, and struck his son with such force that Valerian stumbled backward and collided with a wooden support beam. Blood trickled from the corner of his mouth, and the fires of deepest hell blazed in his eyes.

He didn't say that he hated his father, for there was no need to speak of it. Noah knew a moment of torturous despair, and wondered if things would have been different if he'd made Seraphina call the boys by solid, ordinary names, such as Thomas or John, Gideon or Joseph.

Seraphina screamed, but Noah could not stop himself. He cuffed the lad again and entangled a meaty peasant's hand in that mass of chestnut hair, pulling hard, forcing his firstborn to his knees.

Valerian did not fight back, even though Noah could feel the strength surging inside the youthful, granite-hard body; he endured each blow, each kick, each slap and wrench, all the time gazing upon his father with that ancient, murderous contempt in his eyes. Only when it was too late did Noah realize that this very passivity was Valerian's greatest weapon; by suffering the punishment without struggle, he had assured his mother's undying devotion. At the same time he had sealed Noah's doom, robbed him of the last shreds of Seraphina's esteem. He, this changeling with the face of an archangel, had at last destroyed that which Noah valued above all else.

He drew back his foot, with a mighty moan of sheer agony, and kicked the crouching Valerian as hard as he could.

Seraphina shrieked, kneeling in the rushes to gather her bleeding and now-unconscious offspring into her arms, cradling his head on her bosom. When she raised her eyes to Noah's face, his worst fears were confirmed; the hatred he saw in her gaze would outlive them all.

Though she might lie beside him every night, and even suffer his gropings and groans in the darkness, though she might sit across the board from him for a hundred meals, nay, a thousand, Seraphina was eternally lost to him.

Noah felt tears burning in his eyes, for he loved his wife the way a saint loves God, with fevered and unutterable devotion. He held out one hand to her, unable to speak, and she stared at the twisted, calloused fingers for a long moment, then turned her head away. She buried her face in Valerian's hair and spoke not to Noah, but to their second son.

"Take your brother to his bed," she told Krispin in a bleak, distracted tone. "I'll get a cloth and some water."

Only then could Noah manage one desperate word. Her name.

She rose, helping Krispin lift an insensate Valerian to his feet. She did not look at her husband, and her words sliced through him like a reaper's scythe honed for harvest. "May God curse you, Noah Lazarus," she murmured. "May all His angels despise your name, now and on the Day of Judgment."

VALERIAN

I remember clearly, even after six hundred years, that I awakened sometime after sunset, in the dark, cramped little cell I shared with my brother, feeling as though I'd been trampled by the baron's horses. The straw in my pallet rustled when I moved, and I heard Krispin breathing softly in his own bed, against the opposite wall, but there was another noise tugging at the edges of my mind. It was several moments before I realized what else I was hearing—the sound of my father's drunken, disconsolate weeping.

I closed my eyes, as if to block it out, for although I had never loved Noah, I was not immune to his suffering. I did not revel in his injuries as he did in mine.

"Do you think she's left him at last?" Krispin asked.

"No," I replied, unable to withhold a small groan as I shifted on my bed, disturbing bruised muscles and broken skin. "She'll never leave him. Where would she go?"

There was a brief silence, within the room at least. Without, Father's wails grew louder and more desolate, like the cries of a wounded wolf, and I wondered if his agony would drive him to come after me again.

Although he was not a cruel man in any other respect, there could be no denying that he enjoyed taking off strips of my hide.

"You're not his get," Krispin speculated, with no emotion whatsoever coming forth in his voice. "That's why he hates you so much."

The words wounded me sorely, although they shouldn't have. Certainly I'd had the same thought myself more than once, and I'd often pretended, when I was small, that I had sprung from the loins of someone far more interesting than Noah Lazarus, bootmaker, of Dunnett's Head, Cornwall. A smuggler, for example. Or a poet. Or one of the pirates who plagued the coasts of both England and France.

Alas, I had the bootmaker's broad shoulders and powerful, long-fingered hands; I had his temper and his oddly aristocratic nose, though he probably hadn't noticed the similarities. Oh, I was Noah's seed all right, but he couldn't have despised me more if I'd been begotten by the devil's great-uncle. And rather than try to make peace with him, to win his affection, I had always mocked him instead. Even now, after all these centuries, I'm not sure why I had to defy my father, to constantly rouse his ire; I only know that I could sooner have ceased breathing and stilled my own heart than begged him to love me.

"Valerian?" Krispin sounded slightly irritated; it always annoyed him when he spoke to me and I failed to reply straight away. "What do you think? Are you his son, or are you a bastard?"

I smiled in the fetid gloom, even though I ached in every conceivable part of my anatomy, even though I wanted, on some level of my being, to weep and weep until my body was dry as sun-parched straw. "I am his son," I replied, "and I am most assuredly a bastard."

Krispin did not laugh at my jest, and I was sorry for that. It would have been a comfort to me, his amusement.

Things began to crash against the walls and floors in the outer part of the house where Father kept his shop. He was overturning cherished possessions now, flinging them in rage, and I shuddered inwardly, praying he would not remember me.

"He might have loved us," Krispin said at length, "if we'd wanted to be bootmakers."

I was weeping silently by then, and I didn't want my brother to know, so I didn't speak. But I knew it wasn't our rebellion that made our sire hate us, most especially me. It was the fact that our mother had always taken our part against him.

After a while Father was quiet. Krispin drifted off to sleep, and so eventually did I. On the morrow Mother gave me the book that had started the latest battle, carefully wrapped in her best shawl, and spoke to me in a subdued tone.

"You bring it upon yourself, Valerian," she said, pouring water from a ewer into my wooden cup. Father was not in the shop, and Krispin had gone down to the sea at daybreak to watch for ships, the way he always did, so Mother and I were alone. "Always baiting him, always defying him. Why do you do it?"

I was ashamed, for I knew she had endured much because of my willful nature. "I don't know," I answered glumly, tearing off a piece of coarse brown bread for my breakfast. My lower lip was swollen, and it hurt to chew and swallow. I did not express my fear that if I ever stopped rebelling against Father I would instead grovel at his feet, pleading with him to love me.

She looked upon me sternly, then touched my hair. "Be gone. He'll be back soon, with the things he needs to put the shop to rights again, and he mustn't find you here."

I nodded, snatched up a second piece of the hard, dry bread, took the manuscript shrouded in poor brown cloth, and started for the door. Matthew Challes, Brenna Afton-St. Claire's tutor, whom she generously shared with the bootmaker's boys, disliked laggards and dealt with them severely.

I was the first to enter the schoolroom, that hallowed, light-filled place, with its rush-scattered floors and windows opening onto a vista of the wild sea, and Challes gasped audibly when he saw me. He was a tall man, taller than I was by the span of my hand, with deep-set brown eyes, a poet's sensual mouth, and pale skin. There was a faint smattering of pockmarks across his right cheek.

"So Noah's been at you again, has he, lad?"

I simply nodded and held out the book.

Challes set it aside, with less reverence than I would have expected, and stooped slightly, eyes narrowed, to study my battered face. "Good God, it's barbaric. How do you bear it? Why haven't you run away to London or gone to sea?"

I could not go from Dunnett's Head, though I dreamed of it, because I knew my mother would perish if I abandoned her, and because there was someone else I could not bear to leave, but of course I had too much pride to admit the truth. Blessedly, before I could be compelled to make an answer, the Lady Brenna breezed into the schoolroom, and as always, I felt my steady heartbeat turn to a violent *thud-thud-thud* when I saw her.

She was fifteen that year, nubile and womanly, and it was generally known that her father, the baron, was seeking far and wide for a suitable husband. He had only two requirements in a prospective son-in-law, as I recall—social rank and a respectable fortune. The contents of the baron's coffers, never remarkable, had been dwindling rapidly for a generation or so.

I remember quite clearly that I would have given my immortal soul to be her mate, to bury my hands and face in that wild cascade of lush, red-gold hair, to see myself reflected in those jewel-like green eyes, to press my body against hers, my masculine frame moving in sweet, intimate concert with her soft, lithe one.

To this day I recall that she was wearing a velvet frock that morning, rendered in a deep blue, and that it was no less beautiful for its shabbiness.

Seeing me, and my wounds and swellings, she winced in mingled amusement and sympathy. "My poor Valerian," she said, touching my cheek with a light, cool hand. "When will you learn to steer around trouble instead of sailing straight into the heart of it?"

I had no answer for her question; I was too busy wondering if she knew what even so innocent a caress did to me. Although my tunic fit loosely and hung to the middle of my thighs, thereby covering any involuntary evidence of my desire for milady, a sidelong glance at my tutor told me he'd guessed the true state of affairs.

I blushed and pretended I hadn't seen the mating of mirth and censure in his gaze. I was just opening my mouth to babble something inane to Brenna when Krispin came in, bearing an armload of autumn wildflowers and grasses and beaming.

"For you, milady," he said, holding the gift out to Brenna and following up with a courtly bow. He adored her, as I did, and I wondered if she knew and returned his esteem in even the smallest part.

The light of pleasure blazed in her eyes, and I was bludgeoned by jealousy.

It was Challes who interceded, clearing his throat loudly. "Here, now, no more of this nonsense. Sit down, the lot of you, and we'll begin our lessons."

I couldn't concentrate; the sun was bright and the wind coming up from the sea and swirling through the gapped wooden walls and high windows of the old keep smelled of salt. I dreamed of grand adventures in faraway, exotic lands, with the Lady Brenna at my side, and paid scant attention to my Latin.

When we were through with our studies, Krispin vanished, as he often did, to explore one of his sea caves or walk the shore, and I lingered just outside the great, sagging gates of the keep, looking at the sea. Being a lad of seventeen summers, I was in no significant hurry to return to my home and spend the remainder of the day helping my father in the shop.

I had not heard Brenna's approach, and I was a little startled when she suddenly appeared beside me, holding some of Krispin's now-fading bouquet of flowers and sea-grass to her freckled nose. "Do you dream of leaving here forever, the way your brother does?"

I smiled, even though I felt an infinite sorrow stir in the depths of my spirit. *Yes*, I thought. *And I dream of taking you with me.* "I'd like to see France and the lands beyond," I conceded, cautious in her presence as always, because her opinion of me meant everything. "What about you, milady? Do you imagine being married and bearing children?"

A brief, troubled silence followed, during which I suffered the proverbial agonies of the damned, fearing I'd said the wrong thing. She gazed out toward the sea, squinting against the brightness of the late afternoon sun, her expression so solemn, so mournful, that I wanted to take her into my arms and promise to protect her from dragons and devils and all else she might fear.

Finally she looked up into my face. "I'm to go to Northumberland," she said at last. "Father has found me a husband there. Word reached us yesterday, and he told me as we supped."

I felt a great wail of grief and protest rise in me, pulsing painfully in my throat, but I did not release it. It would have frightened Brenna, and otherwise changed nothing.

Brenna linked her arm through mine. "I don't want to leave you, Valerian," she said. "You love me, don't you?"

I merely nodded, for I would not have dared to speak even if I could have managed it. Without Brenna, my life would be unendurable. And there would be no more lessons in the keep, no more Challes, no more books and poetry and music.

For the first time, I truly wanted to die. In retrospect, that seems an exquisite irony.

She rested her head against my shoulder, and I could smell woodsmoke in her hair, and the sea, and that scent that was, and is, peculiar to her. "I've always pretended," she said in a voice so small that the wind nearly carried it away, "that I would marry you one day. I knew it couldn't happen, and yet . . ."

I turned, staring into her face, bewildered and full of wild, impossible hopes. "What did you say?"

Brenna smiled that same unbearably sad smile that had rested upon her lips moments before. "Is it so difficult to believe," she countered, "that I should love you?"

I swallowed hard, full of sadness and ecstasy. How wrenching it was, knowing that she wanted me as I wanted her and, at the same time, being aware to the depths of my soul that we could never be together. She interlaced her fingers with mine. "How will I bear it?" she murmured, asking herself, not me. Asking the sea and the hard, brittle blue of a September sky.

By then it was all a blur to me, the water, the village, the grassy slope leading down to the shore, for I was blinded by tears. I could not answer her question, or my own, which was exactly the same.

Brenna stepped in front of me, raised her hands to my face. "Perhaps Father would let us be married if I told him how much we care for each other."

I laughed, and the sound was jagged, seeming to tear the flesh of my throat as it passed. "The baron? Bless a marriage between his daughter and the bootmaker's son? Good God, Brenna, he'd have me in chains before day's end, and on the rack not long after!"

She rested her forehead against my chest, and I wanted to push her away, for there were always servants and others about, watching, interpreting what they saw and heard to suit themselves, passing it along to all who would listen. Still, thrusting her from me would have been like expelling the breath in my lungs and never drawing another. I felt her tears dampening my tunic, and laid my hands lightly, reverently, on her slender shoulders.

At last she drew back, sniffling, and her attempt to smile rent my heart. "Perhaps he will be a good man, my husband. Perhaps he will be gentle and think me pretty."

I closed my eyes, remembering the sounds I'd heard so often, through the daub-and-wattle wall that separated my parents' chamber from the one I shared with Krispin. Those were primitive times, and that particular brand of modesty was in short supply in the countryside and the village alike. I had seen men take their wives in the fields, like dogs mounting bitches in the street.

"*Jesu,*" I whispered, shattered by the image of Brenna lying in another man's bed. In that moment I wanted to go to the high cliffs south of the village and fling myself off them, into the sharp rocks clustered below. "Yes," I said finally. "He'll think you pretty. How could he not?"

We parted then—surely it was Lady Brenna who broke away first. I descended the hillside toward the village without looking back. I was still half blinded by tears and thus didn't see Krispin until I'd practically collided with him.

"There's a ship on the horizon!" he cried, fairly dancing with excitement.

I pushed him aside—perhaps I was a bit too rough in my despair. I didn't gave a sacred damn if the shore was lined with Viking vessels, brimming with spear-waving invaders. Brenna was going away, probably before the winter snows, and I would never see her again.

Krispin was not content to let me pass; he clutched the sleeve of my tunic and wrenched me back. I swung at him without thinking, catching him up alongside the head and dropping him to his knees.

I barely noticed the flush of fury in his fine-boned face, or the venomous spark in his eyes. He raised himself and came hurtling at me like a snarling dog, and I cuffed him again, more out of surprise than anger.

He went sprawling once more, in the chilly grass, and then sat up, wiping blood from the corner of his mouth. His face was utterly expressionless as he sat there, looking up at me, thinking God only knew what.

"I'm sorry," I said, extending my hand to him, making no effort to hide the mark of tears on my face.

Krispin allowed me to help him, though oftentimes when we'd had such a scrap, he'd slap my hand away when I offered it. "What's the matter with you?" he demanded, dusting off his leggings and tunic. Like mine, they were poor and ugly garments, rough to the touch and virtually useless against the chill of a cold night. "I was only trying to tell you about the ship—"

I was already striding toward the village again, and the shop, where my mother would be keeping her pitiful vigil, watching for Krispin and me as if we were sailors just home from the sea, while my father watched her, in turn, and seethed. My brother scrambled to get into step with me.

I dragged one arm across my wet face, and we talked no more of ships. We could not have guessed, in our innocence, what monstrous suffering that vessel would bring to us all.

That night Father was in a mood, and Mother had taken to her pallet with some ailment born of the strain between them. Krispin slipped out to mingle with the men from the ship and hear their tales, while I sat in my chamber with my back to the wall, brooding over Brenna's impending departure.

In the morning there was no sign of Krispin. I shrugged at the realization, filled a basin with water from the ewer my mother kept filled, and washed as best I could. During the night I had conceived a plan—I would go to the Baron Afton-St. Claire, Brenna's father, and ask for her hand. If he had me clapped into chains or pulled me apart on the rack for getting above myself, so be it. I had to try.

As it happened, Challes was waiting at the schoolroom door when I arrived, his eyes red-rimmed, fairly bursting with tidings. Dire ones, I could tell.

He grasped my arm, hard enough to leave bruises, and growled, "What in God's name have you done? The baron is demanding to see you, and he is in a towering rage!"

I wrenched free of my tutor's hold, drawing myself up in fury even as terror seeped into every part of my being. In our village and in all the barren lands surrounding it, Afton-St. Claire was the most powerful of men, and my fate was most definitely in his hands.

When I did not answer his question immediately, Challes leaned in close and spat, "Damn you, bootmaker's son, *what have you done?*"

I remembered holding Brenna the day before, while she cried over our parting. Even though I might die screaming for daring to touch her, when I searched my heart I could find no regret. "The Lady Brenna was weeping. She laid her head against my shoulder."

"And you touched her with your hands?" Challes cried in a strangled voice. "Fool! Arrogant, willful fool!"

I straightened. "Where is the baron? In the great hall?"

Challes ran one narrow hand over his face. "We're all finished, you know. Not just you, you young peacock! The Lady Brenna will be locked up until her husband comes to claim her, and Krispin's education will be come to an end, as well as your own. And I will lose my position!"

I wanted to apologize, I truly did. I couldn't bring myself to proceed, though, because in my deepest being I knew I had done nothing wrong. If others suffered because of the situation, it would be by the baron's decree, not by mine.

"Where is he?" I asked again. Stiffly.

Challes's sigh contained all the misery of that difficult and unjust world we lived in. "You'll find him in the inner courtyard—practicing with his sword."

I was no fool, though Challes had called me one. I wanted to bolt from that keep, to run for my life, but there was nowhere to go.

I made my way to the inner courtyard, careful to keep my shoulders straight and my head high. When I arrived, the baron, a muscular, thick-chested man, was indeed wielding a sword, battling a knobby-kneed squire who was plainly terrified. It was little wonder, given the baron's earnest dedication to his task. The nobleman was drenched in sweat and bellowing like an outraged bull.

I stood waiting, and beyond the clanging flash of the swords I saw the Lady Brenna huddled in the shadowy arch of a doorway, watching me.

I was destined to lose her, I knew, and the realization gave me a strange, desolate sort of courage. Facing a lifetime apart from her as I was, years of knowing another man was laying his hands to her, in love and perhaps in anger, I could not but think that death would be a mercy. Any sort of death.

2

VALERIAN
Las Vegas, 1995

S HE was there.
Even before I walked onstage that fateful night, to regale the baffled masses with my illusions, I felt her presence in the grand showroom of the Venetian Hotel. The knowledge that she was nearby left me so shaken that I could barely concentrate on the performance.

Brenna. Dear God, my Brenna . . .

My lusty Elisabeth. And sweet, fragile Jenny. And Harmony. And Sarah.

But of course she had a new identity now, and those other names, all of which had been her own at one time or another, would mean nothing to her. Nor would I, I was certain.

I'd be lying—not that I've ever hesitated to bend the truth should it serve my purpose to do so—if I said I took no joy in the prospect of another encounter with my elusive beloved. Just the thought of speaking to her again, of touching her, was rapture, but there was fear, too, and I already felt the weight of the sorrow that would inevitably follow any bliss we might share.

For my darling and me, the story, played out over and over on the stage of six centuries, had never had a happy ending. Not once.

Invariably, except in her first incarnation, the ruby ring had arrived, out of nowhere, a mysterious thing of splendor and antiquity, and precisely a fortnight later I had been bereaved again. And always, try though I did to discover who had sent that glittering jewel, and with it the curse, the thing vanished while I was caught up in my mourning. The tragic puzzle was no closer to solution that night, when I found Brenna once more, than it had ever been.

I used my powers to hold her in her seat, there in that large and otherwise anonymous audience, sensing her desire to bolt as well as her fascination with my legerdemain, but even after the carriage trick had been completed and all the others had straggled out, I lingered backstage.

I remember wishing I could simply walk away—each time I found her, I entertained that same futile notion, of course—but I am neither fine nor noble enough to make such a sacrifice. I was starved for the sight and sound and feel of her, just as I had always been. It would have been easier to forgo the taking of blood than to turn my back on that particular woman.

So it was that I stood in the wings as the silence lengthened in that great room, watching her fidget at her table, seeing the shadows play in her coppery hair, for some fifteen minutes before one of the dancing girls appeared at my side. Her name was Jillie, and she was still wearing her delectably inadequate costume.

I do enjoy the many and varied facets of my work.

"Someone you know?" she asked with a slight edge of envy to her voice. Jillie was more than passing-curious about me, and I suspect she saw me as a romantic challenge. Being older, to say the least, and infinitely wiser, I didn't encourage her; she could have no way of guessing she was flirting with a bona fide monster.

"An old friend," I said softly, never taking my eyes from the woman sitting alone in the auditorium. She had finished her drink and begun chewing ice cubes, and the crunching sound made me wince.

Jillie lingered a moment, cast a venomous glance toward the object of my attention, and swept off toward the dressing room she shared with the other women in the act.

I allowed myself a fraction of a smile. I'd done Jillie a favor she could not begin to comprehend or appreciate by spurning her naive affections. Would that I could be so gracious with my Lady Brenna.

I had shed the cumbersome cape as soon as the show ended, but I was still wearing my tuxedo when I finally forced myself down the steps at the side of the stage and along the aisle.

If I'd had a living, beating heart instead of an atrophied vestige of one, that organ would have twisted at the sight of her watching me approach. She was helpless, like an animal dazzled by light; I knew that and used it to my advantage.

Fate is cruel, in my experience—except for the modern haircut and clothes, she looked just as she had in each of the previous lifetimes in which our paths had crossed. Her hair was a coppery-gold color, thick and lush, and her eyes were green. Even her face, with its delicate bone structure and impertinent little chin, was the same, right down to the faint smattering of freckles across her nose.

I closed my eyes for a moment, caught up in a spindrift of emotions, and when I looked again, she was staring up at me. Her throat worked, as if she'd attempted to speak and failed, and she offered me her hand. She seemed bewildered, afraid, and perhaps just a bit enchanted.

Her introduction was woven of pure bravado. "Daisy Chandler," she said, offering me her hand. "I'm a homicide detective with the Las Vegas Police Department."

I was taken aback by this flood of information, and arched one eyebrow as I enclosed her hand in my own. I wondered if she felt the chill in my flesh, and puzzled over it. Although I can usually read a mortal mind with embarrassing ease, hers has always been veiled from me, except for a few shifting flickers of discernment here and there—perhaps because I care so much. Creation can be perverse in that way, so often withholding from us the very insights and objects we desire most.

"I am pleased to meet you," I managed to reply, though I have to admit I was as nervous as Daisy. I was just better at hiding what I felt than she was, that was all. I'd had a long time to practice.

She frowned, her pretty brow knitting for a moment in consternation. "Do I know you?"

The answer to that question was better saved for another time. "No," I replied, missing a beat or two. I knew that, deep in her subconscious, she remembered me, and everything we'd been through together, in minute detail. The human mind is a superlative scribe, missing nothing, trundling its uncountable impressions from one lifetime to the next.

Daisy rose, somewhat shakily, and only thought to remove her fingers from mine after she'd gained her feet. She was wearing tight jeans that had seen better days, and her white summer top was airy and ruffled, inviting the eyes to her finely shaped breasts.

I felt a rush of jealous irritation, a downright silly desire to fetch one of my capes and cover her with it. I had had to share her with others when she was Elisabeth Saxon; I could not do so again.

"Your show was fantastic," she said with a tentative smile.

I merely inclined my head once, in acknowledgment of the compliment. There was—and is—no false modesty in my makeup. The performance was indeed "fantastic," and more; my audiences paid for magic, and they got their money's worth.

She looked about, noticed as I did that the waiters and bartenders were gone, replaced by the cleaning staff. "I guess I should be going," she said with a sort of cheerful desperation, and I felt a pang of regret because I knew Daisy wasn't normally a timid person. I was frightening her, and I hated that.

"Yes," I said quickly, at last releasing the mental hold I had taken on her earlier. "Good night, Miss Chandler."

She studied my face, and for a breathless moment I thought she consciously remembered me. In the next instant, however, the pensive expression in her beautiful eyes vanished. Daisy waggled her unmanicured fingers in farewell and dashed out of the showroom without looking back.

I went to my dressing room, where the mirrors were draped and the lights were dim, and stood in the middle of the floor, struggling against the rage and frustration that had arisen in me. I didn't want to go through it all again, loving her, wanting her, losing her, and suffering the soul-crushing consequences once more, but I knew the curse some passing devil had cast over both of us would run its course. The ring would arrive, and Daisy would die.

I was standing there, outwardly still, but with all hell breaking loose inside, when a soft tapping sounded at the door.

My first reaction was fury; I was grieving and did not wish to be disturbed. But then the door opened, and I saw my caller.

Daisy had returned, looking uncertain, as if she'd reached the end of some invisible tether and been drawn back by it. She gripped one of my colorful, printed programs in her right hand and wore a determined if still-fragile smile. There were no photographs of me in the publication, of course, only reproductions of paintings, and she had the booklet open to one of these.

"I was wondering . . ." she began, her eyes straying around the dressing room, taking in the shrouded mirrors and muted lights.

I was so glad to see her that it required the utmost restraint on my part not to wrench her into my arms. "Yes?" I prompted, perhaps sounding the least bit patronizing. My friends, as well as my enemies, tell me that a certain arrogance is native to my manner.

She shoved the program at me, along with a cheap plastic pen. "Would you autograph this, please?"

I did so with a flourish and handed both the booklet and the pen back to her.

Daisy bit her lower lip, and I felt a rush of arousal so keen that I writhed in the core of it, like a man in flames. "Thanks," she said. She hesitated, then went on in a tumbled hurry of words: "I know magicians never tell their secrets, but that carriage trick was—well, it was impossible. You couldn't have used wires or platforms. So it had to be some sort of mass hypnosis—"

"Or," I interrupted gently, "it might have happened exactly as you saw it. By magic." I smiled and spread my hands.

She frowned, and I wanted to kiss the place between her brows where the skin creased prettily. "Something weird is going on here," she finally blurted out. "Who are you?"

I wanted to tell her; it would have been the most delicious relief to explain it all, but I couldn't. For one thing, the story would have taken hours to relate, and for another, I didn't want to frighten Daisy off forever. "You'll understand it all in good time," I replied with resignation. I was beginning to feel restless, agitated; I needed to hunt and feed, and perhaps prowl a bit, before retiring to my lair.

"I'm coming back," Daisy announced, still frowning.

I took a printed pass from the top drawer of my dressing room bureau and handed it to her. "Be my guest," I said.

Daisy accepted the special ticket, nodded her thanks, and left, looking as befuddled as ever. I suspect it wasn't me or my magic that made her thoughtful, but her own unexpected captivation with both. She was clearly not a person given to obsessions and strange fancies.

After she'd gone I mourned her, for even when we parted briefly, I was invariably bereaved. I stood with my forehead touching the door and my hands gripping the woodwork on either side, remembering. Suffering. Loving.

The Lady Brenna
Dunnett's Head, 1348

They were facing each other in the courtyard, Brenna Afton-St. Claire's father, the baron, and Valerian. The autumn sun, though fiercely bright, felt cold, and Brenna shivered.

Her father had been practicing his swordsmanship, though it was unlikely the king would ever again call upon him to serve as a soldier, given his age. For all his four and forty years, however, the baron was strong.

"The bootmaker's son," the baron said, assessing Valerian and at the same time using the hem of his tunic to polish the steel blade of his sword. It caught fire with daylight and flashed like a mirror.

Brenna held her breath, watching Valerian's face. *Jesu*, she prayed silently, *make him hold his tongue. If he doesn't, my father will surely kill him, and with pleasure.*

Valerian only inclined his head, and Brenna nearly swooned with gratitude. The baron's anger was violent, burning hot as the fires of perdition, but it died quickly when it was not fueled.

Sweating profusely from his exercise, the baron held the sword up, between himself and the bootmaker's son, and then pressed the point to the pulse at the base of Valerian's throat.

Brenna gasped and started to bolt toward them, intending to intercede, but Challes, her tutor, gripped her hard by the arm.

"Stand fast," he warned in a whispered hiss, his grasp tightening when she struggled.

Valerian stood still, surely aware that the baron could kill him easily, with no penance forthcoming, looking almost insolently calm. Even from several feet away, Brenna could see that the expression in his eyes was fearless.

With a silent wail of despair Brenna realized that Valerian was courting death—he *wanted* to perish! She tried to cry out, but the only sound that came from her throat was a hoarse, senseless whisper.

The baron broke the awful silence, his words as cold and hard as the blade of the sword he held. "Why did you lay your hands to my daughter, peasant? How dare you touch a noblewoman?"

Brenna squeezed her eyes shut, terrified.

"I forgot myself," Valerian replied. There was no trace of subservience in his tone or manner, but no mockery, either. He was simply stating a fact.

Brenna put one hand over her mouth and swayed slightly in Challes's now-gentled grasp. Her eyes burned with tears as the full measure of her ardor for Valerian Lazarus came down upon her, crushing her spirit as surely as a fallen wall would have done her body. In that terrible moment she knew that she had loved Valerian as long as she had known him, which was all her life, and that they had been together before the stars were born.

"You are bold," the baron remarked, lowering the steel only to beckon to his squire, who was yet trembling from his own encounter with the nobleman. "Fetch a second sword," he told the servant.

Brenna's heart seized with the knowledge that her father meant to challenge Valerian. There could be no contest—despite the lad's youth and strength, he had no experience with weapons. The baron, on the other hand, had wielded heavy swords daily, from earliest childhood. He was a seasoned warrior.

"No!" she managed to shriek. Challes tried to hold her, but in her desperation of fear, Brenna broke free. Her face streaked with tears, she clutched at the sleeve of the baron's tunic. "Don't do this, Father," she pleaded. She dropped to her knees then, grasping his clothing with both hands now, her knuckles white with the effort. "Don't kill Valerian," she pleaded. "Oh, please—I'll do anything—"

Her father's face was terrible, flushed with rage and chagrin, and Brenna did not dare to look at Valerian's. She knew, too late, that she should have listened to the tutor, that she had made a grave mistake in revealing the extent of her devotion.

"You would *beg* like a street whore," the baron seethed in a vicious tone, "for the life of this—dog?"

Valerian stiffened; Brenna felt it, though she still lacked the courage to look into his eyes. It was bad enough meeting her father's condemning gaze.

"I love him," she said.

The baron backhanded her then, so hard that she went sprawling backward into the dust of the courtyard. Valerian made a growling, inhuman sound and lunged at her father.

A furious bellow spilled from the baron's throat, and over it all Brenna's own sobs could be heard, as well as the frantic peace pleas of poor Challes.

The baron raised his sword and neatly sliced open Valerian's poor garment, along with the flesh beneath. The baron laughed, the sound echoing off the inner walls of the keep, like the ravings of a madman. "So you dare to go for my throat, do you?" he roared as the squire returned with the extra sword. "You are brave, as well as insolent, like so many fools." At a gesture from his master, the servant handed the second blade to Valerian. "Well, upon this day, you shall die."

"No!" Brenna screamed, clawing at the ground with spread fingers in her effort to get to her feet and fling herself upon her father. But this time Challes succeeded in forestalling her; he wrapped an arm around her middle and dragged her backward into the shadows. When she shrieked in protest, the tutor slapped her, but it was the words that followed that quieted her, rather than the blow.

"God save us all, my lady, you've already doomed your beloved with your imprudent ways! Will you see him sundered at the joints as well, like a fowl to be served at supper? In the name of all that's holy, *be still*, and perhaps some passing angel will show us mercy!"

Dirty and broken inside, Brenna sagged against her teacher, weeping softly, and he held her.

Valerian took the sword, and though he was not experienced, he was strong. The battle raged for an eternity, it seemed to Brenna. Her father prevailed for a time, then Valerian. Both men were bloodied, their clothes drenched with sweat and gritty with courtyard dirt. At last the baron swung his blade in a mighty arch, and Valerian went down with nary a cry, with a deep, crimson gash in his middle.

He did not rise.

Brenna screamed inwardly, silently.

The baron, unsteady on his feet, breathing hard and bleeding copiously from wounds in his upper arm and one shoulder, looked down upon the half-conscious lad and raised his sword for the kill. For a long time he stood there like that, prepared to run Valerian through and finish it, and for Brenna all of creation stopped, as motionless as a painting.

The baron glanced at her, and she saw the utter absence of love in his eyes, and then looked down at Valerian again. Finally the nobleman spat on the lad and flung the faithful sword aside, sending it clattering across the stone pathway that wove through the courtyard.

"He shall rot awhile in my dungeon, and then hang," the baron decreed, pointing one bloodstained, filthy index finger at Brenna. "You, Daughter of Eve, shall be witness to the fruits of your whoring, and so shall the bootmaker and his wife, and everyone else in the village who cares to witness the spectacle."

"There was no whoring, Your Grace," the tutor said quickly, stunning them all by what he risked. "The Lady Brenna was weeping, and the tradesman's son attempted to comfort her. It was no more than that."

The baron assessed the scholar he had engaged some years before, at the behest of Brenna's late mother, whom he had loved with a slavish devotion. "Get out," he rasped. "Or you shall swing from a gibbet with this dog's get." He kicked Valerian's prone body once, eliciting the first and last moan from him, then stalked away.

Brenna ran to Valerian and placed his head in her lap, stroking his blood-streaked hair. "I won't let him part us," she whispered, cold with shock. "I'll die with you—I vow it by all I know of heaven—before I'll say farewell."

Somewhere, deeper within the keep, she heard her father shouting orders. Too soon, men came, wrenching the dazed Valerian from her arms, roughly hauling him away. Brenna did not fight them, because she was afraid of doing Valerian further injury.

Challes crouched beside her briefly, where she sat in the dust like a beggar, and spoke in a quiet but stern voice. "Go to your quarters, Lady Brenna. Wash yourself, and brush your hair, and don a clean gown. When your father summons you, and he shall, answer his questions respectfully and keep your opinions to yourself. Do you understand me?"

"Yes," she whispered. She didn't see what any of it mattered; all she cared about was saving Valerian.

Then even Challes was gone.

Brenna rose after a while and was met at the edge of the courtyard by her lady's maid, Moll, who clucked and fretted at the sight of her charge. Like a sleepwalker, Brenna let herself be led inside the keep, across the great room, up the broad stone stairs, and along the passageway to her own chamber.

There she stood still and endured while Moll stripped away her gown, along with the shift beneath it, and scrubbed her with chilly water and a rough cloth. Brenna's hair was brushed, then thick tendrils at either side were plaited, with narrow ribbons made from cloth-of-gold woven through. She was powdered and perfumed, like a bride being prepared for her husband. Then, finally, she was laced into a green frock, just a few shades darker than her eyes, and steered across the rushes to the looking glass.

Brenna did not connect herself to the beautiful image wavering upon the murky face of the mirror. She was numb, as insubstantial as a ghost, with no more depth than her reflection.

She turned to look into Moll's eyes and clutched the maid's workworn hands in both her own. "I must go to him," she said. "Where is he?"

Moll's plain, earnest face paled. "The bootmaker's lad? I would imagine he's in the dungeon still, mistress, where the baron had him put, but—"

Brenna's mind was beginning to work again. The servants lived in a world all their own; they knew each other's habits, had their own feuds and romances. Without their help, she could not hope to reach Valerian. "I know Father has already ordered that I am to be closed up in my chamber, after tonight. But you must bring the key and let me out, Moll, as soon as the moon is high."

Moll swayed slightly with fear. "Milady!" she rasped. "Do you know what you're asking of me? Why, if I were found out—"

"You won't be caught," Brenna interrupted, knowing the promise was a rash one even as she spoke. "Please, Moll—I must go to Valerian. Tonight!"

"It's no use, you're putting yourself into such danger!" Moll rarely argued, but she did so now, with fervor. "He's to die one day soon, with the sunrise, is Noah Lazarus's son! And nothing you can do will save him!"

Brenna would not, could not, turn away from her course, though she knew as well as anyone that it was a deadly one. If these were Valerian's last days on earth, then they would be hers as well. If she must see him step into eternity, in the first flowering of his manhood, then she would follow on his heels, and cross the unseen river knowing what it was to pass the night in her beloved's arms.

She tightened her grasp on Moll's hands and looked deep into her old friend's troubled eyes. "My father will have me whipped if he catches me at this," she said softly. "If I can risk that, can you not chance letting me out of my room when the time is right?"

Moll was in anguish, but she nodded just before she turned and left the room.

Brenna's evening meal was served in her chamber, by the light of tallows, for she was well and truly banished from her father's table as well as his heart. He would not forgive her, and the knowledge grieved her sorely, but that night her status in the household was the least of her concerns.

She didn't even pretend to eat; the food on her trencher had grown cold, and she was pacing nervously back and forth at the foot of her bed, her hems whispering in the dry rushes. Moll did not return, and the hours dragged past, with Brenna still a prisoner in her chamber.

She slept in her beautiful gown, and no breakfast was brought when the morrow came. She was given water, that was all, by a servant who would not meet her gaze or answer her questions.

A week had passed, during which Brenna had eaten nothing and heard not a word spoken by another human being, when a burly manservant came and summoned her to her father's chamber. Still wearing the green gown, now much crumpled, she finished the last of a cup of water before stepping into the passageway to follow her silent escort across the stone floors to the other side of the keep.

The baron stood at an open window when she entered, gazing out at the dark sea, and he did not turn to greet her.

Brenna herself heard the song of the tides and felt the cooling mist on her face. She took courage from those things, and straightened her back, for she loved the sea.

"You sent for me," she said with simple dignity. She was light-headed with hunger and worry, but her sense of injustice sustained her. "I am here."

Her father's broad back stiffened, and she felt a stirring of pity for him. He was bound by what and who he was, she realized, and even if somewhere inside himself he truly wanted to show mercy, he would be unable to do so. He had been born to a rigid code, he knew nothing else, and it was not in him to change.

"You have broken my heart," he said starkly, and still he did not face her. "Tell me, have you lain with that devil's spawn or simply lusted after him?"

Brenna swallowed. *Tread carefully*, warned a voice in her giddy mind, one with the timbre and substance of Challes's. "I want him," she admitted without the slightest remorse. "But, no, Father, I have never lain with Valerian or any man. You knew that before you asked me."

At last the baron turned, very slowly, and Brenna's heart quailed behind her rib cage. She was not effortlessly, foolishly bold like Valerian; she had seen her father punish servants and errant villagers, and she knew the ferocity of his rages. Now she was utterly stunned to see that his face was wet with tears.

"Perhaps," he whispered, "your body is indeed pure, just as you say. But yours is the soul of a whore. You have fused yourself to that filthy peasant as surely as if he'd taken you to his bed. And now there is nothing to be done. He must die, and you must go to your new husband in shame."

Brenna interlaced her fingers and bit her lower lip for a moment, trying to think calmly. "There *is* something that can be done," she said quietly, and at length. "Banish us, both of us, Valerian and me. We'll make our way to London, or—"

"Silence!" the baron roared. "Do you argue for him still, when you know I cannot bear any reference to the scab?"

A shrill commotion in the hall beyond the baron's heavy door stopped Brenna's impulsive reply in her throat. It was undoubtedly for the best.

"What in the name of—?" her father muttered as the great door crashed inward.

Seraphina Lazarus, Valerian's mother, filled the chasm, beautiful even in her frenzy. Her flawless skin was white as a corpse's, her violet eyes wild, her chestnut hair loose and untamed, like a witch's tresses, and her simple gown was streaked with ash.

Brenna felt ill, and would have retched if her stomach hadn't been shrunken and empty, as she watched the woman rush to the baron and kneel at his feet.

"My firstborn," Seraphina pleaded, clutching the nobleman's hand and kissing his knuckles and fingers and wrist, frantically, feverishly. "Oh, sir, I beg you, spare my boy—allow me to die in his place—take all of us, my husband, my other son—" The bootmaker's wife paused and made a pitiful, strangling sound, far down in her throat. "There is pestilence abroad in the land," she blathered. "Set Valerian free, I pray you, sir—if it is the will of heaven that he perish for his sin, then surely the plague will take him—"

Plague. Brenna barely registered the word on a conscious level, weakened by her confinement as she was, and sharing Seraphina's agony as she did, but she felt a ripple of fear all the same.

"Damn your indecent soul, woman," the baron seethed, glaring down at Seraphina. "You utter one travesty on top of another, arguing and bargaining for the life of this young devil as if he were a lover!"

Brenna flinched at the cruelty of the words. "Father—" she began in protest, starting toward the pair, but there was no stopping fate.

The baron's rage mounted visibly; he went crimson, temples pulsing, and raised a swordsman's hard fist to strike Seraphina a savage blow. Even after he'd struck her, the bootmaker's wife scrabbled through the rushes to clutch at his garb again, sobbing now, and wailing piteously.

Brenna's father tore himself free with a great curse, and he might have kicked the poor woman if his daughter hadn't stepped between them.

"Her only crime is love," Brenna reasoned with a tranquility that surprised her as much as it did the baron. "Oh, Father, turn from this— please. I'll do anything you say, anything at all, if you'll just unbend this once and show compassion."

The baron eyed her coldly, and then the woman groveling on the floor. He raised his voice to cover the sound of her anguish; she babbled something unintelligible and then fell to whimpering. "Valerian dies," he barked.

Seraphina gave a great, bubbling shriek and fell unconscious onto her side, and a spew of bright red blood burst from her mouth.

Brenna tried to go to the woman's aid, but the baron took a bruising grip on his daughter's arm and flung her out the door. He was shouting for the servants when Brenna started for her chamber, paused, and then slipped into the shadows and made her way to a rear passageway.

The dungeon was unguarded—the baron knew Valerian was injured and probably considered him unworthy of a bailiff's time. Carrying a tallow she'd stolen from the kitchen, along with some cheese, a basin, and a piece of soft cloth, Brenna moved from cell to cell until she reached the last and most cramped of them all. A rat scuttled out of the gloom before she could work the lock. It stopped at her feet to rise onto its haunches and whirl about in a macabre little dance, before falling dead on its side.

A chill trickled down Brenna's spine, and she crossed herself hastily and offered a prayer to the Virgin. Then she stepped over the small, furry corpse and into the cell where Valerian lay.

He was a shadow, curled in the fetid straw. The dank walls dripped with water, and the faint, panicky twitter of other rats reached Brenna's ears.

"Valerian," she whispered urgently.

He stirred. "Milady?" Valerian moaned the word, then sat up, blinking, one arm clutching his wounded middle. "Jesus, Joseph, and Mary," he marveled on a long breath. "Leave me—now—before they find you here!"

Brenna set down the cloth and tallow on a crude bench and knelt beside him in the straw, giving him water from a cup and the morsel of cheese. "This is where I intend to pass the night," she answered. "Here, with you."

He managed to eat just a little, and Brenna went back for the basin. Then, kneeling beside Valerian in the foul straw again, she began to bathe the blood and dirt from his flesh. Even in the dim glow of that one candle, she saw the tears shimmering in his eyes.

"Oh, God, Brenna," he whispered. "How did we get ourselves to this place?"

"Shhh," she said and went on washing him. Her own hunger and weakness floated somewhere above her, suspended.

Presently the loving task had been done as well as it could be, given the circumstances. The tallow guttered out, and Brenna laid herself beside Valerian on the cell floor, and gathered him close with one arm. With the other hand she undid the laces at her bosom and, baring her breasts, offered him the only intimate comfort she knew about.

He was half dead of his wounds, but the blood in his veins was youthful, like the sap in a fierce young tree, and he drank hungrily from her breasts, and kissed her, and spoke pretty, disjointed words while he nibbled at her earlobe. Finally he raised her skirts and took her, with a hard, greedy thrust.

Brenna felt searing pain, followed swiftly by a treacherous pleasure, and she gave herself up to her forbidden lover with all the passion pent up in her innocent soul.

3

DAISY
Las Vegas, 1995

THE victim was a showgirl, no more than twenty years old, and she lay sprawled on the living room floor of her cramped apartment, wearing nothing but a short seagreen robe. Her shoulder-length blond hair spilled over the cheap carpeting and partially covered her face.

She was impossibly pale, even for a corpse. Daisy thought of Snow White waiting for her prince, and shuddered. There was no blood anywhere.

Daisy had been promoted to detective six months before, after the requisite four years on the street, and she had seen her share of murders. No matter how many she investigated, the bile still rushed into the back of her throat, and sometimes she had to run to the nearest bush or bathroom to throw up. On other occasions, especially when the victim was a child, she wept.

This time she felt an ugly sort of shock take hold, deep inside her. Even before her partner, O'Halloran, started filling her in on the details, she knew they were dealing with some kind of monster.

"Look at this," O'Halloran said, crouching beside the body, which had already been outlined and photographed. In fact, the coroner's people were hovering, ready to do their grisly duties. He brushed back a tendril of the dead woman's glossy blond hair with remarkably gentle fingers to reveal a pair of neat puncture wounds, set about two inches apart, in the victim's neck. "If I didn't know better, Chandler, I'd say this was the work of one of them vampires. You know, like in the movies."

Daisy felt a chill trip down her spine. "I know what vampires are," she snapped.

O'Halloran, a wiry, graying man of medium height, with twenty-eight years on the force to his credit, sighed loudly and stretched to his feet. His eyes were either pale blue or pale green, depending on the weather and how things were going at home. This was a blue day. "What's the matter, Chandler—you suffering from PMS or something? Well, take a pill. I got enough problems without you flashing an attitude."

Daisy didn't apologize, though she knew O'Halloran was right. She *was* off track—her meeting with the magician had occupied her every waking thought since she'd left his dressing room the night before. When she had managed to sleep, she'd been plagued by strange, vivid dreams of a medieval courtyard and two men fighting with swords . . .

"Chandler," O'Halloran prompted, poking her with an elbow.

Daisy jumped and shook her head once in an effort to clear her head. "Yeah, I'm with you. Sorry. What's her name?"

"Jillie Fairfield," O'Halloran answered, consulting his notes. "She was nineteen and worked with that hotshot magician over at the Venetian. What's his name—?" He began flipping pages.

"Valerian," Daisy said, feeling jolted.

"Yeah," O'Halloran agreed, tapping his pocket-sized notepad with the end of his stubby pencil. "That's him. You ever catch his show?"

"Last night," Daisy managed.

"I've heard it's really something. According to the papers, there are magicians flying in from all over the world just to see the act and try to figure out how he pulls it off. And he won't let anybody take his picture, either."

"He's good, all right," Daisy said, glancing at the body again. She remembered the dancers coming out of the coach while it was suspended in midair, then sitting underneath, smiling and posing. She wondered if Jillie had been the one who'd brought out the umbrella and gotten a chuckle from the audience. Even to Daisy's trained eye, the performers had looked very much alike.

The older cop led the way toward the gaping front door of the apartment, and Daisy went along gratefully. She'd never gotten used to the smell of death, or the clammy feeling it gave her.

"You look a little peaked," O'Halloran remarked. "You have a bad night?"

She drew in a deep draft of desert air as they descended the wooden stairs outside. The Las Vegas sun was bright, and for Daisy it dispelled some of the chill that had settled into her spirit. "Me? I never have a bad night, O'Halloran," she said with a manufactured smile. "And I never get PMS, either. What's your take on this? What happened to the Fairfield woman?"

O'Halloran shrugged. "I don't know. The coroner will fill us in, though." He paused beside his car, a battered sixty-seven Mustang on its fourth engine, and scratched the back of his head. "This one's different, I can tell you that much. There ought to be blood, and we didn't find a drop. No blow to the head, no visible wounds except for those punctures on her throat. You'd better haul it over to the Venetian and see if you can track down that magician character. See what he can tell you."

Daisy had hoped to encounter Valerian again, though certainly not under those circumstances. "I'm off to see the wizard," she said, heading for her own car, a sporty blue convertible. "Meet you back at the office later."

When Daisy reached the Venetian, Las Vegas's newest and most elaborate hotel-casino, she left her car in the outer lot and stood looking at the place for a few moments, marveling. It was a spectacle in and of itself, bigger and gaudier than the Mirage or Excalibur or even Caesar's, an elegant palace with pillars and fountains. There was a maze of canals in front, traversed by sleek gondolas with costumed attendants.

With a shake of her head Daisy went to the quay and allowed herself to be helped into one of the boats, along with several tourists. Sunlight flashed on the water, dazzling her, and she slipped on her sunglasses, turning her thoughts from the conspicuous consumption that surrounded her to the magician.

Her first reaction, when she'd learned of Valerian's connection with the dead woman, had been to wonder if he'd had something to do with Jillie Fairfield's death. In cases like this one, the murderer often turned out to be someone the victim had known fairly well.

The gondola coursed along the narrow channels, making its way toward the hotel entrance, and Daisy propped her elbow on her blue-jeaned knee and rested her chin in her palm. If Valerian hadn't killed Jillie, and there was no reason to believe he had, he probably wouldn't have heard about her death yet.

Daisy hated being the one to break news like that. She and O'Halloran usually alternated, and when they couldn't remember whose turn it was, they flipped a coin.

Daisy murmured a curse as the gondola struck the dock in front of the hotel. It was O'Halloran's turn, damn it. She'd told a woman, just two days before, that her fifteen-year-old son had been shot in a gang fight.

Inside the hotel was a massive casino, filled with noisy slot machines, blackjack tables, and other accoutrements of gambling. The light was dim, the temperature pleasantly cool. Cigarette smoke made simple breathing a game of chance.

Daisy hurried through, toward the nearest bank of elevators. She hated casinos; they reminded her of when she was a kid. Her divorced mother, Jeanine, had been a cocktail waitress, and every once in a while she'd gotten the gambling bug. When that happened, Jeanine either left Daisy and her younger sister, Nadine, to fend for themselves, often for days at a time, or dragged them along with her. In some ways, that was worse, because Jeanine would either park them on the curb with a hamburger and a bag of french fries to share, or point out the pinball room and order them to stay there until she came back. Only later did she allow the girls to stay with their grandmother for a short time before wrenching them away again.

Snap out of it, Daisy scolded herself as she stepped into a sumptuously appointed elevator and pressed the button for the third floor. The business offices were there, along with a number of conference rooms and hospitality suites.

The receptionist looked Daisy over coolly when she asked where to find the magician. The main entrance to the theater would be locked at that hour, and there were probably big guys posted outside the stage doors.

"You a fan?" the girl asked. Her name tag read "Tiffany."

Daisy wondered how Tiffany could see, since her false eyelashes were the size of whisk brooms. In answer to the girl's question, she pulled her badge out of her handbag and showed it with the appropriate flourish. "Where do I find him?"

Tiffany tapped acrylic nails on the surface of the desk while she thought. From the looks of her, that was no small accomplishment, but a feat involving many wires and gears. "How should I know?"

Daisy braced her hands against the desk's edge and leaned in close. "Look it up," she said evenly.

The receptionist flushed, and her plump lips, no doubt pumped full of collagen, quivered. She left her desk, disappearing into a nearby office, and returned a few moments later, looking resolute.

"We're not supposed to tell," she announced.

"Do I have to get a warrant?" Daisy muttered.

Tiffany vanished again, and when she came back, she brought a man in a three-piece suit. He smiled and offered a manicured hand.

"My name is Jerry Grover," he said. "I'm the assistant manager. And you're Officer—"

"Detective Chandler," Daisy said. "Look, I don't see why this has to be a big deal, Mr. Grover. I want to talk to your headliner—" She pretended that the name had slipped her mind for a moment. "Valerian. It's police business, and it's important."

Grover smiled sleekly. He reminded Daisy a little of a lithe, vicious fish, gliding smoothly through his environment, hunting weaker prey. "If you'll just step into my office, Detective Chandler . . ."

Daisy shrugged and followed him. Jillie Fairfield had had a connection with the hotel, although she'd been employed by the magician. She might as well clue management in before somebody saw it on the news.

Tiffany gave her another haughty once-over as she passed. A look was nothing to Daisy—the names gang members, streetwalkers, and other misguided souls had called her had hardened her sensibilities a little.

"We found a body this morning," Daisy said without preamble when she and Grover were inside his office. Apparently the casino brass believed in looking after middle management—the desktop was black marble, and the view from the wall of windows at the opposite end of the room was panoramic. The carpet swallowed up the lower half of Daisy's purple Keds. "The victim was identified as Ms. Jillie Fairfield. She was one of the dancers in the magic show."

To his credit, Grover paled and sagged bonelessly into the leather chair behind his desk. He recovered quickly, though, and gestured for Daisy to take a seat. "Damn," he said. "What happened?"

Daisy settled herself in the cushy leather chair she'd just pulled up. "We're not sure," she admitted readily, but she had no intention of discussing the details. "Ms. Fairfield was a hotel employee before signing on with Valerian, wasn't she?"

A thin sheen of perspiration appeared on Grover's upper lip. "I wouldn't know that, Detective Chandler, without checking further. We employ a great many people, and as you probably realize, the Venetian hasn't been open all that long. In either case, the publicity won't be good for the Venetian, will it? Any *hint* of crime or scandal can be devastating financially. . . ."

Daisy felt the old impatience surface inside her. A woman was dead, damn it. Jillie Fairfield was never going to dance or laugh or make love again; somebody had put her out like a candle. And all Grover was worried about was the publicity.

"You didn't meet Ms. Fairfield personally, then? Ever?" she asked in a taut voice.

"No," Grover answered quickly, flushing. "And I don't know the magician, either. He's an eccentric—in fact, he gives new meaning to the word *weird.*"

Daisy leaned forward, intrigued. "In what way?"

Grover spread his hands, clearly flustered. "There are rumors, that's all. It's probably just a lot of hype, to bring people in to see his shows. . . ."

"What rumors?" Daisy pressed. There it was again, that odd quivering in the pit of her stomach; her own instincts were telling her, as they had the night before, after the show, that there was something very strange about Valerian. Something far beyond the ordinary mystique of a magician.

"Well, he won't come out in the daylight, for one thing. And for another, he refuses to be photographed—ask our publicity people if you don't believe me."

Daisy thought of the program she'd bought. The text was accompanied by drawings and paintings, but there had been no photographs.

"I believe you," she said, wondering if she should go and get Grover a glass of water or a paper bag to breathe into. He looked really upset.

Grover wrenched a wad of tissues from a box in the top drawer of his fancy desk and daubed at his face with them. "Murder," he muttered to himself. "Oh, Christ—"

Daisy took a deep breath and let it out slowly. "Is there anything else?"

"Yes," Grover burst out, after a moment of consideration. "Even the people closest to Valerian have no idea how he performs his tricks. He has never revealed even the smallest detail."

Daisy was irritated and not a little disappointed. "Of course he doesn't. He's a magician—everyone knows how carefully they guard their secrets." She stood. "If you'll just give me Valerian's home address," she said, nodding toward Grover's computer, "I'll be on my way."

"We don't have one," Grover said.

"What about a Social Security number?" Daisy pressed.

Grover spread his hands again. "Too personal. I don't have to give that out unless you can show me a warrant."

Daisy bit back a nasty remark. Grover was right. "At least get one of your security people to let me into the backstage area, then," she said. Maybe Valerian was in his dressing room meditating or practicing his levitation or something like that. Or perhaps he was onstage, rehearsing.

"All right," Grover agreed at length and with the utmost reluctance. "Come on. I'll let you in myself."

VALERIAN
Dunnett's Head, 1548

Today, I thought when I felt a shred of cold sunlight touch my face, *I am going to die.* I was in such pain, both physical and emotional, that I could not help thinking death would be a mercy.

Then Brenna stirred beside me, in the stale straw, and I remembered all that had transpired the night before, with rising horror as well as desperate love. She had come to me, washed my wounds, and finally lain with me.

We had both been virgins, and for me at least, the experience had been one of almost unbearable bliss. Before Brenna, I had known only the usual furtive satisfactions a lad discovers on his own. Now, having entered her sweet body, moved upon her supple softness in that ancient rhythm, and cried out as she rendered my seed from me, I was a man. And I was more aware than ever that life is precious, poignantly so.

"Valerian?" She raised herself, rumpled and mussed, her lovely hair filled with straw. That same skimpy light that had awakened me, infiltrating that dark hole through some chink in the dungeon wall, played over her face. "I love you. And if you die today, you must wait for me on the other side. I'll soon follow."

I felt tears fill my eyes. The pain of my wounds was nothing to that of loving her, of knowing that an irrevocable parting lay ahead. I cupped her face in my hand, and brushed the pad of my thumb over the lips I had kissed so thoroughly, so hungrily, during the night.

"No, Lady Brenna," I said hoarsely. "You must live."

She shook her head wildly, but I stilled the motion with my hand.

"Listen to me," I growled as we heard an outer door opening, far off in the distance. We both knew that the day had arrived, they were coming for me, and I would soon mount the scaffold. "You must hide, over there in the shadows, until they've taken me out. Don't move until you're certain they've all gone. Return to your chambers when you think it safe, make yourself pretty, and pretend you've never heard of the bootmaker's son—"

She was sobbing by then, incapable, I think, of responding.

"I will find a way to be with you," I vowed, and I meant it with all my youthful soul. "I will curl up in a corner of your heart, and all you'll have to do to find me is turn your thoughts inward. Please, Brenna. Give me this one gift—a living heart to hide in."

Brenna was silent, and the voices grew nearer. Finally she nodded and hid herself in a pile of straw, off in a corner of the cell.

Two of the baron's men arrived to collect me only a moment later. They were murmuring to each other in fearful tones, and I could not make out what they were saying.

Finally they reached the cell door.

"Come along, then, bootmaker's son," said Tom, the largest of the two. He'd often come to my father's shop; they'd been friends, in a manner of speaking, and Tom, like the rest of the men in the village, had enjoyed watching my mother as she went about her daily tasks. "The baron says you're to be set free. Or at least that's what his man-servant told us he said."

Brenna moved, rustling the straw slightly, but I made a surreptitious gesturing, bidding her to be silent. There would be no freedom, and no mercy, for either of us if her father learned what we had done, lying together in the straw.

I stood, painfully, for though my wounds were superficial, they burned like fire. I felt as if I'd been trampled by war horses and then set ablaze, but beneath it all was a thrumming sense of satiation. Brenna had done that with her lovemaking.

"If this is a jest," I said, "it is a cruel one."

Tom opened the cell door, never noticing, it would seem, that the lock wasn't engaged. "It's no jest," he replied. "The baron fell ill two hours ago. Black as a Moor and spewing blood, he is. And there are others, too."

I shivered, despite the wild relief I felt. "What others?"

"Your mother for one," Tom said. "You'd best go home and look after your family. Both Noah and Seraphina are both off their heads with fever, according to that brother of yours."

Alarm mingled with the ineffably sweet knowledge that I was going to live. I would find a way to be with Brenna forever—after the events of the night before, we were certainly bonded, in God's eyes as well as our own hearts—and we would both put Dunnett's Head behind us.

In the meantime, though, I had to go to my parents.

I made my way back to the shop as rapidly as I could, while the sunrise spilled a golden glow to light my way. The village was unnaturally quiet, even for such an early hour, and rife with a hideously putrid stench. There were no dogs barking in the streets, no housewives throwing pots of slop from windows and doorways, no fishermen going down to the sea.

It was eerie.

When I reached the shop, I entered by the back way, peering first into the little room Krispin and I had always shared. I had never expected to see it again, and, humble as it was, my heart lifted at the sight of my pallet, my blankets, my spare tunic and leggings.

There was no sign of my brother, so I went on to my parents' chamber. It was a squalid cell, barely larger than the one Krispin and I shared, and when I stepped over the threshold I was struck by a smell so much viler than the one pervading the village that it sent me stumbling backward a few steps.

"Mother?" I said, speaking to the shadows.

I heard a moan from within, and knew it for my father's cry, not my mother's. I squared my shoulders and forced myself to take a step inside. "Father?"

"No—" he said hoarsely. "Don't—come any closer. We—it's plague. Save yourself. Save—Krispin."

Yet again I wept. And for once in my life I obeyed Noah Lazarus, the bootmaker. "What of my mother?"

"Dead," my father answered. "For your own sake, and hers, you must not look upon her. Please. Flee this—place—"

I turned, unable to bear the stink any longer. My father could not be saved; I knew that. I would find Krispin, if I could, and Brenna, I decided, groping numbly through a welter of disjointed thoughts. We would take horses from the baron's stables and ride away to a new place—London, perhaps.

I stumbled back into the street and encountered Mistress Jane, the cooper's wife. Her face was contorted with grief. "God have mercy on us!" she cried, seeing me and, at the same time, *not* seeing me. "My Will, and my babies—all dead—"

I wanted to offer the poor woman some comfort, but there was nothing I could say that would alter the grim realities in any way. I took her shoulders gently in my hands. "Have you seen my brother?" I asked.

She looked at me without recognition. "All dead," she said again. "Little Mary, and Sam, and my Will, too. All dead, with their skin all black—"

I embraced her for a moment, on impulse, and went on.

All through the village, it was the same. Death raged in every hut and croft, and among the living there was naught but chaos. I didn't find Krispin, though I searched everywhere, and once I stopped, enthralled, to watch two rats rise onto their hind legs in the path and twirl, in a horrible and graceless pirouette, before toppling over in death. Blood spilled, thick, from their muzzles.

Finally I returned to the keep—the shock of all I'd seen instilled a new prudence in me—and I entered through a servant's gate in a rear wall. After a considerable exploration of the place, I found Brenna in her father's room, kneeling beside his bed and holding his hand.

He was blackened, like a statue burned in a fire, his flesh grotesquely swollen, as if his skin would split like a sausage. He stared sightlessly at the beams high overhead. He, like so many others, was dead, and the stench was overwhelming, causing my empty stomach to pitch and my eyes to water.

I hesitated a few moments, then took hold of Brenna's shoulders and raised her gently to her feet. "He's gone," I whispered, and she turned and burrowed into my embrace, burying her face in my tunic and weeping.

I held her until the storm had passed, and spoke to her only when her sobs had turned to soft, heartrending sniffles. "We must take ourselves from this place," I told her. "By some miracle, we've been spared, but if we linger, the plague will surely find us."

She nodded against my chest.

"We'll need horses and food and coin."

Brenna drew back and looked up into my no-doubt bruised and dirty face. "Let's go, Valerian. Now. Let's go and never look back."

I kissed her then. It was just a light, moist touch of our two mouths, but how I treasure the memory of that innocent contact. I hadn't learned, even then, how infinitely precious, and how profound, the simplest expression of affection can be.

"I'll fetch some food from the larder," Brenna said when we drew apart. "And my father won't be needing his purse." She glanced woefully back at the body lying on the bed. A light flickered in her weary eyes; perhaps it was hope for our future. "Hurry, Valerian. I'll wait for you at the servants' gate."

I nodded and hurried out.

At noon Brenna and I sat on a knoll east of the village, our horses nibbling at the sweet grass, saying our own silent goodbyes to the only home we'd ever known. We watched, dry-eyed, beyond horror, while the lucky ones carried corpses into the square and hurled them into a great, roaring fire. Later, I supposed, thinking of my mother and father, already beginning to accept the fact that my brother's body was surely there among those others as well, the charred skeletons would be properly buried. Prayers would be said, and absolutions granted, and heaven would enfold them all.

Please God.

"WHAT of Challes?" I asked, hours later, as Brenna and I rode slowly along the inland road, passing no one. It was the first time either of us had spoken since we'd watched the bodies burn. "Did you see him?"

Brenna, who wore a cloak over a plain kirtle, shook her head. "No. He is probably dead, like Father. I wonder if Moll fell sick."

I knew Moll was her lady's maid, and that she had loved the woman devoutly. Moll, I suspected, had overlooked much mischief in her time at the keep. "It won't serve us to look back," I said quietly, reaching across to squeeze her hand where it grasped her mare's reins. "We have each other."

She looked at me with wide eyes, eyes void of innocence and girlhood fancy, and haunted by inconceivable horror. "Yes."

I reached out, grasped the mare's bridle—I was riding one of her father's geldings—and stopped both horses there in the middle of the road. "I love you, Lady Brenna," I said. It was all I had to give her—a few words, a fragile assurance. We both knew how easily fate could part us—the roads were dangerous in those days, and there was no guarantee that one or both of us would not fall ill with the pestilence at any moment.

Tears pooled along Brenna's lower lashes. "And I love you," she said. "It's enough."

I nodded, and we rode on, but there were clouds gathering on the horizon, and I had a feeling of foreboding. I tried to shake it off, telling myself the events of the day just past were reason aplenty for my gloom.

I was only partially right.

That night Brenna and I slept in an abandoned crofter's cottage, with straw for a bed. We made love, as much to give each other solace and consolation as to appease any physical need, and this second time my thrusts were pleasurable for Brenna. She strained beneath me, offering herself, crying out in her delight, and finally arched like a supple bow, quivering, her eyes sightless, her fingers clawing at my bare back.

I groaned, transported, and spilled myself into her. Soon afterward we tumbled headlong into sleep. It was raining when we awakened, and Brenna seemed uneasy, distracted.

"I want to be near the sea," she said.

I didn't question her, for I knew the waves of a sheltered cove near the keep had been her playmates—she loved the water, and took solace from it. So we ate our poor breakfasts of stale bread, and washed ourselves, running naked in the rain like pagans, and finally turned back, through the gray drizzle, in the direction from which we'd come.

I have tortured myself for centuries with a single question. Would things have been different if we'd pressed on toward London Town instead?

4

W E rode hard all that day, through the gray drizzle and the chill, until we reached the sea. Brenna gave a soft gasp when first she glimpsed that steely, white-ruffled expanse, and drew up on her mare's reins, plainly struck by the harsh beauty of the scene.

The shore was narrow and littered with great stones, and the surf battered the land with such ferocity that huge and glittering scallops of spray arched high against the charcoal sky. The shiver that slipped down my spine like the tip of a dead man's finger had little to do with the cold; no, it was born of the terrible, nameless dread stirring in the darkest reaches of my being. Had I possessed the powers that were conferred upon me later, I would have taken Brenna far from that place, be she willing or unwilling, but I could do nothing then.

She spurred her mare onto a steep, treacherous path that led down to the water, and though I lunged for the reins, I was too late. There was nothing to do but follow—and shout her name.

If Brenna heard my calls over the roar of the surf, she paid no heed. Instead she quickened the mare's pace, driving the frightened beast skillfully between boulders and churning pools toward the jagged shore. My own mount balked at the top of the path and would go no farther.

I sprang from its back and ran after Brenna, stumbling and falling several times before I gained the beach.

I screamed again; I can still feel that cry, swelling sore in my throat, lodging there like the pit of some large and bitter fruit. Brenna looked back at me over one shoulder, and I saw intense joy in her face as she rode, splashing, into the thundering waves. She threw back her head and laughed, and though I could not hear the sound, I saw it, and felt its echo in the very center of my soul.

I dashed toward Brenna, meaning to grasp the mare's bridle and haul the pair of them back to safety, but my sudden motion only frightened the horse, causing it to rear and toss its head in even greater panic. Brenna fought to calm the animal, but there was no fear in milady's magnificent face, only the purest concentration. I don't believe she regretted her recklessness; she surely hadn't guessed what was about to happen. To my torment, for that moment and all of eternity, I foresaw the event with sudden and brutal clarity.

I stood sodden in the cold tide, buffeted by it, blinded eyes stinging from the salt, and I was full of horror. My very breath was battered from me, and when I finally caught sight of Brenna again, she was far beyond my reach. The horse reeled and pitched, and Brenna went hurtling from the beast's back, her slight figure disappearing beneath the relentless waves.

I scrambled toward her, only to be swept back toward the shore by the sheer elemental force of the water. I struggled through the tide once more and was nearly trampled by the terror-stricken mare as it battled its way back to solid ground. I had a glimpse of Brenna's red-gold hair in the surf, and somehow, by strength of will, I reached her and gathered her into my arms.

I wept as I carried her ashore, for I knew, even before I laid her out on the sand, well away from the grasping, murderous water, that she was gone. I knelt beside her, the stony ground biting into the flesh of my knees, and emitted a great, wailing sob that shaped itself into her name. Then I fell forward, my forehead resting against her bosom, and gave full rein to my grief. My cries were wrenching and hoarse and seemingly without end.

Night came; I did not venture far from Brenna's side, even to search for the horses, which had both bolted long before. Instead I gathered what twigs and bits of driftwood I could find and managed to make a small fire—I still believed, in my bewilderment and sorrow, that I might offer my beloved some degree of comfort and protection.

I felt the too-rapid beat of my heart and the raw rasp of my breathing, but I cared nothing for those things. My tunic and breeches clung to my flesh, soaked and icy, and that did not matter, either. Physically I was numb.

I kept my vigil throughout the frigid night, holding her small, still hand in mine, and with the dawn came the devastating realization that this was no nightmare, but the cruelest reality. My Brenna was well and truly dead, and needed burying.

I lifted her into my arms once again and started off toward the place where I had glimpsed smoke rising between the gentle green hills the day before. I did not think beyond the hope that I would find a village, with a churchyard to receive Brenna's fragile remains and a priest to say the holy words that might secure her place in heaven.

I don't know how long I staggered over that barren, windswept terrain, holding my perished angel close against my breast, and I have no memory of reaching the small cluster of huts where I came groping and flailing to my senses some days later.

By that time, according to the aged and crowlike woman who had, by her account, dragged me back from the threshold of death, Brenna had already been laid to rest. Lucky she'd been, too, my nurse proclaimed, not to die of the plague like those other poor souls. *They'd* been flung onto a blazing pyre as soon as they'd breathed their last.

As I lay on my pallet, drenched in the sweat of a recently broken fever and smelling of all manner of base things, I wished with all my being that I, too, might be taken by the pestilence. I realized even then, however, that I was condemned to live, and to my great and secret shame, I also knew I hadn't the courage to put an end to my own misery. I believed too little of my father's grim theology to follow its dictates, and too much to risk the fires and pitchforks of hell.

I turned my face to the dank, daub-and-wattle wall and mourned in silence.

After a while a holy man came to see about me. I would not look at him.

"I am Brother Timothy," he said.

I did not reply.

"You must be grateful and repentant," he persisted. "God has chosen, in His infinite mercy, to spare your life."

I spat, though my mouth was dry.

The man of God sighed and left me to my private damnation.

I might have lain in that wretched hovel forever, despising everything that was holy, waiting to perish of despair, if the crone hadn't finally grown impatient one foggy day and put a foot hard to my ribs.

"Get up, you," she commanded, having apparently passed the outermost bounds of Christian charity. "I can't abide the smell of you, and I'm that weary of spooning gruel and goat's milk into your mouth as if you was a sickly babe. Go on, take yourself out of here."

I groped to my feet with her none-too-gentle help and swayed dangerously before finally catching my balance. I staggered out of the hut with its thatched roof and hard dirt floor into the cold glare of sunlight. For a moment or two I was blinded by the dazzle and raised one arm to shield my eyes.

Mortals are damnably resilient, even when they don't choose to be. Within a moment or so I could see clearly, and my weakened frame supported itself with a shaky determination that came from some unexplored part of my mind. I looked about and saw other huts—pigs and dogs and chickens wandering in their midst—and a few gaunt humans in poor clothes. Not far from the edge of the village was a great firepit, encircled with stones, black and acrid at its center. I was drawn to the place by a horrible fascination that shamed even as it compelled me to take the next step toward it, and the next.

Blackened bones and skulls lay scattered, haphazard, through the ashes, and I recognized a single charred arm, muscles clearly defined, sooty fingers curled. I wretched convulsively and reeled away from that grim sight and the other helter-skelter leavings of death. I could be grateful, at least, that Brenna's mortal remains had not been cast into the pit. That none of those hideous pieces and parts were hers.

I nearly collided with the small, rotund monk who stood behind me.

"What is your name, lad?" he asked, and I was struck, even in my welter of confusion and agony, by the serenity in his expression. I knew this was Brother Timothy, the holy man who had visited me in the witch's hut.

He wore robes of undyed wool, a narrow, frayed rope girding his middle, and his tonsured head was fringed with brown hair. The flesh of his face was tight, but the eyes were old, and I could not begin to guess his age; he might have been seventeen or seventy.

"Valerian," I answered hoarsely. I did not speak of my dead father, nor did I offer the name of my village. I had no home now, after all, and no kinsmen. For me, there was only one question, one concern, in all creation.

"Where did they bury milady?"

Brother Timothy gestured toward a copse of naked birches on top of a small knoll nearby. The branches of those trees looked like white cracks in the smooth, chilly blue surface of the sky. "There," he said. "On the hill."

I moved past him, awkward in my weakness, near collapse, but desperate to look upon Brenna's grave.

"We did not know her name," the monk hastened to inform me. "But there is a cross to mark her resting place. Was she your sister? Your wife, perhaps?"

At his words, the loss of Brenna cut through me anew, fresh and sharp, seeming to sever not just muscle and marrow, but other, less tangible parts of me as well. I locked my knees to keep them from buckling and forced myself to keep moving. "I have no sister," I said. "And the word *wife* is too feeble to contain all that Brenna was to me. If I could have died in her place, I would have done it."

"Such decisions are not ours to make," Brother Timothy replied. "Perhaps that is a blessing in itself. Nor is such a desire unselfish, for its root is merely the cowardly wish to escape your own pain."

A surge of contempt swelled within me and, somewhere deeper, where I was wont to look, shame. "Pray, do not speak to me of blessings," I said without meeting his eyes. "There is no mercy in your God, and I seek no favors of Him."

How glibly I uttered sacrilege in those days of innocence and sorrow, and how very little I knew of damnation and devils, gods and angels! I was yet a lad, after all, with a child's blithe certainty of a multitude of things.

Brother Timothy laid a hand on my shoulder, and though he was smaller in stature, his grasp was forceful enough to stop my progress. "Your grief makes you bitter and angry," he said with a tenderness that made me yearn to sink, weeping, to my knees. "Those feelings will pass one day. The wounds will heal. In the meantime, though, you must turn your heart toward heaven, where comfort and absolution lie."

I shrugged free of his grasp and went on, propelled by stubbornness, not strength. I ached with frailty and fatigue. "No more talk of heaven," I growled, blinking back the stinging moisture in my eyes. "No more."

I knew which plot was Brenna's, even before Brother Timothy pointed it out.

My beloved rested beneath a gentle mound of newly turned earth, with a crude wooden cross to mark her passing. It was a peaceful place, though the sea churned in the near distance, like some tempestuous gift seeking to ungive itself. Light would dance among the shimmering leaves of the birch trees, come summer, and in other seasons the wind and the rain and the sea would sing their varied choruses.

I pressed my palms into the raw dirt and dug my fingers in deep, as if to find her, drag her upward, resurrect her somehow. "Brenna," I whispered. What I wouldn't have given, facing the finality of her death yet again in the moments that followed, to be as she was, unaware, empty of emotion, immune to suffering. Hidden from the gazes of man and God.

I trembled, light-headed from my exertions, and might have pitched forward to lie sprawled across the grave if Brother Timothy hadn't grasped my shoulders and raised me to my feet.

"Come away," he said quietly. "You can do no good here."

I had risen from my sickbed not even an hour before, and I had no power to resist. I allowed that tenacious and good man to support me as we moved away from the village, descending the opposite side of the hill.

Below lay an ancient structure, surely a monastery, with low stone walls and a single crumbling tower. From that height I saw garden plots, a well, a narrow courtyard without fountain or bench. I stumbled, and Brother Timothy tightened his grasp, and once again kept me from falling.

The interlude that followed lies strewn through my memory like dried bones, disjointed and strange. I was taken to a cell, furnished only with a cot and a crucifix, and able hands stripped away my ruined garments. I was bathed in warm water, garbed in a clean, if coarsely woven, robe, given stout wine and broth by spoonfuls.

I slept, wandering in the dark mists of my dreams, searching tirelessly and in vain for Brenna.

WHEN at last I returned to full awareness, body and mind rallying to a semblance of their former vitality, I discovered myself to be a dry, hollow husk of a man. My grief had vanished, but so had my conscience, my better graces, and, indeed, my soul.

I was empty.

"Stay with us, your brothers," Timothy pleaded when, after days of gradual, painstaking recovery, I was well enough to rise from my cot and move about the monastery and the grounds. We were in the courtyard that afternoon and the weather was bright and crisply cold. "Surely it was a sign, our finding you—"

"I am grateful for all you've done," I said, though in fact I felt nothing—not gratitude, not hatred, not grief or joy. What followed, however, was purest truth. "I am not suited to this life, Timothy. I was born a sinner and I shall remain one for all time."

Would that I could have known how prophetic those rashly spoken words really were. But then, I do not believe anything short of Brenna's return from the dead would have changed my course.

Timothy looked pained; tears filled his kindly eyes, and he spread his hands in a gesture of pleading. "Valerian—"

I was unmoved by the monk's sorrow and held up a hand to silence him. In the next moment I looked ruefully down at my borrowed robe. "Have you no breeches in this dreary place? No tunics or belts or boots?"

He drew an audible breath. "We keep a store of such garments, yes," he admitted slowly. "Each of us arrived here as an ordinary man, after all. Our possessions are part of our sacrifice, and as a rule they are either sold for the benefit of the order or given to the poor."

"No one," I said, laying my hands on my chest and looking at Timothy with gentle impudence, "is poorer than I am."

Timothy nodded sadly and left my cell, returning minutes later with a stack of colorless, somewhat ragged garments, neatly laundered and folded. He said nothing as he held them out to me, and I confess that I snatched them from his hands.

I was eager to be gone from that place and those people.

I left the following day, wearing the ill-fitting tatters Timothy had brought to my cell. I also had two coins, of very modest value, that he had provided.

Thus began seventeen years of searching, not for Brenna now, but for that vanished part of myself that had enabled me to love, to laugh, to weep, to mourn.

All hope of that soon perished, and I sought only to meet a merciful death. I was, like the Prodigal, a libertine, a liar, a heretic, and a thief. I wandered, and I committed every sin I could think of without compunction, and a few that were suggested to me. I consumed what wine I could beg or steal, and awakened in pigsties and gaols and the beds of strangers. I cared for nothing and for no one, least of all myself.

Then one momentous gloomy night, when I was four and thirty, and the most devout of derelicts, my old tutor, Challes, quite literally stumbled across me where I lay sprawled, stuporous with drink, upon the filthy floor of a stable.

It was soon after that the dark miracle occurred, and I was forever changed.

DAISY
Las Vegas, 1995

Daisy was not the whimsical type, but it seemed to her that a faint echo of magic lingered in the silence of that empty auditorium. When Jerry Grover flipped on some of the interior lights, the multicolored tinsel curtain threw off a blinding dazzle, and Daisy winced.

Grover smiled, obviously pleased by her discomfort. "You won't find Valerian here," he said with a combination of indulgence and condescension in his tone. "As I told you, he never appears during the daylight hours." He paused to smirk, then added, "Perhaps he's a vampire."

Daisy thought of Jillie Fairfield and her bloodless body and felt a quiver of fear. She quickly squelched it. "No doubt," she answered dryly, widening her eyes, "he's tucked up in a coffin somewhere, fast asleep."

Grover sighed. "Where Valerian is concerned," he said, "nothing would surprise me." He paused to consult his watch, a sporty Rolex, and Daisy didn't miss the point of the gesture.

She folded her arms. "I won't keep you—I can find the dressing rooms on my own," she told him. "In the meantime, I suggest you take another look at your computer files. For a start, I'd like to know where you send this guy's paychecks."

Color seeped up Grover's tanned neck, and he spoke with exaggerated slowness, as though addressing an idiot. "That's easy, Officer Chandler. Like most performers, Valerian has an agent. There are contracts."

"That's *Detective* Chandler," Daisy said, undaunted. "What's this agent's name?"

A pulse pounded in Grover's temple. "I haven't the vaguest idea."

"Then I'd suggest you find out," she answered, turning to start down the nearest aisle. "I'll stop by your office for the information before I leave."

Grover spared her a slight nod, whirled on the heel of one Italian loafer, and strode away.

Daisy lingered for a moment, recalling the events of the night before. She'd never seen a trick that even remotely rivaled the carriage bit, and the mystery of it both intrigued and frustrated her. And there was something else, she admitted to herself, walking toward the door at the right of the stage.

Valerian had touched her, not with his hands, but with his mind. She'd been downright mesmerized by him, and the realization was profoundly irritating. If for no other reason, she wanted to face the magician again and prove to herself, as well as to him, that he had no power over her.

Very little light reached backstage, and the ornate carriage Valerian used in his act loomed in the shadows, ghostly and somehow ominous.

"Hello?" Daisy called out. "Anybody here?"

No answer.

She left the wings and proceeded into the area behind the stage. She immediately encountered a ponytailed young man in jeans and a T-shirt, pushing a rack of costumes along the hallway.

"Hi," she said, pulling her badge from her purse and offering a glimpse before stowing it again.

"Hi," he replied, looking uncertain and slightly flustered. "Can I help you?"

"I hope so," Daisy replied, smiling in an effort to put him at ease. "What's your name?"

He flushed, perhaps with relief. "Joe Fitch. Is—is something wrong?"

Joe hadn't heard about Jillie Fairfield's murder, then. Daisy wished she didn't have to be the one to break the news.

Joe went pale as he took in Daisy's words. "Oh, my God," he whispered when she'd finished, clasping the clothes rack with both hands to steady himself.

Daisy put a hand on his arm. "Would you like to sit down?" she asked.

"I'm okay, really," Joe said, but he fell into a folding chair next to the wall all the same. "Oh, God," he murmured again. "Oh, God—I don't believe it."

Dragging up another chair, Daisy sat down facing Joe. Between the two of them and the clothes rack, they blocked the hallway. "Did you know Ms. Fairfield well?" Daisy asked.

To Daisy's disappointment, Joe shook his head. He looked sick, and he was trembling. "Not really. Neither of us have been here very long. You know how Vegas is—people move around."

Daisy nodded. There was a watercooler a few feet away, with a stack of paper cups on top. She rose to fill one and bring it to Joe. "How about Valerian? What's he like?"

Joe took the cup in both hands and drained it before answering. "He keeps to himself."

"How about the other women in the show? Were any of them friendly with Ms. Fairfield?"

"I think I'm going to puke," Joe confided. Then he bolted, over-turning his chair with a metallic clatter, one hand clasped over his mouth.

Daisy followed him to the door of the men's rest room and waited, leaning against the wall until he came out. His skin, starkly white before, had turned to a greenish shade of gray.

She let her folded arms fall back to her sides and straightened, then reached into her purse for a dog-eared business card. "Here," she said. "Give me a call if something comes to you."

Joe took the card and stared at it like a foreigner trying to read a strange language. "Okay," he agreed. Then he turned and fled back into the men's room.

Daisy heard him retching as she turned away. It was a good thing Joe had gotten the bad news secondhand, she reflected. If he'd actually seen the body, he would have hocked up his socks.

She rapped at Valerian's dressing room door and, when there was no answer, tried the knob. To her surprise, the lock wasn't engaged. She stepped over the threshold and turned on the lights, frowning.

What did you expect, Chandler? she chided herself. *An open casket? Maybe some cobwebs and a pair of six-foot candelabras?*

"Vampires, indeed," she scoffed aloud, recalling Grover's smart-ass remark and what O'Halloran had said that morning at the crime scene. She backed into the hallway, even though she didn't believe in monsters, and her pace was a little faster than usual as she made her way toward a rear exit.

VALERIAN
Las Vegas, 1995

I awakened promptly at sunset, as usual, after a troubled sleep. I'd been tormented by dreams of Brenna—now called Daisy Chandler—throughout the daylight hours, and the terrible images followed me into full consciousness.

I sat up and took in my immediate surroundings, and I was oddly surprised to find myself in my desert lair, even though I distinctly remembered retreating to it just before dawn.

My subterranean palace had been built by a paranoid billionaire with a bizzare imagination and a taste for luxury. I had always found it ironic that the survivalist had not survived, but had succumbed to some relatively minor ailment. I had purchased the place from his widow, who evidenced no desire to live in a rabbit's burrow, however splendid.

The soft strains of Mozart poured into the master suite as I rose from my silk-covered bed. My beloved had returned to me, and I could not help rejoicing in the knowledge, but I felt terror, too. Through the centuries since Brenna's drowning in the treacherous waters off the coast of Cornwall, we had found each other no fewer than five times.

On each occasion, in each new incarnation, Brenna had succeeded in winning my heart, no matter how I resisted. Oh, and I *did* resist, with all the might I possessed, for there was a curse upon milady and me, and it followed us mercilessly, relentlessly, down through the years.

Always, in every lifetime, Brenna's soul remembered our bond, but consciously I was always a stranger to her, a wayfarer who could only come to her in the night. I invariably fell in love with her all over again, and more deeply then ever before, and she returned my affections—for the most part. What bliss it was to hold her, to look upon her face, and what hell to know that she would soon be gone.

It mattered not what efforts I made to protect my darling; my powers were useless against this hex, whatever it was. We were doomed, Brenna and I, to relive the torment of parting, over and over. I could only conclude that it was divine punishment, meted out to me because I had accepted Challes's evil gift all those years before, and used it to the fullest, without the slightest hesitation.

But what sin had Brenna committed, to deserve such a fate? The question angered me, as it had always done.

I went into my glittering bathroom and groomed myself, then selected a starched shirt and a perfectly tailored suit from my wardrobe. A smile, faint and fleeting, touched my mouth. It puzzled the mortals of my acquaintance that I never suffered from the desert heat, no matter how formally I dressed, and I enjoyed their consternation.

Usually.

I affixed my cufflinks and wandered into the vast living room, where the stereo system spilled soft, vibrant notes of music into the air. I silenced the machine with a sort of mental nod and by the same means caused another contraption, an enormous television screen, to fold down from its hiding place in the ceiling.

The set flared with light, and a scene took shape. The images I saw were not being broadcast by any station or network, however. I knew well enough that they sprang from the secret realms of my own mind.

I saw a corpse lying on a matted carpet. The body was that of a woman, and I knew what had killed her even before I focused on the tiny puncture marks on her throat, knew there wasn't a drop of blood left in her veins.

Jillie Fairfield. One of the delectable young creatures who had added so much to my act.

Suddenly weak, I sat down in a soft chair and stared at the horrific vision. This was no ordinary murder, no crime of vengeance or passion. It had been committed by one of my own kind—a vampire. And because of Jillie's connection with me, I could be certain the gesture had been meant as a challenge.

I closed my eyes and willed myself to the scene, materializing in Jillie's small apartment only moments later. The place was dark, a fact that was of no consequence whatever to me, and the body, of course, had been removed.

The corpse had been emptied of blood, but there were traces of that precious stuff everywhere, glittering in the gloom like tiny points of blue light. The scent of it, stale now, and wasted, filled my nostrils.

"Who are you?" I demanded aloud. "Show yourself!"

There was no sound besides the ordinary doings of nearby mortals, which came to me through the walls and the floor as a low murmuring. And yet there was something beneath it, a deeper silence, and not an empty one.

I tried to go back to the moment of the murder—vampires travel through time as easily as men and women pass from one room to another—but my way was blocked. I heard poor little Jillie's muted scream, I felt her terror and then the unholy ecstasy that is a hallmark of a blood-drinker's fatal kiss, but I could not see her killer, and I was unable to help her.

I was swamped by despair, then fury.

The woman's death was the work of another nightwalker, a powerful fiend. But who was this monster? I knew of many other vampires, of course, but of all those, only Maeve was stronger than I. She was a regal creature and did not feed on harmless chorus girls—her prey fell into two distinct categories: those who took pleasure in evil, and those who were already on the brink of death.

Lisette, the former queen, would have done just such a murder, sparing no thought for the victim's youth and relative innocence, but she had been destroyed long ago. Dingdong, the witch was dead—but something else, something equally pitiless, was very much alive.

5

VALERIAN
England, 1365

FORCEFUL hands gripped the front of my tunic, and I was wrenched, half insensible, out of the stinking straw where I'd collapsed earlier, onto my feet. I recognized Challes, my former tutor, in spite of my wine-sodden state.

"By the gods, it *is* you!" he rasped. "What in the name of heaven—?"

I swayed, and he steadied me. I felt a rush of drunken sentimentality, followed by an emotion I had not acknowledged in a long while—hot, searing humiliation. I had liked my teacher and sought his approval, and I found that I wanted it still. My normally quick tongue failed me, and I could say nothing at all.

Challes cursed and released me with such force that I struck the stable wall behind me. The shock cleared my head a little.

"You were the brightest pupil I've ever had," he said furiously, waving with both hands, so that somehow the gesture took in both my disheveled person and my disordered soul. "Now look at you—dissolute, filthy, wasted! Why have you allowed yourself to fall into this shameful state?"

I swallowed, clinging to the last rotted shreds of my pride. "I want nothing but to die," I said in an undertone that was both truthful and defiant.

He stunned me again by slapping me hard across the face. "Weakling!" he whispered vehemently, and when I tried to sidestep him, he grasped my shoulders and thrust me back against the wall once more. "Every day and every night brave men and women beg whatever gods are listening to let them live. And you, you sniveling, pettish little whelp, dare to *throw away* your powers and your gifts like so much rubbish! Well, I won't have it, do you hear me? By God, *I will not allow you destroy to yourself!*"

Tears burned in my eyes, shaming me anew, and I looked away in a vain effort to hide them. "It is too late," I said in a bare whisper. "Too late."

For a moment I thought Challes would strike me again. Instead he tightened his grasp on my shoulders just briefly, then spoke in a gentle, broken voice. "When was the last time you had a decent meal or a real bed to sleep in?"

I had been stealing food, sleeping in ditches and horse stalls, and begging coin for wine for so long that I could barely recall any other life. My childhood in the village of Dunnett's Head seemed unreal, and my brief happiness with Brenna was naught but a pretty tale.

I spread my filthy hands. "When I was with the brothers, I suppose. They took me in after milady died." I didn't remember the old woman and her rough ministrations until much later, and therefore failed to mention her in my hazy account of those wretched days.

"And you've wandered ever since, like some savage lost from his tribe?"

The answer came hoarse from my throat. "Yes." Only then did I notice that Challes was finely dressed—much *too* finely for a poor tutor. His tailored garments and exquisite opera cape would have been more suited to a London theater or a gentleman's club; to say he looked out of place in the stable of a disreputable country inn would constitute an understatement of gross proportions. Odder still, he had not aged in the years since I had seen him last; there was a subtle vitality about him, and yes, he'd acquired an attractive air of quiet menace that made me think of wolves prowling stark and snowy downs.

Challes laid a hand to my shoulder. "Come," he said. "I have a splendid gift to offer you, my misguided friend, but first you must be made ready to receive it."

The strangeness of the remark did not penetrate the dense muddle drunkenness had made of my mind. I believed he was offering food and shelter, perhaps wine, too, and I wanted all of those things. Especially, I am ashamed to admit, the latter.

Challes led me to a carriage, waiting axle-deep in mud on the road. The moon rose around it like a huge and silvery halo, and I felt a shiver at the sight, one more akin to excitement than to fear. A footman opened the door for us, and I sensed the look that passed between him and my tutor rather than saw it.

"How did you know where to find me?" I asked, once settled in the sumptuous leather seat across from Challes.

He sighed. "I will explain that at a later time. For now, it is enough to see that you are fed, scrubbed clean, and rested."

I was already beginning to feel thirsty, and hoped the impressive improvement of Challes's circumstances meant he kept a good stock of wine. Even though I was not particularly alert at that point, I know I didn't give voice to the thought, for I'd guessed that it would not be well received.

Challes heard it all the same, for he responded as if I'd spoken aloud. "Foolish knave. You will crave another nectar soon, but the questionable pleasure of drunkenness is behind you."

I folded my arms, still too fuddled to sort out the fact that Challes had just read my mind. What *was* clear to me was the absolute conviction that I could not bear a lifetime without wine. Such a sacrifice would lay bare my every nerve, physical and spiritual, to agonies beyond my ability to endure.

"Nonsense," Challes said, though again I had not spoken. "You are not about to die, Valerian. You are on the verge of a glorious rebirth."

I frowned. "You sound like my father now, God rest his soul. If it's religion you're peddling, I'll go back to the stable. And how did you do that?"

"I assume you're asking how I interpreted your thoughts. Alas, the divination of mortal minds is the least of my powers. Hardly a challenge at all."

If I'd been sober, I believe I would have been insulted. I started to ask Challes what he was talking about, but he extended an imperious hand in a demand for silence, and I obeyed. My dedicated debauchery had reduced me to less than nothing: I had all the dignity and self-possession of a slat-ribbed hound snuffling through garbage.

"I live near here," Challes told me after a brief silence, during which he gazed pensively through the carriage window, his oddly beautiful face drenched in moonlight. "Our journey will not be a long one."

I studied him, struck by the differences he evidenced and yet unable to define them. "What's happened?" I said. "You've changed."

For the first time my tutor smiled. "So have you," he answered. "Do not trouble me with questions tonight, Valerian. It is enough for now that I have found you."

We traveled the rest of the way without speaking. I closed my eyes and pretended to sleep, and although I was still thoroughly inebriated, I was well aware of Challes's gaze upon me. I knew, somehow, that his regard was pensive, and that there was a certain strange hunger in it.

His home was grand, for that desolate part of England, a small, square keep, made of gray stone and lighted from within. Surely there would be wine in such a place.

I had recovered some of my spirit, so buoyed was I by the mere prospect of a bath and the knowledge that I would not be required to share my bed with vermin. I glanced warily at Challes as a new and disturbing possibility struck me.

My tutor was just alighting from the carriage, tugging at one immaculate white glove as he did so. "Pray do not pursue that ridiculous and insulting thought any further," he said dryly. "I have no designs on your virtue—such as it may be. In point of fact, I shall ask nothing of you behind the joy of seeing you find and exercise your own magnificent powers."

That was all Challes would say, and I had neither the energy nor the will to press him for more. I simply followed him up to the arched wooden door, which was promptly opened for us by a servant bearing a flickering tallow.

He nodded deferentially to Challes, but gave me an oblique look as he stepped back to admit us.

My wits were not about me, so to speak, but I did take note that the place was very clean, and not in the least gloomy. Indeed, moonlight streamed through the high windows in one wall, illuminating the foyer with a glow that was no less beautiful for being eerie.

It seemed that I had been expected. A spacious chamber awaited me abovestairs; there was a cozy blaze snapping on the hearth, and a table had been laid for a meal. A large metal tub steamed in the firelight, and the counterpane on the featherbed had been turned back to reveal linen sheets of the purest white.

I went to the table and checked its contents. There was bread, cold meat, boiled turnips, and even fruit, but alas, no wine.

I sighed.

Challes laughed. "Reprobate," he said, tossing me a bar of hard soap. "You'll find nothing there to fog and foul that splendid mind of yours. I've told you—*no more wine.*"

Not troubling to answer, I raised the soap to my nose; the scent reminded me of my beautiful mother, Seraphina, and for a moment I missed her keenly. I turned from Challes, seeking to disguise my emotions—I had not yet learned that I could hide nothing from him.

"I shall not stay long, then," I answered.

"We'll see," Challes replied. And then he left me.

I bolted the door—in my sorry travels I had learned that what seems like good fortune is often a trap instead—and then stripped off my pitiful clothes and stepped into the tub. I gave a low groan of pleasure as the warm, clean water lapped against my flesh.

I soaked for a long time, then scrubbed my shaggy, red-brown hair and every dirty inch of my hide. When I was clean at last, I rose and stood naked on the hearth, letting the heat of the crackling fire dry the little glittering beads of water that trembled like jewels upon my skin.

A nightshirt of some fine, shimmering fabric—I know now that it was rare and priceless silk—lay spread upon the bed. After I had enjoyed the fire for a time, I pulled the garment over my head and took myself to the table. I ate with remarkable appetite, given the shrunken state of my oft-abused stomach, and no semblance of grace. When I'd finished, I was dizzy with fatigue.

Sated, and able to tolerate my own company for the first time in recent memory, I fell into the lush depths of the bed and gave myself up to sleep. My rest was absolute; I kept no vigil and dreamed no dreams.

It makes me smile to remember that I felt safe.

DAISY
Las Vegas, 1995

Daisy was waiting in Valerian's dressing room when that night's performance ended to thunderous applause and shouts of approbation, and he did not seem at all taken aback to find her there.

So much, she reflected, for the element of surprise.

The magician was a spectacular specimen, not only onstage, but up close as well. Something fast-moving and intangible came to a lurching stop, deep in Daisy's middle, when he looked at her.

She reminded herself that show-business types didn't impress her, and he smiled slightly, as though he'd heard the thought.

But that was impossible, of course.

Daisy's face felt warm. "I'm Detective Chandler," she said.

"I remember," Valerian replied smoothly. He was wearing a majestic black silk cape, lined in red, and he loosened the ties and slipped the garment off, laying it almost tenderly over the back of a chair. There was something intimate and sensual in the way he performed that simple task, and Daisy had taken a hot, dark pleasure in watching him.

"I'd like to talk to you about Jillie Fairfield's murder."

She saw a flicker of grief in the aristocratic face. There was something so regal about the man, she thought, something old-fashioned and almost courtly.

Valerian took his sweet time replying. "What do you want to know?" he finally asked in an abstracted tone, his gaze fixed just above her head as he unfastened his cuff links.

"Several things. Starting with this—did you kill her?"

He met her gaze then, and both pain and annoyance moved in his eyes. "No," he said, and the chill in his voice went straight to the marrow of Daisy's bones, like a wintry wind. "Of course not."

Daisy was unnerved, even disturbed by this guy, though she could not have said why. Even if he had done the murder—and practiced instincts told her he was innocent—she had no reason to be afraid of him. She was a good cop, and she'd learned to take care of herself a long time before.

"Do you know who did?"

Valerian raised one eyebrow and flung his gold and onyx cuff links onto the vanity table, where they landed with a clatter. The wall above, where there should have been a lighted mirror, was empty. "No," he bit out. "It's your responsibility to determine that, isn't it?"

Daisy was stung, and it made her damn mad to catch herself feeling that way. She couldn't afford that kind of vulnerability. "I'm trying to do my job, Mr. Valerian," she seethed. "Unfortunately, that usually involves a lot of spade work."

"Just Valerian," he said, and the very calmness with which he spoke made Daisy feel like a raving hysteric. "Sit down, please," he went on, gesturing toward a velvet-upholstered antique chair, which Daisy promptly took. He drew up a high stool and perched on the seat, arms folded, looking art-deco elegant in his tails, tuxedo pants, and white pleated shirt. "I didn't know much about Jillie," he confided. "We worked together, but that was the extent of our association. I am not a social animal, you see. The other women in the act might be able to tell you something more, however."

Mentally Daisy awarded Valerian a point for referring to the dancers as women and not girls. And it struck her that, although he'd been working under hot lights for a couple of hours, wearing a full suit of clothes and a cloak, he had not broken a sweat. Odd, indeed, she thought.

"I've talked to some of them already. They're pretty upset, though I've got to say they performed well tonight."

Valerian loosened the collar of his shirt, which had probably cost more than the new engine O'Halloran had just put into his car. "I'll pass along the compliment," he assured her. There wasn't a trace of sarcasm in his tone, and yet Daisy knew he was needling her.

Or was she just being oversensitive?

"Where can I get in touch with you during the day, just in case I need to question you again?"

There was a wry twist to his mouth, and a weariness in the set of his broad shoulders that seemed ancient as well as profound. He produced a card, by some sleight of hand, and held it out to Daisy.

"Call my answering service," he said. "I usually spend the daylight hours perfecting my magic, but if you leave a message, I'll be in touch."

Daisy had no reason to linger, and yet she longed to stay. A fragment of a dream she'd had stirred somewhere in her brain, and she heard the terrifying clang of swords clashing in battle. She eased toward the door.

"Well, thank you," she said. "And good night. It was a terrific show."

Valerian bowed. "Sleep well, Miss Chandler."

Daisy went home to her apartment in a complex at the edge of town, heated a frozen entrée, and curled up to watch a news channel. The state of world affairs left her thoroughly depressed, as usual, and she went to the kitchenette and tossed the rest of her dinner into the trash, box and all.

"Maybe I should get out of this business," she said aloud. She was talking to herself more and more these days, but she figured it would be okay as long as O'Halloran didn't find out. He was a good guy and a first-class cop, but he saw it as his mission in life to give her a hard time. That, according to him, was what partners were for.

Daisy kicked off her sneakers as she crossed the gray carpeted floor of her living room, checked her answering machine, and saw that there was one message. She reached for the Play button and then drew back when a vague sense of menace brushed the back of her heart.

She was being silly, she chided herself. The message was probably from her sister, Nadine, who lived in Telluride and was expecting her first baby. Or maybe O'Halloran had called to ask about her interview with the Great Valerian. . . .

Daisy touched the button, and one ominous word swelled from the machine like an evil genie from a lamp.

"Soon," the voice said, and Daisy could not tell whether the caller was a man or a woman.

"What the hell?" she demanded, stabbing the button again.

That time the tape dragged, making the warning, if indeed it *was* a warning and not a prank, that much spookier.

"Damn," Daisy whispered, more irritated then afraid. Was this somebody's idea of a joke—O'Halloran's, for instance? Even as she framed the thought, she knew her partner wouldn't try to scare her. His sense of humor ran toward whoopee cushions, plastic vomit, and hand-buzzers, bless his tacky and totally uninspired heart, but he wasn't cruel.

While Daisy was still standing there, gnawing at her lower lip and wondering whether to worry about this development or have a light beer and go to bed, the telephone rang. It was an ordinary sound, but she almost jumped out of her sneakers, and her hand trembled when she reached for the receiver.

"Hello!" she barked.

"Soon," said that same genderless, robotlike voice she'd heard on the tape only moments before. "Soon you—will—die—again. And again—and—"

"Who is this?" Daisy demanded, furious.

"—again and—"

Daisy slammed down the receiver and shoved a hand through her hair. "Take a breath, Chandler," she told herself in a whisper. "It's just some smart-ass kid, or one of the guys at the station—"

She closed her eyes for a moment, deliberately making her mind a blank, until she was calmer. She started to dial O'Halloran's home number, then stopped in the middle of the process. She had worked damn hard and taken a lot of scary risks to get where she was. She didn't want her partner, or anybody else on the force, to think she couldn't take care of herself.

Daisy went back to the front door and made sure the deadbolt was turned and the chain in place. Then she checked the windows and, on a roll, peeked behind the shower curtain and under the bed.

Finally she washed off her makeup, brushed her teeth and hair, and went to bed. The telephone on her nightstand rang once, but by the time she'd groped for the receiver and put it to her ear, the line was dead.

"Damn," she said again. Then she turned over onto her side, yawned twice, wondered whether or not Nadine suffered from morning sickness, considered getting a big dog, and dozed off.

The dream was remarkably real.

She was wearing strange, simple clothes—medieval, perhaps—and riding a horse. She could hear the roar of the sea and taste its salt in the mist, and suddenly she felt a surge of wild, ebullient daring. With a laugh, she spurred her mount toward the water.

Someone shouted at her to come back, but she had suffered much in recent times, and she had grown up beside the sea, playing chase with the tide. Now the vast ocean seemed to beckon. It was a siren's call, one she could not resist.

She rode down a steep path, wending her way between giant stones, urging the little horse onward when she knew it wanted to bolt.

Another cry found its way over the roar of the waves and made her turn, laughing with delight, to look toward shore. She saw him then, her companion. In that strange way of dreams, she recognized him as the magician, Valerian. And yet he was much younger, hardly more than a boy, and his clothes were ill-fitting and strange.

His face was a mask of terror as he lunged down the rocky path and raced toward the water.

Poor silly darling, she thought indulgently. He's afraid for me. I must tell him that I've ridden into the sea many times before without harm.

She smiled, tossing her head, and raised one hand to wave him back. He was no swimmer, after all, and the sea was more fractious than usual that day.

He shouted to her again, foundering through the surf, and she lost control of the horse. The animal shrieked and reared, and she was flung off, striking her shoulder hard against a rock.

Pain thundered through her. She tried to scream, and water filled her mouth, drove her under, held her there, flailing. The weight of her gown and kirtle pulled her deeper into the smothering darkness, and then a current caught her up and twirled her around.

There was another blow, this time to the head, and then she saw nothing, felt nothing, knew nothing—except for the name she'd been screaming before she died.

Valerian.

VALERIAN
England, 1365

When I awakened that first morning, to find myself in the place I would later know as Colefield Hall, I am ashamed to say that my first conscious sensation was a craving for wine. My mouth was as dry as straw, my stomach felt as though it had withered within me, and every bone and sinew ached in merry time with the slow thud of my heart.

I rose from my bed, relieved myself in the chamber pot provided, and unbolted the door to peer into the hallway. The taciturn serving man was almost to the threshold, his arms laden with folded garments of exquisite quality. Raised in the home of a poor bootmaker and residing, until very recently, in horse stalls, abandoned dovecotes, and pigsties, I had never dared to dream of such things.

"Good morning, sir," said the quiet fellow. "Milord instructed me to provide you with whatever you required." He actually smiled, taking in my nightshirt. "I see I was correct in assuming that proper garb would make a good beginning."

I was delighted and forgot for a moment my deep-seated yearning for the fruit of the vine. I reached out for the garments with a nod of gratitude, barely able to keep myself from donning them right there in the doorway.

"Where is Challes?" I asked, turning away. "I must thank him personally for his generosity."

"I am afraid His Lordship is engaged this morning. He'll be quite busy for the remainder of the day, as it happens. In the meantime, I will look after you—my name, by the way, is Abelard."

I might have been curious about Challes's "engagement" at any other time, but I was still sick and half starved, and those splendidly embroidered tunics and closely woven hose held me rapt. Oh, I was a greedy creature, even then.

Abelard went away, and I put on dark blue hose and a multicolored tunic. When I stepped into the hallway again, intending to explore—and, yes, I confess it, to find Challes's store of wines and spirits—a pair of soft leather boots waited by the door. I snatched them up with joy and paused to pull them onto my feet before proceeding downstairs.

The great house had a curiously expectant air, it seemed to me; as though the very walls and floors and rafters in the ceiling were awaiting some momentous event. I found the kitchen and purloined the leg of a roasted fowl of some sort before continuing to acquaint myself with my tutor's domain.

He owned many manuscripts and even a few bound books—envy flared inside me when I saw those tomes—row upon row of them, brimming with secrets and with magic. I touched their spines reverently, but even I did not dare to take even one down from the shelf to examine it. Those volumes were holy to me in a way crosses and relics and statues had never been, and one does not touch sacred things thoughtlessly.

Besides, my fingers were greasy from the food I'd consumed.

I left the books, albeit reluctantly, and went in search of the wine. Abelard appeared to be occupied elsewhere and did not bother me for the whole of the morning.

The cellar was empty, except for a heavy iron door that would not open when I pulled on the latch. I tried several times and even kicked it once—for I had a more than ordinary dislike for things that thwarted me—but to no avail.

After that small defeat, I searched the pantries, the storerooms, and even the stables and the carriage house. I found nothing except my friend's tidy possessions, all neatly tucked away in their proper places.

Abelard produced a venison stew for the midday meal—he was, it appeared, the only other occupant of the house besides Challes and myself—and sat on the other side of the trestle table talking with me while I ate.

"Has Mr. Challes—his lordship—always lived here?" I asked. It had occurred to me, as my throbbing head cleared, that the gentleman might have deceived us all—Brenna; the baron, her late father; my brother, Krispin—every one of us. Perhaps he had never been a poverty-stricken tutor at all, but a dilettante, merely amusing himself among the poor. Experimenting, perhaps, to find out if country folk were as stupid as mules or if they could learn to reason and work sums.

"He came into an inheritance quite recently," Abelard replied, obviously uncomfortable with the line of questioning. "We have been in residence for perhaps five years."

My mind, ever fitful, had returned to thoughts of Krispin. I did not often let myself remember my brother, for when I did I always imagined how the plague would have changed him. Had his skin turned to a dark, bruised color before he died? Had he risen from his pallet and spun about in a hideous death dance as I had heard of others doing?

I pushed my stew away, my appetite spoiled.

"Where is this engagement of his lordship's?" I asked with an impertinence that causes me to wince when I recall it. "I've looked through practically every window in the keep, and there's naught but empty moors in every direction."

Abelard's patience was not easily strained. "Not empty," he said, drawing a trencher of bread close and tearing off a piece. "There are wolves abroad. Gaunt ones, with ribs showing through their hide, that like nothing better than to happen upon an arrogant fool of a man with more bravado than good sense."

Everyone in England was afraid of wolves in those stark, brutal days, when vast forests still covered the land—the creatures had been known to leap, snarling, into carriages and even to creep into huts and crofts and carry children away in their teeth. The stories about the beasts were rife, told at every cradle and fireside in the country, used, as fear has ever been used, to control those who might otherwise take it into their heads to wander.

Just the mention of the beasts made me go bloodless with dread. In the next instant I blushed furiously, embarrassed by my first reaction.

"We saw no such animals last night while riding in the carriage," I pointed out. The unpleasant images of a dying Krispin had faded from my mind, and I reached for my half-finished stew again.

Abelard made a production of chewing his bread, swallowing, and biting off a new piece. "I suppose they were busy elsewhere, then," he said at long last. "They're out there, though. You can be sure of that, sir."

I could not hide my shudder. "Have you seen them?"

"Oh, yes," Abelard confided in a low voice. "And any man with ears can hear them howling of a night. Calling and calling they are, wanting the unwary to come out and play their dreadful games."

I shifted the conversation away from the subject of wolves. "Is his lordship here, in this house?"

"He might be," Abelard said speculatively, though it was plain, even to me, that he knew exactly where his master was and what he was doing.

"It's damn rude," I blurted out, "making such a mystery of things and leaving a guest all on his own. I didn't ask to come here, after all."

Abelard smiled. "Didn't you?" he asked.

I was completely confused. "By the saints, man, I wasn't so drunk that I can't recall what I said with my own mouth!"

The servant finished his bread and then rose from the table. "There's no need to be afraid, lad," he said gently. "This is where you belong, and you're welcome here, and safe, too, if you mind your manners."

I wanted to point out that I was not some witless youth, that indeed I had lived four and thirty years, but I realized as I shaped the protest in my mind that I would sound foolish if I uttered it.

"Have you any wine?" I wanted to know. Blustering bluff was one of my stock traits; I had relied upon it, among other deceptions and ruses, for a long time.

Abelard sighed. "No," he told me. "And if I did, I would not offer it to you. The stuff might have been your destruction, if his lordship hadn't found you when he did."

I was yet considering the wine, and resenting my host's lack of charity where strong drink was concerned, so I did not stop to wonder how Challes had known where to look for me, or what business he had with me in the first place.

By the gods, I was not only mortal then, I was an idiot. I might have been deaf and blind for all the notice I took of the terrible and magnificent drama unfolding around me!

Abelard brought me one of the precious books that afternoon, and I read hungrily of ancient Greek adventures, hardly noticing when twilight came and the candles were lighted. I was so absorbed that I did not hear Challes enter the room where I sat, my stool drawn up close to the fire.

"This," he said with gruff fondness, "is the Valerian I remember."

"Tell me," I demanded quietly, closing the manuscript with great care. "Tell me why you sought me out, why you brought me here. Now."

He smiled. "I *have* told you, my friend. I have an astounding gift to offer you. If you accept my tribute, you will have powers you cannot begin to imagine now."

I was intrigued. "What is this great and mysterious treasure?" I asked.

Challes reached out to touch my shoulder. There was love in the contact, and reverence. His eyes glowed with affection as he looked down at my face. "Life upon life," he said. "Endless, fathomless, unbounded *life*. Drink from the cup I hold out to you, Valerian—arrogant Valerian, as beautiful as Lucifer in his days of perfect favor—and you will never die."

6

THE light of the drawing room fire flickered over Challes's features as he sat beside me on that momentous night, staring fixedly into the grate. Beyond the windows, on the moonlit moors, I heard the wolves calling sorrowfully to each other like souls just waking to find themselves in hell, and I shuddered.

Nearly imperceptible though the motion must have been, it somehow drew my tutor's notice. He turned his head toward me and smiled, and I remember thinking how remarkably white and even his teeth were. I was more conscious than ever, in that moment, of the dangers that filled the world.

"The time has come, Valerian," Challes began moderately, "to discuss the gift in depth. Preparations must be made, of course, before it can be given. Still, I wish to tell you all that this entails, for you will be called upon to make a choice never presented to most mortals."

I could barely contain my eagerness and curiosity; indeed, I had been in a state of quiet frenzy since he'd made the astonishing claim, a short while before, that I need never die. I find my excitement ironic now, in light of the fact that I had been trying for seventeen years at that point, albeit in a cowardly and indirect fashion, to murder myself.

"Tell me," I pleaded on a scant breath and came near to clasping his arm like a supplicant begging blessings from a saint.

"Be patient, beautiful one," he said fondly. "Once you shed your mortal limitations, you will have all eternity to celebrate what you are."

I waited and held my tongue, but it was the most difficult thing I had undertaken since my failed attempt to rescue Brenna from the merciless surf. I trembled with my need to understand what Challes was offering me, to snatch it from his grasp and hide it in my heart.

He settled back in his great chair, draped now in shadows, now in dancing light, and watched the blaze again. Just when I truly believed I would not be able to restrain myself from lunging like a fevered beast, to somehow wrench the secret from him, Challes began to unburden himself.

"I went to sea after I left Dunnett's Head," he told me, still gazing into the fire. "I know not how I kept myself apart from this cursed plague—it was, and is, everywhere. I saw so many perish, so horribly. I wandered, as you have done, and finally settled on the Continent, in Florence. There I encountered artists, bards, philosophers, and men of science—" He paused and smiled again, not at me certainly, but at some memory he must have glimpsed in the snapping flames of that cheery fire. "Whores and dancing girls, too. Gypsies and princes, and vagabonds, like myself. Those who were drunkards"—he had the charity, bless him, not to look at me when he made this last statement—"those who were saints, and those who were a curious and fascinating combination of the two. I cannot possibly describe the richness and pleasure of my life in that gracious city—and yet I was not truly happy. At times I knew unutterable loneliness."

I bit my lip, feeling no compunction to interrupt now, listening with all my powers of attention. I, too, had known such a separation from others—it was that, more than any other factor, which had spawned my eternal need for strong drink.

"I encountered a magnificent being one night when I was brooding in one of the small piazzas that abound in Florence. We became friends, and then something more than that. Lovers, of a sort, though our consummation was spiritual, rather than physical. Many wondrous nights passed before Christoph told me what he was. What he *is* and will always be—" Challes hesitated again and studied my face with a troubled expression in his eyes, and I thought I would burst with waiting before he went on at last. "Christoph is a fiend, Valerian, as am I. He is a vampyre."

My heart seemed to stop and, just as quickly, start itself pumping again. I drew back a little, I think, though the response was not a conscious one. "A *vampyre*? You mean, a drinker of blood?"

"Yes," Challes answered with a sound that resembled a sigh, but was not.

I bolted to my feet, overturning the stool with a crash, suddenly far more frightened of my old friend and tutor than I'd ever been of the wolves waiting outside in the darkness.

"Wait," Challes ordered calmly, even gently, rising unhurriedly from his chair. I would not have obeyed the command, but there was something in his eyes, something that held me spellbound and stricken, overriding my weak will. "I will do you no hurt, cherished one. There is only pleasure in what I would give to you, only joy." He was silent for a moment, gazing at me, and when he spoke again, it was briskly, in the schoolmaster's tone from days of old. "Sit down, pray, and listen."

Though I was terrified, I righted my stool and slumped onto it, speechless and void of grace, my limbs full of trembling. I made the sign of the cross, and to my horrified amazement, Challes did not recoil. Did not so much as flinch. No, there was only the brief hint of a smile, falling across his lips like a passing shadow, and a deep, pitying sorrow in his eyes.

"Such gestures have their power," he told me, "when there is true faith behind them. But you have none of that, do you?"

I tried to speak, stammered insensibly, and began again. "I believe there's a God—I believe in the Holy Mother, and the Son, and all the saints and angels—"

Challes laughed outright, and the sound echoed, raucous, off the high ceiling of the keep. "Such a hasty and convenient creed!" he exclaimed finally with grim humor. "Even the demons grant the existence of God, Valerian—oh, especially them. Do you think you can fool me—I, who know you so well? You believe now, in this moment, it's true, but only because you perceive your sinful hide to be threatened. Tell me, lovely one, were you so devout when the good brothers bade you stay there to take up the cross and become one of their number?" He shook his head, as if in response to something I'd said, although I spoke not a syllable, for I was too shaken to refute his words. "Let go of what is past, you spectacular idiot, and enter into the glorious future that awaits you."

I could not move or make a sound. I heard the wolves, nearer now, and wished that I might be their prey, alone and unprotected on the moors—that I could be anywhere but in that warm, comfortably furnished drawing room in the company of a devil.

Challes began to speak, his tones the low and measured ones of a father lulling a fretful child to sleep. He told me what it meant to be a vampire—told me of the powers he possessed, the powers *I* would command should I raise the figurative chalice to my lips and drink. I would be able to will myself from one place to another and, eventually, from one century to another. I would become a shape-changer, of sorts, able to present myself to mortals in an endless variety of forms. I should not need food or water, nor would I lack any desirable thing—gold, castles, fine horses, and exquisite garments could be mine by means of simple trickery. And there were much greater gifts and abilities that would come to me over time, with the practice of my art.

"But I must drink blood?" I asked with a slight shiver when Challes had finished painting his grand, glorious images in my mind.

His smile was tender now. "Not in the way you think," he said. And he proceeded to explain that, too—how the blood was drawn in through the fangs, how the victim could be made to feel ecstasy instead of fear and pain if the vampire wished it so, how the innocents need never be touched, because there was such a thriving abundance of truly evil mortals.

I was intrigued, despite my terror. I wanted the terrible magic of which Challes spoke, as he had always known I would. I wanted to fly, to learn, to explore. I wanted to wear rich clothing, always, to hear the music of a thousand minstrels, to traverse the wide seas and continents, to know secrets forbidden to ordinary men.

"Will you accept this gift?" he asked, although he knew what the answer would be. We both did.

I flushed. "Yes," I heard myself say. My old life was untenable now; I truly *would* surrender myself to the wolves before returning to the beggar's existence I had known only the day before. "Now. Tonight."

Challes laughed again and shook his head. "Dear, precious fool! If I changed you now, you would be forever as you are at this moment— gaunt and ill mannered and totally void of the graces. No, Valerian— you must be groomed and prepared for the transformation, as I said before."

I was alarmed—now that I knew what it meant to be an immortal, I could not bear the idea that my tutor might change his mind, might deny me what he had already offered. "How long will it take, this preparation?"

"A month, perhaps two," Challes said. "I will bring you along slowly, lovingly, just as my dark angel Christoph did for me. That way, when you enter in, it will be willingly, and with full knowledge of what you understake. Anything less would be a travesty before hell as well as heaven."

"I must have it now," I muttered, covering my face with my hands. "I cannot bear to wait!" The marvelous gift would be withdrawn, snatched from my fingers for all time—I knew it would. I would suffer that worst of all fates, and remain ordinary.

Challes laid his hand on top of my shaggy, unbrushed hair. "Do not fret," he scolded with gruff affection. "I cannot hurry this process, for it is too important. But I shall show you some of the joy that awaits you, if you're willing."

I raised my eyes to meet his gaze. And I nodded.

Not even Brenna or my poor, ill-fated mother had ever looked upon me with the kind of love I saw that night in Challes's translucent face. It was not a lascivious regard he bore me—even in my ignorance and self-centered naïveté I knew that—but something much deeper and far more complex. The emotion transcended gender, made a mockery of human gropings, and I was in awe.

I could not have known, back then, that one day I would cherish another in just that way, that I would understand completely how Challes felt.

I knew nothing of anything. I craved some blessing from Challes, some unnamed and joyous communion, with an intensity greater even than the wanting of wine.

In the end he dismissed me, to my wretched disappointment, and sent me off to my chamber as if I were a child. Certainly he had power over me, even then, but my obedience was grudging.

Challes came to my room perhaps an hour before dawn—I lay wakeful in my bed, watching the moon through the window and listening to the wolves' song—and suddenly he was simply there. I knew he had not entered by any ordinary means, but I was beyond questioning that. I simply looked at him, silently imploring him for I knew not what, knowing I would perish of grief if he denied me.

Challes knelt beside my bed, smoothed my hair, murmured words I did not comprehend, and bent his head to my throat. The experience was profoundly sensual, but again it was more a thing of the mind and spirit than of the body.

I, who had never knowingly been intimate with a man—I confess there were instances during the dark years after Brenna's death, however, when I was too drunk to know whose pallet I'd shared—was ready to surrender my very soul.

I started when I felt two sharp points penetrate the skin of my neck, and perhaps managed a whimper of fearful protest, but in the next instant, as my very life's blood flowed in Challes's fangs, ecstacy crashed down upon me like a giant wave. I moaned as he drank, only vaguely aware that he wasn't touching me at all, except where his mouth was pressed to the pulsing vein at the base of my throat. It was as though every erotic point, within and without, was being stimulated at once.

It was dark and sweet and violent, my first communion with Challes, like the pleasure I had known when Brenna wooed my seed from me, except that this release encompassed the whole of my being and went on and on, endlessly. At long last I swooned, the exertion and the joy so great that I could not endure them, and when I awakened with the morning sun I believed at first that I'd dreamed the entire episode.

When I touched my throat and felt the two tiny, rapidly healing puncture wounds, however, I knew all that Challes had said was true, that all I remembered was real. And I was filled with a delight, and a terror, of truly infinite proportions.

I did not see Challes that day, and I grieved until darkness fell. It was just after sunset when he returned, and began molding me, ever so artfully, into a fiend's fiend.

DAISY
Las Vegas, 1995

"Why the hell didn't you call me?" O'Halloran demanded the next morning when Daisy had told him about the threatening telephone message. They were riding in his car, on their way to the home of Jillie

Fairfield's next of kin, her divorced mother. Daisy was up to her ankles in empty soda bottles, misfolded maps, and crumpled candy wrappers.

"What would you have done?" she countered irritably. "Hauled yourself over there and sat on my couch all night, holding a .357 in your lap?"

It wasn't the crank call or O'Halloran's gruffly solicitous attitude that was bugging her, she admitted to herself. Mrs. Fairfield resided in a trailer park where Daisy and Nadine had spent six happy months when they were in elementary school, in the care of their paternal grandmother. Inevitably their mother, Jeanine, had returned, rumpled and a little drunk and smelling sour from the bus ride that had brought her back to Vegas from wherever she'd been. She'd reclaimed her daughters, over Gran's fierce but helpless protests, and headed straight for the nearest social worker. A couple of kids made it a whole lot easier to collect welfare, after all, and once Jeanine had dumped or been dumped by her latest boyfriend, a biker with a slipped disk that entitled him to state compensation, she'd suddenly developed all manner of maternal instincts.

"Relax, Chandler," O'Halloran said. "I'm not trying to step on your goddamned feminine rights or anything like that. I just want to make sure this sicko doesn't get too close, okay?"

Daisy wanted to reassure her partner, but she was still distracted by her dread of returning to the trailer park. She and Nadine had never been allowed to go back, even to visit, and after a couple of years the old woman had passed away. Jeanine's boyfriend at the time—Daisy couldn't remember his name and didn't care if she ever did—had shown her the obituary in the newspaper and said maybe they'd get a mobile home out of the deal, "now that Granny has kicked off."

"Chandler?" O'Halloran prompted. They turned a corner on a yellow light, and the door of the glove compartment fell open, slamming against Daisy's knees and spilling a variety of cassette tapes, empty cookie packages, expired registration slips, and unpaid parking tickets into her lap.

She stuffed the whole mess back where it came from and closed the little door with a crash. "What?" she snapped.

"You suffering from a year-round case of PMS, or what?"

Daisy sighed and shoved a hand through her hair. "Why is it that men always think any change in a woman's mood has to be connected with her hormone levels?"

O'Halloran shrugged, running another yellow light, bald tires squealing, and the driver of a tour bus blasted his horn and displayed a specific finger behind the broad tinted window. "After ten or twenty thousand years the evidence starts to stack up," he said. "The thing is, we got this weird case to solve—you know what the medical examiner said—and it's gonna take our undivided attention to work the snarls outta this one. You gotta get all your body chemicals in sync, Chandler, 'cause I need your help."

Daisy tossed him a mock salute. "No problem, Officer Friendly. My mood has nothing to do with chemistry. And slow it down, will you? You take one more corner on two wheels, and I'll have to write you up for driving under the influence of sugar and preservatives."

He grinned, but in the next moment his expression was solemn again. "I don't like this, Chandler," he confided. "This Fairfield thing, I mean. By the time we got to that girl, she didn't have enough blood left in her veins to reach a gnat's ankle. What the sonnabitchen hell *happened* in that place? What about those marks on her neck?"

Daisy shifted in the seat as the entrance to the trailer park came into view. She took a pair of sunglasses from her purse and put them on, telling herself it was because of the glare. "Forensics found blood on the scene when they went over it after the body was removed," she pointed out. "It just wasn't visible to the naked eye, that's all."

"Okay, so there was a little blood. There sure as shit wasn't enough. What happened to the rest of it?"

She shivered, somewhere down deep, and knew her reaction didn't show on the outside. Jillie's corpse, the crank call, the dream, and the magician all sprang out of her subconscious at once to haunt her. "I don't know, O'Halloran," Daisy replied finally in a somewhat testy tone. "Maybe you were right in the first place. Maybe we've got a vampire running loose."

O'Halloran flung her a mildly contemptuous glance and slowed to enter the Lucky Dollar Trailer Park, passing beneath the burned-out neon sign and bouncing down the rutted gravel road between battered mobile homes. "You wish," he said, making a cranking motion with his left arm as he rolled down the window. The air-conditioning had petered out years ago, with the second or third motor. "Better the real thing, for my money, than some psycho who believes with all his diseased little brain that taking a drop of human blood now and then will make him live forever."

Daisy didn't answer. Her thoughts lingered on Valerian. She was comparing the way he looked in real life with the younger, less polished version she'd seen in her dream, wondering if he was gay, straight, or in between, and where he'd learned to do magic. Something told her he was accomplished in the subtler forms of wizardry as well as the spectacular ones he employed onstage.

"Chandler?" O'Halloran barked. "Pay attention, damn it."

Daisy switched mental gears and forced herself to concentrate. "I'm with you, buddy. Let's go make the world safe for humankind."

After asking directions from a gray-haired man mowing a lawn, they found the Fairfield trailer. It was a run-down, two-tone double-wide with a sagging step and a yard made up of crushed gravel and cigarette butts.

Mrs. Fairfield came out onto the dilapidated porch when they drove up, a petite blonde with a leathery tan, wearing white short-shorts and a skimpy red top. She wore high-heeled sandals, her toenails were painted, and her makeup gave rise to speculation concerning the way she earned her living.

"You the cops?" she asked, raising a lipstick-stained cigarette to her mouth.

Just two of them, Daisy thought, flashing her badge, but she didn't say the words out loud because after all, this woman's daughter had just been murdered. Just to the left and a little behind her, O'Halloran flipped out his wallet.

"I'm Detective Chandler," said Daisy, "and this is Detective O'Halloran. We're investigating your daughter's death, and we need to ask you some questions."

"Took you long enough to come around," Mrs. Fairfield replied, giving no sign that she intended to invite them inside.

Daisy was relieved. The place probably reeked of smoke, and worse, it might look too much like Gran's trailer. There might be a loosely crocheted afghan draped over the recliner in the living room, pictures in dime-store frames on top of the television set, cheap shag carpeting with a worn spot in front of the door—

O'Halloran consulted his ever-present notebook, and out of the corner of her eye Daisy saw a short grocery list scrawled on the first page. "According to my log here, I called you myself from the station, about an hour after we left the—er—scene."

Mrs. Fairfield sat down on the top step, crossed her still-shapely legs, and tapped the ashes from her cigarette into a clay pot containing a dead plant. She sounded bored when she spoke again. "If you're going to ask me who Jillie was dating, or who her friends were, I couldn't tell you. She and I didn't get along too well. I do know that she worked for that magician, Valerian something-or-other, in the showroom at the Venetian Hotel. That's some kind of place, isn't it?"

Daisy felt a swift, dizzying fury. Someone was dead, and this woman, the victim's *mother*, for God's sake, was talking about the latest addition to Glitter Gulch. She opened her mouth to comment, but O'Halloran, who could be amazingly perceptive when he tried, silenced her with a touch to her forearm.

"Yeah," he said. "It's something, that hotel. You ever go down there and take in your daughter's show?"

Mrs. Fairfield laughed. The sound was low and throaty, but there was more despair in it than humor. "At the price those places charge for a ticket? Not on what I make serving drinks in a fourth-rate casino. And Jillie sure as hell never found it in her heart to get me comped in. I hear it's a great act, though. HBO wanted to do a special a few months back, according to the papers, but this Valerian character won't let any kind of camera through the door." She tapped more ashes into the planter. "It's all a lot of hype, if you ask me—that stuff about how he's never seen in the daytime and everything. There's nothing like an attitude to generate publicity. You gotta know how to sell yourself in this town, and that guy's a master at it."

Daisy wondered if Mrs. Fairfield was really as crass and unfeeling as she seemed. People handled grief in a lot of different ways, some putting on fronts, some breaking down right away. Daisy had heard more than a few talk all around the subject of their loved one's death, too, just the way this woman was doing. "We need to know if your daughter had any enemies, Mrs. Fairfield," she said, grateful to O'Halloran for running interference until she could get her emotions under control. "In an incident like this, the killer is often someone the victim knew."

The aging cocktail waitress raised a carefully plucked eyebrow. There was something faintly mocking in the motion, and some of Daisy's sympathy ebbed away.

"Is that right? How long you been a cop, sweetie?"

Daisy took a breath, let it out slowly. "We're not here to talk about me, Mrs. Fairfield. Please—tell us whatever you can about your daughter."

"I told you, we didn't get along," came the distracted, slightly hoarse reply. "We didn't speak at all for the last two years."

"Why not?" O'Halloran asked with quiet compassion.

Mrs. Fairfield's eyes were luminous with tears when she raised them to meet his gaze. "It was a stupid thing, really—she was dating a married man, and I told her he'd never leave his wife for her, 'cause they never do, you know—and Jillie and me, we had too much to drink one night, and we got into it good. We tore into each other, right here in front of this pissant trailer, and it was a catfight like you never seen before."

She paused and smiled faintly at the memory, as though proud that she and her daughter were scrappers. "The cops came, too. Look in your computers if you don't believe me. Jillie and me, we was both too stiff-necked to say we were sorry afterwards. We thought we had forever to make things right, you know?"

At this last, her face crumpled, and Mrs. Fairfield gave a small, raw sob that wrenched hard at Daisy's insides.

"I'm so sorry," she said.

Mrs. Fairfield rose gracefully to her feet and tossed her cigarette butt into the gravel. Then she wiped her mascara-streaked cheek with the back of one manicured hand. "Yeah, sure you are, honey. Sure you are."

With that, Jillie's mother turned and went into the trailer, closing the door firmly behind her.

"Back to square one," Daisy said.

"Families just ain't close anymore," O'Halloran philosophized in response as they walked back toward his car.

Later that afternoon a woman ran over her ex-husband in the parking lot of a convenience store, and a fifteen-year-old gang member was knifed to death by his older brother, who had been out of prison just over two weeks. It all seemed to underscore O'Halloran's theory about families, and Daisy was thoroughly depressed when she went off duty at six-thirty that night, got into her convertible, and drove back to her apartment.

There were no messages on the answering machine. That was something, at least.

The blues invariably made Daisy restless, so she dragged her rowing machine out from under her bed—she'd ordered it eighteen months before, inspired to a frenzy of ambition by a late-night infomercial—and into the living room. Usually she worked out in a health club a couple of miles from her building, but that night she just didn't feel like dealing with a lot of people.

She put on her shorts and a T-shirt, switched on the TV, warmed up with a few brisk calesthetics, and rowed up a sweat. The effort relaxed her, as she had known it would, and Daisy showered and put on her chenille robe. She had just put some low-fat fish sticks into the microwave for her dinner when the telephone rang.

Daisy didn't hesitate to answer. Maybe Nadine had picked up on her intent to call and beaten her to the punch.

"Chandler," she said, just in case.

"We got another one," O'Halloran told her wearily.

The bottom dropped out of Daisy's stomach. No matter how many homicides she investigated, she never got over the shock of learning that one human being had killed another. Again.

"What do you mean, 'another one'?" she snapped, though she knew. Damn it to hell, she knew.

"Her name was Susan Cantrell," O'Halloran said. "Miss Cantrell's roommate came back from a long weekend this afternoon and found her dead in the bathtub. No blood, Chandler. And she had those funny little marks on her neck, just like the Fairfield woman did, and the M.E.'s office thinks it happened last night sometime. God, but I hate this job."

"What else?" Daisy prodded, knowing there was more because she could read O'Halloran so well. She didn't argue that he shouldn't hate his job, because he always did when there was a murder. So did she.

O'Halloran gave a deep, sorrowful sigh, and Daisy could just see him running a stubby hand through what was left of his hair. "She worked for that magician, too. The one that's been packing them in down at the Venetian since the hotel opened—" Daisy heard papers rustling. "Let's see here," her partner went on. "His name's—"

"Valerian," Daisy said, leaning against the wall and closing her eyes as tightly as she could.

7

VALERIAN
Las Vegas, 1995

FOR the second time in as many nights, I regained consciousness at sunset to find that there had been another murder. I saw poor Susan's death plainly before I ever opened my eyes—the horrible images were imprinted on the insides of my lids—and I glimpsed the vampire who had done the killing as well. I could not recognize the fiend, for its face was shadowed by a hooded cloak, but I intuited that the creature was male, and for a reason I could not grasp, I felt that I should have known him.

I wept with grief and helpless frustration, although I had not been well acquainted with Miss Cantrell, as I rose from my luxurious pallet and began to dress. This night there would be no performance at the Venetian Hotel—how could there be? No, tonight I would hunt, traverse centuries and continents if necessary, to run this monster to earth and put a finish to him by whatever means that might seem prudent at the moment.

Before destroying this vampire, however, I would extract much in payment for the suffering of my friends. I was furious that the thing had not confronted me directly, for I was obviously the true object of its hatred. The creature was cowardly, however, as well as implacably vicious; it clearly knew that, save Maeve Tremayne, who had not been weakened by her marriage to a fledgling named Calder Holbrook, I was the most powerful blood-drinker on this plane of existence. Better, then, to torment me through those helpless beings close to me, those I valued and, in my way, loved.

I had to find it before another innocent died.

Before it turned to Brenna—now Daisy Chandler—the love of my eternal life.

Before the ruby ring arrived.

I was drawn to the living room of my hideaway, and the television set descended from the ceiling as I entered. I had not willed this to happen, and I felt a mental chill as I watched light flicker in the center of the screen and then spread into an image. My lair had heretofore been sacrosanct, but now it seemed that some other creature dared to work magic within its walls.

Perhaps, I thought, I would not have to search out my enemy after all. Perhaps he had come to me.

The televised picture solidified into an image of Brenna, riding boldly into the surf, laughing, never dreaming that her death was imminent. Before my eyes the scene shifted; Brenna was gone, and the raging sea had vanished to become a shoddy fifteenth-century tavern called the Horse and Horn. Brenna appeared instantly, immediately recognizable for her green eyes and coppery hair, but now her name was Elisabeth Saxon. She was a bold and fiery wench, her cheap dress showing too much of her bosom, flirting shamelessly with the ruffians she served, permitting them to touch her. Driving me half mad with jealousy and frustration. She faded away, and then I saw Jenny Wade, my lovely Jenny, another incarnation of Brenna, though she wore the lush, red-blond hair in a tidy chignon and her green eyes were sightless. I had cherished her especially, because she loved me so completely and so selflessly without ever seeing my face.

Jenny and I were together in the late sixteenth century, for far too short a time.

I heard that gentle angel whisper my name, and when the screen went blank, I was startled to find myself standing in front of the set with both hands pressed to the glass.

"No more," I whispered, for I could not bear to see the other incarnations my beloved had donned, like pretty frocks, over the centuries. It was enough to be reminded of Brenna and Elisabeth and Jenny, of how completely and how hopelessly I had loved them, all different facets of the same glorious, intrepid spirit.

Suddenly another picture spilled across the surface, and I drew back, appalled. The leading lady in this new tableau was Daisy Chandler— the latest incarnation of Lady Brenna Afton-St. Claire. I saw that she lived in one of those bland and anonymous apartments that are so prevalent in the twentieth century, with no more variance between the units than between the cells in a honeycomb.

"Daisy," I muttered, but of course she could not hear me. She was only an image, but a modern version of Brenna nonetheless, projected from the dark depths of my mind—or, more likely, the mind of my enemy, whoever and whatever it was.

I watched as Daisy moved about her small kitchen, preparing a frozen dinner—a peculiarity of the modern age that makes me glad vampires do not require the same sort of sustenance mortals do—and I heard the nerve-jangling ring of her telephone. When she answered, "Chandler," I was touched by the note of bravado in her voice.

I could not discern what the caller said, but I saw Daisy's lovely, impudent face go white with fear and fury. I watched and listened helplessly as she slammed the receiver back into its cradle and then sagged against the wall, trembling.

I wanted to will myself to her side, to draw her into my arms and offer her what comfort I could, but better judgment prevailed. The vignette I'd seen was not occurring at that moment; it was a colorful shadow of the future. If I went to Daisy then, I might find her in the shower, driving her car, doing any one of the millions of wonderful mundane things mortals do. It would be neither kind nor wise to reveal my unique powers to her in such an abrupt way.

Yet I feared for her in those moments as I had never feared for another living being. My unknown foe had shown me all these visions, but most especially the last, to taunt me with the fact that it was stalking Daisy, that it meant to murder her as it had already murdered poor Jillie and Susan.

I closed my eyes. *What was this thing?*

There was no answer, of course—not then. The television screen went dark and returned to its nesting place in the ceiling with a low, electronic buzz.

I was instantly possessed of a brutal weariness, as abject as if my immortality had suddenly proved an illusion or a jest, as if my vampiric powers had been wrested from me and I had been reduced to a fragile, human state. To ask such pitiful flesh and bone to bear the weight of some six hundred years of adventurous living would be like expecting a spider's web to support a cathedral.

With some effort, I collected myself, faced down the consuming panic that threatened me, and centered my thoughts on the one immortal I truly trusted, the only vampire I dared depend upon for help and advice.

I sought Maeve Tremayne, once my fledgling and now my friend and my queen—she who knew our species to be ungovernable, and governed it nonetheless. She who protected us from our foes, be they angels, warlocks, or rogue vampires, and meted out punishment for our crimes.

I found her in the uppermost chamber of her London house. She shared the residence with her mate, Holbrook, who had been a brilliant physician and surgeon in his mortal life. Their remarkable child, Kristina, was grown and far away.

Maeve was at her weaving when I arrived, and alone, as I would have preferred. Calder and I are not particularly friendly; I find him too absorbed in his incessant experiments, and he dislikes me, I suspect, for my superior mind.

Maeve feigned a little sigh when she saw me and said, "Ah, Valerian. What now?"

DAISY
Las Vegas, 1995

Susan Cantrell had died in the same way Jillie Fairfield had, except for a few small details. Her slender dancer's body had been virtually bloodless and unmarked except for the two small puncture wounds at the base of her throat.

The differences were minimal—Jillie was murdered in her living room, and she'd been partially clothed. Susan's body was found naked, and in a ludicrously modest pose, lying in her bathtub.

Two full days after the killing, late in the afternoon, Daisy left the city morgue in a daze. She'd seen corpses before—a lot of them in far worse condition than Miss Cantrell's—but there was something chillingly different about these cases. Even O'Halloran was subdued, and he wasn't given to sensitive contemplation of the deeper mysteries.

"You gonna be okay, Chandler?" he asked when he and Daisy stood between their cars in the parking lot.

She thought of the calls she'd been getting, and a shiver of pure paranoia trickled down her spine and formed a chilly pool in her stomach.

"Yeah," Daisy answered. "As soon as we nail this pervert, I'll be fine."

O'Halloran nodded, opened his car door, and pushed a crumpled potato chip bag off the seat before getting behind the wheel. "You watch out for yourself," he said. "You get any hotshot ideas, you call me. Don't go running off on your own. You hear me?"

Daisy sighed and saluted.

O'Halloran slammed his door and rolled down the window. "And eat a decent dinner for once in your life, will you? Something besides them frozen things with more calories in the carton than in the food."

She smiled. "A nutrition lecture from you?" she said. "I *must* be in a bad way."

"Get outta here," O'Halloran said. "I'm tired of looking at you." With that, he started up his car and backed out with a screech, narrowly missing Daisy's left foot and a UPS truck.

Daisy got into her car and locked both doors with a flick of a button on her armrest. Ironic as it was, she suspected O'Halloran was right about her eating habits. She hadn't had real, unrefined food in days, and she felt like an old beater in need of an oil change.

She went back to her office for an hour, going over reports and statements on the Fairfield and Cantrell cases, looking for something— anything—she might have missed.

Later, on the way home, she stopped at a supermarket in her neighborhood, arriving just after dark, and started wheeling a cart down the aisles. A well-nourished, healthy cop, she reasoned, is a smart and insightful cop. She bought fresh vegetables and fruit, chicken and fish, bread and cereal, and some skim milk. She was standing in the checkout line, reading a tabloid article about space aliens having affairs with members of Congress, when her personal reality splintered.

Suddenly she wasn't Daisy anymore, and at the same time she was, and she was no longer standing in a busy supermarket in one of Las Vegas's more ordinary neighborhoods.

Her name was Elisabeth Saxon, the year was 1457, and she was serving ale in a tavern with the picturesque name of the Horse and Horn. Everything around her seemed real, although she knew it was an illusion, that she was finally cracking—everything from the spit-slickened board floors to the impossibly grubby men seated at tables all around her. They were singing bawdy songs, in a version of English she could barely understand, and swilling ale between choruses.

One of them reached out and pinched her hard on the backside, and she was still Daisy enough to be outraged. She spun around on the heel of her soft leather shoe and clouted the culprit over the head with a pewter trencher.

A *trencher?* She thought frantically, looking down at the weapon in her hands even as her victim swayed beneath the blow. Since when did she refer to platters as "trenchers"?

A raucous cheer rose from the crowd of unwashed revelers, and Daisy—that *was* her real name, wasn't it?—glanced wildly about for an escape route. There was a door open to a starry night, and she dashed toward it, her customers grabbing at her apron and her skirts as she passed.

She collided with a hard form in the doorway, felt strong hands close over her shoulders.

"It's all right," a familiar voice told her gently, and she looked up into the dark blue eyes of the magician, Valerian. "You're safe. I'll take you home."

His clothes were strange—he wore a tabard, belted at the waist, and his silk shirt was puffed at the shoulders and then fitted to his wrists. Woven hose accentuated his muscular legs, and high boots, with cuffs folded down from the top, covered his feet.

All the same, this was the man she knew from her dreams—and from the Venetian Hotel in that faraway world she was already starting to forget.

She fainted, and he caught her up in his arms. When Daisy came around, she was back in the supermarket, and Valerian, incredibly, was there, too. He was holding her.

Daisy stared at him and saw understanding in his eyes, along with sorrow. She was struck in that instant with the dizzying realization that he knew exactly what had just happened to her, that he had indeed shared the experience.

"Put me down," she said, embarrassed by the gathered crowd and the revolving lights in the parking lot. Obviously the paramedics had been called. "I'm *fine*, damn it."

Valerian set her on her feet without a word, but there was a wry twist to his mouth. She stole a sidelong glance at him, half expecting to see that he was wearing a tabard and boots, but his clothes, though obviously expensive, were quite ordinary, quite suited to the twentieth century. Black slacks, a gray silk skirt, Italian shoes.

The paramedics burst through the doors, and Daisy's embarrassment intensified. She knew the majority of these people—worked with them practically every day of her life. The very last thing she needed was for them to think she was losing her grip.

"What happened?" Charlie Cook, the senior EMT, asked Daisy, looking around for the patient.

"Nothing," Daisy said without looking at Valerian, pushing her hair back from her forehead as she spoke.

"Nothing?" demanded a middle-aged checkout clerk with the name Marvella stitched onto her red smock. "This young woman fainted dead away, right here in my line. Went down like a ton of bricks. And look at her—she's pale as milk."

Charlie looked stern, and his co-worker, a rookie Daisy wasn't acquainted with, studied her with a critical eye.

"We'd better check you over, Chandler. After all, it isn't normal to pass out in the supermarket when they haven't even rung up your total yet."

Daisy grinned, though she felt shaky and sick and wanted nothing so much as to be alone with Valerian, so she could ask him what the hell had just happened to her. She was certain that he knew. "Okay," she said, pushing back her hair again. "But just let me pay for this stuff first. I don't want to lose my place in line."

"Funny," Charlie said, and then he glanced at Valerian.

The magician nodded and spoke for the first time. "I'll look after her," he said.

Charlie was apparently satisfied; he cocked a thumb toward the parking lot and told Daisy, "We'll be waiting outside. Follow the flashing red lights."

Daisy paid for her purchases, Valerian standing silently beside her the whole time, and then started to push the cart out of the store. He edged her aside and took over the small task.

"Did you cast some kind of spell over me back there?" she whispered. "Or am I losing my mind?"

"Neither," he answered, with that half smile that tugged at something deep inside her. "What happened to you is called spontaneous regression. You just visited one of your past lives."

"Oh, right," Daisy retorted. She had a headache—stress-related, to be sure.

"Your name was Elisabeth Saxon," Valerian said. "You lived in the mid-fifteenth century. You were a serving wench, and something of a lightskirt, at the Horse and Horn, a tavern on the London road."

Daisy stared up at him as the supermarket doors swished open and they went outside into the dry warmth of the night. "How did you—?"

"I was there, remember?"

He had been.

"I'm having a nervous breakdown," Daisy announced.

Valerian raised one majestic eyebrow. In the glow of stars, streetlights, and the not-too-distant Strip, his skin had a translucent quality. "Are you?" he countered, pushing the cart toward her car without being told which one it was. "If that's the case, then how do you explain my presence there? I was on the threshold of that inn, Daisy, when you hurtled into my chest like a rabbit fleeing a pack of foxes."

Daisy murmured an exclamation. "What is this? Some kind of hypnosis?"

"I'll explain it later," he said, glancing down at the trunk of her car. It sprung open, though neither he nor Daisy had touched the latch, and Valerian began putting the grocery bags inside, that curious little smile playing on his mouth again. "You'd better let your friend listen to your heart, test your reflexes, and look into your ears," he added, nodding toward the ambulance parked only a few spaces away. "He'll follow you home if you don't."

"You'll wait?" Daisy asked. She should have been afraid of this man, she supposed, but she wasn't. Instead she was full of questions she knew only he could answer.

"I'll be right here," he said.

Daisy started to turn away, then frowned down at the trunk of her car, now tightly closed again. "How did you open that without a key?"

Valerian shrugged. "I'm a magician, remember?"

Daisy left him, shaking her head.

She endured the exam, which was perfunctory, knowing all the while that Charlie probably thought she'd fainted because she was pregnant. By this time tomorrow, she figured, the word would be out that Detective Chandler had passed out in the supermarket with a cheap tabloid in her hands. She'd be called into the chief's office, no doubt, and probably taken off the Fairfield/Cantrell case if she didn't talk fast. Her boss was more likely to attribute the fainting spell to stress than pregnancy, and to decide that Daisy needed a break from homicide.

Maybe she did. God knew, she didn't love it.

Valerian waited, as he'd promised, and he insisted on taking the wheel.

Daisy looked around the lot. "Where's your car?"

"I don't own one," he said and offered no further explanation.

Daisy gave him the keys because on that one night she needed to lean on somebody. The fact that he was a stranger, for all practical intents and purposes, and up to his eyeballs in murdered chorus girls, didn't seem to make a difference.

"Where do you live?" he asked, once they were inside the car, though Daisy guessed from his tone that he already knew her address. For some reason, he was going through the motions.

"Are you the nutcase who's been calling me?" she inquired after rattling off directions to her apartment complex.

"No," he said, starting the engine and driving with an easy confidence that made Daisy wonder why he didn't have a car of his own. It wasn't that he couldn't afford one, that was for sure—headliners like him brought home the big bucks.

Maybe he'd lost his license, she speculated to avoid scarier concerns for a little while longer.

"I didn't have a license to lose," he said, as if Daisy had spoken aloud. "And I don't own a car because I have no need for one. Furthermore, the phrase *big bucks*, tacky as it is, doesn't begin to describe my salary. Now, could we talk about the real issue here?"

Daisy sagged back in the passenger seat, knocked breathless by his words. "I wish you'd teach me that trick," she said after a few moments of tumultuous silence, her voice squeaky with bravado. "Mind reading would come in handy when I'm interrogating suspects."

He gave her a sidelong look, then turned his attention back to the road. "Come back in a thousand years or so. By that time the ability will have evolved to the point where ordinary mortals can use it."

The term *ordinary mortals* nettled Daisy, and, besides, it sounded weird, as if Valerian considered himself to be outside the category. "Gee, thanks," she snapped, to hide the fact that she was seriously spooked. "Of course, most of my cases will probably be solved by then, though God knows the paperwork won't be caught up. On the other hand— what will I care? I'll be somebody else."

"You don't believe me?"

"Why should I?"

He smiled. "Why, indeed?" he replied, signaling to turn onto the side street that ran behind her building. "Perhaps our little talk will change your mind—if the incident in the supermarket truly wasn't enough."

"I want to ask you some questions while we're chatting," Daisy said as he brought the car to a stop in her assigned space. Which, of course, was unmarked. She got out of the car and closed the door with a bang. "Like how come the women in your act are being murdered?"

"I don't know," he answered with a weariness on a scale with Daisy's own and perhaps even greater. "Maybe you and I can figure that out together, after you know the truth." He handed her the keys and then opened the trunk, again with no outward motion, and took out both grocery bags.

Daisy led the way up the outside stairs to her apartment.

Inside, Valerian carried the bags to the kitchen and set them on the counter. "Sit down," he said when Daisy started putting things away. "You're still in shock."

With that, he took a head of lettuce and a bag of tomatoes from Daisy's hands and proceeded to put them in the refrigerator. Daisy sat on one of the two stools at the breakfast bar and cupped her chin in one hand.

"Evidently," she said, "your wish is my command."

He grinned at her, and again she felt a wrenching, so far within herself, so far back in her memory, that momentary tears burned behind her eyes. He took a half-eaten entrée, still in its box, and carried it disdainfully from the refrigerator to the trash bin. "Wretched stuff," he muttered.

Daisy was defensive. "I suppose you eat nothing but gourmet fare?"

He laughed and returned to the task of emptying the grocery bags. *"Au contraire,"* he said. "I subsist on a very simple liquid diet. It's the secret of my great longevity, along with a certain talent for evading the consequences of my own actions."

Daisy ran her eyes over Valerian's magnificent physique and discounted most of what he'd just said. Nobody looked like *that* living on fruit juice or vitamin shakes. "I believe that last part—about your evading the consequences of your own actions, I mean," she conceded. "But I'm warning you right now—if you killed those women, I'll get you."

"I believe you would," he answered thoughtfully, having finished putting the food away. "You're very good at what you do, I think."

"So are you," Daisy said, remembering his magic act at the Venetian Hotel, the way he'd opened the trunk of her car, that knack he had of appearing in her dreams. That night he'd even managed to be a part of a psychotic episode.

Impressive.

He brewed tea for her—her favorite English brand, purchased in London in the food stalls at Harrod's by a friend who worked for an airline. Not surprisingly, he didn't ask where it was, where the cups were, or if she wanted tea at all. He simply made it and set it in front of her.

She took a sip, and some of her strength returned. "Am I going crazy?" she asked, addressing herself as much as Valerian.

He leaned against the breakfast bar from the other side, arms folded on the countertop. "No," he said easily, "but there is much I must tell you. You have, to paraphrase one of your better poets, 'miles to go before you sleep.'"

"Talk," Daisy said.

VALERIAN
Colefield Hall, 1365

"You are ready at last," Challes announced one winter night, some three months after he'd found me unconscious in a horse stall. We'd accomplished a great deal in the time that had passed since, but I was young and impatient for the gift to be given, and it seemed then that my tutor had deliberately withheld the joys he'd promised. That he wanted to taunt and torment me.

He had brought me along so slowly, making sure I ate robustly, so that my frame filled out, teaching me to fence, that I might be graceful, pouring the most exquisite music into my ears and inundating me with poetry and numbers, philosophy and science, languages and etiquette.

I was an apt student, perhaps because of my eagerness to be what Challes was, to do what he did, and I was handsome in my fine new clothes, with my trimmed hair and clean-shaven face. I possessed an almost boundless vitality, even surpassing the energies of my early youth, except during the blissfully languid interval following Challes's nocturnal visits to my bedside.

"Tonight, then?" I cried, nearly oversetting my chair by the drawing room fire, where I had learned so many lessons, as I bolted to my feet.

"Tonight," Challes confirmed with tenderness and sorrow in his voice.

I wondered at his sadness, but I was too self-absorbed, too eager to make the change, to ask why he was troubled.

There was a Roman couch beneath the window, with its glittering frosting of ice, and my tutor led me to that and bade me to lie down.

I would have done almost anything he commanded, for by that time I loved him completely. My adoration for Challes was a thing of purity and grace, transcending genders, a joining of spirits rather than bodies. There are those who would call me deviant; instead, I am simply whole.

I did as Challes asked, closing my eyes while he opened the collar of my shirt, listening to the thin, far-off cries of the wolves. I felt their starvation in my own gut, and at the same time my whole being, flesh and soul, hummed with the anticipation of ecstasy.

My joy was terrifying, beyond anything I'd felt before, surpassing every happiness except what I had known in the arms of Brenna Afton-St. Claire. Nothing, before or since, on earth or in heaven, could rival the mere touch of her hand. Still, the pleasure Challes gave me was keen-edged and beautiful.

He had told me that I would die as a man, during this, the greatest of our communions, but when I felt my mortal life ebbing away, I panicked and tried to cry out. By then I was too weak to make a sound, and certainly I could not struggle, but Challes murmured words of comfort and soothed me with gentle whispers. I sank quietly into my death, and all consciousness was obliterated, swallowed up in darkness.

When I awakened, I realized I was in a cryptlike vault, under the earth. I lay on a slab of cold stone, and Challes slumbered an arm's length away on another pallet of rock. I heard rats scrabbling in the corners and shuddered.

A low chuckle sounded, and I turned my head to see that Challes had awakened and lay with his weight braced on one forearm.

"No need to be afraid, Beautiful One," he said. "The rats cannot hurt you. Nothing can, except sunlight or the point of a wooden stake. If you do as I have taught you, you will live forever."

I had wanted this, yearned and pleaded for it, and yet the magnitude of eternity was only then coming home to me. *Never* to die? To never lay down my burdens and rest?

"Now you must learn to hunt," Challes told me, rising from his slab and dusting off his leggings and tunic. "Once that is done, I shall be gone."

I sat bolt upright. He had never spoken of leaving. Did he truly mean to abandon me now, when there was still so much I did not understand?

As he had done so many times before, my tutor laid his hands to my shoulders. "It was worth incurring Nemesis's ire to create such a splendid fiend as you," he said.

I knew, from our studies together, that Nemesis was a warrior angel, greatly feared in the dark realms. "You've had dealings with—" I could barely speak the name, it inspired such terror in me. "With *Nemesis?*"

"In a manner of speaking," Challes replied without flinching. "I have made too many blood-drinkers for his liking, and he is a powerful angel. He vowed revenge, with or without the permission of higher angels, should I make even one more." He feigned a sigh. "Alas, you are so beautiful and so bright—even in your drunkenness, you were magnificent. I could not resist making you immortal, for you were wasted as a mere man. To think of you here a moment, then gone—it was too painful to endure."

"What price have you paid?" I whispered, but I knew the answer already, and it filled me with fathomless grief.

Challes, my teacher, my only friend, was to be destroyed.

Because of me.

I whispered an exclamation that might have qualified as a prayer, had I been anything other than the abomination I was, and wept my first tears as a vampire.

Would that they had been my last.

8

Daisy
Las Vegas, 1995

THE thing that surprised Daisy most about Valerian's story—and it was an incredible tale, spanning some six hundred years—was that she was very much inclined to believe it. She guessed she'd had some glimmer of the truth that first night, in the showroom at the Venetian Hotel, when she'd watched him raise a coach and a team of horses off the stage floor and send them sailing out over the audience members' heads. And while she still didn't consciously remember being those other women he spoke of with such passion and love—Brenna Afton-St. Claire, Elisabeth Saxon, Jenny Wade—the mere mention of their names had struck a resonant chord within her. Perhaps the dreams she'd had all her life had not been dreams at all, but memories of those other lifetimes.

"I've looked exactly the same, in every incarnation?" she asked. "Is that how you recognized me?"

"Yes," Valerian said, his eyes glowing with affection. "You are always your same beautiful self, at least when I've known you—only the costumes and the hairstyles change. Still, I think I would know you even if your looks changed significantly. I felt your presence in the audience at the Venetian long before I actually saw you."

She nodded thoughtfully. "I've read about reincarnation," she said, "like almost everyone else. But I thought people came back in different bodies, sometimes as men, sometimes as women."

"They do normally," Valerian affirmed. "You are an exception, and you needn't ask me why, for I confess I do not know. I can tell you that souls tend to return to the flesh in the company of others they've known and loved or hated in the past."

"You've told me that you can travel through time—back to the point of your own death as a mortal. If that's so, am I in all those other places, as all those other selves, simultaneously? Can you journey back there and see me as Jenny, for instance? Or Elisabeth?"

The magnificent face was drawn for less than a moment with terrible grief. "I don't know," he said. "Some vampires can change the course of events and see and influence the ones they love. Whenever I've tried to find you, however, I've met with utter failure."

She considered that. "Talk about information overload," she murmured. "If you're really Count Dracula, Junior," Daisy reasoned at some length, still sitting at the breakfast bar, elbows on the counter, fingers buried in her hair, "why haven't you tried to bite my neck? And why should I believe you when you say you didn't commit the Fairfield and Cantrell murders? That was a vampire's M.O. if I've ever seen one."

Valerian smiled, and there was just a hint of condescension in it. "Have you?" he inquired. "Seen a vampire at work, I mean?"

Daisy sighed and sat up straight on the stool. "It was just a figure of speech," she said impatiently. "Answer my questions, please."

"I haven't 'tried to bite your neck,' as you so crassly put it, because I adore you—in whatever lifetime I happen to stumble across you. That is my curse. As for why you should believe I'm innocent of these killings—" He paused and shrugged aristocratically. "Because I have told you so. I have done murder in my time, make no mistake, but these poor little creatures? No. I cared for them."

Daisy pondered him skeptically, chin in hand, and said nothing. He had just confessed to the worst crime a person can commit, but she could not picture him taking a life and therefore did not really believe that he had.

"All right," Valerian snapped, waving his arms in a gesture of wild impatience. "Don't believe me. Lock me up in one of your silly jails. But I warn you"—he was shaking his finger now—"that any attempt to detain me is an exercise in futility. If you try, I shall evaporate like so much smoke!"

Daisy looked down at her empty cup and frowned. Her head was still fogged, and it was late. Maybe that was why she believed everything Valerian said; because she was tired and her defenses were down. Or perhaps he'd drugged her. "I'll keep that in mind. Did you put something in my tea?"

Valerian drew himself up, annoyed to a truly imperial degree. "Of *course* not. I have no need of such silly contrivances—I am a vampire!"

Daisy sighed. "Have I missed something? Did Halloween sneak up on me this year?"

He leaned across the counter and bared his teeth with a theatrical hiss.

She bounded off the stool, wide-eyed, her heartbeat making a one-second leap to warp speed. Valerian's incisors, while beautiful like their dazzling counterparts, were longer, and they came to distinct points, sharp as a wolf's fangs.

"Shit!" she blurted, before regaining her courage, easing back to the counter, and raising herself onto the stool again.

"Trick or treat," he said.

Daisy flushed, embarrassed that she'd shown fear. "You could have had that done," she reasoned hastily. "This town is full of people with custom-made teeth. Some of them are probably even crazy enough to think they're vampires!"

Valerian subsided a little, leaning back against the counter opposite the breakfast bar, his hands on his hips, and regarded her wearily. "What do you want, Daisy? How do I prove to you that I'm telling the truth?"

She leaned forward again, studying him for a long time. She was mystified by this maniac, or this vampire, whichever he was. But, oddly, she wasn't afraid of him; underlying all her misgivings was a strange sense of familiarity and the sure knowledge that she was safe in his presence. "I did not say I didn't believe you," she reminded him. "Something weird is definitely going on here. I just need to work through it for myself, that's all." She paused, remembering her impromptu visit to the year 1457, via the supermarket, and how vivid the experience had been. There could be no denying that the episode was more than a dream or a hallucination. "I saw you," she said. "In my—vision, I mean. But you were wearing different clothes. If you were really there, how did you make such a quick change?"

Valerian made a sound that might have been a sigh, but was somehow different. "I merely projected myself into the scene," he said patiently, "complete with costume. You saw me because I wanted you to see me."

Daisy ran her tongue over her teeth, something she often did when she was pondering an enigma. Her headache was starting to come back, and if she didn't get some sleep, she'd be a zombie all the next day. "Earlier, when you were telling me the story of your life, you said you could travel back in time, as far as the point of your own death as a mortal."

He sighed again. "Yes."

"What's to prevent you from meeting yourself somewhere between now and then?"

"Nothing. Occasionally it happens. It's a paradox, like time travel itself."

"I don't understand."

"I'm not surprised. I don't understand, either. I suspect that no one does—at least, not completely. It's a universe of specialties—vampires are vampires, roses are roses, jellyfish are jellyfish. Which of us can grasp the whole of reality, in all its multifaceted complexity?"

Daisy didn't have an answer.

Valerian came around the counter and very gently touched her face, his thumb tracing the outline of her cheekbone. "My poor love," he said. "You've always been this way, you know—wanting answers to impossible questions, tilting at windmills, chasing rainbows. Just as you always have copper-colored hair, green eyes, and a smattering of freckles across your nose."

A shiver of mingled delight and passion moved through Daisy, and strange erotic images stirred in her memory. She did not recoil, although Valerian was still a stranger, and probably a dangerous one at that. Instead, she wanted him to make love to her, she who had slept with exactly three men in her entire life.

The pad of that same thumb strayed sensuously across her mouth. "Soon," he said, apparently reading her mind again. A thoughtful expression darkened his eyes. "But perhaps a small reminder of what we've shared together over the centuries would not be amiss."

He was a hell of an actor, Daisy thought. There were so many things happening in her body, so many sensations bouncing from one part of her insides to another, like laser beams running amuck, that she didn't have the energy to speak.

Valerian smiled ever so slightly, bent his head, and kissed her.

It was only a brief contact, a mere brushing of his lips against hers, but it rocked Daisy to her core. The earth seemed to spin away beneath her feet and shoot off into space, leaving her dangling in a throbbing void. There was no oxygen, and her heart swelled painfully against her rib cage.

She gasped and stared up into Valerian's wise eyes—she could well believe that he was six hundred years old in that moment, for she saw so many emotions reflected there, in that fathomless blue, myriad things that could not have been garnered in a normal lifetime.

"Why aren't I afraid?" she whispered.

He smoothed her hair, and even that innocent motion sent new fissures streaking through her few remaining defenses, caused the last walls to crumble and the innermost doors to swing open. "Because you know, in the essence of yourself, that I would brave hell itself for you." He glanced at the window above the sink. "It will be dawn soon. I must go."

Daisy was disappointed. Hadn't he promised to stay?

He'd read her thoughts again. "I promised a small reminder of what we had together," he clarified with a smile. "And now for one of my more impressive tricks."

With no more preamble than that, he vanished. In the space of an instant—with no drumrolls, no smoke, no mirrors—he was simply *gone.*

Daisy swore and leaped off the stool, as if to pursue the magician into thin air. She thought she heard, far in the distance, the faintest echo of a chuckle.

She stood there for a few moments, open-mouthed, convinced she was certifiable, before her basically pragmatic nature took over. After washing her face, brushing her teeth, and gulping down two aspirin, Daisy fell into bed and slept like a dead woman.

She did not dream.

With the morning and full consciousness came vivid memories of the night before—her "spontaneous regression" to the fifteenth century, Valerian's wild, and undeniably fascinating, tale of living six centuries as a vampire, that soul-shattering kiss, and, finally, his spectacular disappearance.

He was a magician, she reminded herself. But that single fact didn't explain all the things she'd seen and felt. There was more to it—much more.

All right, then, Daisy's highly developed left brain argued, he was a hypnotist as well as a stage wizard. He'd said straight out that he could project his own image into her mind at will, hadn't he? That, supposedly, was how he had joined her in the Horse and Horn, when she was Elisabeth Saxon, erstwhile tavern wench.

Somehow, logical as it was, that explanation didn't work, either.

Daisy tossed back her covers and got up. She was probably getting an ulcer from trying to figure this out—better to let it simmer in her subconscious for a while and think of other things with the everyday brain cells. She'd gotten to the crux of more than one case that way— using what O'Halloran called her woman's intuition.

She smiled. He'd never claimed to be original.

After going to the bathroom, Daisy opened her front door and picked up the newspaper lying on the mat. The headline wiped the smile from her face.

POLICE DUB RECENT CRIMES "VAMPIRE MURDERS."

"What police?" Daisy grumbled, pushing the door shut with her foot and scanning the article as she crossed the apartment to the kitchenette. "Nobody asked *me* about the case."

The piece was peppered with quotes from one Detective John P. O'Halloran, who was, according to the reporter, "in charge of the investigation." Daisy might have been his golf caddie, for all the mention she got, but she didn't care about that. What bothered her, and she knew it was a waste of time to worry about it, was the way the press seemed to *glamorize* what had happened.

Whoever the killer was, he was sure to get off on the attention and notoriety.

When the telephone rang, she was already reaching for the receiver to call the office. She almost hoped it would be the screwball who'd harassed her after Jillie Fairfield's murder; there was a thing or two she wanted to say to him.

Alas, the voice that replied to her brisk "Hello, this is Chandler" was O'Halloran's.

"It's your partner," he said, master of understatement that he was.

Daisy dragged over one of the stools from the breakfast bar and perched on it. "Oh, yes—the dimpled darling of the Fourth Estate. Tell me, O'Halloran, did you have to stay up all night to make the world safe for old ladies and Cub Scouts, or did you just take care of it on your break?"

"Smart-ass," O'Halloran said fondly.

"Have you got something new to tell me about the case, or are we going to go on exchanging sloppy sentiments all morning?"

He cleared his throat, then took a noisy slurp of what was probably coffee. He was stalling, and that was a bad sign.

"O'Halloran," Daisy pressed.

"All right, all right," her partner blurted. "The chief saw the EMT's report on your collapse at the supermarket last night. He wants you to take a few days' leave and get a checkup."

"Are you telling me that I'm suspended?"

"I'm telling you that you have to rest a few days and see a doctor. Don't come unwrapped on me now, Chandler, because this wasn't my idea. It came down from the brass."

"Shit," Daisy muttered, chewing one fingernail.

"You shouldn't talk like that. It ain't becoming."

Daisy struggled to regain her self-control before going on. There was no sense digging herself in deeper. "What the devil did Charlie tell those people?"

"That you passed out."

"And?"

O'Halloran let out a long-suffering sigh. "And the head office got a call from the checkout lady late last night—Marvella somebody. She was worried—said you were talking gibberish while you were out."

Daisy closed her eyes. "They want me to take a drug test, don't they, O'Halloran?"

"Look, it's routine—you know that. Any one of us could be asked to pee in a cup at any time."

She sighed. "I'm not popping pills or shooting up," she said, suddenly feeling as if she could crawl back into bed and sleep for two weeks. "You know that, don't you?"

"Hell, yes," O'Halloran answered gruffly. "Of course I know that. Look, partner, don't try to buck the system, okay? Just catch up on your sleep, get the checkup, and come back to work. If you stay out too long, somebody might get the idea that you're the real supercop and I'm just the sidekick. I've got to think about my image, you know."

Daisy laughed, even though there were tears gathering along her lashes. "Don't worry, fella—your reputation is safe with me."

She hung up the receiver and moved around the apartment in a sort of stupor, showering, brushing her hair and teeth, dressing in jeans and a lightweight sweater, making toast and a poached egg for breakfast. When she'd done those things, she got into her car and drove downtown.

After a thorough examination and a lot of questions, the official department physician announced that Daisy was suffering from exhaustion and recommended that she take two weeks' leave. Her first instinct was to resist, but then she reconsidered. She had all the signs of a classic case of burnout, and if she kept pushing herself, she might just wake up one morning to find that she was an *ex*-cop, with her law enforcement career behind her forever.

With that specter staring her in the face, Daisy filled out the necessary papers, called O'Halloran with the news, and then went back home. For now, she told herself, it was enough that there would be no question that she'd been abusing drugs.

She stayed in her apartment just long enough to pack and call her sister, Nadine, who reported that she was getting labor pains. Within half an hour Daisy was on her way to Telluride, tape deck blaring. The screaming ghosts of all her fears and doubts followed along, staying just inside the outermost edge of her awareness.

VALERIAN
Las Vegas, 1995

I knew Daisy was gone when I arose that evening, rested and ready to feed, and then to resume the hunt for my enemy. Her absence gave me a bereft, hollow sensation, in that dry and atrophied thing that had been my heart, but I thought it better that she was far away. The greater her distance from me, the safer she would be.

I fastened my cuff links, smiling to myself. I had chosen a special pair that night for luck, antique gold ones that had been a gift from a cherished friend, George Bernard Shaw. But it wasn't the jewelry that gave me pleasure, it was the idea of keeping a certain promise to Daisy.

Tonight she would know my magic in a new way, and I hoped it would cause her to remember all we had been to each other over the centuries. She had been a will-o'-the-wisp, flitting from one identity to the next, having the same face and body but a different name in each generation, and having no conscious memory of me whatsoever.

I, on the other hand, had always been Valerian. Endlessly, eternally myself.

I confess that I grow weary of my own company on occasion, fascinating though I am. One gets to know one's self, over the course of centuries, and the utter absence of surprise can grind at the spirit.

"How like you, Valerian, to wax philosophical," observed a cheerful feminine voice, catching me completely off guard.

I whirled to see Maeve standing only a few feet away, gloriously beautiful in her flowing, iridescent robes, her long dark hair falling free around her shoulders, her dark blue eyes like windows into the heart of the universe. She has a penchant for the dramatic, our Maeve, a fondness for spectacular entrances and fiery exits.

But then, so do I. Perhaps it is a trait of vampires, after all, for they tend to be flamboyant creatures.

"You honor me," I said with a slight inclination of my head, "both by your visit and your words."

She laughed. "Still charming as a serpent," she said, putting her hands on her hips. "What a flatterer you are." She paused again, gazing upon me thoughtfully. "I came to ask if there have been more difficulties with this rogue vampire you spoke of the other night."

"I have not been successful in tracking him down," I admitted ruefully. I thought of Daisy again and my resolve to protect her strengthened. "But you have my vow that I will put an end to his mischief, whoever he is."

Maeve picked up one of the pretty glass bottles I kept on my dressing table and examined it with the absorbed interest of one who appreciates fine craftsmanship. "Do not be too hasty, my friend," she warned, returning the bauble to its place before turning her gaze to my face. "This may not be a blood-drinker, but a warlock, for instance, only posing as one of us. I feel certain that this is some sort of trap."

I almost whispered my next words. "Could it be that Lisette has returned?"

"No," Maeve answered with a reassuring lack of hesitation. "She is most certainly dead. You saw her perish—we all did."

"Still—"

"If Lisette had managed to resurrect herself, even in some other form, I would know it. We have other enemies, Valerian. There are many monsters roaming creation—ones we know nothing about. According to Calder, who has been performing some very interesting experiments since his transformation, there could well be other species of vampires, with different powers from our own. He has even uncovered evidence that gaps might exist between dimensions—passageways leading in and out of other realms and realities."

I found the mere prospect so overwhelming that I could not speak. The fiends of my acquaintance were daunting enough, without being joined by a host of other horrors skulking back and forth from one world to another.

Maeve folded her arms and looked at me with sisterly concern. "What is it that you're not telling me?"

I smiled sadly, touched and somehow calmed by this reminder that she cared for me. "I have found her again."

"Not—?"

I nodded, reaching up to straighten my elegant string tie. I often wear formal garb to hunt—a cape and tails, ruffled linen shirt and cummerbund, trousers with silk stripes down the outer seams—due to that theatrical streak I mentioned before, I suppose. And because my victims expect me to resemble the classic media vampire.

Who was I to disappoint the poor wretches?

"Yes," I said. "Same face, same body. This time her name is Daisy Chandler, and she's a homicide detective with the Las Vegas police."

Maeve looked worried. "You know what always happens—the ruby arrives, she dies, and then you are heartbroken. You must avoid this woman at all costs, Valerian, for your own sake as well as hers."

I wanted to weep at the impossibility of the situation, at the injustice and terrible irony of it all. "It's already too late," I confessed. "Besides, there is no avoiding Daisy. It's part of the curse."

"The curse," Maeve mocked. Surprisingly, considering what she is and what she's seen, my revered queen is not in the least superstitious. "That's a medieval idea. There is no dark magic at work here—someone or something is *causing* these things to happen. Find the root of the problem and you will know how to solve it."

"So practical," I said with a sad smile. Maeve is young, in terms of being a vampire, having been made quite recently, in the turbulence of the eighteenth century. "Do you fancy that I've never *tried* to uncover the cause? I have searched for centuries, all to no avail. And every generation or so, the horror repeats itself."

She approached me and put a gentle hand on my arm. "Perhaps Calder can find some remedy in science," she said in an effort to lend comfort.

I laughed, though my feelings resembled bereavement more than mirth. "You have great confidence in that husband of yours."

Maeve nodded. "I have," she admitted. "And it is well placed, I assure you. Now, come with me. We'll feed together, and then search for this mysterious foe of yours."

"It has occurred to me," I said, looking down into her sweet, beautiful face, "that our cause would be better served by keeping watch over the four young women who remain in my employ. I shall sever all ties with them, of course—when I again perform my magic act, I will appear alone—but they seem the most likely targets."

"What about this Daisy woman? I should think she would be in the gravest peril of all."

There could be no denying that, but I had a suspicion that the creature wanted to punish me, to subject me to a lengthy and torturous ordeal. Logically, he was more likely to save Daisy's death for last—and to make it the most grisly of all.

I voiced these thoughts to Maeve, who agreed, though with reservations.

"Still," she said, "you must not leave her unguarded for long."

We linked arms, as though to enter a grand dining room or stroll onto a dance floor for a waltz. "I would like to bring Daisy here to my lair, where she would surely be safe, but mortals balk at such forms of protection—they consider them arbitrary. Remember how Calder hated your efforts to keep him out of danger?"

Maeve winced and then flashed me a guilty little smile. "He was quite impossible as a mortal," she said. "I like him much better as a vampire."

With that, we willed ourselves away.

Feeding was not a challenge—though neither of us had a taste for the blood of innocents—for humans with evil hearts, while in the minority, are still all too easy to find. Prisons abound with them, and so do the world's various halls of government.

When we had taken the necessary sustenance, Maeve and I set out on our search for the demon who had murdered Jillie and Susan.

Our efforts met with failure.

DAISY
Between Las Vegas and Telluride, 1995

Daisy pulled into the parking lot of a well-known motel at ten-thirty that night, too tired to travel even one more mile. After buying half a turkey sandwich and a can of tomato juice in the convenience store across the highway, she locked herself in her room and sat cross-legged on the bed, consuming her dinner and watching the early news.

There was nothing about the so-called "vampire murders" in Las Vegas, but she supposed it was only a matter of time before the wire services and major networks picked up the story. What the tabloids could make out of it didn't bear thinking about.

She got off the bed and threw away the debris from supper, muttering to herself. "Don't think about work, Chandler. Think about Nadine and your niece or nephew. Think about happy things—fun things. Do you want to have a nervous breakdown, for heaven's sake?"

Daisy looked at her reflection in the mirror over the sink. "You're not a crazy person," she said forcefully. "You're smart and strong and brave, and a damn good cop on top of it all. And you *are not* losing your mind. You're just tired, that's all. A week with Nadine and you'll be *thrilled* to rub elbows with homicidal maniacs again!"

She laughed, but the sound lodged in her throat when the telephone rang.

A lesser person wouldn't have answered it at all, Daisy reflected, but she was Woman, and if she had to, she would roar.

"Hello!" she snapped.

A familiar chuckle came over the wire. "I found you," Valerian said. "There are times when I wonder if my magic is a plus or a minus."

Daisy was pleased out of all proportion to reason to hear his voice. Later she would think about the impossibility of his finding her in a motel she'd chosen at random. For the moment she was simply happy that he had.

"I guess it's a plus," she said. "If I asked how you tracked me down, would you tell me?"

"Sure," came the blithe reply. "But you're not going to ask me, are you? Because you already know the answer I'd give."

Daisy wound an index finger in the telephone cord, as wildly happy as a teenager about to be asked to the prom by exactly the right guy. "You'd say it was vampire magic."

"Something like that." He sounded solemn now, almost sad. "Are you all right, Daisy? Have I frightened you?"

She considered. "Yeah, you've done that all right, but in a different way than you probably think. It's a kind of quivery, excited feeling, like I get used to get in high school, when my girlfriends and I would go to a horror movie and then stay up half the night scaring the hell out of each other."

"I honestly don't know whether to be honored or insulted," he said, and the smile was back in his voice.

Daisy sighed. "Take your choice," she said. "You are definitely weird, but I've got to admit, I like you. Maybe it's the old snake-charmer syndrome."

"Maybe," he agreed. "I have to go now, love. But before I hang up, I'd like to ask you a question."

"Okay," Daisy replied.

"Do you remember the promise we talked about last night?"

She felt a shivery, delicious warmth in all the places where she was most feminine. "Yes," she said. "Sure."

"I'm about to keep my word," Valerian told her. "That is, if I have your permission."

Daisy was trembling with anticipation and sweet terror. If this was a sexual fantasy, it was a hot one, and she wasn't about to squelch it. "Okay," she said shakily.

"If you want the lovemaking to stop, you have only to form the thought in your mind, and it will be over."

Daisy was glad he couldn't see her—at least she didn't *think* he could—because she was blushing like crazy. "That sounds fair."

He chuckled. "Good night, Daisy."

"Good night," she whispered, but the line was already dead.

Confused, happier than she'd ever been, Daisy got ready for bed, turned out the lights, and slipped between the sheets. Both the nightgowns she'd brought were still neatly folded in her suitcase.

She lay still for a long time, waiting, half expecting Valerian to appear in her motel room in the same way he'd vanished from her apartment.

Forty-two minutes had passed on the digital clock on her bedside table when the urge to throw aside the blankets and sheets struck her like a sudden fever. She trembled as the cool night air touched her bare skin, making her nipples tighten.

In the next instant she felt hands on her flesh, and she knew the hands were Valerian's, even though she was still alone. Then she felt his lips, warm and wet and soft, on her breasts, on her belly, on her neck and her thighs. It seemed that every part of her, inside and out, was being kissed and caressed, fondled and teased.

Daisy arched her back, giving herself up to the passion that swept around and through her like a storm. She was reminded, in the midst of the wild ecstacy that followed, of a recent dream. She'd been someone else in that dream, living long ago and faraway, and she'd ridden a horse into a pounding surf. The waves had consumed her then; this time, it would be the pleasure, the mounting, excruciating, *glorious* pleasure.

9

VALERIAN
England, 1457

TRUE to his word, Challes had abandoned me after teaching me the rudiments of feeding and protecting myself from certain gruesome perils to which vampires are subject. I was at my most licentious in the years and decades that followed; there were few pleasures I did not sample and even fewer sins I did not commit. In retrospect, it seems that my proclivity for wine had been replaced by an equal devotion to the ever more capricious demands of my senses.

I was beautiful as an archangel and as self-centered as a spoiled child, and I resented my erstwhile tutor bitterly for leaving me to my own devices as he had. I carried cynicism to new heights, and might have continued on this treacherous and unsavory course if I hadn't happened into a seedy roadside inn one spring night in 1457. I'd been traversing the countryside in my coach, pretending to be a mortal, as I sometimes did when I was bored.

I doubt it will surprise you to learn that the place was the Horse and Horn and that I found Brenna within its shoddy walls, clad in a cheap, undyed gown that revealed too many of her charms and carrying pitchers overflowing with ale to tables full of leering louts.

Imagine my astonishment, my joy, my outrage! I had believed her dead—I *knew* she had perished in the waters off the coast of Cornwall—and yet here she was, looking as she had always looked, except for the coarse dress, laughing and bantering with a lot of louse-ridden sailors and highwaymen!

Utter silence descended when I noticed at last, standing there in the doorway of that wretched establishment, a gentleman to all appearances, finely dressed and obviously rich. I heard their jumbled thoughts—more than a few planned to rob me, and most would have done murder for the least of my valuables—but I was interested only in Brenna.

She turned to see what had caught her customers' attention, and the look of speculation in her green eyes was devastating to me, for there was no recognition in them and certainly no love. She, like the bilge-rats and pickpockets seated round the rough-hewn wooden tables, was calculating my worth. The thought that I would pay well for a tumble in the straw, and probably be a pleasant partner in the bargain, flitted across her mind.

This was not my Brenna, and yet it was. The flowing, coppery hair, the slightly freckled and otherwise flawless skin, the sumptuous little figure and the breathtakingly beautiful emerald eyes all belonged to my beloved. The mind and spirit, at least in their deepest recesses, were hers, also; it was the outward character I did not recognize.

She sidled over to me, smoothed the fine silk of my tunic with the palms of her small, grubby hands, and smiled up into my rigid face.

"My, ain't you pretty," she crooned.

Catcalls erupted all over the room, but those men were no more to me than the vermin that crawled among the folds of their ragged garments and skittered behind the walls.

Despair nearly overwhelmed me, and yet I could not help rejoicing. In whatever form I found her, this was my treasured one. The darling of my heart. I would carry her away and, in time, share with her the gift Challes had given me. Together we could explore eternity.

"Brenna," I whispered, catching her fingers in my own.

"You can call me whatever name you want, pet," she simpered, batting her eyelashes and even managing to blush a little. "But I'm Betsey to me friends."

I wanted to carry her out of that place over one shoulder and to throttle her, at one and the same time. In the end I did neither, for I could not move. "Betsey?" I echoed stupidly.

She drew herself up, preening, and her coquetry almost made me laugh, for she was no cleaner than if she'd been thrown down and dragged through a barnyard by her ankles. The poor thing suffered greatly in comparison to the sophisticated mortal women I normally consorted with; in her present state she barely had the grace to slop swine.

"Elisabeth Saxon's me full name," she announced very proudly.

More hoots and crude comments rose from the Great Unwashed, and I ignored them as before. I would deal with any who dared to approach me—or Elisabeth—later.

I placed a small leather pouch in her palm, weighted with gold, and watched with an odd mingling of pleasure and pain as her eyes lit up at the prospect of such wealth.

"Come with me," I said quietly.

Elisabeth did not hesitate; she untied her stained apron and tossed it aside, never noticing that it settled over one reveler's head like a crudely woven shroud. Then she offered her hand to me, and I took it and pushed her out into the dark dooryard of the inn.

Her companions rose almost as one from their benches and stools, and their faces, in the flickering light of the candles and the scant fire on the hearth, were the faces of fiends.

It was pitifully easy to intimidate them, however; no magic was required. I simply swept them up, one and all, in a look calculated to shrivel their very souls. None of them tried to follow as I turned and strode outside, catching Elisabeth's elbow in a forceful grasp as I passed her and thrusting her toward my waiting carriage.

"You're not one of that sort what likes to be rough with a girl, are you?" she asked as I bundled her inside.

"I won't hurt you," I said. I was trembling with emotions I could barely sort through—passion, fury, adoration, disgust. "Great Zeus," I muttered at last when we were settled and I had signaled the driver to be off with a rap of my knuckles on the carriage roof. "What's happened to you?"

Her eyes were huge in the darkness, and she held the small bag of gold tightly against her belly, as though fearing I might snatch it back from her at any moment. "What do you mean by that, sir? I've just been making me way in the world, like any girl would, in me place—"

"When was the last time you had a bath?"

Fire flared in her spirit, and I was heartened to see it. "Baths ain't good for a lady's health," she said with conviction.

I folded my arms and regarded her in silence for a long time. "Don't you remember me, even a little?" I asked at last, unable to keep myself from voicing the deepest disappointment at all.

Elisabeth shook her head. "No," she answered bluntly. "And I'd recall a fine and fancy man like yourself if we'd ever met, now wouldn't I?" She paused to ponder me, though I must have been nearly invisible to her in the thin moonlight, her lovely eyes narrowed. "Why did you call me by that other name, even after I told you it weren't mine?"

I feigned a sigh, wondering what this poor little urchin would think if she knew I wasn't a man, fine and fancy or otherwise, but a beast instead. A creature that ventured out of its vault only by night, loving the darkness, exalting in it, drawing nourishment from the veins of hapless mortals.

"You remind me of someone I knew a long time ago," I answered at length. I believe I realized, even then, that I would not be able to change Elisabeth back into Brenna, but I was not yet ready to accept the fact. I was still caught up in the miracle of finding her at all, and I did not think beyond the easing of my own terrible loneliness.

She held up the pouch and gave it a slight shake, causing the coins inside to jingle with merry solidity. "I guess you'll want plenty for this," she said with what seemed to me uncommon valor, given the circumstances. For all she knew, I meant to make full use of her grubby little body, kill her for sport, and reclaim my gold. She could not have guessed that I wanted only to be near her and keep her safe.

"Yes," I replied, settling back against the upholstered seat and folding my arms. "I will expect a great deal from you. You can start by putting your knees togeher—you look like a bawd, sitting there with one foot on either side of the coach."

Elisabeth flushed, and that raised the vampire hunger in me, though of course I quelled it immediately. Even I had standards, though one would not have guessed it by my behavior in the years prior to that momentous night, and I had no intention of feeding on her.

Which is not to say that the temptation didn't present one of the keenest agonies I've ever had to endure. Elisabeth's vitality, her sumptuousness, filled the interior of that carriage, thrumming like a heartbeat.

I took her to Colefield Hall, the estate that had been Challes's and was now mine. I had not seen him again since his farewell, shortly after my making.

The moon was high when we arrived, and she'd fallen asleep on the coach seat opposite me, curled up like a child.

She did not awaken when I carried her into the keep, or when I laid her gently on the finest bed in the house and covered her with the best blankets.

I stood there, gazing down at her, spellbound by her disheveled magic, stricken by her unexpected reappearance in my life. I had not made the effort to investigate such things up until that time, having been wholly devoted to the pursuit of unceasing pleasure, but now I could only conclude that Brenna had been reincarnated as this grimy, tousled hoyden.

For what purpose, I wondered, if not to find me, her true and only love, once again? That would explain why she looked exactly as she had a century before, in that other, too-brief existence.

She stirred in her sleep, and I smiled to myself. By returning, she had transformed me, I thought—for I, too, was still naive in my fashion, having troubled myself to learn so little of life and love.

I left her to hunt, retracing my steps, so to speak, to the dooryard of the Horse and Horn to feed, and returned to Colefield Hall just before dawn. I was settled in my vault, far beneath the earth, where the acidic light of the sun could not reach my vampire's flesh, when Elisabeth awakened and proceeded, as I later learned, to set the household on its ear.

DAISY
Between Las Vegas and Telluride, 1995

The orgasm was violent, when at last it overtook her, seeming to slam her deep into the mattress even as it sent her hurtling upward to collide hard with the ceiling. She alternately moaned and mumbled incoherently, having no breath for the screams of pleasure that throbbed in the back of her throat, pitching and thrashing and clawing at the sheets with splayed fingers as her body convulsed in spasm after spasm of ecstasy. She longed for peace and stillness, fearing her heart would explode at any moment, it was beating so fast, and at the same time she prayed the release would never end.

Alas, it did, ebbing away slowly, like a tidal wave in grudging retreat, leaving a limp and trembling Daisy behind. She felt the sheen of perspiration cooling on her body, felt her hair clinging wetly to her cheeks and temples and nape. She huddled there upon that strange and anonymous bed, quivering inside an intangible cocoon that still reverberated with the force of her satisfaction. Her breath came in gasps and her heartbeat was still too rapid, thudding like the hooves of a fleet horse racing over hard ground.

She wept, because her mystical union with Valerian had been so unbearably beautiful, and because he was not there to gather her in his arms and hold her close. Then, exhausted, utterly sated, in soul as well as body, Daisy slept.

She awakened with a start, blinking against the bright sunlight sneaking between the blinds at her window, to the sound of someone pounding at the motel room door.

"What?" she demanded, pushing back her hair.

"Five minutes until checkout time," a woman warned cheerfully.

Daisy swore and scrambled out of bed to wash her face and brush her teeth. She wriggled into fresh clothes, grabbed her suitcase and purse, and made a dash for the door, and it was only later, when she had paid her bill, bought a breakfast sandwich, and hit the road again that she let herself think about what had happened the night before.

The languid, limp-muscled sense of well-being was still with her, a warmth that had settled in deep, soothing her nerves, permeating her very bones. As crazy as it was, and as impossible, there could be no denying that Valerian—or someone—had made slow, thorough, excruciating love to her in that motel room.

Without actually being there.

Daisy swallowed another bite of her sandwich. It was hypnosis again, she concluded, chewing. Valerian had known she was attracted to him, and he'd planted the seeds of that session of solitary passion by things he'd said to her, first in her apartment, and then over the telephone. Or maybe the whole thing had been a sort of hysterical hallucination and she'd done it all on her own. . . .

She discarded the idea along with the rest of her sandwich and its paper wrapper, which she stuffed into a plastic garbage bag hanging from a knob on her dashboard. There was no easy explanation for the kind of long-distance lovemaking she'd enjoyed so much, or for Valerian himself.

He'd disappeared from her apartment, vanishing before her very eyes, and last night he'd given her the mother of all orgasms without even *being* there. Those were the facts—unless, of course, it turned out that she was suffering from a major case of self-delusion and had flunked the drug test after all.

Hardly likely, Daisy decided, keeping her eyes on the road. She'd tried to go into denial on several occasions, hoping to escape her problems, and it hadn't worked. She was just too damned left-brained to fool herself for more than a few minutes at a time.

Much as she might wish otherwise, Valerian was real. His magic was just that, and he had really and truly seduced her with his mind, from who knew how far away.

Daisy muttered an expletive and reached out to turn on the car radio.

NADINE, normally petite, was as big as the A-frame she shared with her earnest but quiet husband, a greeting-card artist named Freddy. They both looked sleep-rumbled and a little dazed, and Daisy felt a mild twinge of guilt for awakening them at one in the morning. She supposed she could have checked into a motel, but the truth was that she needed some time to recover. Another bout of psychic sex would probably have killed her.

She kissed Nadine's cheek and nodded to Freddy. "I'm sorry," she said. "I should have let you sleep."

Nadine, bundled in flannel, laughed and shook her head. She was twenty-two, with chin-length dark hair and brown eyes, and worked as a clerk in a supermarket. "Don't be silly. We're glad you're here, and I would have been worried if you didn't show up."

They were standing in the living room, and Freddy went over to fold out the Hide-A-Bed while Nadine helped Daisy out of her coat.

"I thought you said you were in labor," Daisy said, rubbing her hands together. The mountain air was crisp, and the fire in the woodstove had apparently gone out a long time ago.

"False alarm," Nadine said with a cheerful shrug. "Do you want a cup of cocoa or something? Are you hungry?"

Daisy felt a small, sharp twist in the center of her heart. She and Nadine had always mothered each other, except for that short stint when they'd lived with their grandmother, since Jeanine hadn't had a clue when it came to parenting. "No, sweetheart," she said, blinking rapidly and looking away for a moment. "If I find myself on the verge of starvation, I'll get up and raid the refrigerator. You go back to bed. You need your rest."

Freddy, having folded out the couch, proceeded to fling a few chunks of wood into the stove, which was set into an old-fashioned flagstone fireplace. "The bathroom's at the end of the hall," he told Daisy, putting a gentle hand to the small of Nadine's back and pushing her along ahead of him. "Night."

"Night," Daisy replied.

She found the bathroom, which was so cold they could have hung beef carcasses in there without fear of spoilage, and hastily washed and brushed her teeth. The living room was a little warmer, but she figured she would have been able to see her breath in front of her face if there had been enough light.

After stubbing her toe on one of the metal legs of the Hide-A-Bed, Daisy threw back the covers and plunged beneath them, shivering.

She tossed and turned and finally tumbled into a fitful sleep. A sound awakened her sometime later, and she sat up, shoving a hand through her hair. At first she didn't remember where she was, and then she thought there was something wrong with her sister.

"Nadine?"

Silence.

Daisy sat up, groping for the switch on the lamp beside the couch, but before she found it her eyes adjusted to the darkness, and she saw him, standing at the foot of the bed. She didn't scream because she wasn't afraid.

"Valerian," she said softly.

"I'm sorry, love." She heard a smile in his voice. "Did I frighten you?"

"No. Are you really here, or is this one of your tricks?"

He came to sit beside her on the mattress, offering his hand. "I'm here, all right," he said.

"I'd hate to have to explain you to my sister and brother-in-law."

Valerian chuckled. "You won't have to. They're both sound asleep with visions of sugarplums dancing in their heads."

Daisy leaned against the back of the couch. She was wearing long underwear for pajamas in an effort to keep warm. "Last night was pretty spectacular," she told him. "Was I the only one having fun?"

He touched her face, and she saw in the dim light that one corner of his mouth was curved ever so slightly upward. "I knew what you were feeling," he said, "and I took pleasure in that."

"Why did you make love to me from a distance?"

"Because it would be too dangerous up close."

"You certainly take an innovative approach to safe sex. Most people just use condoms."

Valerian laughed, and Daisy was sure the sound would wake Nadine and Freddy, but apparently it didn't, for neither one of them showed up in the living room.

He leaned forward and kissed her lightly, briefly, on the lips. "I was talking about another kind of danger entirely," he said.

"You're afraid you'll pounce on me, in the throes of passion, and bite my neck?"

Valerian shook his head, and she caught a glint of mischief in his eyes, veiled in shadow though they were. "If we were in the 'throes of passion,' as you put it, I would already have pounced." He raised a hand to her face, rubbing his thumb along the length of her cheek. "No, Daisy love, I'm quite capable of making love to a mortal woman. But it's better if I stay away from you—I shouldn't even be here now."

"Because?"

He shoved his fingers through his lush, gleaming brown hair. "Because whoever—*whatever*—murdered Jillie and Susan might come after you next."

Daisy shivered involuntarily, remembering the murder scenes and the bodies of those two ill-fated women as vividly as if she'd seen them moments before. She started to speak, but Valerian stopped her, laying a fingertip to her lips.

"It is vital that you listen to me, Daisy," he said quietly, "that you *believe* what I'm telling you. You are in grave danger, but there is a place where you'll be at least moderately safe."

She closed her hand gently around his and spoke in a soft voice. "I'm a cop, remember? I'm not really safe—moderately or otherwise—anywhere. Hell, I don't even *want* that kind of security. The only risk-free place is the grave, and I'm definitely not ready for that."

Even in the gloom, she saw his magnificent face contort with some powerful emotion—anger? Frustration? Fear?

She couldn't begin to guess.

"You don't understand," he said with admirable control, after a short, tumultuous silence.

"I do," Daisy insisted. "You want to protect me, and that's wonderful. But I'm a big girl, with a badge and a thirty-eight. I can take care of myself, and I won't hide from anybody or anything."

"What use would a piece of metal and a primitive handgun be against a vampire?" Valerian said, leaning in close to make his point. "Don't you see that I—another nightwalker—am your only hope?" He paused, and his struggle to contain his emotions was visible in his face, despite the shadows. "*Damn it*, Daisy," he whispered, "if you won't do this for yourself, do it for your sister and her family. Do you want to draw this creature here, to this house?"

Daisy felt the blood drain from her face, and she raised one hand to her mouth. "Oh, God," she murmured. "Nadine—Freddy—that poor little baby—"

Valerian gripped her shoulders and gave her a gentle shake. "They have guardian angels, Daisy," he said quickly to stem her panic. "Especially the child. But angels are single-minded creatures, almost wholly absorbed in the adoration of their Creator. Sometimes they miss things."

"Oh, great," Daisy muttered.

"You've got to leave here now, tonight," Valerian insisted.

She glanced toward the doorway to the hall. Just beyond it, Nadine and Freddy lay sleeping peacefully in their bed. "I can't just abandon Nadine," she argued frantically. "What would she think if she woke up and found me gone? She's counting on me to help her—she's about to *give birth*, for heaven's sake!"

"That's easy," Valerian said. He was already pulling her to her feet, finding her discarded clothes unerringly in the dark, tugging the garments onto her body, over the bulky long johns, as if she were a child. "I'll simply remove all memory of your arrival from both their minds."

"That's crazy," Daisy protested and he closed her suitcase and shoved it at her. "You can't actually do that, can you?"

"I can," Valerian said, "and I have. Tonight your sister dreamed you came for a visit. In the morning she'll feel a little wistful and wonder how you are and if you're taking good care of yourself."

He pushed her out the door, closed it quietly behind them, and ushered her straight to the car.

"What about Freddy?"

"Same thing. 'Strange,' they'll say, 'that we both dreamed about Daisy. Do you suppose it means anything?' "

Daisy was pressed into the driver's seat. "Won't they hear the motor?"

"They might," Valerian said, relaxing at last, "but they'll just think it's one of the neighbors' cars."

"But—"

"Just drive, Daisy."

"Terrific. After all this, I don't even get to travel by broomstick?"

She could see his face clearly in the moonlight, and his expression was downright reproving. "That was beneath you, Daisy," he said. "Just go home before I lose my patience."

"Okay, genius, I will. It's not like Super-ghoul would think of looking for me *there* of all places. And what happens if you lose your patience?"

"Leave," Valerian said evenly, "before you find out."

With a sigh Daisy started the engine, backed out of Freddy and Nadine's driveway, and headed back in the general direction of Las Vegas.

VALERIAN
Colefield Hall, 1457

Elisabeth let out a bloodcurdling shriek, not of fear but of fury, as I ripped away the last of her clothes—no better than rotted rags, they were—and hoisted her off her kicking feet and into the brimming tub before the fire.

"This is foul treatment, sir!" she shrilled, hammering at my chest with her fists and splashing enough water over the sides—and down the front of my breeches—to fill the long-empty moat outside. "And it weren't no part of our bargain, neither! Don't you know I could catch me death? And you don't care, neither, do you, you bloody mother-loving—"

"In the name of whatever deity you worship, Elisabeth," I said through my teeth, "stop this mewling and thrashing, or I swear I'll take you to the nearest nunnery and leave you there to rot!"

She fell silent, and I felt pity for her, seeing the look in her eyes, but I wasn't fool enough to show it. She'd have been raising the roof again in a trice, the little imp.

"That's better," I said with what would have been a heartfelt sigh, had I been a mortal man. "You've been laboring under a delusion, my dear. Being clean is a most desirable state."

Elisabeth's expression was one of pure bafflement, and I realized, with both tender amusement and weariness, that she hadn't grasped my meaning at all.

I tried again. "No one has ever died from taking a bath," I assured her quietly. I scrubbed her from head to foot, for it was plain that she hadn't the vaguest idea how to scrub herself, then wrapped her in a blanket.

She knelt in obedient silence by the fire while I sat in the hearth chair, gently combing the tangles from her copper-gold hair.

At last she turned and looked up at me, letting the blanket fall away, revealing her exquisite, creamy body with a combination of shyness and pride.

"Will you have me now?" she asked.

I could not help myself; I reached out to touch her damp hair, her smooth, fire-warmed cheek. "Not yet, love."

"But I am a—a whore. You paid for me."

"You are not a whore. You are a princess. And if I paid for you, then I have the right to decide when to take you to my bed. Is that not so?"

The perfect column of her neck moved slightly as she swallowed. No sound came from her lips.

I pulled the blanket around her again and raised her to her feet. "Are you afraid?" I asked, holding her in my arms because I could not resist doing so. Not after loving her, wanting her, mourning for her for so many long, empty years.

Elisabeth nodded.

"Don't be," I whispered. "Because I would sooner destroy myself than do anything to hurt you. All I want is to look after you—"

"I'm not a fine lady, like you're used to," she murmured. "Is that why you don't want me?"

I laid an index finger to her nose, remembering so many things we had done together, things I knew she could not recall. "But I do want you," I said softly. "I want you desperately."

"Then, why—?"

I bent to kiss her lips, but only lightly. Only briefly. "We have time," I told her.

She trembled against me. "Well, I can't stay away from the Horse and Horn forever, you know," she protested, drawing back in my embrace. "There be those who'll be asking after me. I've got to look out for me lads, or some other girl will have them—"

An unholy rage surged through me at the thought of her giving herself to another man, whether for love or for money.

I caught her chin in my hand, perhaps a touch too roughly at first, and immediately relaxed my hold. Still, I knew from the fear that rose in her eyes that I had hurt her a little, and that she had not missed the look of fury I had been unable to disguise.

I closed my eyes for a moment, cursing myself for a rash, intemperate fool.

"I'm sorry," I said hoarsely. "I didn't mean to hurt you."

Her lower lip quivered as she gazed up at me. "I'm not that other girl—the one you used to know. I'm just plain Betsey Saxon, who lifts her skirts for them what can pay."

I should have listened to her. It might have saved us both so much pain.

Instead, I turned furiously away. "Don't ever say that again," I rasped, and she made no other attempt to reason with me for the rest of that night.

10

ELISABETH SAXON
Colefield Hall, 1457

ELISABETH lay alone and puzzled in Valerian's enormous bed, watching the firelight flicker across the ceiling. It was unheard of for a man to offer coins and then not take his pleasure, and she was troubled. Perhaps the gentleman did not think her fetching—the idea nettled her sorely—or perhaps she just wasn't fine enough for the likes of him.

Well, come the morrow, she'd take her bag of gold—it was tucked safely away beneath her pillow—and go straight back to the Horse and Horn. There were men there what appreciated a sweet-natured woman, and they wouldn't try to drown her in hot water or burn her eyes out with soap, neither.

She stretched, enjoying the feeling of the clean, smooth sheets against her bare skin, and sighed. She'd known a queer sense of recognition, when Valerian had entered the inn, as if she remembered him from somewhere beyond the reach of her memory, but she'd worked out why he'd seemed familiar. He was the living specter of a figure in a painting she'd seen, up in London Town, when she was a girl of eight.

Her father was still alive back then, and they'd gone to the city, the pair of them, hoping to sell off a cartload of cabbage in one of the marketplaces. They'd done well and shared an eel pie to celebrate, but as they started back toward home, a storm had come up, washing the cobbled streets and stinking gutters with rain.

They'd left the cart and pony in the mews and taken refuge inside a vast church, where there were paintings on the walls, and statues all about, and what seemed like thousands of candles. The place was empty, except for a priest and two or three old women kneeling in prayer, and as Elisabeth looked about, she marveled at the grandeur of it all.

The biggest painting loomed on the rear wall of the sanctuary, and Elisabeth's father, cap in hand, had told her in a whisper that it represented the aftermath of the great battle between God's angels and those who followed Lucifer. They'd been tussling on and off ever since, the good sorts and the bad, by his reckoning.

The eerie reality of the picture fascinated Elisabeth. The sky was filled with angels that appeared to fly, wings fluttering gracefully, while below their dangling, snow-white feet, amidst leaping flames, hideous demons thrust their pitchforks upward and leered in defiance.

On an outcropping of rock, well below heaven, but not quite in hell, or so it had seemed to Elisabeth, stood a magnificent figure, gazing up at the angels with a look of such sorrow and yearning that she'd wanted to weep for him. "Who is that?" she'd whispered and would have touched the image with a small, dirty finger if her father hadn't grasped her hand to stop her.

A monk had crept up behind them, leathershod feet moving soundlessly over the cold stone floor, and it was he who answered Elisabeth's question. "That, my child, is Lucifer—once God's favorite angel."

"Why does he look so sad?" she'd asked.

The monk spoke briskly and without compassion. "He knows that he is forever damned. As are all who willfully disobey God. Have a thought for the well-being of your soul, or you also will know the wrath of heaven."

Elisabeth had shuddered and moved a little closer to her father, who had put an arm about her shoulders. He had often remarked, in the privacy of their poor hovel in the outmost edge of the village of Lower Bilby, that kinder gods had once ruled in England, before the Christians came, bringing their devil with them.

Now, lying in a warm bed, with her belly full of good food, Elisabeth realized only too well why the master of this grand house had seemed familiar.

He looked exactly like that beautiful, solemn being in the church painting.

She shivered and pulled the covers up under her chin.

"Don't be a dunce, Betsey Saxon," she murmured to herself. "The master's a strange one, I'll give you that, but he's no more than a man."

A shadow moved next to the window, took on solidity and shape. "Ah," said that cultured, resonant voice she had come to recognize. "But I am 'more than a man,' Elisabeth. So much more."

Valerian.

Elisabeth's heart thundered; indeed its beat seemed to reverberate into every part of her body, but she couldn't rightly say she was afraid. "Where did you come from?" she demanded. "You wasn't here a minute ago."

He laughed, and the sound, rich and masculine, moved over Elisabeth like an intangible caress. "No, I wasn't," he said. He took the candle from its pewter stick, carried it over to the hearth, and squatted to touch the wick to the embers.

Thin, golden light gilded his face, his hair, and the fine, strange cut of his clothes as he crossed the room again. He stood at the foot of her bed, holding the tallow at chest height, seemingly unaware of the hot wax dropping onto the flesh of his hand. In the candle's glow, and the silver wash of the moon, it seemed he'd been sculpted from alabaster or ivory, like the statues in that London church.

"I just wish you'd make up your mind, that's all," Elisabeth said. "About whether you want a tumble or not, I mean."

Something moved in the exquisite, shadowy face at her words. Some fleeting emotion she supposed was better left unrecognized.

"Must you speak like a common trollop?" he asked after a moment's silence.

Elisabeth sat bolt upright in bed, and it never occurred to her to cover her full breasts. Modesty had no place in her life; she survived by enticing men with coppers to spend. And she had not been unhappy or ashamed, for she'd only done what she must.

Her cheeks were as hot as the last coals tumbling through the grate. "That's what I am, sir. Who else would I talk like now, besides me own self?"

Valerian looked as though she'd struck him, then he whirled suddenly and flung the candle into the fireplace. The tallow melted and caught fire before he turned to face her again.

"I can't bear it," he murmured, rubbing his temples with a thumb and forefinger. "This is worse than if I'd never found you at all."

Elisabeth felt a sudden, sweeping sympathy for him, just as she had for that lonely fellow in the painting, standing on the very brink of hell. Rising onto her knees, she made her way to the end of the bed. "For tonight," she said softly, "I can try to pretend that I'm her. I ain't been around so many ladies as some others might have been, but I think if I just kept quiet—"

He made an odd, strangled sound that might have been either a sigh or a sob. Then he came to where she knelt, placed his hands on either side of her head, and pressed her close against his chest.

"No," he whispered brokenly. "No, love. You needn't change to suit me. I adore you—I always will, no matter what you do. Yours is a splendid and brave spirit, and the truth is, you are far better than any woman, anywhere—"

She raised her hands to his shoulders and gazed up into his magnificent face. She didn't understand a great deal of what he said, it was true, but she knew how to console a man. "Let a girl lend a bit of comfort, won't you?" she said. "It won't be so bad, I promise."

He gazed into her eyes, idly smoothing the pads of his thumbs over her cheekbones. "Such charity," he marveled, and she knew by the tender despair in his voice he wasn't mocking her. "Have you no inhibitions at all?"

She was eager to lift his spirits. "I don't know," she said quickly, "but if you'll just explain how that's done—"

Valerian threw back his head and gave a shout of laughter, and when he looked at her again, it really did seem that there might be tears glistening in his eyes.

Elisabeth flushed, closing her hands into fists against his chest. "What's the joke?" she demanded.

He lifted her until she was standing, her feet sinking into the feather ticking as her knees had done before, her face on a level with his own. "Stay here with me," he pleaded quietly. "I'll give you whatever you want—all the gowns and kirtles you could wish for—a bucket of gold to celebrate the setting of every sun—anything."

Elisabeth relaxed her hands. No man had ever spoken to her that way, as if she had the option of granting or refusing his petition, when he was willing to pay so dear a price for her company. "And I don't have to be her—that other woman?"

Valerian lifted his face for a few moments, as though silently begging some favor of heaven, and then lifted her into his arms. "You only have to be Elisabeth," he said in a husky tone. "Tomorrow, after the sun goes down, you and I will be off to London, and we'll buy you so many baubles and ribbons that you won't be able to carry them all."

"You wouldn't make a promise like that and then change your mind, would you?"

He smiled and shook his head. "No, sweet. A promise is a promise."

She thought he would lie with her at last, since he carried her around the bed and set her so gently atop the smooth covers, but instead he just stood there, looking down at her.

Elisabeth caught hold of his hand, realizing that she wanted very much for him to stay. A peculiar state of shyness had overtaken her, though, and she could not confess what she was thinking.

"Couldn't we go in the morning?" she asked eagerly. "To London Town, I mean."

"I shall be busy then," he answered, and his words had just the faintest edge. "Have your evening meal early. We'll set out as soon as the moon rises."

Something compelled her to argue, to stall, so that he might stay longer. "But there's wolves about then, ain't there?"

"I am not afraid of those poor creatures," Valerian replied, "nor should you be. They'll do you no harm."

Despite the gentle tone in which he spoke, Elisabeth knew he would not change his mind. For reasons of his own—only the saints knew what they were—he did not wish to travel the road to London by day.

In Elisabeth's opinion, it was daft to take such a chance, for there were not only wolves to lie in wait along the way, but brigands, too. She told herself it was for the gowns she was going, and the gold he'd promised—a bucketful of it for every day at sunset, he'd said! Of course, he was probably bluffing about that.

She sighed. If things didn't turn out to her liking, why, London was a big place, and it would be easy to slip away and make a new start for herself. Especially with money saved and good clothes to wear.

"Won't you stay?" she said, still clasping his hand, which felt strangely cool and hard.

Valerian bent just far enough to brush his lips, shiver-light, across her knuckles. "Some other night, my love. When you've learned to trust me. And don't think of running away once you get to London—there are creatures far deadlier than wolves wandering its streets."

Elisabeth gasped, for she'd only *thought* of losing herself in that great city—she certainly hadn't spoken of it aloud. "You're a warlock!" she accused, meaning to sit up again, to flee the room, nay, the castle itself, and take her chances with the wild animals and thieves she might well meet on the road.

She could not move. Valerian held her with nothing but his gaze, and yet she was pinioned to the bed.

"I pray you," he said evenly, "do not insult me so again. I am no such creature."

Tears, more of wonder and amazement than fear, sprang to Elisabeth's eyes. She had given up struggling beneath his invisible hold, having found it futile to do so. "What are you, then?" she persisted, barely breathing the words. "You said yourself, when first you came out of the shadows beside the window, that you are more than a man!"

"Brave, foolish Elisabeth," he said, withdrawing a little way into the darkness. "That was your fatal flaw before as well, you know. You were not wise enough to be afraid, and that's why the sea took you from me."

"What do you mean?" Elisabeth might have been bound by visible ropes; the spell he'd cast over her was that strong. "What are you, if you ain't a man or a warlock? And what do you mean, saying the sea took me away from you? What have you done to me?"

Valerian did not reply, but simply retreated another step, and then another. In the next instant he was gone, without so much as stirring a draft.

The enchantment was broken; freed from whatever mysterious power had held her pressed to the mattress, Elisabeth leaped off the bed and rushed to the place where Valerian had been until a mere heartbeat before.

Furious because she could not comprehend his trick, she stomped one foot and let loose with a string of curses that would have turned the River Thames back upon itself.

Valerian did not return that night, although Elisabeth kept her eyes open as long as she could, waiting for him.

DAISY
Las Vegas, 1995

The trip back from Telluride was never quite clear in Daisy's memory. One minute she'd been driving down the highway in the predawn darkness, sensing rather than seeing the mountains and Christmas-scented forests all around her. The next, she found herself cruising through the Nevada desert in the bright afternoon sunlight, only a few miles outside her hometown.

Either she really was losing her mind, or Valerian had come through with a version of broomstick travel after all.

Turning onto the roadside, Daisy put on the brakes and shut off the engine. Then she just sat there, trembling, her forehead resting against the steering wheel, until she was sure she wouldn't a) hyperventilate or b) go into hysterics.

After a few moments of recovery, she reached up and wrenched the rearview mirror toward her, peering into her own eyes, noting the shadows beneath them and the pallor of her skin.

"You're not crazy, Chandler," she said aloud and with conviction.

"Have you got that? If you saw a guy disappear, he damned well *disappeared*! And if you think you made the trip between Telluride and Vegas in practically the blink of an eye, then that's what happened!"

A swirling blue light flashed across her reflected image, and she sighed and tilted her head back against the seat to take a deep breath, hold it to the count of five, and release it slowly. It was an antistress technique she'd read about in a magazine article while waiting in the dentist's office.

The state trooper approached the car on the driver's side and rapped on the window.

"You feeling all right, ma'am?" he inquired through the glass.

Daisy rolled it down. The trooper was young, and probably still convinced he could change the world, and her heart went out to him. According to the plastic tag on his uniform shirt, his name was Wilson.

She nodded and smiled. "I'm okay. I guess I'm a little tired, though—I just drove over from my sister's place in Telluride."

Okay, so that might have been a small lie, Daisy conceded to her twitching conscience. What was she supposed to have said—that she'd been zapped from Colorado to Nevada, without even touching down in Utah? Badge or no badge, she'd wind up in a room with upholstered walls if she told the truth.

"I'd like to take a look at your license and registration, please," Wilson said, with an endearing all-American smile.

Daisy reached for her purse, but slowly. She was a cop herself, after all, and she knew well enough how a quick move would look from the trooper's perspective. She handed him the requested license along with her badge and was removing the registration from the clip on the visor when he cleared his throat.

"That's all right, Detective Chandler," he said, returning the laminated card with her mug shot on it, along with the small leather folder containing her police ID and badge. He was blushing a little. "You know how it is."

"Yeah," Daisy said good-naturedly, "I do."

"I could drive you into town if you're too tired to go on."

Daisy shook her head. "I'm okay. I just needed to take a breather, that's all. Thanks."

The trooper nodded, touched the brim of his hat, and strode back to his car. Daisy watched his retreating figure in the mirror, grinning slightly and thinking there was nothing quite like a man in a uniform.

Except maybe a vampire magician in a tux and a flowing cape, she reflected, starting the ignition, signaling, and pulling back out onto the freeway.

Trooper Wilson chivalrously escorted her all the way to the Las Vegas city limits.

She sighed when he took an exit and headed back in the other direction. So much for the police escort.

At first Daisy's apartment seemed to be just the way she'd left it. She called Nadine right away, ignoring the blinking light on her answering machine, and heard her sister's cheerful "Hello?"

Daisy closed her eyes. Would Nadine remember her visit, or had Valerian wiped it out of her mind, and Freddy's, as he'd claimed? "Hi, sis," she said in a rush of breath. "How are you?"

"Daze! Hi! Freddy and I were just talking about you this morning—it's the darnedest thing. We *both* dreamed you showed up late last night and slept on our Hide-A-Bed! Isn't that wild—the two of us having the same dream?"

"Wild," Daisy agreed, feeling a bit sad and very disoriented. By now she half believed she'd dreamed her part of the experience, too. "When's that baby planning to be born? When interest rates go down? When there's another Republican in the White House?"

Nadine laughed. "I'd ask her, but I think she's busy doing aerobics. This kid never sleeps."

Daisy felt bruised inside. It was, and would always be, a sharp disappointment that she couldn't be there for Nadine at this important time. "Have you and Freddy managed to agree on a name yet?"

"No," Nadine admitted. "He wants to call her Carmen Miranda. Trust me, Daisy, no child of mine is going to go around with half the produce department piled on top of her head."

Now it was Daisy who laughed. "What do you want to call her?" she asked when she'd recovered.

"Whitney," Nadine replied in a wistful voice. "It's such a classy name, don't you think? But Freddy says it's pretentious."

"I'm sure the two of you will come up with something suitable."

There was a short silence. "When are you coming over to see us?" Nadine finally asked.

Daisy's eyes burned. *When we've found this Thing, this murdering fiend, and driven a stake through its heart. Or shot it with a silver bullet.*

"Soon," she said aloud, after what she hoped was an inaudible sniffle.

"Are you catching cold?"

It was Daisy's day for telling lies, among other things. "Yeah," she said. "Maybe I'll take a few days off to drink chicken broth and watch soap operas."

"Good plan."

"You'll call? When it's time, I mean?"

"You bet," Nadine said gently. "You're destined to be Carmen Miranda's favorite aunt. Besides, I'm expecting a really good baby present from you."

Daisy smiled. "Don't worry about that," she said. "I've been poring over catalogs and prowling through malls for weeks. I'm going to send something that will make Miss *Whitney* Donaldson the envy of the disposable diaper crowd."

"Why don't you bring the gift in person?" Nadine asked.

Daisy's smile faded. "I can't get away just now, sweetie," she said. "Trust me when I tell you that some very big things are going down around here right now."

Nadine let out a long, martyrly sigh. Evidently she figured it was her turn to be the mother hen of the pair. "I worry about you, Daze. You take too many risks. And it seems like every time I watch one of those reality shows on television, some police officer gets killed."

"Nadine? There's an easy solution to that—stop watching reality shows."

"Promise me you'll be careful. God knows where Mom is—we're probably happier not knowing. But you're all I've got, Daisy, and I can't bear to lose you."

A tear slipped down Daisy's right cheek, and she dashed it away with the back of her free hand. "I'm not all you have," she reminded her sister. "You've got Freddy and that little one doing a high-impact workout under your rib cage." Images of Jillie's and Susan's bloodless bodies filled her mind and made her stomach pitch. She'd try her damnedest, she vowed silently, not to end up like them. "Look, just focus on the business at hand, okay? I'll be fine."

Nadine didn't sound reassured, but they said their goodbyes and hung up. Daisy immediately called O'Halloran on his cell phone, guessing that he wouldn't be in his office if he could help it.

She was right.

"O'Halloran," he barked. "Don't tell me there's been another murder," he rushed on before Daisy could even identify herself, "because I don't want to hear it!"

"*Has* there been another murder?" she demanded.

"Shit," O'Halloran snapped. "This is Chandler, ain't it? You're already back in town."

There are moments when I'm not sure I ever left in the first place, Daisy thought, with a sort of fatalistic whimsy. "It's your winning personality and your movie-star body, O'Halloran," she said. "You drive me mad with passion. How could I stay away?"

He swore again, more creatively than before and with considerably more venom. "You're on leave, damn it!" he growled once he'd finished reciting the long list of colorful epithets and expletives he'd learned in nearly three decades of public service.

Daisy smiled into the telephone receiver. "Don't talk like that," she said sweetly. "It ain't becoming."

O'Halloran sighed heavily. It wasn't easy, the sound seemed to say, single-handedly thwarting evil and holding back the tide of crime.

"All right," he said. "You'll read it in the papers or see it on the tube anyhow. Somebody else was killed last night."

Daisy leaned against the wall, her eyes closed. "Who?"

"It wasn't another one of that magician's showgirls, if that's what you're thinking," O'Halloran said, his voice gruff with suppressed emotion. "But the M.O. was the same. Lady named Janet Hurly."

Daisy knew her partner well. "There is a connection, though, isn't there?"

"Yes, damn it, for all the concern it is of yours right now, with your badge in limbo. You stay out of this, Chandler, or I swear to God I'll go to the chief myself and tell him you think you've been to Mars twice on an alien spaceship. And he'll believe me, too, after the way you went T.U. in the supermarket."

"*O'Halloran.*"

"She was this Valerian guy's agent and business manager," he finally admitted. "The victim, I mean."

Daisy muttered a favorite swearword of her own, rubbing her right temple with two fingers. "Getting information out of you is like getting a congressman to admit he wears lacy underwear. I feel like I've just dragged Lake Tahoe with a hairnet!"

"Why should I make it easy? This one's my problem."

"That's what you think, O'Halloran."

He hung up.

"O'Halloran!" Daisy screamed into the mouthpiece. Then she disconnected with a belated bang, knowing it was useless to try to reason with the man. He thought he was protecting her.

Instantly the phone rang again, and Daisy snatched it off the hook.

"What?" she demanded, thinking it was O'Halloran calling back with another reason why she shouldn't try to do her job. He might fancy himself her knight in shining armor, but she'd be damned if she'd let him trample her career beneath the hooves of his trusty charger.

"Dai-sy." The voice was the same mechanical, androgynous drone she'd heard before. "Time—to—die—soon—"

"Why did you kill Janet Hurly?" Daisy interrupted acidly. She was too furious to be afraid; that would come later, she supposed, when she'd had time to think. "I thought I was supposed to be next." She drew out the last words, mimicking the caller's tinny monotone.

"I left—a—message—for you," the thing said. There was no soul behind the voice, no emotion. "I'll be sending—a special gift—very soon."

Daisy felt a familiar chill. "Gee, thanks," she replied, revealing none of the cloying, elemental fear that was climbing her backbone, vertebra by vertebra. "I was beginning to think it was over between us."

"Goodbye, Dai-sy/Bren-na/Elis-a-beth/Jen-ny. See—you—soon."

Daisy hung up and dashed into the bathroom as bile surged into the back of her throat. She was bending over the toilet, shivering and retching convulsively, when out of the corner of one eye she caught a glimpse of a still form behind the shower curtain.

With a cry Daisy whirled, automatically reaching for her service revolver—which was tucked away under the front seat of her car. There was a baseball bat in the towel cupboard—she'd never really recovered from seeing *Psycho* on the late-late show—and Daisy grabbed it and prepared to swing.

The shape behind the shower curtain didn't move or speak.

Bravado was all she had, besides the baseball bat. Reason and experience told her that if she tried to run, the intruder would be on her before she got to the front door. If he happened to be bigger or stronger, she'd be in deep sewage.

"If you have a weapon," she said forcefully, "drop it. Now."

Nothing.

Daisy took a deep breath, let it out, and then, on one of those rash impulses that sometimes earn cops their own segment on the local news, reached out and wrenched the plastic curtain to one side.

A life-size blowup doll, the kind that can be purchased in any sleazy novelty shop, dangled from the shower head by a noose fashioned from the belt of Daisy's bathrobe. For a dramatic touch, two small red marks had been drawn onto the neck.

Daisy turned back to the toilet and threw up in earnest.

When the heaving stopped at last, she rinsed her mouth, washed her face, and called O'Halloran on his car phone again. "Get over here," she said calmly. "Now."

She hung up and went down to her car for the thirty-eight. While she waited for her partner to arrive, Daisy inspected the rest of the apartment. None of the windows had been forced, and she remembered clearly that the front door was locked when she'd arrived home from a trip she probably hadn't gone on in the first place.

Daisy sat down on the couch in her living room, the revolver in her lap, and heard the echo of the caller's robotic voice in her brain.

I left a message for you. . . .

O'Halloran didn't bother to knock. He just walked right in. Daisy thought numbly that she should be grateful he hadn't kicked the door open, movie-cop style, weapon drawn. She might have shot him if he had.

"What's going on, Chandler?" To his credit, O'Halloran looked genuinely concerned. "You space out again or something?"

"Just go and look in my shower," she said.

I left a message. . . .

O'Halloran did so and bellowed an exclamation. When he got back to the living room, his face was heart-attack gray, and sweat beaded his forehead and upper lip.

"Jesus, Joseph, and Mary," he rasped, shoving one hand through his sparse hair. "That's just plain ugly."

Daisy knew there was more. Maybe she was psychic. "And?"

O'Halloran sank into a chair, pulling his cell phone out of his jacket pocket in almost the same motion. "Janet Hurly's body was found hanging from a showerhead," he said as he dialed headquarters. "The killer used what looked like the belt of a bathrobe for a rope. What we got here, Chandler, is a real reasonable facsimile."

11

VALERIAN
Outside Las Vegas, 1995

THE taillights of Daisy's car, glowing red as the eyes of a demon in a bad painting, dissolved into the predawn gloom. I worked a mental trick that would cause the journey to pass quickly for her and withstood the temptation to set my beloved on a path leading anywhere except back to Las Vegas.

How I yearned to lock her away in some enchanted tower—if such a place existed—or hide her like a treasure in my desert lair. The ruby ring, the harbinger of her death, would arrive soon, I knew, and I was full of terror.

I dared not attempt to shield her, though, however noble my intentions, for Daisy cherished her freedom in this life, as she had in all the others before it. I had learned from bitter experience that she would despise me for imprisoning her.

I was, by that time, utterly desperate. I had searched for my ruthless enemy, along with Maeve, and all to no avail. I think I realized, even then, that if I found the fiend I sought, I would also find the one who had stalked my beloved and me, down through the centuries, making a deadly gift of the bloodred gemstone I had come to hate and fear.

As I saw it, I had no choice but to awaken Tobias, the slumbering one, who had been among the first vampires created. The rest of that strange fellowship had perished by their own choice, in the womb of the earth, except of course for Lisette, the first queen. She'd died by Maeve's hand, and rightfully so, far away on a moonswept moor.

But those are other tales, for other vampires to tell.

I willed myself to Tobias's lair, barely reaching that gravelike pit ahead of the consuming sunlight, and sprawled beside my elder. Before I could even attempt to rouse him, by word or touch, the consuming sleep bore me down and down, into darkness.

I was trapped inside my dreams, where I saw Janet Hurly, my mortal manager and something akin to a friend, savagely murdered in her apartment. I was unable to come to her aid, mired as I was in the vampire sleep, and it was perfect torment to look on helplessly. When it was over at last, when he'd strangled Janet, this creature I couldn't quite recognize, and then left her body hanging from the showerhead by a strip of cloth, it seemed her staring eyes were fixed on me.

Accusing. Asking why.

I flailed mentally, trying to regain consciousness and thus escape the smothering weight of the nightmare, but it was no use. Sometimes I was wakeful during the daylight hours, though I could never tolerate the sun, but it was not a feat I could perform at will. The phenomenon happened on its own, generally after I had been feeding with uncommon appetite for a long period of time.

At last, at last, the blessed caress of twilight reached me, stretching fingers of shadow down through the soil, and I was again in command of my body and mind. I sat up in Tobias's cramped coffin of a lair, pebbles and the bones of some hapless mortal scrabbling beneath me as I moved.

"Tobias!" I shook his slender shoulder. He resembled a lad, having been made while still a youth, but in fact he was, as far as I knew, the oldest vampire in existence.

He mumbled and stirred slightly, making a groping motion with one hand, to dismiss me.

I straddled him and grasped both his shoulders now, and the rotted fabric of his tunic crumbled in my hands, fragile as curls of ash on a cold hearth.

"Damn you, Tobias, wake! I need your help!"

Even in a stupor he was powerful, and with no physical effort at all, with nothing more than a half-formed thought, he cast me from him. I slammed against the side of our joint tomb with a jarring impact, mentally revising my earlier supposition that only Maeve Tremayne was stronger than I.

"Go—away," Tobias muttered.

For Daisy's sake, I would brave Tobias's rare but formidable wrath. I would plead, bargain, lie.

Anything to keep Daisy from the unknown monster.

I knelt at his side. "Please, Old One, hear me. There is a fiend, a vampire, I think, but perhaps a warlock—"

Tobias interrupted in the expressionless tones of one entranced. "Return to Dunnett's Head," he said slowly without opening his eyes. "The answer is there—and not there. That is the riddle."

With that, he settled deeper into his nest of death, looking for all the world like a child curling up on the nursery couch for his afternoon nap. I knew I would get no more from him no matter how long or how forcefully I persisted.

Dunnett's Head. My ancient home.

I sat back on my haunches. I had not been near that accursed place since the day Brenna and I left it, while I was yet mortal. Crouched there in Tobias's grave, I doubted that even a trace of the village itself had survived the passing centuries, though there might well be ruins of Baron Afton-St. Claire's austere keep.

I covered my face with both hands for a moment, hating even the thought of returning to the scene of so much tragedy and pain, knowing at the same time that I must go immediately. Tobias had said its name clearly.

Dunnett's Head.

I dared not even take the time to hunt and feed, for any delay might rob me of my determination to find my foe before he completed his plan of revenge. I did not need to be told that his designs included Daisy.

Daisy. She would have been doomed anyway, like Brenna and Elisabeth and Jenny and the others before her. There was no escaping the curse, no matter what I did or said or thought, but my desperate delusion was also a part of the mysterious evil that had tormented us both for six hundred years. Each time I stumbled across my beloved, in each new incarnation, I believed I could save her. I *had* to cling to that vain fancy, or go stark, screaming mad at the prospect of losing her again.

I turned the powers of my mind upon Dunnett's Head, and in the length of a mortal's heartbeat, I was there, standing among the moonlit stones that had once formed the baron's keep. I shivered in the night wind that surged upward from the sea, although a vampire does not feel that kind of chill, and turned slowly to look around me.

In a few paces I stood where the courtyard had been, in the exact spot where Brenna's father had bested me in swordplay. I bear the scar of that conflict still, a tidy line across my middle.

Soon I found the remnants of the great hall and the chapel, and there was still a ditch, though so shallow now that it was hardly discernible, where the moat had been.

Memories assailed me, striking my spirit like stones hard-flung, and I found I could not bear to stand in this place where Brenna had been and was no more.

I walked down the hillside to the site of the village, traversing the short distance as a mortal man would have done, instead of willing myself to my destination, for I was in no hurry to arrive.

Not even stones remained to mark where the cluster of humble huts and shops had been, but it didn't matter. I found the location of the bootmaker's shop, with our pitiful rooms at the back, where I'd been born as a human child, where I'd nursed at my mother's breast and endured my father's resentment as I grew. I knew the places where Krispin and I had played as boys, the spots where peddlers had sold their wares and tinkers had made their bright, noisy camps. I looked out upon the dark sea, watching the moonlight dance in ever-changing patterns of gold and silver, and wondered why Tobias had sent me here.

I had found memories, yes. But what of the answers I sought? What had I gained by returning, beyond another increase in my capacity to endure pain?

I might have left then, in frustration and disappointment, were it not for a stray thought of my poor mother. I knew that she, like my father and Krispin, like most everyone in the village, had died in the pestilence. Brenna and I had looked on from the hillside while corpses, blackened by that foul plague even before they burned, were flung onto the blazing pyre.

Someone must have buried the bones afterward, I reasoned, for the majority of our neighbors had been Christians, and they will go, I have found, to great lengths to dig proper graves and say holy words over them.

While I did not mourn my father, I had loved my mother and brother quite devotedly in my way. I wanted to find their last resting place and stand beside those long-forgotten plots for a brief interval, remembering, hoping they had fared well in the next world.

They deserved that much, I reflected, after all their suffering.

When I had made considerable explorations, striding this way and that, dredging my memory and all my senses, I divined the presence of a large, common grave, well away from the place where the village had been, and hurried toward it, gliding silently through the grass like a specter.

Standing beside that unseen tomb, with its great, dry jumble of bones, I closed my eyes and fixed my concentration on days so long past that only immortals remember their like. After a time I began to see images of the bodies in that grave as they had been before the plague struck.

I saw Old Tom, the tanner, and Ben Willy, who milled the corn into meal. I saw their wives and their children, and so many others as well—fishermen, crofters, the baron himself. They were ghosts, some joyous, others full of sorrow, and they cast dancing shadows into my mind.

I saw my mother, the uncommonly beautiful Seraphina, and knew her remains lay disjointed and brown within the pit. My father's bones were there, too, far from hers and reaching out to her even in death, but I felt no impression of Krispin, no echo of his laughter or his quick fury.

I frowned. If he did not lie here with the others, then where? Had he escaped to the sea, onboard one of the ships he was forever sighting on the horizon? Had he gone to London, or taken up the Christian cross, as the good brothers had bade me do so long ago?

I heard Tobias's voice in my head.

Return to Dunnett's Head. The answer is there—and not there.

I frowned, and another chill struck me, coming not from the cold and treacherous sea but rising from within my own being.

Could it be? Was this my enemy, then—my own brother, Krispin? No, I insisted to myself. He loved me, and I loved him.

Krispin would have been unable to keep his existence from me for so long. Besides, we had been brothers, friends. He had followed me everywhere, looked up to me, laughed with me . . .

And wanted to do everything I did.

Everything.

I shuddered and tipped my head back to search the starry sky with eyes that burned. "No," I whispered. "Not Krispin."

But I knew even then that my brother had not returned to dust, like our father and mother. He was aboard, and he was my avowed foe. Some vampire, most likely Challes, had transformed Krispin into a blood-drinker.

My despair was absolute, all-encompassing. It drove me to my knees, there beside that mass grave, where I wept with fresh grief.

"Krispin," I whispered. "Why?"

There was, of course, no answer, for my brother, as it happened, was very busy elsewhere.

ELISABETH
London, 1457

The house was fine indeed, with a cozy fire burning in every room and paintings on the walls. Elisabeth had a chamber of her own—that was what the master called it, a "chamber," and she liked the way the word sounded—and even a servant whose task it was to look after her. The maiden, named Kate Crown, plainly disapproved of Elisabeth and her country manners, but she was a canny soul and showed her misgivings only when Valerian wasn't about.

Elisabeth saw neither hide nor hair of the master during the day, and even at night he often had business abroad. She didn't mind dealing with Kate and the other servants of the household, for she could hold her own against that lot right enough, but she'd become somewhat attached to Valerian and was always anxious for his return.

He joined her at the table most nights, and an abundance of roast meat and boiled vegetables was always served, along with fruits and potatoes, but Elisabeth never saw him take so much as a bite to eat. She asked him once why he didn't touch his food, and he said he'd had all he needed somewhere else. She didn't raise the subject again, but she'd often gone hungry in her brief and difficult life, and she still thought it was a queer thing never to take up a spoon or a knife in your own house.

There were other odd things about the household and its master.

For one, Valerian was never addressed as Mister This or Mister That—the servants called him sir or master, and kept their eyes down. His friends, of whom there were a great many, and who always visited at night, were every bit as strange as he was, and greeted him in odd ways. They scolded him indulgently, as if he were a child, and yet they seemed to revere and even fear him.

Elisabeth was frankly jealous and wished they wouldn't be so familiar. She especially hated the women, in their grand gowns and jewel-trimmed capes, for to them he was "darling" and "beautiful one," and they kissed him and smoothed his hair.

Sometimes, when he was home of an evening, he read to Elisabeth from manuscripts and bound volumes by the fire in the drawing room. He took her to see a puppet show once, and every night, when she was ready to go to bed, she found a handful of shimmering gold coins waiting on her pillow.

She hoarded them against a future that might be less bountiful, hiding them under a loose board in a corner of her room. She had learned long since that good fortune was no more trustworthy than spring weather or a tinker's promise, but there could be no denying that she was in luck.

Not that Elisabeth was entirely happy, for she wasn't. She had come to want Valerian, as a woman wants a man, but despite his generosity, he still had not come to her bed. In fact, he hadn't even entered her room since the second night, when he'd appeared as if by conjuring and asked her to stay with him.

One evening, after a month of high living in London Town, Elisabeth was alone by the drawing room fire. She kicked away her slippers to warm her toes and wished it was so easy to take the chill off her heart. She was a woman, not a child, as the master seemed to think, and she longed to be touched and held and spoken to in soft words.

Elisabeth had enjoyed her work at the Horse and Horn, both upstairs and down. It was worth enduring the occasional bad night for all the times when she'd taken comfort from the warm presence of another person.

She wanted that again.

The guest came in the early evening, when the master was out, and asked expressly for Elisabeth. He was fair and handsome in a prissy sort of way, and he would not give his name. He'd brought a packet for her, he said, a splendid gift.

The package was small, a sheet of parchment tied with a thin blue ribbon. Pleased, Elisabeth opened the bundle and found a golden ring inside, set with a great, glittering red stone.

Elisabeth closed her fingers around the jewel, wanting it for her own and yet strangely afraid, too. "What do you want in return?" she asked, for she knew the ways of the world well enough.

The stranger slipped the exquisite ring onto her finger, and the square stone winked, red as an ox's blood, in the firelight. "Only for you to wear it," he said.

Elisabeth was speechless.

He touched her forehead with light, cool fingers, and then he was gone. Within five minutes Elisabeth had no memory of the encounter, and could not explain, to herself or anyone else, how she'd come to have such a ring.

When Valerian returned home, it was late, for the moon had fitted itself into a high corner of the window, and it was so pale Elisabeth could almost see through it, like an onion skin. There were two young men with him, their eyes bright, their beautiful skin white as new milk, their clothes rich and elegantly cut. To another person, they might have seemed drunk, but Elisabeth was an expert on that, and she knew they were sober as Saint Peter, the pair of them.

The master stopped on the threshold when he saw Elisabeth curled up in his favorite chair, and she realized with a start that he was surprised to see her. That was an odd thing in itself, since he usually knew not only where she was, but what she was thinking.

The two knaves squeezed into the doorway behind Valerian, peering over his shoulders at Elisabeth.

"The rumors are true," one of them said. "What a vision she is!"

"However do you resist her?" asked the other.

Valerian's gaze was fixed on the fiery jewel gracing Elisabeth's finger, and a small frown creased his brow. There ended the theory that the costly bauble had come from him.

She hoped she hadn't taken to stealing in her sleep.

Elisabeth rose, with a dignity she'd learned by watching the master's female guests, and put her hands on her hips. "I'll thank the both of you not to talk about me as if I had neither ears nor wits!"

Valerian's mouth twitched at one side, but Elisabeth didn't know whether he'd suppressed a smile or a scowl. And she wouldn't have cared, whichever one it was.

"Go to bed, Elisabeth. It is late," he said evenly. She noticed that he didn't move out of the doorway, but effectively blocked his friends from entering the room.

"I ain't a little girl and I won't be ordered about," Elisabeth replied with a lift of her chin.

The master raised one eyebrow. "Ah, but this is my household," he countered in the same smooth tones as before. "Here things are done as I command."

"Are they now?" Elisabeth pressed. She had doubts about the wisdom of what she was saying, but she couldn't seem to stop herself. She folded her arms and raised her chin. "For all I care, you can take your bloody commands and bugger yourself with them, one right after the other."

The lads laughed uproariously at this, but Valerian did not look pleased.

"Leave us," he said, without sparing his guests so much as a glance, but they knew he was speaking to them. Elisabeth recognized that right enough, because they almost collided with each other in their rush to back away.

"Wait!" Elisabeth called to them, not in fear, but in defiance. "I'll go with you, lads. It's that dull around this place—"

She started to pass Valerian, as if to follow them, and he caught her arm in a firm but gentle hold and stopped her. It was hard not to smile; silly of him, not to realize that she'd never leave without her store of gold coins and at least one woolen cloak.

"You're not going anywhere," he said. "And we'll discuss that little trinket you're wearing later."

Elisabeth hid her triumph, and the flash of fear that streaked through her like lightning, as she had hid her amusement. He'd read her mind often enough in the past, the master had, but he seemed to have lost the knack.

Still holding her arm, Valerian glanced at his guests and repeated his earlier request in blunter terms.

"Get out."

They obeyed without further ado, and the door slammed hard behind them.

"What is this about?" the master demanded of Elisabeth when they were alone.

Her chin quivered, and she thought she might cry. Damned if she would, she vowed in the very next instant, she who hadn't shed a single tear since the day her father died of a fever, when she was but fourteen.

"I want to go back to the Horse and Horn," she said, hugging herself tightly with both arms.

He did not release her until he'd marched her back over to the chair and pushed her into it. "You want to do *what*?" he rasped, pacing the length of the stone hearth several times and then stopping suddenly to stand there glaring at her. "In the name of all that's holy, why? Haven't I treated you well—given you food and coin and garments fit for a princess to wear?"

"You've treated me," Elisabeth said bravely, though in truth her courage was starting to crumble, "like I was your sister!"

The master stared down at her, clearly astounded. "My behavior has been impeccable!"

"Whatever that means!" Elisabeth flung out her arms in exclamation. "Talk like a plain man for once, damn you, and not some walking book with skin and hair and eyeballs!"

He closed his eyes for a moment. "What would you have me say?"

Elisabeth swallowed. "I wouldn't have you say nothing," she replied boldly. "You don't only talk too fancy, sir—you talk too *much* as well!"

He watched her in pointed silence, his arms folded.

A terrible thought occurred to Elisabeth, a reason why he had never touched her in any intimate fashion.

"No," Valerian said before she could voice the possibility, "I do not prefer boys to women."

It was almost a relief that he was reading her mind again; at least he was paying attention.

Elisabeth blushed, holding his gaze, fierce and intimidating though it was. "I need somebody to lie down with me," she said. "I need to be held real tight in somebody's arms." And then she began to cry. Noisily, with a great deal of snuffling and heaving of shoulders.

Valerian hesitated, then stepped forward and, without a word, pulled her into his embrace. She wailed into his fancy tunic, the fabric bunched in her fists.

Presently, when she'd expended most of her great sorrow, he lifted her gently off her feet and carried her up the stairway and along the passage to the door of her chamber. She was certain she wouldn't be able to stand it if he left her alone, feeling the way she did, but he stayed.

He undressed her slowly and with reverence, admiring and caressing her breasts as he bared them, lightly touching her soft white belly and the tangle of skin beneath, where her legs met.

Elisabeth lifted her hands to his face and drew his head down. When their lips touched, he moaned, somewhere deep inside himself, and for Elisabeth it was as if there were stout ale mingling with her blood, racing through her veins.

After a while he pulled back from her, just far enough to look into her eyes. His hands, though cool, seemed to set her flesh ablaze with sensation.

"Is this what you want?" he asked. "The choice must be yours, beloved, not just mine."

She nodded, frantic and feverish, and pressed herself close to him. *Beloved.* The word found its way into her very soul and tolled there, like a bell. "Yes," she whispered. "Oh, yes."

He laid her gently on the bed and took off his clothes without hurrying. Moonlight streamed in through the windows, making his splendid body glow like polished marble, and as she watched him, it occurred to Elisabeth that he was too beautiful, too perfect, to be human.

Valerian was indeed, as he himself had once told her, more than a man.

"Touch me," she said, and he lay down beside her on the soft mattress, taking her into his arms. There was a single flaw, she saw, as he poised himself above her, a long, thin scar, pink against the alabaster whiteness of his skin, spanning the width of his torso.

"I have wanted you for so long," he told her, and she believed him.

Elisabeth had never known such piercing desire, never dreamed of feeling the way she did that night. She could not lie still and, putting her arms around Valerian's neck, she moved her hips in a circular motion beneath him.

He groaned, and somewhere far off a hound bayed in primitive harmony.

Their joining, too long delayed, was neither gentle nor ordinary. One moment they were separate, the next they were a single being, with a shared heartbeat, breathing the same air, thinking with one mind, one soul entwined with the other.

There was a sense of the inevitable, of a destiny that could not have been avoided. They moved together, their pace rapid, urgent, fierce.

Elisabeth pitched beneath Valerian, her hands moving wildly over the smooth flesh of his back and the flexing muscles of his buttocks, as if to take the whole of him inside her, as she had taken his manhood. She had pretended with other men, but with Valerian there was no need; her rising cries were born of the purest pleasure.

Valerian did not try to quiet her; instead he thrust harder and deeper. Although he made no sound at all, Elisabeth saw ecstasy in the planes of his face and felt it in the way he trembled upon her.

She reached satisfaction first, sobbing and breathless, soaring into a new place, far above the reach of her own mind and soul.

When Valerian followed her into the flames, only moments later, he gave a long, low cry, and started to spill himself into her. Then his body jerked convulsively, as if to leap to some new and unexpected height of pleasure. He closed his eyes, his head thrust back, and gave a raspy, triumphant shout.

The name he called was not her own. It was Brenna's.

Elisabeth didn't care, for he'd given her what she wanted, and she had never aspired to earn his love, never so much as hoped for such a thing. She cradled him in her arms and soothed him with light fingers and whispered words while he shuddered in the aftermath of a climax that had been emotional as well as physical.

Presently he slid downward upon her warm and welcoming body, still trembling, to rest his head between her breasts, and she stroked his hair. He turned and took her nipple, tentatively at first, and then with greed. Elisabeth felt something reawaken inside her and coil itself tighter and tighter.

She moaned and arched her back, offering herself, and he took her eagerly, gratefully, running his hands down her sides and then lifting them to her breasts again.

When he claimed her for the second time, Elisabeth exploded immediately, a fiery spiral unfurling within her, the circles ever-widening, flinging light with every revolution, warming the parts of her soul she'd kept secret even from herself.

Valerian loved her over and over that night, satisfying every desire, meeting every need. Sometime just before dawn, he let her sleep at last, and when she opened her eyes at midmorning, he was gone.

She got up, washed, donned a clean gown and overskirt, and silently dared Kate Crown, who brought her breakfast on a tray, to speak so much as a word.

Kate did not take the challenge, but the fine ring on Elisabeth's finger caught her eye, and there would be talk about it in the kitchen for sure. The maid left the food on the table next to the bed with its tangled covers and left the room again.

Elisabeth ate fruit and brown bread and some cold meat, then used her knife to pry up the loose floorboard. She took out the hoard of gold, which was tightly bundled in a bit of cloth pinched from the kitchen, and marveled at how heavy it was.

There was enough there, she guessed, to keep her for years, if she was careful, and she wouldn't have to go back to the Horse and Horn, either, or to any place like it. The night just past had changed her, in some way she didn't fully understand. She knew now that she would never lay with another man in the whole of her life. She had made a serious mistake in wooing the master to her bed, for she had fallen in love with him in the course of their time together, but she knew he couldn't return her regard.

Valerian cared for a woman named Brenna, and Elisabeth, wise in the ways of men, knew it was an eternal bond. There was no room in the master's heart, generous as it was, for the likes of Betsey Saxon.

A tear fell onto the back of Elisabeth's hand as she replaced the board in the floor. She could have stayed, if only she'd left well enough alone and contented herself with what she had. She might not have discovered what love was, might not have learned to need and want the impossible.

Everything was different now.

The servants were busy, and it was easy to creep out of the house into the shifting morning fog, with the bundle of gold coins rattling beneath her skirts and bumping against her thigh as she walked.

She didn't know which way to go, and it didn't really matter, as long as she got away.

Elisabeth wandered all that day, growing more frightened and confused with every passing moment, and finally took a room above a seedy, dockside tavern. She lay curled on the filthy bed, the gold clutched to her middle like an unborn child, and watched the eerie dance of the fog outside the high, narrow window.

She slipped into a strange reverie, and a fever followed, with terrible cramps in her bowels.

Valerian found her that night, just after sunset, and brought her home, holding her even in the carriage, and she felt his tears on her face and in her hair.

He bathed her himself, tenderly, and sent for a physician, but Elisabeth was dying. She knew it, and so did Valerian.

He asked her about the ring once when she was lucid, but she could not recall where it came from, and said she was sorry if she'd pinched it from one of his lady friends. He wept silently at her words and did not speak of the ruby again until the following night when he was feeding her spoonfuls of broth.

"Kate said a gentleman brought it, the evening before you ran away," Valerian said gently. "That would have been a fortnight ago, as of tomorrow. Do you remember a caller, Elisabeth?"

She sensed that the ring had meaning, as well as value, that it was terribly important in some way, but she couldn't recall any man. She wished she did, for that would mean she didn't have to die a thief, with the fires of hell licking at her toes.

"No," she replied, her eyes filling with tears, and she saw by Valerian's expression that he believed her.

Just before dawn Elisabeth awakened to see an angel of death standing over her. He was very beautiful, and a tear left a glittering streak on his cheek.

Despite her weakness, she became aware of a probing sensation, and felt his mind searching hers, reaching past the fever, the confusion, the pain, into that place where her spirit lived.

"We can be together for all time," he said. "Let me give you the gift—"

Elisabeth had risen out of her body, and she could see so clearly now that her physical eyes had closed. She knew what Valerian was, knew he was damned, as surely as Lucifer and his fallen angels. She loved him without reservation and without regret, but the price of that love, her very soul, was too dear.

She came back to herself briefly and with an agonizing effort. "No," she said. "I cannot."

Valerian held her tightly, and she rested her head against his shoulder, inexpressibly weary. She felt his grief and wished she could console him or simply say good-bye, but her consciousness was fading, stretching and spreading itself thin like smoke, until finally it became part of the fog stroking the window glass with white, shifting fingers.

Dying, it turned out, was easy. A simple matter of letting go. . . .

12

VALERIAN
Las Vegas, 1995

I was remembering Elisabeth Saxon when I returned to Daisy at sunset of the following day, having taken my fitful rest in a burrow far beneath the ruins of the baron's keep. Remembering, with punishing clarity, that I had not watched her closely enough, not protected her. Perhaps I had even cursed her with my lovemaking. I suffered greatly over her passing, certain that she would not have fallen ill and perished after much suffering if I had left her alone, instead of dragging her away from that wretched tavern to live in a city where disease flourished. I forgot about the mysterious ring in my frenzy of bereavement and did not notice that it was gone until the undertaker and his helper had come to take her away.

Elisabeth's death had been my doing, of that I was certain. And now Daisy was doomed as well, if Krispin had his way.

Beneath that terrible certainty was another brier, caught in the tenderest part of my psyche and festering there—my fragile, cherubic brother, whom I had loved, despised me and wished me harm. That pup, who had frolicked at my heels, who had emulated my every word and move and aided me in all forms and fashions of mischief, had somehow become a ravening wolf, bent on tearing out my heart.

Thus distracted, I failed to concentrate and bungled into Daisy's apartment with an ungraceful crash, finding myself in the shower stall.

The running water instantly drenched my hair and the dusty suit and cloak I was wearing, and I roared in surprise and dismay, reaching for the plastic curtain and shoving it aside. There was a simultaneous scream from beyond.

Daisy stood on the cheap pink-fluff rug, dressed in a pair of oversize pajamas, with mayhem in her eyes and a baseball bat poised at shoulder level, ready to do serious damage.

"Oh, for God's sake," she spat, "it's only you." For a moment I thought she was going to take a swing at my head anyway, and although it would not have done me any lasting injury, I was still relieved when she lowered the bat.

Belatedly, I confess, I turned off the shower spray and stepped out of the stall, snatching a towel from a nearby rack and sponging gingerly at my sodden, mud-streaked cloak.

"Who were you expecting?" I demanded somewhat impatiently. "Norman Bates?"

Some of the air seemed to go out of Daisy, and I thought I discerned the faintest glimmer of tears pooling along her lower lashes.

She recovered quickly, as she had always done, for among the many sterling qualities she tended to carry from lifetime to lifetime was a perfectly astounding capacity for resilience. There had been many occasions when, in my opinion, cowardice would have served her better. When she rode into the sea as Brenna, for one example, and she fled my house in London as Elisabeth, for another.

A corner of Daisy's mouth tipped upward in a cocky little grin. "Are you losing your touch?" she asked, looking me over with a slow impudence I wouldn't have suffered from anyone else. "Frankly, I'd come to expect a little more subtlety and grace from you."

I don't doubt that the sheer heat of my annoyance could have dried my sodden garments, but I chose instead to construct another suit of clothes entirely, by means of my will. In the figurative blink of an eye, the tails and cloak and trousers were gone, and in their place were tailored slacks and a cashmere turtleneck sweater, both black. On my feet, instead of the former water-spotted spats, were a pair of the sleek boots I have made in a certain elite shop in Milan.

I must admit I enjoyed Daisy's round-eyed reaction to the transformation, which had been virtually instantaneous.

"I'm not even going to *ask* how you did that," she informed me after closing her gaping mouth and swallowing a few times. "I don't suppose it's a trick we poor, bumbling mortals can learn?"

I touched the tip of her nose, with its faint golden trail of freckles, and smiled. "Sorry, love—I believe that particular feat will require a few more millennia of evolution. Don't feel badly, though—the ability *is* there, slumbering away in a rather gelatinous portion of your brain."

Daisy gave me a spook-house smile, purposely grim and humorless. "Thanks so much for setting me straight," she said with mild irony, then turned on one bare heel to march out of the bathroom. "Every once in a while I lose touch with the fact that I'm Only Human."

I had no choice but to trail after her, and I don't mind saying that it galled me. It has always been my habit, and my distinct preference, to lead, not follow.

"Is that about poor Janet?" I demanded, hastening along that shoddy little hallway behind Daisy. "Is that why you're so peevish tonight?"

She turned so quickly that I nearly collided with her at the entrance to her uninspired living room. "I'm not peevish!" she insisted, folding her arms. "I'm *scared*, damn it! I'm scared shitless!"

I hated it when she, or any woman, talked like that. Call me a male chauvinist vampire, but I miss the old-fashioned female virtues, gracious speech among them. Sometime, I vowed to myself, I will tell her about her incarnation as Jenny Wade, when she'd been so sweet-tempered and ladylike.

But this was not the time for lectures. I put my hands on Daisy's shoulders to steady her and was struck anew by the fragility of her tender flesh and delicate bones. *Ashes to ashes,* I thought with a stab of sorrow, *and dust to dust.*

"I cannot endure this again," I muttered, speaking more to myself than to her. Even then, of course, I knew I had no choice but to endure, to suffer, to pass through the very fires of hell, and, worst of all, to survive it.

Daisy reached up and touched my mouth with the fingertips of her right hand. "What do you mean by that?" she asked in tones so gentle that they splintered my dry and hollow heart. "You left out some things the other night when you told me about our past lives together, didn't you?"

"Not 'our past lives,' darling," I replied, closing my hand around hers, because I couldn't resist, and brushing her knuckles across my lower lip. "Yours. I have been who I am—Valerian Lazarus, the bootmaker's son—since my birth in the fourteenth century."

"What is it that you haven't told me?" she persisted. She might have been Elisabeth then, or Brenna, or any of the other saucy, dauntless minxes she'd been through the endless and dreary march of years that lay between our first encounter and this one. In each successive encounter I have loved her more deeply than before. "Speak up, please."

I had not told her about the curse, of course. Or about the ruby ring that always heralded the end of another bittersweet episode between us. And I would not burden her with those things now, for there was nothing she could do to change the future.

"Do not ask," I said, and the words came hoarse from my throat. "I cannot and will not answer."

For a long moment Daisy simply stared up at me, working some old and potent magic of her own. She looked incredibly small and breakable in those blasted pajamas, and yet I sensed in her some mysterious power that I would never understand or possess.

"He was here," she said. "The killer."

I could not have been more horrified or taken aback if Daisy's bat, which she'd left in the bathroom, had suddenly materialized in her hands and slammed into my middle. How could I have failed to sense such a threat? *How?*

"When?" I rasped, grasping her shoulders again.

Daisy turned beneath my hands and walked away, into the kitchen. She took some modern horror from the freezer and slid it into the microwave before deigning to meet my gaze and answer my anguished question.

She shrugged, leaning against the counter while the oven whirred behind her. "While I was visiting—make that *not visiting*—my sister in Telluride. I came home and found a life-size doll hanging from the showerhead, with an improvised noose around its neck. There were two red marks on the throat—for dramatic effect, I suppose. It was overkill, if you'll forgive the pun."

I stopped myself just as I would have smashed one fist through the cheap plasterboard of her living room wall. "Here? Krispin was *here*?"

The bell on the oven chimed, and Daisy opened the door and took out something evidently intended to pass for a pizza. "Ah, so Superfiend has a name now. How interesting."

I was still struggling to regain my inner—and outer—equilibrium. The scent of the wretched thing she'd cooked and was now preparing to eat—oh, yes, vampires have the sense of smell in abundance, and all the others, too—nearly gagged me.

"I discovered the truth only last night," I said, curling my lip and trying to distance myself from the culinary travesty, which Daisy was now balancing atop a folded paper towel and raising to her lips. "My brother, Krispin, lives."

Daisy took a bite and had the effrontery to chew as she answered. "So does my sister, Nadine."

I went to stand on the other side of the living room and opened a window to the still desert air. "The difference," I said coldly, "is that Krispin, like me, was born in the fourteenth century. He is a vampire."

"I take it the two of you haven't kept in touch," Daisy observed.

I thrust a hand through my hair in exasperation. "I believed him dead all these years, and he never troubled himself to disabuse me of the notion."

She shrugged again, raising just one shoulder, and gazed at me over the expanse of the half-eaten pizza. "Maybe he didn't know about you, either," she suggested.

I glowered at her. "He veiled himself from me. He could have no honorable reason for doing that. We were brothers, after all, dragged, bloody, from the same womb."

Daisy made a face and dropped what remained of her food into the trash. "Maybe he—what was his name again?—Krispin, that's it. Maybe *Krispin* simply doesn't like you? Did you ever consider that possibility?"

She started to lick her fingers—a habit I cannot abide—but stopped when I fixed my gaze on her and projected my disapproval.

"Clearly, to say that Krispin 'doesn't like me' is an understatement of truly enormous proportions. I believed, however foolishly, that he cared for me while he lived, as I did for him."

Daisy raised an eyebrow and, to my relief, wiped her hands clean on a dishtowel hanging from the refrigerator handle. "It couldn't have been easy to be your brother," she said. "You've got to admit you can be a bit overwhelming. A hard act to follow, in more ways than one."

"Be that as it may," I said, struggling again to control my impatience, "I believe Krispin is the killer. I must find him."

She paled slightly and came a step nearer. "And then?"

Such sorrow welled up within me that I could barely withstand it. "And then I shall destroy him."

Daisy drew closer still and laid a hand on my arm. I hoped she did not feel the involuntary tremor that spilled through what passes, in a vampire, as flesh and muscle.

"How?"

I saw my brother in my mind's eye, as a small, coltish boy, with sunlight gleaming in his bright yellow hair and mischief shining in his eyes. I heard him running after me, imploring me to slow my strides so that he might keep pace.

The memories caused me pain the like of which I have known only a handful of times—always in connection with this woman—and the images of what the future might hold for me and for Krispin were so horrible that I could not hold them in my mind.

I said nothing, because I was incapable of speaking at that moment.

"Is it like in books and movies?" Daisy asked with a tenderness that made me long to lose myself in her arms for a little while, to nestle in her warm heart like a dream and hide from all that was mine to do. "Do you have to drive a stake through his heart?"

"Something like that," I managed to say. "I would almost rather destroy myself than Krispin. Great Zeus, Daisy, if you could have seen him as a child, as a youth—he was beautiful."

"Like you," she said. "But smaller, I think, and perhaps not as quick, or as bright, or as bold."

I looked into her eyes, surprised by her insight. "My father used to say I took the best of my mother's nurturing—that my craven hungers made my brother weak and robbed the children who came after him of the very marrow of their bones and the potency of their blood."

"Father of the Year," Daisy said with gentle sarcasm, putting her hands on my shoulders.

I wanted to melt beneath her warm, soft palms and supple fingers, but there was, regrettably, no time to waste on such sweet indulgences.

"You are not safe, Daisy," I began.

"Tell me about it," she interrupted before I could go on. "I'm a cop, remember? And we've had this conversation before. There is no safe place, Valerian—maybe not for any of us."

"My brother will come for you in earnest. The thing you found in your shower was only his calling card."

She lowered her lashes briefly, then looked up at me again. I saw in her eyes the shimmering courage that was woven into the very fiber of her spirit long, long ago, at some celestial loom. "Where shall I hide, Valerian? Name the place that you, or creatures like you, cannot enter."

I could not answer her challenge, for besides heaven itself, there was nothing that could keep me out, no place I could not go if I so wished. The same, of course, applied to Krispin.

I was forlorn in those moments, filled with hopeless despair, but then a stray thought caught in my mind. "This mannequin he left for you—where is it?"

She drew back a little way. "O'Halloran—my partner—took it in for evidence. He thinks we're dealing with an ordinary human being, you see, so he wanted the thing dusted for fingerprints, after Forensics looked it over, of course."

I would get the dummy if I had to—I needed to lay my hands on something Krispin had touched—but I preferred to avoid dealings with the police for as long as possible. Now that Janet had been killed, they were almost certain to lay the crimes at my door, and it would be awkward to vanish from their midst when they attempted to detain me.

"The tie to your robe," I said. "The one that was used as a noose. Did your partner take that, too?"

She frowned and shook her head. "No. I was afraid I wouldn't get it back."

I might have laughed, had the circumstances been different, for I admit to a certain macabre amusement at her reluctance to separate a bathrobe from its matching belt. And never mind that the thing had been used like a hangman's rope.

"Where is it?" I demanded, but I did not wait for her reply. No, I was already homing in on her bedroom, and the closet within it, and the brass hook on its inside wall.

I snatched the robe from its peg and pulled the terrycloth belt through the loops, holding it in my two hands as I might have held a tame snake. Instantly I had a strong impression of Krispin, and I knew, with both elation and despair, that my theories were correct.

I felt his hatred for me in that bit of cloth, I felt his jealousy, his madness, his fury.

I was more afraid for Daisy than ever before, previous lifetimes included. My brother would not hesitate to kill her—indeed, he *relished* the prospect. He was saving that act for last, the way a child hoards a favorite sweet.

"Why?" I whispered, in case he had linked his mind to mine and could discern my words. "Why?"

Krispin did not choose to answer.

Not then, at least.

I was compelled to hunt, for I had not fed the night before, due to my visit to Dunnett's Head. But I could not bear to leave Daisy alone in that apartment, like bait in a trap, tempting Krispin to punish me with her death.

Even in those silly, oversize pajamas, which had probably been left behind by an earlier lover, Daisy was a vision. Her copper-gold hair tumbled around her shoulders, and her eyes were like antique gems I had once admired in a shop window—impossibly green, but opaque with tension. The smattering of freckles stood out against the creamy paleness of her skin.

"How can I leave you here?" I whispered, stricken to the heart.

She drew a step nearer, and I saw the flash of memories in her mind—she was recalling, of all things, the somewhat one-sided lovemaking session in that tacky motel along the road to Telluride. Her desire for me burned bright, like a flare, and such longing seized me then that I uttered a small cry of protest and need.

"Take me with you," she said. "Let me sleep where you sleep."

I had not consciously cast a spell over Daisy; to do so would have been an abominable liberty, tantamount to rape. No, it was not magic, but plain fear that made her want the scathing comfort only I could give her. "But when we spoke of safety, you said—"

"I said I would not be your prisoner," she interrupted gently, putting her arms around my neck. "But I will be your lover."

I ached to have her, even to make her into my true mate, but of course I could do neither. The recollection of Elisabeth's death, following so soon after our intimate union, was preying upon my mind. Too, the need to hunt was urgent—were I to encounter Krispin or some other enemy before feeding, I would be too weak to protect either Daisy or myself. Once I had taken sustenance, I must immediately resume the search for my brother.

"This is not the night," I told her gently. I am certain that my disappointment was greater than hers.

"Take me with you, then," Daisy urged, running one fingertip down the chilled, pale planes of my cheek and upper jaw. "Please. I can face this killer—this thing—I know I can. But not tonight."

I kissed her forehead and wrapped her in a loose embrace, and she tucked herself against me like a nestling seeking shelter beneath the wing of a larger bird. "Very well," I said and fixed my mind on the lair hidden well outside the city's bright, tattered edge, beneath the desert sands.

We were there in an instant, standing in my gracious living room. Daisy swayed a little, from shock no doubt, and I steadied her.

"You are probably safe here, for the moment at least," I said, aware that time was passing at its usual merciless and inexorable pace. "Vampires are not gregarious creatures, and they are, therefore, most uncomfortable in a stranger's lair." I stepped back, left her teetering there in her pajamas, and moved one arm in a broad gesture intended to take in the whole of my splendid hiding place. "I must go now, Daisy. Explore to your heart's content. I'll be back an hour or so before dawn."

With that, I vanished, carrying with me the look of unadulterated surprise I had glimpsed on her face, smiling a little over it. Mortals have such a difficult time accepting new realities.

DAISY
The Vampire's Lair, Outside Las Vegas, 1995

At first Daisy was so overwhelmed by Valerian's latest flashy disappearance and her own recent introduction to broomstick transport that she sank onto the leather couch and stared blankly into space. Her next coherent thought, coming some time later, was the wish that she'd taken time to change her clothes.

Trust her to show up for the experience of the aeons in the pajamas O'Halloran had given her for Christmas the year before. He'd been making a point about equality between the sexes at the time, but Daisy couldn't quite recall what it was.

She levered herself off the expensive sofa, once she'd recovered the required muscle control, and stood shakily, her knees trembling. Valerian might have spurned her seduction attempt, however politely, but he had flat-out invited her to check out his house, and she wasn't about to miss the opportunity.

Daisy soon realized that the whole place was underground, a gigantic and very luxurious bomb shelter. The light was artificial, of course, but of such clear intensity that it might have sprung from the sun itself. Besides the living room, which appeared to be equipped with every modern electronic plaything in existence, there was a large, lagoonlike swimming pool and smaller hot tub, both surrounded by a jungle of lush plants, and a kitchen containing every conceivable appliance but no dishes, silverware, pots and pans, or food. There was nothing in the giant refrigerator except a lightbulb and a box of baking soda.

Daisy considered calling out for a pizza, just to see if the delivery driver could find the place.

The master bedroom was a suite, decadently appointed with antiques, paintings, and sculptures, all priceless. Besides a huge bed with a canopy and velvet draperies, and a working gas fireplace, there was a marble tub of truly decadent proportions set right into the floor. The faucet and spigots were gold, and the exquisite tiles surrounding the bath were hand-painted and very old.

Daisy found six other bedrooms opening off the same hallway, all sumptuously furnished and obviously unused, all with their own marble-and-gold bathrooms, spectacular enough to suit the most hedonistic guests. She hoped to find clothes to borrow—Daisy took care not to think too much about who might have left such garments behind, and not just because she felt proprietary about Valerian's attentions—but there was nothing.

Finally she returned to Valerian's room and helped herself to one of his pleated dress shirts. The tails reached almost to her knees, and she finished the ensemble off by taking a tie from his vast collection and knotting it loosely around her waist for a belt.

She was just entering the living room again, planning to stretch out on the leather sofa and try to sleep, when the biggest television screen she'd ever seen—and there were some enormous ones in the casinos—slid down out of the ceiling with an electronic purr.

Daisy looked around, thinking she must have touched a button inadvertently, but there was nothing like that in sight. She stared at the screen, and a peculiar sensation of mingled terror and excitement stirred in the pit of her stomach.

She made her way to the sofa as the great expanse of glass flickered and then brightened into light. Sliding both hands along the back of the couch, Daisy made her way to one end and collapsed into the deep cushions.

A field of flowers nodded on the screen, breathtakingly beautiful, bending and bowing gracefully in a twilight breeze. Daisy waited for credits, for any explanation of what was happening, but in some half-conscious part of her brain she'd already grasped the truth.

The image she was seeing wasn't being transmitted from any television station. This was vampire magic, but the trick wasn't Valerian's. He wouldn't have frightened her like that.

She watched the flowers, daisies mostly, bathed in the lavender of approaching night and at the same time reflecting a peculiar crimson glow. When she saw someone in the upper right-hand corner of the screen, she felt tension coil in her stomach, and when that figure drew near enough to see clearly, she gasped aloud.

The woman was a stranger, a tall, brown-eyed blonde, and yet Daisy knew she was looking at herself. Valerian had not told her about this incarnation, and she suspected that was because he hadn't known about it. By some mysterious cosmic fluke, she'd gotten past him that time.

Watching the screen, fascinated and terrified at the same time, Daisy struggled to remember being this person, but not so much as a glimmer came to her.

She stood up, squinting, realizing only then that the living room, so dazzlingly bright before, was now lighted only by the flickering glow of the screen. A chill dripped down the center of her back, like a trickle of icy water, and she shivered, studying the face of that other self.

She sank down onto the cushions again a moment later, when her knees would no longer support her.

She forced herself to stay calm, to watch. Daisy was in danger, and she knew it, but her years of training and police service stood her in good stead. If she panicked, if she failed to pay close attention, she would not survive.

Daisy took careful note of the image on the screen—studied the reflection of this being who was and yet was not herself. The clothes her double wore were ragged and old, garments a peasant woman might have worn in any one of several different centuries.

She scooted forward, gripping the edge of the couch with both hands, heart thrumming, upper lip moist with perspiration.

The woman on the screen began to call out for someone, raising both hands to cup her mouth, scanning the field with worried eyes. There was no sound except for the faintest murmur of circuitry, but Daisy recognized the name on those lips so similar to her own.

Shock rocketed through Daisy, and her heart began to beat painfully fast; she barely overcame an elemental urge to cover her eyes with both hands.

The flowers were wilting, and a garish light had arisen in the background, crimson and orange, leaping, hot to the eye as it would be to the touch.

The fire was drawing nearer.

She watched herself begin to run, and realized that the flowers and grasses, all fainting beneath an undulating, glimmering tide of heat, grew in a graveyard.

Suddenly Daisy was not sitting on Valerian's couch, watching the scene—she was in it. *She* was the pretty woman-child running between tilting headstones. *She* felt the heat of the approaching fire scouring the flesh of her back, even through the rough weave of her shift. The earth was rocky and uneven beneath her feet, her lungs burned fit to burst, and she was scared enough to pass water without slowing down.

Between one instant and the next she forgot that she'd ever been called Daisy Chandler, would not have recognized the name except as one she might have heard long ago in a dream.

"Krispin!" she screamed, tripping, falling, and rising again, all in a virtually simultaneous motion. The blaze roared as it ate up cottages and fields and churches behind her, gaining on her like the fleetest of runners.

She ran on, making a whimpering sound when she wasn't choking on the rolling black smoke, until her legs gave out a second time. She toppled to the ground and crawled behind a great huge monument with a French name chiseled into its side.

It was coming on dark now—or was it just the smoke darkening the sky?—but where was her beloved? He'd promised to meet her here, to take her far away from London—perhaps to Paris, he'd said, or Rome or even Istanbul.

"Here's the truth of it, Maddie Goodtree," she whispered to herself, choking on the thick, acrid air between words. "Either he's gone up in flames like a scarecrow, your fancy man, or you've been made the fool."

Maddie leaned around the end of the monument, which felt hot as brimstone to the touch, and peered toward the line of thundering crimson on the horizon. London was gone, that it was. And at the rate the flames were traveling, they would gobble up the rest of England as well. Paris might have gone up, too, if it weren't for the waters of the channel blocking the way.

She tried to rise, to run again, but all the feeling had gone out of her knees. Other folks, fleeing the city, scrambled past, dragging carts, mewling children, and the doddering old behind them.

No one stopped to help.

The fire drew nearer, and Maddie found it more and more difficult to breathe. She managed to gain her feet at last and stumbled after the others. The sun had set, but one would never have known it, with the sky so hellish bright.

Then suddenly he was there beside her. He smiled and took her hand, her beautiful lover, and told her not to be afraid.

There were shrieks puncturing the darkness all around them, cries of terror and of pain, and Maddie would have thought she was lost in hell itself if her beautiful, fair-haired angel hadn't been walking beside her, showing her the way.

Krispin had found her at last.

They escaped the fire in a twinkling, it seemed to Maddie, taking refuge inside cool, dank walls, where there was no light at all. He drew her close, and their lips and bodies seemed to melt into one as they celebrated the darkness. . . .

Slowly, slowly, Daisy returned to herself.

The television screen had disappeared, and every light in the place was blazing, and she heard a soft, seductive voice that should have come from anywhere except within her own head.

"You were mine in that lifetime. Not Valerian's. *Mine.*" There was a pause, no longer than a heartbeat, followed by a throaty chuckle. "He didn't know you were alive, and you belonged to me. As you shall again."

13

VALERIAN
The Vampire's Lair, 1995

I returned to my underground lair just before dawn, exhausted and frustrated beyond measure. I had combed the earth, from one pole to the other, over the last few nights, and found no sign, no hair or trace, of my prey. Krispin had hidden himself very cleverly indeed.

Daisy was lying on the couch when I returned, clad in one of my handsewn shirts, artfully belted with a necktie. She was pale as a medieval snow.

I extended a hand and swayed slightly on my feet, for I was already beginning to succumb to the vampire sleep. I had sought my brother with little regard for the thinning darkness, and dawn was only moments away.

I could barely focus my gaze on her, and speaking was a greater effort than I could manage. I struggled to regain my tenuous grip on consciousness, knowing all the while that the attempt was hopeless. Yes, there had been times in my past when the mysterious slumber had not wrestled me downward, into inner darkness, but this night I would not be spared.

Daisy rushed toward me, and I sagged against her. She supported me with surprising strength, speaking rapidly, but by then her words were no more than an unintelligible murmur. The last thing I was aware of was the couch beneath me, still pulsing with the sweet warmth of her body.

DAISY
The Vampire's Lair, 1995

Daisy knelt on the floor beside Valerian's resting place, holding his cold hand in both of hers, both horrified and fascinated. His flesh, always unusually fair, was white as alabaster, and there was a stillness about him, so absolute that he might have been dead.

She laid her head to his chest and heard no heartbeat, felt no rise and fall of ribs and muscles and flesh. Had she not experienced Valerian's magic for herself, over and over, she would have mourned, believing she'd lost him forever. She remained as she was for a long while, her ear chilling against his hard breast, struggling with the knowledge that she not only knew a vampire personally, she'd fallen in love with one.

She cried softly, silently, her tears wetting the fine fabric of the shirt he wore. Lots of women, even when they happened to be cops, lost their hearts to practicing alcoholics, philanderers, compulsive gamblers, and assorted other losers, but falling for a vampire was carrying dysfunction to a new level.

Here was an idiosyncrasy even Geraldo hadn't encountered before.

After mourning for a time, Daisy raised her head and sat back on her heels, sinking her teeth into her lower lip. She needed to tell Valerian about Krispin, and the episode with the television set, but she dreaded the task to such an extent that she was almost glad for the respite sunrise provided.

She would be reasonably safe in the interim, she supposed, for if Valerian was incapacitated during the daylight hours, then Krispin, being a vampire himself, was surely curled up in a coffin somewhere, motionless as a corpse and temporarily harmless.

She hoped.

Daisy kept her vigil until her knees went numb, then made herself get up and walk around. There wasn't a scrap of food in the house, and she was violently hungry. To keep her mind off the problem for a little while, she went out to the pool, which, like everything else, was underground. Building that place had been a real feat of engineering, and yet

Daisy, living all her life in Las Vegas, had never heard so much as a rumor of its existence.

She removed the tie belt and the shirt purloined from Valerian's vast wardrobe and slipped into the warm, sapphire-colored water. The chamber housing the pool and hot tub had a cavernlike ambience, and reflections danced across the dark ceiling, but the air was humid rather than dank and cool.

The water seemed to cradle Daisy as she turned, naked, onto her back, to float. Her hair spilled out around her, and the tips of her breasts hardened, reminding her of how desperately she had wanted—and *still* wanted—Valerian's lovemaking. The desire was deep-rooted and instinctive, a consuming need beyond explanation or understanding, something so powerful that it frightened her and so compelling that she could not resist.

It was as though some ancient vow would be fulfilled in the act, some promise made before the stars were shaped. For good or ill, they would be joined, if only for a night.

Daisy permitted herself to remember the scene she'd witnessed on the television screen earlier. She'd felt the throbbing heat of the great fire, the rough ground beneath her feet, and with them the terror, somehow her own as well as Maddie Goodtree's. She had known relief at the sight of Krispin—or Maddie had—and experienced every nuance of their tempestuous lovemaking as well.

She blushed, floating there in Valerian's pool, to recall the sheer physical intensity of her satisfaction. And yes, she must claim that glorious, forbidden release as her own, because she had *been* Maddie Goodtree. As well as Brenna Afton-St. Claire and Elisabeth Saxon. She had vague, gauzy memories of those lifetimes, and she knew they had often touched her dreams.

Daisy sighed, lying still upon the water. As pleasurable as Krispin's intimate attentions had been, in that other life so recently recalled, they paled by comparison to the psychic sex she'd had with Valerian. He had driven her out of herself, the magician had, without even being in the same room.

She kicked her feet and tossed back her wet hair. If Valerian made love to her in person, the pleasure would probably kill her.

It would almost be worth dying young, she decided with a smile, making her way toward the tiled edge of the pool, if the last experience was anything to go by.

Daisy climbed out of the water and found a stack of fragrant white towels on a glistening brass stand next to the wall. Only then did it occur to her to wonder who cleaned this strange, hidden house—surely Valerian, vampire of legend, star of stage if not screen, did not scrub toilets and mop floors.

"Curiouser and curiouser," Daisy muttered, wrapping the towel around herself like a sarong and leaving the borrowed shirt and tie where she'd left them, flung across the back of a lounge chair.

There was a strange freedom in her confinement, though by rights the place was nothing more than a luxurious grave. She could walk about stark naked if she wanted to, and know that no one, including Valerian, would see her.

She dropped the towel at the doorway to the living room and went to stand over the exquisitely handsome vampire sleeping on the sofa. He was beyond a doubt the most beautiful creature, man or woman, she had ever seen, a subject worthy of Michelangelo or any of the masters.

How long, she wondered, had she loved him? A thousand years? Ten thousand?

Daisy turned away, the question heavy in her heart, and wandered into the kitchen, still starved. Maybe she'd overlooked a box of crackers or a can of sardines, kept on hand for that rare visit by a mortal.

The telephone caught her eye as soon as she flipped on the lights, and Daisy went to it and lifted the receiver with a slight smile playing at one corner of her mouth. She dialed O'Halloran's cellular number, knowing he was going to give her a ration for disappearing the way she had. He wouldn't be able to handle the truth—that she was standing naked in a vampire's kitchen. In fact, he'd probably go straight to the chief and have her badge pulled—permanently.

"Yeah!" he barked over the roar of air rushing past an open car window, plainly annoyed at the interruption. O'Halloran carried a cell phone, but not for status. He hated the things and tolerated them only because they helped him stay in touch with his contacts.

"O'Halloran?" Daisy asked sweetly, although she would have known that voice anywhere.

The howl diminished into nothing as O'Halloran rolled up his window. "Chandler? Is that you?" He sounded anxious. "Where the hell are you?"

"I'm staying out of sight for a few days, that's all." She thought of the layers of earth between the cool tiles beneath her feet and the surface of the Nevada desert. "Laying low, you might say. If you've been worrying about me, stop. I'm okay."

"Is somebody forcing you to say that?"

"No, O'Halloran. Nobody is forcing me to do anything. I just need a little time to get my head together, that's all. You were the one who suggested that in the first place, remember?"

"You're really all right?"

Daisy felt a surge of affection for O'Halloran; he and his wife, Eleanor, were like family to her. All she had, except for Nadine. "Yes," she said, blinking back tears because there was so much she couldn't share. "How's the investigation going?"

"No progress," O'Halloran said with a raspy sigh. "We can't find this Valerian character, for one thing. He's let his personal staff and the surviving performers go and closed down the show at the Venetian, but the management says he plans to return soon, so they haven't booked anybody else. His name is still on the marquee, and the press is clamoring for him. If I was a cynical guy, I might just figure it was all a publicity stunt."

"You think he'd murder those women just to get attention?" Daisy demanded, feeling cold all of a sudden in her birthday suit. "You can't be serious, O'Halloran. He has to know he'd be number one on the suspect list." She glanced toward the living room where Valerian was sleeping. "Nobody in his right mind would expect to commit a crime like that and then just go merrily on with his career!"

"That's just it, Chandler. You saw the bodies. We ain't dealing with somebody who's in his right mind."

Daisy wanted to tell him that it was Krispin, not Valerian, who had done the killings, but there was simply no way to explain the realities of the situation. "That's right," she agreed somewhat testily, "we're not. Look beyond the obvious, O'Halloran. Dig deeper. You're missing something."

"I wish you were here to help out," the older cop confessed. "You got good instincts, Chandler."

"I take it I'm still suspended, then?" Daisy asked, unable to hide the sadness and frustration she felt. Her work was such a large part of her identity that she wasn't sure who she was without it. "The chief hasn't blown a brass trumpet and shouted, 'Bring me Chandler, she of the good instincts and negative drug test'?"

O'Halloran was quiet. Too quiet.

"Talk to me," Daisy ordered when she could stand his silence no longer.

"The brass wants you to talk things over with a shrink."

"They think I'm crazy."

"They think you're under a lot of stress, like every other cop in the country."

"Yeah, well, they're not making 'every other cop' see a head doctor, are they?"

"Chandler? Do yourself a favor, take some advice from an old veteran. Don't fight this one. Just do what they ask. It ain't so much, you know—the doc will probably want you to look at a few ink blots and play some word association games, that's all."

Daisy swore.

"More advice," O'Halloran said crisply. "Don't use that word in front of anybody above the rank of lieutenant."

"I'll keep that in mind," Daisy allowed. It was hard, she discovered, to be naked and angry at the same time.

"Okay, Chandler, give me a number where I can reach you, and we'll wrap this conversation up. I'm on my way over to the Venetian— again—to see if I can track down this magician of theirs. I'll say one thing for this Valerian fella—he's got the disappearing act down pat."

Daisy smiled and dashed at her cheek with the back of one hand. All of the sudden she felt vulnerable, rather than free, and she was anxious to put Valerian's shirt back on. In the meantime, though, O'Halloran wanted a number.

She thought quickly. "I'm staying in a lake cabin," she lied, "and I have to use a pay phone whenever I want to make a call. I'll be in touch within a day or two."

"Just give me the name of the resort, then."

"Sorry, partner—that's a secret. I'll call again soon." With that, her stomach twisted into a knot of guilt, Daisy hung up the telephone.

Next she called her apartment. She listened patiently to her own voice, droning the usual spiel about leaving a name and number, and punched the pound sign when it was over. At the other end of the line the tape rewound with a high-pitched squeaking sound, and then the accumulated messages began to play.

The first was from Nadine, saying she was in labor and had checked into the hospital.

The second was from Freddy. Nadine was yelling a lot, he said frantically, and he wished he'd never gotten her into this mess. Could Daisy please come to Telluride as soon as possible?

Fresh tears brimmed in Daisy's eyes. She wanted desperately to be with her sister and lend what support she could, more now than ever, but it was too dangerous for Nadine and Freddy and the baby. She couldn't bear even the thought of what Krispin might do to them, for whatever insane reason of his own.

The next voice was the same painfully slow, inhuman drone she'd heard before, and she knew now that it was some trick of Krispin's—a robot, maybe, or a computer, or his own private brand of magic. "Come out, Daisy. You cannot hide from me forever. If you don't show yourself, I will kill again."

Bile surged into the back of Daisy's throat; she squeezed her eyes shut and struggled to keep her empty stomach from convulsing. "Dear God," she whispered. "Help me."

The line went dead, and then she heard Nadine's voice again. Daisy's sister sounded weary but full of joy. "Daze? The baby came this morning, and mother and daughter are doing great. Freddy suffered so much angst over all the pain I went through that he gave a little ground on the name business. We're calling our daughter Whitney Miranda. Fruit not included. What do you think, Auntie? Call me soon—I'm going to tell you more about childbirth than any sensible woman would want to know."

That was the end of the tape, and Daisy was weeping softly as she hung up the receiver. She had a niece—her only flesh-and-blood relative besides Nadine and the long-lost Jeanine—and she couldn't even make a pilgrimage to Telluride to admire her.

It wasn't fair.

"Not much is fair in this life," a female voice observed.

Daisy was so startled that she whirled and pressed herself to the wall. She had expected some stray fiend; instead, she was faced with an attractive woman of about her own age. The visitor had short dark hair, stylishly cut, and enormous gray eyes. She was sleekly trim and clad in black corduroy slacks, a white poet's shirt, and a vest of charcoal velvet.

"Who are you?" the pixie demanded, taking in Daisy's bare body with a frown of disapproval.

Daisy swallowed. "I was going to ask the same question of you," she said, just resisting a futile urge to cover herself with both arms. "Are you a vampire?"

"Of course not," was the brisk answer. "I couldn't be abroad in the daylight if I were. But I'll give you my name in trade for yours—it's Kristina Holbrook."

The surname was faintly familiar; Daisy thought Valerian might have mentioned it in passing. "Daisy Chandler," she said. "I'm a detective with the Las Vegas Police Department." She regretted that last part the moment the words had tumbled from her mouth—in her present unclothed state, she wasn't exactly a credit to hard-working law enforcement officers everywhere.

Ms. Holbrook's lips twitched. "Perhaps you'd better call for backup, Detective Chandler. It would appear that someone has stolen your clothes."

Daisy flushed with embarrassment. "I was wearing pajamas when I came here," she blurted out. "And then I went swimming, and it just seemed, with Valerian asleep and no one else around or anything—"

"It's okay," Kristina said quickly with a full-fledged and quite dazzling smile. "I'll get you something to wear." She pondered Daisy thoughtfully again, then said with conviction, "I think blue is your color."

With that she closed her eyes, and within the instant Daisy felt cloth against her skin. She looked down, speechless with amazement, to see that she was wearing an indigo silk jumpsuit with a hammered gold belt.

"I was right," Kristina boasted with a good-natured grin. "You look fantastic."

"Who—" Daisy lapsed into incoherence for a few moments, then made another attempt. "Who are you?"

"I told you. I'm Kristina Holbrook."

"And y-you're not a vampire."

Kristina's forehead crumpled slightly as she frowned. "Definitely not. But both my parents are. It's very complicated—my father was still mortal when I was conceived, so I'm human. Mostly."

Daisy swallowed hard. *"Mostly?"*

Kristina laughed, and the sound was like the peal of distant bells. "I'm mortal, essentially. But I'm not sure when I'll get old, if ever, and I do have certain powers, as I've just illustrated." She paused for a beat or two, then took the conversation in a whole other direction. "Would you like something to eat?"

Daisy was breathless—and surprised to discover that she was still hungry. "Yes—please."

The other woman pointed dramatically at the island in the center of the kitchen, and a picnic basket appeared, accompanied by the tantalizing aromas of fried chicken and freshly baked apple pie.

"Come on and join me," Kristina urged pleasantly, pulling a stool over to the island and sitting down. "You said you were hungry, didn't you?"

Daisy hesitated a moment longer, then approached the food. The fine silk of her jumpsuit brushed softly against her skin as she moved.

"Would you like some jewelry to go with that?" Kristina asked, pulling a drumstick out of the basket and biting into it with relish.

"No, thanks," Daisy said, standing on the other side of the island and helping herself to the food. There were plates inside the elegant basket, along with sterling silver, crystal wine flutes, and a very fine Bordeaux. "The outfit's enough. Is it going to melt at midnight?"

Kristina's grin was puckish. "Are you accusing me of slipshod magic?"

Daisy didn't bother to answer. "Why are you here?" she asked between bites of delicious chicken, potato salad, and coleslaw.

"Mother has been worried about Valerian. She asked me to look in on him."

By now Daisy's head was reeling. Maybe the higher-ups on the force were right, she thought in a brief flurry of hysteria. Perhaps she was losing it, and she needed intensive therapy. But no—deep inside, where it counted, Daisy knew she was all too sane.

Delusions? Hallucinations?

She should be so lucky.

"Is he—family? Valerian, I mean?"

"He's like a godfather, I guess," Kristina answered. "Or a favorite uncle. We're quite close, he and I. He spoiled me outrageously when I was a child—take the dollhouse he gave me, for example. It's a perfect replica of the palace at Versailles, down to the last light fixture."

Daisy had been standing up, but now she groped for a stool, dragged it over, and sort of collapsed onto it. Now that she knew it wasn't romantic, she had no pressing interest in Kristina's relationship with Valerian. "So you just sort of zapped yourself here from somewhere else?"

"Seattle," Kristina said. "I own a small antiques shop there." She frowned at Daisy over the rim of a carton of mashed potatoes. "I'm sorry. We must be quite overwhelming, Valerian and I. Have you met any of the others?" She paused to shudder. "Canaan and Benecia Havermail, for instance? They're little girls, beautiful as dolls, and hardly any bigger than they were five hundred years ago, when they became vampires. What vile little creatures they are—but you needn't worry about them. They wouldn't dare bother anyone Valerian befriends."

Daisy had been left behind, like a piece of luggage tossed from a moving train. "Five hundred years—"

Kristina shrugged. "That's not uncommon," she said. "My mother was born in the eighteenth century, you know, and my father served as a surgeon in the American Civil War when he was mortal. And as for me—"

Daisy held her breath, bracing herself to absorb yet another stunning revelation.

"Well, just between us, I've been around a while myself. How old would you say I am?"

It was the kind of question Daisy hated, but she'd had a lot of experience at gauging such things as a police officer, and she was fairly confident of her abilities. "Twenty-nine or thirty, I'd say."

"Bless you." Kristina beamed. Then she leaned forward to confide in a cheerful whisper, "Andrew Johnson was President when I was born."

"No," Daisy said, but the fall-away sensation in the pit of her stomach told her it was true.

"Yes," Kristina insisted. Then she sighed sadly. "It's hard, when your friends get old and you stay just the same, year after year, decade after decade. Naturally they wonder why."

"Naturally," Daisy croaked, at a loss for anything sensible to say.

"I take it you're completely mortal?"

"Completely," Daisy said.

"I envy you. I'd trade all my magic, you see, for a real home and a family of my own. How lovely to marry and grow old with a man you cherish and respect—"

Daisy pushed away her food. "Don't envy me," she whispered, and then she made the unthinkable confession. "I'm in love with a vampire. And that isn't the worst of it. It would seem we've been together in other lifetimes—"

"Oh, no!" Kristina interrupted, covering her mouth with one hand and widening her already huge gray eyes. "*You're* Valerian's ladylove—the one he keeps finding and losing, finding and losing!"

Daisy nodded glumly. "I think so, yes."

Tears of sympathy glistened in Kristina's dark lashes. "It's true, then—there is some sort of curse."

Valerian had told her about their star-crossed encounters in various centuries, and she was beginning to remember the odd detail, but he hadn't said anything about a curse.

"Tell me what you know," she pleaded.

Kristina shook her head. "You'll have to ask Valerian, Daisy. This is a personal matter, and I have no business interfering. Besides, the plain truth is I don't know much about it. I've heard whispers through the years, that's all."

Daisy supposed she should have been afraid of Kristina Holbrook, but instead she liked and trusted her. She wanted her for a friend, though it seemed unlikely that they'd have much in common.

"Okay, I can respect that," Daisy said. "Thanks for the food, anyway, and the jumpsuit."

Kristina got off the stool and started toward the kitchen door, and Daisy followed her into the living room. The dark-haired woman went to stand beside the couch and touched Valerian's forehead with such tenderness that Daisy felt an involuntary stab of jealousy.

"Is he all right?" Daisy asked, because it was plain that Kristina knew.

"Valerian is very strong and not a little stubborn," she replied, but there was a small, worried crease between her eyebrows. "We must all be tried and tested in the crucible, mortal or immortal, and it would seem that his time has come."

"What do you mean by that?" Daisy could barely get the words out, she was so stricken by the grisly array of possibilities invading her imagination.

Kristina withdrew her hand from Valerian's opalescent flesh, but did not look away from his face. Her expression was full of sorrow and hope, trust and fear. "Everything changes. Perhaps the curse has finally run its course—perhaps everything can be resolved, one way or the other."

Daisy thought about Krispin, and the murdered women, about the horrible dummy she'd found hanging in her shower, and the scene played out on Valerian's television screen. She'd watched those strange images and, at the same time, been a part of them.

Yes, she reflected, Kristina was right. Events were building toward some sort of crescendo, and she was caught up in it all, not only because of her past lives, but through her growing love for Valerian.

She stayed silent, because there was nothing to say.

Kristina bent again and kissed Valerian's forehead, then straightened and turned to Daisy. "Here," she said, taking a pendant from around her neck and putting it around Daisy's. It was an exquisite golden rosebud suspended from a priceless chain. "This has been in our family since my mother and her twin brother, Aidan, were mortal children. Over the centuries, it has gained power from the love of those who wore it against their hearts. You'll need all your wits, all your love, all your faith to fight the battles ahead, but this talisman will lend you strength."

The necklace felt warm beneath Daisy's fingertips. "Thank you," she said. She was aware that, in giving away the pendant, Kristina was making a sacrifice. Whether that sacrifice was large or small, Daisy could not guess.

Kristina smiled somewhat sadly. Or so it seemed to Daisy. Almost as an afterthought, as she was preparing to leave, the pixie-witch asked, "Do you want to leave here? Or is your vigil a willing one?"

"I want to stay," Daisy said.

Kristina nodded. "Please tell Valerian when he wakes that I was here to look in on him." At Daisy's smile of acquiescence, Kristina raised both hands over her head and vanished with a showy little puff of smoke.

"Wow," Daisy couldn't help remarking. Then she stretched out beside Valerian's still form, there on that roomy leather sofa, cuddled up close, closed her eyes, and drifted into a fairy-tale sleep.

She dreamed she rested in a crumbling castle, its walls obscured by thistles and thorns, its parapets and baileys and courtyards overgrown with vines.

Only the kiss of a certain prince could awaken her.

VALERIAN
The Vampire's Lair, 1995

I opened my eyes at dusk to find Daisy sleeping beside me. My strength was flagging, despite the rest I'd taken and last night's hasty feeding outside one of my favorite haunts, the Last Ditch Tavern, but I could not leave her. Not yet.

I shifted slightly and brushed her lips with a tender kiss, and her eyes opened, wide and startled and so green that the sight of them made my heart clench like a fist within me.

Then she smiled and put her arms around my neck. She did not need to speak; the invitation reverberated through her supple, warm little body and pierced me like lightning.

"You don't understand," I began. My vampire senses, a thousand times more acute than those of an ordinary man, were leaping to life, pulsing beneath my skin, promising agony if I denied them, ecstasy if I gave in.

I have ever cherished my pleasures.

I made one last attempt, however. "Daisy—" I began, my voice no more than a raspy whisper.

She touched my lips with a fingertip and wriggled beneath me. "I want you," she murmured. "I don't care what comes after that."

I groaned and fell into her kiss, willing to burn in hell for her, to offer myself as a sacrifice—anything, so long as I could taste again the joy I had mourned these many decades since I had seen her last. And I wanted the joining of our two souls even more, for I was only whole when her spirit and mine were fused by the fire of our love-making.

Daisy whimpered beneath my mouth as I opened the front of her garment—a curious thing it was, trousers and a blouse fastened together—and took gentle sustenance at her full breasts, one after the other. Her fingers, buried in my hair, pressed me closer, and I felt her hips arch under mine, wooing and tempting me in the age-old way, tormenting me with the promise of pleasure so intense a mortal could not have endured it, setting my bedazzled senses ablaze.

"Take me," she pleaded, and hers was not one but a chorus of sweet voices—her own, of course, and Brenna's, and Elisabeth's, and Jenny's. And more.

I refused to grant her such easy gratification, sliding down from her quivering, well-suckled breasts, over her smooth belly, damp beneath my lips. There was much I wanted to remind Daisy of, before our joining, and much I wanted to teach her.

14

DAISY
The Vampire's Lair, 1995

DAISY thrashed beneath Valerian, in a delirium of need, but he withheld satisfaction long after she had begun to plead. He tongued the peaks of her breasts until she felt her heartbeat throbbing in that taut flesh, and kissed her stomach and her hipbones, the insides of her thighs, the backs of her knees. She might have been a goddess, so thoroughly did he worship her, with tenderness and fire for his offerings.

She uttered a primitive, groaning sound when he burrowed through the veil of moist silk to take the hidden nubbin of flesh between his lips and begin to draw upon it, ever so gently. While he teased and nibbled and savored, at his leisure, Daisy writhed, soaked with perspiration, her hair clinging, in wild strands of copper, to her temples, her cheeks, her shoulders, and the upper swell of her breasts.

In desperation, she tore open Valerian's shirt, as brazen and untamed as a she-wolf in her season, and spread her hands over his marble chest. It was as if Michelangelo's *David* had come to life and was making love to her, so splendid was he, so soul-wrenchingly beautiful.

Mankind, she thought frantically, had never been meant to look as Valerian looked, or feel as he felt. Such magnificence could not be imprisoned in mortal flesh any more than lightning could be confined to a teacup or the music of a symphony to a single seashell.

Valerian groaned at her touch, and she slid her arms around him and stroked his perfectly sculpted back with warm palms. At the same time she murmured to him—softly, insensibly, for she was not capable of reason—and knew that her love was balm to his spirit as well as his body.

His clothes vanished with a mere blink of his hooded, sapphire eyes, and then Daisy's were gone, too.

"May the Fates forgive me," Valerian whispered, and then he found the entrance to her body and took her in a single deep, swift stroke.

Daisy's arousal, already ferocious, convulsed her whole being in cataclysmic release, and she screamed, not from pain, but out of a pleasure that went beyond any conceivable agony or delight. Each time she reached a new peak, she was sent spiraling upward, toward another, until the last measure of response had been wrung from her. Throughout that sweet odyssey, Valerian whispered to her, stroked her face and her breasts, smoothed her hair.

When at last, with a faint whimper, she sank back to the sofa in exhaustion, he gave her a few moments to catch her breath. Then, at long last, Valerian was overwhelmed by his own passions. He reached beneath her to grasp her buttocks in powerful hands and raise her like a sheath to the sword.

Valerian's strokes were long and slow and smooth; he plucked at Daisy's senses, tuned them, like the strings of an exquisite violin, and soon she was playing a fevered rhapsody for him. They reached the crescendo simultaneously, with hoarse shouts of beleaguered triumph, and collapsed into the stillness that lay beneath their passion.

A long time had passed when Valerian broke the mystic silence with a low chuckle. "I didn't plan for us to make love on the living room couch like a pair of teenagers," he said. "Frankly, I had something a little more romantic in mind."

Daisy nuzzled his neck, putting off the moment when she would have to tell him about her message from Krispin and the lifetime as Maddie Goodtree. "Don't give it another thought. If that had been any better, I would have gone up like a campfire doused with kerosene."

He laughed. "It was good, then?"

"It was better than good. It would be an improvement on 'perfect,' in fact."

Valerian kissed her, but lightly, mischievously. He knew, without being told, that she had given him everything she had to give, and that she would need time to recover before they made love again.

"And what secrets are you keeping from me?" he asked.

Deep within Daisy, small muscles continued to contract as the last and strongest orgasm ebbed away, and she tucked her face into his shoulder. "I'm still coming," she whispered.

"I knew that," Valerian said with a smile in his voice. "We are yet joined, in case you've forgotten, and I can feel you tightening around me. What exquisite torture it is."

Daisy whimpered and then gave a little sigh as the resonance grew softer, and more distant. "There aren't any other—secrets."

"Don't lie to me, Daisy." Valerian groaned and shifted his weight slightly, but made no move to withdraw from her. He was still hard, and she was exulted to sense a new tension rising quietly and steadily within him. This time she would be in control.

She taunted him with an almost imperceptible motion of her hips, and he threw back his head, the muscles of his neck corded with the effort of holding back.

"You will pay for that impertinence," he vowed.

Daisy drew him deeper, and his majestic body flexed once, twice upon hers. He moaned, as if in pain, and spilled himself into her a second time.

"You will pay," he repeated, but he was kissing her as he spoke, tasting her eyelids, searching out her mouth with his own.

Daisy toppled back into sleep, so sated was she; her muscles were limp, and it seemed her very bones had melted. When she awakened, she was lying in Valerian's bed in the master suite, and he was standing at its foot, clad in his magician's garb and just donning his cape. He looked gaunt somehow, and she wondered if it was her lovemaking that had sapped his strength, or some experience he'd had the night before.

"Why didn't you dress by magic?" she asked, putting off the moment when she would have to tell him about Krispin.

His smile was slight, distracted. "I sometimes enjoy the mechanics of simple tasks."

She sighed. Now or never, she thought.

"I need to tell you something before you go," Daisy said bluntly, sitting up and drawing the linen bedsheets up to cover her breasts.

Valerian crossed to the bed and uncovered them again, and a shock of fresh desire sizzled through Daisy's system as he looked at her with an expression of wry appreciation. "Your body is far too lovely to hide," he said. "Besides, it's a little late for modesty, don't you think?"

Daisy clung to her resolve, but decided to start small. She would save the news about Krispin for last.

"Kristina was here, while you were sleeping today. She gave me this." She held out the antique pendant for him to see.

"I noticed that, as it happens," Valerian said.

Daisy blushed. He'd been up close and personal—of *course* he'd noticed. "She's worried about you. Kristina, I mean. So is her mother."

He was straightening his elegant string tie. "She has always been a perceptive child," he replied evenly. "Likewise, Maeve."

Daisy dropped the bomb, blurting out the words in a rush. "There's something else. Krispin's been tampering with your television set. He played a few stirring scenes from what I assume was one of my past lives and said I belonged to him then and I would again."

Valerian's hands fell to his sides, and he stood utterly still. His expression was cold, and his eyes seemed to pierce Daisy's very soul. "Why didn't you tell me this before?" he asked evenly, and with ominous softness.

"We were busy," she reminded him, refusing to be cowed.

"Tell me what you saw."

"Myself, running away from what was probably the London Fire— 1666, I think it was. My name was Maddie Goodtree, and I didn't look anything like I do now."

Valerian frowned ever so slightly. "Maddie Goodtree?"

It was as Daisy had feared; Valerian had not known about that particular lifetime. He might even hate her when he learned the truth, and believe she'd betrayed him by loving Krispin.

"I don't know much about her," Daisy said bravely, "except that she was involved with your brother."

There followed a towering silence, much more intimidating to Daisy than any that had gone before it. *"She was what?"*

Daisy gulped. "In love with Krispin," she said miserably.

He turned away, but his rage was like a swell of heat, filling the room, pushing at the walls and the ceiling, glimmering and undulating all around him, miragelike.

"There was a message on my machine when I called home, too," Daisy went on, wanting to finish, to get it all out in the open so they could go on from there. "He—Krispin—said he would kill again if I didn't come to him." A decision she had not consciously made rose to the surface of her thoughts. "I can't let that happen, Valerian—I can't let someone else die when it's me he wants."

Valerian turned to her again, and his face, though as beautiful as ever, was terrible to see. *"You will not go to him,"* he decreed in a furious undertone.

"It's my job," Daisy insisted, equally angry. "And blink me up some clothes, will you please? I'm tired of running around naked, like some sultan's personal plaything."

A black formal materialized on her body, fitted, with a pleated flair at the bottom and diamond clasps holding the bodice together.

"Very funny," Daisy said. "I want jeans, damn it, and a T-shirt."

Valerian complied, but grudgingly. The gown disappeared, replaced by Levi's that were two sizes too big and a lime green T-shirt with the name of a fertilizer company emblazoned across the front.

She folded her arms. "You can do better."

Scowling, he made the jeans fit and changed the shirt to a plain red one, tucked in at the waist.

"Thank you," Daisy said wearily, rising at last from the bed and looking down at her magic clothes. "I could have used your help when I was in high school. It took me forever to dress, and I was late for everything."

Valerian was seething, and he glared down at Daisy as she moved close to him and laid her hands lightly on his chest.

"Listen to reason," she pleaded quietly. "I'm a cop. Before I made detective and was assigned to the Homicide Division, I worked Bunko and Vice, and I was the bait in every kind of sting. I was damn good at what I did, too."

Valerian's frown deepened, and Daisy felt his fury and his fear coursing beneath her hands. "Do you honestly think you—or any other mortal—could prevail against a monster such as my brother surely is?"

"Not by myself," Daisy conceded. "I was counting on you to help."

Reluctantly, with a sound like a sigh, but deeper, and seeming to rise from his soul instead of his lungs, he put his arms around her. "I shall deal with Krispin alone, Daisy, and in my own way. With no interference from you. It is hard enough to concentrate now, when you are in such danger. I could not bear to take the risk you are suggesting."

"I might just do it on my own, then. I have the pendant to protect me."

"The pendant," Valerian scoffed, giving her a slight shake within his embrace. "It has no more power than a prize from a second-rate carnival."

"That isn't what Kristina said."

"Kristina is a fanciful sort, given to wild imaginings. Stay out of my way and let me handle this, Daisy, or I vow I will lock you up somewhere."

Daisy knew he meant what he was saying. She also knew she couldn't stand back and let more innocent people fall victim to Krispin's madness. "Take me with you," she begged. "At least that way you'll be able to protect me."

He closed his eyes for a moment. "Daisy, I must feed. And the places I go are unfit for a mortal woman."

"Well, I won't stay here. I don't think I could handle another one of Krispin's impromptu television productions, and besides, I'm not a vampire. I get hungry for real food, and even though I pull my share of late shifts, I'm not used to sleeping during the day."

Valerian smiled sadly. "This has ever been your flaw, Daisy—you are stubborn beyond all reason." He drew her very close, and his black silk cape encircled her like a whisper from another world. "Close your eyes and hold on tightly."

She looked up into his magnificent face. "Could I fall?"

"No," Valerian replied. "The request was strictly lascivious."

Daisy laughed despite her grief, and the sound had barely left her throat when she found herself standing in Valerian's dressing room, behind the stage of the main showroom in the Venetian Hotel. She was still safely cossetted in the magician's cloak, but she was alone.

"Valerian!" she yelled, letting the cape fall into a shimmering, inky pool at her feet and resting her hands on her hips. "You come back here, damn it!"

After fifteen minutes there was still no sign of him. Muttering, Daisy let herself out of the casino by a back way into the warm night, walked around front, and boarded one of the gondolas ferrying tourists back and forth to the hotel.

Although Valerian had eventually provided her with the requested jeans and T-shirt—he'd thoughtfully included a pair of sneakers, too—she didn't have a quarter for the telephone, let alone cab fare back to her apartment.

Once she'd reached the street, Daisy started walking toward home. With a little luck—if it could be called that—Krispin might make an appearance.

VALERIAN
The Last Ditch, 1995

I grew weaker, it seemed, with every passing moment, as though a cancer had taken root inside me, sapping my strength. I felt unsteady and somewhat disoriented as I made my way through the crowd of warlocks, vampires, and other monsters who filled that wretched bar. The place was outside the normal barriers of time, an anteroom to hell itself, and I despised it for a reminder of my own damnation. I went back only because I knew that, eventually, every rumor found its way there, to circulate among the creatures who sat around the tables, lined the bars, and shuffled on the dance floor.

Sooner or later there would surely be word of Krispin.

I found a place in a shadowy corner and sat down to listen and to watch.

Dathan, a warlock I particularly dislike, immediately made his way through the seedy throng to join me. I had had an impression of his presence, an instant's knowing, but I had shoved it aside, hoping the perception was in error.

With an insolent smile, not waiting for an invitation, he drew back a chair and slipped into it.

He would have made a very striking vampire with his fair hair and cherubic features, I thought, but appearances were indeed deceiving. Dathan was a warlock, with poisoned blood flowing through his veins and a stock of evil tricks comparable to my own.

"You seem sickly, my old friend—as if you've taken a draft of warlock's blood," Dathan remarked with a crooked smile.

I made no effort to hide my contempt. While it was true that Dathan and his followers had been helpful during a recent conflict between Maeve Tremayne and the late, great vampire queen, Lisette, I for one was not prepared either to suggest a truce or to accept one.

Not that the warlock intended to offer an olive branch.

"I am not a fledgling," I said coldly. "I know better than to consume so wretched a substance."

"Do you?" Dathan taunted in a soft voice. His eyes danced with mockery.

I considered my lethargic state, which had subsided temporarily, borne away on a tide of annoyance. Inside of an instant my hands were gripping the lapels of the warlock's finely tailored coat and, without leaving my chair, I had drawn him halfway across the table.

"Have you poisoned me?" I demanded in a whisper audible only to the two of us. "Confess, warlock, or I shall sunder your liver from your chest and burn both parts while they still quiver with life!"

Dathan, to his credit, was unruffled. He made no move to resist my grasp or to answer with a threat of his own. Instead, he sighed, for unlike vampires, warlocks have breath.

"I am not without defenses, blood-drinker," he said cordially. "For both our sakes, I pray you—keep that in mind."

I knew well that Dathan could ignite infernos by the power of his mind, and vampires can be destroyed by fire, as by sunlight and the point of a stake, but I was reckless, caring nothing about my own fate. Daisy's future was all that mattered.

I released Dathan with a summarial unflexing of my fingers, and he sank blithely back into his chair. There was not so much as a flush of irritation pulsing on his high, fine cheekbones, or a twitch at his temple.

Either I had not made him angry, or he was keeping his emotions veiled. I expect it was the latter, for Dathan's affection for me was then, and remains, no greater than mine for him.

"You have been searching for a vampire called Krispin, have you not?" he asked, as prim and proper as an English butler.

I regarded him in silence for a few moments, pondering the fortuitousness of his appearance in that place. I had come to the Last Ditch Tavern hoping to hear even a scrap of information concerning my brother's whereabouts, and here was someone very likely to know. Still, I mistrusted all warlocks and indeed most vampires as well. If I stumbled into a trap of some sort, Daisy would be at Krispin's mercy.

"Yes," I allowed at last, offering no more.

"There is an old one who can tell you what you need to know. A vampire called Challes."

I drew back slightly, feeling as if I'd been slapped. "Challes? He was destroyed centuries ago, felled by the hand of Nemesis himself."

Dathan raised his eyebrows. "How certain you seem. And yet you believed your brother to be dead, only to learn that you were wrong. I should think such an oversight would cause even you to think twice thereafter and avoid hasty conclusions."

"Why are you telling me this?"

The warlock's smile was beatific. Had I not known him for a fiend, I might have thought he was an angel. "Rest assured, vampire," he said, laying a hand to his chest, "this heart bears you no love, but only malice, as ever. I bring you this news because I want something in return."

I relaxed a little, for this was a philosophy I understood and subscribed to myself, but with this more temperate mood came a new flagging of my vitality. I could have laid my head down on that scarred, ugly table, closed my eyes, and slept like an ingenuous child, but of course I resisted the compulsion. It would be safer to make my bed among vipers or plague-bearing rats. "Explain," I said.

"You have been careless," he scolded in an indulgent tone, letting me know it was not my curt one-word command that had moved him to reply. He and his kindred are prideful creatures, and vain. "There were warlocks among your victims. Think, twin of Lucifer—do you not recall a faint difference in the blood you've taken these past few nights?"

I did, but I wasn't about to admit it. I simply folded my arms and waited. Dathan sought a favor from me; let him pay for it in advance, in coin of appropriate value.

"Challes, the old one, wishes to talk with you. But he feared your anger with him would be too great, that you would be beyond his control, so he took steps to weaken you. He succeeded, probably because you were distracted by the need to find your brother."

"Where is he?" I demanded. My surroundings were a thunderous void by then, and I could barely keep my head up.

"You have only to wait," Dathan answered implacably. "He will come to you."

The floor seemed to shift and roll beneath me; I feared to rise from my chair, lest I lose consciousness entirely and become yet more vulnerable to my many foes.

"Are you in league with him?"

"No," Dathan said. "Challes is a vampire, after all." He paused, and I could see that he was studying me intently, even though his image seemed to recede to a pinpoint and then rush toward me, looming and huge. "Have you fed this night, blood-drinker?" he demanded.

I had not, and I was glad. Another tainted feeding might have been the end of me—assuming I had not already taken the fatal dose.

I managed to shake my head.

"If I help you save your ladylove," Dathan said, "will you repay me by doing what I ask?"

I gripped the edge of the table with both hands. "I will do anything to break the curse," I whispered, my eyes bedazzled by flashes of bright light inside my head. "Anything."

"I have your word? Heed my warning, vampire—betray me, and I will seek out your Daisy Chandler and exact vengeance even your most rabid enemies would not wish to witness."

"My—word—" I vowed. And then I collapsed and never felt myself strike the floor.

* * *

CHALLES stood over me when I opened my eyes, and I knew we were back in the chamber beneath Colefield Hall. I lay on the slab that had been my bed in my earliest days as a vampire, stripped to the waist, my hands and feet lashed not by ropes or thongs of leather—those could not have held me—but by my tutor's magic.

"Why?" I asked. He had infused me with good blood while I slept; I was stronger, though still not powerful enough to break my bonds, and I felt a vague sting where his fangs had punctured my throat.

He smiled benignly and stroked my forehead and hair with a fond hand. "I have not meant to frighten you," he said in a near croon.

I was very afraid, but not of anything Challes might do to me. No, my terror was for Krispin's unguarded prey—my Daisy. "If it's true that you mean me well," I countered, "then set me free. Now."

Challes set his hands palm to palm, bringing to mind a saint or, at the least, a devout monk, and the noble sorrow in his pretended sigh told me he would refuse.

"I cannot. I am a powerful vampire, in my way, but you are youthful and filled with the passion of rage. Your body is still, but your mind prowls like a panther—do you think I haven't felt it circling, probing, ever seeking an opportunity to strike and rip out my throat?"

I closed my eyes for a moment, subduing an urge to struggle wildly. "What the devil do you want with me?"

He began to stroke my face and my hair again, and I could not hide my shudder of revulsion. "I have come to take you away, sweet child, into that other world where you shall see an end to your suffering. After all, it was I who laid the vampire curse upon your soul. It is my duty to lift the burden from you."

My interest was caught, though not by the promise of an end to pain. Was there indeed a way to change, to be redeemed, to live in the light again? I had seen a blood-drinker made mortal once, but it had been an agonizing, deadly process, and afterward the Old Ones had destroyed the means of transformation forever.

"You are mad," I whispered.

Challes smiled again, briefly, indulgently, as though dealing with a spoiled but basically good-hearted child. "I shall show you."

"Were God to forgive me for all my six hundred years of sin," I told him, "and that, as you know, is not going to happen, I would still refuse to set foot in Paradise without my beloved."

An instant after I'd spoken, I regretted mentioning Daisy, even indirectly.

My ancient tutor raised his brows again and withdrew his hand in a quick, spasmodic motion. "Leave the wench to Krispin," he said, and for the first time since he'd first brought me to Colefield Hall, and begun to train me for the vampire's life, I saw profound anger in his face.

"You made Krispin a blood-drinker," I accused, my whisper as ragged as my hopes, "even before you found me lying in that horse stall, half dead of drink. Why didn't you tell me then that my brother was alive? Why?"

"He begged me not to do that," Challes answered. "And I, having had an elder brother myself once upon a time, was not unsympathetic to his plight. Krispin yearned to live outside your shadow, and he knew that would be impossible if you learned of his existence."

I was more wounded by these words than I would ever have allowed Challes to see. Had my brother always hated me, then? Even when we were mortal boys, playing and working together? Apparently I had only imagined that Krispin had borne me the same deep affection I had harbored for him.

In the next moment even my illusion that I had hidden my feelings from Challes was dashed.

He leaned over, so that his face was close to mine, and spoke softly. "It was because of Seraphina—she was the reason Krispin loathed you as he did. When the baron pronounced your death sentence, you see, your sweet mother offered up your brother's life in payment for yours. Krispin heard an account of it later from a servant."

"No," I murmured, but the image of Seraphina kneeling and pleading before Brenna's father was vivid in my mind, as if I had witnessed it myself. It might have been only moments past, instead of lying in the far and dusty reaches of long, long ago. "She couldn't have done such a thing."

"Ah, but she did. And there's more. After Seraphina collapsed, and the baron's men carried her home, Krispin tried to comfort her. She spat at him and screamed like a madwoman, imploring her saints one after another to take him instead of you."

No wonder Krispin had abhorred me, I thought. No doubt the other children born of our mother, the doll-like twin girls with the transparent eyelids, the boy called Royal, would have been my enemies, too, had they survived. Oh, I remembered the little ones, the lost ones, with cruel clarity, even after so many centuries, remembered my father's ravings, his insistence that I had robbed them. My cursed soul, Lazarus the bootmaker had snarled, reeling with mead, had been greedy, consuming my mother's strength to weave for its pauper-self a nobleman's body and a demon's mind. . . .

I could not bear to remember.

"Where—where has Krispin been all these centuries?" I managed to ask with difficulty. "Surely he could not have veiled himself so completely—"

"No," Challes said. "Nor could I. You were always quite quick—about most things, if not all. There are other dimensions, pet, other worlds, if you will. Layer upon layer of them, as a matter of fact, on and on into infinity. And passages exist between them, though of course those byways are known to very few."

I was reminded of a conversation I had had with Maeve, concerning experiments her mate, Calder Holbrook, had been performing. He had found evidence of such phenomena, although I had been too concerned about other matters at the time to ask questions.

It is my curse, it would seem, to be either too curious or not curious enough.

"Is it far away, this place where you've been hiding?" I spoke softly, trying to lull Challes a little so that he might relax his mental hold on me. I was regaining my normal powers, quickening inwardly on the sustenance my tutor had given me even as I ached for all the grief my mother's misguided adoration had caused.

Challes extended a hand. "You will know soon enough," he said, dropping his voice to a whisper, as though fearing that we weren't alone in that dank, gloomy crypt under the crumbling floors of Colefield Hall.

"I have no wish to be mortal again," I confessed. The statement was purest truth, I realized, and it was shattering to face. I knew without asking that Daisy would not wish to become the very thing I gloried in being—a vampire. We were doomed, she and I, even if I managed somehow to save her from Krispin's vengeance, to be parted yet again.

"But you would not be mere flesh and bone and blood," Challes exulted quietly, laying a loosely knotted fist to his bosom. "Not you."

I was mystified. "Speak sense, vampire!" I commanded. "I have no patience for your damnable doubletalk!"

Challes laughed. "It pleases me to see that you are as arrogant as ever, Valerian Lazarus. Has it escaped your notice that you are a prisoner? It is I who govern the night, not you." He paused and regarded me gently, as though memorizing my features. "Hush, now. Be not afraid. I have returned to fetch you home—we shall enter Paradise together."

15

DAISY
Las Vegas, 1995

DAISY walked quickly toward home, as though pursued.
The night was hot and dry, thrumming with sound and with silence. Las Vegas twinkled all around her, a bright, gaudy tangle of emeralds and rubies, diamonds and sapphires, tumbling over the desert sands like loot spilled from a treasure chest.

Daisy wondered if Krispin would be waiting for her when she reached her apartment. If he meant to kill her that night, he'd have to be quick about it—dawn was less than an hour away.

Loneliness and fear made a swelling ache in Daisy's throat. If there had ever been a time in her life when she needed someone to talk to, it was then, but there was nobody to confide in really, besides the elusive Valerian. She dared not tell her sister—to do so would worry Nadine and, worse, endanger her, as well as Freddy and the baby. Nor could Daisy open up to O'Halloran. One word about vampires, except in jest, and he'd personally see that she was put on medical leave.

Daisy couldn't blame her partner; if someone had come to her with a wild story like her own, just a few weeks before, she would have recommended long-term therapy, if not shock treatments.

Her apartment building was in plain sight when the shift occurred.

In an instant reality altered itself with a sickening lurch. The sidewalk beneath Daisy's feet turned to cobblestones, and the desert air was suddenly dank and somehow sour. Fog layered the ground, alive with shifting, wraithlike shapes, and Daisy made out old-fashioned street lamps and heard the rattle of carriage wheels and the clatter of horses' hooves on the pavement. The vibrations rose through the soles of her feet.

Daisy sagged against the nearest wall, the brick cold against her back, closed her eyes, and tried to slow her runaway heartbeat and rapid breathing by sheer force of will. It didn't help, knowing this wasn't real, that it was only another "spontaneous regression," as Valerian would say.

Normal, healthy people did not have experiences like this.

When she was sure she wouldn't hyperventilate, or faint dead away,

Daisy opened her eyes, cherishing even then the vain hope that she would find herself back in Las Vegas where she belonged.

Nothing had changed—except to become more intense.

The stench of the gutter at her feet swelled and then broke over her in a nauseating wave, and the passersby, clad in rags like fugitives from the cast of *Les Misérables*, were still more aromatic.

Daisy swallowed a scalding rush of bile and murmured an incoherent sound, meant to be a cry for help, but Valerian did not appear as he had the last time, when she'd found herself waiting tables in a fifteenth-century tavern.

It seemed the noxious fog was seeping through her skin, penetrating her skull, settling heavily into her mind and finally causing her memory to dissipate like steam. She was forgetting things, and remembering others that had never happened.

She clung desperately to the last shredded recollections of the person she'd been only moments before . . . her name had been Daisy once, in a fever or a dream, but she had no idea who she was now. Or where she was.

It was getting darker and colder by the moment.

She reached out and caught at an old woman's tattered sleeve. "Excuse me—what is this place?" she asked. "Where am I, please?"

The crone jerked free with a fierce and fearful motion and bustled on without answering, grumbling as she went.

"It's London Town, miss," said a small voice at her side. She looked down to see a child gazing up at her, an impossibly thin boy wearing torn clothing and a filthy cap. "You lost?"

She clung to the last memory, the name, repeating it to herself . . . *Daisy, Daisy* . . . though even that was struggling to escape her, squirming in her mind like a greased pig.

"Do you know me?" she whispered, terrified. "Can you tell me who I am?"

The boy shook his head. His enormous gray eyes were at once pitying and shrewd as he regarded her from beneath a fringe of dark, shaggy hair. "The peelers'll take you away that quick," he warned with a snap of his grubby fingers, "if they hear you talkin' such ways as that. You got fine clothes on, so you must be a lady. Here—let me have a look inside that bag you're carryin'—maybe we'll find your name inside."

She extended the bag—a frilly black drawstring affair with fringe and jet beads—but before the street urchin could take it from her, an elegantly gloved hand interceded. She caught a glimpse of a dark waistcoat, a silken vest, the merest impression of pale blue eyes, and then her vision faded completely. Rather than a cruel surprise, this state of blindness seemed somehow a return to the norm, and in its way it was comforting, even empowering, in its very familiarity.

"Away with you, you thieving little wastrel, or I'll drag you off to Newgate myself," the man said in a tone that was at once refined and mildly savage, and she heard the boy's quick steps on the stones as he fled. There was a gentle reprimand in that cultured voice when he went on, and she felt his strong arm slip around her waist. "Jenny," he scolded, and with the name came a torrent of remembrances, almost too many to sort through, and all sense of disorientation left her. "How many times must I warn you not to wander off by yourself?" He paused to emit an elegant sigh. When he went on, there was an edge to his voice. "Perhaps Adela is right in her assertion that you would be better off in an institution of some sort, where allowances could be made for your affliction."

The reference to a hospital sent a little chill skittering along her spine, and she distracted herself by aligning all the things she suddenly knew about herself and the man beside her.

This was Martin, her elder brother and guardian, holding her arm so firmly, ushering her into a waiting carriage. He was a prominent man of business who kept offices in High Street. Her name was Jenny Wade, and she lived with Martin and his wife, Adela, in a spacious town house only a few streets away. She was nineteen years old and a spinster, much to her grievous disappointment, for her greatest ambition was to marry and bear children. Her "affliction," as Martin called it, had come upon her in the course of an illness suffered when she was seven. Their parents were both dead, and the year was 1722.

Jenny heard Martin rap at the wall of the coach, and the sleek and costly vehicle jostled into motion, creaking and smelling of rich leather. "You won't send me to an asylum, so don't threaten," she said cheerfully, acutely aware of so many things—the varied texture of her gown, her gloves, her cloak among them. Over the years Jenny had learned to let her other senses compensate for the loss of her eyesight, and she could determine much from touching, hearing, smelling, and tasting.

She sensed her brother's smile, knew it contained reluctance as well as affection. "No," he confessed, "I wouldn't. But you're a scamp all the same, and I can't think why I put up with you."

"That's easy—it's because you love me," Jenny said. She was not spoiled by her brother, she reflected, but still he often indulged her. Out of affection, it was to be hoped, and not pity.

Martin laughed, but there was sorrow in the sound, and worry. Several moments passed before he spoke, and when he did, his tone was serious. "Why were you handing your bag over to that little street rat back there?"

Jenny squirmed, uneasy. She'd suffered some kind of spell, she supposed, forgetting who she was and where she lived, and behind that realization were other memories, nebulous ones she couldn't quite grasp, so fantastic that they would surely come up in her dreams.

"I was a bit confused, that's all," she said. Jenny seldom lied to Martin, for he was far more perceptive than most sighted people, and he had an almost unerring knack for recognizing an untruth. Deception by omission was another matter, however, and she often employed it. "You were too hard on the child. He only wanted to look in my bag for a name of someone who might come to my aid."

"Piffle. Do you think the little wretch can read? If you'd handed him the bag, he would have run off with it," Martin said with smooth conviction. "The world is a treacherous and deviant place, Jenny. You must be more cautious in the future."

"Why?" Jenny teased as the carriage rounded a corner. The swaying sensation was unique to this particular turn in the road, and she knew they'd entered their own street. "Are these coppers all that stand between us and penury?" She gave the handbag a little shake, causing the coins inside to rattle.

Martin's reply was snappish, impatient, but Jenny was not deceived by the show of anger. She'd frightened her brother, and the thought filled her with remorse.

"Don't be silly. Do you think I give a damn about a handful of pocket change? You were in *danger*, Jenny. And now you're telling me you were 'confused.' I'm summoning the doctor as soon as Mistress Peach has given you supper and put you to bed."

Jenny's regret was swept aside by a rush of impotent fury, though she harbored an abiding affection for Mistress Peach, who had once served as her nanny and was now referred to as her companion. "I'm not a child, Martin, to be tucked up with a dolly, and no one has to 'give' me my supper. I can feed myself!"

Martin's only answer was an exasperated sigh. The carriage stopped, and cold air buffeted Jenny's cheeks when the door was opened from the outside. She descended without waiting for help from her brother, pushing aside the coach driver's hand, and strode toward the house with the certainty of long practice.

She was greatly troubled, though she wouldn't have admitted as much to Martin and certainly not to Adela, who was bound to nag, or

Mistress Peach, who would fret herself into a sick headache. Jenny had been blind for twelve years, and yet she'd *seen* the fog and the boy and even Martin, though only for a moment. Furthermore, there were things she should remember, things she desperately *needed* to remember, about the moments prior to her fit of forgetfulness, important matters struggling behind a heavy veil at the back of her mind.

Jenny's devoted companion met her in the foyer, muttering, bundling her briskly in a knitted coverlet, while Adela stood by, silent except for the slight, familiar wheezing sound she made when she was irritated.

"Where did you find her?" she demanded sharply of Martin. Adela was a fine woman and good wife to Jenny's brother, considering her somewhat intractable and obstreperous nature, but she collected disappointments, slights, and minor injustices the way some people garnered seashells or buttons or bits of bright ribbon. The habit rendered her tiresome indeed, and pettish.

Jenny stiffened inside the coverlet. "Kindly do not speak as if I were deaf, Adela, as well as blind. If you have a question, then ask it directly!"

"That will be enough, both of you," Martin said wearily, and Jenny's ears caught the faint whisper of kidskin brushing flesh as he removed his gloves—more an impression than a sound, really. She felt a draft as he removed his waistcoat with a habitual flourish that was uniquely his own. "Jenny became distracted while I was doing business with the tailor, that's all. I'm sure she merely stepped out of the carriage to get a breath of air and did not realize how far she'd strayed."

Jenny's face flamed with heat—Martin was as bad as Adela, in his way, making excuses for her behavior as though she were a slow-witted child—but it would be futile to argue. Besides, she was exhausted, and vaguely unwell in the bargain, wanting only to sit by the fire in her room and sip strong tea.

She endured Mistress Peach's seemingly interminable fussing, and when that good woman finally left her alone, Jenny's gratitude was profound. She felt oddly insubstantial, like a character in an oft-told tale, and she was deeply frightened. Pictures flashed inside her head, shifting, jewel-like images of a strange and faraway place, that pulsed with activity and with unaccountable noises. How, she wondered, could such things have found their way into the mind of a sheltered blind woman?

The sense of displacement grew as the hours passed; it was as if she were not entirely real, for all the solidity and substance of her surroundings. Jenny herself might have been a shadow, or a reflection.

Was she the dreamer—or the dream?

The doctor came at nine and was shown to her room by Adela.

Jenny did not confide in the aging physician, but endured his fumbling examinations in silence. She was, by that time, convinced that she was fading, like a figure in an old and weathered portrait, and would soon vanish entirely.

VALERIAN
Colefield Hall, 1995

I had almost freed myself from the unseen shackles my tutor had used to restrain me. In the meantime, while I continued the struggle I hoped was imperceptible, I spoke moderately to Challes. "Paradise," I murmured in a thoughtful tone while he loomed over me in an avid and singularly unnerving fashion. "The place where there are many mansions."

"Yes," he whispered, his face translucent with some maniacal ecstasy.

"I would not dare to cross the threshold of any one of them," I told him, and while I lent the words a regretful note, the unflattering truth was that I had no desire to be anything other than what I was—not angel or devil, specter or saint, and certainly not a mortal man.

Challes looked as though I'd struck him, and recoiled.

I had broken my bonds and bolted upright on the slab, but before Challes could react or I could get to my feet, the chamber trembled as if the very walls would give way. There was a strange, implosive feeling all around, as if the air had been replaced by a vacuum, and then he was there.

My brother.

Krispin gripped Challes from behind and flung him cruelly aside. "Fool!" he rasped.

I studied him, my head tilted slightly to one side. Krispin was not a large fiend, neither broad through the shoulders nor long of leg, like me; he had, instead, the lithe agility of a trapeze artist or a dancer. His hair was fair as moonlight, his eyes a soft, deceptively fragile blue, his skin so flawless that he appeared to have no pores.

"Enough," I said quietly when Krispin moved to stove in Challes's ribs with one booted foot. Granted, a mortal could not have done a vampire injury by such a blow, but Krispin, of course, was not human. He was plainly much stronger than the blood-drinker who had spawned us both.

Krispin listened—evidently there was still enough of the flesh-and-blood boy in him that his first instinct was to respond to an elder brother's command—and Challes crawled, crablike, into a corner, there to whimper and mewl in a manner that made me want to kick him myself.

Still seated on the slab, I spread my hands. "Here I am, Krispin," I said mildly, belying my true feelings, which were myriad and complicated, bittersweet and excruciatingly painful. "Destroy me if you can."

For a long interval Krispin simply stared at me in silence, and I watched a kaleidoscope of emotions flash across his Dresden face. I saw hatred, along with the ghostly and shimmering reflection of an adoration it shamed him to recall, and finally, a sort of terrified triumph.

He shook his seraphic head. "No, my brother," he said with the vaguest of smiles. "Your death will be neither quick nor merciful. You have much to suffer before the gates of hell swing wide to grant you entrance."

What I felt was more revulsion than fear, more sorrow than hatred. How I despised Challes in those moments for taking that naive, mischievous child Krispin had been and turning him into this monster! Had I not been occupied, perforce, with my brother's presence, I believe I would have carried Challes to a churchyard, laid him at the feet of a holy statue, and driven a stake through his heart.

"Do you think there will be a welcoming parade?" I asked with no trace of guile. "When I finally meet with damnation, I mean?"

Krispin might have flushed, had he been mortal. I saw the anger flood his face, although it did not alter the pristine white of his flesh, but instead rendered it more transparent still, like cloth woven of spun moonlight. "You are in grave trouble, brother," he said quietly. "Pray, do not make light of it."

"You would prefer pathos? Pleading, perhaps, with copious tears? Sorry." I paused for the length of a heartbeat. "I won't be humbling myself in any significant fashion, Krispin. Pride is my curse, as well as your own. We are, after all, begotten of the same dam and sire, God rest their misguided souls."

Krispin flinched, though not, I thought, from the mention of the Supreme Being. No, I believed it was my reference to our mother, however generically, that disturbed him—and his response confirmed my suspicions.

"Do not speak her name," he warned. "Your lips, your tongue, would defile those revered syllables merely by shaping them!"

I rolled my eyes. "Great Zeus," I said on what would have been a long breath, had I been human. "You are fixated—perhaps that good woman kept you too long on the breast. Or, mayhap, not long enough—"

"Be silent!"

I stood at last and crossed the few feet that separated us with an easy, unhurried gait. "Why?" I asked, knowing he saw only the insolence and disdain I willed him to see, and not the heartbreak and confusion churning behind the facade I presented. "Why did you murder those poor women, instead of bringing your rancor straight to me in the first place?"

His lips curled slightly, and I was struck by the realization that any female, mortal or otherwise, would find him vastly appealing. He could seem ingenuous if he so wished, and even virtuous. Perhaps he had not simply killed his victims, but gotten to know them first, methodically seducing their minds. . . .

"I told you before," Krispin said with elegant contempt, "I would not make this easy for you. I want you to pay."

I rested my hands on my hips, realizing only after the fact that it was an old gesture, from our days as corporeal youths, a posture of superior power for me, but a subtly daunting one for him. "Even considering my multitude of sins, mortal and otherwise," I began, "your loathing of me is somewhat disproportionate to reality, don't you think?"

Challes had risen to his feet, and he was no longer making pitiful noises, but he cowered against the wall of the vault, watching Krispin as though he were the Devil incarnate or, far worse from a vampire's perspective, Nemesis, the angel of sublime vengeance. I began to speculate that my teacher had not been trying to usher me into Paradise at all, but merely to hide me from my brother's madness, which appeared to be even greater and more virulent than his own.

I was touched, and decided not to stake Challes after all. Not immediately, at least.

"It is more than Seraphina's betrayal," Krispin said, and I felt the searing cold of his agony flicker across my spirit, like shadows cast by flames of ice. "You have taken my mate. Over and over again, you have stolen her."

All sympathy deserted me in that moment, for it enraged me that Krispin dared to regard himself as a rival for Daisy's affections. We had been created to live side by side, she and I, through all the ages; had it not been for my transformation from man to vampire, we would have been incarnated together, again and again, until we stepped over the farthest boundary of time.

"Your mate?" I shaped the words softly, insolently, on my tongue.

"You were never anything more than an interloper, Krispin. She is mine—now and forever, time without end, amen and amen."

He raised one finely shaped eyebrow, and his mocking expression made me want to close my hands around his polished marble throat and choke him. "Is she?" Krispin paused to feign a luxurious sigh. "Ah, yes—our lady of many names. How lovely she is. You call her Daisy now, but you have known her as Brenna, as Elisabeth—poor whoring little wretch—and as sweet Jenny. Unfortunate how quickly she took sick and died, wasn't it?" Another sigh, still theatrical, if almost inaudible. "And there were other lifetimes, of course—she was the fetching woman who ran the boardinghouse in that little western town, wasn't she?"

Harmony Beaucheau. I closed my eyes against the memory of that particular incarnation—for it remained acutely painful, even after more than a century—and opened them again only out of an instinct for self-preservation. "What is the point of this?" I whispered. "Are you leading up to telling me that Daisy cared for you once, when her name was Maddie Goodtree and the two of you made love in a gravedigger's cottage, with the Great Fire of London licking at your—heels?"

"So she told you," Krispin said with a self-satisfied and somewhat distant little smile. "I hoped she would, once I'd revived the memory for her."

I felt sick, just to think of Krispin's hands on Daisy's flesh, in this lifetime or any other, but I did not allow the aversion to show. I had no way of reckoning the extent of my brother's powers, but I sensed that they were formidable, and quite different from my own. Whether his abilities were greater or lesser than mine, I could not guess, but they were unquestionably heightened by my ignorance of their nature.

"You could not have her, except by trickery," I said. "So you murdered her, over and over again."

The cherubic mouth twitched with barely contained amusement. "Not the first time, when she was Brenna," he disclaimed blithely. "That happened quite on its own. But I admit to helping justice along a little, now and again, in this or that lifetime. Elisabeth's fever, for example. It's easy, you know, to plant the germ of an illness in mortal flesh. They're so fragile. So vulnerable to any passing malady."

I flung myself upon my brother, knowing all the while it was what he wanted, what he'd goaded me to do, but unable to restrain the poisonous fury swelling within me. I made a sound that was at once a guttural growl and a shriek as I throttled him; I was as frenzied as a wolf in a trap, and as dangerous.

Krispin screamed, but it was a cry of hideous pleasure, even of ecstasy, like some hell-beast in climax. Even the hurt I caused him gave him joy, however heinous; he had surely dreamed of this moment, planned and schemed for it, for nearly the whole of his existence.

He melted in my hands like vapor, and vanished, but we had renewed our brotherly bond, malevolent as it was, and I sensed his destination and pursued him, leaving a disconsolate Challes behind to weep into his palms.

Krispin took me to a high plain, somewhere on the coast of Cornwall, and the sea was within our hearing if not our sight. There were standing stones, garish in the frigid, silvery glow, casting their lengthy shadows toward the moon, instead of away, in an eerie juxtaposition of nature.

His laughter was the keening of a mad creature, and he ran between the stones, his cape trailing absurdly behind him, as if he expected to take wing and fly. I would not have been surprised if he had.

I waited until he had expended some of his demented energy, watching him spin and cavort, now perched crowlike atop the highest of the ancient stones, now pirouetting in the center of the circle, arms outstretched, head tilted back, beautiful face bathed in moonlight.

The pagan revels continued for some time. Then, at long last, Krispin was still, smiling and beckoning for me to join him inside the stones.

I did not hesitate, though I was certain a trap was about to spring. I would have followed him into the very heart of hell, anywhere, because as long as I was with him, watching him, Daisy would be safe. When the time was right, when I had discovered my brother's greatest vulnerability, I meant to destroy him.

"There were countless sacrifices on this spot," he told me when I stood beside him. "So much passion, so much terror—the place reverberates with it even after all this time. Can't you feel it?"

I kept my repugnance to myself. Temporarily. "I have terror and passion enough of my own," I said. "I do not require that of others."

Krispin smiled at me and seemed, for a moment, almost like his old self. That facet of the experience stood out in sharp relief, wholly separate and more frightening somehow than anything that had gone before. "You were always damnably self-reliant, a law unto yourself—Valerian, the archangel made flesh, the saint with fangs."

I ignored the jibe. I would not allow him to glory in my attack again until I was ready to drive a pointed stick through his crumbling, rotted little heart. He could take all the perverted pleasure he wished in that. "You want my life," I said quietly, "and I will give it to you."

He stared at me, plainly baffled, and I was relieved to know he could not read my mind the way some fiends could. "On what condition?" he asked, suspicious.

"That we face our end together," I said in all sincerity. It was, I saw, the only way to put a finish to the curse that had pursued Daisy and me for so long. If I perished, and Krispin with me, the cycle would be broken at long last. Never again would I find Daisy, fall in love with her, hold her in my arms as she gave up the ghost yet another time. She would be left to live out this life, and any others that lay ahead, in relative peace.

Krispin studied me in silence for a long time. I could feel dawn hovering beyond the hills, ready to spill over the horizon and consume us. I wanted that death, although I knew it would be agonizing, and only a prelude to the suffering waiting beyond the veil.

"Suppose there is no judgment and no hell," Krispin reflected. "Would you welcome death? Would you yearn to rest, at long last, in the dark arms of oblivion?"

I felt the sting of impending morning on my cool flesh and wondered if I would die bravely, or in a screaming, writhing frenzy of anguish. I had never seen a vampire burned to cinders by the sun, but I *had* witnessed other demises—all of them ghastly.

I shivered.

"Oblivion would certainly be preferable to eternal suffering in the flames of Hades," I confessed, "but I have no particular wish to rest forever, either."

"You care for her so much, the lovely Daisy, that you would submit yourself to any fate?" Krispin paused to smile. Then, before I could offer a reply, he went on. "How noble you are. Imagine it—Valerian Lazarus, the bootmaker's whelp, willing to sacrifice his glorious self to save a woman. Why, it's almost Arthurian!"

I hadn't been callow enough to hope that Krispin would fail to guess why I wanted him to die with me. An idiot could have figured it out. Nor had I taken any great risk in letting him see how very great my love for Daisy truly was—he had known all along. He had tormented me with it, without my ever guessing, for hundreds of years.

I glanced uneasily toward the eastern horizon. It was still dark, and yet there was enough light hidden in the gloom to sear my sensitive eyes. For the first time, it occurred to me that one of the differences between Krispin's powers and mine could be the ability to withstand sunlight. "You have made your point," I said irascibly. "I know that you hate me, that you hold me in utter contempt. And I grow weary of your self-pity. Great Scot, to grieve and wail all these centuries over the slights of a vain, selfish, and utterly ignorant woman like Seraphina—to cry over spilt mother's milk—it's madness, Krispin. It's obscene!"

The light was coming closer, getting stronger, burning. Burning.

Krispin glared at me and gave that harrowing animal shriek of rage again, but then he turned to smoke, like a movie vampire, and seeped into the ground, there in the center of the circle, which yawned around us like the jaws of some great beast.

I did the same, and found myself, along with my brother, in a pit of tangled bones covered by the hard, windswept earth. These, no doubt, were the remains of those poor scapegoats who had been sacrificed to ancient, greedy gods. I felt their emotions, especially their fear, and heard the silent, protesting cacophony of their voices.

Krispin burrowed in among them, curled into the same position I'd seen him take as a small child, and, with a beatific smile curving his lips, tumbled abruptly into the vampire sleep. I would have killed him then, despite multitudinous compunctions, using one of the martyr's bones for a stake and another for a mallet, but my own nature betrayed me—I succumbed to the dark waters swamping my mind and slipped down and down, into the valley of the shadow.

16

Jenny Wade
London, 1722

IN her dreams Jenny could see as clearly as she had before her illness, and the images flashing through her mind were alive with clamor and bright, vibrant colors, pulsing and infused with light.

Everything moved at impossible speeds, and she was surrounded by purposeful people clad in odd, abbreviated clothing. They were strangers, and yet, conversely, she felt she knew and understood them, in a general way at least.

When she awakened, with a violent jerk, the scenes and the actors who had played them out vanished into the part of her brain where unremembered things were hidden. Her breathing was rapid and shallow, and she sank back against her pillows, willing herself to be calm. When she had achieved that, she focused her sharpened senses and discerned, by the coolness of the air against the flesh on her arms and by the deep, settled stillness of the house, that it was not yet morning.

She ached with a sudden, terrible loneliness, worse than anything she'd felt before, and was too distraught even to weep. She was young, she was blind, and she would never have a home of her own, or a loving husband to laugh with, or children to tug at her skirts and plead for sweets and stories.

Jenny waited patiently for the familiar sounds that meant the others were awake. Then she rose and washed, and was seated at her vanity table, brushing and plaiting her waist-length hair, when there came a rapid knock at her bedroom door. Before she could call out in answer, Adela swept in, her scent and the essence of her nature going before her like unseen heralds.

"Good morning, Jenny," she said without warmth.

Jenny felt a stirring of pity for her sister-in-law, for there was no poetry in her, no sunshine or humor. "Good morning," she replied and went on weaving her hair into a single thick braid.

Adela came to stand just behind her. "Martin tells me you suffered an episode yesterday."

A small muscle, hidden somewhere deep in Jenny's heart, seized with the renewed fear of being sent away to some awful place, where mad-women would be her only companions. "It was nothing," she said, hoping she sounded sane, as well as cheerful. "I was just thinking of other things, that's all."

Her sister-in-law was rigidly silent.

Jenny imagined that she could see her reflection in the vanity mirror, but the only image she could recall was that of a scrawny, red-haired girl with green eyes dominating a freckled face. She did not know how she looked now, though she often plagued Peach to describe her, and begged to know if she was beautiful.

Dear, loyal Peach always answered that she was lovely enough to capture and break the heart of any gentleman alive.

"What have I done, Adela?" Jenny asked in a soft voice, "to make you despise me so much? This is a large house—a palace by anyone's standards, and yet I invariably feel as though I'm in the way."

Adela did not answer—perhaps she did not know what to say, or refrained out of kindness—and left the room.

Jenny finished dressing, descended the broad staircase, and made her way into the parlor. There she sat down at the harpsichord and made music while a gentle rain pattered upon the windowpanes, making itself part of the song.

There were callers after luncheon, and Martin came home early from his offices and sat in the parlor with Jenny, reading aloud from a new

French novel. It was during that pleasant interlude that the simple truth came to her—Adela was jealous of Martin's affection for his young sister, and no doubt wished for more attention from him.

A great sorrow filled Jenny, and when Martin had finished reading, she ventured a suggestion. "Perhaps you should take Adela to the seaside. It would be romantic, just the two of you."

"And what would become of you?"

Jenny was mildly incensed. "I have Peach to look after me, Martin," she said in a moderate tone. "And don't say you must concentrate on your work, because I know it isn't true. You could manage your business in your sleep—I've heard you complain of it before."

Martin chuckled, but there was an undercurrent of sadness in his mirth. "I must stop buying these damned sentimental novels," he said. "They give you unseemly ideas."

"Adela needs you," Jenny insisted gently. "You neglect her."

"Leave it alone, Jenny," Martin said, and his tone was sharp enough to sting. He set the book aside with a telling thump, got out of his chair, and strode out of the room.

Jenny had dinner alone that evening beside the fire, for Martin had gone off to his club, and Adela had taken to her bed with yet another headache. And still the rain fell, though it wasn't singing now, as before. It was dreary, and Jenny's loneliness was such that she wondered how she could bear a lifetime of such feelings.

After her meal she returned to the harpsichord, closing the great doors behind her to muffle the sound, and sat down to play.

It was that night, in the soft swirling center of her music, that Jenny heard the angel's voice for the first time.

"Jenny," it said softly, almost reverently, from just behind her right shoulder. Whether born of heaven or of hell, the visitor was male. To a disturbing degree.

Jenny was not afraid, but she did wonder if she was having another spell. She craved comfort and reassurance; mayhap her active imagination had conjured a being to meet that need. She knew, because her blindness had made her introspective, and she'd spent a great deal of time exploring the fascinating and mysterious corners, closets, and crevices of her own inner world, learning that the mind was capable of all sorts of trickery, pleasant and otherwise.

She did not move from the little bench, or speak, but simply stopped playing and held out one hand.

"I have found you," said the visitor, and she heard weeping in his voice, as well as joy. Felt the air stir as he bent to kiss her lightly on top of the head.

An exquisite passion swept through her, and she felt herself flush. "You're not real," she said. "You were born of my longing and my need."

His hands rested gently on her shoulders; his grasp was gentle, but not warm as Martin's would have been, or Peach's. His flesh felt as cool and smooth as a polished gem, even through the fabric of her gown, and she reasoned that heaven must of course be a temperate place, the logical opposite of hell.

"No, precious," he said. "I'm not an illusion."

"Are you an angel then?" Jenny managed to ask.

His laugh was low and richly masculine, but contained none of the mockery or mild contempt she sometimes detected in Martin's mirth. His lips brushed the side of her neck, and they were cool, too, and soft like the petals of some exotic flower. "Perish the thought," he said. "But I am not a demon, either, so please do not fear me."

Jenny was convinced now that she must be having a waking dream— she could not hope for such tender attentions in reality, given her affliction—and the realization was a keen stab of sorrow, piercing the heart.

"I can't bear to think I've imagined you," she said wretchedly.

"I'm all too real, my Jenny. And I have loved you for longer than you can imagine."

Something leaped within her, something primitive and treacherous and wildly improper. She wanted to believe, wanted desperately for this phantom lover to be genuine, formed of flesh and blood, loving her, needing her, despite her flaw. A name, she thought, would give him substance, so she asked for his in a quiet, hopeful tone.

"Valerian," he answered somewhat hoarsely, and he squeezed her shoulders with his long fingers, and once again Jenny felt a deep and unholy pleasure slamming through her veins and muscles. At last, after finding its way into every part of her, the sensation shaped itself into a fiery coil and spun, tightening with every turn, just beneath her stomach.

"I've been so lonely," Jenny confessed. It was all right, because she was surely dreaming, and because it wouldn't have done to confide such a stark truth to Martin, or Adela, or Peach. They would have thought it untoward for an innocent young woman to desire an intimacy deeper than the brisk, blithe affection they themselves displayed for her.

"As have I," Valerian replied. In her mind she could picture him— he was tall, as stately and handsome as a prince from a storybook. She imagined his eyes to be blue, intensely so, and his hair to be the warm and rich color of chestnuts—and she was quite sure of these things, though she did not know how she could have discerned them.

Jenny reached up and interlocked her fingers with his. "Will you stay with me?"

He chuckled, though the sound was like a sob, too, and raised her from the seat before the harpsichord to kiss her ever so softly on the mouth. At this contact, an entirely new experience for Jenny, the wicked flame in her depths, only then dwindling, flared once more into a brilliant, consuming blaze.

"I must go," Valerian told her while she was still swaying in his arms, giddy from the kiss. "But I'll return soon, lovely Jenny. I promise."

She put her arms around his neck, perhaps a little desperately. "Stay," she pleaded, unashamed.

He rested a fingertip on her still-tingling, slightly swollen lips. "It is almost morning, beloved—I cannot stay."

Jenny clung, but he seemed to dissolve in her very embrace, as dream people are able to do, and she was alone again, but not so sad. The beginnings of a sweet and fragile hope kindled in her breast, and she hummed softly to herself as she went upstairs, moved confidently along the passageway to her room, and got herself ready for bed.

On the morrow she awakened to the joy and prevailed upon Peach to take special care in arranging her hair, with ribbons and dried flowers woven through the plait before it was wrapped round her crown in a coronet. She donned a cheerful dress of yellow silk, too; Jenny knew the color because of its unique, buttery warmth beneath her practiced fingertips, and could recognize red and blue and green and white, when the need arose, by similar means.

Before tea that afternoon, Adela read to Jenny from a volume of classic Greek poetry, perhaps as a gesture of peace. Dinner was served at eight, and when it was over, Jenny pleaded fatigue and retired to her room, unaccompanied because it was Peach's night to visit her sister.

Jenny had not lied when she'd claimed to be tired, but beneath her weariness flowed a wild, anticipatory emotion she could not define, an elemental, unfettered *something*, careening along like a river, under no command but its own. Jenny could no more have stopped the rushing torrent than altered the course of the Thames, so she sat down in the chair by the hearth in her room and waited.

The house settled slowly around her—servants shuffled sleepily in the halls, doors opened and closed, floors creaked. She heard Martin's voice, and Adela's, as they said their good-nights and parted in the passage to enter their separate rooms.

Jenny had led a sheltered life, but she was not ignorant of the ways of men and women, thanks to Peach's frankness and the scandalous gossip she sometimes overheard the maids exchanging when they thought no one else was about. It puzzled her that Martin and Adela did not share a bed, and had never done so within her memory. Perhaps, she speculated, they did not wish to have children, like other couples of their age and means.

Guilt washed through Jenny in the wake of the great flood of indefinable excitement that had nearly drowned her moments before. Other couples did not have a blind and indigent relation to look after, she thought with chagrin.

The summons from her angel, when it came, was a trill of silent music, a burst of harp strings too subtle for the ear to catch, but something felt instead, like a feather passed close to the skin but not quite touching. Jenny moved quietly and competently toward it, unhampered by the darkness that slowed others' steps, responding to the piper's call.

There could be no doubt that she was awake this time, she reflected with a sense of soaring joy, when she entered the misty, fragrant garden and knew that he was there waiting.

"Valerian," she said softly, and he drew her, by some faculty of mind, or perhaps by the shimmering thread of her most private desires, along the brick walk and into his arms.

It was the first of many such visits. Sometimes Valerian told wonderful tales, and on other nights they danced together in the garden, and it was as though Jenny's feet skimmed above the flat stones surrounding the fountain.

Nearly a year passed before they became lovers.

On that eve of sweet surrender Valerian wrapped her in something silken and whispering—a cloak, she thought. Jenny clung to him when they were caught up by the wind and became part of it, and of each other, and were carried away to another place.

"What are you that you can work such tricks?" she asked when Valerian laid her on a soft couch in a room she couldn't see, and she knew by sound and motion that he knelt beside her. At last, after all the courting, all the subtle preparation, she would give herself to her phantom.

It would not have mattered what reply he made to her question—be he devil or fairy prince, Jenny thought, he was the answer to all her longings. She had been waiting for him since before her first memory.

"A fallen angel," Valerian said with tenderness and sorrow mingling in his wonderful voice. He hadn't made the music that had drawn her to the garden so many nights, she realized then—he *was* that music. "Don't trouble yourself with who I am, sweet. It is enough, isn't it, that we've found each other again at long last?"

Jenny raised trembling fingers to the bodice of her gown, guided by the same inner instinct that made her heart pound and caused a heavy, aching warmth to settle over her. She undid the ribbon ties of her camisole and parted the fabric to reveal her plump breasts, because she knew that he wanted to see and touch them, because she longed to nurture him somehow.

He groaned, and the sound bore her high on fragile wings, and she soared upon it, triumphant, and murmured his beautiful name— Valerian. The utterance itself was a caress, echoing back to her, lodging in deep, forbidden places.

She felt his lips on her nipple, hungry and wet, and cried out, not in fear or in horror, but in that singular, innocent lust at which only virgins can be truly proficient. Her fingers found their way into his thick, silken hair, and she pressed him closer, whimpering, urging him on in his gentle greed.

The pleasure was unspeakable, not to be borne, exceeding even the fitful and licentious fantasies that had caused Jenny to toss restlessly in her bed when she first reached womanhood. She had never even guessed that the mating process could be so fiercely delightful.

Jenny wanted to give herself up to Valerian, wanted it more than the return of her eyesight, more than a husband or a child or a house where she was mistress, and not Adela. These last were, after all, impossible dreams, but this other pleasure was within her grasp. The joy of it would sustain her, even if he should abandon her, through all the bleak years of spinsterhood that might lay ahead.

She could barely speak, so intense was the ecstasy he offered and withdrew and then offered again, with his light, musician's fingers and his seeking mouth. "Valerian—where have we known each other before? I do not—remember—" She paused to give a shuddering sigh as he raised her far enough off the couch to remove her clothes.

To be naked to his gaze was as heady as a surfeit of summer wine. For the first time ever, Jenny felt lushly beautiful and womanly—and whole.

Valerian was nibbling at the delicate flesh on her neck. "Your heart remembers," he said softly. "Look into your heart."

"I can't—*think*," she protested with a throaty laugh.

He gathered her breasts in his strong, gentle hands, chafing the taut peaks with his thumbs, and she wondered distractedly why she did not feel his breath upon her flesh, for his face was very near to hers. "How like a woman to want to think at such a time," he teased. "The heart does not have thoughts, beloved—only feelings. Search there, among them, and I promise you will find recollection, some shadow, of what we have been to each other."

Such a search could not be made, Jenny knew, while her blood was thundering through her veins and her breathing was racing out of control. Still, she sensed that Valerian was right—they were not strangers, but companions of old; each belonging to the other in some elemental and enigmatic way.

To lie with Valerian was to return home after a long and difficult journey, to be safe after a spell of unrelenting danger.

"Please," she said. "Make love to me."

"Yes," he replied, and after parting her legs tenderly, to either side of the couch, he mounted her. "There may be pain—"

Jenny's slim, supple form arched like a bow, taut and humming. "I don't care," she said, and it was true. Nothing mattered but their joining, the reunion of their bodies and souls.

Valerian lunged into her, and she cried out, in a virgin's distress, yes, but also in profound welcome. She was exultant, alive with sensation. At last, at last, she was truly herself.

In the meantime, Valerian murmured endearments to her, and half-formed prayers of adoration, his magnificent body flexing powerfully, reaching deep inside Jenny, causing her to sob softly even as her spirit took fire and burned.

It ended, finally, as must all joys and all sorrows, and they lay together, entwined, exhausted, reunited after a separation so long that Jenny could not remember their parting. Later, when she'd gathered her scattered wits, she would examine her heart, as Valerian had said she must, and surely she would find him there. . . .

DAISY
Las Vegas, 1995

"Chandler!" The voice was snappish, insistent. "Damn it, Daisy, you gotta come out of it!"

She stirred. Daisy? Who the hell was Daisy?

"Open your eyes, Chandler," her tormentor commanded.

She ached all over, yet a sweet languor possessed her, as though she had just made love, and been thoroughly, skillfully satisfied. She did not want to surface, to leave the sensation behind.

"I ain't got all night, Chandler!"

Was this the man who had been her lover, who had carried her to heights she only faintly remembered?

It couldn't be, she thought. Reluctantly she opened her eyes.

Seeing O'Halloran looming over her brought everything back with all the subtly of a train plunging off a high trestle. He had cookie crumbs on his chin, what hair he had left was standing on end, and there was a rumpled air about him, as if he hadn't changed clothes since the Carter administration.

She sighed and closed her eyes again, just for a moment. At least that much was normal—her partner was the same sweet slob he'd always been.

"Daisy, don't veg out on me now," O'Halloran rasped. "You looked right at me a second ago. I saw you."

"Super-cop," she said, trying on the name he'd called her by— Daisy—in her muddled mind and finding that it fit comfortably, like a favorite T-shirt or a roomy pair of sweat pants. "Nothing gets by you, does it, O'Halloran?" She paused, wanting to cry but too proud to give in to the urge. "Damn it, this is a hospital, isn't it?"

"University Medical Center," O'Halloran confirmed. "But don't get your panties in a wad, Chandler—it ain't the psycho ward. You collapsed on the sidewalk, that's all, and somebody called an ambulance."

Daisy's temples were throbbing, and she thought she might stick her head over the side of the bed and heave all over O'Halloran's shoes. Chances were, nobody would notice if she did.

"Am I hurt?"

"Nope," O'Halloran said proudly, as though he'd participated in her salvation or even engineered it single-handedly. "But you were definitely out of it. Talked about some guy named Martin and twitched a lot."

She raised a hand to her forehead, to push back her hair, and noticed for the first time she was on IV. "What the—?" she said, starting to sit up.

O'Halloran pushed her back onto the pillows. "Take a breath, Chandler," he said. "It's just sugar water. No big deal. And don't even think about getting up, because you ain't going noplace, not tonight."

A tear escaped, despite Daisy's determination, and zigzagged down her cheek. "They think I'm crazy or on drugs, don't they? The brass, I mean."

Her partner smiled, produced a chocolate cookie from somewhere, and bit into it with relish. The crumbs dropped onto Daisy's bedsheet. "Nobody thinks you're using," he said. "You've already had the necessary blood and urine tests. And you're probably only mildly deranged, which puts you in the normal category."

"I'm not having a breakdown," Daisy said. But she was remembering so many things—being blind, living in her brother and sister-in-law's house in eighteenth-century London, Valerian carrying her away by magic and making love to her, and wondering if she'd imagined all of it. She wouldn't be the first cop to crumble under stress, though that didn't make the idea any easier to deal with.

O'Halloran found her other hand, the one without the needle and tube protruding from the large vein, and gathered it awkwardly between his own. "If you say your head's on straight, Chandler, I believe you," he told her. "You just need to rest for a while, that's all."

"They've suspended me."

"You're on medical leave," O'Halloran corrected.

Daisy took a few moments to gather her composure. "Permanently?"

The other cop hesitated just a moment too long. "Until further notice," he said finally, still holding her hand. "You'll have to have some counseling and some tests, and then you'll go up before a review board. Happens all the time."

"Not to me, it doesn't."

O'Halloran shrugged in an effort to appear nonchalant, but she saw the concern in his eyes. "Okay, Chandler, so you got stepped on. Things ain't too cool just now. That's reality, and you gotta deal with it. You have sick leave, and some savings, maybe?"

Life with—or without—Jeanine had made Daisy pragmatic at a very young age. She had sick leave, vacation time, and a year's wages tucked away in the bank. "Don't sweat it, O'Halloran," she said. "I won't have to move in with you."

He laughed. "You're still a smartass. That's got to be a good sign."

"How's the case going, hotshot? And before you come back with, 'what case?', let me just say you know damn well which one I'm talking about."

"The vampire thing?"

"That's the one."

O'Halloran sighed. "We ain't made a whole hell of a lot of progress with that one, Chandler." A nurse appeared on the other side of Daisy's bed and gave the veteran cop a meaningful look. "Tell you what, ace. I'll stop by in the morning and fill you in, okay?"

Daisy had neither the strength nor the will to argue. It was late, and she felt as if she'd been trampled by a herd of tap-dancing burros. Besides, once O'Halloran and the nurse had gone and the lights were out, she'd be able to cry in private.

Her partner left, and the nurse, whose nametag read 'Betty,' gave Daisy a pill to make her sleep, checked the flow of glucose through the tube, switched off the light, and went out.

Daisy lay perfectly still, staring up at the ceiling, trying to make sense of all that had been happening to her since that first fateful night, when she'd shelled out big bucks to watch a magic show at the Venetian Hotel. Everything had gone to hell as soon as she'd met Valerian.

He was a regular sort of guy, if you were willing to overlook the fangs and the fact that he was six hundred years old. Far be it from her to fall in love with a normal human being, somebody with a last name, at least. Oh, no. She had to lose her heart to a *vampire*.

She was, for a time, so caught up in her private lament that she did not notice the elegant form leaning against the metal rail at the foot of her bed. When she did, her heart spiraled into the back of her throat, blocking the cry of alarm that would have escaped a moment later.

"It's only me," Valerian said.

Daisy's relief was so intense that it seemed to melt her bones and muscles like sunshine on snow. She squinted as he came to stand beside her, his handsome face clearly visible even in the darkness, because of its pale translucence.

"For a moment, I thought—"

"That I was Krispin, come to kill you at last?"

She could only nod.

He touched her face, and she was reminded of his lovemaking, as she'd experienced it in this lifetime, and as Jenny Wade, the blind girl. "My precious love," he said in a ragged whisper and bent to kiss her almost fitfully on the forehead. "I've come to bid you farewell."

Once or twice, since the vampire odyssey had begun, Daisy had wished she could have her old, comparatively uncomplicated life back. Now, faced with the prospect of losing Valerian forever, she discovered she was willing to risk almost anything to continue the relationship, weird as it was.

Maybe she *had* gone over the edge, and the department had been right to pull her badge.

"No," she said, her eyes filling with fresh tears. "I don't want you to go."

"Daisy," he whispered, and there was anguish in the way he said her name. "This is the only way I can protect you, and it's difficult enough—"

"*What* is the only way? What are you talking about?"

Valerian deflected the questions with a statement. "Krispin won't bother you again."

"Damn it, Valerian, I have to know what you mean. I *love* you—that alone probably qualifies me for megatherapy—but there it is. You can't just walk out of here, or turn into a bat and fly away, or dissolve into a mist and seep through the wall—by God, you owe me more than that!"

He regarded her silently for a time, and she saw his pain clearly in those moments, though the room was as dark as ever, and felt the weight of his sorrow descend on her own heart. When he spoke, his voice was only a raspy murmur.

"All right," Valerian said tonelessly. "I've made a bargain with Krispin. We will both perish, together, and the curse will be broken. You'll be free."

Daisy wanted to blurt out a protest, but she stopped the words in her throat and swallowed them. Then she waited until she could trust herself to speak in a rational manner. "How?" She waved her good hand, precluding interruptions. "I'm not asking about the curse. I want to know how you intend to 'perish,' as you put it. What tragic elegance that word has!"

His eyes glistened as though he might be weeping, as she certainly was, but there was no tremor in his voice. "We'll be burned."

Such horror engulfed Daisy that she nearly fainted. She sat up at last and groped for the small stainless-steel pan on the bedside table, certain her stomach would fling up its contents. "*Burned?* Good God, Valerian, you can't be serious!"

He managed a brief, crooked smile, full of grief. "It's hardly a suitable subject for a joke," he pointed out.

"I won't let you!" Daisy cried and tried to scramble out of bed.

Valerian pinned her to the pillows, as surely as if he'd grasped her shoulders, though he was not physically touching her. "You can't stop this, Daisy," he said reasonably, gently. "And you wouldn't try if you really understood the situation."

Daisy's face was wet with tears, and they kept coming, as if there were no end to them, and she didn't give a damn. "That's bull, and you know it," she argued furiously. "I *do* understand the god-damned *situation*. What I don't get is how you could be such an idiot! Can't you see that this is a trick—that Krispin has no intention of going up in smoke with you?"

In a graceful motion that was at once firm and heartbreakingly tender, Valerian gathered Daisy into his arms and held her close against his chest. "Shhhh," he said, stroking her hair with one hand as she gave way to great, silent, shuddering sobs. For a long time he rocked her gently in his embrace, and when the worst of the storm had passed, he crooked a finger under her quivering chin and made her look at him. "Why are you here, Daisy?"

She laid her head against his chest, listening for a heartbeat that wasn't there. She was kneeling on the mattress now, the IV tube still dangling from her left hand, with one arm around Valerian's neck. Haltingly she answered his question, told him how she'd been walking home from the Venetian Hotel when the second spontaneous regression had overtaken her. Daisy went on to recount her brief experience as Jenny Wade, finishing with, "You were there, too. You carried me away, and we made love. I was a virgin."

She felt him tremble. "Yes," he said.

"Did I travel through time, the way you do?"

"No," Valerian replied at length. "You were only remembering. It was all an illusion."

"Even you?"

"Especially me."

Daisy was disappointed; she'd wanted the experience to be real. "Can vampires make women pregnant?"

He stiffened but did not pull away, as it had seemed for a moment that he would. "I don't know," he answered after another long interval. "Pray that such a thing cannot happen. Any child of mine would surely be a monster."

Daisy turned her wet face into his shirtfront and indulged in a loud sniffle. "Only during the Terrible Twos," she said, because if she spoke seriously, or let go of Valerian, the world would end.

Valerian laid a hand to either side of Daisy's head and tilted it back to look into her eyes. "Stop, Daisy," he pleaded. "I know what you're trying to do, but it won't work. We can't put off the inevitable."

"Please—stay."

"*I can't.*"

"It's a trap—Krispin means to let you die and save himself at the last moment!"

"I know that, Daisy," Valerian said patiently, glancing uneasily toward the window. The darkness seemed to be thinning, losing its depth. "He won't succeed."

"Yes, he will. He'll come back here and carry me off, and there'll be no one to protect me—"

Valerian laid a finger to her lips, effectively stopping the rising tide of hysteria. "I love you," he said, and then he was simply gone. It was as if she'd only imagined him, only dreamed he was there.

Daisy knelt on the bed for a few moments, frantic, her mind full of horrific images of Valerian burning. She reached for the pan again and retched convulsively.

When the spate of illness passed, Daisy switched on her reading lamp and reached for the telephone on the bedside stand. She called information in Seattle and asked for Kristina's number.

Ms. Holbrook answered right away, though she sounded sleepy. "This had better be good," she said without preamble.

Daisy had had to make a lot of difficult calls in the course of her work. By comparison, telephoning the daughter of two blood-drinking monsters in the middle of the night was tame. "Valerian is in trouble," she told Kristina. "I need your help."

"Who is this?"

"Daisy Chandler. We met in Las Vegas, at Valerian's house."

"Oh, yes—the naked cop. Tell me—just what kind of fix has my Guardian Vampire gotten himself into this time? He does have a regrettable gift for generating chaos, our Valerian. Not to mention scandal, usually accompanied by high drama."

Daisy closed her eyes, gathered her courage, and began to talk.

17

VALERIAN
London, 1875

I found Calder Holbrook in the lab beneath the London house he shared with Maeve, his mate. Like many vampires, he preferred the century of his mortal birth and, having that option, passed much of his time there.

"Valerian," the doctor greeted me, with more resignation than affection, when I appeared at his elbow. He was an ideal partner for Maeve, though like a great many doctors he tended to be taciturn to the point of abruptness. He was quiet and steady, providing a perfect counterbalance to her more spectacular personality. Though I had transformed Holbrook from mortal to fiend myself, and was thus, in a manner of speaking, his sire, and although it had been I, and no one else, who had taught him the rudiments of navigating the world of the supernatural, there was, as the saying goes, no love lost between us.

For it was I who made Maeve a vampire, albeit long before he knew her, and he was jealous of that undeniable intimacy.

I stood with my hands clasped behind my back, peering over Calder's shoulder at the concoction bubbling in a bottle heated over a small brazier. "Have you discovered the cure for what ails us?" I inquired, for I knew that was what the doctor sought—a way to circumvent a night-walker's needs for blood-sustenance and protection from the sun, while retaining the glorious powers we possess. Unhampered by the kind of idealism that plagues men and vampires of Calder's ilk, I envisioned a plethora of such creatures ranging over the earth and, subsequent to that thought, hoped for a resounding failure.

Holbrook turned his head to regard me archly for a moment or two, one eyebrow raised, then uttered a gruff *harumph* and turned back to his work. "Mysteries, mysteries," he muttered. "Even vampirism cannot explain what ails *you*, Valerian."

I had just parted from Daisy, probably forever, and I faced an eternity of damnation—unceasing punishment so terrible, so brutal, that only a medieval mind could truly grasp its portent—and I was not in the mood to exchange jibes with the queen's consort. "Please—spare me your hysterical expressions of admiration and tender regard."

The stuff in Calder's glass vial turned to an interesting shade of amber, and he raised it high to peer through it and murmur again.

"What do you want?" he asked when he'd left me quivering on the hook a little longer.

"I have been told that you've discovered parallel dimensions and passages into those other worlds."

At long last Calder turned and granted me his full, if somewhat grudging, attention. "I have uncovered the existence of such phenomena, yes, but I have only theories as to how they are reached."

I resisted the urge to grasp the doctor's collar and haul him onto his toes as I might have done with a mortal, for I knew Calder wouldn't suffer such an affront lightly. He must have glimpsed the intent in my face before I quelled it, for the shadow of a smile fell across his mouth.

I had amused him. Oh, joy.

"The way must be sealed, whatever and wherever it is," I said at last in an angry rasp. My temper was not helped by the sense of hopelessness that pervaded my being like an unseen vapor, bruising every cell and sinew, even in their atrophy. "Don't you see? That's how he—my brother, Krispin—has been able to hide himself from me all these centuries. Suppose there are others like him? Suppose—"

"What in hell are you talking about?" Calder interrupted.

Dawn was approaching; I could feel it tugging at my consciousness, pulling me downward into a maelstrom of nothingness, although the doctor did not seem to be affected. "There is so little time!" I cried, desperate to make him understand.

"Tell me," he said, this time with a note of gentleness in his voice. I imagined that Dr. Holbrook had been a comfort to his patients, as a mortal physician. He was not generally so delicate with the sensibilities of vampires.

I told the tale, as best I was able, my words faltering and tumbling over each other as I attempted to resist the grasping, smothering darkness rising around me. I explained the danger Krispin represented, or at least I hoped that was what I had done, for it all sounded garbled to me, and disjointed. All the while I was speaking, I wondered vaguely why my fledgling was not succumbing to the great sleep as I was.

Finally the moment came when I could no longer think, or speak, or wonder. I had been dragged under, into the oblivion of my innermost being, there to slumber, witless and unstirring, until the sun sank into westerly seas.

DAISY
Las Vegas, 1995

The sleeping pill must have taken hold soon after Daisy had finished her call to Kristina, for she wakened to full sunlight and a breakfast tray, with no conscious memory of hanging up the receiver.

The ageless Ms. Holbrook was standing by the window, her cap of dark hair gleaming richly in the dazzle of morning, clad in a cream-colored pantsuit of impeccable tailoring, Gucci shoes, and a matching bag of soft, supple leather. Her jewelry, a single heavy golden chain, was real, and Daisy wondered if she'd zapped the outfit out of thin air or simply bought everything in stores, like anyone else.

"Why didn't you awaken me?" Daisy demanded, frowning at the food on her tray and reaching reluctantly for a piece of toast. She had no appetite, but she knew she would need her strength for the challenges ahead, and that meant she had to eat.

Kristina raised one shoulder in a slight, elegant shrug. "There's really no hurry. Valerian is a vampire. He's burrowed down somewhere, sleeping off the day."

Daisy nibbled at the toast. "And Krispin?"

"Who knows? From what you told me on the telephone last night, he may be the proverbial horse of a different color. An unknown quantity, if you will."

A shiver cartwheeled down Daisy's spine, and the words she spoke were born of pure bravado. "Can you take me to him?"

"Oh, that's a brilliant idea," Kristina muttered, ignoring the nurse who came to see if Daisy was eating her breakfast. "If this *thing* didn't kill us both for our trouble, my mother well might. Or Valerian himself." She shoved a hand through her hair, and it immediately fell back into perfect array, a soft cascade of ebony spun to silk.

In her next life Daisy wanted hair like that.

She settled against her pillow, an unwilling patient, dolefully spooning stewed peaches into her mouth. A nurse had taken the IV needle from her hand; that was some progress, at least. And O'Halloran hadn't been in with any further news flashes on the dismal state of her career. A person had to focus on the positive whenever possible. "Okay. Then just tell me how to find the creep," she said between bites of spongy fruit, "and I'll go by myself."

"Absolutely not," Kristina said. "I'm taking you to my place in Seattle. You can stay there until all this is settled, one way or another."

Daisy couldn't bear the thought of sitting by passively and leaving everything to fate. She had too much to lose—and besides, there was really no place to hide. Krispin would close in for the kill when he wanted to—up until now, he'd only been toying with Daisy, using her to torment Valerian.

"Hiding out is no solution, Kristina, and you know it," she replied with as much firmness as she could muster under the circumstances. "Some things can't be avoided, and this is one of them. There has to be a confrontation."

"Between Valerian and Krispin, yes," Kristina insisted. "But you should stay out of it. You can't begin to understand what you're dealing with here."

"Would *you* turn away and pretend nothing was happening? If you were in love with a man—excuse me, a vampire—could you hide out somewhere until it was all over?"

Daisy thought she saw a shadow of sadness move in Kristina's eyes, but the expression was so fleeting that she told herself she'd imagined it.

"Daisy, the important thing here is for you to stay alive. The relationship isn't going to work anyway, because in case you've forgotten, you're a mortal woman and Valerian is a vampire. How could the two of you ever hope to have anything even remotely resembling a normal life? You'll get old and die, for instance, but Valerian, if he survives, will look the same a thousand years from now as he does today." She paused to walk over and close the door on the hustle and bustle of the hospital corridor before continuing. "He wouldn't change back into a mortal, Daisy, even if such a thing were possible. Valerian *revels* in what he is. Would you be willing to become a vampire?"

Daisy shrank back, repelled by the idea and more than a little stricken because Kristina's points were valid ones. "Of course not," she said.

Kristina spread her hands wide as if to say, "Well, then?"

"I love Valerian," Daisy insisted in a fragile tone. "And I don't care if everybody thinks I'm his mother someday—or if I don't see him in the daytime, or any of that. It would be enough just to be with him."

The other woman raised one delicate eyebrow. Her eyes were an intense shade of silvery gray and so expressive that few words were needed. "Of all vampires, Daisy, Valerian is the most fickle, the most outrageous, the most flamboyant. His passions have a range you cannot begin to appreciate."

Daisy closed her eyes, just briefly, against the keenest ache she had ever felt. "If you are saying he has loved others—"

"He has," Kristina said, though not unkindly.

"Whose side are you on, anyway?" Daisy demanded, regretting that she'd turned to this woman—if indeed she *was* a woman and not some kind of spook—for help in saving Valerian from himself as well as from his brother.

"Your side, Daisy," Kristina answered sadly. "And Valerian's. Just now my only aim is to keep you both alive. Still, if you're smart, you'll take my advice, forget our splendid friend and find a nice, ordinary mortal to love."

Daisy pushed away her food and folded her arms stubbornly. "I'm afraid knowing Valerian has spoiled me for 'nice, ordinary mortals,' " she said. "Besides, there's something bigger than all of us going on here. It's as if we've come to the crux of it all, the *X* on the map, after centuries of blunders and near misses. The situation has to be resolved—I feel sure of it. There is something we're supposed to do to make things right."

"No wonder you keep reincarnating as Valerian's lover, over and over again," Kristina remarked with some irritation. "You haven't the *sense* to learn your lesson."

"Which is?" Daisy asked tartly, swinging her legs over the side of the bed and testing a privately held theory that she could stand on her own if she tried, despite the bone-melting weakness that still afflicted her.

"That you must let go of Valerian, once and for all. And the same goes for him. The two of you are obsessed, following each other from continent to continent and century to century, as if you could thwart karma by mule-headed persistence!"

Daisy stood, wavered, clutched the bed, indulging in a few deep, steadying breaths before replying. "Maybe it's just that we know we belong together," she said. "Damn it, aren't we entitled to one lifetime of happiness, after all we've been through?"

"None of us is entitled to anything," Kristina countered, folding her arms. "We're here on sufferance. Mortal and monster, saint and sinner—we could all be obliterated at the whim of heaven."

"How nice that you came to visit," Daisy said with acid sweetness. "To think I was actually depressed before!"

Kristina smiled tentatively and approached Daisy's bedside. "Sorry— I tend to be a little overrealistic sometimes," she said and laughed a little. "I get that from my father, I think. He's pragmatic to a fault."

Daisy, steadier on her feet now, began to make her way slowly around the bed, with a goal of reaching the closet. She didn't ask Kristina to blink her up an outfit, like before at Valerian's house; it had occurred to her since that the clothes might have been woven of fancy and little else, like those of the fabled emperor. There was also a possibility that the garments could vanish, being magical, like so much smoke, leaving her standing in some public place clad only in her good intentions.

"Nothing wrong with taking a sensible approach to things," she said, because she liked Kristina and because she, being a cop, albeit a suspended one, was inclined toward a practical view herself. Her knuckles whitened where she gripped the steel rail at the foot of the mattress as she inched along. "Are you an only child?" she inquired, sensing that Kristina was about to order her back into bed and anxious to deflect any concern, however well meant, that might be coming her way.

"To say the least," Kristina answered, folding her arms and watching Daisy's slow progress with her head tilted slightly to one side. The expression on her exquisite face was at once pitying and wry. "As far as I know, my mother was the first vampire to give birth in the human fashion. Nightwalkers generally create their 'children' by transforming favorite mortals."

Daisy stopped, trembling with weakness, grasping the footrails as if to keep from dropping over a precipice. She laughed, but the sound was one of pain, not merriment. "I thought I'd heard everything, until I fell in with your crowd. The confessions of serial killers and street hoods pale by comparison."

Kristina moved silently to her side, as lithe and graceful as a cat, and put a strong arm around her. "Back into bed, Daisy," she said with kind insistence. "You're not ready to ride to the rescue quite yet."

Daisy wanted to resist, but there was a hypnotic quality to Kristina's touch, as well as her voice, and besides, she was tired. So unbelievably tired. "Can't just—give up—" she protested, amazed to find that she was already lying down again. Kristina was covering her gently with the sheet and thin blanket.

"I can't imagine you doing that," Kristina said with amusement and a touch of sorrow, too. "In fact, I don't believe you know how to quit—even when it would be the smartest thing to do."

Daisy felt the bed spinning beneath her, felt herself spiraling down and down, like Alice tumbling into the rabbit hole, to land, bouncing, on a dream. . . .

VALERIAN
London, 1875

I awakened from my enforced rest to find myself sprawled ingloriously on the floor of Holbrook's laboratory, with the good doctor gone. I was not alone, however—Kristina, child of my soul, was sitting nearby, slender legs elegantly crossed and arms folded, awaiting my return to consciousness.

"Bloody hell," I rasped, sitting up and shaking my head. I felt rather like a pugilist felled by a stronger opponent.

Kristina smiled sweetly. "Hello, lazybones."

I stood shakily, grasping the examination table with one arm to steady myself during the process. "Where the devil is that no-account father of yours?" I demanded.

She sighed. "When I turned a hundred and thirty, I stopped keeping track."

"He didn't sleep," I marveled.

"What?"

"Calder. Your father—he didn't sleep."

"I know Calder is my father," Kristina said patiently, leaning forward in her chair but not rising, as a more mannerly and respectful child might do. "And how do you know what happened after you dropped off? Papa could have willed himself to some other lair the moment you closed your eyes."

My practiced instincts, coupled with the memory of a wide-awake, completely alert Dr. Holbrook, argued against Kristina's theory. "He's found a way to circumvent the vampire sleep—by all the old gods, he's done it!" Fury scorched through me, consuming the last wisps of insensibility lingering in my brain. "And *damn him*, Calder means to keep the secret to himself!"

Kristina folded back the slim, tapered fingers of one hand and gazed thoughtfully at her nails. "You aren't being fair," she accused mildly. "Papa does not number among your more ardent admirers—we both know that. But he would never withhold any knowledge that could be used to accomplish something good."

I began to pace, muttering to myself as I moved. Although I had awakened refreshed, my thoughts were again jumbled and fragmentary, and I quite literally did not know which way to turn.

The woman who would, in any other society except our own, be called my goddaughter, rose at last from her chair. "I've seen Daisy," she said, stopping me in midstride. "There's a crazy scheme cooking in the back of that mortal brain, Valerian—she figures she can save you, your Daisy, if she surrenders herself to Krispin before your heroic sacrifice can be made."

The mere idea chilled me. I grasped Kristina's shoulders and hauled her onto her toes, giving her a little shake in the process. "You talked her out of it, of course," I said.

Fire kindled in Kristina's pewter-colored eyes, but she did not use her singular magic to punish me for the effort. "I tried," was her response. "Right now Daisy is too frail to try anything very dramatic, but there can be no question that she's determined. I expect she'll do something stupid the moment she's worked up the necessary stamina. Now, let me go before I turn you into a garden slug and bury you in salt."

I released her, wincing at the image, and at the same time smiling a little. "Not very imaginative," I scolded, bending forward to plant a soft kiss on her forehead. "Help me, Kristina. Please. If you know anything about Calder's experiments, I beg of you, tell me now."

She looked at me with a sheen of tears glimmering in her eyes. "You're asking me to betray my father's trust."

I shook my head. "I'm asking you to save Daisy, and others probably, from Krispin's madness. If I can find the passageway between this world and his, I can find *him*."

Kristina was silent for a time, obviously torn, but then she turned and crossed the room to a wall lined with neatly arranged volumes on sturdy shelves. She ran an index finger over the spines with affection and finally selected one particular book and took it reverently from its place among the others.

She held the tome against her chest for a moment, then extended it to me.

It was a diary of sorts, a complex record of Calder's most recent explorations of science. In it were all his theories concerning parallel dimensions, and I absorbed the words greedily by running my right hand down every page.

When I was finished, I had a very good idea where to find my brother. The solution, in fact, was almost ludicrously simple. I might have thought of it myself, or at least asked a certain friend who writes screenplays for horror films to suggest possibilities, if I had been in a calm frame of mind rather than a mild state of hysteria.

"Thank you," I said to Kristina and pressed the volume back into her hands.

I went from there to my favorite part of nineteenth-century London for a hasty feeding, leaving my victim anemic but otherwise ecstatic. Then I proceeded to a certain burial mound not far from modern-day Dunnett's Head, a place where Challes had taken Krispin, Brenna, and me long ago while in the throes of a scholarly passion for antiquities. We were all fascinated by the area, for the bones secreted beneath that manmade hillock of stone and rubble and grass had been ancient even in our medieval time. According to our tutor, the occupants of that underground chamber had lived and died before the Romans came to Britain.

When I reached that bleak, moon-swept monument, it looked so strange, so eerie, that it might have been the landscape of some lesser planet, knowing neither snow nor fire, catching only the chill, straying beams of some wasted star. It was difficult to believe that any cogent being, human or otherwise, had ever trod this hard, unyielding ground, let alone toiled there, and given birth, fought battles, and built small, leaky ships to brave the treacherous seas.

For me, that night, as well fed and strong as I was, it seemed to be the loneliest, most desolate place in the universe. I reminded myself of the information I'd absorbed from Calder's notes—in order to move between our world and the alternate one Krispin apparently frequented, one must undergo another birth, with the grave for a womb.

I was drawn to that particular site by an impulse born in some unexplored region of my being—no doubt there were still bonds linking

Krispin and me, however tenuous they might have been. We had been brothers once, after all.

I closed my eyes as an infinite sadness encompassed me, but my resolve was not shaken. If I found Krispin before the appointed time of our mutual destruction, I would destroy him, thus evading the ambush he most assuredly planned for me and, at the same time, making certain that Daisy was safe.

I was willing to risk anything to succeed in that one aim, and with that certainty in mind, I dared to call upon the most fearsome angel in all heaven's uncounted legions.

"Nemesis!" I shouted into the night. "Pay heed to the bargain I offer!"

Even though I had just summoned him, it was still a profound shock when the night was rent by a narrow strip of light, no product of the sun or the moon, but of some inner universe. It broadened, a gleaming doorway to a realm I would never see, and the great warrior angel appeared. He was quite ordinary-looking, was Nemesis, a fact that probably served him very well during his frequent interactions with the mortal race.

The chasm vanished, but Nemesis seemed luminous, as though light flowed through his veins instead of blood. Perhaps it did.

He looked at me with contemptuous interest. "You dare to command me, vampire, as though I were a genie in a lamp instead of a warrior of the One God? What is your purpose?"

"I seek your assistance."

Nemesis chuckled to himself, and that sound, too, was disdainful. "What perfidy is this?" he demanded after a few moments of silence. "Vampires do not seek favors of angels."

"This vampire is desperate," I replied with resignation, and then I told him my lengthy story, which was also Daisy's, leaving nothing out beyond those things that would offend a celibate creature. Aside from that, I spoke the absolute and unvarnished truth, describing Krispin and all the havoc he could wreak if he wasn't stopped.

The angel listened without interruption, I will give him that, but when I had finished, he was plainly still doubtful of my motives for calling him to that barren place and relating such a tale.

"You would ask me to help destroy this vampire?" Nemesis inquired, after considering my words in silence for a long interval. When I merely nodded, he went on. "If it were up to me," he said, "you may be certain I would put a finish to the lot of you. Abominations, that's what you are. Since I have yet to reduce you to ashes, to be swept away by the wind, it should be plain that the choice is not mine."

"You have a certain autonomy, I suspect," I ventured to insist, though quietly and very, very carefully. "Were that not so, you couldn't have risen to a position of authority."

Nemesis studied me, his eyes narrowed in distrustful curiosity, and I marveled that, for all his terrible power, he clearly could not look into my mind. Had he been able to do so, he would have known that I was sincere, and there was no treachery afoot.

"I cannot destroy any creature, save demons," he said, but with less certainly than before.

"Perhaps," I conceded moderately, "but you are allowed, I trust, to escort surrendering fiends into the welcoming arms of hell."

The statement caught him off guard, I was pleased to see, but only for a moment. "What are you saying?"

"If you will help me to capture the one who bore the name of Krispin Lazarus, as a mortal, then I shall go willingly into the pit."

"You cannot begin to guess what you are suggesting," the angel said, but I knew he was intrigued by my proposal. To rid the world of two troublesome vampires was surely, in his view, a worthy aspiration.

I recalled the things I had been taught about hell as a human child, and shivered involuntarily. "Oh, but I do," I said at last. "I was mortal in the fourteenth century, and the torments awaiting the damned were described to me in vivid detail from the time I could make sense of such matters. I know well what I shall suffer."

"And you are willing to face such punishment for the sake of one woman?"

"Yes," I answered without hesitation, but I was full of dread and sorrow, for there has never been another creature that loved life as I did.

"Remarkable," the angel said, rubbing his chin thoughtfully between a thumb and index finger as he pondered my countenance. "Either you lie, which seems most likely, or you are indeed a rare vampire. It hardly wants saying that your kind is not noted for generosity—especially when the required sacrifice is one of such magnitude." He paused. "It is known that you have made a bargain with your brother, the renegade Krispin. You have agreed to accept the help of a warlock, as well. Why, then, do you come to me?"

I smiled sadly. "You have a remarkable intelligence system."

"The best," Nemesis agreed. "Speak, vampire. Do you dare attempt to deceive me?"

I shook my head. "No. You are a fierce warrior, Nemesis. You will surely rejoice when I fall into the hands of Lucifer. But unlike Dathan, the warlock, unlike my misguided brother, you can be counted upon to honor any bargain you make. Truth is your nature, and there are no lies in you."

"How beautifully you speak. And what a waste that you have cast your lot with fiends and devils. Yes, vampire—I would delight in putting an end to your evil, and that of all others like you, but you mistake me in one point. I take no pleasure in the suffering of any creature, no matter how heinous it may be. Why do you think I despise you so much? Because you cause pain and fear, because you make the sweet sanction of darkness, where humankind is meant to take rest, a foul and unholy thing."

I was not armed for a philosophical discussion, nor was I in the mood to undertake an argument. Still, Nemesis had the upper hand in this scenario; his was the power to grant or deny my entreaty, and I was merely the supplicant. "You are misinformed," I answered, maintaining my dignity but giving the words no edge of contempt or sarcasm. "The attentions of a vampire are not painful. They foster only ecstasy. Furthermore, we rarely frighten a mortal deliberately—they manage to scare themselves nicely, with their silly legends and superstitions."

Nemesis was still, measuring me with his eyes, and I could not discern from his expression whether I had roused his ire or his sympathy. Common sense caused me to dismiss the latter possibility entirely.

I waited, having said my piece, gazing back at the great angel in silence, using all my strength to veil the terror I felt. Yes, I loved Daisy— enough not only to surrender the myriad pleasures and powers of my existence, but to consign myself to eternal torment as well. And yet everything within me, every instinct, every mental pulse, clamored for life.

"Very well," the angel agreed after a long while. After a moment's hesitation, during which his distaste showed clearly in his face, Nemesis laid a hand to my shoulder. "The covenant is made. I confer upon you the power to capture and bind your enemy, and I warn you—do not abuse this gift, for it will turn on you like a viper if you attempt such a thing. When your quest is achieved, I will come for you."

18

VALERIAN
New York, 1995

AFTER taking my leave of Nemesis, there on that cold and empty plain, I traveled immediately to New York, a favorite city of mine, to feed. I was greedy that night, and perhaps a bit less delicate with my "victims" than I would normally have been. The ordeal ahead, the covenant I had made with the warrior angel notwithstanding, would require the fullest use of all my powers. Proper preparation demanded that I take more blood than ever before.

I did not kill; indeed, I was not even unkind. Furthermore, knowing how Challes had tricked me into taking the wine of warlocks before, I was unusually cautious in selecting my prey.

It was an intoxicating feast—I imbibed the blood of a teenage gang member, a hot and heady brew, vibrant with youthful anger, passion, and frustration. I took sustenance from a baglady and left her swooning in the warm night, remembering me as a generous and tender lover rather than a fiend. The roll of bills I tucked into the pocket of her ragged coat would provide for her needs from then on.

There were others, too—I don't recall exactly how many, for after the youth and the old woman, I was in something of a frenzy. When the first light of dawn rimmed the New York skyline with gold and apricot and crimson, I was still bursting with energy and power.

I would not sleep this day away, I knew, and yet I dared not let the sun find me. Beneath the ebullience I could not seem to quell was the grim and ironic awareness that perdition itself, Dante's hell and my own, awaited my surrender. There I would know fires that burned eternally, but never consumed the anguished, screaming creatures writhing within their flames.

It seemed pointless, in the face of such suffering, to avoid the light of one minor star, whirling through space with nine odd and insignificant planets in its thrall.

Nonetheless, I was a prudent monster when the situation called for the virtue of circumspection. I took myself to the center of the stone circle, where Krispin had danced and reeled with such demented abandon, drunk on moonlight and evil, and I became mist, slipping into the ground only moments ahead of Old Sol's fiery fingers.

I scrabbled through the bones I found there—strong and wakeful, I was—but Krispin was nowhere to be found. Even through some twelve feet of earth and rubble, roots and bones, rodents and worms, I could feel the clawing warmth of the sun, seeking and groping and prodding. Searching me out.

I had once seen a vampire who had been caught abroad in daylight, shortly after Challes transformed me, and the recollection still causes me to shudder. It was a living monstrosity, a blackened skeleton, ludicrous and pathetic. I wondered what had happened to the poor wretch in the centuries since, but only briefly. I reminded myself that I must focus and find Krispin.

I closed my eyes and concentrated on my brother. In my mind I saw him in the same way I always had: as a fragile, eager boy, forever following me about, admiring me despite my arrogance, desperately tolerant of my impatience with him. A tear slipped down my face as I mourned that child, lost to me for all time, and the remorse I felt for the way I'd treated him made me heartsore.

My musings took me to Krispin's side, as I had hoped they would. Imagine my amazement in finding him not only awake, but standing on the darkened stage of the showroom in the Venetian Hotel, examining the carriage I used in my magic act.

He did not seem surprised by my appearance, but then, he wouldn't have been, would he, for he had surely expected me. I had a peculiar idea that, indeed, he might actually have *summoned* me there somehow.

"Did you think to find me lying on a slab somewhere, Valerian?" he asked with amusement, running an artist's hand over the fancy gilded cupids and flowers carved into the coach door. "Just waiting for you to plunge a stake through my heart and put an end to me for all time?"

"Yes," I said, for there was utterly no point in lying. "How is it that you, a vampire, are up and about while the sun shines?"

"I took a great deal of blood over the past night or two, as you undoubtedly did," Krispin replied, sounding almost bored. He crouched beside a wheel now, touching it with those white minstrel's fingers and tipped his head back briefly to gaze upward into the rigging for the stage lights. "It's so dark and cool here," he mused. "One wouldn't guess that the morning has come."

I did not take a step closer to him, as reflex bade me to do, but instead folded my arms. My posture was idle, shoulders at a slight slant, head tilted to one side, but I doubt Krispin was fooled by these mannerisms. Being my sibling, he knew all my ruses, shams, and affectations.

"Tell me about this place where you've been hiding all these centuries."

Krispin smiled, met my eyes for a moment, then returned to his thoughtful examination of the carriage. Such things had fascinated him as a lad, I remembered with a vague pang; he'd loved carts and coaches and wagons as a mortal, as well as ships.

"It's a world almost indiscernible from this one. Rather like passing through Alice's looking glass. Everything here has a counterpart there."

"You have no special powers, then?"

Krispin laughed, stroking the ornate spokes of one wheel as a mortal lover might stroke a shapely limb. "I have many unique qualities, Valerian, as you do. Like most vampires, I sleep during the day and cannot bear the light of the sun. I must take blood or perish of a truly agonizing hunger. I can travel through time, change my shape, veil myself from all but the most discerning eyes—the usual."

"And move between dimensions."

He feigned a sigh and straightened, hands in the pockets of his impeccably tailored tuxedo slacks. There was a look of the 1920s about him, a certain dissolute elegance. With his slicked-back blond hair and lithe figure, he resembled a character from one of F. Scott Fitzgerald's novels.

"Yes," he said, "I can move between dimensions. Even a mortal can do that, albeit usually by accident. Many of your so-called missing persons have merely slipped over onto our side." Krispin paused to smile indulgently, reminding me of a fond uncle recalling an outing with a precocious niece or nephew. "Their reactions are interesting—oft-times they don't realize they've made a transition and try to return home as if nothing had happened. They make odd little discoveries along the way. Their house is suddenly to be found on the opposite side of the street from where it was before, that sort of thing. Of course, that's nothing compared to the shock of opening the front door and encountering their equally bewildered double on the other side."

I was fascinated, in spite of myself. I was also vigilant, expecting treachery at any moment and, I admit, watching for any opportunity to execute a trick of my own. "Interesting," I said. "When someone dies in this dimension, does his counterpart in the other world perish as well?"

"Not necessarily. The two planes are quite separate, even though they seem to reflect each other. If that weren't the case, then a person who disappears here would immediately vanish there, too."

"Do immortals have counterparts, as humans do?"

Again Krispin smiled. He kicked the carriage wheel lightly with the toe of one gleaming shoe, as if testing a tire. "Not exactly. Your reflection died some five hundred and sixty-eight years ago, as well he should have, being mere flesh and blood. You might be interested to know that he lived quite a saintly life, for his time. He was all you might have been, without your greed and arrogance."

I felt an empathy with that long-gone Valerian Lazarus, a soft but poignant wrenching sensation, as if we had shared a soul, he and I. The two of us, I knew, had been one being, even though we had never guessed at the other's existence, and it gave me a certain comfort to know he had been a force for good in his world. Perhaps some mercy would be extended to me, when I presented myself to Lucifer for punishment, on account of that other Valerian's fruitful life.

"And your counterpart?" I inquired.

Another sigh. "I'm afraid he died as a small child. His elder brother— your other self, if you will—was strong and smart and very healthy, like you. And like you, he left his mother with little or nothing for the children who came after him." Krispin stiffened, and his eyes glinted with a hatred he took no trouble to disguise. "You took it all, Valerian. You sapped the very marrow of Mother's bones. You had her complete devotion—by the gods, it was unholy the way she cared for you!"

"Stop," I warned quietly, "before you say too much."

He swayed slightly, as though buffeted from within by the sheer force of his emotions, and covered his eyes for a moment. When he looked at me again, however, he seemed strong again and utterly defiant, thriving on some poison of the soul even as it consumed his sanity. "If she could have rid herself of our father and me, and lived only with and for you, she would have done it."

Disgust raised a scalding gorge to the back of my throat. "Enough," I reiterated. "There can be no profit in such talk."

"No profit?" Krispin came nearer, moving as silently and sinuously as a cat. When he was within my reach, he stopped and gave a hoarse, harrowing cry of laughter. "May Apollo and Zeus and all the old gods of Olympus forbid! No profit, indeed!"

"You are mad." I could not keep the contempt from my tone. Among our kind, madness is a choice, not a sentence conferred by a random fate or an illness, as it is with humankind. This particular aberration requires careful, vigilant nurturing, for our wounds, be they emotional or physical, are quick to heal. Barring blood-starvation, sunlight, fire, or the point of a stake, wooden or otherwise, driven through its heart, a vampire cannot be killed.

Krispin reached out to straighten my lapel, as any brother might do, and his hand lingered lightly on my chest. I felt the hard chill of it even through my clothes. "Alas," he said, "I have not been able to put the grief of Seraphina's negligence behind me. Do you realize that she never kissed me good night, or ruffled my hair as she passed, or told me she loved me? Not even once?"

I recalled many instances when our mother had shown me those simple affections, and I knew that Krispin did, too. In a way, I understood his obsession with that deluded woman—fiend or mortal, we always long for that which is withheld from us.

"I'm sorry," I said, and I meant it. I regretted all he had suffered, on my account and on that of our mother. "If I could change things, Krispin, so that you were the favored one, the beloved, I would. But even we cannot go back that far, as you know. It is done. Over."

For the merest flicker of a moment I saw Krispin's true self in his pale blue eyes and knew the cosmic extent of his loneliness and his yearning for a time and a love that would unknot the ancient, ever-tightening ache inside him. "That's the worst irony of all, you know," he said in a voice so soft it might have been a breath or the faintest of sighs. "For all Seraphina's adoration of you, you never loved her at all. I think, in fact, that she amused you, with her foolish fascination and never-ending attempts to please you."

Krispin's words were close enough to the truth to wound me a little, but he was not entirely correct in his assumptions. "I did love our mother," I said quietly, and it was true. "But she expected too much of me. I was her son, not her husband or her lover. Her fixation with me was tantamount to emotional incest!"

Although my brother had implied this very thing himself, he clearly could not bear to hear the words spoken aloud. He drew back one of those slim, ethereal hands and struck me a blow that sent pain trammeling through me.

I did not move to retaliate; indeed, I did not move at all. Nor did I speak. I felt a grinding pity for Krispin, but it was not sympathy that motivated me then. I knew my brother's weakness lay in his volatile emotions, and I sought, God forgive me, to undermine him further.

The offending fist knotted at his side now, Krispin gazed up at me, weeping silently and without shame, porcelain flesh aflame with color. Like me, he had fed well in preparation for this skirmish, and the blush beneath his skin was not truly his own, but that of his most recent victims.

"It wasn't enough," he went on after a long time, "that Mother worshiped you. You had to have Brenna, too."

My voice, when I spoke, was hoarse with disuse and with sorrow. "Yes," I agreed. "Of all creatures, on earth or in hell or heaven, I love Brenna best. It has ever been so."

"You would die for her, in fact."

I smiled, though there was no mirth in me. It was a reflex, I think, a grimace masquerading as a grin. "Dying would be a merciful end, in comparison to what I would—and will—do for milady."

"Daisy," Krispin mused distractedly. "She's called Daisy now."

I did not reply, knowing as I did that Krispin was not communicating, but simply thinking aloud.

"I'm going to kill her, you know," he announced presently in a conversational tone. We might have been discussing the prospect of snow or the price of a good cigar for all the animation he displayed in those moments.

I shook my head. "I won't allow it, Krispin," I said. And then I put my right hand to his throat, at first caressing, regretting what I must do. My fingers tightened, however, when I thought of Daisy dying by his whim, and of those other women—Jillie, Janet, and Susan. Their only crime had been working for and with me.

Again Krispin gave that ghastly shriek of mingled pleasure and pain, seeming to enjoy the punishment I meted out. I felt his throat crumple like papier-mâché beneath the pressure of my fingers, and yet he did not collapse, or even struggle. His mad, glistening eyes were fixed upon my face as I crushed his windpipe, at once adoring and despising me.

I let him go, shaken and revolted, and he sank, coughing, onto the floor, there to kneel like some forlorn supplicant.

"You forget," he said after several seconds had passed, "that we are not mortal. I cannot be killed by strangling."

Violence surged up within me; I yearned to kick Krispin, to stab and tear and pummel him. I suppressed my rage, but it quaked and burned within me, like lava roiling deep in the bowels and belly of a mountain, and I knew it would rise soon and spew out of me, destroying everything in its path.

My brother half reclined on the floor now, supported by one elbow, his mouth bleeding, his right cheekbone bruised purple, watching me.

"You're right," I said at last. "As much as I enjoyed the exercise, any attempt to choke you is, of course, futile." I crossed to a chest standing in the shadows, raised the lid, and took out the jeweled sword I used in the performance of one of my favorite illusions. The blade made a whispering sound as I pulled it from its scabbard and went back to stand over Krispin.

Even in my state of agitation I found his calm attitude remarkable. It wasn't like him simply to lie there, like a concubine on a sultan's couch, awaiting his fate. Which meant, of course, that he was up to something.

I raised the sword, clasping the handle in both hands, so that the point was suspended an inch or so above Krispin's chest.

"Go ahead," he chided softly. "Kill me."

I cannot explain my hesitation even now. By that time, all filial sentiment had been exorcised from me; I neither loved nor hated Krispin. I was as coldly indifferent as if he'd been a snake, writhing beneath the tip of my blade.

He laughed suddenly, and then to my amazement the sword turned to silvery flames in my hands. I gasped at the pain, and the flames became sparks, showering the floor. My weapon was gone.

Krispin was on his feet in an instant. "Does it hurt, big brother?" he crooned. "Oh, I do hope it does."

The injury had been excruciating, but it is the nature of vampire flesh to heal rapidly, as I have already recorded, and the wounds were little more than memories by then. Likewise, Krispin's throat, crushed in my hands only minutes before, was whole again. Neither was he bleeding any longer, and the bruise that had marred his perfect face was gone as well.

"No, Krispin," I said quietly. "The flames did me no lasting harm. It is your hatred that hurts most."

He laid splayed fingers to his bosom in a theatrical gesture of chagrin, truly meant, of course, as mockery. "And yet you would take me to hell with you, if you could, and endure that loathing, along with the unceasing torment, for eternity? And all to save your ladylove?"

"Yes," I answered.

He laughed again. "So noble," he said. "And so vain a notion. You *will* go to hell, Valerian, but alone. That will be part of your punishment, won't it? Knowing that I'm with your beloved—bedding her and finally dispensing just punishment for her betrayals?" Krispin paused to reflect. "Who knows? Perhaps your Daisy-Brenna has been a bad girl and will end up burning beside you. It's a romantic picture, isn't it?"

I might have been ill, had I been mortal, so vile was the image of Daisy suffering that way. I had earned my damnation, even before the bargain with Nemesis, but she was an innocent and deserved none of what I had brought upon her.

"Your jealousy has made you ugly, Krispin," I said moderately. "You've wasted your life, your looks, your power, everything. You could have known such pleasures, and yet you threw it all away in order to spin your petty plots and schemes of vengeance."

Krispin's fine features contorted for a moment, and I knew that I'd been right. Even in that shining other world, the one where Challes expected to find salvation for us both, my brother had nursed his grievances and counted the injustices he'd suffered. Thus he had squandered six centuries that might have been given over to adventure, to beauty, to laughter, to love.

"Damn you," he rasped. "Do not presume to pity me!"

"I cannot help it. You are the most wretched of beings." I took the lapels of his fine coat in my hands and raised him slightly. "We shall both spend eternity in hell," I told my brother in a furious whisper, "but I, at least, will have the comfort of knowing that I have *lived*! I have loved, sometimes unwisely, but always with verve and passion. I have explored the world, known angels and warlocks, felt agony and ecstasy and everything in between. I *used* the gifts that were given me. I drank the wine."

When I released him, Krispin straightened his clothes and produced a crooked, cocky grin. "As I shall do, when you have gone to reap the harvest you have sown. But never fear, cherished brother—I will send pretty Daisy along to you, probably somewhat the worse for wear, when I am through with her."

I moved to advance upon him again, but before I could cross even the small distance between us, he raised both hands, palms out. The words he said rendered me as stiff and still as a mastodon surprised by the first Ice Age.

"Before you make another of your hasty and awkward attempts, Valerian," he said, "allow me to tell you that I have already visited Daisy, during the night just past. She was released from the hospital in the afternoon, you know. Unfortunately our lady of the badge has, as they say, taken a turn for the worse."

I could not speak.

Krispin smiled, pleased by my paralysis, temporary though it was. Hands clasped behind his back, he rocked on his heels and watched me like a mischievous child who has just played an exceedingly clever prank.

We passed several moments thus, before I found my voice.

"What have you done?" I demanded.

"Do you recall the fable about the sleeping princess?" he countered. "Daisy is—asleep. In her apartment, I mean. The doctors, of course, will think she's in a coma."

I whirled away from him, ready to will myself to Daisy's quaint little home, realizing only at the last instant that I could not take the risk. After all, the sun could reach me there, and a shrieking vampire, wreathed in flames, would hardly improve matters.

I have rarely felt more desperate.

Alas, when I remembered my brother's presence and turned again to confront him, he had vanished.

DAISY
Las Vegas, 1995

Daisy had known him, of course, when he entered her apartment with no more fanfare than a summer breeze ruffling the curtains. He had come to kill her at last.

She waited, expecting to hear herself scream, oddly detached from the situation, and found that she wasn't even especially afraid. She did, however, reach for her thirty-eight, which was lying loaded on the bedside table.

Krispin chuckled, folding his arms. Moonlight glimmered in his hair and flashed from his strange, pale eyes as if they were mirrors. "That won't do anything but alarm the neighbors," he said, nodding toward the pistol wavering in Daisy's hands.

"Get out of here. Right now."

He stood still in the middle of her bedroom floor, smiling. "What a splendidly audacious thing you are. No wonder my brother finds you so endlessly fascinating."

"I've been wanting to speak with you anyway," she said, as if Krispin hadn't spoken, amazed by the steadiness of her voice. "I guess now's as good a time as any."

"How interesting," Krispin responded smoothly, taking something small from the pocket of his vest and tossing it once, triumphantly, before tucking it away again. "I do hope you aren't trying to trick me, though. There's no forestalling the inevitable. I shall have to put you out of commission, just temporarily, while I settle things with Valerian."

Daisy lowered the pistol to her lap. "You want me, don't you?" she asked in a matter-of-fact tone.

"Oh, yes," Krispin admitted. Although Daisy had not actually seen him move, he was no longer standing, but sitting on the foot of her bed.

"Then why don't you take me away with you—to your den or lair or whatever it is?"

There was a barely discernible but very frightening change in Krispin's face; too late, Daisy realized she'd made a mistake. In the next instant he lunged at her, and she managed nothing more than a single hoarse gasp before he was upon her.

"Whore!" he growled, hurting her everywhere, crushing her beneath him. "You would sacrifice anything to save my wretch of a brother!"

Daisy struggled fiercely, and she was strong, but her efforts to fling the vampire off were in vain. Her last conscious emotion was fury, the final physical sensation that of sharp teeth puncturing her throat. . . .

Daisy sank down and down, deeper and deeper into herself, and found shelter and sanction in the memories tucked away there, like keepsakes. . . .

She was that other woman again, standing at a window, gazing out on a vista her blind eyes could not see. She had the ruby ring he'd sent her a fortnight before; surely it meant he would return. . . .

JENNY WADE
London, 1722

Jenny had no more than formed the thought when she heard his voice, heard him whisper her name.

Joy surged through her. Her angel had returned to her, her Valerian. She did not need her eyes to recognize him, or any of her other senses, either, for her heart knew him as its own. She turned to face him, unconcerned by his sudden arrival in her room. He had always come and gone like a ghost.

Jenny had almost succumbed to despair in days past, but now that he was here, everything would surely be all right. He would take her away with him, marry her, give their child a name.

There need be no scandal now, as Martin and Adela feared.

She turned to face her beloved, realizing only as he took her into his arms that something was very different. Instead of discerning him by her own senses, as she usually did, it seemed that impressions were being forced upon her mind.

"You've been unfaithful," he murmured, stroking her hair. "That was very foolish indeed. What possessed you to betray me the way you did?"

Jenny trembled, too stricken by the accusations to speak. It didn't occur to her to call for help, for a part of her still believed that this was her beloved, the mate of her soul. He would never do her harm.

He drew her head back, very gently, and kissed her with a heartrending tenderness. "Do you love me, my Jenny?" he whispered.

"Y-Yes," she replied. Her strength had drained away, and she felt as though she might swoon, and that was quite unlike her. Jenny prided herself on her vigor and resilience; she was not given to spells of fainting and weeping, like so many females of her acquaintance. "Of course I love you, Valerian. How can you say—how can you even think—?"

"Then why did you do it? Why did you lie with another?"

Jenny's heart was racing, though not in the pleasant way it usually did when her lover held her close, and she was wildly dizzy. "I did no such thing," she managed to say.

"You did." His voice was so quiet, so calm, the same one she knew so well, and yet so terrifyingly different. "You're carrying someone's child. And it isn't mine."

She wanted to thrust herself away from him, for she was angry, but although she had the will to do it, she did not have the strength. Instead, to her horror, she found herself clutching his coat to keep from sinking to the floor. "That's reprehensible," Jenny said. "Leave me, please. And don't ever come back."

He did not release her. "You don't mean that."

Jenny was trembling, and the despised tears were threatening. It was not in her nature to love a man who was cruel to her, but she mourned the beautiful feelings she'd once had for him, the dreams she'd cherished. . . . All her hopes for a home and children and simple happiness lay in pieces at her feet, like shards of stained glass from a church window.

"I do mean it," she insisted, struggling now to pull away from him. "I don't need you, nor does our child. Go away now, before I call my brother in to give you a thrashing and hand you over to the police."

He laughed. "Call for him, it will do you no good. This night, at least, your dear Martin is as deaf as the fabled post, and so are Peach and that irritating sister-in-law of yours. We have business to settle, Jenny-love, and we will not be interrupted."

She began to be terribly afraid. She was barely conscious, such was her mental state, and yet she found a scream within her brave heart and released it. Her lover was amused by the effort, and as he'd predicted, it brought no one rushing to her aid.

He swept her up into his arms, and though his embrace felt like the one she knew so well, she had a curious feeling that the perception was not her own, that it had been suggested to her somehow.

"Such a pity, a beautiful, intelligent young woman like yourself, hurling herself from an upstairs window," he said calmly. "Of course, everyone will be sorely grieved, and the gossips will say it's no wonder, is it, considering the shame and scandal the poor girl was facing."

Jenny stiffened and tried again to free herself, but it was no use. He was too strong.

"Don't do this," she whispered, barely conscious, wanting desperately to stay alive, to protect the unborn child nestled within her. "Please—"

She heard the window creak on its hinges, felt the cool night air touch her.

"Don't beg, my sweet. It's demeaning, and altogether futile in the bargain."

Jenny felt her nightgown brush the window ledge, felt the yawning space beneath her, and uttered a sob, clutching at his coat. He kissed her once, very lightly, and then, with considerable reluctance, flung her from him.

She fell, flailing her arms and legs, and struck the cobblestones in the courtyard below with an impact that shattered her bones. Her death was instantaneous, but she perished with a name quivering in her heart like an arrow.

Valerian.

Her lover. Her murderer.

IT was Peach who found the body lying broken and bloody on the stones of the courtyard, early the next morning when she went out for the master's newspaper. Her screams were heard all over the neighborhood, shrill as fire-bells, and brought a passing constable through the front gate on a run.

Martin was the next to arrive on the scene, followed by a pale Adela. She stayed back a little distance, one bony hand pressed to her throat, while Martin let out a low, plaintive groan of sorrow and dropped to his knees beside Jenny. He gripped her shoulders in both hands, as if he expected to awaken her.

The constable looked up and saw the second-story window, still open. He'd seen such things often enough in his line of work, and he had an idea or two about what might drive the daughter of a wealthy household to take her own life. Probably she'd had a dalliance with a groom or a footman, and nature had taken its course.

Poor girl.

"It's a shame, that's what it is," he said, for he was not without compassion, nor was he a man inclined toward the judgment of others.

Peach continued to shriek and wail and blubber, while Martin, seemingly aware of nothing and no one else, gathered his dead sister into his arms and, holding her close against his breast, carried her into the house without a word to anyone.

The funeral was held two days later, and the church was brimming with mourners, for Jenny had been a kindly, cheerful girl, well liked by those who knew her. Rain fell hard all that morning, and well into the afternoon, too, and Mistress Peach said it was only fitting that the very heavens should weep when an angel was put into the ground to molder away to nothing. Adela stayed at home, taking to her bed with a violent headache, but Martin went doggedly from home to the church to the cemetery, heedless of the downpour, and would not leave his sister, even when the coffin had been lowered into the earth on ropes.

Several concerned gentlemen from his club had to lead him away in the end, so that the gravediggers might finish their labors.

They shoveled hastily, these unwashed and unsavory men, for they were superstitious, and despite their vocation, they had no wish to be found among the dead, recently passed-on and otherwise, when darkness fell. They'd heard so many stories, and made up a few to give their friends a turn, that they no longer knew which were fable and which might possibly be true.

It was just as well, for their sakes and for his own, that the vampire did not arrive until they'd gone, to grieve in solitude for the woman he had loved and lost, again.

Through discreet inquiries over the coming nights, he learned that Jenny Wade had disgraced herself by taking a lover. He'd given her a fine ruby ring, so he must have been a man of means, but it had disappeared before the poor girl was even buried.

19

VALERIAN
Las Vegas, 1995

I hurried to Daisy the instant the last feeble rays of sunlight had faded into darkness, and found her sprawled, unconscious, on the floor of her bedroom. Kristina's pendant, intended as a talisman of protection, lay coiled on the carpet beside her, offering mute testimony that my brother would not be thwarted by such fragile magic.

Krispin's ring was upon her finger; I removed it and cast it aside.

"Daisy, sweetheart—" I gathered her up and held her close, breathing in the scent of her. She was alive, but pale as wax and deeply unconscious. It would require more than a kiss of a prince to awaken my sleeping beauty, for Krispin had taken blood from her, as vampires do before transformation. He had only to infuse Daisy with that same fluid, which had surely undergone the mysterious change while flowing through his veins, to make her a fiend.

I stroked her hair back from her gray-white face with a gentle motion of one hand. He planned to turn her into one of us, thus consigning her to the eternal damnation that awaited all our race. Perhaps, I concluded in my despondency, we vampires were in reality no less fragile than humans, but merely a little better at staving off the inevitable.

Carefully I lifted my beloved into my arms and stood. She was clad only in an oversize shirt, and fearing that she might catch a chill, I wrapped her in my cloak and pressed her close against my chest. How I wished in those moments that I had a mortal's warmth to offer her, but my flesh was as cold and ungiving as that of a statue.

Closing my eyes, I took myself, and Daisy, to the only vampire I knew who might be able to help. Calder Holbrook.

His laboratory was empty when I reached it, for this was modern-day London, and Calder, of course, favored the nineteenth-century. I would not have risked taking Daisy back through time, for mortals have yet to evolve the ability to make such journeys in safety, and I might have lost her somewhere along the way.

I laid her tenderly on the examination table, still cossetted in my cloak, and began rummaging for blankets.

Calder sensed my presence in his domain, as I had hoped he would, and appeared posthaste, wearing a scowl that would surely have intimidated a lesser vampire than myself. "What the—?"

"I've brought you a patient," I interrupted, finding a covering that looked like a relic from the American Civil War and giving it a shake before draping it over Daisy's motionless form. "I'd like you to save her."

The good doctor flung an irritated glance in my direction, but his attention was soon centered on the slender nymph lying, near death, on his table. I saw what I had hoped for in his face—a physician's compassion. "What happened?" Calder asked, though he must have guessed some of the tale, for he had already laid gentle fingers to the marks of Krispin's fangs defiling her throat.

I told him what my brother had done, and why, sparing no detail.

Calder worked on Daisy as he listened, examining her for other injuries, listening to her heart through a stethoscope, taking her blood pressure. This laboratory, unlike its counterpart in the last century, of course, was equipped with a number of modern medical implements.

While I watched, in vigilant silence, Calder took plasma from a refrigerator in the corner and administered the initial transfusion. For the first time since I had found her, Daisy made a sound and stirred slightly.

My eyes blurred with tears, for I knew it was pain that had moved her, and finding myself powerless to spare her this suffering, however subliminal, was agony.

I tried to mask my emotions with words, for I was not at ease in Calder's company, nor he in mine. I could not wail and sob in despair, as I needed to do, as I might have done in Maeve's presence, or even Kristina's. "Human plasma," I observed as the precious liquid dripped slowly through a tube and into Daisy's veins. "Do you keep it around for those nights when you just don't feel like hunting?"

Calder did not look at me; he had produced a small penlight from his pocket and was peering into one of Daisy's glazed and sightless eyes. "Hardly," he replied with quiet disdain. "I have a supply on hand because I am a doctor, and because the occasional hapless human being finds his or her way here and has need of it."

"How did you know her blood type?"

Now he did meet my eyes. With a scathing glare. "Being a vampire, I am an expert on the stuff," he said pointedly and with intolerance. "If you must blather to distract yourself from your worries, Valerian, at least find something worthwhile to say."

I swallowed a cry of grief and fear and fury. "Will she die?" I asked when I felt I could speak coherently.

"Perhaps," Calder said, going back to the refrigerator and rummaging through a number of clear plastic pouches filled with blood. "We know the alternative—allowing your brother to finish the process he began— and somehow I don't think that's what you want for her. Or what she would wish for herself." He turned to look at me curiously. "Could it be, Valerian, that for once in your debauched and utterly self-serving life, you are actually putting the desires of another before your own?"

I did not refute his assessment of my character; it was, after all, accurate. "Daisy has never wanted to become a vampire," I said, defeated. The multiple feedings I had taken in New York were beginning to wear off, and my strength was flagging. "And while I would like nothing better than to have her at my side forever, as you have your glorious Maeve, and show her all the wonders we are heir to, I won't change Daisy against her will."

Calder made a sighlike sound. "Suppose that is your only choice? Would she prefer a mortal's death to the everlasting life of a vampire?"

I found a stool and perched upon it, lowering my face to one hand. "Yes," I said. "I have offered her the gift before, in other incarnations. I cannot think her wishes have changed. Daisy's is a pure and noble spirit, unwilling to be counted among the damned."

The doctor said nothing, but simply stood beside the table, watching his patient with a solemn and thoughtful expression. I would have given all the considerable wealth I had accrued over the centuries to know what he believed Daisy's true prognosis to be.

We kept our vigil in silence after that, with Calder giving Daisy more blood at intervals. Slowly her color began to improve, and she stirred more often beneath her blanket, and made soft, disconsolate sounds that wounded me as nothing else could have done.

I had to feed, for Calder's store of plasma, while life-giving for Daisy, was but thin gruel in relation to my hunger. With the greatest reluctance I left her in the doctor's care and went out to hunt.

As before in New York, I was gluttonous, prowling the dark streets of London and filling myself, like a leech, until my tissues were swollen with the stuff.

When I returned to Calder's laboratory to resume my watch at Daisy's side, I found her virtually restored and sleeping soundly. The doctor had gone, probably to take his rest in some dark vault in the bowels of that very house, as dawn would soon be upon us, but Kristina was there, the talisman pendant clutched in one hand.

The last time I'd fed so copiously, I had not succumbed to the vampire slumber, but this occasion was different. I felt myself fading, losing my grip on consciousness. Stubbornly I lay down on the table beside Daisy and drew her into my arms, flinging Kristina a glance that dared her to protest.

"Sleep, Valerian," Maeve's child said quietly. "I will keep watch for you."

I struggled to remain awake those few extra moments, nodding toward the pendant Kristina grasped. "A fat lot of help that was," I complained. "Why didn't you just make her a necklace of garlic?"

"Don't be tiresome," Kristina said. "The pendant would have protected Daisy if she'd been wearing it."

It was then that Daisy opened her wonderful, fathomless eyes and looked straight into my hell-bound soul.

"*You,*" she said in an odd voice. "You killed me."

I had no chance to reply before the darkness overtook me.

DAISY
Seattle, 1995

The room where Daisy awakened was filled with light and color. She did not know where she was, nor did she have any idea how she'd gotten there.

She sat up in the strange bed, with its linen sheets and exquisite lace spread, and looked around in amazement. There were six floor-to-ceiling windows opposite, affording a stunning view of dark blue waters and snow-draped mountains, and the furniture was light, lacquered stuff, painted with flowers. Italian antiques, probably, and beyond expensive.

Before Daisy could toss back the covers and rise, Kristina appeared in the doorway. She was wearing jeans and a loose white shirt with flowing sleeves and a cut-work collar.

"Welcome to Seattle," she said with a smile.

"How did I—what—?"

"I brought you here, from my father's lab in London. How are you feeling?"

Daisy settled back against the pillows, reassured by the presence of her friend and the normality of her surroundings. "Confused, light-headed, and hungry."

Kristina laughed. "I can't do much about the confusion and the dizziness, I'm afraid. But food I've got. Sit tight, and I'll bring you a tray."

"You're not going to zap it up out of nowhere?" Daisy asked, a little disappointed.

Her hostess sighed. "I only do that in emergencies. I like to cook, and besides, I try to live as normal a life as my predicament allows." She nodded toward another door. "The guest bath is that way."

Fifteen minutes later, when Daisy had used the facilities, washed her face and hands, and made her somewhat shaky way back to bed, Kristina returned with the promised food.

The dishes were heavy squares of brightly colored pottery, painted with whimsical flowers and checks and stripes. There was a tiny pot of steaming tea, along with pasta, warm bread, and green salad.

While Daisy ate, Kristina pulled up a large blue hassock, imprinted with smiling golden suns sporting pointed rays, and sat down.

"Papa and I discussed the situation and decided you would be better off here, in a more familiar environment."

Daisy poured tea with a somewhat unsteady hand and raised the cup to her lips. The brew was strong and sweet, laced with milk. Just the way she liked it. "He can still get to me here, you know," she said after several bracing sips. "Krispin, I mean."

"Yes," Kristina answered. "I'm sure he can. But he won't find you alone and defenseless, like before."

"No," Daisy said with a mild note of irony. "This time he'll be able to attack you, as well as me." She shuddered, remembering Krispin's assault in her apartment. She'd honestly thought, in those moments of violence just before losing consciousness, that she was about to die.

Seeing that Daisy didn't intend to eat any more of her meal, Kristina rose from her perch on the hassock, took the tray, and carried it out of the room. She returned almost immediately, this time taking a seat on the edge of Daisy's bed.

"I'll do everything I can to keep you safe," she promised.

"Why? Why would you put yourself in so much danger?"

"Because I care about Valerian, and about you, Daisy. Do you realize you're the only friend I have who knows who and what I am? How do you think my neighbors and business associates would react if I suddenly announced that my parents are vampires, for instance? Imagine me confiding, say at a chamber of commerce luncheon, that I'm well into my second century." She paused to smile sadly. "You're not going to bail out on me now, are you, Daisy? Just when I've started to think I might have run across somebody I can really talk to?"

Daisy's heart warmed, despite the mess she was in. She'd never had a close female friend, except for Nadine and their late grandmother, and she found the prospect appealing. "No," she said. "I'm not going to 'bail out,' as you put it. If you want to talk, I'm ready to listen."

Kristina smiled and squeezed Daisy's hand briefly. "Thanks, friend, but even listening is work, and right now you need to rest. Go back to sleep."

There were a lot of questions Daisy wanted to ask Kristina, but she had apparently lost a lot of blood during the incident with Krispin, and she was exhausted. She stretched out, closed her eyes, and tumbled into a waiting memory. . . .

HER name was Harmony Beaucheau, and she was twenty-three years old. The year was 1878, and the town was called Poplar Hill, though it stood in a dusty corner of the Arizona Territory and boasted neither poplar nor hill.

Oh, damn it, thought that part of her that was still Daisy. *Here we go again.*

Harmony was standing in front of a cracked mirror, and with some relief Daisy saw herself looking back from the glass. She was wearing a worn dress of brown calico with a high neck, and her reddish-brown hair was pinned up in a loose, fluffy style. Stubborn tendrils trailed at her neck and on her temples and cheeks.

She turned away from the mirror and from all consciousness of herself as Daisy Chandler. Reluctantly Harmony left her small, sparsely furnished room and made her way down the narrow passageway leading to the stairs. The saloon below was filled with swirling blue-gray smoke, tinny music from the piano, which was missing a few vital parts, and the raucous, vulgar talk of cowboys, drifters, and various locals. There were a handful of tawdry women, too—they entertained men in private, and Harmony herself paid their wages.

She hesitated on the stairs, one hand resting on the crude rail, and sighed. Harmony was not a whore, and never would be, for she'd been raised in Boston by a maiden aunt and educated to be a lady. Before she could marry, however, her elderly guardian had passed away, and when dear Aunt Millicent had been properly buried, and all accounts settled, there was a small but respectable sum of money remaining.

Harmony had barely recovered from Millicent Beaucheau's death when an old friend of the family appeared, bearing a packet of old letters. In them was irrefutable proof that Millicent had been Harmony's mother, and not her aunt, and in staid Boston to be illegitimate was hardly a social advantage.

Despite her fine looks, cultivated mind, and more than adequate dowry, no one who knew the truth was going to marry the likes of Harmony Beaucheau. She was tainted forever.

A resilient sort, Harmony had taken herself to an establishment dealing in properties. These were the very people who had sold Millicent's house, which, it turned out, had been bought for her by her lover and not bequeathed by a doting father, as she'd always maintained, and Harmony had no reason to mistrust them.

She had inquired about the West and promptly purchased a hotel, sight unseen, in the Arizona Territory. On her arrival, Harmony discovered that she'd bought a brothel, not an inn, and used her last nickel in the process. The place was thriving—that was one consolation.

Still lingering on the stairs, Harmony scanned the saloon with eyes squinted against the smoke, and a smile broke over her face. He was there again, playing faro at the table nearest the door, the handsome gambler with the fancy name.

Valerian, he called himself. Harmony was already half in love with him, and practical as she was, she'd had no success in disabusing herself of the fancy. Men like him never stayed in one place long; they dallied a while, drank and gambled and told lies, and then moved on.

He was wearing a long duster made of soft leather, high black boots, well-cut trousers, and the kind of shirt only a man like him could get away with. His hat was pushed to the back of his head, and he sensed Harmony's presence somehow, for all the hubbub between them, and raised his fathomless indigo eyes slowly to her face.

She felt a charge of emotion go through her, feelings so complicated, so tangled and interwoven with each other, that she could not begin to sort them through. She had never seen Valerian before his appearance in Poplar Hill one night a month or so before, and yet it was as though she'd always known him. She knew, for instance, how his hands would feel on her body, and his mouth on hers. She, who was a virgin despite her spoiled reputation, knew the powerful flex of his hips as he took her, and the tug of his lips on her nipples. . . .

Harmony went to him, like a creature enthralled, and her life began that very night. He vanished often, her lover, often for days at a time, and she never once saw him when the sun came up. When he was with her, in her ugly little room, they made love, but he told her stories, too, about other countries and other times in history, and he was full of poetry.

She knew he loved her truly—he admired her strong spirit and asked her opinion on important things, something no man had ever done before. And although his lovemaking transported her, she suspected its absence would not have changed her feelings or his. There was an old bond between them, as though their souls had been fused by some ancient and forgotten god, and if there were many mysteries about her Valerian, she didn't care.

He had been away nearly a month when the ruby ring arrived by stage with three weeks' worth of mail. It was wrapped in gold foil and tied with a scarlet ribbon trimmed in lace, and Harmony's heart brimmed with happiness as she slid it onto the ring finger of her left hand. Surely this was his pledge that they would be together, ever after. . . .

But Valerian did not return, although Harmony watched for him every night on the tiny balcony outside one of the upstairs rooms, anxiously scanning the moonlit trail that snaked away into the desert.

It had been two more weeks, and she was beginning to despair. Perhaps the wonderful ring had not been a promise, after all, but a farewell.

That night three men rode into town, liquored up and shooting. Harmony got her shotgun out from behind the bar and stepped out onto the sidewalk, her jaw set and her eyes narrowed. There was no law in Poplar Hill, not yet, and folks had to look after their own property and their own hide, whether they were women or men.

The drunks howled and carried on, firing their six guns and spurring their terrified horses onto the sidewalk. They were headed for Harmony's saloon, and she was ready for them. . . .

DAISY sat bolt upright, gasping and drenched in perspiration, clutching her chest. A bullet had struck Harmony, exploding in the center of her heart, and Daisy had felt it as though it had penetrated her own flesh.

"Oh, God," she whispered, falling back against the pillows, her face wet with tears of sorrow and fear. She was strong, though, and presently the trembling stopped and she drifted back to sleep, this time finding only sweet oblivion.

She did not awaken again until sometime after the moon had risen.

The house was quiet, except for a low murmur of conversation in a nearby room and the soft strains of a Mozart concerto flowing from the stereo system.

Daisy rose, relieved to find herself stronger, and donned the terrycloth robe she found lying across the foot of the bed. She walked slowly out of the bedroom and found herself in a well-lit hallway with a shining oak floor.

Kristina and Valerian were in the living room. The vampire stood, imperious and grim, beside the cold fireplace. Kristina sat cross-legged on an overstuffed sofa, a glass of wine in her hands. Their quiet but earnest exchange ended abruptly when they realized that Daisy had joined them.

Valerian came slowly toward her, took her hands in his, and gazed down into her eyes. "Kristina told me you were better," he said hoarsely, "but it is good to see for myself."

Daisy wanted to hurl her arms around him and cling in a very un-Daisy-like way, but she resisted the urge. "Yes," she said, thinking how well she had loved him, not only in the present, but during her lifetimes as Brenna and Elisabeth and Jenny and Harmony as well. "I'm almost myself again, if you'll forgive the expression."

He smiled and cupped a hand under her chin, and Daisy closed her eyes for a moment, against a rush of emotion. He brushed her lips with his thumb, and sent liquid fire surging through her system.

"I must know, Daisy," Valerian said with tender sorrow, "what you meant in Dr. Holbrook's lab when you said I killed you. Come, sit down and talk to me."

Daisy nodded, for suddenly she recalled uttering those words, recalled the experience that had made her speak them. She knew now, too, that it had been Krispin who had murdered Jenny Wade, Krispin pretending to be Valerian. And he had been behind Harmony's shooting, too, and Elisabeth's fever.

Kristina left the room, and Valerian settled Daisy into a comfortable chair and carefully covered her legs with a knitted afghan. How could she have believed, in this lifetime or the one lived as Jenny Wade, that this tender creature would ever do her deliberate harm?

Daisy spoke softly, hesitantly, as she related what she knew of Jenny's story. Valerian, seated on the arm of her chair, listened in absorbed silence.

When she'd finished the tale, he did not speak for a long time. The expression on his aristocratic face was one of quiet torment.

"I'm sorry," Valerian said at last. "I should have guessed that you were in danger, and been there to protect you."

Daisy rested her head against his arm. "Did you believe the stories? That Jenny ended her own life, I mean?"

He met her gaze. "Yes," he replied. "I was unable to visit her—you—for a considerable length of time. She—forgive me, but I find I cannot say 'you' when we are speaking of death—she was a porcelain rose, my Jenny, though she fancied herself to be as sturdy as a summer weed. I was convinced that she had sunk into despair because of my neglect."

Daisy bit her lower lip, then spoke quickly before she could lose her courage. At the same time, though, she touched Valerian's hand in an effort to reassure him a little. "There was something else. Something Krispin knew, but you apparently did not."

Valerian did not speak, but simply waited for her to go on, one eyebrow slightly elevated.

"There was to be a baby," she blurted. "You and Jenny—you and I, Valerian—conceived a child together."

"No," he said, quickly, gruffly. It was a plea, that solitary word, echoing with regret and incomprehensible pain. "That couldn't be—" He stopped, glancing in the direction of the doorway through which Kristina had disappeared minutes before. Obviously he was recalling the circumstances of another birth—Maeve Tremayne, a vampire, and Calder Holbrook, still mortal then, had had a daughter.

Daisy gave Valerian a few moments to collect himself before going on. "Times being what they were," she said quietly, "Jenny's family feared there would be a ruinous scandal. They were going to send her away somewhere, I think, but she never doubted that you would come back for her."

"And she died thinking I had murdered her. Along with our child." The controlled agony, so visible in Valerian's face as he spoke, found its way into Daisy's heart and burrowed down deep.

"Jenny sensed that something was wrong," Daisy said, for that flimsy assurance was all the solace she had to offer him just then. "I think she knew, on some level at least, that it wasn't you who visited her that awful night."

Valerian threaded his fingers through hers, and his attempt at a smile was even more painful to look upon than his stark grief had been before it. "Krispin," he muttered, making a curse of the name by his tone and manner. His gaze, as he stared into the fireplace contained such sulphurous fury that Daisy fully expected flames to leap from the ashes in the grate. "Flesh of my flesh, bone of my bone, soul of my soul— Krispin, Krispin. *What have you done?*"

Daisy shivered. An unspoken vow coursed beneath the anger and despair of the vampire's words. Valerian meant to destroy Krispin—but at what cost?

Before she could give voice to her concerns, however, another visitor joined them, nearly startling Daisy out of her skin.

He appeared in the middle of the room, with no smoke or fire to herald his coming, but for all the strange experiences she'd had since meeting Valerian, Daisy still wasn't used to such surprises. She longed for the company of other mortals, human beings who knocked on doors and telephoned and wrote letters but never, *never* simply materialized out of the ether!

Valerian stood, but he seemed annoyed, rather than afraid. Daisy was touched—and irritated at the same time—by the way he put himself between her and the unexpected guest, like a barrier.

"Explain yourself," he snapped.

Daisy leaned out over the arm of her chair to get a better look at the new arrival. He was remarkably good-looking, she decided, with his golden hair and soft brown eyes. His clothes were courtly and old-fashioned, and formidably expensive, like Valerian's—he wore a splendid cape of dark blue wool, high boots, breeches, and a frilly shirt. In one gloved hand he grasped the handle of a carved walking stick—a weapon, Daisy decided, not merely an addition to his costume.

He smiled at her, and at the watchful Kristina, and bowed, ever so slightly and ever so gracefully to each, pointedly ignoring the seething Valerian.

"Allow me to introduce myself. I am called Dathan, and I do apologize for making an unannounced entrance. I trust I am forgiven?"

Kristina replied with a brief, tentative smile, but Daisy was too fascinated to respond to him at all—except, of course, to stare.

"You left out your title, Dathan," Valerian interceded in an acidic tone. "Warlock."

Daisy was now so far out over the chair arm that she nearly fell. At her quick, scrambling motion of self-rescue, Valerian turned to glower down at her over one shoulder. The look was unmistakably a warning, and it both angered and intimidated Daisy.

She subsided a little, though only temporarily.

"Yes," Dathan allowed, only then acknowledging the vampire looming within pouncing distance. "I am indeed a warlock." The twinkling brown gaze found Daisy's face, despite Valerian, and lingered for a moment, admiring. When he looked at Valerian, however, there was no gentleness anywhere in his countenance, and the mischievous, cherubic eyes were suddenly hard. "I grow weary, blood-drinker, of waiting. Did we not speak of a bargain?"

Valerian glanced back at Daisy again, then returned his gaze to the warlock. "I will not discuss this here."

"Oh, yes, you will," Daisy argued, tugging at the back of his coat. "I want to know what's going on."

"We don't always get what we want, do we?" Valerian retorted, frowning again, this time with such heat that she felt like paraffin going soft in the sun. "Stay out of this, Daisy, or I swear by all the old gods that I will stop up your ears and still your tongue for a fortnight!"

Daisy was furious, but she was still too tired to wage a proper battle, verbal or otherwise, so she sank back in the chair, trembling. Kristina flung her a sympathetic look but contributed nothing to the conversation.

It was Dathan who broke the oppressive silence. "You know where to find me," he told Valerian cheerfully, tugging at his elegant gloves and then bowing once more to the ladies. "I shall expect you forthwith."

With that, he vanished without sound or flurry, just as he had appeared.

Valerian did not bid Daisy farewell or even look at her again. In the blink of an eye he was simply gone.

VALERIAN
Last Ditch Tavern, 1995

I arrived in the back room of the Last Ditch Tavern a fraction of a second after Dathan, and found him seated at one of the felt-covered poker tables, hat and cloak tossed onto a chair, feet up and crossed at the ankle.

"What took you so long?" he asked with a grin.

I overcame a whimsical desire to kick his chair over. I had not wanted him to see Daisy, to know her, for he represented yet another danger to her. Too, warlocks are notorious seducers, and while I held Daisy's personal scruples in high esteem, I wondered what use they could be against the charm of such a fetching monster.

"How dare you intrude that way?" I rasped.

Dathan cocked an eyebrow. "Intrude? I'm trying to do you a favor, vampire. But it seems you no longer want my help."

I drew up a chair, probably with more clatter than necessary, and dropped into it. I *didn't* want the warlock's help, had never wanted it, but I was in this instance a beggar, not a chooser. I could no longer afford to indulge my dislike of this particular antagonist.

"What can you do?" I asked with a dismal lack of faith in Dathan's powers. "After all, if you could destroy vampires, you would have wiped out every blood-drinker in the universe by this time."

Dathan chuckled fondly at the image. "Yes," he agreed. "With the possible exception of Maeve Tremayne. Splendid female. Her daughter is very like her—beautiful, brave, intelligent—"

"Leave Kristina alone," I warned. The warlock now had my undivided attention. "If you go near her, I'll drain every drop of your poisoned blood into the nearest gutter!"

He took a glass of whiskey from the table, without putting his feet down, and indulged in a thoughtful sip before replying. "Let us confine ourselves, for the moment, to the business at hand. The two of us, I fear, are prone to endless disagreement on an infinite number of points. Do you still want my help in destroying your brother?"

I did, but the very necessity of the act struck me like a blow to the solar plexus. Would I never get used to it? Would I grieve for Krispin even as I burned among the very coals and embers of hell?

"Yes," I said in a miserable whisper.

"Then let us lay a plan."

My eyes were narrowed, for I was recalling the previous encounter with Dathan, there in the Last Ditch. He wanted something in return for his assistance, of course, but he had yet to say what it was he meant to require of me, in the event of our success. "First," I said, "tell me what you hope to gain by this."

He took another draft of the whiskey, and I envied him the warlock's ability to eat and drink like a mortal, momentarily at least. A glass of wine—nay, a tubful of the stuff—would have been a blessed comfort just then.

"It is time," he said at considerable length, "to join our two races. To produce a being that is part vampire and part warlock."

I was so horrified that I forgot the craving for wine that had been clawing at my core only a moment ago. "Great Zeus—it's an unspeakable thing you're suggesting!"

"Is it? Consider a creature with your powers and mine. A vampire able to walk in daylight, for instance. A warlock with the propensity for time-travel. The possibilities are truly staggering."

"You've lost your mind, such as it was!"

Dathan laughed and raised his glass in a mocking toast. "There are those of both our species who will hasten to agree. To hell with them all." He drank again and made a sound of satisfaction afterward that grated on my every nerve. "Here's the bargain, blood-drinker: take it or leave it, as the mortals say. Inventive, these humans, and oft-times amusing, though given to the odd cliché. In any case, as payment for my help, I want a vampire for a mate."

I shot to my feet. "What blood-drinker would have a warlock?" I demanded. Alas, tact, even in situations where it was crucial, had never been my forte.

Dathan's brown eyes, which could shine with a saintly glow when he looked upon a woman, flashed with restrained temper. "Sit down and listen, you incredible fool. My own kind isn't going to rejoice over the union, either, after all. But it must be done."

"Why?"

"Because I want it."

This, for better or worse, was an attitude I understood. I sat down again despondently, reminded that I had no choice in the matter. With Dathan's assistance I might succeed in tracking down and destroying Krispin. Without it, though it galled me to acknowledge the fact even to myself, I could very well lose the battle.

And Daisy.

"So I am to become a matchmaker," I muttered. "By the gods, though, I don't know how I'll manage it."

Dathan laughed. "Am I so wretched, so offensive, as all that?"

"Yes," I answered.

The warlock smiled. "Never fear. You are the most persuasive of creatures—and you have so very much at stake, don't you?"

Again I thought of Daisy. "Oh, yes," I replied, reaching for a deck of cards that lay in the center of the table, among neat pillars of blue, white and red poker chips. "Everything, in fact."

"You also have an agreement with Nemesis, I understand."

I began to deal. "You've done your homework," I said. "He promised me the power to put an end to Krispin, though I must admit I haven't seen any sign of it yet. Which, of course, accounts for my willingness to cooperate with the likes of you." The warlock took up his cards, and I gathered mine, frowning as I pondered the possibilities they presented. "Our bargain, warlock, will not hold good unless you are instrumental in my brother's destruction. And I believe you can be, or I would not be sitting here now."

"I'll take two cards," Dathan replied. "And none of your tricks."

I smiled. "You expect too much of a mere vampire," I replied. And while I systematically divested him of two castles, a horse, and a pocket watch, we discussed our strategy.

20

VALERIAN
Colefield Hall, 1995

THE warlock and I found Challes at Colefield Hall, half buried by the stacks of musty books he had left to me so many years before, along with the property itself. At his side sat a magnificent white wolf with pale blue eyes.

Upon our appearance, the beast raised himself to his haunches and growled.

"Be still, Barabbas," Challes said with firm affection, and the wolf whimpered once and dropped at his master's feet, resting his muzzle on his paws. "These are friends."

I did not correct Challes on this point, though I certainly wouldn't have counted myself among his friends just then, and I felt no fear of the great wolf, only admiration. Had my business not been so urgent, in fact, I think I might have envied my tutor the company of such a fantastic creature and wanted Barabbas for my own.

"It is time to make restitution," I said without expression in voice or in manner. "We know from Calder Holbrook's experiments that it is possible to track Krispin into the other dimension through a grave. You will show me where that particular tomb is, please. Now."

Still seated, with the wolf lying watchful at his side, Challes looked up at me with mingled sorrow and amusement. "Still the same officious, haughty brat you always were. Ah, but what—or who—could ever have changed you? Nothing and no one, that is certain. And I think I should not have wanted you to be different—you would have been so much less interesting."

An ancient clock ticked loudly on the mantel, reminding me of the need for haste, and I was mindful, too, of Dathan's impatience. "Please," I said again. I would kneel to him if I had to, and beg, but of course I hoped to be spared that humiliation.

"At one time I wanted to take you through the looking glass, Valerian, and show you the other world. You refused—quite adamantly, as I recall."

"I was afraid."

"Poppycock. You've never been truly afraid in your life. But you will be. Your bowels will turn to water, beautiful one, when you see what awaits you beyond the veil, where Nemesis will take you." He spoke without rancor, and he took no pleasure, it seemed, in my fate. He was, however, resigned, and he made that sighlike sound that I had learned from him long before. "I am so tired, Valerian. So very tired."

I went to Challes's chair and crouched beside it, opposite the wolf. The animal raised his head, then lowered it again, having decided, apparently, that I represented no significant threat to his master. "Will you make me plead?" I asked softly. "Is that what you want?"

Challes's face, once beloved, crumpled with some emotion I could not recognize. "No." He reached down to pat the wolf's huge, silvery head. "It is wrong to humble such creatures as you, and as Barabbas here."

"Take me to Krispin's hiding place. Or simply direct me there. I implore you."

He put aside the volume that had been resting in his lap and stood at long last. A muttered command kept the wolf from springing up with him, but the beast gave a low, chilling whine to declare his displeasure.

"It is day in that other world," Challes warned. "Krispin lies resting in a vault, deep beneath the earth, but I cannot promise the light will not reach you there."

I was willing to take that chance—to take any chance. My smile, I fear, was on the rueful side. "Do not worry, Master," I said. "I cannot be destroyed. I must survive to endure my damnation, remember?"

Tears glittered in Challes's eyes, and I remembered when I had loved and admired him. "Nemesis is to have the both of us, then."

"Both of us?"

Challes smiled, though the tears had not lessened. "I made a bargain of my own long ago with the great Warrior Angel. I have eluded him, thus far, by trickery, but I daresay he will prevail." He took one of my hands in both of his. "Forgive me, Valerian, for making you what you are."

"Forgive you? I will always be grateful, Challes. Even in hell."

"Come, then," he said with another sigh. And we were gone from that place in an instant, leaving the wolf to snooze placidly on the hearth.

When we materialized again, we were inside a tomb whose headstone had long since crumbled to dust. Still, I was chagrined to recognize the place, for I sensed immediately that it was at Dunnett's Head, on the grounds where the baron's keep had once stood.

"By Apollo," Dathan grumbled, making a fruitless and disgruntled attempt to shake the dust from his costly cape. "Who but a vampire would pass even a moment in such a place?"

"Feel free to leave at any time," I offered with biting politeness.

"We must make of ourselves a single mist," Challes said, taking no notice of the tension between Dathan and me.

"Is the warlock capable of such a trick?" I asked of my teacher, not to bait Dathan, but merely because I was curious.

"The warlock," Dathan interjected in an angry whisper, "is quite capable!"

I said nothing further, but simply concentrated on Challes's instructions. We became as one entity, we three, in the moments that followed, and solidified again, mercifully separate once more, in a vast dark chamber beneath a great castle or fortress of some sort.

"Where are we?" Dathan asked, sounding for the first time in our acquaintance as though he might be suffering a few doubts where his conviction of eminent superiority was concerned.

"Second Earth," Challes replied in a weary tone. For one who had once wanted so badly to bring me to this place that he would hold me prisoner and try to force me to accompany him, my tutor seemed reticent.

I offered no response, for I was drawn to the dusty silver outline of a large mirror covering the whole of a nearby wall. I crossed to it, touched the glass with splayed fingers, and gave a cry of alarm when, in the length of a heartbeat, it was filled with dazzling light.

"This looking glass once graced the ballroom on the third level of the castle," Challes said, standing beside me. As he spoke, the light faded a little, and I saw dancers beyond the smooth surface. Women in colorful, full-skirted frocks whose hems swept the floor, men in waistcoats and breeches and ascots. I could almost hear the music to which they whirled, smiling, talking, full of joy.

"They are of this world—Second Earth?" I wondered aloud, somehow stricken by the tableau, and sorrowing that I was not among those happy dancers, with Daisy beaming in my arms. Oh, to be mortal, for just one lifetime!

Challes touched my shoulder, as if to console a mourner. "No, lovely one. They are of the world we just left. Come—we much reach Krispin before he awakens."

Although I was as intent on the task ahead as ever, I found I did not wish to leave that mirror. I wanted to go on looking at those people, sharing vicariously in their innocent felicity.

Challes led the way out of the chamber, with Dathan following after him. I brought up the rear, reluctantly, gazing back often at the fading images in the glass.

It was remarkably easy to find Krispin's resting place.

Too easy.

He was lying, like a slain statesman in the rotunda of some great government edifice, with his arms crossed over his breast and candles burning all around. He wore a white suit, reminiscent of *The Great Gatsby*, and his golden head gleamed in the dim light.

I stood over him, remembering so many things.

"Make haste, Valerian!" Challes muttered. "If Krispin awakens, he will make a formidable foe."

I was trembling as I held out my hand for the stake and mallet Dathan provided. Whether the warlock had carried those implements with him, conjured them, or simply found them along the way, I shall never know. Never care to know.

I took the stake first and placed the point over my brother's heart, holding it there with my left hand. In my right I held the mallet.

"Do it," Dathan said. "Kill him!"

We had underestimated Krispin's cleverness, for beneath my stake and raised hammer, he suddenly became the little fair-haired boy I had known as a mortal. He looked as peaceful as a sleeping cherub, the child of angels.

"Do not be fooled," Challes warned quietly.

I was weeping now, though in silence. I prepared myself to drive in the stake, and Krispin changed shape again. This time he took on the image of our mother, Seraphina. I had forgotten how lovely she was, how fragile and small.

"Valerian!" Challes spoke more sternly this time. "Can't you see what's happening? He is a chameleon—there is no end to the forms he can take! In the names of all the old gods, *destroy him* before—"

I was about to wield the mallet at last when Krispin took on still another guise. This time he was the perfect image of Daisy, and he had awakened to gaze up at me, imploring, with her emerald eyes.

I gave a roar of rage and torment. I could not plunge a stake through Daisy's heart—I could not!

Dathan spoke. "This is not your beloved," he said with uncommon gentleness. "If you cannot kill the dragon, then pray, step aside and allow me."

I dropped the stake and the mallet, though I had made no conscious decision to do so. I was beginning to feel the first biting sting of the sun, despite the thick walls and floors that sheltered us, just as Challes had warned I might. I was, however, oblivious to the pain; it was nothing beside my horror and grief.

"Stand back," Dathan commanded, and Challes grasped my arms and pulled me away from the high marble slab where Krispin lay, posing as Daisy, pleading with me now, in her voice, to save her.

I had seen the warlock work his magic before, but nothing could have prepared me for what happened next. He glared down at the lovely monster, still prone on the slab, and murmured some kind of incantation.

Fire seemed to explode in that chamber, to leap from the candles and catch on Daisy's—Krispin's—clothes. He shrieked, did Krispin, more in fury than in pain, as the fire enveloped him, leaping, crackling, consuming. He abandoned Daisy's shape, and became himself again, but the spectacle was still torture to watch.

I felt a scream of my own swell, shrill and sharp-edged, in my throat, and I struggled, compelled by some animal instinct to go to my brother's aid, but Dathan and Challes restrained me.

Krispin writhed and shrieked upon his pyre, his gaze fixed on me all the while, hating, using even his agony to taunt me.

I cried out again, hoarsely, and fought to free myself, but my tutor and my unlikely ally were stronger. I sank at last to my knees, sobbing, as the warlock's fire devoured the monster in flames of ever-changing colors.

And there were other flames, too—the invisible ones, spawned by the sun around which Second Earth revolved. I, too, was burning, and it was an unspeakable agony, but I did not care. I wanted to suffer, to atone for the anguish my brother had endured.

I was soon to have the opportunity, as it happened.

DAISY
Seattle, 1995

After three days at Kristina's house, being spoiled, coddled, and overfed, Daisy was, for all practical intents and purposes, completely recovered. There had been no sign of Krispin, and she had not seen Valerian since he and the warlock, Dathan, had vanished in tandem from Kristina's living room.

"I'm going back to Las Vegas," Daisy announced that sunny morning, finding her friend on the large deck overlooking the waters of Puget Sound, a magazine resting in her lap. "I've got some loose ends to tie up there, but then I'd like to come back."

Kristina looked surprised and pleased, then solemn. "You've felt it, then. That Krispin is gone?"

Daisy nodded, fighting back tears. "Yes. Valerian is gone, too, in a different way. I don't know how to explain it, but—it's as though he has died."

"I know," Kristina said. She had less success in suppressing her tears; her silver eyes glistened with them. "Maybe he's only resting somewhere."

"And maybe not," Daisy replied. She supposed she was in shock— she'd dreamed a horrid death scene in the night and watched Krispin burn, twisting and turning like a twig, but the cries of torment she had heard had been Valerian's. . . .

Kristina stood facing her. "What made you decide you want to live here in Seattle?" she asked. Gulls squawked in the sky, and in the distance a ferry horn sounded.

"I need a change," Daisy said, moving to stand at the rail. She'd regained most of her strength, but it helped to lean on something. "I figured out one thing, at least. I don't want to be a cop anymore."

Kristina was beside her, looking at the view. "What then?" she asked.

"You'll laugh."

"I promise I won't."

Daisy sighed. "I've got some money saved, and it would be a shame to let my talents and all that training and experience go to waste. I'm going to rent an office somewhere and hire myself out as a private investigator."

Kristina grinned. "I can see you doing that," she said. "You know you're welcome to stay here until you find a place to live."

Daisy shook her head. "Thanks, Kris, but I don't want to wear out my welcome. After all, you're the only friend I've got in Seattle, and I'm going to need somebody to talk to. Somebody who believes in vampires, for instance."

Kristina slipped a friendly arm around Daisy's shoulders. "I also believe in ghosts, werewolves, warlocks, and a few other dysfunctional types, but I don't suppose you're up to hearing all of that just yet."

Daisy smiled, though she wanted more than ever to cry. "Save it until I get back," she said. "Unless, of course, you're going to tell me that Santa Claus, the Tooth Fairy, and the Easter Bunny really exist?"

"Sorry," Kristina said, and they both laughed.

VALERIAN
Colefield Hall, 1995

"Remember," Dathan told me the instant I opened my eyes, "you owe me."

I was lying on a cool slab in that familiar cellar where I had spent many nights, following my transformation. I lifted my arms, and that gesture raised a storm of pain that reached deep into my flesh like the white-hot claws of a million ravening rats. My hands were scarred and misshapen, and I must have made a pitiful sound at this discovery, for Challes appeared, fussing like an obsessed nanny, to give me blood in a silver cup.

"Don't fret," Dathan taunted me as I drew the desperately needed fluid in through my fangs. "You look like the ugliest of Lon Chaney's thousand faces, but you'll be your usual pretty self again soon enough, I vow."

I might have spat at him if I hadn't needed the blood so badly. The worst of my ordeal—an eternity in hell—still lay ahead of me. I spared no grief over my lost beauty.

"Krispin—?" I spoke to Challes when the cup had been taken away.

"His body was destroyed," my tutor replied. He looked shrunken, did Challes, as though he were dissolving from the inside, caving in upon himself like an ancient mummy, disturbed by some bumbling archaeologist, callously subjected to sunlight and air. "Krispin's soul, on the other hand, surely awaits us both in hell."

"Yes," I said. I would have given much to see Daisy then, but I knew I would only grieve her, especially in my present repugnant state. I wanted her love, not her pity. "Nemesis will be here soon, no doubt."

"You can't go to hell without keeping your end of the bargain," Dathan protested vigorously. He'd been leaning against the wall, but with these words he sprang at me like a wire coil released from a matchbox. "Damn you, vampire, you must pay this debt!"

I smiled at him and saw in his pitying eyes what a ludicrous picture I made, with my distorted face and hairless head. "Very well," I said. "There is a vampire—Roxanne Havermail is her name. Her mate has left her for a fledgling, I hear—and I think she'd grown weary of him anyway, given the number of times she's tried to seduce me. Go to her, warlock, and make your monster children—if you can."

He looked as though he might stretch out his hands and strangle me for a moment, but then he must have realized the futility of such a gesture, for he whirled away with a curse, and struck the wall with one fist.

I laughed—there were so few pleasures left to me at that juncture that I could not spare even one—and the warlock came back to my side, seething with fury.

"You'd damn well better go to hell, vampire," he spat, "for no other place will hide you from my revenge!"

"Tut-tut," I scolded, groaning a little as the tide of pain rose up within me again. "You have no one to blame but yourself. 'Never trust a vampire.' Was that not your motto, your credo, the very litany of your black heart? Besides, I gave you the female you requested. It is not my fault if poor Roxanne is not to your liking."

Dathan did not reply, for he was too angry—with himself, I suspect, as well as me—but simply shoved splayed fingers through his hair and turned away again.

I groped for Challes's hand. I was weakening again, slipping into sleep, but even there I could not escape the relentless pain of my burns.

"The murders—in Las Vegas—the police will never understand about Krispin—must be some resolution—"

My tutor smiled and smoothed my scarred forehead with gentle fingers. "A few memories erased, a few changes made in the department's central computer, an idea planted here and there—"

I nodded, murmured a few disjointed suggestions of my own, and gave myself up, once again, to the ravenous, tearing teeth of torment.

DAISY
Las Vegas, 1995

Daisy arrived in Las Vegas at five-thirty in the afternoon, climbed into a cab at the airport, and headed straight for the police department. *Do not pass Go,* she thought, *do not collect two hundred dollars.*

O'Halloran was in his office, laboring over a stack of paperwork, when she walked in. He beamed at the sight of her, shot out of his chair like a dolphin going for a hoop at Sea World, and threw both arms around her.

"Chandler! Damn, it's good to see you."

Daisy gave him an awkward kiss on the cheek, and they stepped apart. "How's the vampire case going?"

O'Halloran's smile grew broader, if that was possible. He gestured for Daisy to take a seat and sat down in his desk chair, making a steeple of his plump, unmanicured fingers. "Don't you read the papers no more, Chandler? We got the psycho, dead to rights. Already arraigned."

Daisy knew the man behind bars wasn't the real killer—Krispin had gone on to his reward—but she had a hunch that he was guilty of other murders, whoever he was. The situation smacked of vampire justice, but there was no point in trying to tell O'Halloran that, of course.

More important, if her theory was right, it meant Valerian was around somewhere. Didn't it? The tricks would be simple to him—a memory or two wiped clean of certain facts, a couple of strokes to a computer keyboard, linked by modem to the department's mainframe, a deserving criminal to take the rap for a certain renegade vampire. Easy stuff.

Don't risk it, Chandler. Don't let yourself hope.

"That was good police work," she said with a purposeful smile of congratulations and admiration. "I wish I'd been part of it."

"So do I," O'Halloran said. "I missed you, partner."

Daisy's smile faded. She hadn't thought it would be so hard, explaining her change of plans. "I've turned in my letter of resignation," she said. "I need to do other things—have a change of scene. You know."

"Yeah," O'Halloran replied sadly. "I know. Sometimes I wonder why I hang around myself. For every creep we nail, it seems like there's fifty who get off on a technicality or something."

Daisy told him about her plans to open a detective agency in Seattle and finished with, "I can always use a good partner. If you get burned out on the beat, give me a call."

O'Halloran grinned, and his chair creaked as he sat back, hands clasped behind his head. "You know, Chandler, I can see myself as a gumshoe. The question is, can my Eleanor? She's been after me to retire for a long time, but I don't think living with Sam Spade is exactly what she had in mind."

Daisy stood, ready to leave, and O'Halloran stood, too, offering his hand across the cluttered desk.

"Why don't you ask her?" she retorted as they shook hands. It was as close as they came to saying good-bye.

VALERIAN
Colefield Hall, 1995

There was no fanfare when Nemesis came to collect me, no bolts of lightning, no crashing thunder, and certainly no trumpet. He simply appeared in the vault at Colefield Hall one night, standing patiently beside the bolted door until I took note of his presence. Or, more properly, until I ceased pretending I didn't know he was there.

I was quite alone, as are we all, I daresay, when we face our unique doom.

Challes, having brought me blood like a mother bird nurturing a nestling and flown off again, on some errand of my invention, would not return for many hours.

Dathan, for his part, had decamped sometime before, I think to pursue the deceitful Roxanne Havermail. It was a great comfort, knowing that those two, who deserved each other so richly, were very likely careening, even then, along a collision course. My deepest solace naturally came from the knowledge that I had broken the curse and saved Daisy from Krispin and his madness.

She might mourn me for a while, my Daisy . . . Brenna—I would surely grieve the loss of her throughout eternity—but our tragic dance through the corridors of time had ended forever, and the orchestra was silent.

Alas, I digress. I was recounting Nemesis's arrival.

The most feared of all angels found me reading peacefully in my underground chamber, and looked at me with obvious pity, though I was by that time quite myself again. My hair had grown back, and my flesh and features were as flawless as ever, except for a stubborn scar here and there.

I closed the book. "It is time to go?" I said. It was an observation, a statement, more than a question.

"Yes," Nemesis replied. I thought I saw regret in his unremarkable face, then dismissed the idea as pure fancy. There would be no reprieve for me.

I rose from my chair, and the angel reached out and touched my forehead, very lightly. I remember that his fingertips felt cool, and that the contact was strangely soothing, considering all that lay ahead.

We were transported, the two of us, in a way much like the means I had employed since my transformation in the fourteenth century, except that it was somehow swifter and more graceful.

We stood on a dark ledge, looking down upon a pit of fire that seemed to have no bottom and no borders, but to be infinite. I felt its heat and heard the screams and shrieks of its inhabitants, and I admit that my very heart quailed with fear. I recall a sense of mild hysteria, and a flurry of meaningless thoughts bursting from my head like a flock of crows. I know I told myself it was good that, as a vampire, I had no bladder.

Nemesis gestured toward the inferno. "Hell," he said, raising his voice a little, to be heard over the hideous din, "is what each man or woman decides it should be. This, Valerian Lazarus, is your hell. It is an illusion, in truth, but it will be no less real for that."

I thought of Daisy and took a faltering step toward the fires, ready to hurl myself in, but Nemesis caught my arm in one hand and stopped me. I felt his great strength and knew then that neither Challes nor I had ever deceived or eluded him; he had merely been biding his time until the appointed moment.

"You would truly suffer torment, throughout eternity, for the love of one mortal woman?"

I did not hesitate. "Yes," I replied.

Nemesis did not release me but instead stared deep into my eyes. I felt him probing my very soul, exploring every corner and shadow, seeking I knew not what. The only thing that was really plain to me, besides the terrible fear gnawing at my gut, was the fact that I could hide nothing from him.

"You speak the truth," he said, marveling. He raised his free arm, still gazing at me, and in one gesture caused my spectacular medieval hell to vanish in a twinkling. We were back in the vault, at Colefield Hall, before I could quite credit that I had been spared.

"Why?" I whispered, trembling, when I realized I was safe. The memory of that dreadful place we'd visited together would haunt me for all I knew of time. "Why did you bring me here instead of—?"

"There is truth in you," Nemesis said. "For all your evil, there is an element of good, though I confess I like you no better than I ever did."

I could not contain my joy, my relief. But my delight was quick to fade as I felt again the unceasing heat of hell, heard the shrieks of the damned, saw the hungry flames leaping against the darkness.

"That place—will I have to go back there someday?"

Nemesis gave me another searching look. "Perhaps. Perhaps not. What really matters, vampire, is the moment at hand. Nothing else is real."

Having made this pronouncement, the angel vanished, and I was alone once more.

I wanted to will myself to Daisy's side, but I was far too shaken. After all, I'd just had a close call, one of truly cosmic proportions, and the next few minutes were given over to gratitude.

VALERIAN
Las Vegas, 1995

Jerry Grover, assistant manager of the Venetian Hotel and Casino, trembled in his expensive leather shoes as the magician loomed over him. "What the devil do you mean?" Valerian demanded in a lethal undertone, looking damned scary in those Count Dracula clothes of his. "How could she have left town without telling me?"

Grover swallowed. All around, slot machines whirred and clinked, swallowing tokens with melodic greed. Bells clamored and lights flashed, and Jerry wished he didn't have to dance attendance like a flunky, but Valerian was a headliner, and the board of directors wanted to keep him happy. Nobody packed in the paying customers like this guy, and what the star wanted, the star got. Or somebody's head, specifically Jerry's, was going to roll.

"I checked on Miss Chandler, as you asked me to do, sir," Grover said in a squeaky voice. God, he hated it when he sounded weak and effeminate like that. "My contact in the police department told me she's resigned and moved to Seattle."

The magician glowered down at him for a long moment, during which time Jerry honestly thought his best suit might spontaneously combust, then whirled and stormed off through the casino, his black cape trailing majestically behind him. As he passed, every slot machine in the place suddenly went beserk, clanking like old-fashioned fire bells and spewing coins into the trays and onto the floor. Happy gamblers shouted for joy, scooping up their winnings with both hands.

It was the damnedest thing Jerry Grover had ever seen, and he didn't even want to think about trying to explain it to the corporation.

21

DAISY
Seattle, 1995

THE ancient elevator in Daisy's office building clanked and jerked as it made its dogged climb to the twelfth floor. It was late, and there was probably nobody else on the premises except the janitor, but that didn't matter. Since coming to Seattle two weeks before, it seemed to Daisy that she did her best work at night.

That, she thought, with a pang and a rueful smile, was what she got for hanging around with vampires.

The cage lurched ominously, and Daisy looked up at the numbers above the ornate iron bars, feeling the first flicker of fear. If the cables were to snap . . .

She gave herself a mental shake. Since encountering Valerian and some of his crowd, she'd become fanciful, even skittish. If she wanted to succeed as a private investigator, and she most assuredly did, then she would have to put all that behind her and get back her old pragmatic nature.

The lights blinked off, then came right back on again. The needle on the indicator above the door bounced between two brass digits— seven and eight.

Daisy bit her lip. After arranging the move from Las Vegas, she'd driven to Nadine and Freddy's place in Telluride and spent a week there, fussing over the baby and playing Auntie Mame to the hilt. All the while, she admitted to herself in the privacy of that antique elevator, she'd been waiting to hear from Valerian, to see him again.

He was alive and well and back at the Venetian Hotel, drawing crowds like never before—the newspapers and magazines were full of him. Daisy could only conclude that, after dealing with Krispin he had decided a mortal lover was a troublesome lover. Perhaps he had taken up with one of his many old flames, some splendid monster like himself.

There was a grinding sound, and then the elevator stopped completely, and the lights went out.

"Shit," Daisy muttered.

"Not very ladylike," Valerian's voice responded.

Daisy's heart stopped, much as the elevator had, then started again. *Valerian.* Had she only imagined hearing him speak to her? The cubicle was dark, but she could see well enough to know that she was still alone.

She felt a sweet heat stir in the depths of her femininity. She'd been alone in that motel room, too, midway between Las Vegas and Telluride.

"Do you love me, Daisy?"

There was no mistaking it. Valerian was speaking to her, if only inside her head.

The stress of the past few weeks had finally caught up with her.

"Yes," she murmured nonetheless. "Do you love me in return?"

"Let me show you," he responded.

The files fluttered to the floor as Daisy felt his lips touch hers, lightly at first, and then with passion. His hands caressed her everywhere at once, stroking her back, cupping her buttocks, weighing her breasts, teasing the nubbin of flesh between her legs.

"Damn you," she whispered when he'd freed her mouth to let her take a breath. "Why can't you make love to me in person?"

"Do you want me to stop?"

Daisy's pride battled needs too long unfulfilled, and suffered a resounding defeat. "No—please—don't stop."

She felt her clothes dissolve like smoke, felt the heat of her desire in every tissue and fiber and pore, and sobbed for joy when he entered her in a single powerful thrust. He was neither tentative nor gentle, seeming to sense that Daisy needed a primal mating.

Satisfaction came swiftly, tumultuous and fierce, and left Daisy clinging to the handrail in the elevator with all ten fingers, barely able to breathe. The lights came back on, and the lumbering box resumed its climb to the twelfth floor with a shuddering jerk.

Daisy was still alone and frankly surprised to find her jeans and T-shirt on her body instead of in a crumpled heap on the floor. She knelt, blushing, and hastily gathered up the files scattered at her feet.

All the while, satisfaction thrummed within her, deep and abiding and utterly undeniable.

Reaching her office, she was forced to lie down on the couch where clients were meant to sit, for small, sweet explosions were still rocking her from within, and she could not trust her knees to support her.

She fell asleep, bathed in silver light and feeling the lack of her lover's presence, and was awakened sometime later by a shadow crossing the moon.

Daisy sat bolt upright with a little cry, for seated on the edge of her desk, resplendent in his magician's garb, was Valerian himself.

"You should have been here for the lovemaking," she said. "It was pretty good."

He smiled and raised one aristocratic eyebrow. "Only 'pretty good'? Maybe I'd better try again."

"No!" Daisy said quickly and with conviction. "Another session like that, and I'll be stimulated to death."

Valerian laughed and opened his arms, and against her better judgment Daisy went to him.

"Where the hell have you been?" she whispered. It was safe to be angry within his embrace.

He laughed again. "Exactly," he said.

Daisy reared back to look into his eyes. "What—?"

He laid a finger to her lips. "Shh," he whispered. "It's over now, and we can be together. If you still want me, that is."

"I was thinking you didn't want me," Daisy said, stiffening a bit but making no move to withdraw from his arms. "What kept you so long, damn it?"

Valerian smiled and kissed her forehead lightly. "I had a few scars that I didn't want you to see, and I thought we both needed a little time to regain our balance."

Daisy nodded. "I'd gotten mine back, but you just threw me off again. Now what?"

"Now we go about making some sort of life together."

"I'm going to get old," Daisy reminded him. "And when I'm ninety, you'll still look just as you do tonight. People will think I'm your great-grandmother."

"I have never cared, overmuch, what mortals think. Or immortals, either, come to that. Such things don't matter, Daisy, when two lovers have been torn apart as often as we have in the past several centuries."

Daisy rested her forehead against his chin. "Okay. But how exactly are we going to work this? I like it here, and you like Las Vegas—"

"In case you haven't noticed, I find it easy enough to commute."

This time it was Daisy who laughed, but there were tears blurring her vision when she looked up at him again. "What about that guy the Las Vegas police department arrested for the murders Krispin committed? Isn't he a scapegoat, of sorts?"

Valerian shrugged elegantly. "I guess that depends on your perspective. The fellow has killed eight people, three of them children, and he's always prided himself on pulling off the perfect crimes. Some might say that justice was done here, however indirectly."

Daisy accepted that reply, although she knew it could have been debated for a long time to come, and returned to the original subject. "I don't see how we're going to manage a relationship," she fretted. "Do vampires even marry?"

"They mate, though to a much more profound degree than you probably think. Ours would be an eternal pledge, understand. Yes, you will grow old and eventually die. Then you will be born again, and I will be nearby, waiting for you to grow up and rejoin me."

The idea was bittersweet. "What about kids? What about a house and a dog and all that?"

Valerian feigned a sigh. "Any natural child of mine, Daisy love, would be a monster in both the subjective and literal senses of the word. Still, there are plenty of children alone in the world who would be happy enough to join our unconventional little family. As for a house, you have only to tell me what you want, and I will provide it." He paused. "The pet can be managed, too. It just so happens that an old friend has recently given me a splendid animal as a gift. You'll like him—his name is Barabbas."

Daisy considered her beloved's checkered past and the multitude of romantic involvements he readily admitted he'd enjoyed. "You won't get—restless? I should think a mortal might be pretty dull, over the long haul, when a guy's used to lady vampires."

He brushed her lips with his own. "If you knew what I have been through, just to be with you, you would never doubt my fidelity," he answered at his leisure. "One day—or one night, rather—I shall tell you all about it. Furthermore, while usually beautiful and always fascinating, 'lady vampires,' as you so generously describe them, can be the coldest and most heartless beings in all creation."

Daisy didn't reply, but simply slid her arms around his neck and raised her face in the shimmering moonlight to invite the vampire's kiss.

"Remember this night," she whispered.

"Because we can be together at long last?"

She smiled. "And because it's the beginning of always."

Tonight and Always

For love is a smoke raised with the fume of sighs;
Being purged, a fire sparkling in lovers' eyes;
Being vex'd, a sea nourish'd with lovers' tears:
What is it else? a madness most discreet,
A choking gall and a preserving sweet.

ROMEO AND JULIET

Prologue

London
Winter, 1872

THE new governess leaned down from what seemed to the child a great height, smiling her brash American smile. The woman was pretty enough, with her auburn hair and shining green eyes, and smart, too, or Mummy wouldn't have engaged her in the first place. Still, a stranger was a stranger.

"Kristina Tremayne Holbrook, is it?" Miss Phillips inquired in a nonobjectionable tone of voice. "Such a big name for so small a girl."

Kristina came out of the voluminous folds of her nanny's skirts to correct an apparent misconception on the part of the newcomer. "I am not so very little," she said. "I'm five—six next April—and I can already read and count to a hundred. You may be on your way now—we won't be needing you because I shall learn all I need to know from Mama and Papa and Valerian."

Mrs. Eldridge, the plump nurse with whom Kristina spent the majority of her time, laid a fond and encouraging hand atop her charge's head. "Hush now, child," she scolded benignly. Then, to the governess she confided, "You mustn't mind our Kristina. She's too bright by half, she is, and sometimes it makes her a mite saucy, but she's good through and through." She paused to emit a heartfelt sigh. "Now, come right in and settle yourself next to the drawing room fire, Miss Phillips, and welcome to you. It's a blustery day out, isn't it, and I daresay a nice cup of tea would go well with you just now."

"Thank you, Mrs. Eldridge," Miss Phillips said, removing her dowdy bonnet and cloak, both of which were dappled with snow, and handing them off to Delia, the handsome downstairs maid, whose duty it was to greet and announce guests and look after their belongings while they were being entertained. Delia collected Miss Phillips's battered carpet satchel—it was dripping on the Persian rug—and bore that away as well.

Kristina lagged behind as Mrs. Eldridge and Miss Phillips hurried into the drawing room, arms linked, whispering to each other. She lingered just inside the double doors, half hidden behind the marble pedestal that supported a bust of Socrates, while Miss Phillips was made comfortable beside the coal fire.

When Mrs. Eldridge went out to arrange for tea to be served, Miss Phillips put her small feet in their scuffed black boots on the chrome rail edging the hearth, and sighed contentedly.

"I do like to toast my toes on a winter's day," she said cheerfully. "Don't you, Kristina?"

Kristina had believed herself invisible, dwarfed as she was by Socrates and his pillar, and was both disgruntled and pleased that her new teacher had taken notice of her. Mama and Papa were loving and attentive, but they were never about during the daylight hours, and both of them were very busy—Papa worked in his laboratory belowstairs, and Mama was the queen of something, though Kristina didn't know exactly what.

"Yes," she said tentatively, drawn to the young woman with bright hair and shabby clothes and a gentle voice.

"Won't you join me by the fire? I feel a little lonely, sitting here all by myself."

Kristina understood loneliness well, though she was but five. It was a mysterious ache in one small corner of her heart, and always with her, even when Mama or Papa or Valerian or Mrs. Eldridge was nearby. Most of the time she felt as though she were lost from someone she did not yet know, and must find that person to be truly happy. Given her age and size, and the fact that she was not allowed to go farther than the wall at the rear of the garden by herself, the objective seemed very daunting indeed.

She stepped nearer to the hearth, leaning on the arm of Papa's wing-back chair. Miss Phillips sat smiling in the matching seat, which was Mama's. The approach was concession enough, for the moment—Kristina did not speak.

Miss Phillips smoothed her skirts, which were clean but frayed at the hem and mended in at least two places. "I do not think you are really so shy as you pretend to be," she said. "Are you afraid of me, Kristina?"

"No," Kristina said in a sturdy voice. "Not now. I was for a few moments, though."

"Why?"

"Because I don't know you," Kristina responded reasonably. "I've been told never to speak to strangers."

"Good advice," Miss Phillips agreed. "We shall be fast friends, you and I, as well as student and tutor. I think you like to learn, and there is much I can teach you. I would like to begin our association by taking you to St. Regent's Lecture Hall tomorrow afternoon. The topic is the mythology of ancient Greece."

Kristina felt her eyes widen. She rarely left the house, except with Mrs. Eldridge for carriage rides through the park in good weather, and she loved the sights and sounds and smells and people—so *many* people—that made up the great city of London.

"I don't know anything at all about Greece," she confessed solemnly. "Or mistology, either."

"All the more reason to attend a lecture," replied Miss Phillips, tucking away a smile.

THAT night, after Mrs. Eldridge and Miss Phillips and Kristina had taken their supper by the nursery fire, the nanny and the governess went off to their own quarters, and Mama came to help Kristina get ready for bed.

It was her favorite time of the day, for Mama was beautiful, and full of stories, and she could do all sorts of marvelous tricks, like making dolls dance with each other, or causing real snow to drift down from the ceiling. She never entered or left the room in the customary fashion, either, but simply appeared and disappeared. Kristina wondered, when she took the time to ponder such questions, why Mrs. Eldridge and the maids didn't move from place to place the way Mama did, instead of bothering with stairs and doors and other such ordinary things.

"I'm going to hear a lecture on ancient Greece tomorrow with Miss Phillips!" Kristina blurted, so excited that she bounced on her feather bed and wheeled her arms.

Mama laughed as she wrestled Kristina's warm flannel nightgown over her small head, which was dark like her own. "Well, now," she said. "I shall want to hear all about that adventure." She paused to smooth Kristina's silken hair. "Do you like Miss Phillips, darling?"

"Oh, yes. She's wonderful." Kristina's happiness faded a little as she considered a possibility that had not occurred to her before. "Will Mrs. Eldridge be going away, now that I'm big enough to have a governess?"

Mama kissed her forehead, her blue eyes shining with love, and embraced her daughter tightly. "No, sweetheart—she'll stay. Since Papa and I can't be with you in the daytime, it's important that Mrs. Eldridge be here."

Kristina was relieved, for the nanny had been her constant companion for as long as she could remember, and it would be terrible indeed if she ever went away. "Why is that, Mama?" she ventured to ask. "Why are you and Papa never at home before dark?"

Mama hesitated, then answered in a soft and somewhat wistful voice, "I'll explain that soon, when you're just a little older. In the meantime, you must be patient."

After a grave nod, Kristina sat down on the bed and pulled the warm covers up to her chest. "All right," she said. "But I want to know the *instant* I'm old enough."

Her mother laughed again, and Kristina was struck anew by her loveliness; she was a magical creature, with her pale, flawless skin, her flowing ebony hair, her exquisitely fitted white gown. "I promise to tell you all the family secrets as soon as I think you're ready to hear them," she said.

Kristina snuggled deeper into the bedclothes, already fighting sleep but determined to make the time with Mama last. "Make the puppets tell a story," she whispered. "Please?"

Mama drew a chair up beside Kristina's bed, sat down, and gestured grandly toward the ornate toy puppet theater, a gift from Kristina's uncle Valerian, which stood on the window seat. Instantly the tiny stage was flooded with light, and the small, colorful figures rattled to loose-jointed life and began to perform.

Kristina was asleep before the end of the first act.

THE lecture was fascinating, full of gods and goddesses, minotaurs and mazes. Kristina perched on the edge of her chair throughout, and even though she did not understand much of what was said, she left the public hall with a storm of bright, strange images raging in her mind.

She and Miss Phillips rode home together in the carriage, with a heavy quilt over their laps and warm bricks tucked beneath their feet, chattering excitedly about all they'd heard.

It was that night after supper, and after Papa had come to the nursery to read a chapter from a novel by Mr. Mark Twain in his deep and somehow reassuring voice, that Kristina first realized that she was different from other children.

She'd been sleeping, and dreaming of Athens, the city that had figured so prominently in the lecture, when the warmth of her bed was suddenly gone, replaced by a chill that seemed to wrap itself around her very bones. She opened her eyes and found herself standing in the middle of a vast marble pavilion, an eerie place, splashed with cold silver moonlight and utterly silent.

This, Kristina knew, was no dream. The cool stone beneath her bare feet was solid and real, and so were the chipped columns and fractured statues looming all around her. This was certainly not London, and she did not know how to get home.

She cried out in fear.

Instantly Mama appeared and knelt to draw a trembling Kristina into her arms. "It's all right, darling," she whispered. "Don't be afraid."

Kristina clung tightly to her mother. "How did I get here?" she pleaded. "What is this place?"

Mama cupped Kristina's face in her cool, soft fingers and looked into her eyes. "This is Greece, my love. You were dreaming about it, weren't you? And your thoughts brought you here."

"My thoughts?"

Mama smiled and gave Kristina a tight hug before rising to her full height again and taking her daughter's hand. "Yes. Come, let's go home—think hard about your room and your toys, sweetheart, and we'll be there in a trice."

It happened just as Mama said; in a twinkling the two of them were safe in the nursery, and Greece was far away, where it belonged.

"The time to speak of magic and mysteries came sooner than I expected," Mama began, sitting down by the dying fire and lifting Kristina onto her lap. They rocked together, Kristina's head resting against her mother's shoulder. "A long time ago there were two small children, your uncle Aidan and me. One day our mother took us to see a gypsy, and we had our fortunes told. . . ."

1

KRISTINA found the packet of letters tucked inside a small cedar box, in a far corner of her attic, while searching for a ceramic jack-o'lantern to set out on the front porch in honor of Halloween. In an instant the witches' holiday was forgotten; the mere sight of those heavy vellum envelopes, with their faded, curling stamps, struck her a bitter-sweet blow to the heart. She had not thought of her beloved governess, Miss Eudocia Phillips, in at least fifty years.

Now, in that cramped and dusty chamber where bits and fragments of the past were stored, memories nearly overwhelmed Kristina. She sat down on the arched lid of an old steamer trunk, heedless of potential damage to her white silk slacks, and was only mildly surprised to find the ribbon-bound stack of letters clasped with fevered gentleness in her hands. She did not recall reaching for it.

For a long time she simply sat there, holding the letters, remember-ing. There was no real need to read the words, some penned in her own handwriting, some in Miss Phillips's ornate Victorian script. Just touch-ing the paper evoked those vibrant, colorful, and often painful days with breathtaking clarity, bringing tears to Kristina's eyes and stealing her breath.

Presently Kristina looked up, blinked several times, and saw her re-flection in the murky surface of the large antique mirror she'd purchased in Hong Kong. She looked just as she had for upwards of a hundred years, except that she'd worn her dark hair long before the nineteen-twenties, like everyone else. Her skin was still unwrinkled, and her figure remained slender and supple.

Pretty good, she thought, with a slight and rueful smile, *for a woman of my maturity.*

Kristina shifted her attention from her image to the ornately ugly contours of the mirror itself, pressing the back of one hand to her face. She'd gone traveling after her husband Michael's death in the 1890s, roaming the world like a restless wind, never staying in one place for long. One bleak and rainy afternoon she'd found the piece in a seedy back-street shop and bought it.

To this day Kristina had no idea why she'd wanted the monstrosity. She'd done a number of strange things after Michael was killed—and many of her experiences and emotions were recorded, in great detail, in the letters she held. Miss Phillips's private nurse, engaged by Kristina, had returned her letters after the old woman succumbed to pneumonia in 1934.

A distracted thought flitted through Kristina's mind: She ought to clean the mirror and have it moved to her exclusive and suitably snobbish little antiques and fine art shop on Western Avenue. One woman's junk invariably proved to be another's treasure, as the success of Kristina's business proved.

The correspondence resting in her fingers reclaimed her attention, and with uncommonly awkward fingers she opened the first envelope. The fragile paper was turning to dust, and Kristina held it carefully. Reverently.

The faintest scent of lemon verbena, the fragrance she'd favored then, rose delicately from the vellum, arousing other remembrances, effectively carrying Kristina back to a time that no longer existed for her . . .

Cheltingham Castle
Somerset
June 14, 1897

My very dear Phillie,
By now, I know you will have heard of Michael's death, but I find I must recount all of it, as I could to no one else, in order to lay down some of the burden. A mortal's death is a mere trifle to my parents, though they have respected my pain and grief and done what they could to lend me comfort, but their kindness does not reach deep enough to soothe the bruises upon my spirit. As for Valerian, who is, as you are well aware, my confidante and friend— well, suffice it to say I believe he secretly thinks me better off without Michael. He always believed my husband was weak, and thus utterly unworthy of my affections. He would, of course, have had that same opinion of virtually anyone, for such is his devotion to me.
Valerian could never understand, as you always have, beloved Phillie, that one need not be especially worthy to be cherished by another. So often love simply occurs, *all on its own, like an earthquake or a case of the grippe, and to seek rhyme or reason in*

such an event is to seek in vain. That, of course, is how it was with Michael and me.

But I must start at the beginning, if I am to tell the tale properly. . . .

My memories spin so beautifully in my mind just now, Phillie, bright-hued and vivid, brimming with sorrow and joy and all the emotions in between. Life is, as you always asserted, rife with paradoxes.

I was already twenty-two the day I met Michael Bradford, an old maid by anyone's standards. You had long since gone to live with your sister, far away in Boston, and I had completed my formal education in Switzerland and London. I visited you sometimes, though I was careful not to draw your notice, out of fear that I might frighten you. I had not yet learned to trust my magic in those days, and there are times when I doubt it still.

But I digress.

I was alone at Refuge, my parents' cottage near Cheltingham Castle, except for the servants, and it had been raining all that morning. The house, spacious as it was, seemed close and dark, and I was fitful, with the beginnings of a headache throbbing in my temples. Just after lunch the blessed sun came out at last, and I asked a groom to saddle my pony, Pan, thinking a ride would clear my muddled brain.

Pan, you may recall, was a wretched beast, spawned no doubt in some corner of hell where the devil himself will not venture, and we hadn't traveled a mile before he'd pitched me headlong into the ditch alongside the road. I was not injured, but my favorite riding habit, a lovely gray velvet with a divided skirt to match, was torn and muddied beyond repair.

I was livid and barely resisted the impulse to turn that odious creature into a tree stump teaming with termites as he raced back toward the stables at Refuge, where the stable hands would no doubt reward him for his villainy with grain and perhaps even a lump of sugar. It was the way of grooms, I supposed, standing there covered in wet dirt, my hair straggling and my hat still floating in the ditch, to care more for horses than for people.

I could have willed myself home, or exchanged my spoiled garments for fresh ones in a twinkling, of course, but even then I liked to do things in the ordinary human way, wherever possible. You taught me that, Phillie, that I was more mortal than monster, and may heaven bless you for it. (And for so many other kindnesses that I can't begin to count them.)

Michael came round a bend in the track, mounted on a spectacular dapple gray gelding, just moments after I'd shouted a particularly ungracious malediction to the retreating Pan. I had known Michael to be a pest and a bully when we were children— he was the second son of the Duke of Cheltingham, and his resentment of his elder brother Gilbert's splendid prospects had fostered a corresponding nastiness in his nature—but there could be no denying now that he had changed.

Or so I thought, at the time, in my naiveté. Even though I was unquestionably a woman grown by then, I had led a very sheltered life, as you are certainly aware, and there was so much I did not know.

Michael had grown into a spectacular man, with golden hair and eyes of the palest green—just the color of the tree-shaded pond behind our house. He sat his horse well, for he, like most young men of his social class, had spent virtually every free moment in the saddle from earliest childhood, and was an expert rider. I knew from the servants' gossip that he won every race he entered, that he drank and gambled with a vengeance, and had been put out of several schools for unseemly behavior.

He had many shortcomings, my Michael—there is no denying that. Being apprised of these imperfections, I should have fled the scene with all haste and spared myself much suffering, but in that curious way of females, I was instantly and powerfully attracted to him instead. I am otherwise quite intelligent, as Valerian has since and often pointed out, always with a telling emphasis on the word otherwise.

Michael reined in his horse just short of trampling me and smiled indulgently at my dishabille. "Are you hurt?" he inquired with what I deemed an unnecessary note of delight in his voice. I did not think, from his tone and manner, that it would dampen his spirits in the slightest if I said I'd fractured every bone in my skeleton, and I was stung to flushing fury. A few weeks spent as a toad, I reflected uncharitably, might have a salutary effect upon his character.

"No," I said, giving him one of my most quelling looks. "I'm fine, though it's no credit to you that I wasn't stomped to a bloody pulp in the mud! How dare you ride in so reckless a fashion?"

Michael laughed, and his steed danced beneath him, but he

*managed the beast with no more conscious effort than he would
have ascribed to breathing or causing his heart to beat. "You were
in no danger from me, Miss Holbrook. I am, after all, an
accomplished rider." He leaned down, the rich leather of his saddle
creaking as he moved, to offer me his hand. "Come along, then,
and I'll see you safely home."*

*"I can take myself home," I insisted, still blushing. My heart
pounded like the hooves of a great horse passing over hard ground,
and I thought I'd be violently ill, right there in the road. For all of
it, I knew a rash and heated pleasure at the prospect of pressing my
person against his.*

*I gave him my hand, after wiping it hastily on my skirts—I can
hear your voice now, Phillie dear, saying,* Life is paradox,
Kristina—*and I confess I used just a smidgeon of magic to mount
the horse behind Michael, thus allowing him to fancy that he'd
raised me up by means of manly strength alone. Little is required,
I have discovered, to surfeit the masculine ego, but once again I
stray from my subject.*

*We rode back to Refuge, and my arms were round Michael's
lean waist, and that innocent contact stirred the most wondrously
wicked feelings within me, desires that I had only read about and
imagined until then. And alas, Phillie, knowing better all the
while, I began to fall in love. . . .*

"Not one of your more salient moments," a male voice intruded,
wrenching Kristina out of her reverie and back to the dusty attic.

She looked up to see Valerian towering between her and the mirror,
then glanced toward the fanlight set high in the outside wall. Sure
enough, full darkness had come, without her noticing. Where had the
time gone?

The vampire was majestic, as always, clad in his magician's cape and
impeccably tailored tuxedo and carrying a walking stick that doubled as
a wand when he was onstage. His Las Vegas act was sold out for a full
year in advance, and he obviously planned to perform that night. A
mortal would have been justifiably concerned, being in Seattle with
curtain time only minutes away, but for Valerian the commute was no
more difficult than a blink of his sapphire eyes.

"Falling in love with Michael, I mean," he clarified when Kristina
failed to respond to his original remark. "I can't think what happened
to your judgment."

"How fortunate," Kristina said dryly, "that I did not require your approval then any more than I do now."

The vampire smiled, his shaggy chestnut hair gleaming in the moonlight. "It is a relief to find you as insolent and willful as ever. I should not know how to react if you were the least bit sensible."

Carefully Kristina folded the letter she had been holding and slipped it back into its envelope. She did not set the packet aside, but instead held it close against her middle, as if she feared her formidable friend would snatch it from her. "I have gotten by these many years," she commented, "despite my ineptitude."

"I did not say you were inept," Valerian pointed out, twirling the wand idly between his long fingers, like a baton. "Never that. You know full well, Kristina, that I could not adore you more if you were my own child."

She stood and felt an odd and unaccustomed ache in her knees. Was she beginning to age at last, like a normal woman? She dared not hope it was so; she hadn't changed significantly, after all, since she was thirty.

Except to become lonelier.

"What brings you here?" she asked, making her way toward the stairs.

Behind her Valerian muttered and grumbled. He, like her mother—and even her more practical father, to some extent—could not comprehend why she so seldom used her powers to move from place to place. To want mortality was an enigma to them, she knew, though her uncle Aidan would certainly have been sympathetic.

"I sensed that you were in a melancholy mood," he replied, "and I came to see what could be done about it. You're very lonely, aren't you, Kristina?"

She felt her shoulders slump a little, despite her effort to be strong. Valerian had recently found his soul mate, a mortal by the delightful name of Daisy Chandler, and the experience had turned him into something of a romantic. "What good would it do to deny it?" she asked, gaining the second floor landing and taking the rear stairway that led to the kitchen. "You know me better than I know myself. Tell me, O Guardian Vampire—what is your sage advice?"

Valerian loomed near the table, looking pensive, imperious, and vaguely annoyed, while Kristina took a pot from the cupboard and filled it with water for pasta. "Find yourself a nice mortal and settle down," he said at length.

Kristina laughed, but she was painfully conscious of her heart, which felt cracked and brittle, and as fragile as translucent porcelain. "Don't look now, but I *am* a nice mortal, and I have long since settled down.

Look around you." She gestured with a distracted wave of one hand. "I have a house filled with antiques and exquisite art. I have a successful business."

"You are not a mortal," Valerian insisted quietly, disregarding everything else she'd said.

Kristina felt fresh tears sting her eyes. "Then what am I, will you tell me that? Not a vampire, not a woman. Neither witch nor angel, fish nor fowl—"

The magician's magician crossed the room in his faster-than-light fashion and enfolded her in his arms, and she wept disconsolately onto the white linen ruffles of his shirt. "You are unique, Kristina," he told her tenderly. "There is no other like you."

"But I want to be a woman!" Kristina wailed, tilting her head back to look up into the aristocratic face. "I want to love and be loved, to marry and have a baby and gain too much weight and get stretch marks. I want to grow old with someone special and die when it's my turn and be mourned by my children and grandchildren and great-grandchildren!"

"I know," Valerian replied, and this time his voice was sorrowful. He was almost certainly thinking of Kristina's uncle, Aidan Tremayne, whom he had loved with devotion and singular passion. Aidan, made a vampire against his will in the eighteenth century, had wanted nothing so much as to be a flesh-and-blood man again. His transformation had separated him forever from those who had known him as a fiend, for he had no memory of his original existence.

Kristina collected herself quickly, sniffling and turning from Valerian's fatherly embrace. He could do nothing to change her situation, and it was not only wrong but unkind to burden him with her grief.

"I'm sorry," she said.

Valerian was silent for a long moment. Then he made the pretense of a sigh—being an immortal, he had no breath—and said, "You're bound to meet someone—or something. Just be more careful this time, if you don't mind. I will not tolerate another wenching wastrel like Michael Bradford."

Kristina welcomed the anger that surged through her, knew Valerian had deliberately inspired it in an effort to give her a way out of her gloomy mood, if only for a little while. "*You* won't be asked to tolerate anybody," she said, dumping a handful of tortellini into the water boiling on the stove and slamming the lid onto the pot with a heartening, cymbal-like crash. "My love life, pitiful as it may be, is none of your damned business!"

The vampire shook an imperious finger under her nose, but she saw fond amusement in his eyes. "You only wish it were so," he warned sternly. "And see that you don't take up with that warlock Dathan, either!"

"Go to hell!" Kristina yelled, vastly cheered.

"I've been there!" Valerian retorted at equal volume, his nose within an inch of hers. "It's overrated and they *don't* take American Express. Good-bye!"

With that, he vanished.

As always, it was an impressive exit, smoky and sudden.

Kristina smiled, shook her head, and turned back to her tortellini. Just this one night, she decided, she would indulge herself and have pesto with her pasta instead of marinara.

IT was beyond a doubt the most ferociously hideous piece of furniture he'd ever seen, Max Kilcarragh reflected, circling the antique mirror once more. It would do nicely.

He reached for the price tag, turned it over, and winced.

A woman came into the main part of the shop from a back room, and Max caught his breath when he saw her image in the highly polished looking glass. She was truly lovely, with her short ebony hair and intelligent silver eyes, and he couldn't help thinking that her reflection had transformed the awful mirror into a thing of beauty.

He smiled as she approached. Attractive she definitely was, but she wasn't his type. He liked wholesome, athletic women, and this one exuded sophistication and class. She looked, he decided, sort of art deco, as though she'd just slinked out of an Erte print.

"May I help you?" she asked. Her voice reminded him of the tiny silver chimes Sandy had hung in a corner of the girls' bedroom, just weeks before she died. Musical, delicate, somehow magical.

Max cleared his throat. *Get a grip,* he told himself. *Even if she was your type, which she isn't, a woman like this wouldn't be attracted to a high school football coach.*

"I think I may be beyond help," he confided. "Anyone who would even consider buying this mirror definitely qualifies as a serious case."

She raised one dark eyebrow, and he watched the hint of a smile tug at one corner of her heart-shaped mouth. "Oh? *I* bought it, a long time ago, and I hardly consider myself a lost cause."

Max raked his brown hair with one hand, oddly nervous. It was just plain ridiculous, he thought impatiently, to be so damned edgy. After all, he'd never see this woman again after today.

"It's a vengeance present," he said.

"I beg your pardon?"

Max grinned, feeling awkward and even bigger than his six-foot, four-inch frame. "The mirror, I mean. I'm thinking of giving it to my sister Gweneth for her birthday. To pay her back for the moth-eaten moose head she gave me at Christmas."

Now she didn't suppress the smile, and Max felt as though he'd just run, at full speed and head down, into a goalpost. "I see. On gift-giving occasions each of you tries to present the other with a truly ugly object."

Suddenly the tradition seemed slightly sophomoric, though the antiques dealer had not implied that in any way. "Yes," Max said wretchedly, wishing he'd gone somewhere else to shop, like that store down the street, with the rubber snakes and the souvenirs and the mummy on display. A nice, tacky ashtray in the shape of Washington State would have been just the ticket, or maybe one of those floating plastic eyeballs.

She laughed, and the sound made something ache, deep down in Max's gut. "That's wonderful," she said. "Tell you what. It just so happens that I share your opinion of this particular piece, though it's quite old and—mercifully, I think—rare. I'm willing to let you have it on a very slim profit margin."

"How slim?" Max inquired. He wanted to ask her name, if she was married or otherwise involved, if she liked Chinese food and old movies and Christmas. But he didn't. If there was one thing Max prided himself on, besides his daughters, it was self-control.

She named a price, and he agreed to it, producing a credit card.

While she was writing up the purchase and arranging for delivery, Max idly took a business card from a small brass holder on the counter and scanned it. *Kristina's*, the raised script read. *Antiques and Fine Art for the Discerning. Kristina Holbrook, Prop.* This was followed by the shop's address and a phone number, and Max tucked the information into the pocket of his brown sports jacket.

"Max Kilcarragh," Ms. Holbrook read aloud from his Visa card. "That's a very unusual last name. I don't believe I've ever heard it before."

Was she trying to prolong the conversation?

He couldn't be that lucky.

"It's Irish," he volunteered, and immediately felt stupid. Anybody with a brain in his head would know *that*, for God's sake. He just hoped he wasn't blushing, like some pimply second-stringer with a bad case.

She smiled. "Yes," she said, handing back his card along with a receipt. "I'll have the mirror delivered to your sister's house this afternoon, if that's suitable. Heaven help the poor woman."

The wisecrack put Max at ease again, but he felt giddy, as if he'd just downed a six-pack of Corona in a few gulps. He grinned like a fool and leaned against the counter, his big linebacker's hands leaving smudges on the gleaming glass.

"Was there something else?" Kristina Holbrook asked.

Max cleared his throat again and realized he was sweating. "No," he said hoarsely and turned to leave the shop.

"Thank you," Ms. Holbrook called after him, soft laughter playing like a chorus of distant harps in her voice. "Come back soon."

Come back soon. The words were innocent, ordinary—merchants said them to departing customers every hour of every day. Especially the ones who were dense enough to pay good money for a mirror so ugly that even Sleeping Beauty's stepmother wouldn't have believed a word it said.

Max went to the door and pulled it open, feeling the late-October chill rush up from the busy sidewalk to turn his perspiration to ice. The little brass bell overhead tinkled merrily to indicate that the big, bad jock was leaving at last, but Max just stood there.

Kristina was at his side before he'd finished telling himself he was an idiot.

"Are you all right?" she asked. She really cared, really wanted to know, he could see that. And he was so touched by that one small sign of tenderness that the backs of his eyes began to burn.

"Yes," he replied, closing the door. "No. I don't really know."

Kristina touched his arm, and he fancied that he could feel her warm fingertips even through the fabric and lining of his jacket and shirt. "Maybe you'd better sit down for a few minutes. Or I could call someone—your wife, perhaps?"

The word *wife* wounded Max like an arrow fired from a crossbow at close range. It had been two years, and he'd worked through his grief. When, he wondered, would he stop stepping into emotional booby traps?

"Sandy is dead," he said, as though he were telling Kristina that it was about to rain.

"I'm sorry," she replied.

"So am I," he answered, and then he opened the door again, stepped over the threshold, and strode off down the sidewalk.

He hadn't gone a block when he found himself turning around and retracing his steps to the door of Kristina's shop. He hesitated for a moment, then stepped inside.

"I'm back," he announced.

"Good," Kristina said, with a smile that tugged at Max's insides. "I rather expected you."

He looked around, out of his element and yet wishing to be nowhere but exactly where he was. "Do you have a husband?" he asked bluntly, for it was not his nature to beat around the proverbial bush. "Or a boyfriend?"

"Neither," Kristina responded, gesturing toward an elegant old wing-back chair upholstered in dark crimson velvet. "Sit down. I'll make tea—or would you prefer coffee?"

Max had that bull-in-a-china-shop feeling again; he was a big man, broad in the shoulders and muscular, and he was afraid he'd smash the spindly legs of the chair. "I'll stand, if you don't mind," he said.

Way to go, Max, he mocked himself silently. *You've got all the style of a high school freshman trying to make time with a cheerleader.*

"If you're worried about breaking the chair," Kristina said from the doorway that led into the rear of the store, "don't be. They don't make 'em like that anymore, as the saying goes. That thing would support a Sumo wrestler."

Max figured he'd only imagined that she'd read his mind, and sank gingerly into the seat of an antique that probably cost more than he made in a month. He was pleasantly surprised when it withstood his weight without so much as a creak.

"I'll take coffee," he said belatedly in answer to her question. "Please."

She smiled and left him alone with the paintings and chairs and breakfronts and figurines.

He felt clumsy, off balance, as if there should have been prom tickets in his pocket and a corsage wilting in his hands. It was crazy; even Sandy hadn't affected him like this, and he'd loved her as much as any man had ever loved a woman. Even now, two long years after her death, he would have surrendered his own life gladly if that would bring her back.

Kristina returned, carrying a tray with two steaming cups on it, and sat down on a footstool with a fancy needlepoint cover. She handed Max his coffee and sipped from a mug of her own, surveying him with those remarkable silvery eyes of hers.

He tasted the brew and was startled to find that just the right amount of sugar had been added, along with a little milk. "How did you know how I take my coffee?" he asked.

She took her time answering, still watching him with that expression of gentle speculation. "I'm a good guesser," she finally replied, and he had an odd and completely unfounded suspicion that she knew all his secrets. Right down to the fact that he wore his wedding band on a chain around his neck, tucked under his shirt.

"You're very kind." Max drank more coffee and was almost his old self again.

Kristina's wide eyes twinkled. "It's the least I could do, now that you've taken that dreadful mirror off my hands. Your sister can return it if she really hates it."

Max beamed. "She will," he said. "Hate it, I mean. But she won't bring it back because that's against the rules. The only legitimate way to unload a vengeance gift is to find somebody who really wants it and give it to them."

"A tall order, in this case," Kristina observed.

"I got rid of the moose head," Max boasted with a shrug and spontaneous grin.

Kristina leaned forward slightly, and Max basked shamelessly in her warmth and her innate femininity, breathing in the faintly spicy scent of her hair and skin. "Who would want something like that?" she demanded, eyes narrowed, hair glistening like onyx in the muted light of the shop.

Max couldn't remember for the life of him.

2

KRISTINA was working out on the stair climber in her family room the next morning when Daisy Chandler arrived, wearing blue jeans, worn-out running shoes, a pink-and-white-striped shirt, and an oversize letterman's jacket with the name *Walt* stitched onto one sleeve. Her beautiful copper-gold hair was pulled into a ponytail, which cascaded through the hole in the back of her blue baseball cap in a wild profusion of curls.

"You're demented," she told Kristina, who was still diligently climbing, and sweating in the bargain. "You couldn't get fat if you tried. Why exercise?"

Kristina was asking herself that same question just about then, but she kept going. "You know why. I want to be normal."

Daisy flung her arms out in a gesture of exclamation. Looking at her in those crazy clothes, it seemed ironic that she was the center of a certain very sophisticated vampire's life. "What's normal?" she railed with good-natured irritation. "I haven't met anybody yet who really qualifies."

Kristina was in no mood to discuss her penchant for doing everything she could in the ordinary human way. She'd been thinking about Max Kilcarragh ever since their encounter at the shop the day before, and the temptation to use her singular powers to explore every nook and corner of his life and psyche had been nearly overwhelming.

"I have," she replied in a somewhat bleak tone. Mr. Kilcarragh was *wonderfully* normal, sound and stable and genuine, yet strong, too, and utterly masculine.

Drying her hairline with the white towel draped around her neck, Kristina continued the workout and changed the subject. Daisy was her best friend, but she wasn't ready to talk to anyone about Max because there was too much—and nothing at all—to say. "I trust Mrs. Prine let you in," she said. "Or did you pick the locks?"

Daisy, who had been a police detective, now ran a thriving private investigation service. She beamed, shrugged out of the secondhand athletic jacket, and tossed it onto the couch. Her cap sailed after it. "I'm still working on basic breaking and entering. In this case, your housekeeper is the culprit." She crossed to the refrigerator in the small kitchenette and helped herself to a bottle of sparkling water. She frowned. "I must have rung the doorbell ten times. Does Prine always go around with earphones stuck to her head?"

"Yes." The timer on Kristina's stair climber started to beep, and she shut it off and stepped gratefully down from the machine. Mrs. Prine's name didn't suit her; she was not a plump and proper matron, as one might expect. She appeared to be in her late forties, had a body like Jane Fonda's, wore well-scuffed cowboy boots and big belt buckles with an assortment of old jeans and tank tops, and had a tattoo on her upper right arm that read *Garth Forever*. She bleached her hair and probably hadn't said more than half a dozen sentences to Kristina in the five years she'd worked for her.

Daisy watched Kristina towel her leotard-clad body and shook her head once in apparent disbelief. "Aren't you going to ask if there's a point to my visit?" the gumshoe inquired, plunking down on the overstuffed sofa with her bottle of water.

Kristina shrugged. "You're my closest friend. Friends drop in on each other." She sighed and hung the towel over the handrest on the stair climber. "But since it seems important to you, I'll ask. What are you doing here, Daisy?"

"Tonight is Halloween," Daisy said, "and I've decided I want to have a party for some of the kids in our neighborhood."

Daisy's neighborhood was one of Seattle's poshest; she and Valerian shared a marvelous, spooky old mansion with seven gables and at least that many secret rooms. The property was surrounded by a high brick wall, and there were gardens and fountains everywhere. Instead of being intimidated by the place, however, children came from blocks around to peer through the high wrought-iron gates, waiting for Daisy or Valerian to appear. They fed the white wolf, Barabbas, tidbits from their brightly colored lunch boxes and tucked letters written in crayon into the ornate mailbox out front.

What delicious irony, Kristina thought. The vampire and his ladylove throwing a Halloween party for a horde of miniature mortals. "It's a terrific idea," she said in all sincerity. "I suppose Valerian plans to set a coffin in the center of the parlor and lie in state?"

Daisy made a rueful face. "I suggested it, and he nearly bit my head off, if you'll forgive the expression. Once I'd really thought the thing through, I had to admit that a coffin with a real vampire in it would probably be a touch too scary."

"A touch," Kristina agreed with a slight twitch of the lips. "I have to shower and hie myself to the shop. Could we fast forward to the part of this that has something to do with me?"

Daisy reached for her baseball cap and jacket. "I'd like you to be there, that's all," she said happily.

"And do what?"

Daisy bit her lower lip. "Stir a cauldron. And it would help if you wore something long and black—"

"No doubt I could borrow an outfit from Morticia Addams," Kristina teased. "But where would I get a big pot of foul and bubbling brew?"

"I thought you could conjure one up," Daisy said, pulling on her jacket.

"You know how I feel about doing things like that."

"Come on, Kristina—you don't have to be stuffy just because you're old."

"Thanks."

"Will you do it?"

"I must be crazy," Kristina said with a nod of acquiescence. Daisy was a hard person to refuse.

"Great!" Daisy cried, adding the cap to her jaunty ensemble. Then she gave her friend a quick hug. "Come at four-thirty if you can. It'll be dark by then."

Kristina promised to be on time, suitably garbed and in possession of a large cast iron pot emitting green steam. When Daisy had gone, she asked herself why she didn't spend Halloween in seclusion, as did most of the vampires, warlocks, and other supernatural creatures she knew.

As she stepped under a shower of hot water minutes later, Kristina answered her own question. She participated in mortal holidays for the same reason she exercised, traveled by car, cooked her own meals, and bought her clothes in stores. When she did those things, she could pretend to be fully human.

THE old Tarrington estate was a great place for a Halloween party, Max thought as he led his small daughters, in their masks and costumes, through the open gates and up the long brick driveway to the front door. Eliette, seven years old and dressed as Princess Jasmine, chattered happily about any number of things, while Sabrina, better known as Bree, age four and garbed as a clown, was unusually quiet.

"Everything okay, shortstop?" Max asked, crouching to tweak Bree's red foam nose when they'd reached the front steps.

Bree glanced nervously in one direction and then the other. "They have a big dog," she confided. *"I think it's a wolf."*

"That's only Barabbas," said Eliette, who feared neither man nor beast. Her reckless acceptance of everyone and everything worried Max; for obvious reasons, he wished she were not quite so brave.

"Listen," Max said, holding Bree's gaze with his own. "If you're scared, I'll take you home. You can help Aunt Elaine pass out treats while your sister the party animal and I bob for apples and swig cider."

The tiny clown shifted from one floppy orange foot to the other and cast a yearning glance toward the elegant brick porch, which was lined with the flickering smiles of at least a dozen jack-o'-lanterns. "What about Bob's apples?"

Max suppressed a grin. "That's *bobbing* for apples, honey—"

"It's a game, stupid," Eliette grumbled, impatient to get in on the action. The house emitted an intriguing combination of moans, shrieks, and maniacal laughter—none of which seemed to frighten Eliette in the least.

"Bad choice of words," Max told his older daughter. "Your sister isn't stupid."

"Sorry," Eliette said with limited conviction.

"I guess I want go in," Bree announced. "But if we see that dog—"

Eliette had forged ahead and was already stomping up the steps. "I already told you Barabbas wouldn't hurt you," she reiterated.

Bree slipped her tiny hand into Max's and looked up at him with Sandy's solemn brown eyes. "You'll save me if the wolf comes, won't you, Daddy? You won't let him gobble me up?"

Max swallowed, and though he tried to sound casual, his voice came out hoarse. "Count on it, babe," he said. "You're safe with me."

He was thinking, while Eliette rang the doorbell with verve, that Barabbas was a damned strange name to give a mutt.

One of the twelve-foot double doors swung open with a theatrical creak, and just like that she was there—Kristina Holbrook, the woman he'd been thinking about almost nonstop since yesterday.

Even with green paint on her hands and face she was elegant, and her gray eyes sparked with surprise, then humor, as she recognized Max.

"Come iiiiiin," she said in a very witchy voice. Eliette went past her like a shot, eager to join her friends, but Bree stood still at Max's side, staring up at Kristina in awe.

"You can do magic," the child said without a trace of fear.

"Yes," Kristina replied simply. Max had a brief, odd flash that she wasn't kidding. "Won't you come in?"

Bree released her sweaty hold on Max's thumb and padded past Kristina into the shadowy hall.

The lovely witch smiled and gestured for Max to step inside as well. "Hello, again. Did your sister hate the mirror as much as you hoped?"

Max grinned, getting over the shock of seeing her again so easily, and so soon. He wondered, as he had for the past twenty-four hours, what she'd say if he asked her out for dinner. "More," he replied. "Gweneth has sworn vengeance."

Kristina laughed. "I'd watch it if I were you," she told him. "It's Halloween, after all. She might find a way to cast a spell over you."

Max took a chance. "Somebody already did that," he told her quietly. "You're looking at an enchanted man."

She might have blushed—he couldn't tell, because of the dim light and her green makeup—but she did lower her eyes for a moment. "Do you like it?" she asked in a voice so soft he barely heard it. "Being under a spell, that is?"

"Yes," Max answered. "Which isn't to say I'm not scared."

Before Kristina could say anything in reply, the doorbell rang again, and she went back to being a witch and greeting guests. Max stood and watched her for a few seconds, then found an assemblage of adults in a nearby room, where a mob of noisy, delighted kids was watching a magician perform.

After helping himself to an hors d'oeuvre and a cup of mulled wine, Max chatted amiably with a few neighbors and then went to the doorway of the parlor to watch the magician. All the while his mind was full of Kristina—her scent, her voice, her supple, shapely body.

Their host and hostess hadn't spared any expense, he thought, watching the conjurer. This was no hobbyist or clever college kid moonlighting; the guy was a definite pro. His tuxedo was custom made and probably cost about as much as a midsize car. Over it he wore a black silk cape, lined in glistening red, and his skin had a pearlescent quality Max had never seen before. His hair was brown and somewhat shaggy, lending him an oddly old-fashioned look, as if he actually belonged to another time and was just visiting the present.

While Max watched, the wizard gestured toward a tall vase of carved jade, which was probably priceless, with a graceful, white-gloved hand. A sparkling light surrounded the piece, which stood alone in the middle of the floor, glowing more and more brightly until it dazzled the eyes. The children—Max had long since located Eliette and Bree—were spellbound and utterly silent. A feat in itself, he thought with amusement.

The curious, electrical mist dissipated as Max watched, and a small monkey wearing a red velvet fez and a matching vest perched where the vase had been.

The kids shrieked and clapped with joy, believing. Accepting it all at face value.

Max frowned, stumped. No trapdoor, no table, no box on wheels. How the hell had he done that?

"It's a night for magic," commented a feminine voice, and he saw Kristina standing beside him.

"Who is that?" Max demanded in a whisper as the fog of light returned and the vase reappeared. There was, of course, no sign of the monkey.

"His name is Valerian," Kristina said, watching the magician with pride and affection shimmering in her eyes.

"He's damn good," Max allowed, but he felt grumpy all of a sudden. Especially when all the kids, including his own, turned as one to shush him.

Kristina took his arm and pulled him away, into the hall. Her cauldron was there, doubling and bubbling, toiling and troubling. "I didn't realize you lived in this neighborhood," she said.

Max felt a surge of crazy, drunken joy. God, it was pathetic when a thirty-five-year-old man could be this grateful just because an attractive woman made small talk with him. He needed to get out more.

"Our house isn't quite this fancy," he replied. "It's just an ordinary colonial with green shutters and a fanlight over the door."

"Your wife must have loved it," she said dreamily. Then she put a hand to her shapely chest, plainly embarrassed, and gave a sigh. "I'm sorry. I don't know why I said that."

Max wanted to put her at ease, and more. He wanted to ford rivers and scale peaks for her, to slay dragons and build cities of gold that she could rule over.

Get a grip, he told himself. "It's okay," he said aloud. "Sandy never saw the house—we lived in a condo on Queen Anne Hill when she was killed. After—afterward, well, Eliette and I seemed to stumble over a memory every time we turned around, and we weren't making much progress with the grief, so I bought this place—" He stopped, flustered, wishing he could refill his cup. He hadn't said that much about the move to his parents, his closest friends, or even Gweneth. "I guess I told you more than you wanted to know."

She touched his arm with gentle albeit green fingers and smiled. "No," she said softly. There was a brief, tender pause, then she went on. "Eliette is a beautiful name—I don't think I've ever heard it before."

"My wife's father was with the diplomatic corps, and the family spent a lot of time in France. Sandy spoke the language fluently and loved everything about the place—the people, the food, the music, the art. We were going to take a trip to Paris the next summer—"

Damn it, he'd done it again.

"It's all right," Kristina insisted. "What about your other daughter— the little one?"

Max smiled. "That's Sabrina—we call her Bree," he said. "She thinks you can do magic."

"Maybe I can," Kristina replied with a smile and the slightest of shrugs. "Unlike most adults, children know enchantment when they see it. The lucky ones have yet to be blinded by disbelief—they still trust themselves."

Max cleared his throat, went to take a sip of his wine, remembered that the cup was empty, and blurted out, "I like you." He was wondering if there was such a thing as classes for the dating-impaired. "I mean—"

She laughed that wonderful, chiming laugh. "I like you, too, Max," she said, and waited, her eyes dancing, her makeup beginning to run.

Beneath the green grease-paint, her skin was very fair and cameo-perfect.

"I thought maybe we could go out to dinner somewhere. Tomorrow night, I mean." He held his breath.

"I'd enjoy that," she said. "I keep the shop open until seven on Friday nights. Would you like to pick me up there, or should I meet you at the restaurant?"

Max was wildly pleased and wanted to run outside and dance on the lawn like a kid celebrating the first snowfall. Fortunately he managed to subdue those urges. "I'm an old-fashioned guy," he answered. "I'll pick you up at the shop."

"I knew that."

"That I'd pick you up at the shop?"

"No," she said with a twinkle. "That you were an old-fashioned guy."

It sounded like a compliment, so Max took it as such.

KRISTINA waved stained fingers as Max left the party sometime later, carrying a sleepy Bree in the curve of one strong arm. His free hand rested lightly, affectionately, on Eliette's small head. He nodded to Kristina, and she felt a sweet pull, deep down, that was both physical and emotional.

Daisy, aka Marie Antoinette, stood next to her, holding her head in the curve of one elbow. Her green eyes peered at Kristina from inside the French queen's latex bosom, above which rose a stump of a neck.

"Good-looking guy," said Marie's cleavage.

Kristina sighed. She didn't know why she was letting herself dream about dating Max Kilcarragh, let alone marrying him and having children by him. He was mortal, and she was God-only-knew-what. Things could never work out between them.

"Yeah," she said sadly. "He's good-looking all right. Even better, he's decent, and funny, and kind."

Daisy shifted the plastic head from one arm to the other and shifted uncomfortably. Evidently Marie's dainty satin slippers were beginning to pinch. "Shall I run a check on him for you? You know, find out if he's got any bad habits—more than one wife—stuff like that?"

"Don't you dare," Kristina said, prodding at the bloody stump of Her Highness's neck with one finger and frowning. "Max and I are having dinner together, not getting married. If he's got any bad habits— and I doubt it—I don't want to know about them."

Daisy pulled off the top part of her costume, to Kristina's relief, so that her own unsevered head was revealed, and tossed the debris onto the hall table. "Don't you read pop psychology or watch talk shows?" she demanded. Her copper hair was wildly disarrayed, and the look in her green eyes said she was serious. "You can't go around *ignoring* bad habits in a man. That's denial!"

The house was empty except for the two of them and Barabbas, who was upstairs somewhere, sleeping under a bed. Valerian had already done his vanishing act; he would want to feed before materializing in his dressing room at the Venetian Hotel, in Las Vegas, to prepare for that night's performance. So Kristina spoke freely. "Don't talk to me about denial, my friend," she said cheerfully, taking her coat and purse from the hall closet. "The love of your life is a real, live, card-carrying, neck-munching *vampire*, remember? Talk about bad habits!"

Daisy shoved fingers stained with novelty-store blood through her hair and grinned. It had been hot inside that costume, apparently, for her face glistened with perspiration. "I never said I wasn't kinky," she said, and they both laughed.

"Good night," Kristina said moments later, pulling on her coat and rummaging through her drawstring bag for her car keys. "And thanks for a sensational party."

"Thank you," Daisy countered. "You made a really great witch. But, uh—" she glanced back at the cauldron. "What am I supposed to do with the brew? Is it toxic, or can I pore it down the storm drain?"

"Not to worry." Kristina looked at the pot and snapped her fingers, and it obediently disappeared.

Daisy smiled. "You've got a future with the Environmental Protection Agency," she said, following Kristina out onto the porch, where the jack-o'-lanterns still projected gleaming grins into the darkness. "Could you just make the stuff in the landfills disappear, for a start?"

Kristina waggled a finger at her friend, walking backward while she spoke. "You know the rules, Daze. No interfering with the course of history."

Daisy leaned against one of the pillars supporting the porch roof. "At least your attitude is better than Valerian's—when I ask him questions like that, he says something like, 'You mortals made your bed, you can lie in it.' Who makes these rules, anyway?"

Standing beside her car, a white Mercedes 450SL, Kristina shrugged and pushed a key into the lock on the driver's side. "I haven't the faintest idea," she called back. "All I can tell you is, I was born knowing I'd better obey them. Good night again, Daisy. I'll see you soon."

"Let me know how the date goes," Daisy replied with a nod and a wave.

When Kristina looked into her rearview mirror, as she drove down the driveway, she saw the white wolf join Daisy on the porch, its coat gleaming in the moonlight. One by one, the faces of the jack-o'-lanterns winked out.

THE girls had both washed their faces, brushed their teeth, said their prayers, and gone to sleep. No doubt they were already dreaming magic dreams, Max thought as he closed the door of the room they shared, and turned to go back down the hall to the head of the stairs.

Elaine, Sandy's sister, was standing by the front door, wearing her coat. She was wrapping a muffler around her neck when Max reached the bottom step.

"Thanks," he said. "For holding down the fort while we were visiting the neighbors tonight, I mean. Did you get a lot of trick-or-treaters?"

Elaine resembled her late sister, but only physically. She was shy and uncertain, while Sandy had been a dynamo, full of opinions and ideas and eager to express them. "Not so many," she said, pulling the muffler up over her head like a shawl. "I guess most of the kids were at the party."

Max nodded. He always felt vaguely guilty around Elaine, as though there was something he was supposed to do or say or notice—something that eluded him completely. "I'll walk you to your car," he said.

Elaine smiled, and for a moment she was almost pretty. "It's in the driveway. Just watch me from the porch, if you would—"

Max opened the door and took her elbow lightly in one hand. He saw Elaine to the late-model Toyota parked behind his red Blazer, despite her earlier suggestion, and waited until she'd locked the doors, started the engine, and driven away. The neighborhood was a peaceful one, but crime was on the rise in Seattle like everywhere else.

Turning to go back inside, Max saw the sleek, silvery-white form of a dog streak across the lawn next door. In mere moments the animal leaped the fence, trotted over, and sat on its haunches on Max's front walk.

Standing still, more fascinated than afraid, Max saw that this was no dog, after all, but a wolf. The creature's eyes were an uncanny blue, and they glinted with an unnerving intelligence.

"If you aren't the infamous Barabbas," Max said, slipping his hands into the pockets of his brown corduroy slacks, "you're certainly a candidate for the all-around best costume."

A shrill whistle pierced the night, and Barabbas perked up his ears in response.

"Damn it, Barabbas," a female voice called, "do you want to end up in the pound?"

Barabbas made a whimpering sound and then uttered a dutiful yelp, and an attractive woman in jeans and a plaid flannel jacket appeared on the sidewalk in front of Max's house. He recognized her immediately as his neighbor, the party-giver, and he was happy to see her. Relieved, too.

The wolf trotted over, took the fence in another graceful bound, and proceeded to lick one of the woman's hands.

"I'm Daisy Chandler," she said, holding out the other hand over the fence. "I saw you at the party tonight, but we didn't get a chance to talk."

Max walked to the gate and shook her hand. "Max Kilcarragh," he said. "It was a terrific setup—especially the witch." He was embarrassed all of a sudden, fearing he'd revealed too much about his attraction to Kristina. "The magician wasn't bad, either."

She laughed. "I guess that's a matter of viewpoint," she said. "Sorry about Barabbas, here. I hope he didn't scare you."

Max saw the humor of the situation, now that White Fang was on the other side of the fence and completely enthralled by his mistress. "It was the first time I ever had an aerobic experience without moving anything on the outside of my body," he said. Mindful of recent chilling headlines concerning wolves kept as pets, and of Bree's fear of the animal, Max turned serious. "Maybe it isn't—well, maybe it's dangerous, keeping a wild animal in a residential area."

"Oh, Barabbas isn't wild," Ms. Chandler said with supreme confidence. "He wouldn't hurt anybody unless they deserved it."

Eliette had said a similar thing earlier, Max recalled. He wondered what made his daughter—and Ms. Chandler—so sure the wolf was tame. "All the same, I wonder—"

"Trust me, it's okay," Ms. Chandler broke in, speaking as cheerfully as before, and Max found that he wanted very much to believe her. Some instinct, born long, long ago in the mind of some distant ancestor and passed down to him through uncountable generations, told him that this woman was a friend. "Barabbas loves children."

Max felt his mouth slant into a grin. "That's what I'm afraid of," he said. But in truth he really wasn't worried about the wolf any longer. Maybe some passing witch had cast a spell over him. "My daughters enjoyed the party, and so did I. Thanks for inviting us."

"Thanks for coming," she said. "It was a nice turnout, wasn't it? I would have been disappointed if nobody had showed up." She flashed him another smile. "Well, Barabbas and I had better be getting back now. See you around, Mr. Kilcarragh."

"Max," he corrected, starting toward the house. No need to fear for Ms. Chandler's safe passage home, with a wolf to escort her.

"Daisy," she answered and went her way, with the Hound of the Baskervilles trotting along behind her like a puppy.

Max went back inside and wandered into the living room, which had been cluttered when he left for the party earlier in the evening. Now, thanks to Elaine, the place was as tidy as an old maid's parlor—except for the pumpkin.

The jack-o'-lantern, which he had carved a week before, with close supervision by Eliette and Bree, sat forlornly in the middle of the coffee table, caving in on itself and smelling like what it was—a scorched squash.

Max took it in both hands, carried it into the kitchen, and dropped it into the trash. "Sorry," he told the discarded vegetable as he washed his hands at the sink, "but that's life. Ask last year's Christmas tree."

"Who are you talking to, Daddy?"

Max turned to see Bree standing in the doorway, clutching her "blankie." "Myself," he said, scooping the child into his arms and giving her a quick hug. "What are you doing up, anyway? It's late."

"I was thinking about the witch lady," Bree answered, rubbing one eye with the back of a dimpled hand. "The pretty one we saw at the white wolf's house. Do you think she's green all over?"

Max started up the rear stairway, still carrying Bree. "No," he replied, hiding a smile. "She isn't green anywhere, Poppet. She's a regular woman, not a witch. Her name is Kristina, and she's very, very nice."

Bree laid her head on Max's shoulder and sighed sleepily. "Maybe she isn't green, and maybe she's nice, too. Maybe she's even regular, but she *is* a witch."

Max kissed his daughter's downy temple. "No, honey. She was only pretending. For Halloween."

Bree yawned big and gave his cheek a sympathetic pat. "Grown-ups," she said with another sigh. With that, she promptly fell asleep again.

3

AFTER blitzing her costume back into the nothingness from whence it came, and scrubbing off the green greasepaint in the shower, Kristina brewed herself a cup of herbal tea. Bundled in the comfortable cocoon of her favorite robe, a pink terry-cloth number with deep pockets and a zipper in front, she sat in her darkened living room, watching the moon through the huge leaded-glass windows opposite her chair.

"Here's to you," she said, raising her teacup in a friendly salute to all things lunar. The massive translucent disk almost seemed to be hovering just beyond the glass, hoping for an invitation to tea.

Kristina settled back in her chair and closed her eyes, haunted by images of Max and his beautiful children. Her yearning to be mortal was, in those moments, so poignant, so deeply rooted in the center of her being, that it threatened to splinter her very soul.

If indeed she *had* a soul, Kristina thought as one tear slipped down her cheek.

"Depressed, my darling?"

Kristina jumped and opened her eyes wide to see Dathan, the golden-haired warlock, standing next to the fireplace. Of late, he had taken to wearing capes and tuxedos, à la Valerian, though the two politely despised each other.

"Don't call me 'darling,' " Kristina snapped, nearly upsetting her tea as angry adrenaline surged through her system. "And I won't have you just *appearing* in my house, either. It's bad enough when my mother and Valerian do it."

Dathan's smile was charmingly rueful and quite heartrending—if one didn't know him for the scheming wastrel he was. Despite his guileless brown eyes and choir-boy looks, his capacity for devilment rivaled Valerian's own. "Sorry," he said. "I was passing by and—"

"Flying across the moon, you mean," Kristina scoffed. She remained in her chair and held her teacup in both hands to keep from spilling the contents on her bathrobe.

He pressed one palm to his chest and splayed his fine, tapered fingers. "You wound me," he said. "I'm here out of concern for you, Kristina."

"Right."

"And it is Halloween, after all. Surely I can be forgiven for popping in on a friend." He crossed to a table inlaid with marble, a piece Kristina had acquired at Sotheby's in 1921, and helped himself to a handful of brightly colored candies.

"You are not a friend," Kristina pointed out coolly. "I hope the candy corn will suit. We're fresh out of dead rats and flies' wings."

"A second blow," Dathan cried around a mouthful of treats, clutching his chest again. "More crippling even than the first!" He swallowed with a tragic gulp. "I've come here expressly to save you from making a dreadful error, and how do you repay me? With insults!"

Kristina sighed. "Please do not add bad acting to your other crimes," she said. "Just tell me what you want and get out."

He executed a sweeping bow, eyes twinkling, and began to pace the length of the room in long, aristocratic strides, showing off his cape to excellent advantage and putting away more candy corn with every step. "You may know that I seek a vampire bride," he said. "Imagine the possibilities, the powers that might result, if a warlock and a blood-drinker were to mate!"

Kristina rubbed her temple. "Well, you're barking up the wrong tombstone this time," she said wearily. "Despite my illustrious heritage, I'm definitely not a vampire. And even if I were—"

"Stop," Dathan warned, halting, with a majestic, rustling swirl of silk in the center of the room. "You've made your disinterest in my romantic attentions plain enough already. I wasn't suggesting that we get together, I merely hoped that you might have a friend—"

"Ah," Kristina said, her headache intensifying. "You want me to fix you up. I thought you and Roxanne Havermail were an item. How's the family, by the way?"

Color surged into Dathan's face. "Kindly do not mention that creature, or her horrible children, again!"

Kristina smiled, recalling Benecia and Canaan Havermail, Roxanne's five-hundred-year-old babies, who were vampires in their own right and all the more savage for their doll-like, little-girl beauty. "Valerian will be disappointed that his matchmaking didn't work out," she said. "And since Avery Havermail ran off with that fledgling a few years ago, Roxanne and the girls have been—lost."

Dathan seethed in silence for a few moments, then, with admirable resolve, regained control of his temper and spoke in a moderate, even cordial, tone. "Kristina," he began again, in slow, measured tones. "Do you know any unattached vampires?"

She couldn't help it—she laughed. His phrasing had been unfortunate but highly visual. "No," she said when she'd recovered. "Except for my mother—who is madly in love with my father and will be for all eternity—and the Havermails, I am not acquainted with any female nightwalkers." Her tea had turned cold, but she took a sip anyway. "Now, before you go, please explain that comment you made earlier, about saving me from making a terrible mistake."

The warlock looked so defeated and so forlorn that Kristina almost felt sorry for him. Almost, but not quite. She'd been around long enough to know a first-class flimflam artist when she saw one. "You shouldn't become involved with the mortal," he said. "Max Kilcarragh, I mean."

Kristina stiffened. Valerian, her parents, the Havermails—all of them could defend themselves against the warlock if the need arose—but Max was different, of course. He had no magical powers and would thus be no match for the likes of Dathan. "What do you know about Max?"

The magnificent warlock toyed with one of the emerald cufflinks glittering at his wrists. "Enough," he replied gruffly, "and stop worrying. I'm no threat to him or to his children. It's just that he can't give you his heart, my dear—it's buried with his dead wife. He adored her, you see."

Kristina's eyes stung, and she blinked a couple of times in an effort to hold back tears. "Stay away from Max Kilcarragh," she said evenly and quietly. "If you dare to bother him in any way—"

Dathan held up both hands, immaculately gloved, in a bid for peace. "I give you my word, Kristina. I mean him no harm."

"Valerian has told me about the word of warlocks."

The splendid, graceful creature sighed. "Your friend the vampire is hardly objective where we are concerned, is he? Be fair, Kristina—what have I ever done to deserve your rancor, except admire you and make a fool of myself over you?"

Kristina was not good at holding grudges, especially against beings, human or otherwise, who had never hurt her in any way. She let Dathan's plaintive question pass unanswered, however, and countered, "How would you know anything about the state of Max Kilcarragh's heart?"

He shrugged. "I saw you with him earlier, and flipped through a few mental files, that's all. Poor Max. He'd give up his own life, even after two years, if it would bring his Sandy back."

Kristina ached inside, because she understood Max's pain, had felt something similar herself, once upon a time. Far from putting her off, Max's devotion to his lost wife increased his appeal. Along with all his other fine characteristics, he was loyal.

"Yes," she said softly, "I'm sure he would do that. That's part of what makes him Max. Now, if you don't mind—"

Dathan uttered another sigh, gave his cape a dashing swirl, and vanished.

Kristina carried her teacup into the kitchen and set it on the drainboard. Then she climbed the rear stairway and moved along the hall toward her bedroom. On the way she passed one of her favorite pieces of furniture, a small lacquered chest purchased long ago in Florence, and ran her fingers lightly over its smooth surface.

The thick packet of letters from the attic waited on the nightstand in Kristina's bedroom, in the cedar box, and she did not need to open them, or even touch the dried, crumbling paper, to bring their contents flooding into her mind, word for word. . . .

. . . and you can probably imagine, Phillie dear, how my beloved parents reacted to the news that I was in love with Michael Bradford. Why, they hardly took it better than Valerian did—he was in a terrible rage for weeks, and when that finally passed, he remained inconsolable for some time.

But I'm getting ahead of myself again. I'm afraid I've never quite broken that habit, despite all my efforts to slow down and take matters one by one.

It began to rain again, that afternoon when Michael brought me home to Refuge after my tumble from Pan's back, and we were quite drenched by the time we reached the stables. Naturally I offered the hospitality of our cozy drawing room, where there would be a warm fire burning, with hot tea and biscuits close at hand, and Michael accepted graciously.

I still recall the mingled and not unpleasant scents of damp wool, brandy, horseflesh, and some manly cologne as my childhood enemy stood before the hearth, smiling down at me while he waited for his clothes and hair to dry.

"You've grown up to be a very lovely woman, Kristina," he said.

My heart rate quickened at his words and so, however imperceptibly, did my breathing. I wondered how lovely I could be, sitting there on Papa's leather hassock with my garments torn and wet and covered in mud, and my tresses straggling untidily from their pins. Only then did it occur to me that I might have gone to my room to wash and change and do something with my hair before sitting down to tea with a gentleman.

I fear the social graces were not emphasized in our home after your time with us came to an end. Mama would have thought it demeaning for a woman to prink and preen for a man, and Papa was only interested in Mama, then as now, and in his endless scientific experiments. Manners and conventions seem silly to him, I'm sure.

But Michael had paid me a compliment, and I was charmed and quite smitten even then. I had to set my tea aside, for fear of spillage, and my face felt much too warm, considering the distance between myself and the fire.

"Thank you," *I said, as you taught me, keeping my eyes down.*

"You're here all alone, in this vast house?"

I made myself look at Michael and replied, "Not really. The servants are here, and it's not a large place, really. Not like Cheltingham."

"That haunted ruin," *Michael scoffed, dismissing several centuries of very distinctive history with the wave of a hand.* "It's a cold dungeon of a place, filled with drafts and dust motes and wailing specters, and I abhor it."

The word haunted *did not intrigue me, as it might have done another girl, for I knew a thing or two about such phenomena, of course, and in fact found them so commonplace as to be boring.* "But Cheltingham is your home," *I protested.* "Your family lives there, after all."

Too late I recalled Michael's antipathy toward his elder brother, Gilbert, the future Duke of Cheltingham. He turned away quickly, ostensibly fascinated by a small figurine on the mantelpiece, but not before I saw the look of wretched misery flickering like dark flames in his eyes. "So they do," *he said, trying to sound disinterested and failing utterly.*

I rose from my hassock and went to lay a bold hand on his arm, whispering his name, wanting to offer him some small comfort, some reassurance.

He turned suddenly and took me into his arms and held me close, out of some secret desperation rather than passion. I felt him tremble against me as he struggled to contain his emotions, and although I am ashamed to admit it, I wanted him to go on holding me like that forever.

Alas, Michael remembered himself and released me within a few moments, and I stood tottering on the hearth, speechless and flushed, while he stepped away, shoving a hand through his rain-dampened hair. "I'm sorry, Kristina," *he said.* "I had no right to take such a liberty."

I did not speak; I could not have done so for anything, for my foolish heart was wedged into my throat, and my eyes were filled with the tears of a besotted virgin. Which, of course, is exactly what I was.

He apologized again and promptly took his leave, and I was left behind to adore him in hopeless solitude, as I would be many times in the future. But I knew nothing of heartache then, nothing of suffering.

I was so very innocent.

The following day, Phillie, he was back—Michael, I mean—to bring me a blue hair ribbon and invite me to go riding with him. I accepted happily and sent a maid to the stables to speak to one of the grooms. I would not ride Pan again, I had decided. The fractious beast could just stay in his stall until he'd learned to behave himself, as far as I was concerned. If he toppled over from old age first, so be it.

A fine palomino mare was brought around for my inspection—Mama had probably acquired it for one of her adventures—and I was more than pleased. Here was a mount that would not embarrass me.

I allowed Michael to assist me onto the saddle—being in the company of a gentleman, I did not sit astride as I normally would have done but perched demurely on the animal's back, hoping I looked pretty.

I was such a fool in those days, but I don't mind it so much now—looking back on that time, I mean. I was absurdly happy, you see, and the dazzling sunshine of that day will surely warm my heart whenever I remember how it was.

Michael came to call often in the weeks and months that followed, and on those occasions when he was occupied with other things, I missed him so badly that I could not eat or sleep. I might have gone to him, by means of my powers, but even then I was determined not to take unfair advantage of those around me.

Since then, as you might imagine when you've heard the whole account, I have often wished I had not been so noble.

Michael proposed marriage exactly eight weeks after our first rainy encounter on the road between Refuge and Cheltingham, and I accepted eagerly.

I did not need to go searching for Mama and Papa to tell them my news; they appeared that very night in the drawing room, where I was sipping tea and sketching wedding gowns for the dressmaker in the village.

"Kristina Holbrook!" Mama said, so sternly that I started in my chair. I had not noticed my parents' arrival until she spoke, for they had long since foresworn the flamboyant entrances and exits Valerian generally employed.

"What is this nonsense about your marrying Cheltingham's younger son?" Papa demanded.

I held out my hand to show the promise ring—a sizable sapphire brought from some far-off country many years before, for Michael's great-grandmother to wear—and smiled. I was pleased to see my mother and father, and not even faintly intimidated by their obvious displeasure. "His name is Michael," I said, well aware that a certain stubborn light had come into my eyes. "And I love him very much."

"This will not do!" my father informed me. "The boy is a waste of skin—Cheltingham's been threatening to make a remittance man of him for years!"

"I shall be his salvation," I said.

I recall that my beautiful mother rolled her indigo-blue eyes at this pronouncement. "All he needs is the love of a good woman," she muttered in clear disdain.

"Well, it's true!" I cried, leaping to my feet.

Papa folded his arms. "Kristina, I forbid you to see this young man again. Do you understand? I forbid it."

"Don't be a fool, Calder," Mama said, nudging him lightly with one elbow. "Kristina is an adult. You cannot forbid her to do anything." She drew close to me and laid cool, calming white hands on my cheeks. "You are infatuated with the lad, darling," she reasoned. "But that will pass in time, I promise. In the meanwhile, you mustn't do anything rash."

I was to think of my mother's wise counsel often in the years to come, but at the time I thought she only wanted to spoil my fun and keep me a spinster forever.

"I'm tired of being alone," I said with some bitterness, pulling away and establishing a little distance between myself and the splendid vampires who had raised me with love. "Good heavens, I'm already older than most girls are when they marry."

"We're not saying you shouldn't take a mate, my dear," Mama said cautiously. Papa was glowering at me in silence, his hands in the pockets of his trousers, his sleeves rolled up for laboratory work, as always. "It's simply that Michael is——"

"A mortal?" I demanded rudely. "May I remind you, Mama, that Papa was human, too, when I was conceived?"

"Kristina," my father warned in a quiet voice I had long since learned to obey. "Have a care what you say. No one, not even you, is permitted to address your mother without respect."

I swallowed hard, closer to tears now than tantrums. "I'm sorry. It's just that I do love Michael and I want my own life. I've waited long enough."

We had the same conversation many times in the following weeks, but I was immovable. Finally, in despair, my parents gave up the cause of dissuading me from marrying Michael Bradford and told me sadly that they loved me, that I had only to summon them if I needed anything.

They did not attend the wedding, nor did Valerian, whom I had adopted as an uncle when I was very small. I wept secret tears, before and after the ceremony, because my cherished family refused to share my joy.

I confess, Phillie, that I went so far as to hire a man and woman from a neighboring village to pose as my parents, lest I be shamed before my bridegroom's kin. Yes, I know it was a cheap and even reprehensible deception, but what else should I have done, old friend? Should I have told the aging duke and duchess, the heir apparent, and my own proud young husband, before their friends and relations, that my mother and father never went abroad during the daylight hours because they were vampires?

Of course I could not. And I must close this letter now, dear, before it becomes too fat for its envelope. I shall write more soon, and I warn you, Phillie, I mean to leave nothing out. You must brace yourself for some ugly truths.

Love always, Kristina

Max paused outside the door of Kristina's shop at exactly seven o'clock the next evening, loosened his tie, which felt like a noose, and asked himself what had made him think he had anything in common with this woman. He was an exceptional father, a good football coach, a loyal American, and an all-around regular guy, but Kristina Holbrook was way out of his league. He wasn't even sure what to say to her.

He forced himself to cross the threshold, and the tinkling of the small brass bell heralding his entrance vibrated in his head like the toll of an enormous gong.

Kristina was standing behind the counter, wrapping an exquisite rosewood music box for an upscale woman with a stylish haircut. The silly thought flashed in Max's mind that Bree would be glad to hear that Kristina was no longer green.

"Hi, Max," she called with a friendly wave. "I'll be with you in a moment."

"No hurry," he said, and turned away to browse while Kristina and the customer finished their business.

He was pondering a grotesque bronze monkey when Kristina joined him a few minutes later.

"This might be perfect for Gweneth," he mused. "Christmas is coming, after all."

To Max's surprise, Kristina snatched up the monstrosity and carried it into the back room. She was pale when she returned, and there was a stubborn set to her jaw.

"That thing is not for sale," she said.

"Why not?" Max asked, puzzled. He didn't know Kristina well—there hadn't been time for that—but he *had* figured out that she wasn't given to mood swings.

"Because it's evil, that's why," Kristina replied, and immediately looked as though she regretted explaining.

"Evil?"

"Never mind, Max," she said, her silver eyes softening with some old sorrow as she linked her arm with his. "It's late, and I'm hungry and very anxious to lock up and leave."

He smiled down at her, noting the lingering sadness he saw in her delicate features and wondering what he could do, or say, to drive it away. "I tend to be too curious for my own good sometimes," he said. "Come on, let's go get something to eat."

He took her to his favorite restaurant, just off Pioneer Square, where a jazz band played on weekends and the food was Creole and Cajun. It was a loud jumble of waiters and customers, always jammed to the baseboards. The wooden floors were uneven, and the pipes in the rest rooms were exposed and you had to pass the supply closet to find them.

As they followed the hostess through the throng, Max felt a wild stab of doubt. What had he been thinking, bringing a woman like Kristina to a place like this? She was probably used to quiet, elegant restaurants with sweeping views and parchment menus with no prices.

He glanced down at her face, and his heart hurtled upward on a swell of relief because her smile was brilliant. She *liked* the noise, the crowds, the rickety tables, and the vinyl-backed chairs.

Glory be.

Max put a hand to the small of Kristina's back, and his touch was light but undeniably protective. Perhaps even a little possessive.

He wished to God he knew how to act.

Kristina was still smiling when they were seated at their table. Although there were plenty of well-dressed people in the restaurant, along with the jeans-and-T-shirt crowd, she stood out in her slim dress of glimmering gray velvet. Her hair was like polished onyx, catching the light, and Max wanted to slip his fingers through it, find out if it felt as silky-soft as it looked.

"This is great!" she shouted across the Formica tabletop, opening the menu.

"I'm glad you like it!" Max yelled back, smiling, but he was thinking about the music, which was so loud that he felt his liver quivering. Why hadn't he noticed that before, when he came here with the kids, or Gweneth, or his buddies from school and the gym? He reached for his own menu and pretended to examine it carefully, even though he always had the Seafood Étouffée.

Kristina ordered first and chose the special, Craw-Dad pie. It was impossible to talk with all the noise, and Max wondered if he hadn't subconsciously chosen the place for just that reason. He hadn't been this fascinated by a woman since he and Sandy had met and fallen in love when they were in college, and he was scared because the depths of what he felt were uncharted ones. Because he didn't want to say something stupid that would make her dislike him.

They ate, and Kristina smiled and moved her head in time with the music, and Max thought, *Even if this is all there is, it's enough. Just let it last forever.*

It didn't, of course. They finished their meal, Max paid the bill, and they left the restaurant, making their way through a crowd of new customers swelling in from the sidewalk.

"Nice night," Max said.

Kristina pulled her camel-hair coat closer and laughed. "I was about to say it was unseasonably cold, even for the first of November."

Max debated with himself. Should he slip an arm around her, or was it too soon to touch her at all? "Well," he said from the horns of his dilemma, determined to strike a positive note, "at least the stars are out."

"You're an optimist, Max Kilcarragh," Kristina told him as he took her hand and pulled her across the street, between honking cabs, smoking clunkers with dragging mufflers, and BMWs polished to a blinding shine.

They reached the opposite sidewalk safely, but Max didn't let go of Kristina's hand. There were a lot of panhandlers on the street, he reasoned, and even though most of the poor devils were harmless, you couldn't be too careful. Not these days.

It was ironic, his thinking thoughts like that when Kristina had just accused him of being an optimist. "What's wrong with looking on the bright side?" he asked as they approached the parking lot where he'd parked the Blazer earlier.

Her expression was serious in the neon glow of Pioneer Square and the streetlights. "It can be so dazzling that it blinds you, that's what," she said.

Frowning, Max opened the passenger door, helped Kristina in, and walked around to the other side. He was behind the wheel, with the engine started, when he spoke again. "Where did that come from?" he asked.

She settled back against the seat with a sigh so deep and so weary that Max wanted to put his arms around her. Even more than he had before, that is. "I found some old letters in the attic the other day," she said. "I guess they've brought back a few feelings I thought I'd already dealt with."

"The past can sneak up on a person, all right," Max agreed, switching on the lights and pulling out into the brisk Friday-night traffic. "Sometimes it's tough to stay in the present."

"Yes," Kristina said, turning her head and looking at him with those spectacular gray eyes of hers. They reminded Max of the sparklers he always bought for the kids on the Fourth of July. "You're a nice guy, Max Kilcarragh."

"Thanks," he answered with a touch of regret in his voice. "Just once, though, I'd like some woman to say I was—"

"What?" she prompted, grinning, as they drove up one of Seattle's many one-way streets.

"Dangerous," Max admitted with a grin of his own. "I'd like for mothers to say to their daughters, 'Watch out for that one. He's trouble.' "

Kristina's laughter pealed through the car like the chiming of a celebratory bell. "No, you wouldn't," she said when she'd calmed herself a little. "You're sweet and you're strong and you're good, and trouble, my friend, is definitely *not* your middle name."

Max was mildly insulted. "You make me sound like a real wimp, to use today's vernacular."

She touched his arm, and Max felt the proverbial electric shock snake through his veins and explode in his biceps. "Never," she said quietly. "Don't you understand, Max? You're the complete opposite of a wimp. You're a genuine, grown-up, secure-in-his-masculinity *man*."

He was grateful that it was dark inside the Blazer, because he blushed. He hadn't reacted quite like that since the beginning of adolescence, when his hormones, dormant one moment, had been running amok the next.

"Max?" She wasn't going to give him time to think of something clever to say, which was just as well, because it might have taken the rest of his life.

He cleared his throat. "Yeah?"

Kristina's fingers brushed the side of his face, so lightly, so briefly, that he was afraid he'd only dreamed it. "I'm not what you think I am."

Max turned his head, smiling with his eyes as well as his mouth. "You used to be a man," he teased. "You were born on another planet." He snapped his fingers, as if struck by a sudden revelation. "I've got it. Bree was right—you're a witch."

Kristina's silver eyes shimmered, and when she answered, her voice was hardly more than a whisper. "Close," she said. "You almost guessed it, Max."

4

KRISTINA turned in the passenger seat of Max's car and regarded him solemnly, so he'd know she hadn't been joking when she'd said his guess that she was a witch was close to the truth. Their brief evening together was about to end, she thought with dismal resignation, and once he'd heard what she had to say, there wouldn't be another date.

The thought stirred an unbearable sadness in Kristina. How had she come to want so much from this man, so soon?

Max glanced at her, navigating the traffic with a skill born of long practice. He was a good driver, yet another trait Kristina admired in him, for she herself had never really gotten the knack of motoring. Probably because of her nineteenth-century beginnings, she still yearned for horse-drawn carriages and spirited riding ponies.

"What is it?" he prompted in a gentle voice.

Kristina sighed. "I'm different," she said.

Max kept driving, but he was plainly listening, waiting for her to go on. There was something very nurturing in his attentiveness, something Kristina had craved all her adult life, without being aware of it until that moment.

She folded her arms, gnawed briefly on her lower lip. "A moving vehicle is hardly the place to discuss something like this," she observed, thinking aloud more than addressing Max in any specific way. "Could we go to my place for coffee?"

"I'd like that," Max answered simply, apparently ascribing no other meaning to the invitation, as many men might have done. Another point in his favor: He didn't think buying dinner entitled him to spend the rest of the night in Kristina's bed.

She murmured directions, and they soon pulled into the driveway of her house. Without thinking, she turned on both the interior and exterior lights with the flip of a mental switch. Despite her unique heritage, or perhaps because of it, Kristina did not care for dark places.

A bright glow spilled around them, pouring through virtually every window. Max, in the midst of helping Kristina out of the Blazer, merely grinned. "These electronic motion-detectors are great, aren't they?"

Kristina nodded in reply. Her resolve to tell all was already waning. The deep, unutterable loneliness that had plagued her since her disastrous marriage to Michael would surely return, once Max had taken his inevitable leave, and she dreaded that empty ache the way mortals dreaded death.

She did not normally lock her front door; vampires and other immortals could not be kept out by such simple means, and she was more than a match for human criminals. Kristina gave a moment of thought to a certain doorstop on display at the shop, an ugly brass monkey that had once been a living, breathing man—a thief and a would-be rapist. He'd broken into her store one night when she was working late, going over the books, and threatened her with a knife. She'd dealt with him accordingly.

One of these days, of course, she would have to change him back and hand him over to the authorities. For the time being, though, he could remain a brass monkey, quietly contemplating the error of his ways.

Kristina pretended to use a key, for Max's benefit, and stepped into the house. "This way," she said, and set out for the kitchen.

Max followed. "This is a beautiful place," he remarked as they passed through the large living room, with its elegantly faded Persian rugs and French antique furniture.

"Thank you," Kristina replied, proud of her possessions, which she had gathered from all over the world, in nearly a century of travel. "That writing desk in the corner next to the fireplace belonged to Marie Antoinette." Naturally she did not add that Valerian, whom Max knew only as a neighbor and a magician, had been personally acquainted with the queen and indeed been a member of her court until, inevitably, he'd managed to offend her.

Max gave a low whistle of appreciation, pausing to examine the workmanship of the piece, and then they proceeded into the kitchen, where lights blazed and the large refrigerator, with its stainless-steel door, hummed.

"Have a seat," Kristina said, gesturing toward the tall stools lining the breakfast bar, which overlooked the family room. It was there that she exercised, read, and occasionally watched television. "What will you have—coffee or tea?"

He perched on one of the stools, looking a little awkward there because of his size, though he was not an ungainly man.

"Coffee sounds good," he said quietly, watching her. He was surely waiting for her to confide in him, as she had promised to do earlier, but he didn't press. There was something so restful about him, so easy. With Max, Kristina thought, there would be no games, no subterfuge, no guessing. He was exactly who he appeared to be.

She sighed inwardly, envying him a little. If she were ever so open about herself, her life would become a circus in short order. "Regular or decaf?" she asked in order to fill the silence, comfortable though it was, opening cupboard doors and taking down cups with brisk clatters and clinks.

"Regular," he answered with a smile in his voice. "Nothing keeps me awake."

A vivid image came to Kristina's mind, unbidden and fierce; she saw herself and Max making love, and sudden heat suffused her, beginning in the very core of her being, in regions at once physical and spiritual, and surging to the surface to throb beneath her skin. She was very glad that her back was turned to Max, that he couldn't see her high color or trembling hands. "You're lucky," she said, hoping she sounded even remotely normal.

"Kristina." Max spoke calmly but firmly, causing her to turn toward him before she'd thought about it. "What is your terrible secret?"

She hesitated, imagining herself saying, "Well, both my parents are vampires, you see. I'm a hundred and thirty years old, and I have magical powers. Except for those things, I'm perfectly normal."

Her considerable courage failed her in that instant, and she said the first thing that came to mind. "I was married once."

Hardly a shocking confession in this day and age, she reflected, wishing she'd thought of something more dramatic.

Max shrugged, his hands still resting comfortably on the countertop, fingers loosely intertwined. "So was I," he said.

The four-cup coffeemaker began to chortle and hiss. "I know," Kristina answered, thinking of his beautiful children, the little girls she'd seen at Daisy and Valerian's Halloween party. "Please—tell me about her."

"I thought we were going to talk about you." It was an unvarnished statement, with no underlying meaning and no hint of secrecy or irritation.

"We will," Kristina said. She felt shame, because she wasn't sure she could manage complete honesty with this man. Not if it meant driving him away.

"Her name was Sandy," Max said, and a certain sorrow came into his brown eyes, as though he were looking inward, seeing some tragic scene. And no doubt he was. "She was killed two years ago, just before Christmas, in a car accident."

Kristina felt his pain in a shattering rush, making it her own, and steadied herself by moving close to the breakfast bar and grasping the counter's edge in both hands. "You loved her," she said. It wasn't a question, or an accusation, or a protest. Just a plain fact.

"Yes," Max answered. "We were very happy together. I met Sandy in college, and we were together from then on."

The coffee had finished brewing, but Kristina did not move to fill the cups. "I'm sorry," she said and then blushed again. "Not that you were happy, of course—I only meant—"

Max smiled and reached over to brush calloused fingertips across the backs of her knuckles. "Relax, Kristina," he said. "I know what you meant."

She looked down at his hand, now resting lightly upon hers, and marveled that such an innocent contact could rouse so many violent sensations. Nerve endings crackled in every part of Kristina's body, as if she'd grasped a lightning bolt, and her heart felt like a smooth stone, skittering over ice.

"It's just that—well—I don't want to say the wrong thing," she admitted. That much, at least, was true. Kristina could not remember a time when making a good impression had been so important to her.

"I don't think you could," he replied. "You have to be the most elegant, well-spoken woman I have ever met." With that, Max got off the stool, came around the end of the breakfast bar, and took Kristina's arm. Once he'd seated her at the table in the family room, he went back to the kitchen, poured coffee into the two cups Kristina had gotten out earlier, and then rejoined her.

These small ordinary courtesies pleased her to a ridiculous degree, and so did the compliment. In all her long life Kristina had never known a man quite like Max Kilcarragh. She thanked him for bringing the coffee, lowering her eyes, feeling shy and awkward and anything but well spoken.

"I'd like to see you again, Kristina," Max said when a long but untroubled silence had unfurled between them.

Kristina met his eyes, swallowed hard. *Tell him*, commanded some sensible inner voice, but she couldn't bring herself to comply. "I'm a pretty good cook," she said. "Would you like to come to dinner tomorrow night with the girls?"

He grinned. "Just tell me what time to be here," he said.

"Seven-thirty?" Kristina replied, even as she called herself a reckless fool. It was bad enough to risk her own heart, but there was much more at stake than that. Through her, Max and his children would be exposed to creatures they couldn't begin to imagine—vampires and warlocks for certain, and possibly other monsters, too. She did not have the right to unleash such forces, she knew that, and yet she seemed unable to stop herself.

"Seven-thirty," Max confirmed. Then, glancing at his watch, he sighed and rose from his chair. "I'd better go. It's a school night, and I don't want to keep the babysitter out late."

Kristina stood up, too, and walked with him to the front door. There he kissed her gently on the forehead, said good night, and went out. She watched until he'd gotten into the Blazer and backed out of the driveway, her heart brimming with contradictions—guilt, longing, sorrow, and hope.

Once Max was gone, Kristina climbed the stairs to her bedroom and took the packet containing her old letters to Phillie, her governess, from the top drawer of her writing desk. Then, after mentally shutting off all the lights in the house, except for the lamp beside her chintz-covered chaise lounge, she sat down and began to read . . .

My dearest Phillie,
    I am certain that my last letter must have caused you considerable worry, and I do regret any anxiety you may have felt while waiting for me to continue my tale.
    Michael and I were married in the family chapel at Cheltingham, under a shower of colors from the splendid medieval win-

dows of stained glass that grace the wall behind the altar. My fraudulent "parents," engaged by Valerian (because I pleaded and wept until he gave in), sat on the bride's side of the church, along with the servants from Refuge and a few mortal friends I'd managed to make along the way. They were well behaved and fashionably dressed, this hired mother and father, but given the circles Valerian travels in, I shudder even now to think who, or what, they might have been.

But that is beside the point. Our vows were exchanged, and there was music and great merriment on the south lawn of Cheltingham, my new home, where pavilions of silk had been erected for the occasion. Never, since the days of the dissolute Romans, has there ever been so much food and wine arrayed in one place. There was dancing and laughter, and I felt welcome and wanted, despite the fact that most of the wedding guests had been invited by Michael's family. I actually believed that I belonged, at long last.

After the sun went down, I began to look for Mama and Papa and Valerian, though I knew none of them would appear. They did not approve of the marriage, and besides, they were notably different from everyone else and would have attracted unwanted attention.

Still, I was wretchedly disappointed.

Michael's brother, Gilbert, Lord Cheltingham, had arranged for fireworks. When the last of the day's light had truly gone, and only the stars and the red and blue and yellow Chinese lanterns suspended from wires crisscrossing the lawn offered any illumination at all, Gilbert gave the order for the fuses to be lit.

Oh, Phillie, it was splendid! The sky was black and cloudless, and suddenly there were great bursts of brilliantly colored light blooming overhead, like massive celestial flowers. I was awestruck, my arm linked with Michael's as we, like everyone else, gazed up at that incredible spectacle.

Michael was a bit drunk by then, for he and his friends had been offering toasts to marital bliss ever since the ceremony ended, but I didn't think much of it until later. I had only one concern, as I have told you, and that was the marked absence of my own, true family.

The fireworks ended, and Michael staggered off somewhere, leaving me quite alone. Before I knew what to make of that—it was our wedding night, after all, and I had been looking forward to being deflowered, though I admit I was fearful, too—an argument erupted between my bridegroom and one of his guests.

I could not have guessed then how serious the repercussions of what seemed like a simple disagreement would turn out to be. Gilbert broke up the shouting match before it could become a brawl, and gave his younger brother a subtle push in my direction.

I suppose it is indelicate to speak of what happened next, but I must if I am to tell the story in an accurate fashion. Michael put his arm around my waist and guided me toward the darkened house, with only a candle, plucked from one of the Chinese lanterns, to guide our steps.

I was shivering with excitement and the peculiar sort of dread all innocent brides must feel, and by the time we had entered the castle and gained Michael's room on the second floor, my husband had sobered considerably.

In light of future events, I suppose it would make more sense if the evening had brought disillusion, even pain, but it did not. I loved Michael thoroughly, and I believe he felt the same toward me, insofar as he was capable of tender sentiments. He was uncommonly gentle as he removed my wedding gown and all the many troublesome garments beneath, each in its turn and its own good time. He caressed me, and whispered pretty words, and though there was some hurt when, at last, he took me as a husband takes a wife, pleasure soon followed. Am I wanton, Phillie? I enjoyed the things Michael did to me in his bed that night—I thrashed upon the mattress. I moaned when he promised that strange, sweet satisfaction I craved without understanding, cried out when at long last he gave it.

I understood, after that introduction to marriage, the tremendous passion my parents felt for each other, a caring that transcended time and space, existing in a dimension of its own creation. I actually believed, in my naïveté, that Michael and I shared such a love.

When I awakened, my bridegroom was gone, though it was not yet dawn. I had sublimated my powers in my desire to be human, but that morning my intuition would not be ignored. I threw back the covers, full of a sick and sudden terror, and pulled on my silk wrapper. I might have gone to him then, disregarding all the care I had taken to hide my magic, but for the sound of a single shot echoing through the air.

I froze, there in the bedroom I was to share with my husband,

*while the whole terrible scene unfolded before my eyes, as clearly as
if I'd been on that fog-shrouded hillside to witness the tragedy. . . .*

"And still the rascal wasn't dead," said an imperious male voice, startling
Kristina out of the lost world of the letter. "More's the pity."

Kristina folded the fragile vellum pages carefully and put them aside
on the lamp table. Her father, Calder Holbrook, stood at the foot of
the chaise, looking both spectacular and miserable in his formal evening
clothes. He fiddled with one of his diamond cufflinks—a gift from her
mother, of course, since he would never have purchased or conjured
such a frippery for himself—and glowered down at his daughter.

"Mother often appears unannounced," Kristina said, with a wry, af-
fectionate smile, while he took off his top hat and laid aside his heavy
silk cape. "Valerian, too. But this isn't like you, Papa. Is something
wrong?"

He was beside her in much less than an instant, bending to kiss the
top of her head in greeting. "I simply wanted to look in on you, that's
all," he said, drawing up another chair to sit down. Calder glanced
uneasily at the letter Kristina had been immersed in when he arrived.
"I didn't mean to intrude, but your thoughts were so plain that you
might as well have been reading those words into a bullhorn."

Kristina smiled. She did not want to discuss the letter. "How is
Mama? Or should I ask *where* is Mama?"

Calder sighed, looking exasperated. "There is a ball tonight, to honor
Dimity. I have promised to meet your mother there, though I dislike
the prospect heartily."

She laughed. "If it weren't for Mama," she pointed out, "you would
never leave that laboratory of yours, except to feed. Tell me, Papa—
have you found what you've been looking for all these years?"

At the mention of his singular quest—to find a means of curing
vampirism, while retaining the best of that creature's powers—Calder
Holbrook beamed, and Kristina was struck by how handsome he was,
with his dark hair and patrician features. He had been a doctor in mortal
life, and a good one, serving in the American Civil War. He'd become
a vampire, according to her mother, because he wanted to explore a
blood-drinker's singular gifts and use them, if possible, for the good of
his beloved humans. Kristina knew that had only been part of the reason; Calder adored Maeve and could not have borne being parted from
her.

"I am making progress," he said.

Kristina thought of Max and his children, and the babies she wanted so much but would probably never have. "If you come across a way to make me normal, let me know, will you?"

Calder's smile faded to an expression of intense concern. " 'Normal'?" he echoed. "You of all people, Kristina, should know that no such blissful state exists." He regarded her even more closely. "You've met someone. A mortal."

There was no sense in denying it. Vampires were perceptive creatures, and they read the secrets of those with lesser powers easily. "Yes," Kristina admitted, bracing herself for the same sort of censure she'd gotten when she fell in love with Michael, over a century before. "His name is Max Kilcarragh," she said almost defiantly, "and he's a high school football coach."

To her surprise, Calder looked excited, even happy. "That's wonderful!" he enthused. "Just wait until I tell your mother."

"Tell her mother what?" demanded Maeve Tremayne Holbrook, appearing out of nowhere in typical fashion. She too was dressed for Dimity's ball, in a white gown shimmering with thousands of tiny diamonds. Her black hair, showing not a strand of gray, flowed down her back in a gleaming fall of curls, and she stood imperially erect, as always, with her hands resting on her hips.

"Kristina has fallen in love," Calder announced before his daughter could move, let alone offer a greeting. He was already on his feet, in that quicker-than-a-wink way vampires had, gazing with fond triumph upon his wife.

The Queen of all Vampires turned slightly, to regard her daughter with thoughtful, ink-blue eyes. In a trice she'd read the complete story from Kristina's mind, just as Calder had moments before.

Kristina loved both her parents beyond measure, but she resented the lack of privacy their tremendous powers afforded her. Rising at last from the chaise, she faced her mother, her stance as regal, in its way, as Maeve's own. "I hope neither of you will take it upon yourselves to interfere," she said.

As if she had any recourse should these two magnificently beautiful monsters decide to turn her entire life inside out and upside down! Her magic, though formidable by mortal standards, was nothing in comparison to theirs. They could travel back in time, for one thing, which meant they could change the present significantly, and that was only the beginning of their abilities.

Maeve drew herself up, looking more queenlike than ever. "If we didn't step in when you married that wretch Michael," she pointed out, "what makes you think we would involve ourselves in this new romance?"

"It isn't a romance," Kristina said wearily.

Calder cleared his throat to get his wife's attention and offered his arm in that elegant, old-fashioned way so rare in modern times. "We are late for the ball, are we not?" he inquired.

The tension was broken, for both Maeve and Kristina knew he had no wish to attend the event, and they laughed.

Maeve linked her arm with Calder's. "So we are," she said, smiling up at him in plain adoration. A moment later her gaze shifted to Kristina. "We are not through discussing this situation," she warned. Then, in the merest shadow of a moment, the two vampires vanished.

Kristina felt more alone than ever. She was neither vampire nor mortal, and in certain ways both worlds were closed to her because of that.

She glanced back at the letter she had been reading before her father's arrival, but she suddenly felt too downhearted to go back to it. She'd been kidding herself, inviting Max and his daughters to dinner, letting her heart go wandering where it would, dreaming dreams that could never come true.

What had she been thinking of? Her attraction to Max Kilcarragh meant trouble at best and, at worst, absolute calamity for all of them.

Tomorrow, Kristina promised herself, she would telephone Max, make up some excuse, call the whole thing off before any harm had been done.

The trouble was, she suspected that it was already too late.

"DADDY?"

Max was standing in front of the living room fireplace, staring at a framed photograph of Sandy, the children, and himself, and he turned at the sound of his youngest daughter's voice.

Bree was in the doorway, clad in pink footed pajamas, her dark hair a-tumble, clasping her beloved teddy bear in one arm.

"What is it, sweetheart?" he asked. "Bad dream?"

Bree shook her head. "How long till Christmas?" she asked.

Max shoved a hand through his hair, feeling mildly exasperated. Halloween was barely over, and Thanksgiving was almost a month off, but the commercials on TV were already pushing toys at every opportunity. "It's quite a while," he answered, crossing the room to lift the child into his arms, teddy bear and all. "Why?"

"I have to get in touch with Santa Claus," Bree said with the special urgency of a four-year-old. "Do you think we could send him a fax?"

Max grinned, already mounting the stairs, Bree solid in his arms. "When I was a kid," he said, "we just wrote the old boy a letter."

"A fax is quicker," Bree reasoned. "Besides, this is an emergency."

He wondered where she'd picked up a fancy word like *emergency,* but only for a moment. Bree was smart, like her sister, and she spent most of her time with adults. "Okay," he said. "You tell me what you want to say, and I'll get a message to the North Pole first thing in the morning. There's a fax machine in the office at school."

They had reached the upstairs hallway. Bree yawned in spite of herself, then rested her head on Max's shoulder. "Ask Santa to please bring back Mommy," she said. She yawned again, more broadly. "Do you know his number?"

Max could barely speak. He'd been ambushed by his emotions again; his throat was thick with tears he dared not shed, and his eyes burned. Where had Bree gotten the idea of asking for something like that? She'd been barely two when the accident happened and couldn't possibly remember Sandy the way Eliette did. "Sure," he said gruffly. "I know his number. But there's a problem here, button."

Bree raised her head and looked at him with Sandy's eyes. "What?"

Max swallowed hard and blinked. "Nobody can bring Mommy back, honey. Not even Santa."

"Oh," Bree said.

"Shhh," he whispered, carrying the child into the room she shared with Eliette, putting her gently back into bed, tucking the covers under her chin and kissing her forehead. "You don't want to wake your sister, do you?"

Bree shook her head. "What do you want Santa to bring you, Daddy?" she asked, barely breathing the words.

Max thought of Kristina Holbrook. Try as he might, he couldn't imagine her living in this spacious but essentially ordinary house, sharing his life, helping to raise two little girls. Nor could he picture her accompanying him to high school football games and social gatherings for the faculty members.

"I've got everything I want," he answered. "Now go back to sleep."

Obediently Bree closed her eyes and snuggled down into her pillow with a soft sigh. Max checked Eliette, who was sleeping soundly, and then slipped out of the room, closing the door softly behind him.

In the hallway he stood still, collecting himself. He'd told Bree he had everything he wanted—two fantastic kids called him Daddy, his health was good, his extended family really cared, and he worked at a job he loved—but he had to admit, at least to himself, that he'd stretched the truth a little. For a year after the accident he'd concentrated on just getting through the days and nights without cracking up from grief. Then, at his friends' insistence, he'd started to date again.

God, that had been terrible at first. He'd felt awkward and somehow guilty, as though he were cheating on Sandy. Dating had become tolerable, though, little by little, and then he'd actually begun to enjoy it. He hadn't expected to care deeply about any woman, ever again, however. He'd thought he'd lost the capacity for the kind of passionate, romantic love he and Sandy had shared.

Now, after one evening with Kristina, he wondered.

He made his way down the hall to his own room. They'd moved to this house after Sandy's funeral, when the memories at the condo had become too much for him and for Eliette, and no one had ever slept in his new bed except him. He was grateful now that there were no memories lurking there, because that night it wasn't Sandy he was thinking about, it was Kristina.

Max hauled his sweater off over his head and tossed it onto a chair. He'd been faithful to Sandy, from the day he met her, and even though he'd dated several women in the last year, he'd never gone to bed with any of them. Now he wanted someone else, and the fact was difficult to face and even harder to square with his personal code.

He took off the rest of his clothes and stepped into his bathroom, reaching for the shower spigot. After just a moment's hesitation, Max turned on the cold water, full blast, and stepped under the spray.

THE next morning, despite a restless night, rife with disturbing dreams, things looked brighter to Kristina. She was simply cooking a meal for Max, not marrying him and promising to raise his children, and she'd made too much of the whole matter. Surely there was no danger from the supernatural world, either—the vast majority of mortals lived their whole lives without encountering anything but other human beings.

Coolly, while she got ready to go to the shop, Kristina considered the menu for that evening's meal.

Pasta, she decided, donning a loose dress of rose-colored silk, purchased on a buying trip to the Orient. After studying her reflection in the vanity mirror, she added a long strand of pearls and touched her lips with soft pink lipstick. A person had to keep things in perspective, that was all, she thought. Max was an attractive man, and there was no denying that she was drawn to him, but they really didn't have much in common, and after a few dates they would probably lose interest in each other.

Half an hour later Kristina entered the shop. The weather was cold, but the day was unusually bright for Seattle in November, and as she was opening the cash register, a stray beam of sunshine struck the brass doorstop.

Kristina frowned. Valerian had warned her that such flamboyant spells were unpredictable; he'd said that the ugly monkey might turn back into a criminal at an inconvenient moment. Suppose that happened, he'd asked, and her magic failed, as magic sometimes will, just when she needed it most?

She took a moment to ponder again the foibles of the justice system, which would probably set the man free to hurt other, more defenseless people, and promptly put the whole matter out of her mind.

Business was brisk that morning, with Christmas just appearing on the far horizon. By noon Kristina had sold a set of sterling silver combs, a lacquered bureau made in China in the eighteenth century, and a painting of two young girls in frilly gowns, weaving flower crowns in a Victorian garden.

She was just beginning to think about lunch when Daisy came in, wearing her customary jeans, letterman's jacket, T-shirt, sneakers, and baseball cap. It amused Kristina that, for all his sophistication and incredible power, Valerian loved this particular woman. Every time she thought about it, in fact, she gave thanks for his good judgment.

"I hope that contains food," Kristina said, indicating the large, greasy bag Daisy carried with a nod of her head.

Daisy smiled. "Fish and chips," she said. "With extra tartar sauce."

"Let me at it," Kristina answered. She put the *Closed* sign in the window, locked the door, and led the way to the back room, where a gracious old table stood, surrounded by crates and boxes.

"I resent the fact that you can eat stuff like this without worrying about the fat content," Daisy said a few minutes later, holding up a french fry as Exhibit A. "Some of us can actually gain weight from what we eat!"

Kristina didn't laugh, as she might have done another time. Her thoughts had taken a serious turn again, because food had reminded her that Max and his daughters were coming to her house for dinner that night. "You and Valerian seem to be making your relationship work," she mused, swirling a piece of deep-fried fish in the tartar sauce. "Even though he's immortal and you're human."

Daisy widened her eyes at Kristina in mock surprise. "Now, there's a quick change of subject," she said. Then she sighed in a way that revealed deep contentment and caused a flash of envy in Kristina. Her smile was dreamy and faintly wicked. "Yeah," she went on after a moment of mysterious reflection. "It works, all right."

"How?" Kristina pressed. "You're so different from each other."

"An understatement if I've ever heard one. You know the story, Kris," Daisy replied gently. "It was fate. Valerian and I have been together before, in other lifetimes and all that mystical stuff." She paused and grinned devilishly. "Of course, it helps that the sex is only terrific."

Kristina blushed. "I don't even want to know about that, so don't tell me."

Daisy laughed. "Okay, I won't."

"It doesn't bother you that he—that he's a vampire?"

"I think of it as a mixed marriage," Daisy said, eyes twinkling. "As for the thing about his having to stay out of the sun, well, I just tell people my husband works the graveyard shift."

Kristina thought about Max again—actually, she'd been thinking about him all along, on some level—and tried to imagine making a life with him. It seemed impossible, given the fact that he was a down-to-earth sort of guy who probably didn't believe that vampires and other such creatures existed, outside of movies and books. Meeting up with one, an inevitability if he spent much time with her, would probably have him rushing out to consult the nearest mental health professional.

And he certainly wouldn't want his children to encounter such monsters.

Suddenly tears sprang to Kristina's eyes, and she covered her face with both hands and sobbed.

"What's the matter?" Daisy asked quickly, full of concern. "Kris, what is it?"

Kristina struggled to compose herself, but the effort was a failure. "The most awful thing has happened," she wailed. "I've met a wonderful man, and I think I'm falling in love with him!"

Daisy raised her eyebrows in mock horror. "That *is* terrible," she teased. Then she went to the water cooler, filled a paper cup, and brought it back to the table for Kristina. "Drink up, kiddo," she said. "There's no 'I think' about it. You're crazy about the guy, whoever he is. And all I can say is, it's about time."

5

MAX surveyed his varsity football squad with pride as they finished their daily laps and trotted off the field toward the locker rooms. None of them would ever play college ball, let alone get a crack at the pros, but they were good kids who knew how to set goals, think on their feet, and work as a team. To Max, implanting those qualities in his students was the most important part of his job. Winning was a secondary consideration, as far as he was concerned, but because the boys were so focused and so dedicated, they took their share of games.

Max himself had been preoccupied for much of that day—once he'd gotten Eliette and Bree off to school and play group respectively, he'd found his thoughts continually turning to Kristina Holbrook. Although he loved his children more than his own life, he found himself wishing they weren't invited to that night's dinner.

It wasn't that he was ashamed of his daughters or afraid they would misbehave. It was pure selfishness on his part; he wanted Kristina to himself, wanted to concentrate on getting to know her, with no distractions.

Inside the locker room, Max ignored the noise, towel-snapping, and good-natured bickering—it was standard adolescent stuff—and walked through to his office. A pink message slip lay on his desk amid the general clutter of diagrams of potential plays, evaluation forms, magazines and mail.

Max picked it up, feeling a small tremor of fear as he did so. Since the accident, and Sandy's instantaneous death, he had been well aware of the fragility of human life. On some level he was always braced for disaster, and knew it could come from any direction. Even a simple telephone message could sometimes shake him up.

"Dr. Kwo called," one of the clerks in the high school's reception office had written in a neat, loopy hand. "Don't forget your appointment."

Max realized that he *had* forgotten, probably because he'd been thinking about Kristina all day. He glanced at his watch and considered foregoing the visit to his chiropractor because he still had to pick the girls up and get them ready to go out again. Then he thought of the pain he might suffer in his neck and shoulders—residual effects of the wreck, after which he had spent more than a month in the hospital—and rummaged for the telephone.

Fortunately his mother, who was in her third year of law school at the University of Washington, happened to be at home. She agreed to collect Bree and Eliette, take them to Max's place, and wait with them until he arrived.

He thanked her with genuine sincerity—if it hadn't been for his mother and Gweneth and Elaine, Sandy's sister, the transition to single parent would have been even more difficult and wrenching than it was.

When he arrived at his chiropractor's professional building, Stan Kwo was ready for him. They were old friends, having gone to college together, and Max had been visiting Stan's office ever since the accident. Kwo's treatments, which he called adjustments, had enabled Max to recover without an undue dependence on drugs. He had begun with three adjustments per week and was now down to a couple of sessions a month.

"You seem to be doing well," Stan observed, watching Max through the lenses of his wire-rimmed glasses. "The last few years have been rough, but maybe now you are coming out on the other side of your grief?"

Max sighed, remembering the way Bree's inquiry about faxing Santa Claus had broadsided him the night before. "Sometimes I think so," he agreed. "Other times?" He shrugged. "Who knows? Maybe you never get over it completely."

"Maybe not," Stan allowed. "But I see something new in you, old buddy. There's a light in the back of your eyes that hasn't been there since before Sandy died."

Because of Kristina, Max thought, but he wasn't ready to talk about her yet, even with a close friend. Things were still delicate, and he sensed in Kristina a reluctance to let down her guard that was equal to, or even greater than, his own trepidation. "One day at a time, allowing for a step back every once in a while, things get better," he said.

Stan slapped him on the shoulder. "See you again in two weeks. I'll have Doreen call with a reminder. And how about a game of racquetball one of these evenings?"

Max grinned. "Sounds good," he said and took his leave.

Traffic was thick, since it was the height of the rush hour, but Max was in no hurry. He'd called the house on his cell phone as soon as he climbed into the Blazer, and the kids were home, having milk and fruit with their grandmother, Alison Kilcarragh, future attorney.

When Max pulled into the driveway, Bree burst out of the house to hurl herself toward him, her little face bright with joy. He swept her up in his arms and swung her around once, before planting a smacking kiss on her forehead. "Hi, monkey," he said. "How's my girl?"

Bree wrapped her arms around Max's neck and held on tightly. "I'm being *really* good," she said. "Because Santa Claus is coming to this very house!"

Max hoped they weren't going to have a discussion like the one the night before; he wasn't sure he could handle explaining again that Santa couldn't bring Sandy back. "I'd say it's a safe bet that he'll show up," he answered. "But Christmas is still a ways off. Why don't we think about Thanksgiving first? Aren't you painting turkeys or pilgrims at play group?"

They had reached the gaping front door, where Eliette stood, reticent and serious. Max suspected his elder daughter was already wise to the Santa gambit and hoped she wouldn't spill the beans to her little sister. Kids had to give up believing in magic all too soon, he reflected, saddened by the thought. Maybe he'd go to the video store, a week or two after Thanksgiving, and rent a copy of *Miracle on 34th Street.* . . .

"Can we go out for pizza tonight?" Eliette asked as they went inside.

Max ruffled her mop of curly brown hair. "Sorry, sweetnik," he replied. "We're invited to have dinner with a friend of mine."

Eliette wrinkled her freckled nose. "Who?"

Max's mom appeared in the doorway that led to the dining room, chin-length silver hair sleekly cut, clad in a beige wool skirt, a long maroon sweater, and high boots. Her arms were folded and her brown eyes were twinkling.

"Yeah," she said with an inquisitive smile. "Who?"

"Her name is Kristina Holbrook," Max replied, setting Bree down and getting out of his jacket. He met Eliette's piercing gaze. "You met her the other night at the Halloween party. She was dressed as a witch."

"The green lady!" Bree crowed, obviously delighted.

Eliette said nothing, but merely looked thoughtful. She was a very bright kid, and damnably perceptive at times. Max suspected there was a wicked-stepmother scenario going on in that little head.

"I take it she's only green when she's dressed as a witch?" Alison inquired of her son, putting an arm around Eliette and holding the child close against her side for a moment. Perception ran in the family, at least on the female side.

Max gave his mother a look in reply and rubbed the back of his neck with one hand. Again he wished he'd hired a sitter, or arranged for the girls to spend the evening with Gweneth or Elaine. Alison had class that night, had probably brought her textbooks along, so that she could go straight to school.

"I don't want to go," Eliette announced. "To dinner, I mean."

Here was a convenient out, but Max's instincts told him not to take it. In his experience, things that seemed easy in the beginning often turned into major snags later on. He stifled Bree's rising protest by laying a gentle hand on top of her head and addressed the eldest of his daughters.

"Why not?"

"Because my stomach hurts."

Max glanced at Alison, but her expression said, *You're on your own with this one.*

"Is that really true," he began, "or are you just trying to get out of going to dinner at Ms. Holbrook's place?"

Eliette lowered her gaze for a moment. She was an honest child, and Max could usually get to the bottom of whatever happened to be bugging her by simply asking a few direct questions. He sat down on the lower part of the curved stairway and made room beside him for Eliette. Alison took Bree by the hand and led her back toward the kitchen.

"It's really true," Eliette said in a very small voice.

Max put an arm around his daughter. "Are you just nervous, or do you figure you're coming down with something?"

Eliette scooted a little closer to her father and looked up at him with wide, worried eyes. "I don't know," she confessed.

Max gave her a gentle squeeze. "Fair enough," he said. "Ms. Holbrook is a very nice person, you know. There's no need to be afraid of her."

"She's not Mommy," Eliette pointed out.

Another stab of mingled pain and guilt struck Max's heart and splintered into shards. "No," he said gruffly. "Mommy's gone, and there's never going to be anybody just like her."

"Are you going to marry Ms. Holbrook?"

Max frowned. Kristina certainly wasn't the first woman he'd dated, and yet Eliette had never asked that particular question before. "I don't know," he replied presently. "Why?"

"Marcy Hilcrest's dad got married last summer. Now Marcy doesn't get to visit him as much as before, because he's always busy. She says he doesn't love her anymore—that he only cares about his new wife."

"Ah," Max said, understanding at last. "You must be worried that I wouldn't love you and your sister as much if I got married."

Eliette swallowed hard, then nodded.

"That isn't going to happen, sweetheart. Whether I get married or not."

The child smiled tentatively. "Marcy's dad is a jerk," she said.

"Yeah," Max agreed. "I think you're probably right about that. But don't quote me, okay? That would only make Marcy feel worse."

Eliette leaned close and whispered. "I won't tell."

Max kissed her forehead. "I'll give you a dollar," he whispered back, "if you can persuade your sister to take a bath and put on a dress."

Delighted to be a part of the conspiracy, Eliette nodded again and bounced to her feet. "Bree!" she shouted, hurrying into the kitchen.

Both his daughters were upstairs when Alison got into her coat, with Max's help, then gathered her purse, notebook, and books.

"You are a good father, Max Kilcarragh," she declared, pausing beside the kitchen door.

Max thrust a hand through his hair and sighed. "Thanks."

"Gweneth showed me the mirror you gave her," Alison said, grinning as she reached for the doorknob. "It truly is ugly. I think you should know your sister has sworn revenge."

He chuckled. "Has she found anybody to palm the thing off on yet?"

Alison shook her head. "That little rule about the other person having to want the item is getting in her way," she answered. "Have a good evening, Max."

He went to her and kissed her forehead. "Thanks, Mom. For everything."

She patted his cheek. "I think it would be wonderful if you fell in love with the mysterious Green Lady," she said. With that, she left, carrying her books. Max watched through the kitchen window until he saw her get into her silver Volvo and back out of the driveway.

For perhaps the thousandth time that day, Kristina's image took shape in Max's mind. He could hardly wait to see her again.

THE last customer of the day entered the shop at 4:45, just fifteen minutes before closing time. Kristina, anxious to get to the Pike Place Market for fresh pasta, vegetables, and a bouquet of fresh flowers, wished she'd put the *Closed* sign in the window of the front door at 4:30, as she'd been tempted to do.

The woman was well dressed, perhaps forty years old, with graying blond hair and dark, inquisitive eyes. Kristina did not need her magic to guess that the visitor was related to Max; despite the difference in hair color and her diminutive size, the resemblance was marked.

"May I help you?" Kristina asked. Family relationships and resemblances had always fascinated her. As the only child of supernatural parents, she had been lonely for much of her life, even though Maeve and Calder had given her all the love and guidance anyone could want.

"My name is Gweneth Peterson," the woman said, holding out a gloved hand. Her cloth coat was beautifully made, and her general appearance implied an upscale profession, such as medicine, academics, or law. "I'm Max Kilcarragh's sister. I believe he bought that terrible mirror from you?"

Kristina couldn't help smiling a little, though she suspected Ms. Peterson was about to ask for an exchange, if not a refund. "Yes," she said. "He told me you would hate it."

Gweneth laughed. "And of course he was right."

"Perhaps you'd like to choose something else," Kristina offered, gesturing toward her large and varied stock of antiques.

Gweneth sighed, but her eyes were still sparkling. "Alas, that's against the rules. I came here seeking something equally hideous—a present for my dear brother, naturally. What do you have?"

Kristina was amused; Max had this coming, after inflicting that monstrosity of a mirror on his own sister. "Believe it or not, Ms. Peterson, I don't specialize in horrendous merchandise. But if you look around—"

"Please—call me Gwen," she said.

"And I'm Kristina."

Gwen scanned the shop, her attractive features narrowed into a speculative frown. Then, as luck would have it, she zeroed in on the brass-monkey doorstop, the one item in the place that Kristina wouldn't have sold.

"Perfect!" Gwen cried, bending over to hoist the thing from the floor and set it carefully on a table to examine. "It *is* dreadful, isn't it?" she marveled. "What possesses people to make such atrocious things?"

Kristina remembered the vicious young man who had broken into her shop, intending to rob, rape, and perhaps even kill her. "You might be surprised," she replied, hovering. Valerian was something of an alarmist, and he enjoyed pondering the unthinkable, but if he was right in maintaining this thing could come back to life unexpectedly . . .

"I'm afraid the doorstop isn't for sale. I've—I've promised it to another client."

The next time Kristina saw Valerian, she would ask him to dispose of the brass monkey, no questions asked.

Gwen looked disappointed, but took the refusal sportingly. "Do you mean to say there are other people in this world who play the same game Max and I do? Surely no one would actually *want* to own it."

"There's no accounting for taste," Kristina answered, carrying the heavy piece into the back room. Was it her imagination, or did the thing feel slightly warm to the touch? When she returned to the shop, Gwen was still there, pondering a vase with the roller coaster at Coney Island painted on one side. After a moment Max's sister shook her head and turned back to Kristina.

"I can see surpassing that mirror Max bought is going to take some real effort," she said.

Kristina smiled. "I think you're up to the challenge," she said. "Max told me about the moose head you gave him in the last round. How did this contest get started, anyway?"

"It was Max's bright idea," Gwen replied, tugging at her gloves and lifting the collar of her coat against the twilight chill outside. Her smile was genuine, full of happy, hilarious memories. "When he was eleven and I was turning fifteen, he gave me a neon beer sign he'd bought at a flea market as a birthday present. I was about to throw it away—or better yet, break the thing over his head—but Mom and Dad wouldn't let me. They said a gift was a gift, and I had to find someone who wanted it. I did, though it wasn't easy. And after that I prowled the thrift shops and souvenir stores, a woman with a mission. I retaliated at Christmas with a bronze statue of a hula dancer with a clock in her belly. Our little competition became a family tradition."

Once again Kristina felt a whisper of envy, far back in the darkest reaches of her heart. Then she brought herself up short, ashamed. Her own childhood might have been unconventional, to say the least, but she'd been deeply loved, and she'd had everything she needed and most of what she wanted.

She almost confided that she was having dinner with Max and his daughters that night, but in the end she held her tongue. It was fragile, this thing with Max, and she didn't want to jinx it with too many words, too many expectations.

Gwen took a card from her handbag and laid it on the polished counter. "Here's my number," she said. "Please call immediately if you get something in that I might be interested in." She glanced wistfully toward the storeroom. "Or if that misguided soul who bought the monkey doesn't come back for it."

Kristina barely suppressed a shudder as she reached for the card. "That particular client is pretty reliable," she lied. "But I will keep an eye out for something that would suit."

Gwen, according to the card, was a CPA with a highly respected

Seattle firm. She smiled and raised one hand in farewell before leaving the shop.

Kristina glanced at the clock on the shelf behind the cash register— five-fifteen. She still needed to stop at the market, and there was a good chance she would be caught in traffic on her way home. She drew a deep breath and released it slowly, in order to calm herself. It was silly to be so stressed out over a simple dinner.

Hastily she reversed the *Open* sign to say *Closed*, then locked the door. She put the day's cash and checks in her purse, snatched her coat from the peg in the storeroom and almost tripped over the brass monkey as she passed it. Yes, indeed, it was time to get rid of the reprehensible thing once and for all.

She'd speak to Valerian soon.

"YOU'RE not wearing your green makeup," the smaller of Max's daughters remarked, the moment Kristina opened the front door to her guests. The child sounded somewhat disappointed.

Kristina exchanged a grin with Max and stepped back to admit the Kilcarragh family to the warmth of her living room. It was chilly out that night, though the sky was clear, with a few determined stars winking through smog and city lights. Once the door was closed, she stooped to offer her hand, careful to speak as she would to an adult.

"I'm afraid I've run out of green makeup," she confided, as though sharing a secret, noticing that the elder sister was just as interested as the younger one, though not so willing to trust. "I used it all up on Halloween."

"For what it's worth, I think you look terrific, even without the greasepaint," Max offered quietly as Kristina straightened again, tugging self-consciously at the hem of her white angora sweater. Her tailored wool slacks matched perfectly and her only jewelry was a polished sterling medallion on a long chain.

"Thanks," she said and blushed. It was such a small compliment, and yet she felt as moved as if Max had knelt at her feet, like a knight pledging fealty to his queen. "Is everybody hungry?"

The girls nodded shyly, and Max helped them out of their coats. Kristina summoned their names from her memory—the little one was Bree, short for Sabrina, and the eldest was Eliette.

Kristina had set the glass-topped table next to the breakfast bar, instead of the formal one in the dining room. She wanted Max and his children to be comfortable, rather than impressed.

Bree and Eliette were well behaved during the meal, though it was soon apparent that tortellini in pesto sauce was not their favorite dish. Max didn't urge them to eat, but it was all Kristina could do to keep from offering them sugared cereal, pizza, or hamburgers. Whatever it was that kids liked—she hadn't had enough experience with them to know.

Max seemed to sense her concern; at one point, while they were talking about a recent development in local politics, he touched her arm lightly and said, "Relax, Kristina. They won't starve."

The remark took the pressure off; Kristina let out a mental breath and stopped worrying. Max was right; his daughters were well nourished and would no doubt survive one scanty meal.

"May we be excused, please?" Eliette asked, her expression sweet as she took in both Kristina and her father in a single glance.

Max deferred to Kristina with a slight inclination of his head.

"Of course," Kristina said.

"Sit quietly," Max told his daughters with another nod, this time toward the family room sofa. "An in-depth report on any goofing off will be faxed to Santa the minute I get to work tomorrow morning."

Eliette smiled coyly at this threat, but Bree looked impressed.

Kristina and Max finished their meal in peace, chatting cordially, and then cleared the table together. Once Kristina had convinced Max that the dishes could wait until morning, she approached the two little girls, perched side by side on the couch. Eliette was paging through a travel magazine, while Bree peered over her shoulder, her tiny brow furrowed with concentration.

"I have something I'd like to show you," Kristina said.

Both children looked up with interest.

"Is it magic?" Bree asked, brightening.

"Don't be silly," Eliette scolded.

Kristina felt, rather than heard, Max's inward sigh. He didn't say anything, though, but simply waited.

"I think we'll save the magic for another time," Kristina replied. "Follow me, and I'll show you the things I played with when I was your age."

Both Bree and Eliette complied eagerly, and Max trailed behind them. When Kristina glanced back at him once, as they all mounted the rear stairway leading to the second floor, their gazes met and held, and Kristina felt a powerful jolt of emotion.

Upstairs, she opened the door of the atticlike room where she kept the priceless memorabilia of her childhood. There were dozens of dolls, most with painted china heads and elaborate dresses, along with miniature furniture of the finest craftsmanship. One end of the room was dominated by the magnificent dollhouse Valerian had given her for her seventh birthday—it was a close replica of the Palace of Versailles, complete with a Hall of Mirrors and the Queen's sumptuous boudoir. The creation was seven feet wide and over five feet tall, and it dwarfed the intricately made puppet theater resting on the floor beside it.

Bree and Eliette were plainly enchanted, but Kristina felt immediate chagrin. Maybe it was macabre for a grown woman to have a room full of toys, however precious they might be. Suddenly her treasures seemed more like artifacts in a museum or an ancient tomb than the innocent belongings that had brought her so much joy as a little girl.

"Wow," Max said.

"Can we touch something?" Bree cried, almost breathless with excitement.

"Please, Ms. Holbrook?" Eliette added in a soft, awed voice.

"Everything is very sturdy," Kristina said, "specifically made to hold and touch." She sounded a little shaky, to herself at least—she had referred to these things as her own, mentioned playing with them when she was small. How was she going to explain the rather obvious fact that they were priceless antiques?

Max bent to look inside the gigantic dollhouse, with its paintings and marble fireplaces and velvet-draped windows. Bree lifted a porcelain baby doll from its hand-carved cradle and held it as gently as if it were a newborn, while Eliette crouched to examine the puppet theater, her eyes wide and luminous with wonder.

"Where did you get this?" Eliette asked, touching the tiny stage curtain, made of heavy blue velvet and trimmed in shimmering gold fringe.

"It was a gift from my mother. I had the measles and couldn't leave my nur—my room, so she put on puppet shows for me." Kristina didn't add, of course, that Maeve had made the puppets move and speak and dance without touching them.

"Our mommy died," Bree confided, holding the baby doll, in its exquisitely embroidered christening gown and matching bonnet, close against her little chest. "I don't remember her face."

Kristina's throat tightened, and her eyes stung. "I'm—I'm sorry," she managed to say.

Max, standing just behind her, laid a gentle hand on her shoulder.

"All you have to do to see Mommy's face is look at her picture, silly," Eliette taunted, still concentrating on her examination of the puppet theater, but the words were spoken with affection, not rancor.

"Is your mommy still alive?" Bree asked, standing very close to Kristina now, and gazing up into her face. She continued to cradle the doll.

If the situation hadn't been so touching, Kristina might have smiled at the singular irony of that question. *Alive* was probably not the precise word to describe the reigning Queen of the Vampires, but it was close enough, she supposed.

"Yes," she said simply.

"This stuff is really old," Eliette commented. There was nothing critical in her tone; she was merely making an observation. A very astute one, for such a small child. "You couldn't get these things at Toys "Я" Us."

Both Kristina and Max laughed at that, and Kristina's tension eased significantly.

"Some people like old things better than new ones," Max told his daughter a moment later. "And I think it's time you ya-hoos were home in bed." Both girls joined him in comical chorus to finish the statement with, "Tomorrow is a school day, after all."

Kristina laughed again, wondering why she was so dangerously close to tears. It had been a wonderful evening, even if it was ending too quickly. For this little while, she'd felt part of a normal mortal family, and the sensation was sweet and warm.

"I've raised a couple of smart alecks," Max confided out of the corner of his mouth, to the enormous delight of his daughters.

Kristina led the way back downstairs, blinking hard and sniffling once or twice, so Max wouldn't guess what a sentimental fool she was. "I'm sorry to see you leave so soon," she said in the entryway, while Max helped Bree into her coat. Eliette would have scorned assistance with such a task, Kristina thought—she was trying very hard to be a big girl.

"We had a great time," Max said, straightening, towering over Kristina now and looking straight down into her eyes. "I'd like to see you again—without the entourage."

"He means us," Eliette said.

Max rolled his eyes, and Kristina found herself laughing yet again. She couldn't remember the last time she'd felt such a range of emotions in such a short interval.

Bree tugged at her dad's leather jacket. "I want Santa to bring me a doll like that one upstairs," she crowed. "*Exactly* like it!"

"Oh, great," Max murmured, but his eyes hadn't strayed from Kristina's face. There was something so strong in his expression, and yet so tender. What manner of man was this, managing two small girls with such love and skill? Kristina had been married to a mortal, and had dated any number of others, over a very long period of time, but Max Kilcarragh was different from them all. Evidently he was so confident of his masculinity that he didn't need to assert it at every turn.

Charming, Kristina reflected, more intrigued than ever.

Max caught her by surprise when he bent his head and brushed her lips lightly with his own. The girls, already out the door and headed for Max's Blazer, which was parked at the curb, were engaged in a lively conversation of their own.

"Thank you," he said in a low voice. "May I call you?"

Kristina wondered if there were stars in her eyes. "If you don't," she said, "I'll call you."

He grinned and turned away to follow Bree and Eliette, who were arguing by that time over who got to sit in the front seat.

"The answer is: nobody but me," Max told them in a game-show host's exuberant tone of voice.

Kristina watched, smiling, until he'd settled both children in the backseat and made sure their seat belts were fastened. Then, after a wave to her, Max got into the Blazer and drove away.

Suddenly the big house echoed around her, full of nothing. At that moment, as she closed the door, Kristina would have given all her possessions and the fortune she'd accrued over the decades for a family of her own.

She allowed herself to dream as she winked off the lights.

Oh, to be getting children off to bed, reading them a story, making sure they'd brushed their teeth and washed their faces and said their prayers. And once they were asleep, to talk quietly with a man like Max, to share the events of the day with him, to be held in his arms . . .

"Stop it," Kristina whispered brokenly, standing there in the darkness, alone, just as she would always be alone. There was no place for her in the flesh-and-blood world of mortals, nor in the realm of supernatural beings, for she was neither one nor the other. Forgetting that fact would not only be rash, but also dangerous.

6

THE nightmare was upon Max, like some monster lying in wait, the moment he drifted off to sleep. He knew he was not awake, and yet the dream was excruciatingly vivid, in color and dimension and sound. He struggled to escape its hold, to rise to the surface of consciousness, but he was trapped, entangled, like a diver flailing in seaweed. . . .

He was riding in the passenger seat of the late-model van he and Sandy had just bought, to accommodate their growing family. It was a Saturday in mid-December, around seven o'clock in the evening. They'd spent the day shopping at one of the area's major malls, and the rear of the vehicle was jammed with Christmas presents, mostly toys and clothes for Bree and Eliette, who were with Sandy's parents for the weekend.

Max and Sandy were tired, triumphant, and very, very happy. They were fortunate people; they knew that and were grateful. They had each other, their children, their career plans and personal goals, their home. And in six months Sandy was going to have another baby.

Max was hoping for a boy.

They'd had dinner at their favorite Mexican restaurant after braving the crowded stores, and Max, feeling unusually festive, had consumed two sizable margueritas along with a plate of enchiladas. After the meal, they'd discussed stopping off to see a movie, but in the end they'd decided to spend a romantic evening at home instead.

Although Max did not feel drunk, he and Sandy had agreed that it would be best if she drove home, and she had gotten behind the wheel. He recalled that she'd adjusted the seat and the mirrors before carefully fastening her seat belt.

That was Sandy—responsible, conscientious, competent. The best of wives, the most devoted of mothers, somebody who took being a good citizen very seriously. Although she'd taken a few years off from her own career as an elementary school teacher, she made a point of keeping up with every new development in the field of education. When the time came to go back to work, she would be ready. Max had not only loved Sandy, he'd admired her, too.

Again he tried to wake up, to break out of the dream. Again he was unsuccessful. Sandy was about to die, and there was nothing he could do to prevent it. No way to warn her, or even to say good-bye.

He was caught inside his smiling, dreaming self. He tried to memorize the look of her—slender, tall, with laughing eyes and curly light brown hair—the clean, fresh-air scent of her, the sweet sound of her voice.

They left the restaurant parking lot, cruised along city streets, pulled onto the freeway. Traffic was fairly heavy and moving at a moderate pace as a consequence.

She winked at him and checked the rearview before signaling and changing lanes. There was no rain, no thick fog, no ice on the pavement.

It should have been perfectly safe.

Should have been.

Waking and sleeping, Max wanted to weep at the serenity he saw in Sandy's face in those final moments of her life, of their life together. She looked so happy, so trusting. She had no reason to think the future was about to be canceled.

The semi-truck, loaded with Christmas trees, roared up beside them, appearing suddenly, then pulled out to pass. In the next instant there was a terrible metallic screech, the only warning they had, followed by a fleeting interval, surely only seconds long, of what seemed like suspended animation. That pulsing void was shattered by a thunderous crash, a bone-jarring impact, a spinning sensation so violent that Max did not have the breath to cry out.

And then, darkness. Pain, fierce and heavy.

Voices—horrified, reassuring. Disembodied.

Sandy.

The grief and terror gave Max the impetus he needed; he lunged upward out of the nightmare, breathing hard, his flesh chilled beneath a cold sweat. Groping for the switch, he turned on the bedside lamp and lay gasping in its thin light for several moments, waiting for the shock to subside. Finally, when he was no longer trembling, when he had freed himself from the last tentacles of the dream, he got up, reached for his robe, and pulled it on.

He hadn't had that particular nightmare in months, but its return wasn't exactly a surprise, he thought as he descended the rear stairs leading to the kitchen. Max didn't need a shrink to explain the situation—he was deeply attracted to Kristina Holbrook, and he had some conflicts about it.

He flipped on the light over the sink, poured himself a glass of milk, and leaned against the counter. He still felt the chill of the dream, and there was a lingering ache in the pit of his stomach. His strongest instinct was to push the memories out of his mind, but he made himself walk through them instead.

Max had awakened in the Intensive Care Unit of a Seattle hospital some four days after the crash. His parents had been there when he opened his eyes, his mother on one side of his bed, his father on the other. And the sorrow he'd seen in their faces had been far worse than the relentless pain in his body.

He'd known before either of them spoke that Sandy was gone. His dad had wept unashamedly as he related the grim facts of the accident. Sandy had died instantly.

Max had spent what seemed like an eternity in the hospital, staring up at the ceiling, enduring, undergoing constant physical therapy. He'd missed Sandy's funeral, and Christmas, and when he was finally able to go home, he needed crutches to walk. It would have been easier to go under, body and soul, in those dark days and even darker nights, if it hadn't been for his daughters. Eliette, only five but formidably bright, had been bewildered and hollow-eyed. Bree was just a baby then, barely two, and she'd cried for Sandy at night, and searched every room and closet of the condo by day, as though hoping this was only a game. She clearly expected her mother to pop out of some hiding place and say "Boo!", the way she'd done when they played.

Max had done his share of weeping, though always in private, so that the children wouldn't see or hear. And it had often seemed to him that Sandy *couldn't* be dead—that she would breeze in one morning or afternoon or evening, saying it had all been a mistake, making everything all right just by being back.

He finished the milk and set the glass in the sink, but he wasn't really seeing the spacious kitchen around him. Instead he saw himself going through Sandy's things with help from Elaine and Gweneth and his mother, giving some of her possessions away, keeping others for the girls to have when they were older. He'd finally sold the condo, when he knew in his heart, as well as in his reasoning mind, that Sandy was never coming home. It was simply too painful to stay.

Even now, as he remembered, Max's throat tightened, and his eyes burned. If he had problems squaring whatever he felt for Kristina with all he and Sandy had shared, it was his own fault. Had his wife lived, Max was sure they would have grown old together, for their commitment to each other had been the kind that lasts. But Sandy was gone, and he knew that she would want him to find someone else.

"You're not cut out to be alone, Max," he recalled her saying, one winter night when they were newlyweds, snuggled before the cheap fireplace in their first apartment, neither one guessing how brief their time together would be. "You need somebody to love and protect."

Max flipped off the light. There was no question that he'd loved Sandy, but in the end, when it really counted, he hadn't been able to protect her or their unborn child. He climbed the stairs slowly. If he'd been driving the night of the accident, instead of Sandy, maybe she would have survived. He would have gladly died in her place.

Pausing on the threshold of his empty bedroom, Max sighed and shoved a hand through his hair. He'd been over the tragedy a million times, second-guessing fate, tormenting himself with the inevitable regrets—if only he hadn't had drinks with dinner he would have been the one driving. If only they'd lingered in the restaurant for even another five minutes, or gone to the movies instead of heading straight home.

If only, if only, if only.

As Max climbed back into bed and stretched to turn off the lamp, however, he found himself thinking about Kristina again, and wondered if he was ready for all the things she made him feel.

AFTER Max and the children had gone, the house seemed emptier than ever. Kristina, though fond of her elegant home, suddenly felt a need to leave it, at least for a little while.

She focused her thoughts on her parents' London residence, the stately mansion where she had passed much of her childhood, and arrived there in the blink of an eye. It was around five A.M. in England, and dawn was not far off.

Her mother might still be hunting, Kristina knew, but her father would have fed early, in order to spend as much time as possible in his lab.

Having assembled herself in the kitchen, still empty at that early hour, Kristina reverted to human habits, went to the cellar door and descended the steep stone steps. There was grillwork on the windows, which were just above ground level, and the area was in no way spooky, as a more fanciful soul might expect. No cobwebs, no coffins, no candelabras or ghostly shrouded furniture.

"Papa?" Kristina rapped at the door of Calder's lab as she called to him. Only her mother and possibly Valerian would have dared to enter unannounced.

The heavy panel swung open on well-oiled hinges, and Dr. Holbrook stood in the opening, wearing a lab coat, his dark hair rumpled. He was plainly surprised to see her, which in turn surprised Kristina, for vampires are perceptive creatures, rarely caught off guard.

"Hello, sweetheart," Calder said, a glorious smile dawning in his handsome face as he took her hand and drew her into his inner sanctum. He kissed her forehead. "What are you doing here?"

"I couldn't sleep," she said.

Calder glanced at his watch, hastily drawn from his vest pocket, and frowned. In truth, he did not need such a mechanism to discern the time for, as a blood-drinker, he was always intuitively aware of approaching daylight. Dr. Holbrook still practiced many small, mortal rituals, though whether out of habit or preference Kristina didn't know. "What I wouldn't give for the luxury of insomnia," he said, and his serious expression was replaced in an instant by a wry grin. "I could accomplish so much."

Kristina raised herself on tiptoe to kiss her father's cheek. He had not aged, since becoming a vampire in his mid-thirties, and thus did not look much older than his daughter. "You work so hard," she chided gently. "Why can't you be self-indulgent, like Valerian? Or adventurous, like Mother?"

Calder chuckled and shook his head. There was no love lost between her father and the vampire she thought of as an uncle, although he had been the one to transform Calder to an immortal more than a century before. "Heaven forbid," he said, "that I should be anything like Valerian, beguiling monster that he is. As for adventure—I get all I need just living with Maeve Tremayne."

Kristina saw that Calder was growing wearier by the moment as morning drew near; he spoke slowly and seemed unusually distracted. She smiled. "You need to rest now," she said, "so I won't keep you from your bed. It's all right, isn't it, if I spend some time here?"

He squeezed her shoulders lightly. "Of course it is—this is your home." Discreetly he guided her toward the door of the lab. "Perhaps you'll still be here at sunset, and we can talk further."

Eased out of her father's private domain, Kristina waggled her fingers in temporary farewell. "Sleep tight, Papa," she said and took herself back up the stairs to the kitchen.

Mrs. Fullywub, the housekeeper, was there, standing in front of the open door of the refrigerator. She was clad in a yellow chenille robe, and her gray hair was tied up in the old-fashioned way, with many little strips of cloth.

"Mercy, child," she protested, laying one hand to her heart, "you scared me!"

Kristina was fond of the woman; though mortal, Mrs. F. had been with the family for many years, and she knew what was what in that unconventional household. "I would have thought you'd be used to people appearing and disappearing by now," she observed. The refrigerator was still open, and she reached past the housekeeper for a bottle of mineral water. "I use the word *people* loosely, of course."

Mrs. F. took packages of sliced cheese and cold cuts from the shelves and carried them to the counter, where she began making a sandwich. "It's very good to see you again, Miss Holbrook," the old woman said warmly. "I hope I didn't make you feel unwelcome or anything like that."

Sipping her water, Kristina pulled back one of the stools at the breakfast bar and sat. "I could never feel unwelcome here," she replied. "And I'm sorry for startling you."

Mrs. F. rolled her wise, merry eyes. "I'm getting too old for this job," she confessed, still busy with her snack. "A body never knows who—or what—she'll meet in the passage."

Kristina chuckled. "Valerian, perhaps?"

"Oh, him," Mrs. F. muttered, discounting one of the most powerful vampires in existence with a motion of one hand. "He's gentle as a lamb, that one, if you know how to manage him." She paused and shivered. "It's creatures like those dreadful Havermail children—Benecia and Canaan, I believe they're called—that I dread."

Kristina's amusement faded; she felt a flicker of alarm. Benecia and Canaan were hardly children, as each had lived more than five centuries as a vampire. "They've been here?" she asked in surprise.

"Oh, yes," Mrs. F. answered. "Are you hungry, dear? I must be sleep-fogged—it only occurs to me now that you might like something to eat as well."

"No, thank you," Kristina said automatically. Her mind was still on the Havermails—two ghouls all the more hideous for their appearance. They looked like little girls, exquisitely beautiful ones at that, because they had been transformed as children. "When were Benecia and Canaan in this house?"

Mrs. F. trundled across the kitchen and took a seat at the table, a few feet from where Kristina sat, her sandwich on a china plate before her. "Just the other night, dear," she answered after pausing to make mental calculations. "Don't you worry, though—they came in response to a summons from your mother. I doubt they'd dare to show their awful little faces under this roof unless Maeve invited them, though I admit it gave me a turn to stumble across them the way I did."

Kristina was not reassured. Benecia and Canaan might be afraid of Maeve, the acknowledged queen of all blood-drinkers, but they probably wouldn't fear a half-mortal like herself. Suppose their deadly attention was drawn to Max and Bree and Eliette through Kristina? Just the thought of that made her raise one hand to her mouth in a mute expression of horror.

"Oh, dear," Mrs. F. fretted, pushing away her food. "You mustn't be frightened, Kristina—horrid as they are, those creatures wouldn't have the gall to trouble you. They know your mother would finish them if they did, and she'd have to get to the little demons before Valerian found them, at that."

Kristina swallowed hard, her eyes burning with hot, sudden tears. "If only it were that simple," she murmured. She wanted desperately to speak to Maeve, but by now the sun had risen, and her mother would be sleeping, probably side by side with Calder in the special vault beneath the house. "It's not myself I fear for, Mrs. F. There are—there are mortals I've come to care about. And by that caring, I've made them vulnerable."

Mrs. F. rose and went to stand beside Kristina, patting her hand once with cool, aged fingers. "Here, now. Human beings are *born* vulnerable. Yes, your love may endanger these special mortals of yours, but you are also in a unique position to protect them. You must not forget your own powers."

"I've sublimated my magic," Kristina confessed, still near tears. "All this time I've wanted so much to be fully human—I've pretended—"

"Then you must become strong again. You must be what you are, Kristina, and stop resisting your own nature."

Kristina nodded. "Yes," she said after a long, reflective silence. "You're right, Mrs. F. It's time I explored my powers, found out what I can and cannot do."

"Your mother will help," the housekeeper agreed gently. "And I have no doubt that Valerian could advise you in the matter, too."

Valerian. It was eight hours earlier in the western United States. He would still be awake, if he had not gone abroad to hunt.

Yes, Valerian was definitely the vampire of the hour. Kristina stood, stepped back from Mrs. F. and the breakfast bar, smiled, and gave the old woman a nod of farewell.

Her thoughts took her not to Seattle, as she had expected, or even to Las Vegas, where Valerian still mystified the masses with his magic act four times per week, at the Venetian Hotel. Instead she found herself on a moonlit street, in a tropical clime. The paving stones were broken and uneven, the houses squalid and close together. The stench of raw sewage mingled with that of ripe garbage, and Kristina wrinkled her nose.

There was no sign of the vampire, no sign of anyone, though she sensed the slumbering residents of the hovels crowding both sides of the narrow street. She heard rats rummaging in the mountains of refuse crammed into every alleyway, piled outside every door. Somewhere, a couple made sleepy love; from another direction came the faint mewling of a hungry baby.

What is this place? Kristina asked herself, standing still on the street, waiting, listening to her intuition.

"This is Rio," a familiar voice answered from just behind her. "Great Zeus, Kristina—you *are* rusty."

She turned to see Valerian an arm's length away, looking spectacular and arrogant, as usual. Perhaps for the drama of it—he was impervious, of course, to the smothering heat—he wore one of his many tailored tuxedos and a voluminous cape lined with cobalt blue satin.

"This is a really depressing place to hunt, if that was what you were doing," she said, in a futile effort to deflect his attention from her neglected skills.

"*All* the places where I hunt are depressing," Valerian retorted, looming over her now, his patrician nose nearly touching hers. "Did you think I would go to Disneyland?"

Kristina felt uncomfortable, though she had traveled to virtually every part of the world, sometimes with the aid of a train or airplane, sometimes without. "I don't like it here."

"The answer to that is so obvious I can't bring myself to utter it."

She sighed, then a new thought occurred to her, and she studied the imperious vampire with narrowed eyes. "So help me, Valerian, if you're hunting something besides your dinner—"

He drew himself up, so that he seemed even taller than his already intimidating height, folded his arms and glared. "Have a care, snippet," he said, seething. "To insult me in that manner—or any other—is most imprudent."

"Before Daisy came into your life, you were a notorious rake," Kristina reminded him.

"The key words in that statement," Valerian replied evenly, his tone no less lethal for its softness, "were *before Daisy*. I am here, if you must know, because there is a child—"

Kristina's eyes widened in surprise. "*You've* sired a child?"

Valerian bristled, then smoothed his countenance by means of his will, like a majestic bird settling ruffled feathers into sleek array. "Please," he snapped, thereby dispensing with the possibility, as though his word were universal law.

"Well, you can't just snatch one off the streets," Kristina retorted, growing impatient. "Kids are people, you know, and they have rights."

Valerian arched one eyebrow, which made him look, if possible, even more imposing. Then, a moment later he relented, and Kristina saw sorrow in his magnificent face. He might have been sculpted by Michelangelo, a statue brought to life at the whim of a favored angel, so perfect were his features, his build, his graceful manner. "Thank you for that sermon," he said, but then he took Kristina's hand and drew her along the street, through an alleyway, up a set of crumbling stone steps to a wretched, atticlike room.

The heat was sweltering, the air close and fetid.

On the floor sat a little boy, probably three or four years of age, though it was hard to tell. His clothes were mere rags, he was filthy, and he raised great, luminous brown eyes to the vampire.

"His mother is a prostitute," Valerian said to Kristina, without taking his eyes from the child. "Tonight, in a cantina not far from here, she sold him, her own son, to a procurer who specializes in pretty boys. They'll be coming to fetch him at any moment."

Kristina felt sick. Her own problems were forgotten, at least temporarily. "What are you going to do?"

Valerian did not reply. Instead he dropped to one knee and addressed the boy in rapid, facile Portuguese. The child raised his arms to the vampire, obviously wanting to be held. He spoke to Valerian in the same language, and although Kristina did not speak it, she got the general drift.

Valerian meant to take the boy away, perhaps even home to Daisy in Seattle, to be raised as their son.

As Kristina watched, the magnificent vampire drew the little boy into his arms and rose to his feet.

"His name is Esteban," he said to Kristina as the lad nestled against Valerian's broad shoulder and buried his face in his neck. With a shudder of relief, Esteban gave himself up to sleep.

She was moved by the sight of the monster cradling the frightened child. "Valerian," she whispered, "he's *mortal*. This is very dangerous—"

"Are you implying that I would do him harm—this—this baby?"

"Of course not," Kristina replied, annoyed. The situation had reminded her, however, of her own concern for Max and his daughters, and the singular dangers she might have brought into their lives. "But you have enemies. He could be hurt."

"Would any fate be worse than what awaits him this night, at the hands of his mother?" Valerian affected a sigh, having no breath to fuel a real one. "He will be my son," the vampire added patiently. "The fiend who dares to touch him will suffer a reprisal that would make hell itself seem trivial by comparison."

Kristina had no answer, for she knew that Esteban's world was a place where children such as he could be shot in the streets like vermin.

Despite the perils he might face, even with Valerian to protect him, he would undoubtedly be better off in Seattle.

A woman's laughter sounded from the street outside, shrill and somehow ugly. Instinctively Kristina took a step closer to Valerian and touched the child's matted ebony hair with a tender, protective hand.

Valerian gave Kristina a meaningful glance, covered the sleeping child with his cape, and vanished. She had no choice but to follow on the vampire's coattails.

They popped into the mansion in Seattle simultaneously, and Esteban was still sleeping, undisturbed, when Valerian laid him gently on the plush sofa in the large front room Kristina thought of as a parlor. There was a fire crackling in the grate of the beautiful chiseled marble fireplace, and Barabbas lay on the hearth, his muzzle resting on his paws, his eerie eyes watchful.

There was no sign of Daisy, but it was a vast house, and both Valerian and Kristina knew she was around somewhere.

Kristina felt awkward, but she held her ground. It was important that she speak with Valerian.

"What is it?" the vampire asked without looking at her, covering Esteban's small, thin body with a cashmere afghan as he spoke. "I know you didn't seek me out for nothing."

"I wanted to speak to you because I'm—I'm afraid."

That statement drew Valerian's gaze straight to Kristina's face. "Afraid? Of what?"

"Of Benecia and Canaan Havermail, to name just two of a great many ogres."

He raised an eyebrow in that familiar expression of irritation. "If those soulless chits have threatened you, I shall put stakes through their miserable, atrophied hearts!"

Barabbas rose from his warm resting place on the hearth to pad over to the couch and sniff the little boy's grubby face. Kristina shook her head. "I'm not afraid for myself," she said. "It's Max and his children. Without meaning to, I've made them vulnerable."

"Without meaning to?" Valerian echoed, somewhat skeptically. "Come now, Kristina—you may have let your powers go to an alarming degree, but you are not stupid. You must have known, from the moment you met this man, that he was only a mortal, and thus prey to all manner of fiends, human and otherwise."

Kristina could not refute Valerian's claim. She had been selfish, wanting Max and the girls to be part of her life, however briefly, but she had not admitted unwittingly. "All right!" she snapped, panicked. "I knew! I was lonely—Max is so gentle and kind and intelligent and—"

"Shhh," Valerian said, taking her shoulders in his hands, as her father had done earlier in London. "You needn't justify what you feel, my sweet."

"But what about the dangers? It will be my fault if—"

"It is your task to protect those you love, Kristina. And you have the means to do so—you were born with a great deal of your mother's magic."

Before Kristina could argue that she was no match for ancient vampires like the Havermails, Daisy entered the room, clad in a blue and white flannel nightshirt and fuzzy slippers. Her gaze went straight to Esteban, as though drawn there by a magnet, and Kristina marveled that she had not seen how much her friend wanted a child until now.

"Who is this?" Daisy asked in the softest of voices, kneeling by the couch and smoothing the boy's hair back from his forehead with feather-light fingers. He stirred and made a fearful, whimpering sound, but did not awaken.

Valerian was watching Daisy with a tenderness so poignant that it wrenched Kristina's heart. She knew she could not stay another moment; to do so would be an inexcusable intrusion.

She did not feel like blinking herself back to London, however. She'd done enough traveling for one day, and wanted only to return to her own house.

She used no magic to do so, but simply let herself out and walked the short distance. Once there, she gathered all the letters she'd written to her aged governess over the years, settled herself in the big, cozy chair in the family room, and began to read.

MAX entered the shop at four-twenty the following afternoon, carrying a bouquet of snow-white peonies in one hand.

"For you," he said, laying the perfect flowers in front of Kristina. The glass counter was a barrier between them. He spoke shyly, though there was something in his brown eyes—an invitation, or perhaps a promise—that roused desires in her that she'd thought she'd forgotten how to feel.

Kristina could not resist the peonies. She gathered them up, held them to her nose for a moment, enjoying their scent. "Thank you," she said, and went to fetch a small crystal vase to put them in.

Max followed her into the back room, watched as she filled the vase with water at the sink, then arranged the flowers. They were breathtakingly beautiful, in their simplicity and purity, and Kristina felt another surge of emotion as she admired them.

"I thought all the peonies were gone for the season," she said. The comment was the least of what was in her heart, but all she could manage at the moment.

"My sister has a greenhouse," Max answered, standing in the doorway with his hands braced on either side of the frame. As big as he was, he did not look intimidating, only solid and strong. "I stole them from her."

"Great," Kristina replied with a smile, carrying the vase in both hands as she approached, meaning to go back to the main part of the shop.

Max did not step aside, as she had expected him to do. Instead he took the flowers from her and set them on a shelf next to the door. "Kristina, there's something I need to say," he told her. "The problem is, I'm not sure you want to hear it."

Kristina's heart missed one beat, then careened into the next. She couldn't speak, so she nodded, looking up into Max's eyes.

"I care about you, Kristina," he said quietly, returning her gaze unflinchingly. "I don't know if what I feel is love, or if it will ever turn into that, but it's there, and I can't ignore it, even though I've tried." He paused, as if gathering his courage, and then went on. "I'm a high school football coach and I like what I do, but I'm never going to make a lot of money. I have two kids, one of whom still misses her mother very much. I guess what I need to know is, do I have a chance with you?"

Here was her chance to do the noble thing, to end a potentially disastrous romance with Max Kilcarragh before it got started. Kristina took a step closer, when she knew she should retreat, and put her arms around Max's neck.

"Oh, yes," she answered. "You've got a chance. In fact, I'd say you're a sure thing."

He smiled and bent his head to kiss her, tentatively at first, then in earnest. And all that had slept within Kristina awakened, full of yearning.

7

To Kristina, Max's kiss seemed like a miniature eternity, during which she was born as a new creature, to live, to die, and then to begin the magical cycle all over again. She was breathless when the intimate contact ended at last, and clutched Max's upper arms with both hands to steady herself. Her heart was thundering, as if to escape her chest and take wing, and there was a vibrant quickening in all her nerve endings and pulse points, accompanied by a warm, tightening sensation deep between her pelvic bones.

She had never felt so much before, even in her wildest, most abandoned moments with Michael, and did not know what to make of this new capacity, this new depth of response. If a simple kiss could stir her so profoundly, what would happen when—if—she and Max made love? The thought was both worrisome and alluring, for while Kristina yearned for the sort of soul fusion she knew Daisy and Valerian shared, she was also afraid of baring not just her body, but her very being, to another person.

Max sighed, his brown eyes dancing with mischief and undisguised pleasure. "Wow," he said, and wrapped his arms loosely around her waist, keeping her close but not crushing her.

Kristina let her forehead rest against his rock-hard shoulder. He was wearing a corduroy sports jacket, and the fabric smelled pleasantly of cologne, misty rain, and man. She was moved, almost overwhelmed, by the realization that Max had found the kiss special, too.

He rested the fingertips of one large but incredibly gentle hand at her nape, sending a tremor through her entire system. "Kristina," he murmured. That was all, just her name, and yet she was stricken with joy, as though some part of herself, long missing, had been restored.

She struggled not to weep from happiness and wonder, and with effort looked up at Max, her eyes shimmering. "Oh, Max," she said softly, "it is dangerous to care for me—I'm not what you think—"

Max cupped her chin firmly in one hand, ran a calloused thumb over her mouth in a way that sent sharp quivers of sensation into every part of her body. He spoke tenderly, but his eyes were dark with passion— Kristina knew that, like her, he wanted very much to make love, then and there.

"What are you, Kristina Holbrook, if not a beautiful, intelligent, fascinating woman?"

She did not want to tell him, could not bear the prospect of his horror, his rejection, but she had already let things go too far. "You'll think I'm mad when I tell you," she said fearfully. She had known Max for such a short time, but already he had a place in her life, and when he left, she would be devastated.

The shop bell tinkled before Max could reply; he looked exasperated and amused at the same time.

"I'll—I'll take care of this customer and then close up," Kristina promised. "We have to talk."

Max didn't reply verbally, but the sparkle in his eyes indicated that he had more than conversation in mind. Clearly he did not expect Kristina's impending confession to be anything too dire.

Still feeling aftershocks from the kiss and at the same time dreading the task that lay ahead, Kristina left Max in the back room and proceeded into the main part of the shop.

She stopped in her tracks when she found the warlock, Dathan, standing next to the counter. He looked quite ordinary, despite his suave good looks, like a lawyer or an accountant or perhaps a professor. He wore a beautifully tailored camel-hair coat over a dark suit, and carried an umbrella and a briefcase. His guileless eyes twinkled as he met Kristina's startled gaze; he knew he had taken her unaware, and he was enjoying that small triumph.

Kristina stifled an impulse to turn him into a piece of bric-a-brac—he would surely resist, and his magic, unlike her own, was state-of-the-art.

"May I help you?" she asked, for Max's benefit rather than Dathan's or her own. With her thoughts, she warned the warlock not to make a scene, unless he wanted yet another eternal enemy. "We were just about to close, but if you have something particular in mind—"

Dathan's gaze slipped past Kristina, went unerringly to the door of the back room. He smiled impishly and had probably known Max was with her even before his badly timed arrival.

"My card," he said, extending one expensively gloved hand. "I was hoping to find a silver snuffbox, like one I'd seen in London. It was inlaid with ground malachite and the interior of conch shells, in the fashion of Italian marble."

Kristina accepted the bit of heavy card stock, frowning. Reading it, she realized that, of course, Dathan had conjured it for the occasion. *I must speak to you in private,* it read. *I will visit you this evening.*

Kristina shook her head. "I'm sorry," she said in the most ordinary tone she could manage. "I don't have anything like that in stock." She had several similar items, but that was beside the point. "I'll get in touch with you if I ever have reason."

She hoped the message was clear. *Don't call me. I'll call you.*

Dathan merely smiled and inclined his head slightly, indicating the card Kristina still held. The print had been changed. *This is serious, Kristina. I will arrive at midnight.*

Kristina let out a long breath in frustration. If Dathan wanted to pop in on her at the witching hour, there wasn't a great deal she could do to prevent him. Here was yet another obstacle between herself and any reasonable life she might have shared with Max or any other mortal man—gregarious warlocks who couldn't take a hint.

"You arrived just at closing time," she said sweetly, ushering Dathan toward the door.

His eyes twinkled merrily. "What a pity," he replied, and went out.

Kristina promptly locked the door behind him—a useless gesture if ever there was one—and glanced once again at the card. *Be there,* it read.

She crumpled the bit of paper and tossed it into the trash, where it dissolved with a chiming sound, like the thinnest crystal.

Show-off, Kristina thought, and made another vow to practice her magic.

Max was sipping herbal tea from a mug as he came out of the storeroom. Just looking at him reawakened all the physical hungers Kristina had felt before when they kissed. Obviously their relationship—if indeed it *was* a relationship—had undergone some subtle but very important change.

The knowledge filled her with a strange mingling of joy and guilt. There was no question that she loved Max Kilcarragh, but it was a selfish love, promising fulfillment and even rapture for Kristina, and terrible danger for Max and his daughters.

She had no choice but to give him up, she knew, and she was swamped with sorrow at the thought. Once he knew the truth, he would no longer want her—in fact, he might well recoil in disgust and horror.

Kristina gazed up at Max with tears of grief welling in her eyes. She could not help thinking of her uncle Aidan, her mother's twin, who had been made a vampire against his will, and so hated what he was that he had undergone a truly torturous process in the hope of becoming human again. He had succeeded, though barely, and made a life for himself with the mortal woman he loved, but he was forever separated from Maeve, from Valerian, from Kristina herself. All memory of his existence as a vampire had been eradicated from his mind for all time.

She thought she understood now, longing for complete union with Max, why Aidan Tremayne had been willing, even eager, to make such a sacrifice.

She took his hand, led him to a corner of the shop and the lovely Victorian settee that was part of a nineteenth-century parlor display. It was a private place; they could not be seen from the shop windows.

When Kristina would have withdrawn her hand from Max's, out of a nervous need to smooth her lightweight woolen skirt, he did not let her go. His patient expression nearly broke her heart.

She drew a deep breath, let it out slowly, and began. "You remember the first time we went out—I started to tell you how I was different—"

Max merely nodded. The shop telephone rang, but neither of them paid any attention; they were, for that brief interval at least, in a world of their own.

Kristina forced herself to go on, dreading the inevitable reaction with her whole soul. Michael, she recalled, had laughed at her when she finally confessed her secret, and accused her of taking too much laudanum.

"I have never been as attracted to another man as I am to you," she said.

"That's good news," Max interjected quietly.

Kristina shook her head. "No. No, it isn't," she replied. "I'm not human, Max—not exactly."

Now he looked worried. It would be a short leap from there to outright abhorrence—or mockery—or, worst of all, pity. His grasp on her hand tightened ever so slightly, and he waited in silence for her to go on.

"It's all too incredible for any sensible person to believe—I know that—but it's very important that I tell you because—because being closely associated with me could be deadly." She paused and closed her eyes for a moment while she gathered her courage. When she looked at Max she saw only compassion in his rugged face, and incredible tenderness. "My father was mortal when I was conceived, but now, like my mother, he's—he's—" Max squeezed her hand again, lending encouragement. "He's a vampire."

Max stared at her; his expression revealed amazement, but no other emotion. No revulsion, no judgment—yet. "A vampire?"

"I know how it sounds," she said miserably, feeling as though she would shatter, fall apart into a thousand irretrievable pieces. "Ridiculous, impossible, even ludicrous. But nevertheless, Max, it's true. I'm a sort of half-breed—I have powers, but I'm not a—I'm not like my parents—"

He let out a long sigh and shoved a hand through his hair. "You're right, Kristina. It's hard to comprehend. I mean, *vampires*?"

"Yes." She waited a beat, struggling to hold on to her composure. "I know that most people don't even believe in such creatures, and in most cases the vampires prefer that. But they are real, Max—as real, maybe more so, than you or I."

Max didn't bolt and run, or jump to his feet and form a protective cross with his index fingers, but he was plainly confounded all the same. He had surely decided that Kristina was deluded, and therefore to be avoided from then on. He was right on one count, anyway.

"My God," he said.

"You don't believe me," Kristina replied with resignation. "You must think I'm insane. Sometimes, Max, I truly wish I were."

Slowly, Max Kilcarragh shook his head. "No," he insisted calmly, still making no effort to flee or even to release Kristina's hand. "No, you're no more insane than I am. Still—"

She was going to have to prove that she was telling the truth; it was, after all, the least she could do under the circumstances. Focusing her attention on a small Dresden figurine, standing on an intricately crocheted doily in the center of the coffee table before them, she raised it several inches off the green marble surface, let it hover in midair for a few moments, then carefully lowered it.

Max frowned and raised his eyes toward the ceiling, clearly looking for a string of fishing line or some other form of trickery. Kristina knew, without invading the privacy of his mind, that he was thinking of Valerian's magic act at the party on Halloween night, no doubt concluding that hers was a family of necromancers.

"Impressive," he said.

"But obviously not enough to convince you," Kristina said with another sigh.

He laced his fingers through hers. "I'm a skeptic," he conceded mildly.

"Brace yourself," she murmured. Then, by mental means alone, she raised Max himself some six inches off the settee.

To say he was surprised would be a supreme understatement, but, to his credit, Max did not flail or cry out as another man might have done. He had to know Kristina would never hurt him—not intentionally, at least.

Gently she lowered him back to the cushioned seat of the small sofa.

He was pale and understandably somewhat ruffled. "I know this is a mundane question, but I have to ask it. How in hell did you do that?"

"By what you would call magic," Kristina answered with great reluctance.

"And what would *you* call it?"

Kristina shrugged slightly. "Actually, such things are natural functions of the human brain. It's just that most mortals haven't evolved the ability to utilize all their faculties."

Max's dark brows came together in a thoughtful frown. "Are you saying that we all have the potential to do things like that?"

She nodded. "Some mortals naturally use more of their mental capacities than others, of course—and can do things that would appear magical to the average person. The Russians, in fact, were making significant strides in opening new frontiers of the mind until their political structure finally collapsed under its own weight."

Max narrowed his eyes. "This is truly fantastic."

"You do believe me, then?" A brief, shining hope lighted Kristina's spirit before logic snuffed it out. "By your association with me, Max," she forced herself to say, "you and your children would be in peril from other supernatural beings. I would of course do everything I possibly could to protect you, but—"

He laid an index finger to her mouth to quiet her. "It isn't your job to protect me, Kristina, or my daughters. I have no idea what I'm dealing with here, but I do know from personal experience that life can be very fragile, and that all human beings are in constant jeopardy. But evil isn't the only force in the world—there is good as well."

Kristina didn't know what to say, so she just sat back against the settee and looked at Max, waiting for him to go on.

"Obviously my first priority is to make sure Eliette and Bree are as safe as possible. We're going to have to take this situation one step at a time and move slowly. But I care about you, Kristina, and I'm not willing to just walk away—it's too late for that."

Kristina's eyes were beginning to smart, but she didn't cry. "Where do we go from here?" she asked, letting her head rest against his shoulder.

He chuckled ruefully. "I guess I don't need to tell you where I'd *like* to go from here," he replied, "but I don't want to scare you off."

She laughed at the amazing irony of that statement, but her heart felt tremulous and very, very fragile, like a bubble of newly blown glass, still shivering and insubstantial. "There is so much I need to explain," she said. "To begin with, there's my age. Then my marriage. And my family."

"I think my brain circuits are overloaded," he said with a grin. "Let's have some dinner in some quiet place and talk about ordinary things, just for a little while. I'm still getting over my first experience with personal levitation."

She watched him, marveling, wondering at her good fortune in encountering such a man.

"I hope you weren't frightened," she said.

"More like baffled," Max admitted. "That was a really weird feeling." He stood and offered his hand to Kristina, helping her up.

They had an early supper in a small, secluded restaurant down the street from Kristina's shop—Bree and Eliette were spending the evening with their aunt Gweneth—and after coffee they drove in separate cars back to Kristina's house.

After starting a cheery fire in the family room fireplace and offering Max a seat at the table, she went upstairs for the stack of letters she'd written to her governess, Miss Phillips, over a span of some fifty years. Reading them would explain more to Max about who—and what—Kristina was than anything she might say.

Noting the date on the initial page of the first letter, and probably the worn, fragile state of the paper, Max looked at Kristina and grinned. "There's a slight age difference between us," he remarked.

"Almost a century," Kristina confirmed. She wasn't smiling.

"This is incredible," Max muttered, and turned his attention back to the letters before him. He read through her meeting with Michael, her marriage, the account of her wedding night, all without flinching. Kristina, for her part, was painfully aware of one particular passage.

> . . . *He was uncommonly gentle as he removed my wedding gown and all the many troublesome garments beneath, each in its turn and its own good time. He caressed me, and whispered pretty words, and though there was some hurt when, at last, he took me as a husband takes a wife, pleasure soon followed. Am I wanton, Phillie? I enjoyed the things Michael did to me in his bed that night—I thrashed upon the mattress. I moaned when he promised that strange, sweet satisfaction I craved without understanding, cried out when at long last he gave it.*

Finally Max reached the incident of the shooting, and Kristina, seated across the table from him, saw those neatly penned words as clearly as if she were reading over Max's shoulder. . . .

> . . . *with the blast of a pistol still thundering in my head, I dressed hastily in a simple chemise, slippers, and a loose gown—I could not trouble myself with corsets and the like—and raced out into the passageway and down the main staircase.*

The great house was abuzz with consternation, for it seemed that all within those thick, august walls had heard the report of gunfire, though it was still so early that the sun had not yet risen. At that hour even the servants would not have arisen, but for that dreadful, singularly ominous noise.

I encountered Gilbert in the entry hall—Lord and Lady Cheltingham, my mother- and father-in-law, were nowhere to be seen. Gilbert wore rough huntsman's clothes, and his brown hair had not been tied back but instead fell loose around his face. I glimpsed pity in his eyes when he spared me a glance, and despair.

"There has been a duel," I said, grasping one of his arms as though I thought he could somehow undo the morning's tragedy. I knew that was impossible, of course, and I had seen the incident by means of my magic, even before leaving the bedchamber. "Michael is hurt—"

For a moment Gilbert's strong jaw tightened, but his mind was veiled from me, and I could not discern his thoughts. "You must stay here, Kristina," he told me. "It is unseasonably cold this morning and raining. Besides, there may be more trouble."

With that, he turned and hurried out, joined by several rumpled male wedding guests summoned from their beds by the clarion of calamity.

I obeyed my brother-in-law's edict, not because I was daunted by his authority, but because I knew I could be of no real help on that dismal knoll behind the parish church, where two men lay bleeding on the dew-dampened grass. One was dead, having taken a bullet through the heart; the other, my Michael, had been shot in the right knee.

I hurried back upstairs, breathless in my urgency, went straight to the main linen cupboard, and began pulling out Lady Cheltingham's finely stitched sheets with their borders of Irish and Italian lace. When I had torn a sufficient supply of bandages, I carried these back into our bedroom and sent a mewling maid to fetch hot water, a large basin, and a selection of whiskey from the cabinet in Gilbert's study belowstairs.

While she was gone, I stripped the linens from our marriage bed and replaced them. Then I ran back downstairs again and waited fitfully by the stables, heedless of the drizzling rain, for the men to return.

Michael was astride his own horse when they arrived, drenched with blood and rain, plainly only half-conscious. After reining in

the great stallion, my husband promptly collapsed and would have
landed in the mud of the stableyard if Gilbert and another man
hadn't been there to catch him. A litter was brought from one of
the sheds, and Michael was placed upon it, out of his head now
and raving.

Concern for my badly injured husband was, of course, my para-
mount emotion, but I did not fail to notice the other man, draped
over the back of a horse led by one of the other guests. I recognized
him with a pang of sorrow—he was the eighteen-year-old cousin,
come all the way from London to celebrate the marriage, with
whom Michael had argued so vociferously on the lawn. His sister,
even younger at fifteen, ran sobbing through the rain in bare feet
and a wrapper, her hair unbound, trailing and sodden, her pretty
face twisted into a mask of unfathomable anguish. She flung herself at the lad's narrow, lifeless back and clung to him, wailing.

Gently one of the men drew her away, lifted her into his arms,
and carried her back toward the house.

I returned my attention to Michael, prostrate on his litter, but I
knew I would never forget what I had just seen. I believe my feelings toward my husband began to change in that very moment,
Phillie, for I had seen the confrontation between the two men, remember; I was well aware that Michael had been the instigator of
these sorrows.

They carried Michael to our room, where Gilbert and I stripped
away his coat and boots, his muddy shirt, and bloodstained
breeches. My new husband was groaning, and though he could not
have left our bed more than an hour before, and the sun was just
then topping the eastern horizon, he reeked of ardent spirits.

"Damn you," Gilbert said to his brother, soaking one of the
cloths I'd torn earlier in the basin the maid had brought, as requested. He sat on the edge of the plump feather mattress and began gingerly to clean the terrible wound to Michael's knee. "You've
killed poor young Justin, and for what cause? In the process, it appears that you've made a cripple of yourself!"

I could not feel anger toward Gilbert, righteous or otherwise.
"Has the doctor been sent for?" I asked stupidly—for of course the
village physician would have been summoned immediately—and
moved to the opposite side of the bed, where I knelt and held Michael's pale, long-fingered hand in both my own. I desperately
wished for my father in those moments, for there was no finer surgeon in all of creation, but daylight had come, and I knew that

Papa would have gone underground to sleep, as all but the oldest vampires do. . . .

Max stopped reading to rub his eyes with the thumb and forefinger of his right hand. Kristina had made a fresh pot of coffee, and she carried two cups to the family room table, once again sitting down across from him. There must have been a thousand questions he wanted to ask; Kristina watched his expressive eyes as he sifted through his thoughts, sorting, trying to assign reasonable priorities.

"What kind of man was your husband?" he asked at last. It would have been unnecessary to ask if she had loved Michael, for it was obvious that she had—just as Max himself had cherished his lost wife, Sandy.

"He was rich and handsome and very spoiled." Privately Kristina compared the two men—Max was attractive, but in a rugged, straightforward and intensely masculine way. Michael had been the boyish type, charming and superficial and selfish.

"I'm surprised you were interested in him," Max said without rancor before taking a sip of his coffee.

Kristina smiled; remorse might come later, but for now she was happy because Max had heard her terrible secret, and he was still around. "I was younger then," she said.

Max laughed. "I'll say," he replied, squinting at her. "But you're very well preserved." Some of his amusement faded. "Will you ever age, Kristina? I mean—and this is hypothetical, of course—if you and I were married, would you get old, as I will?"

"I don't know," Kristina replied, and suddenly she felt like crying again. She sipped some coffee to steady herself. "Vampires, theoretically, that is, are immortal. I don't—er—hunt, or sleep during the day, and I can't travel through time the way my parents and Valerian do—"

Max held up one hand. "One second, please. Valerian is a vampire? That guy who was doing magic tricks for the kids on Halloween night?"

Kristina drew a deep breath and let it out slowly. "Yes," she answered. She thought of Esteban, the urchin Valerian had rescued from the mean streets of Rio only the night before. She would never forget the sight of the illustrious vampire cradling that scared, wretched little boy against his shoulder. "But you needn't worry—he would never harm a child."

"I had already figured that out," Max said. "You're obviously fond of him, and that is as good a character reference as I need. But knowing what Valerian is explains how he pulled off all those fantastic tricks at the party the other night."

"You're in on a world-class secret now," Kristina said, feeling a bit less weary, a bit less ancient. She leaned across the table a little way. "But you must swear not to tell, for your own sake—no one will believe you, and your sanity will be suspect—and because magicians fly in from all over the world to watch Valerian's act in Las Vegas and try to figure out how he manages such fantastic feats. It's all part of his mystique."

Max frowned, looking down at the letters scattered before him in peculiar neatness. "This is all so personal—are you sure you want to share it?"

Except for her feelings for Max, Kristina could not recall the last time she had been so certain of anything. "It's important for you to understand," she said.

He began to read again, taking up where he had left off.

. . . and while I knew a great many pretty tricks, levitation, altering the form of things, making objects and people disappear and then appear again, I was ignorant of the healing arts.

Michael started to come round, once the doctor had arrived and set himself to sorting out that shattered knee. Gilbert, for all his fury with his younger brother, looked as though he would have changed places with him in a moment and borne the pain himself. I know I would gladly have done that, but I wonder if it was generosity that prompted me. Watching a loved one suffer is perhaps the greater agony, making the desire to usurp that pain an act of cowardice, rather than nobility. It was no comfort that Michael had brought this anguish upon himself, that he might even have deserved to bear it, after taking another man's life.

I do not know.

The surgery was dreadful to witness, and yet I could not leave Michael's side. I absorbed each scream, each moan and curse, in my spirit, every one like a violent shock, and when it was over, and he collapsed again, however mercifully, into a near comatose state, I also swooned.

Gilbert, poor, beleaguered, stricken Gilbert, carried me to another room, where I was to be looked after by a maid. I was exhausted by Michael's ordeal, and went immediately to sleep.

But I must leave the tale here for a little while, dear Phillie, for I fear I have run on too long, and my story, while dramatic, is also grim. I do not wish to tire you overmuch, so I shall wait a week or so before I write another letter.

Thank you, beloved friend, for your understanding heart and

gentle comments. You cannot know what comfort your wise letters
have brought me.

Love always, Kristina

Max folded the aged vellum pages carefully, almost reverently, and
tucked them back into the appropriate envelope. Instead of reaching for
another, he looked at Kristina, seeming to see into the farthest corner
of her bruised heart, and she knew he saw her loneliness, her pain, her
doubts. He pushed back his chair a little way.

"Come here," he said gently. "You look like somebody who needs to
be held."

Kristina didn't require a second invitation. She was around the table
and seated on Max's lap, with her arms encircling his neck and her head
resting on his shoulder, almost before her next heartbeat.

Max held her tightly. He smelled good, and felt good, too—hard
and strong and yet incredibly tender. Although Kristina wanted him
powerfully, she appreciated that he did nothing in those moments except
to keep her within the warm circle of his embrace.

"You're too good to be true, Max Kilcarragh," she said against his
neck.

He chuckled. "I wish I could keep you thinking that for the rest of
your life," he replied, his breath a soft caress at her temple as he spoke,
one that set her tingling and roused the legion of needs that had been
slumbering within her. "Unfortunately it won't be long before you find
out the truth. I have a temper. I'm opinionated, especially when it comes
to politics. And somewhere deep inside, I have to admit, I wish women
still wanted to stay home, cook, and raise kids. How's that for a shocking
confession?"

Kristina sat back far enough to look into Max's face, albeit reluctantly. No man had ever held her so lovingly without expecting, even
demanding, something in return, and she loved the intimacy of it. "In
comparison to my being one hundred and thirty years old and having
vampires for parents, you mean?"

Max sighed heavily, but his eyes were still warm, still smiling. "I
don't think I've absorbed that yet," he confessed.

"When you do," Kristina predicted, suddenly sorrowful again, "you'll
never want to see me again. You'll tell me to stay away from you and
your beautiful children."

He brushed her mouth with his. "It's more likely, lovely Kristina,
that you will become bored with me one day."

The sound of clapping and the chiming of the mantel clock in the parlor were simultaneous. It was midnight—where had the evening gone?—and Dathan stood in the kitchen doorway, still applauding.

"An accurate prediction, I'm sure," the warlock said, ignoring Kristina's murderous glare. "What, I pray you, is duller than a mortal?"

8

MAX, always so unflappable, in Kristina's experience at least, tensed at the sight of the warlock and moved without hesitation to confront him. Kristina put out an arm to prevent that. There were any number of ways an immortal could defend himself against a human being, no matter how brave that feckless mortal might be, and most of them were unthinkable. Especially in connection with Max.

Dathan was at his most charming—but with an edge. "Oh, dear," he said with a sly glint in his eyes and a soft exhalation of breath. "Here we have that most foolhardy of all creatures—a *brave* mortal. Perhaps I was too hasty, Mr. Kilcarragh, in declaring you to be dull. Though you would be oh-so-much better off as a dullard than a martyr, it's true."

"Enough," Kristina said firmly, her gaze never leaving Dathan's face. She still had the palm of one hand pressed against Max's chest, as though that would stop him if he decided to pounce.

"Who the hell is this guy?" Max demanded.

Dathan chuckled. "Who indeed?"

Kristina sighed. "Max Kilcarragh," she said, "meet Dathan—warlock among warlocks."

Max seemed to feel a grudging fascination, rather than fear. He narrowed his eyes, studying the splendid beast who stood before him; Dathan's manner was almost as imperious as that of Valerian. "Is that your religious persuasion," Max asked, "or were you born that way?"

Dathan's deceptively soft brown eyes gleamed with delighted amusement. "Religion has nothing to do with it," he replied at some length. "And, yes, I suppose I was born a warlock, but I couldn't say when that momentous event occurred. I've quite forgotten."

"Vampires are made," Kristina explained, looking back at Max over one shoulder. A deep sorrow possessed her; the understanding he had displayed earlier would be short-lived, once he really comprehended the full spectrum of fiends he might encounter, just by association with Kristina. "Created by other vampires, I mean. Warlocks"—she tossed a malevolent glance toward Dathan"—probably *hatch*, like reptiles."

"I'm getting a headache," Max said. He looked as though every muscle in his body was poised for a fight. "Just tell me, Kristina—is this guy welcome here?"

"*Welcome* is hardly the word I would use," Kristina answered, and Dathan pretended to be wounded by her remark. "He's quite harmless, however. Where I'm concerned, at least."

Max looked skeptical, assessing Dathan again with undisguised dislike and suspicion in his eyes. "Are you sure?"

Kristina spoke lightly, her tone, as well as her words, calculated to irritate the arrogant warlock. "Dathan wouldn't dare do me mischief," she said. "If he did, he would have my mother to contend with, not to mention Valerian."

Dathan flushed. "I am not afraid of that—that *stage magician!*" he snapped. He and Valerian were sworn adversaries, actively antagonistic toward each other.

Kristina noticed that he had not raised the same protest in regard to Maeve. As queen of the nightwalkers, she was among the most powerful beings in this dimension and several others. Dathan, while an accomplished necromancer, was no match for the legendary vampire, and he was smart enough to know it.

She linked her arm with Max's. "It would be better if you left," she said. "I'm in no danger, and the sooner I hear Dathan out, the sooner he will leave me alone."

The warlock adjusted his diamond cufflinks, somewhat huffily, but offered no comment.

"You're sure?" Max asked, looking deeply into Kristina's eyes.

She nodded and stood on tiptoe to kiss him lightly on the mouth. "We'll talk tomorrow," she said.

"Count on it," Max replied. Then, with the utmost reluctance, he collected his coat from the back of one of the chairs at the table in the family room, gave Dathan a long, unfriendly once-over, and left.

"The nerve," Dathan complained when Max was gone.

"Go near him," Kristina answered evenly, "ruffle one hair on his head, bother him in any way, and I promise you, Dathan, I will find a way to destroy you if it takes my share of eternity. Do not take my warning lightly, thinking my magic small, either, for I have not begun to explore the extent of my powers."

"A stirring speech," Dathan said, removing his cloak with a graceful gesture. "Though, alas, all for naught. You have nothing to fear from me, Kristina—I shall not trouble your mortal."

"Then what do you want?"

"You touched upon the purpose of my visit yourself, just a moment ago. Your magic is rusty, and woe betide you, my dear, if you find yourself in need of it, without your mother, myself, or a certain ill-tempered vampire within rescuing distance. I have appointed myself your tutor."

The idea was not without merit, though Kristina would have dearly loved to hurl the suggestion right back in his face. The nearly unpalatable truth was that she desperately needed to polish her skills. "What's in this for you?" she asked warily. "And don't say you're willing to offer your time out of simple generosity. You're not the charitable type, and we both know it."

Dathan released a long sigh. Unlike Valerian's sighs, which were always feigned, for vampires do not breathe, Dathan's was quite genuine. Warlocks, unlike their blood-drinking counterparts, had beating hearts and functioning lungs, among other humanlike appurtenances.

"I wish to find a mate," he said.

Kristina recalled that Dathan had once made some unholy bargain with Valerian, to that end. The warlock did not wish a union with another witch, or even a mortal; he sought a vampire. Part of the antipathy between the two was based in the indisputable fact that Valerian had tricked Dathan.

She felt herself softening a little toward the warlock, for she certainly understood what it was to be lonely, to yearn for love. "I don't know how you think I can help," she said, after mulling Dathan's announcement over for a few more moments. "It may have escaped your notice, but I don't exactly have a wide circle of friends—or even acquaintances—in the world of nightwalkers. And I'd prefer to keep it that way."

"You are your mother's daughter," Dathan insisted with a quiet earnestness Kristina did not think was a pretense. "As such, there are doors open to you that would be closed to me."

Kristina turned away, went to the table where she and Max had been reading the letters she had written so long before about her marriage to Michael Bradford, and began gathering them together. She felt a need to be busy.

"Why don't you take a witch for a mate?"

"Witches are notoriously independent," Dathan answered in a

vaguely defensive tone. "They tend to regard intimate relationships as bothersome."

Kristina barely suppressed an urge to roll her eyes. She was not without sympathy—toward the viewpoint of the female of the species, that is. If Dathan was a representation of the average warlock, they could be obnoxious creatures.

But then, so could vampires. And men.

"What can you teach me?" she asked.

"Virtually everything, with the probable exception of time travel. That is quite tricky—requiring either a great age or a conversion from mortal to blood-drinker, as in the case of your parents, for example."

Kristina raised one eyebrow slightly and indulged in a crooked smile. "I'm a hundred and thirty," she said. "Isn't that a great age?"

"Not in this crowd," Dathan replied, folding his arms. His cloak lay over the back of the family room couch in a familiar way, as though he'd tossed it there a thousand times. Which, of course, he hadn't. "Put an end to my suspense, Kristina. Do we have an agreement or not?"

"With reservations," she answered, standing still now, the gathered letters in her hands, watching him. "I run an antiques shop, not a preternatural dating service. I'll do my best to help you out, but I can't promise miracles."

Dathan snatched up his cloak in a practiced motion of one hand. "I hardly think it should be that difficult," he said. "I am not, after all, ugly or otherwise objectionable."

"You are definitely not ugly," Kristina agreed, sensing that, at least temporarily, she had the upper hand. "Whether or not you could be described as objectionable is certainly open to debate. But if finding a mate were not difficult, you would have done it yourself by now, wouldn't you?"

The warlock donned the cape in a theatrical swirling motion reminiscent of Valerian, although Kristina judiciously refrained from pointing out the similarity. "As you know," he said coolly, "vampires and warlocks do not commonly interact."

"Perhaps because the blood of warlocks is poisonous to nightwalkers, and so many have been tricked into partaking," Kristina commented. "Why are you set on attaining this? Vampires are among your oldest and most ardent enemies."

"It does not have to be so," Dathan replied with faint umbrage rather than acquiescence. "Between us we could create a new race of beings." There was a hint of the crusader in the warlock's bearing, putting Kristina in mind of her father, who spent practically every spare moment in his laboratory, searching for a way to enhance the positive side of vampirism while eliminating the negative aspects.

"I'm not sure I want to participate," Kristina said.

"Consider my proposition well," Dathan advised. "I will return for your answer tomorrow."

Kristina inclined her head in silent agreement, and Dathan vanished within the instant.

She went slowly up the stairs, carrying the letters, tucking all but one away in the drawer of the night table beside her bed. She wanted very much to consult with her mother, but it was eight hours later in London, which meant that Maeve had taken refuge in her lair.

Leaving the letter that took up where the account of the duel, Michael's terrible injuries, and poor Justin's death, had left off, Kristina went into her bathroom to indulge in a long, soothing shower.

The flow of warm water calmed her, helped her to think more clearly. She faced a paradox in considering Dathan's bargain; on the one hand, she would be better able to protect Max and his children, not to mention herself, if she took instruction from the warlock. On the other hand, that same crucial training would inevitably lead her deeper into the very world she found so threatening and so abhorrent.

She might have asked her mother for help, of course, or even Valerian, but Kristina had lived thirteen decades, not thirteen years. She had loved and lost, she had traveled the world, she had built a highly respected and lucrative business. Always, always, Kristina had steered her own ship, albeit with more success at some times than others. Now she found that she did not relish the prospect of asking either vampire to lead her through the elementary steps of magic like a preadolescent stumbling through a lesson in ballroom dance.

As she stepped out of the shower, toweled her body and her hair dry, Kristina allowed herself the indulgence of thinking about Max again. He could not have guessed what it meant to her, his readiness to believe in her, to share her memories by reading the letters. While he had certainly been shocked by her revelations—who wouldn't be?—he had also gone to remarkable lengths to understand. Even more important, he hadn't shown disgust, or any sort of judgment.

Nothing had really rattled Max, she reflected, until Dathan had materialized. At that point, Max had been ready to protect her, a noble if highly imprudent act.

While the memory definitely troubled her—the range of horrible things Dathan might have done in response was almost unlimited— Kristina couldn't help feeling a little pleased by Max's gallantry. She did not recall another instance, in all her adult life, when she'd been the object of such reckless chivalry.

She pulled on her white terry-cloth robe and ran a comb through her cap of sleek, dark hair, which was already drying nicely. She was smiling as she went through her bedroom and into the hallway, intending to brew a cup of herbal tea.

Her amusement faded as she passed the room where she had taken Max and Bree and Eliette, to show them the toys from her childhood. She heard two chilling, little-girl voices through the door.

Kristina froze in the hall, almost too startled to think, let alone act. Then, summoning all her paltry powers, she reached for the knob.

The lock clicked before her hand closed on the brass handle and the heavy wooden panel swung silently open. An eerie wash of moonlight lit the otherwise darkened room, but Kristina could see only too clearly.

She stood on the threshold, torn between fury and terror, unable, for the moment, even to speak.

Benecia Havermail, demon-child, all blond, blue-eyed perfection, with her ringlets and ruffled dress, was perched on the cushioned window seat, holding the very baby doll Bree had so favored during her visit. She smiled, showing tiny, perfect white teeth. Teeth capable of tearing the throat out of a rhinoceros.

"Hello, Kristina," she chimed.

Canaan, the younger of the two monsters, was dark-haired and smaller than her sister, though just as exquisitely beautiful. And just as deadly. She was seated cross-legged on the floor, in front of the toy theater, while the puppets whirled in a ludicrous, drunken dance. This, like Benecia's attentions to the baby doll, was a subtle but effective parody of the Kilcarragh children's visit, for Eliette had been fascinated by the little stage, with its colorful, inanimate players.

"What are you doing here?" Kristina managed to croak. She knew it was unwise to show fear—and fear wasn't precisely what she felt—but hiding her emotions from these two ancient blood-drinkers was more than she could manage at the moment. "How dare you?"

Benecia smiled sweetly, but did not stir herself from the window seat. She might have been a mannequin, a model of Alice in Wonderland come to life, Kristina thought with an involuntary shiver. So flawless were her features. "You mustn't be rude," Benecia scolded in that musical voice. She glanced toward the array of priceless porcelain dolls Kristina had collected, displayed in a cabinet on one wall, behind glass doors.

Silently the doors opened. The dolls climbed daintily down from their shelves, murmuring among themselves.

"Stop it!" Kristina gasped.

The treasured dolls joined hands and made a circle, going round and round in a stiff-jointed caricature of some schoolyard game. Their voices were a singsong, chantlike sound that made the hairs on Kristina's nape stand upright.

"Stop!" she said again. "Now!"

Canaan only laughed, but Benecia gave a somewhat petulant sigh, and, at some mental command from her, the dolls returned to their cases, closing the doors behind them, striking their familiar poses. Their small voices, however, seemed to echo in the room for a long time.

"We didn't mean to frighten you," Benecia said.

"The hell you didn't," Kristina shot back. "I want you out of my house—now. And don't ever come back!"

"What will you do—complain to Valerian? Or to your mother? Or perhaps to your father, the mad scientist?"

Kristina ignored the jibe at Calder Holbrook's fascination with mysterious experiments, but she was incensed by the idea that she needed Valerian or Maeve to protect her. Even though that was, in essence, the truth of the matter. "Valerian is just looking for an excuse to drive a stake through your rotten little hearts, and as for my mother—"

Canaan got to her feet. "Valerian won't have time for you now that he has Daisy, and that filthy, awful little street urchin he's brought home from Brazil," she said. "And Maeve happens to be quite busy, if you haven't noticed. There is another political problem, you see, between vampires and angels, and Her Majesty"—she gave these last two words a note of mockery—"spends every waking moment trying to resolve it."

Kristina felt a stab of guilt, as well as trepidation. Relations between the realms of darkness and light were always dubious, of course, but a conflagration, if serious enough, might well bring on the cataclysm mortals referred to as Armageddon. Kristina had not even suspected that her mother was facing another such crisis. "Why did you come here?" she asked. If she could not keep the panic out of her psyche, perhaps she could at least sound normal. "What do you want?"

As usual, Benecia, being the eldest, was the spokesperson for the dreadful duo. "We have heard that the warlock, Dathan, desires a vampire wife."

Kristina's stomach rolled. Surely even such fiends, such ghouls as these two, would not, *could* not, suggest . . .

"I should like to offer myself," Benecia said.

Kristina barely kept her dinner down. "You have the body of a child," she pointed out in what she hoped was an even, reasonable tone.

"I am nearly as old as Valerian," argued the ancient woman imprisoned forever in the size and form of a little girl.

"No," Kristina said, retreating a step.

"Do you know what it is like, Kristina?" Benecia demanded bitterly, advancing with a delicate tread. "Can you even guess what it means to be trapped for all of time? If I had been left alone, I would have grown to womanhood, married, lived, and died, and then been born again, through a procession of lives. Instead I must spend eternity just as I am!"

Kristina stopped retreating; this was her house, damn it. But before she could say anything, Canaan entered the conversation, addressing her sister. It was well known among immortals and their consorts that the two, though invariably together, were not always in accord.

"Do stop being so dramatic about it, Benecia," Canaan said without a trace of tenderness or sympathy. "It's not as though you were made a vampire against your will, like poor Aidan Tremayne. You begged Papa until he changed you, and you knew full well what you were doing!"

Kristina stood her ground, frantically trying to figure out a way to use the sisters' antipathy toward each other in order to defend herself. "I have no desire to listen to an account of the Havermail family history," she said with bravado. "You will both leave this house immediately and stay away."

Benecia and Canaan looked at each other and laughed. The sound was like crystal chimes, dancing in a soft breeze, and it raised a cold sweat on Kristina's skin.

"If you don't do as I say," Benecia said sweetly, patiently, as though explaining something elemental to a slavering idiot, "Canaan and I shall simply have to strike up a friendship with—what were their names again?—oh, yes. Bree and Eliette. I'm sure we could convince them we were angels—mortals are such gullible creatures, and we've made good use of that trick in the past."

Kristina was outraged. She was also more convinced than ever that she needed to bring her magic skills up to speed ASAP. "Dathan is a warlock," she said when she could trust herself to speak without shrieking in uncontrollable fury, "but he is not a deviate. If I suggested such a vile thing to him, he would be as revolted as I am."

Benecia had evidently fed copiously earlier in the evening, for a blush rose beneath her nearly transparent ivory skin. "I have told you. I am not a child, I am an adult!"

"Then go find someone else whose development was arrested in a similar fashion," Kristina replied. She did not know where she got the audacity, for here was a creature who could burn her to cinders with a mere glance. And that would be one of her more merciful punishments.

"We could transform a small boy," Canaan said thoughtfully.

"Fool," Benecia spat. "I have the mind of a woman. I desire a mature mate, not a child! Besides, the making of vampires is forbidden, by Maeve's order."

Kristina was silent, hoping the argument would escalate, carrying the Havermail sisters away—*far* away—on a swell of indignation or at least sibling rivalry.

"I thought you weren't afraid of Maeve," Canaan taunted.

So far, so good, Kristina thought.

"You know, Canaan, sometimes I wish I'd been an only child."

Unfortunately the phrase *only child* turned their attention back to Kristina. They assessed her with glittering, gemlike eyes.

"I am not going to forget this, Kristina Holbrook," Benecia said. "You have made an enemy by insulting me."

Kristina refrained from saying that she had been an enemy for a very long time. She simply gestured toward the door, tendering a silent invitation to leave.

Benecia and Canaan disappeared in a blink.

Kristina, for her part, gave up all hope of getting a good night's sleep. She dressed in dark jeans and a matching cashmere turtleneck, then added a long, buttonless cardigan in the same ebony color. After only a moment's hesitation, she willed herself to Max's house.

Invisibility, being a fairly simple trick compared to some others, was still part of Kristina's repertoire. The dark clothes were a safeguard, in case she had overestimated her talents.

Her reasons for paying this late-night, uninvited visit were altruistic— she meant to watch over little Eliette and Bree until dawn, when the Havermails would be forced into their lairs by the light of the sun— but she still felt like a trespasser, a sort of inverse Peeping Tom.

Perhaps it was not an accident, on an unconscious level at least, that Kristina first projected herself into Max's room. He lay sprawled across the large bed, sound asleep, his naked athletic body only partially covered by a sheet. She admired him for a long time, hoping his dreams were sweet but suspecting otherwise by his restlessness, and then sought and found the room his daughters shared.

It was a spacious chamber, nearly as large as Max's own quarters, furnished with two canopied beds in the pseudo-French Provençal style so popular with little girls, matching dressers, a desk, and a miniature vanity. On Bree's side of the room was a toy chest, overflowing with vinyl dolls in various states of undress, a scattering of clothes, a coloring book, still open, with crayons in the seam like logs in a flume.

Eliette's territory, on the other hand, was almost painfully neat. The desk and vanity were tidy, and even in sleep the little girl looked as though she were bracing herself, expecting tragedy. Kristina knew that this child had felt the loss of her mother more deeply than anyone suspected, including her very caring father.

Kristina's heart ached; she almost made herself solid again, so strong was her desire to smooth Eliette's little brow with her fingertips, to kiss her and tell her that everything was all right, that she was safe now.

But that promise could not be made, in honesty, to any mortal on earth, no matter how beloved, for inherent in the glorious miracle of life, of course, was the certainty of death.

Kristina moved to stand beside Bree's bed and saw with an inner smile that the younger child was utterly relaxed in sleep, still trusting and vulnerable. She had only deep-seated, almost instinctual memories of her lost mother and did not yet suspect that love could be treacherous.

In those moments a new sort of love was born in the very center of Kristina's being, one she had never known before. The fathomless devotion a mother feels for her children.

It was silly. Even preposterous. But there it was. She cared so much for these little girls that she would have laid down her own life for them.

It was no great leap, from that conclusion, to the realization that she loved Max, as well. Truly and completely, in an adult fashion that bore no resemblance at all to the reckless, superficial and somewhat fatuous fondness she had felt toward Michael.

Kristina settled in to keep her vigil, reflecting upon these revelations while she waited for the dawn.

Perhaps an hour had passed when Bree awakened, groped her sleepy way into the bathroom, and crawled back into bed. She sat up for a few moments, a tousled moppet gilded in silvery moonlight, as though she sensed someone's presence. Then, with an expansive yawn, she collapsed onto the pillows and tumbled back into the sort of consuming slumber Kristina suspected only vampires and small children can attain.

The remainder of the night passed quickly for Kristina. After a last stolen look at Max, who was sleeping peacefully now, she willed herself back to her own house, her own bedroom.

The letter she had intended to read the night before lay on her bed, where she had left it before her shower the night before. Still wearing the dark clothes she'd put on after the encounter with Benecia and Canaan Havermail, she hurried down the hall.

Stepping over the threshold, Kristina scanned the room. The dolls were in their cabinets, staring and silent, and there was no sign that the tiny vampires had ever fouled the place with their presence.

"Behave yourselves," Kristina told the dolls before closing the door and returning to her room to dress for work.

Dathan was waiting inside the shop when she arrived, making himself at home on a Chippendale chair and reading the current issue of *USA Today.* He smiled benevolently, like an indulgent husband whose docile wife has just brought his breakfast on a tray.

"Well?" he said, laying aside the newspaper and rising. He was wearing battered jeans and a tweedy brown sweater, but he bowed as elegantly as if he were clad in a coat and tails.

Kristina was more than irritated at his presumption—he could at least have waited until she'd arrived at the shop herself instead of entering like a common thief—but she put her annoyance aside. Last night's visit from the Havermails had convinced her that she needed someone's help, and at the moment Dathan was the best available candidate.

"We have a bargain," she said, extending one hand to seal the agreement.

Dathan looked mildly surprised. "Acquiescence? So easily and so soon? Great Zeus, Kristina, I confess I'm almost disappointed!"

He deserved a jab, she decided. "You've already had one offer of marriage," she said, "though I doubt you'll find it suitable."

"Was it a vampire?"

"*It* is certainly the appropriate word and, yes, Benecia Havermail is indeed a vampire."

Dathan all but spat his response. "Why, that's revolting—the creature is a child!"

"She only looks like one," Kristina replied. "Apparently she's decided she made a bad bargain in becoming a vampire and passing up her chance to go through the normal sequence of lifetimes. In addition, she seems to be smitten with you."

Dathan's expression was a study in revulsion. "Needless to say, my dear, that particular monster will not do."

Kristina went to the back of the shop to hang up her coat, set her purse on a shelf, and put a mug of water into the microwave for tea. She had not taken the time for breakfast and felt the beginnings of hunger in the pit of her stomach. "I completely agree that Benecia is not suitable. I hasten to remind you, however, that all vampires are monsters, in one way or another."

"As are all witches and warlocks," Dathan said, though he glossed over the concession pretty quickly. He gave Kristina a pointed look as she took the mug out of the microwave and swirled a teabag around in the hot water before discarding it in the trash bin. "Lesson one, Ms. Holbrook," he said. "Why do you brew tea in the mortal way, like a common scullery maid, when you could simply conjure it up in the first place?"

Kristina considered her long-cherished preference for doing things in human fashion. "I wanted to live as normal a life as I could," she said.

"Normal for you, Kristina? Or normal for the mortal you wish you were? 'This above all,' as the Bard so wisely said, 'to thine own self be true.'"

"Point taken," Kristina replied, deflated. "I've been playing make believe for a long time. The problem is, I'm not sure *what* I am—clearly I'm not human, but I'm no vampire, either."

"You are Kristina Holbrook," Dathan said, touching the tip of her nose with an index finger in the same fond way that her father and Valerian had often done, while reassuring her. "You are utterly unique, and you should celebrate that, *glory in it*, rather than fretting and trying to pretend you're someone else."

Kristina knew he was right, but just knowing didn't mean she could change right away. After all, she'd been posing as a mortal woman ever since that long-ago day when she'd taken a spill from her horse on an English country road and just as surely fallen for Michael Bradford. A habit of more than a century's standing would take time and effort to break.

"Okay," she said. "What do I do first? How do I start?"

Dathan studied her speculatively. "I assume you know the basics—appearing and disappearing, changing the outward appearance of simple objects and all that?"

Kristina flushed with indignation. "I'm not an idiot," she said.

"Now, now," Dathan scolded, waggling a finger under her nose. "The mark of a good student is humility. To achieve mastery, one must assume the attitude of a beginner."

Indignation gave way to a singular lack of enthusiasm. "Terrific," Kristina muttered.

9

FOR the first time in his life, as he drove the short distance between Kristina's house and his own, Max Kilcarragh questioned his sanity. He cared—more than cared—for a woman who professed to be one hundred and thirty years old, with vampires for parents. He had seen a genuine warlock pop into the room like a character on *Bewitched*.

Seeing was believing, they said. He didn't know which was crazier— that he'd seen, or that he believed. Even more insane was the fact that he wasn't running as fast as he could in the other direction.

He was at risk. More important, so were his children.

Yet there was something inside him, a part of himself he'd never explored, that urged him to stand his ground.

Stand his ground? How could one mortal, however athletic, hold his own against creatures with magical powers? Maybe it was already too late to protect his daughters, himself, and Kristina.

Now *there* was a grandiose idea—that he, a high school football coach just five years short of turning forty—would have so much as a prayer against the likes of that warlock, Dathan, or any of the other monsters Kristina had so haltingly described.

He was nearly home, but suddenly there it was—the neighborhood church he had avoided assiduously since the accident. Although he'd sent Bree and Eliette to Sunday School every week, knowing Sandy would have wanted them to stay in touch with their personal heritage, he hadn't set foot in the place himself. Hadn't been inclined to worship a God who would take somebody like Sandy out of the world, though he guessed he still believed. Grudgingly.

Maybe, he thought, pulling over to the curb and staring up at the darkened structure, it wasn't a case of not having a prayer after all. Maybe, in fact, that was *all* he had.

He gripped the steering wheel in both hands and lowered his head, motivated mostly by discouragement, rather than reverence. His supplication was silent. *Show me how to handle this. I don't care what happens to me, but I'm asking You to look out for Kristina and Eliette and Bree. Please.*

That was the extent of Max's entreaty; he hoped it would be enough.

When Sandy was killed, he hadn't had time to ask for help; everything had happened too fast.

He shifted the Blazer back into gear and went home.

Elaine was there to babysit, and her face brightened as Max entered the house. He greeted her with a nod and bounded up the stairs without taking off his coat or asking how the kids were. He had to see his daughters for himself; a report from his sister-in-law wouldn't suffice.

They were safe.

Bree was tangled in her blankets, though the expression on her little face was one of sweet repose. Eliette seemed to be on guard, even in her sleep, but that was normal for her. Max's heart ached because he couldn't take away the pain, make up for the loss that had wounded her so terribly.

She awakened, this elder daughter of his, who remembered the death of her mother all too clearly, and looked at him with large brown eyes. "Hi, Daddy," she whispered, conscious, as always, of Bree. Eliette was too serious, too responsible, but he didn't know how to help her.

"Hi," he said in a gruff, gentle whisper.

"I'm glad you're home."

"Me, too. Everything go okay tonight?"

Eliette nodded soberly. Max wondered if she was thinking what he was—trying to reason out how things could be okay in a world in which your mom could be snatched away forever, without a moment's notice. "You were with Kristina," she said.

It was only a statement, not an accusation. Not a protest.

Max felt a twinge of guilt all the same. What new kind of suffering might he have brought into Eliette's life, and Bree's, by involving himself with Kristina Holbrook?

"Yeah," he said.

"Bree says she's going to be our mommy now. Miss Holbrook, I mean."

Max tucked Eliette in, in an approximation of the way Sandy had done it. "Just a second here," he said softly. "Mommies come one to a customer, and yours is gone to heaven. Miss Holbrook—if I did marry her, and trust me, things haven't gotten that far—would be your step-mother."

Eliette's nose crinkled. "Like in *Cinderella*?"

The word *stepmother* had been a poor choice, Max thought. While he knew in the center of his soul that Kristina wasn't wicked, she was no Mary Poppins, either. "No," he said quickly. "Kristina isn't mean."

"Would she get to boss me around?"

Max suppressed a smile, in spite of the fact that the evening's events had left him feeling as though he'd been pushed five miles by a snowplow and then run over. "If you mean could she tell you to do your homework, quit picking on your sister, or clean up your room, yes. Now, go to sleep. We'll talk about this in the morning." He kissed Eliette's forehead and left the room.

Elaine was lingering downstairs, sipping herbal tea. She always lingered, it seemed, but then Max wouldn't have wanted her to walk to her car alone. She was a good friend to him, an attentive and loving aunt to the children, and she had been Sandy's sister. But she got on his nerves sometimes.

She looked at him with big, soulful eyes, and Max was confronted, yet again, with a fact he usually managed to deny. Elaine wanted more from him than he was willing to give. She wanted to step into Sandy's shoes, raise the girls, share his bed every night.

"Bree and Eliette were good, like always," she said.

Max shoved a hand through his hair, much rumpled because it had been a night for that sort of gesture, and manufactured a smile. "I really appreciate your coming over here on such short notice to take care of them," he said. "But it occurs to me that I've been taking advantage of you by asking. I'm sorry, Elaine—I haven't been very thoughtful."

She drew nearer, and Max unconsciously stepped back.

Her smile was tremulous. Her hair was like Sandy's, her face and body were similar. It would be so easy to pretend . . .

And so unfair. So cruel.

Besides, it was Kristina who occupied his mind and heart these days, for better or worse. He didn't even want to think about the worse part.

"Max," Elaine said quietly as if she were holding out a handful of seeds to a bird on the verge of taking wing, "the girls need a mother."

While Max privately agreed, the remark rankled. In an ideal world, every child would have two loving, nurturing parents, but this one was another kind of place entirely. He'd done his best in spite of that, making sure Eliette and Bree knew that he would be there for them, no matter what. If there was a single thing he was sure of, in a universe full of surprises, it was that he was a good father.

"I don't think we should pursue this, Elaine," he said with a sigh. "I'm really tired and . . ." *And tonight I found out that vampires and warlocks, to name just two of a variety of fiends, are real. Not only that—I learned that I'm in love with a woman who is a hundred and thirty years old.*

Elaine did not advance, but neither did she retreat. Max was developing a pounding headache, and he was still wearing his coat. The room felt hot and close, though he knew the temperature was set at sixty-eight degrees, as always.

"I've been patient," she said.

Max felt a chill. Patient? Her sister had died violently, tragically, instantaneously. He said nothing, but started toward the door, hoping to lead Elaine in that direction. Her coat, a simple one of gray tweed, hung on the hall tree. "It's late," he said, offering the garment, holding it out so that she could slip her arms into the sleeves.

She smiled somewhat sadly and got into the coat. Max wished he loved her; it would have made everything so much simpler. Elaine looked like Sandy. She cherished the girls, and they were fond of her. And there were, to his knowledge anyway, no vampires in her family tree, no warlocks amidst her small circle of lackluster friends.

"I've watched you," she said with her back still turned to him, her hands busy with the buttons of her coat. "First you grieved, like all of us, of course. Then you started dating . . ."

Max closed his eyes for a moment. *Damn. She was going to push it.*

"Elaine—" he began awkwardly, reluctantly.

She turned and placed a finger to his lips. Her eyes were brimming with tears, and her chin trembled. "Just listen," she said. "I've always loved you—even when you and Sandy were first dating. I kept hoping. But then you married her."

He had an image of Elaine as a shy, knock-kneed kid in a bridesmaid's dress. Sandy had tossed her bouquet to her younger sister. Elaine had had too much champagne at the reception, he recalled. She'd sobbed and made something of a scene when he and Sandy left for their honeymoon.

He'd felt sorry for the kid, ascribing her behavior to excitement and the champagne she and some of the cousins had been sneaking all afternoon, but Sandy had touched his arm and shook her head. A signal that she didn't want to discuss the matter.

"Don't," he said now, in the entryway of his home. "Please. Don't."

She ignored his plea. "I can make you happy, Max."

He let out a long, raspy sigh and put a hand to the small of her back, ushering her to the door, turning the knob. "Come on," he said as if she hadn't spoken. "I'll see you to your car."

"Max."

He didn't push her over the threshold, but he did guide her a little, increasing the pressure just slightly. "No, Elaine," he said firmly. Wearily. "I won't talk about this with you. Not tonight, not ever."

"Couldn't you just pretend I was Sandy?" They were in the middle of the front yard. Only a few more feet to her car.

"My God," Max answered, opening the car door for her, waiting for her to slip inside. "I'm going to forget you even suggested that. You don't mean what you're saying, Elaine." He felt compelled to offer a reason, an explanation, for her behavior. "It's the grief that's making you say these things. You haven't worked through losing Sandy."

She got behind the wheel, but Max couldn't close the car door because she hadn't swung her legs inside. "You think I didn't love her, don't you? Well, I did. I do. And I miss her as much as you do."

Max shivered, but he didn't think it was the cold November wind that was biting at him, even through his coat. "I know you loved her," he said patiently, carefully. "We all did."

"It's what Sandy wants, you know," she told him. "For us to be together. A family. She told me so."

Max didn't speak. He wouldn't have known what to say.

"In dreams," Elaine explained, all the way inside the car now, at long last. Switching on the ignition. "Sandy comes to me in dreams. Talks to me. Tells me things."

Max still didn't answer. He was a pragmatic man who did not believe the dead spoke to the living, waking or sleeping, but that night he'd learned, in an unforgettable way, that there were indeed other realms, other realities besides the one he knew.

"I'll ask her to visit you. Sandy, I mean. Maybe that will convince you." Having uttered those incredible words, Elaine closed the door, clicked the electric lock button, and backed out of Max's driveway.

He was scared, and not just because of what had been revealed to him at Kristina's house earlier that evening. Nor did he believe that his late wife would show up in his dreams, at Elaine's behest or for any other reason. He knew because he'd tried often enough to summon Sandy, during the early, dark days, when the loneliness had been almost too much to bear. No, what worried Max was the state of his sister-in-law's mind.

He stood in the driveway long after Elaine's car had disappeared around the corner.

"SLOW," Dathan said critically, "but a little better than your last try."

Kristina glared at him. She'd willed herself to China and back—the whole process couldn't have taken more than a minute—but she felt as if she'd made the journey on foot. "I'm half mortal, you know," she said.

"No excuse," Dathan replied. They were standing in the center of her living room, where they had materialized moments before; Dathan first, of course, then a disgruntled and somewhat breathless Kristina. There was a subtle change in his expression as he studied her. "You know," he said, "maybe I don't need a vampire for a mate after all. You might do very well."

Kristina felt herself flush with indignation and something not unlike revulsion, although the warlock was a beguiling creature if she'd ever seen one. "Forget it," she said. "My family is weird enough without stirring you into the mix."

Dathan's tender brown eyes flashed with annoyance, and he spread one long-fingered hand over his chest in a gesture of injured pride. "You lack grace," he said. "Verbally, as well as in regard to your magic."

Kristina was exhausted. She wanted to crawl into bed and lie there for a hundred years, like Sleeping Beauty. When she woke up, Max and his sweet, innocent children would have lived out their lives and gone on to some brighter, safer realm where she would no longer be a danger to them.

"I'm not going to apologize, if that's what you're waiting for," she told Dathan.

"Don't you see that it's your very insistence on pretending to be mortal that has gotten you into this mess?" the warlock demanded. "And yet you persist. You're in love with, of all things, a *high school football coach*. A jock, Kristina. That's what humans call men like him, isn't it? Jocks?"

She felt incredibly defensive. "There is nothing wrong with being athletic," she said. "Besides, Max is smart. And sensitive."

Dathan rolled his eyes. "You may already be beyond hope," he said, folding his arms. He looked magnificent, standing there in the center of Kristina's beautifully appointed living room, but she felt nothing except irritation.

"Maybe I am," she said. It was only too true. If anything happened to Max and the girls because of their association with her, she would not be able to bear it. It was the one prospect with the impetus to drive Kristina to destroy herself.

"No," Dathan insisted. "I won't let it happen."

She wondered if he'd been reading her mind, hoped not. There were a great many things she didn't know about warlocks and their singular powers. Or those of vampires, for that matter. "Won't let what happen?"

she asked suspiciously. She kept some very private things in her mind and didn't want Dathan or anyone else rifling through them.

"You're not going to give up on your magic, Kristina," Dathan decreed. He tilted his handsome head to one side, considering. His exquisite features were taut with concentration. "Come with me," he went on after a long and, for Kristina, uncomfortable silence. "Be my bride. You will learn to love me in time, and forget your little mortal."

Little was hardly the word Kristina would have used to describe Max; he was well over six feet tall and probably weighed better than two hundred pounds. And that didn't take the size of his spirit into account; she had known from their first encounter that Max had the soul of a gentle warrior. Even if he'd been small physically, his character would have made him a giant.

"If I thought going with you would keep Max and his daughters safe, I would probably do it," Kristina said. She hadn't considered her words ahead of time; they simply came tumbling out of her mouth. Straight from her heart. "But it's too late now. The damage has been done."

"Exactly whom do you fear so much?" Dathan asked. He was standing behind a Queen Anne chair now, his elegant hands grasping the back. "Surely it can't be Valerian. He dotes on you."

"It's the Havermails," Kristina said, and shuddered superstitiously, lest mentioning the little demons' names might summon them from whatever hellish pursuit they'd chosen for the night. As soon as Dathan was gone, in fact, she would go to Max's house and keep watch again.

"Avery? Roxanne?" Dathan raised one eyebrow, and his fine, angelic mouth twisted slightly in a delicate expression of contempt. "Those cowardly creatures? Neither of them would dare cross Valerian, let alone your mother."

Kristina shook her head. "Benecia and Canaan."

"The devil's children," Dathan said. The contempt in his face changed to revulsion, and there was nothing delicate about it. "Surely they, too, would be afraid—"

Kristina recalled the recklessness of Benecia's taunts the night before when she'd found them in the room where she kept her childhood toys, her collection of dolls. "Something is different. I don't know about Canaan, but Benecia is—well—it's almost as if she wants to be destroyed." Before Dathan could offer to oblige, Kristina held up one hand to stay his words. "Which isn't to say she won't fight to defend herself, Dathan. She is five hundred years old, remember, and her powers are beyond reckoning."

"Maybe for you. Compared to me, she is but a babe."

"But she is powerful."

"She must sleep in the daytime, like most other vampires. Warlocks suffer no such disadvantage. I have only to find her lair and drive a stake through her heart to put an end to her."

"Not good enough," Kristina answered. "Canaan would avenge her, and even if you managed to destroy her as well, other vampires would seek retribution, if for no other reason than that a warlock had given them cause."

"They would defy your mother's command, that there must be peace between vampires and warlocks, lest Nemesis and his angels be sent to destroy us all?"

"Eternity is a long time," Kristina answered. "I believe some vampires—perhaps many of them—are weary like Benecia. Maybe destruction, even damnation, would be a welcome release after century upon century of being just what they are. Humans pass through a variety of lives, you know, shedding each body like a skin when they are through with it. They go on, change, make progress. I've never spoken of it with my mother, Papa, or Valerian, but I suspect that sometimes a blood-drinker hates being trapped in one identity for all of time. Perhaps they've denied themselves the very thing they sought in the first place, in becoming vampires—life."

"They live forever," Dathan reminded her in a quiet voice.

"No," Kristina replied. "They *exist* forever, or until they are destroyed. There is a big difference."

"I will concede that, if for no other cause than courtesy. What does it have to do with the hideous Benecia Havermail and her equally charming sister?"

"They have nothing to lose," Kristina said. The realization weighed so heavily on her spirit that it threatened to crush her. "They may be desperate enough, lonely enough, bored enough, to risk hellfire on the chance that they could encounter oblivion instead. Valerian says the afterlife is what each one of us expects it to be, and he has reason to know."

In a blink Dathan was standing before Kristina, his hands resting lightly on her shoulders. "Let me show you wonders beyond your greatest fantasies, Kristina."

She smiled, though the last thing she felt was amusement. "Let you take me away from all this? No, Dathan. I don't care for you and, anyway, as I told you before, it's too late."

"Then I shall find Benecia's lair, and that of her sister, and before the first crow of the cock—"

"No," Kristina said quickly. "You mustn't interfere, Dathan. Not in that way. No conscious, reasoning creature kills with impunity."

"More philosophy?"

"Call it a hunch," Kristina replied. "Now, will you please leave? I need some time to myself."

Dathan snapped his fingers; the cloak he'd worn earlier, when he arrived, appeared in his grasp. He donned it with the customary flourish, his soft eyes fiery as he regarded Kristina. "Don't forget our bargain," he warned. "I will train you in magic, and you will find me a suitable mate. In the meantime, I intend to woo you by any means I can devise."

She suppressed an urge to slap her self-appointed mentor across the face. Kristina might have let her powers slip, but she was no fool. "That last part wasn't in the deal," she pointed out. "I don't love you. I don't want you. In fact, I wouldn't have anything to do with you if I didn't need your help. How's that for philosophical?"

Dathan smiled, though both her words and her manner had been poisonous. One warlock's venom was another's ambrosia, she supposed.

"You have your mother's magnificent spirit," he said. "That only makes you more desirable, as far as I'm concerned." He executed a suave little bow, more a motion of his head than his body. "Farewell, lovely Kristina. For now, at least."

With that, he was gone, leaving no trace of smoke or sulphur in his wake.

Kristina hesitated only a few moments before willing herself to the Kilcarragh house. The children were sleeping soundly, but Max was in his living room, sitting in the dark, without even the television screen to provide light.

He sat in a recliner, a drink in one hand, looking rumpled but plainly not intoxicated. Kristina's heart ached as she stood a few feet away, hopefully invisible, watching him. Little wonder that he was upset, she reflected. He'd just been introduced to a world where things that went bump in the night were real, not just imagined. He'd lost that precious mortal innocence because of her.

As if Max sensed her presence, he set the glass aside and peered into the gloom.

Kristina retreated a little way; he knew she had powers, but she didn't want him to think she was going to pop in on him for no reason, like some supernatural stalker. Maybe he could see her; maybe what was developing between them made that possible.

"Kristina?"

She did the mental equivalent of biting her lip and said nothing.

"Damn," Max muttered, rising from the chair with a sudden motion that almost startled Kristina right out of her spell and into full visibility. "You're not that lucky, Kilcarragh."

Had Kristina been solid, she knew tears would have filled her eyes.

He started toward the stairway, moving confidently in the familiar darkness.

Kristina waited until he was asleep before following him up the stairs and slipping into his room. She was tired from her session with Dathan, and her invisibility was shaky at best. At any moment, she might be seen, and explaining would be difficult.

She stood at the foot of Max's bed for a long while, watching him sleep, searching her mind and heart for a way to keep him and his children safe. But no one was really beyond harm except the dead; Kristina knew that and so, surely, did Max.

Reluctantly Kristina finally turned away, forgetting her spell, opening the door, stepping into the hallway.

Bree was standing there, just outside the bathroom door, wide awake and staring in Kristina's direction.

"You really *can* do magic," the child said in a tone of awe rather than fear.

"Or you could be dreaming," Kristina suggested, somewhat lamely, and in a very soft voice. She hadn't planned on being caught, and now that she had been, she didn't know what to say. It would be cruel and foolish to tell an innocent little girl that monsters, whether hiding in the closet or otherwise, were not necessarily imaginary. That sometimes children needed guarding.

"I'm not dreaming," Bree said firmly. She took a few steps toward Kristina, dragging her blanket behind her, holding a worn teddy bear under one arm. "I can sort of see through you. Are you a ghost, like my mommy?"

"No," Kristina answered. "I'm not a ghost, and neither is your mommy."

"How do you know? About Mommy, I mean?"

Kristina shrugged. She didn't know how she knew that Sandy Kilcarragh had gone on to better things, but she was as sure of that as she was of anything else. "I guess by magic," she said. "Now, don't you think you'd better go back to bed?"

Bree wasn't ready to cooperate, though she yawned broadly. "You're getting pretty solid." She reached out, touched Kristina's hand to test the theory. "Yep. How come you're here? Walking around in our house in the middle of the night?"

"I just wanted to make sure you were all right," Kristina said. It was as close to the truth as she dared to venture, at the moment.

Bree pulled, so that Kristina bent down to her level. "I'm okay," she confided in a stage whisper, "but Eliette is really sad. And Daddy needs somebody grown up to talk to and stuff like that."

"I understand," Kristina whispered. "Why is Eliette sad?"

"She thinks about Mommy a lot," Bree explained. "It makes her lonesome."

Kristina shared the sleeping Eliette's sorrow, felt it keenly in that moment. Her own upbringing had been anything but normal, but Maeve had been a devoted mother, for all her temperament and dramatic flair. Kristina could barely imagine what it would have been like to grow up without her. "It's good to remember people we love," she said gently. "Even if it hurts sometimes."

Bree frowned, her small, pixie-like face solemn. She clutched both blanket and bear just a little closer. "Is it bad that I can't see Mommy's face in my brain, even when I close my eyes?"

Kristina kissed the little girl's cheek. "No, darling, it isn't bad. And deep in your heart, you do remember. I promise."

Bree smiled brilliantly. "I do?"

Kristina nodded, no longer trusting herself to speak. She watched in silence as the little girl toddled back into the room she shared with her sister, there to sleep and, Kristina hoped, to dream sweet dreams.

Not bothering to cloak herself in invisibility again, not even sure she could manage the spell if she tried, Kristina waited a while, then followed, sitting in the wooden rocking chair in the corner of the room, keeping her vigil and waiting.

The night passed without incident, and Kristina went home a few minutes before sunrise, marveling at the weariness she felt. Was she finally beginning to age, after all these years? It seemed too much to hope for.

Only after Kristina had filled the glass carafe with water and started the coffee machine in her kitchen did she turn and see the note resting prominently on the counter. It was written on expensive, handmade parchment, and the elegant, flowing letters could only have been shaped by one hand.

Her mother's.

Come to London at once, Maeve had written. *I must see you.*

Kristina frowned. Sunset was still a few hours away in England, so she didn't have to hurry. It wasn't the summons that troubled her, either, but the fact that Maeve had not simply come to her at Max's house. Why had her mother left a note, instead of seeking Kristina out, or wrenching her home again, by means of her formidable magic?

In the end, it didn't matter why. Maeve had commanded her, as a daughter and as a subject, to make an appearance at "court." There was never any question of disobeying.

Kristina showered, applied careful makeup, and put on a suit of dove-gray silk. Then, after taking a few minutes to psyche herself up for the task, she blinked herself to London and the lovely old house where so many secrets lived.

It was not yet sunset when Kristina arrived. Having materialized in the outer hallway—she was grateful it hadn't been the coal bin, considering the strain she'd been under lately—she made her way to the library, which was situated at the back of the first floor. The room was spacious, overlooking the garden, and a polished suit of armor, empty as far as Kristina knew, guarded the double doors.

She stepped inside the vast chamber and went straight to her mother's collection of volumes on the subjects of alchemy and general magic. The tomes were very old, some still in manuscript form and in danger of turning to dust at a touch, and the language was strange. Kristina was puzzling out a spell to forestall evil spirits when a voice startled her out of her contemplation.

"You are here," Maeve remarked, sounding at once imperious and relieved. "I daresay I feared you would not obey."

Kristina laid the book gently aside and smiled at her mother. Maeve was a splendid creature, with flowing dark hair, flawless ivory skin, and eyes of a singular indigo shade. She wore a gossamer white gown, as was typical of her, for she loved spectacle and glamour. Which was not to say that she didn't have a somewhat raunchy side, uncontested queen of the vampires though she was.

"Of course I am here," Kristina answered. "When have I disobeyed you?"

"When you married that mortal—what was his name?—Michael Bradford."

"Mother, that was more than a century ago. I was young and foolish."

Maeve came near, bringing the scent of jasmine with her, and kissed her daughter's cheek. Her smile was warm, full of love and humor, but also tinged with worry. "I fear, from what I am told," she said, "that you are *still* foolish."

10

MAEVE'S words trembled in the air.

I fear, from what I am told, that you are still *foolish.*

Kristina was not intimidated by her mother; she knew Maeve would never hurt her. Would indeed perish to protect her daughter, if such a sacrifice were to prove necessary. Still, she was unsettled by the troubled expression she saw in the queen's dark blue eyes, behind the welcome and the joy.

"Foolish?" Kristina echoed, in a tone of false innocence, stalling.

Maeve's brilliant eyes flashed with impatience and temper. Creatures of every sort quailed before that look, and not without reason, but Kristina held her ground. She was about to hear a lecture about her involvement with Max, and she fully intended to fight back.

"Yes, foolish," Maeve snapped. "You've been consorting with warlocks! Kristina, how could you?"

Kristina was taken aback. While she had certainly known that there was a polite rancor between her mother and Dathan, she was also aware that the two had once joined forces to destroy a particularly evil vampire called Lisette. "This is about *Dathan?*"

"Yes," Maeve said with a little less impatience this time. "How can you be so foolhardy as to trust that—that viper?"

Kristina sighed. She had the beginnings of a headache, though she didn't know whether the tension behind it stemmed from her transatlantic blink or the stress she'd suffered of late. Perhaps both. "I expected you to rail against Max," she said, turning, finding a chair and sinking wearily into it.

All her life she'd been able to go days, even weeks, without sleep, but she had never been sick. Still, something was wrong; she wasn't herself.

Maeve was beside her in an instant, seated gracefully on a hassock, holding Kristina's hand in both her own graceful, chilly ones. "He's done something to you," the great vampire fretted. "I swear, if he's poisoned you, I'll find him and make him long for the mercies of hell!"

"Dathan hasn't harmed me, Mother," Kristina said patiently, gently. "He's helping me with my magic, that's all. Frankly the strain is getting to me."

Maeve narrowed her eyes. "Why should a warlock wish to help the child of two vampires?" she demanded suspiciously.

"We have a bargain," Kristina answered. She conjured a cup of tea, hoping that would restore her a little, and while it appeared in her hands, as ordered, it proved slightly bitter and none too warm. She sipped it anyway. "My part is to find him a mate."

Maeve frowned at the teacup, which rattled against its saucer as Kristina set it aside. "Why doesn't he find a partner from his own species?"

"He says witches are too independent," Kristina explained. "He wants a vampire."

"Why?" Merely suspicious before, Maeve was now a study in irritated disbelief. "Does the arrogant bore think *us* weak and pliable?"

"It's something about blending the powers of warlocks and blood-drinkers." Kristina had no intention of mentioning that Dathan had suggested *her* as a romantic possibility. Maeve would have come unwrapped if she did, and that was an event to be dreaded by monsters and mortals alike.

Disbelieving annoyance had finally turned to rage. "That *idiot!*" Maeve hissed, letting go of Kristina's hand, surging to her feet. "How can he think Nemesis would tolerate such an aberration for so much as a moment?"

Nemesis, Kristina knew, was a powerful angel. A warrior feared, and rightfully so, by the very demons of hell. For centuries, Nemesis had been straining at the celestial bit, wanting to destroy the supernatural world once and for all. Maeve, Valerian, and Dathan had barely prevented that from happening before Kristina was born. Clearly the danger was still very real.

Kristina made another attempt at conjuring tea and this time got it right. She supposed caffeine was a mistake, given the situation, but she needed something to raise her energy level. "I ran into Benecia Havermail the other night," she said cautiously. "She implied that you have your hands full with some new crisis. What's going on, Mother?"

As easily as that, the tables were turned. Kristina had become the inquisitor, instead of the one being questioned. Maeve began to pace smoothly and gracefully, as she did everything. But she was clearly agitated.

"There has been an—incident."

"What sort of incident?" Kristina pressed.

"Do you remember Dimity?"

The image of a beautiful vampire came to Kristina's mind. Dimity was fair of hair and flesh, and she'd played a stringed instrument of

some sort, a small harp or dulcimer. Her most distinguishing charac-
teristic, however, was her friendship with Gideon, an angel under the
command of Nemesis himself.

"Yes," Kristina said. "I remember." She'd always thought Dimity
looked more like an angel than a fiend, but then that was an attribute
of evil—it was so often gentle of countenance, beguiling to the eyes,
deceiving the heart.

"They have vanished, the pair of them."

Kristina made no further attempt to drink her tea. The ramifications
of her mother's words were earthshaking. If Gideon had been destroyed
or wooed to the dark side, there would literally be hell to pay. Dimity,
for her part, would be on her own as far as her fellow vampires were
concerned, but angels were protected, each one accounted for and cherished by their Maker. As were mortals.

"Surely Nemesis would know where—"

Maeve interrupted her with a shake of the head. "That's the mystery
of it. There's no sign, anywhere, of either of them."

Kristina let out a long breath. "What's your theory, Mother? And
don't say you haven't one, because I know you too well to believe it."

The vampire queen ceased her pacing and gave her daughter a level
look. "I've discussed the matter with your father, of course. And the
only possibility we've been able to come up with is that they've gone
into some other dimension, some alternate reality."

Kristina was nearly speechless. "A place even Nemesis doesn't know
about?" The implications of that were staggering, because the warrior
angel was privy to the greatest secrets of heaven itself. How could there
possibly be a place, a realm, that was beyond his ken, out of his reach?

"You've been searching for them."

Maeve nodded. "To no avail, obviously. Nemesis has been turning
the universe upside-down as well, and he is fit to be tied, as you can
imagine. He thinks we're plotting against the Light, we vampires, planning to take over, extinguish the sun—" She flung her hands wide in a
gesture of bewilderment, an extremely rare emotion for her.

"Are those things possible?" Kristina asked, awestruck as well as
frightened. If they were, she had underestimated her mother's powers
and Valerian's by an immeasurable margin.

"No," Maeve said, "but Nemesis can be utterly unreasonable when
his temper is roused. The fact that his every effort to locate Gideon has
failed only compounds his frustration, of course."

"Dear heaven," Kristina murmured.

"I wish you wouldn't use that word," Maeve replied crisply. She gathered herself, as imperious as ever, and stood before Kristina, willing her daughter to rise. Kristina could no more have resisted than a jonquil bulb could defy the warm, incessant tug of spring sunlight. "We must still discuss the warlock."

Kristina thought of Max and Bree and Eliette, how vulnerable they were. "I have reasons of my own for forging an alliance with Dathan," she said evenly. "Just as you once had. Besides, I doubt that a warlock and a vampire *could* conceive a child in any case."

"Do you?" Maeve asked, arching one ebony eyebrow in an expression that might have been disdain, had it been directed at anyone else except her daughter or her beloved mate. "You forget, then, that you yourself were born of a nightwalker and a mortal. That, too, was thought to be impossible."

Kristina sighed. "I haven't forgotten," she said. "But my conception was a rare occurrence, wasn't it? There has been no other birth like it, before or since—isn't that true?"

"Yes," Maeve admitted, but only after a long and stubborn silence. "It's true."

"Then we can safely assume that any union between Dathan and a vampire would be childless."

"We can safely assume nothing," Maeve said fiercely. "But you are right about one thing—I simply cannot concern myself with this affair, not at the moment. The other situation must take precedence over virtually everything else."

Kristina faced her mother and kissed her cool, alabaster white forehead. "I will be very careful," she promised. "Don't expend your energies worrying about me."

Maeve made a sound that might have been a sigh in a creature with breath. "Warlocks are the most treacherous of monsters," she said. "And they are the natural enemies of vampires."

"Yes," Kristina replied, "but it isn't only politics that makes strange bedfellows. I need Dathan's help, and apparently he needs mine. Never fear, though—I won't make the mistake of trusting him."

"That will have to be good enough, for the moment at least," Maeve conceded. "I *am* glad to hear that you are giving up this silly pretense of being human and finally exploring your powers. It's about time you came to your senses."

Kristina bit her lip and gestured toward the shelves behind her, where the manuscript she had been perusing still lay. "May I borrow some of those volumes? There are some interesting, if ancient, spells recorded there—difficult to decipher but worth the effort, I think."

"Of course," Maeve said. She made a gesture with one hand, and the books Kristina wanted to read vanished into thin air, to land neatly on her desk at home, no doubt. Express mail, vampire style. "I must go now, darling," the queen continued. "First to hunt, then to seek the ever-illusive Dimity. Your father is probably in the laboratory if you'd like to see him."

Kristina smiled and nodded. "Good luck in your search."

Maeve vanished in a draft of cool air and a whiff of jasmine.

Kristina hesitated only a few moments before heading belowstairs, to her father's favorite place. Still oddly weary, knowing she would need her energy for the return trip to Seattle, she took the stairs in good mortal fashion and knocked at the laboratory door.

Simultaneously a lock clicked, and Calder's voice called out, "Come in, Kristina."

She entered to find her father busy at one of his tables. He appeared to be performing an autopsy on something, and Kristina felt bile surge into the back of her throat. "What is that?" she asked, holding back.

Calder grinned at her over one shoulder. He was handsome, and more than one female vampire had dared to flirt with him over the years, but he cared only for Maeve. "Sorry, I should have warned you," he said. "This is—was—a vampire."

Kristina's revulsion was overruled by her natural curiosity, much of which had been inherited, no doubt, from Calder himself. She stepped closer, looking down at the creature on the table, saw a humanoid shape with fangs and sunken, staring eyes. There was none of the gore that would have accompanied such an examination of a mortal, however— the vampire, a female, was dried out and crumbling, like a wasp's nest long abandoned.

"Who—who was she?"

"No one you knew," Calder said, returning his attention to his work.

"How was she killed?"

"An infusion of warlock blood, I would guess. There have been a number of such cases lately, though Dathan and his underlings deny all knowledge of the matter."

Kristina shivered. "Why the autopsy?"

"Part of an experiment," Calder said.

Of course. He was still trying to find the method and the magic that would "cure" blood-drinkers of their ghastly obsession, without robbing them of their singular powers.

She spoke quietly, gently, because she needed for him to look at her, needed his full attention. "Papa, I want to be mortal—I want to have babies, get gray hair, and eventually die. Can you help me?"

Calder's splendid face contorted for a moment with pain and perhaps with understanding. He said nothing just then, but left the autopsy table to cross the room where he shed his lab coat and scrubbed his hands with disinfectant soap and a brush, like a surgeon.

Kristina followed him, stayed close by his side. "Can you?" she repeated.

"I don't know," Calder answered. She saw true suffering in his eyes as he looked at her. To do what she asked would be, in his view, to kill her.

"Don't you ever get weary, Papa?" Kristina pressed. "Don't you long sometimes for peace, for oblivion, for cool, dark nothingness?"

Calder was drying his hands on a starched, spotless towel. He tossed the cloth into a hamper beside the sink before replying. "I am young, as vampires go," he said. "There is still much I want to accomplish."

"But someday—?"

He closed his eyes for a moment, this vampire who had once been a man, a surgeon on the bloody battlefields of the American Civil War. He had seen anguish, of both the flesh and the spirit, and despite his intense focus on his experiments, he was not insensible to the shared sorrows of men and monsters. "Perhaps someday I will grow weary, yes. Kristina, why do you ask these questions? Is it because of that mortal you have become enamored of?"

"Mostly, yes," Kristina admitted. There was no use in lying to Calder, even if she'd felt the inclination. Because of the scientific bent of his mind, he was far more focused than Maeve, and attempts to dissemble were lost on him. "I love Max very much, Papa. You of all people"— they both smiled at the misnomer—"er—vampires—should understand."

"I do," Calder said with a nod. He frowned and narrowed his eyes, studying Kristina more intently than usual. "You do not look well. What is wrong?"

Kristina shrugged. "Love, I suppose," she said. "And I am so very tired."

Calder's frown deepened. "Sit down," he said, indicating a nearby stool. Behind him, the half-dissected vampire was clearly visible, lying still on its gleaming stainless-steel autopsy table. Calder took a syringe from its sterile packaging and skillfully drew blood from the vein in Kristina's right forearm.

"What's the diagnosis, Doctor?" Kristina asked with a wan smile.

He set the vial of blood carefully on a countertop and smiled back, but there was a shadow of consternation in his dark eyes. "Probably nothing," he replied, "but it will take some time to determine the exact nature of the problem."

Kristina felt a little shiver of uneasiness. Was it possible for her to be ill? She'd never had so much as a case of the sniffles, in almost a century and a half of life, though she did occasionally suffer headaches. Even those tended to be more psychic in origin, however, rather than physical. "You'll be in touch as soon as you know?"

He came to her and laid a comforting hand on her shoulder. "Of course, and in the meantime, I don't want you fretting. I took that blood sample as a precautionary measure, and for no other reason."

Kristina stood. "But there is another reason. You must study the specimen closely, Papa." She paused to draw a resolute breath. "Please. I want to know what I am, if there's a definition."

Calder squeezed Kristina's shoulder lightly before letting go. He did not speak again but simply nodded.

Kristina summoned all her strength and willed herself back to Seattle. Although she had aimed for her house, she materialized in the shop instead. Then, too tired to do anything more, she curled up on a settee in the back of the store and tumbled into a deep, all-encompassing sleep.

The shop remained closed that day. The telephone went unanswered, and so did the postman's knock at the door. Kristina was oblivious, almost comatose.

When she awakened, it was dark, and for a few moments she could not remember where she was. She felt groggy and disoriented, as though she'd been drugged, and the thin light coming in through the windows cast eerie shadows all around her.

Only then did Kristina recognize her surroundings.

She pushed splayed fingers through her hair. The Victorian settee was hard, stuffed with bristly horsehair that smelled faintly musty, anything but comfortable. She sat up slowly, shaken and filled with a strange sense of urgency, as though there was somewhere she was supposed to go. Something she needed desperately to do.

But she couldn't think, couldn't concentrate. What was wrong?

Kristina made herself stand and flip on a light. She still had enough magic for that, at least, but the effort sapped her strength all the same, made her feel dizzy.

Someone rapped at the shop door; Kristina made her way through the maze of old furniture and umbrella stands and statues to peer through the glass.

Jim Graham, a policeman who patrolled the area on foot, greeted her with a concerned smile after she'd fumbled with the locks and opened the door to the chilly night breeze.

"Everything okay, Ms. Holbrook?"

"I'm just working late," Kristina said. She hadn't really shaped the excuse; it just fell from her tongue, ready-made.

"You look like you could use some rest." The cop was a nice middle-aged man, and Kristina liked him. She wished it was so simple, that all she needed was a day in bed or a short vacation.

"You're right." A smile fluttered near her lips, but she couldn't quite bring it in for a landing. "But you know how it is these days."

Jim nodded sagely. "You want me to walk you to your car? I could wait while you get your coat and lock up."

Kristina's car was parked in her garage at home, her coat still hanging in the hall closet. She didn't explain, of course. "That's really kind of you," she said, and meant it. "But I have a friend picking me up in a little while."

"Well, just make sure you keep the place locked up tight until he gets here," the officer said. "Can't be too careful, you know."

Kristina thought belatedly of the intruder who had broken into the store some months before. She'd turned him into a doorstop, handily enough, but she wondered now how trustworthy her magic had been, even then, and shuddered to think what might have happened if her skills had failed her. "That's for sure," she agreed as the policeman stepped away from the door. He waited, she noticed with appreciation, until all the locks were in place again.

The brass monkey was still on his shelf in the back room, where Kristina had left him. Dredging up all the strength she could summon, she reinforced the original spell, and promptly sank to the floor in a faint.

When Kristina opened her eyes, only moments later, she found herself at home, lying on her own bed. Dathan bent over her to lay a cool cloth on her forehead.

"What's the matter with me?" she asked in a small voice. She wanted Max, wanted to go to him, to make sure he and the girls were all right, but she couldn't seem to move, except in slow motion.

The warlock sat down beside the bed. He looked incongruous in the delicate, chintz-covered chair, given his size and his almost regal elegance. "It's only a guess," he said, "but I'd say that all these years of pretending have finally caught up with you. You've allowed your magic to be depleted and, thus, the very essence of your being."

"Am I going to die?"

Dathan smiled. "Probably not. You come from sturdy—not to mention stubborn—stock."

Kristina wasn't sure whether to be relieved or disappointed, and the dilemma made her slightly testy. "What are you doing here?"

"You're welcome," the warlock said pointedly.

"Thank you." Kristina gave the words a grudging note. "What happened?"

"You swooned. I dropped by on a lark, and did the—er—gentlemanly thing. Lifted you into my arms, brought you here, all that."

Kristina closed her eyes for a moment, trying to absorb what was happening to her, to make some sense of it. Dathan's theory, that she had expended vital powers in her efforts to live as a mortal, seemed the most likely. "I'm in big trouble," she said.

"That's true," Dathan agreed, but lightly.

"My mother warned me not to trust you."

He smiled as beatifically as an angel. "Maeve is a suspicious vampire."

"She is also a *smart* vampire. I need a spell, Dathan. Something to keep the Havermails away from Max and the children, at least until I can get myself together. Will you help me?"

"It is a good thing for you, my dear, that you are virtually irresistible." The warlock sighed in a long-suffering fashion. "Yes, I'll arrange to shield your precious mortals, for tonight at least, though I don't think Benecia and Canaan will trouble them."

"I can't take the chance." But Kristina knew there would have been nothing she could do if Dathan had refused to help. She simply had no strength left.

MAX paced. He'd tried to call Kristina intermittently throughout the day. There was no answer at her shop or at her house.

She was a businesswoman, an adult with a life of her own, and he had no claim on her, no right to obsess about where she was or what she was doing. Yet something in his gut, some instinct he had never felt before, was telling him there was trouble.

He shoved a hand through his hair. It was late, and the girls were already in bed. He couldn't leave them alone and, after the exchange with Elaine the night before, he wasn't about to ask his sister-in-law to come over and babysit. The teenager he hired when Elaine wasn't available was probably sound asleep, and if he called his mother or Gwen in the middle of the night, they would be frightened, not to mention angry.

Max returned to the telephone on the desk in his study and punched the redial button; there was no need to go through the sequence of numbers that would make Kristina's home phone ring, because he'd been calling there since six o'clock.

This time she answered. Her voice sounded small, fragile.

"Hello?"

"It's Max." He closed his eyes, feeling both relieved and foolish.

"I guessed that," she said. There was a smile in her softly spoken words.

"By magic?"

The smile came through again, though Max knew in his heart of hearts that all was not right with Kristina. He was scared.

"No," she answered. "I was just hoping."

He wanted to hold her, to draw her into his arms and shelter her against whatever threatened her. He had never felt so protective before, even with Sandy—but then, he'd been naive in those golden days before his wife's death. He hadn't known how quickly and finally tragedy could strike. Hadn't dreamed.

"Are you all right?"

"Just tired," she said.

Max's gut clenched hard. He was torn between his children and the need to go to this woman who had finally caused him to put away Sandy's wedding band, which he had worn on a chain around his neck ever since his wife's death. He ached to see with his own eyes that she was safe and well.

"Do you need anything?"

He could almost see her shaking her head. He knew she was in bed, though he wasn't sure how, and he felt guilty because the image stirred him in a profoundly sexual way. So much for the altruistic wish to embrace Kristina and lend his manly strength. Max wanted more—a whole lot more—and he wasn't proud of the fact, given that she was so obviously vulnerable.

"No," Kristina replied. "I'm all right, Max, really. What about you? Are you okay? And the girls?"

"Don't worry about us," Max said firmly. "We're fine."

There was a short, pulsing silence, during which their hearts communicated.

I need you, Max told Kristina.

And I need you, was her reply.

"Can I see you tomorrow?" Max finally asked aloud. He was leaning against the desk now, the receiver clutched in his hand, still wanting to go to her right then. Not in an hour, not the next day, after football practice.

Now.

"I'd like that," she said. "I'll be at home, taking it easy. I've been meaning to read through the rest of those letters anyway."

Just the prospect of seeing Kristina again made Max ridiculously happy, even though he still wished he could go to her immediately. "Couldn't you just—well—blink yourself over here? You could stay in the spare room—"

"Not tonight, Max," she interrupted gently. "I need to sleep now."

A thick knot formed in his throat; he wanted to weep, could not imagine why. "Yeah, okay, me, too," he said. "Good night."

Another pause. "Good night, Max." Kristina had not just spoken to him, she had caressed him. He replaced the receiver, crossed the room, and switched out the lights before heading toward the stairway.

If he'd looked out a window, he might have seen the strange, cloaked sentries standing guard in the night, but Max was thinking only of Kristina that night.

"TAKE this," Dathan said, holding out a spoonful of something.

Kristina, resting against her pillows and still fully dressed, eyed the offering suspiciously. "Like I told you, my mother warned me to be careful of warlocks and their tricks."

"Give me a little credit, will you?" Dathan demanded. "I didn't bring you here and tuck you into bed just to destroy you. I could have done that at any time if that was what I wanted."

"What is this stuff?" The spoon was closer; Kristina saw that it contained a brownish fluid, some herbal concoction, judging by the noxious smell. One she had never come across before and hoped never to encounter again.

"Call it witches' brew if you must," Dathan answered with a touch of impatience. "It will make you sleep, and thus restore some of your strength. Not a cure, but it's a start."

Kristina deliberated a moment longer, then opened her mouth and took the medicine. It tasted bitter, but she swallowed it. "I'm not going to grow horns, am I?" she asked, falling back against her pillows once more.

Dathan's expression said he wasn't about to dignify such a question with a reply.

"You'd better not take advantage of me while I'm sleeping, either."

He bent close and smiled wickedly. "I hadn't thought of that. What a delightful prospect—thank you for suggesting it, Kristina."

Already she was drifting, spinning, sinking. *This,* she thought, *must be how it is for vampires when they lie down in their lairs, far out of the sun's reach.*

Kristina did not dream and awakened many hours later, in the same position in which she'd fallen asleep, in the same clothes. There was no sign of Dathan, but Max was standing at the foot of her bed, wearing jeans and a bright blue sweatshirt, his face beard-stubbled and his hair rumpled.

"How long?" she asked. "Since we talked, I mean?"

"About twenty-four hours," Max replied.

She sat up, yawning. The room was brilliant with sunlight. "You're missing work."

"It's Saturday."

"The girls—"

"Forget about Bree and Eliette," Max said gently. "They're with my folks for the weekend. Kristina, what's going on with you? What knocked you out like this?"

She sighed. Dathan's potion, whatever it was, had certainly done its work. She felt strong again, energetic, almost her old self. Almost.

"Maybe it was the supernatural equivalent of the flu," she said. "In any case, I feel fine now."

Max grinned. He looked tired, though, and she wondered how long he'd been watching over her. "If you don't mind, I'd like to borrow your shower," he said. "And a razor, if you have a spare. I forgot mine."

There was a certain intimacy in sharing space with Max, letting him use her shower, her things. She felt a sensual, stretching sensation deep inside, just looking at him. "Okay," she said. "Help yourself to whatever you need."

Another silence ensued, rife with possible interpretations. Then Max turned and went into the bathroom, carrying a gym bag he'd apparently brought from home.

Kristina heard the water go on, imagined Max stripping off his clothes, stepping naked and muscular under the spray. He was so blatantly, unapologetically male.

She wondered what he would say, what he would think, if she joined him.

In the end she didn't quite have the courage. She took a peach silk robe from her closet and went down the hall to the guest bathroom, where she took a long, hot shower of her own. The flow of water did nothing to soothe the ache inside her, the one only Max Kilcarragh could reach and assuage.

Kristina toweled her hair dry, ran a brush through it, and then dried her body. The silk robe clung a little as she stepped out into the hall.

Max was there, clad in a pair of clean, worn jeans and nothing else. The encounter seemed accidental, but Kristina knew that it wasn't, that they'd both wanted to be together. That had been in the cards from the first moment of history.

Slowly, deliberately, Kristina untied the belt of her robe.

11

MAX did not move from where he stood, just outside Kristina's bedroom door, until she was near enough to touch, her robe untied, hanging loosely from her shoulders. He put his hands on either side of her face and, with a low sound, part growl and part groan, took her mouth with his.

The kiss was passionate from the first; there was no hesitation this time, only a hunger that had been denied too long. Max entered her with his tongue, conquered her, his silent command presaging all that was to come.

Kristina sagged against him, weakened by her own wanting, by a yearning she had never felt before. When at last he drew back and lifted her into his arms, there were tears of wonder in her eyes.

He kissed her lids, her cheeks, and carried her over the threshold of her bedroom.

"Are you sure you want this?" he asked, still holding her.

Kristina was in a daze. "Oh, yes," she said. "Yes."

Max set her on her feet, ever so gently, and smoothed the robe back off her shoulders, down over her arms. He tossed the garment aside and consumed her naked form with his eyes, arousing her to a fever pitch of desire just by admiring and cherishing her.

"You are so unbelievably, impossibly beautiful," he said.

Kristina leaned forward, brushed his hairy chest with her lips, teasing hard brown nipples with the tip of her tongue. Her fingers strayed to the zipper of his jeans; he halted the motion with both hands, though he did not put her away from him.

"There's a problem," he confessed. "I didn't plan—"

She smiled. Her magic might be rusty, but it was still magic. She held out one hand, in a rather cocky gesture, and a small packet appeared on her palm.

Max chuckled, took the condom, and laid it on the nightstand, within easy reach of the bed. "Impressive," he said.

"Thanks." Kristina slipped her arms around his neck and tilted her head back to look up into his eyes. She knew she was casting a spell, and that it had nothing to do with supernatural powers. In that moment, in that private place, she was not a freak, but a woman, pure and simple.

He unfastened his own jeans and shed them, along with his underwear, and then simply held Kristina against him for a long, heated interval. Just that simple intimacy nurtured her on the deepest level of her being; she could have stood there, cradled in Max's arms, for an indeterminate length of time. Even that small contact was better than anything she had ever felt with Michael.

Finally, however, Max raised his hands to cup Kristina's small, firm breasts. A searing shiver went through her at his touch, for the contact was at once possessive and inexpressibly tender. Hard-edged thumbs stroked her nipples, causing them to stiffen into little peaks.

Kristina emitted a long sigh and closed her eyes. Max bent his head and kissed her again, teasing now, tasting and tempting.

She was still standing, was amazed that her legs would support her. She moved her hands up and down the muscled length of Max's back, in a slow yet conversely frantic motion. She had waited so long, suppressed the yearnings of her body so often, that patience was nearly beyond her.

"Max . . ." she pleaded against his mouth.

"Shhh," he whispered, and continued to caress her, to adore her with his hands.

Kristina made a soft, whimpering sound; it was all she could manage because he had stolen her breath, stilled her heartbeat, frozen her in one fiery moment of time.

Max laid her down on the bed and stretched out beside her. She wanted him to take her, but he was conducting some primal ritual; she knew he would make her feel every nuance of their lovemaking, that her responses were, to him, a vital part of the encounter.

He kissed her again and again, until she was drunk with the need to have him inside her, but it still wasn't enough. While Kristina entangled desperate fingers in his hair, Max brushed her earlobes with his lips, nibbled at her neck, finally moved down over the quivering rise of her breasts.

She gasped with pleasure and arched her back in an ancient, instinctive gesture of surrender as he took one nipple into his mouth and drew at it greedily.

He went on suckling, meanwhile parting her legs with one hand. She ached to accommodate him; her hips rose and fell as he parted the moist curls at the junction of her thighs and teased her with a soft, plucking motion of his fingers.

Kristina sobbed, with joy, with triumph, with frustration. Her body arched, again and again, seeking, reverberating like the strings of a fine instrument drawn tight.

At last, Max relented. He reached for the condom on the bedside table while kissing Kristina's belly. Once he was ready, he cupped both hands under her buttocks and raised her to receive him.

His eyes searched hers one last time, and then he plunged into her, delving deep, as if to touch the very core of her.

Kristina thrashed beneath him, in a physical plea for him to move faster, to thrust himself even farther inside. She wanted all of him, not just his powerful body, but his mind, even his soul. She did not wish to own Max, it wasn't that, but to be a part of him, to meld the very essence of her being with his.

Max set an even pace, driving Kristina insane with long, slow, methodical strokes.

Finally, as she flung herself up to meet yet another thrust, a cataclysmic orgasm exploded within her, thrusting her legs even wider apart, splintering the heavens, altering the path of uncounted planets orbiting innumerable stars. While Kristina flexed beneath Max, seized by spasm after spasm, he stiffened upon her, and cried out in hoarse ecstasy.

Kristina lay still, stunned, spent, but Max got up and disappeared into the bathroom. He was back in a few moments, stretching out beside her again, gathering her close against him. She was trembling, even then, in the aftermath of satisfaction.

Max kissed her temple. "What are we going to do now?" he asked.

She snuggled even closer, loving the feel of him, the substance and power and the scent of him. "After that, anything else would be anticlimactic."

He groaned at the play on words, but there was a smile in the sound.

Kristina laughed and buried her face in his neck.

"What?" Max prompted.

She lifted her head to look into his eyes. "You're the first man I've slept with in a hundred years," she said. "That's got to be some kind of distinction."

Max rolled over so that she was pinned beneath him, his brown eyes bright with mischief and the beginnings of fresh desire. "Was I worth waiting for?"

Kristina put her arms around his neck, kissed his chin and then his mouth. "Oh, yes, Mr. Kilcarragh." She felt him growing hard against her thigh, while her own body prepared itself to receive him again.

"Do you think you could work that little trick again? This time without the package and all the groping around?"

She nodded, and Max was instantly outfitted with a fresh condom.

"Pretty fancy," he said, grinning.

"Stop talking," Kristina replied, putting her arms around his neck. "And let's skip the foreplay."

Max wouldn't hear of it; he worked Kristina into another fit of longing, and by the time she was in the throes of her second climax, a pleasure even keener and more strenuous than the first, she was glistening with perspiration and completely incoherent.

Much later, when Max was dozing, Kristina got out of bed, took another shower, and put on jeans and a T-shirt. Her earlier exhaustion was gone; making love with Max had restored her, it seemed.

She was in the kitchen, humming and filling the teapot at the sink, when Valerian appeared at her elbow, unheralded as usual. Kristina was so startled that she nearly dropped the kettle.

"I wish you wouldn't do that," she snapped.

Valerian folded his arms and glowered at her. "Wish away," he replied.

Kristina sighed. There was no reasoning with him when he was in one of his moods, and she could only guess at what was bugging this most temperamental of vampires. Her controversial arrangement with Dathan or her blossoming affair with Max? Or perhaps Valerian was finding parenthood to be less than wonderful.

"Okay, I give up," she said. "What is it now?" She moved around him to set the teakettle on the stove and switch on the burner.

"If you wanted to polish your magic, you might have come to me. I do know a thing or two about the craft, as it happens!"

Kristina hid a smile. She'd injured Valerian's formidable pride, without meaning to, of course. "You've been busy," she said reasonably. "With Daisy and your magic act in Las Vegas and now Esteban. I didn't want to bother you."

"So you took up with a *warlock*!"

"You sound just like Mother," Kristina answered, no longer smiling. She was an adult by anyone's definition of the word, and she was getting tired of being scolded about the company she kept. "I didn't 'take up' with Dathan. We have a bargain, that's all."

"What sort of bargain?" Valerian's magnificent face was thunderous, and his cloak and tailored tuxedo made him resemble some great, beautiful bird of prey.

Kristina sighed, hoping Max wouldn't awaken and come downstairs. He'd already met a warlock; it was too soon to introduce him to a vampire. "You know damn well what sort of bargain," she retorted. "He's tutoring me in magic, and I'm—I'm going to help him find a bride."

Valerian loomed, in that singular way he had. Kristina drew herself up to her full if unspectacular height, trying not to seem intimidated.

"Great Zeus, is he still harping on that?" the vampire demanded. "I thought I'd cured him of the obsession by setting Roxanne Havermail on his trail."

"Dathan is as stubborn as you are. He won't rest until he has what he wants."

"You realize, of course, how dangerous he is—that he is the leader of all warlocks everywhere? That his mate will share in that power?"

Kristina knew only too well that Valerian could read minds when he tried; she hoped he was too annoyed and distracted to focus on hers and learn that Dathan had proposed an unholy marriage. "He has been an ally in the past," she said to deflect the vampire's attention. "It seems to me that you welcomed his help at one time."

"That was an armed truce," Valerian snapped. "There was never any question that we would be enemies again, once the common threat had been eliminated."

The common threat, of course, had been the vampire Lisette, who had reigned over the nightwalkers before Maeve. "That's silly. If vampires and warlocks made peace once, they can do it again."

Surprisingly Valerian subsided a little, and Kristina had a sudden insight. It wasn't just her relationship with Dathan that was troubling him, but something deeper and much closer to home. *His* home.

"Things aren't going well with Esteban, are they?" she said softly, touching his arm. She had been so occupied with her own concerns that she had not had the time to visit Daisy or Valerian.

The vampire, so imposing, so fearsome, suddenly appeared vulnerable. "He sleeps on the floor like an animal," he said. "He hides food in his room and won't acknowledge anyone except Barabbas."

Kristina considered the environment from which the little boy had been rescued. "Things like this take time," she said.

Valerian was downright crestfallen. "I wanted to give Daisy a child," he whispered, staring off into some realm Kristina couldn't see. "She's so beautiful, so smart and so good. She deserves a normal life."

Kristina felt a wrench far down in her heart. Whatever his faults, and they were many, Valerian adored Daisy. He had sought her out through lifetime after lifetime, only to lose her again and again. Clearly he feared that history would repeat itself. "Daisy loves you," she reminded him gently.

"Yes," he said, his tone dark with misery. "She loves a fiend, a monster, an inhuman ghoul who dares not sire a child for fear of creating something far worse than himself."

Kristina bit her lip. "I was conceived by a vampire and a mortal," she pointed out, "and I didn't turn out so badly, did I?"

Valerian touched her cheek, not as a lover would, but in the way of a devoted uncle or a godfather. His smile was beautiful, and full of sorrow, and Kristina began to fear for him. He had been known, in his long history, to succumb to terrible fits of melancholia, during which he could lie dormant for decades. One of the oldest vampires, Tobias, had gone underground long ago and never resurfaced.

"No," Valerian said. "You are a miracle, Kristina. But your splendid mother and honorable father are far better creatures than I have ever been."

Kristina willed Max not to come downstairs, but she sensed that he was stirring in his sleep, soon to awaken. Although he had seen Valerian at the Halloween party, meeting the legendary vampire up close and personal was something else again. An experience for which any human being would have to be carefully prepared.

She couldn't help thinking of her private theory that some vampires must grow weary of their existence, of watching mortal loved ones live and die. Though they were predators, blood-drinkers were fascinated by human beings and often became enamored of them, appointing themselves as their guardians or wooing them as lovers. Perhaps Valerian, who had been born as a mortal in the fourteenth century, secretly yearned to rest in peace.

"Do you ever wish you'd never become a vampire?" she asked. The kettle was whistling insistently on the stove, but they both ignored the noise.

"Yes," Valerian answered. "Each time I've found Daisy in a new incarnation and loved her, only to lose her again." For a moment a haunted expression clouded his fathomless sapphire eyes. "It is always with me, Kristina. The knowledge that she will grow old and die, and that I will live on, alone, and wait for her, search for her yet again—"

Kristina thought with sorrow of all the people she'd cared about throughout the years she'd lived—a very short time in comparison to Valerian—her beloved governess, Miss Phillips, for instance. Gilbert Bradford, her husband's brother, and certain mortal friends she'd made along the way. She'd seen all of them age and finally leave her behind. It would happen with Max, too, if they managed to make a life together, and the dread of that pierced her heart like a shard of ice.

"I would gladly surrender my immortality, if indeed that's what I have," she confessed, taking the kettle off the burner at last, pouring hot water over loose tea leaves she'd spooned into a crockery pot earlier. "To me, it's a curse."

Valerian closed his eyes for a moment, as though she'd struck him. "And yet you would suggest that I sire a child by Daisy," he said, meeting her gaze again.

"I would not presume to advise you one way or the other," Kristina answered, "except to say that I think you should forget your Las Vegas show for a while and concentrate on Daisy and Esteban. You yourself said that human life is fleeting—why spend so much time away from them? You certainly don't need the money or the notoriety."

"You're right," he conceded, though somewhat ungraciously. Valerian preferred to play the mentor and guide, not the pupil. In the next moment he assumed a stern expression. "Remember my warning. Warlocks are not to be trusted."

Upstairs, the shower was running. Max was out of bed; he would be downstairs within a matter of minutes.

Valerian arched an eyebrow. "The mortal?"

"Yes," Kristina said with a hint of defiance.

"Is it for him that you are willing to risk so much?"

Kristina knew Valerian was referring to her contract with Dathan. She nodded. "Do you dare to chastise me for that—you who have pursued one woman, one human being, down so many crooked corridors of history?"

"No," Valerian said softly, almost tenderly. "But I sympathize. It would almost be better, I think, if you took a warlock for a mate. At least then you'd be spared the terrible grief, the vulnerability."

"But that would mean giving up the joy as well," Kristina pointed out.

At last he smiled, and when Valerian did that, he was as much a work of art as Michelangelo's *David*. "Wise words," he said. He kissed her forehead and vanished.

There lingered a faint draft in the room, from the vampire's passing, when Max came down the rear stairs and into the kitchen, fully dressed, his hair still damp from the shower. In that moment of simplicity and silence, Kristina knew for certain not only that she loved Max Kilcarragh, but that he had been chosen as her beloved long, long ago, in a time before time, and a place neither of them remembered.

He approached, laying a hand to either side of her waist. He smelled pleasantly of soap, shampoo, and toothpaste as he bent to kiss her lightly on the mouth.

"Hungry?" Kristina asked.

Max drew her against him, gently but firmly enough that she could not doubt his attraction to her. He slid a second, featherlight kiss from the bridge of her nose to the tip. "Yeah," he answered, eyes twinkling, "but I'll settle for food."

Kristina laughed softly and turned in the direction of the refrigerator. Max caught her hand and pulled her back. "Sit down," he said. "I'll cook."

She was amazed again; so much about this man surprised her. In her adult life, especially during her marriage to Michael Bradford, Kristina had never been taken care of by a man. She had essentially looked out for herself, with occasional interference from her mother or Valerian.

Kristina allowed Max to seat her at the breakfast bar. The tea had finished brewing by then, and he brought her a cup before opening the refrigerator door and taking out the ingredients for an omelette— onions, peppers, mushrooms, fat-free cheese, and a carton containing an egg substitute.

"Is it possible for you to develop high cholesterol?" he asked, frowning at the collection of healthy foods.

Kristina flushed a little, embarrassed at this small, harmless reminder of just how different she was from Max himself and virtually everyone else on earth. "I don't know," she said. "I guess it's all part of the act."

Max's expression was thoughtful as he explored the cupboards, finally producing a nonstick skillet. "The act being your need to be—how shall I put it—ordinary?"

She nodded. Her cheeks still felt warm, and she was just a touch defensive. "I've wanted that all my life," she said.

He set the skillet on the stove, turned on the appropriate burner, and began mixing and chopping with a deftness that indicated long practice. There was a twinkly smile in his brown eyes when, at last, he looked at

Kristina. "You've been overlooking one very important fact," he told her. "You, Kristina Holbrook, could never be ordinary, in any sense of the word. Even if you were mortal, you would still be utterly unique."

Kristina looked away for a moment, wanting to believe he meant what he said, but skeptical. He was trying to be kind, to spare her feelings. "I know what I am, Max," she said a little impatiently.

But it wasn't true, of course. She wasn't a witch, woman, angel, or vampire. What did that leave? Were there creatures on other planets like her? In alternate universes and parallel dimensions?

He poured the omelette concoction into the pan and added pepper and salt from the shakers on the back of the stove. He didn't reply to her statement, which made her uneasy.

"What do you think I am?" she asked, trying to hide the vulnerability she felt. When Michael, her husband, had learned of her powers, he had said she was unnatural, a bestial freak. Even after more than a century, the memory had the power to wound her.

"Beautiful," Max replied without hesitation, managing the omelette while at the same time meeting her gaze directly. "Intelligent. Generous. Responsive. Shall I go on?"

Tears gathered along her lower lashes; she blinked them back quickly. Her reaction was contradictory—on the one hand, she was relieved, but Max hadn't really had time to absorb and assimilate the various realities of the situation. It was too soon, even for a man as bright as Max, to comprehend what it meant to be involved with her.

Again he nodded, smiling a little now, dashing at her eyes with the back of one hand. "Yes," she said in a raspy whisper. "Tell me more."

"You have the elegance of a goddess and the mind of a philosopher. Making love to you was like being taken apart, cell by cell, and then put back together, but better than before. Stronger."

Kristina sniffled and then gave a soft laugh. Her hand trembled a little as she reached out for her teacup. "You either have a poetic soul or one hell of a line," she said.

Max found plates, divided the omelette, and slid the halves expertly out of the pan. "And you have a trust problem," he answered without rancor. "I guess that's pretty common these days, with both sexes."

She didn't point out that she didn't really qualify for the analogy; there was no sense in harping on the fact that, for all practical intents and purposes, she was some kind of mutant. "How about you, Max? Do you have a trust problem?"

He set the plates on the breakfast bar, found forks, and joined her, taking the stool next to hers. "No," he said after a few moments of thoughtful silence, during which he surveyed his half of the omelette as though he thought it might offer some sort of input. "I was raised in one of the few functional families in America. Nobody drank, gambled, or hit anybody else. We all went to church every Sunday, yet neither Mom nor Dad could be described as fanatical in any way. I was still in college when I fell in love with Sandy, and she happened to be an emotionally healthy individual, too. The toughest thing that ever happened to me—to all of us, really—was her death."

Kristina took up her fork, more because Max had gone to the trouble to cook for her than because she was hungry. It was a terrible injustice that someone talented and beautiful, with a loving husband and two precious children, could be taken in her youth, while jaded vampires yearned for the solace of death and were denied it.

"I'd like to know more about your life with Michael," Max said in that straightforward way he had that so often caught Kristina off guard. "What happened after the duel?"

Kristina started to rise from the stool, her food forgotten. She wanted, even needed, to share the remaining letters, and the story they contained, with an objective person. If indeed Max could be described as objective, after the way he'd made love to her.

"I'll get the letters," she said.

Max stopped her, taking her wrist in a gentle grasp. "Not now, love," he said. "After breakfast."

Kristina realized that she was hungry, and returned to the omelette. "You're a good cook," she said with some surprise after she'd taken a few bites.

Max grinned. "I'm a nineties kinda guy," he said. "I also do laundry, clean bathrooms, and scrub floors. Once I even mended a tutu fifteen minutes before Eliette was due to perform in a dance recital. Naturally I wouldn't want the guys on my team to find out about that last part."

She smiled at the image of this large, powerfully built man stitching a little girl's ballet costume. The thought stirred a poignant sweetness in the bottom of her heart. "You're a good man, Max Kilcarragh," she said.

He sighed. "Don't give me too much credit. I didn't say I *liked* sewing and cleaning. It was just that somebody had to do it."

Because Sandy was gone, she thought sadly. It was almost as if Max's late wife were there in the room with them, and only then did Kristina fully realize that even if she herself were a normal mortal woman, there would still be an obstacle to overcome. Max had loved Sandy with a rare intensity. Perhaps he did not have the emotional resources to care so deeply again.

"Was—was Sandy that sort of wife?" she asked in a cautious tone. It wasn't really any of her business, she knew, but she still wanted to know what Sandy Kilcarragh had been like. She, who had always had servants, traveled the world, and, in recent decades, concentrated almost completely on building a business that was international in scope. "The domestic type, I mean?"

Max didn't take offense to the inquiry, didn't seem to mind it at all. He took his plate and Kristina's, seeing that she was finished eating, to the sink. "We shared the housework in the beginning," he said, "but once Eliette was born, Sandy decided to take a few years off from her teaching career and stay home. She did more than her share after that, but I helped with the kids as much as I could."

Kristina got off the stool, ready to go upstairs for the other letters. Her throat felt tight, painfully so, for she would probably never be a mother. She and Michael had never conceived a child, and besides, like Valerian, she was afraid of producing a monster of some sort.

"I—I don't think I can have children," she said very softly. She had very good reason to believe as she did.

Max, who had been running water over the breakfast dishes, left the sink to cross the room and take her shoulders tenderly in his big hands. "That hurts you, doesn't it?" he asked. And then, without waiting for her answer, which was probably visible in her eyes, he drew her close and held her tightly for a moment.

Kristina was starved for tenderness; she did not trust her judgment or her perceptions, so great was her need. She was intoxicated by Max's caring, it affected her like opium. She allowed herself to cling to him, just for a few seconds, then pulled away and went upstairs.

She found the letters where she had left them, hesitating only briefly before going back down to the kitchen again. Max was in the family room, sipping from a mug of steaming coffee, probably brewed in the microwave, and gazing out the window, watching a ferry head out of Elliott Bay, lights blazing.

With a smile, Max put down his coffee, went over to the fireplace, and built a crackling fire. It was still dark; dawn was at least an hour away, and there was a certain trenchant intimacy in being together when much of the city was still sleeping. A silent resonance echoed between them, too—a lingering sense-memory of their lovemaking, as though their passion had imprinted itself forever, in the very cells of their flesh.

Kristina stood still, watching Max, allowing herself the fantasy that there could be a thousand other mornings like this one. A lifetime of days and nights.

Max rose to his feet, dusting his hands together, and turned to face Kristina. He ignored the packet of letters in her hand. "Did you ever have one of those moments that you wished could last forever?"

"I think I'm having one right now," Kristina replied.

Neither of them moved.

"It scares me," Max confessed.

"What?"

"Caring so damn much. Kristina, I don't know if I can let myself feel what I'm starting to feel. I don't know if I can risk it."

She understood, or thought she did. "You don't have to be afraid of—of warlocks and vampires. I'll find a way to protect you—"

Max shook his head, and she fell silent. "That isn't what I meant."

Kristina swallowed hard. "Oh."

"I think I'd lose my mind if I loved a woman the way I believe I could love you and then lost her. I've been down that road before, and if I hadn't had Bree and Eliette to live for, I'm not sure I would have made it."

Kristina didn't remind Max that she was already a hundred and thirty years old, that she would probably be the one to grieve, not him. That would have been self-pity, even martyrdom, and those were states of mind she tried hard to avoid, though it wasn't always easy.

She might have said that there were no guarantees, that everyone takes chances, that caring is worth the risks involved, but all those things were too easy, too glib. Max's concerns were valid, and so were her own.

There were so many questions, and so few clear answers.

12

M Y *beloved Phillie*, the next letter began. Max had settled comfortably on the overstuffed leather sofa to read, with Kristina beside him, her eyes following the lines she herself had penned so long before. For her the experience was almost equivalent to reliving those dreadful times, and yet she knew she had to do it, in order to put that most disturbing part of her past to rest . . .

I had intended to write sooner, my patient friend, but it is not so easy remembering those dark days, even now, when considerable time has passed.

When last I put pen to paper, Michael had killed his own cousin, Justin Winterheath, in a pointless duel, whilst doing terrible damage to his own person as well. My husband's knee was shattered, never to heal properly, always to cause him inexorable pain. His drinking, already a problem even before we were married—I had seen that in him and yet refused to accept it as truth— became much worse. He now had the excuse of his injuries.

Phillie, you can imagine the gossip that followed the tragedy at Cheltingham, but I wonder if even you, clever as you are, can anticipate what a web of suffering Michael wove that early morning in the fog.

It was said that Michael was a murderer and should be tried and hanged for his crime. Lady Cheltingham, my mother-in-law, was a fragile wisp of a woman in the first place, and after the tragedy she went into swift decline. Her consumption of laudanum increased by increments, it was said, until she wasn't even bothering to get out of bed. Her husband, the once-blustering Lord Cheltingham, had never been an attentive spouse—I believe some of Michael's more pronounced character flaws came from him—but after Justin was buried, the duke gave up his gaming clubs, his hounds and horses, even his mistress. He shut himself away in his library, not to read, a pursuit which might have done much to mend his spirit, but simply to sit, or so the servants whispered, staring morosely out the windows.

Only Gilbert and I remained strong—Gilbert, because that was his nature, I because Michael needed me. (I was so foolish, Phillie, thinking I could save him, if only I loved him enough!)

Michael became more impossible with every passing day.

He tried over and over again to ride—that had ever been his passion, and love for me had never supplanted it—but his stiff knee made the pursuit wholly impossible. He was thrown on each attempt, and then there was more pain, followed by more drinking, and then more railing and cursing.

In those days when I might still have been a bride, had I wed myself to a more suitable man, I became instead a reminder of all Michael had lost. By that time, he saw himself as the victim of Winterheath's ungovernable temper, and although he must have known what venomous things were being said about him, he never showed a moment's shame or remorse. He hated me, it seemed, as if I'd brought the whole catastrophe down upon us all, and would often mutter the most vile curses at me, or shout. He even accused me of being faithless, Phillie—of betraying him with his own brother.

I don't doubt that you are wondering why I stayed. I am not sure I can answer that question, even now, when I have gained a modicum of perspective. I can only say that I loved Michael completely; my error, no doubt, was in cherishing the man he might have been, instead of the man he was.

At night I slept in a room adjoining Michael's—I did not want him to touch me in a drunken and hateful state. But he came often to my bed and claimed me roughly, and I grew to hate that aspect of marriage that I had so enjoyed at first. I didn't need my magic to disassociate myself from what Michael was doing to me—and I had almost forgotten that I possessed any powers at all.

One spring morning Lady Cheltingham's serving woman woke the household with a shrill scream. The duchess had died in her sleep and lay shrunken and staring in her lacy nightcap and high-necked gown. The ever-present bottle of laudanum stood upon her bedside table within easy reach.

A pall of gloom seemed to settle over the whole of the estate after that, even though the hillsides of Cheltingham were green with sweet grass and the ewes were lambing. Trout stirred in the streams and ponds, and the sky was that fragile eggshell blue that I have only seen in the English countryside. I wanted to be happy, but I could not.

Within a month of Lady Cheltingham's funeral, her husband went into the family chapel in the middle of the afternoon, put the barrel of his favorite hunting rifle into his mouth, and pulled the trigger. The small, ancient church where countless children had been baptized, where eulogies had been said and vows exchanged, was thus fouled by the literal and figurative carnage of Lord Cheltingham's furious despair.

Demons seemed to pursue Michael as never before, to stare out of his eyes, to torment him from both sides of his skin. Gilbert tried but could not reason with his brother at all. Michael was beyond both our reaches.

He disappeared for days on end, commandeering one of the carriages and leaving Cheltingham Castle, and me, in temporary peace. During those intervals, Phillie, I prayed that he would *never come back. God forgive me, I hoped that he would die. But he always returned, angrier, uglier than before, full of terrible accusations.*

By then Gilbert was the Duke of Cheltingham. Though grief-stricken, and bitterly furious with Michael, he was determined to make the estates prosper, to be a good steward. He had long loved one Susan Christopher, a young woman of excellent social standing, and they had planned, since childhood, to marry.

In the wake of the "Cheltingham Scandals," however, Susan's family withdrew their support of the marriage, and Susan herself offered no protest and wed herself to another. She was not steadfast like Gilbert, but I assign her no blame. Although I believe that my own father, as a mortal, was such a man, I have not known another like my brother-in-law.

If you are guessing that I at last knew the worst truth of all, that I had joined myself, under the laws of heaven, to the wrong brother, you are right. I came to love Gilbert, and I believe he bore me some tender sentiment, though of course something within him was broken with the loss of Susan.

Gilbert and I might have taken some comfort from each other, and perhaps not been blamed too much by a merciful heaven, but we did not. Gilbert was far too honorable, though he often looked at me with the same yearning I felt, but it was no such noble notion as honor that stayed me from sin. I might have seduced my husband's brother, so much did I want him, if the act wouldn't have given weight to Michael's constant and otherwise unfounded reproaches.

During this period, Mother, Papa, and Valerian kept their distance. They might have been figures from a mythical tale, for all I knew, and I resented their absence completely, and often summoned them, aloud and in tears. Later, of course, I came to understand that they had stayed away in part because these were battles I had to fight for myself, but there was another reason as well. All of them feared that they would render Michael some unholy punishment, in a moment of uncontrollable fury, and earn my undying hatred in the process.

And so I was alone, except for Gilbert. . . .

The shrill ringing of the telephone jolted both Kristina and Max out of the paper world of the letter; Max leaned his head back on the sofa and closed his eyes, while Kristina went to answer.

"Ms. Holbrook?" an unfamiliar voice asked.

Kristina was watching Max, wondering what he thought of her now, how the information in the letters had affected him. "Yes," she said into the receiver.

The caller gave his name and identified himself as a dispatcher for the alarm company that monitored her shop. "We've had a signal from your place of business, ma'am, and we've sent the police to that address. We're calling to notify you that there may have been a break-in."

Kristina sighed, thanked the man, and hung up. Max was looking at her with raised eyebrows.

"That was somebody from the electronic security firm I deal with," she said. "They've sent the police to my shop. It's probably just a false alarm, but I've got to go down there anyway."

Max laid the unfinished letter carefully on the coffee table and got to his feet. "Let's go," he said.

Kristina luxuriated in the knowledge that Max wanted to go with her, even though she knew it didn't necessarily mean anything. He was a nice guy, raised to be polite and considerate. Silently she blessed his parents—what fine people they must be.

"You don't seem very worried," he commented when, after helping her into her coat and donning his own, he opened the front door. It was tacitly agreed that they would take his Blazer, which was parked in the driveway beside her Mercedes. "About the shop, I mean."

Something was tugging at the edge of her mind, but she couldn't quite identify it. "Like I said, it's probably just a false alarm. And even if somebody did break in, everything is insured."

Max raised the collar of his coat. An icy breeze was blowing in from Puget Sound, and the promise of a rare Seattle snowfall darkened the eastern sky. "Money doesn't matter much to you, does it?" he asked, opening the Blazer's passenger door for her. There was no surprise in the question, and no criticism. Apparently he was just making conversation.

Kristina waited until he was behind the wheel before answering. "I've always had more than enough," she said.

"And what you wanted, you could conjure," he replied, backing carefully into the street.

"But I didn't," Kristina confessed. "Even in the early days, I wanted so much to be—well—normal."

Max shook his head and smiled. "A lot of us would have taken advantage of that kind of power," he said. "Weren't you ever tempted to strike back at Michael when he treated you so badly?"

Kristina considered for several moments, not weighing the answer because she knew that immediately, but deciding whether or not to make such a confession. "I imagined a thousand sorts of vengeance," she said. "Frankly, I've never been sure it wasn't my anger that finally finished him."

Max glanced at her. A few fat flakes of snow wafted down from the burdened sky. "Are you going to tell me about that?"

She bit her lip. "You'll come to it in the letters," she said.

"Fair enough," Max answered.

They reached Western Avenue and the shop within a few minutes. There were two police cars parked out front, and Max tucked the Blazer neatly between them.

Kristina's uneasiness, barely the fragment of a shadow before, rose a notch or two and would not be denied. She got out of the car without waiting for Max to open the door and approached the front door of the shop, which was broken. Huge, jagged shards of glass littered the steps and the sidewalk.

There went the false alarm theory.

"I'm Kristina Holbrook," Kristina told the uniformed officer guarding the door. "This is my store."

He asked for ID, and she fumbled in her purse, found her driver's license.

The officer nodded, and both Max and Kristina entered the shop. There was almost no glass on the floor, and a quick sweep of the room revealed that very little had been disturbed. The cash register, an antique in its own right, had been slammed through the top of the jewelry counter, probably when the robbers discovered that it was empty.

A plainclothes detective approached, flashing his badge. "Ms. Holbrook? Detective Walters."

Kristina nodded in acknowledgment. Max said nothing, but he stood very close to Kristina, and she was grateful.

"We've got an odd case here, Ms. Holbrook," Detective Graham said. He was a clean-cut sort of guy, nice-looking and neatly dressed. "Looks like it was an inside job. You have any employees? Somebody who might have a key?"

Kristina thought of the glass on the sidewalk. Of course. The door had been broken from the inside. Her uneasiness grew, though she still couldn't pinpoint its cause, and bile burned the back of her throat. "No," she said. "I've always run the shop by myself."

"Any chance somebody could have hidden in here somewhere, when you closed up last night?"

"I wasn't here then," Kristina said, blushing a little. She didn't want to have to explain that she'd been with Max; that was precious and private.

Detective Walters didn't press. After all, one of the advantages of owning a business lies in setting one's own hours. "You having any financial problems, Ms. Holbrook?" he asked instead, in an almost bored tone of voice.

Kristina felt Max stiffen, willed him not to defend her. And at the same time relished the fact that he wanted to protest the implications of the policeman's question.

"No," she said. "I don't need the insurance money."

Walters had the good grace to look mildly embarrassed. "Have to ask, Ms. Holbrook. Fact is, it's an easy thing to check out anyway. Matter of a few strokes to a computer keyboard."

That didn't come as any surprise to Kristina. Her best friend, Daisy, was a private detective, and Daisy had long since filled her in on just how easy it was to invade a person's privacy, with or without their knowledge. "I'd like to look around, if you don't mind," she said.

The detective produced a small notebook and a pencil stub from the pocket of his ski jacket. He was wearing jeans, a sweatshirt and sneakers, in lieu of the trench coat Kristina would have expected. "Here," he replied. "Make a list of everything that's missing, if you would."

It finally came to her then, what she had been fretting about ever since the telephone call from the security people had alerted her to the possibility of a robbery.

She headed directly for the back room, where she'd set the doorstop, the ugly brass monkey.

It was gone.

Kristina's knees sagged beneath her; Max caught her elbow in one hand and steered her to the little table nearby, where she took tea breaks in the mornings and afternoons. She sank into one of the cold folding chairs and laid her head on her arms, trembling.

Max touched her shoulder, then crouched beside her chair. "Sweetheart," he said softly. "What is it?"

"The brass monkey," she whispered miserably, turning her head to look into his concerned eyes. "Oh, God, Max—the doorstop is gone!"

"Did this piece have some special sentimental value?" Detective Walters asked, from the doorway. Kristina resented the intrusion, though she did not dislike the man himself.

How could she explain that one night, nearly a year before, a young man had entered the store, bent on rape and robbery, and she'd changed him into a brass doorstop? Obviously she couldn't—not until she and Max were alone, of course.

"Yes," she lied, making herself sit up straight, still dizzy. She knew she was wretchedly pale, and thought she might actually throw up. She hadn't known she was quite human enough to do that. "It wasn't valuable but I—I liked it." She turned imploring eyes to Max, who was still on his haunches beside her chair, watching her closely. "Would you please call my friend and ask her to come down here as soon as she can? Her name is Daisy Chandler." She gave Max the number.

"I'm afraid the perpetrator broke the telephones," Detective Walters said.

Of course. The thief—she'd never troubled herself to learn his name—would have been filled with rage when the spell wore off. It was a wonder he hadn't trashed the whole shop, or even come to Kristina's house to avenge himself. Her home address was printed on the personal cards she kept in her desk, among other places.

"I've got a cell phone in the Blazer," Max answered, and went out to get it.

"What about him?" the detective asked, cocking a thumb in Max's direction. "He have a key to this place?"

"No," Kristina said, unable to keep a note of annoyance out of her voice. "Max is the original solid citizen." She got up, filled a mug with water from the cooler, added a tea bag, and put the whole shebang into the microwave. Nausea roiled in her stomach and seared the back of her throat; maybe chamomile would soothe her nerves.

"Had to ask," Walters said. "Not much more we can do here, today at least. We'll write up a report and ask you to sign it. You probably should get somebody over to either replace that glass or board the place up."

Protecting the rest of her merchandise was the least of Kristina's worries. "Thank you," she said. She didn't exactly mean it, but that was the closest thing to sincerity she could manage at the moment.

Max returned as Walters and the others were leaving. "Daisy's on her way," he said. "While I was on the telephone, I called a friend of mine, a contractor. He'll see what he can do about the door."

Kristina had collected her tea from the microwave. She made her wobbly way back to the table and sat down. She used both hands to raise the cup to her lips, she was still shaking so badly.

"Do you want to tell me what you meant by that remark about the doorstop?" Max asked when they had both been silent for some time.

The police were gone, and a cold draft blew in from outside. Both Max and Kristina were still wearing their coats.

She shook her head. "When Daisy gets here," she promised. "I can't stand to tell it twice."

Max drew back the other chair and sat down across from her. "Daisy would be the woman who gave the Halloween party for the neighborhood kids. The one who keeps a white wolf for a pet and considers herself the wife of a vampire."

It might have been funny, so ludicrous was the situation, if it weren't for the fact that an angry robber and rapist had been turned loose. Kristina couldn't find it within herself to smile. "That's her. She's also a private investigator."

"Figures," Max said wryly. "Never let it be said that your friends and relations lead dull lives."

Kristina managed a ghost of a grin. "Before she came to Seattle, Daisy was a homicide detective in Las Vegas. The word *dull* is not in her vocabulary."

Max pushed his metal folding chair back on two legs, his arms folded, regarding Kristina in thoughtful silence for several seconds. "I'm almost afraid to ask this question," he began. "But what can Ms. Chandler do that the police can't? Isn't she mortal, just like them?"

Kristina let out a long breath. She nodded. "Daisy is quite human. She's also very, very good at what she does."

"And she, like you, has some very powerful allies."

"Yes," Kristina replied. She was counting on Valerian and perhaps Dathan for some aid and advice, but she didn't plan to bother either of her parents with the problem. Calder was doing important work of his own, and Maeve was occupied with the search for Gideon and Dimity.

"How about some more tea?" Max asked, seeing that Kristina's cup was empty.

"Are you always such a nice guy?" Kristina countered, surrendering her mug. "I keep expecting to find out something awful about you."

Max grinned as he dropped a tea bag into water and set the cup back in the microwave. "I leave dirty socks around sometimes," he confessed. "And I'm a sore loser at racquetball."

Kristina spread a hand over her upper chest in mock horror. "Oh, no."

Max leaned down, while the oven whirred behind him, and kissed Kristina lightly on the mouth. "I'm a long way from perfect, okay?"

Suddenly Kristina felt the weight of the ages settle on her slender shoulders. "Maybe," she admitted sorrowfully, "but there's a definition in the dictionary for what you are. I'm something that doesn't even have a name."

The microwave bell chimed; Max took the tea out and set it down in front of Kristina and dropped back into his chair across from her before grasping her hand. "You're a woman," he insisted quietly. "Trust me. I know."

A tear trickled down Kristina's cheek; she dashed it away with the back of her hand. Before she could say anything, however, there was a stir at the front of the shop and the sound of a familiar voice.

"Kris?" Daisy called. "Are you in here?"

"Back here," Kristina replied, rising shakily to her feet.

Max followed her into the shop, where Daisy stood near the broken counter, surveying the damage.

"What happened?" she asked. She was wearing jeans, a turtleneck sweater, hiking boots, and a baseball cap, and her adopted son, Esteban, was perched on her hip. He, too, was bundled against the cold, and his enormous brown eyes were wide as he looked around.

Kristina shoved her hands into the pockets of her coat. Max stood beside her. "You know Max Kilcarragh, don't you?" she asked, stalling.

Daisy nodded. "He came to the Halloween gig," she answered. "Hi, Max. How are the kids?"

"Great," Max replied with another grin. "How's the wolf?"

It was a rhetorical question; no one expected a reply, and Daisy didn't offer one. She was already prowling around the shop, looking at things, assessing the situation. Finally she turned to Kristina again. "Obviously the guy didn't break in, he broke out. What the hell happened here?"

Kristina led the way to the settee and chairs on the other side of the shop, where she and Max had sat talking on another occasion. Daisy took one of the chairs, Esteban settling against her chest and pushing a thumb into his mouth, and Max sat down beside Kristina, on the settee.

Slowly, quietly, Kristina told her friends about the night she'd turned the unwelcome visitor into a doorstop. She admitted that Valerian had warned her that the spell could wear off, and that she had always meant to do something about the thing, but she'd procrastinated.

Now it was only too obvious that the brass monkey had come back to life, torn the shop apart, and left.

"He'd be scared to bother you again, wouldn't he?" Max reasoned. His elbows were braced on his knees; he'd interlaced his fingers and rested his chin on extended thumbs.

Daisy sighed. "As a rule, these guys aren't real smart. That's one of the reasons they commit crimes—because they can't work out the cause-

and-effect equation—i.e., 'If I knock off this convenience store, the cops are going to catch me if they can, and then I'll end up in prison.' They don't think beyond what they want at the moment."

Kristina shivered. She hadn't seen the last of her would-be assailant; he'd be back. And now her magic was so weak as to be almost nonexistent. Was she finally going to die, after a hundred and thirty years? And what if Max got in the thief's way, trying to protect her?

She covered her face with both hands and groaned. "Valerian warned me. I should have listened!"

"It's going to be okay," Daisy said. She sounded so certain. Daisy was that kind of person; she never seemed to doubt anything. "First of all, I'm going to bring Barabbas over to keep you company for a while. You could use a pet anyway. And when Valerian—" She glanced briefly at Max, then went on. "When Valerian wakes up, I'll ask him to find this guy."

Max took Kristina's hand and held it tightly between both his own. She felt strength and reassurance surge into her. She saw such love in his eyes that her heart ached with the effort to receive and contain it all.

"My folks could keep Bree and Eliette for a few more days—until this is resolved," he said. "In the meantime, I'll stay at your place. I don't want you alone, even with a wolf to protect you."

Kristina promptly vetoed the idea. "Not a chance, Max," she said. "I won't allow you to endanger yourself that way. Valerian will have some suggestions, and, besides, Barabbas is no ordinary wolf. He'll be a perfectly adequate bodyguard as long as I need one."

Daisy nodded in agreement, but said nothing. There was new respect in her eyes as she looked at Max.

"What are my options here?" Max demanded. "Where this lame-brained plan is concerned, I mean?"

"You don't have any," Kristina said. "If you refuse to let me do this my way, then I'll have no choice but to find this guy and confront him. I have to act, Max. I can't sit around and wait."

A look of horror dawned in Max's handsome face. *"You expect this bastard to come to your house,"* he rasped.

"It won't go that far," Daisy interjected. But she was the only one who felt confident. She stood, easily lifting the now-sleeping child in her arms.

"How do you like motherhood?" Kristina asked, desperate to change the subject. Max's friend, the contractor, had arrived. Max went to join him at the front of the shop, where the two men conferred about the broken door.

Daisy beamed and kissed the dark, silken hair on top of Esteban's head. "I like it fine," she answered. "Valerian is having fits, though—it upsets him that the little guy sleeps on the floor and hides food and stuff. You'd think in six hundred years he'd have learned some patience."

"Not Valerian," Kristina said, with a wan smile. She was anxious to see the vampire again, although she knew a heated lecture was inevitable. He had warned her, after all, about casting frivolous spells and failing to follow up on them. "What about your work as a PI? Are you going to give that up?"

Daisy shook her head. "I'll be cutting back a little for a while, but I'm a career woman at heart," she said. "We've hired a nanny, through one of those swanky agencies. She came from Brazil, so she speaks perfect Portuguese, as well as English, of course. And Valerian has given up his magic act in Vegas, at least for the time being." She paused and grinned mischievously. "He'll come as quite a shock to the PTA once Esteban starts school, won't he?"

Kristina chuckled, grateful for a few moments of distraction from the new and difficult problem she faced. "I just hope the nanny can deal with your—er—unconventional lifestyle." She thought of the loyal Mrs. Fullywub, who had worked for Kristina's parents for many years, and been fully aware that her employers were vampires.

Daisy shrugged. "Given what we're paying her, I doubt she'll ask all that many questions. Besides, we're not half as weird as some of the people you see on TV talk shows. Listen, I've got to go, but I'll have Barabbas at your place before the sun goes down, I promise. And you can expect a visit from Valerian, too, of course."

Kristina thanked her friend, and Daisy left.

Max introduced Kristina to the contractor, whose name was Jess Baker. Arrangements were made, and Jess prepared to board up the door, until it could be replaced with a new one the following day.

Back at Kristina's house, Max insisted that she sit in the Blazer until he'd gone through the whole place, room by room and closet by closet, to make sure it was safe. Finally he came to the door and signaled that she could come in.

"Are you sure you won't let me move in for a day or two?" he asked, helping her out of her coat.

"Positive," she answered. "Max, we can't keep seeing each other. It's too dangerous—"

He put his arms around her and drew her very close. "Just try to get rid of me," he replied, and kissed her.

Kristina lost herself, lost her troubles, in that sweet, brief contact. "Oh, Max," she said when it was over. "I need you to hold me, to make love to me."

"I think we can arrange that," he answered gruffly.

They went upstairs then, Kristina leading the way, returning to her room. The bed was still rumpled from their last encounter.

Slowly, garment by garment, savoring every moment, every stolen kiss, they undressed each other and lay together on the musk-scented sheets, having flung the covers to the floor. Beyond the windows snow fell, great, fat flakes swaying from side to side, taking their time.

Kristina was filled with a sense of peace, unwarranted as that was, for while Max was touching her, kissing her, holding her, there was no sorrow in the universe, no pain or treachery or vengeance.

"I love you," she said on a breath as Max moved over her.

His body spoke eloquently, but he did not say the vital words, and even in her need, Kristina took note. And she grieved.

13

IT was still snowing when nightfall came, and Valerian appeared soon after the earth had reached that crucial degree of turning, the white wolf at his heels. Max felt his hackles rise, but he wasn't sure whether it was the animal that provoked this primitive response in him or the vampire. He suspected there wasn't a whole lot of difference between the two of them—both were ferocious, both were cunning, both were wild, and, as hard as it was to admit, beautiful in a lethal sort of way.

There had been nothing particularly dramatic about their arrival, however—the vampire rang the front doorbell, and the wolf crouched at his heels. The animal's silver-white pelt glistened with flakes of snow; Valerian, too, wore a dusting of the stuff, glimmering in his shaggy chestnut hair and on the shoulders of his expensively cut overcoat. Both the wolf and the vampire studied Max with a hungry glint in their eyes, as though ready to pounce.

He stepped back to admit them. "Kristina is in the living room," he said, gesturing. He was sure Valerian knew the way, and that he had never bothered to ring the doorbell before. Popping in unannounced was more his style, according to Kristina.

The vampire stepped over the threshold and shed his coat in a graceful, shrugging motion, then handed the garment to Max, as though he were a footman or a butler. Amused rather than offended, and understandably fascinated, Max offered no protest.

The wolf, in the meantime, shook himself off in the middle of the entryway's Persian rug, then trotted, puppylike, toward the living room. Valerian gave Max a long, assessing look, then followed the beast.

Max hung up the coat, next to his own ratty ski jacket, and went to join the party.

Valerian stood with his back to the living room fire, which Max had built to a comforting roar, warming his hands. Kristina rested on an elegant Victorian chaise, the pages of an ancient manuscript spread across her lap. The wolf had taken his place on the floor beside her, strange blue eyes watchful, muzzle resting on paws as white as the snow drifting past the windows.

Max bent over Kristina and kissed the top of her head. "You're sure you don't want me to stay," he said. It wasn't a question really, but a statement. He hated the thought of leaving her, but she'd already made her wishes more than clear.

She looked up at him, touched his lips and then his chin with one index finger. Hours had passed since they'd made love, showered together, and gotten dressed again, but he still felt the aftershocks of passion deep in his groin.

"I'm sure," she said.

He met the vampire's gaze, which was level and patently unfriendly, then looked down at Kristina again. "You'll call if you need me?"

"I'll call," she promised, trying to smile. She was looking fragile again; Max wondered if their lovemaking had merely added to the strain of her other concerns, rather than lending comfort.

With a nod to Valerian, Max turned and left the room, collecting his coat and the gym bag containing his dirty clothes on the way out of the house. He sat in the Blazer for a long time before turning the key in the ignition, backing out of the driveway, and heading toward home.

"YOU'VE really done it this time," Valerian said when the front door closed behind Max. The vampire's nostrils were slightly flared, and Kristina knew he had had trouble containing his temper until they were alone.

Barabbas whimpered.

Kristina closed her eyes. She'd found the volumes she'd asked to borrow from Maeve's personal library waiting on her desk, when she and Max had come downstairs after making love, and searched the pages for a spell that would get her out of this mess. "How do you mean?" she asked with exaggerated innocence, finally making herself meet Valerian's furious glare. "By letting the doorstop come back to life, or by getting involved with Max Kilcarragh?"

"It's obviously too late to do anything about your infatuation with that mortal, and, as you pointed out the last time we talked, it would be hypocritical of me to condemn you for loving a human being." He paused, pacing along the edge of the hearth, striving hard to retain his composure. "Great Zeus, Kristina—I warned you about that damnable, silly spell, didn't I? Have you tried to find this—this doorstop of yours?"

Kristina bit her lower lip and nodded. "No luck," she said. She tapped the manuscript. "But I did come across an incantation that might turn him back into a brass monkey. At least for a little while, until we, or the police, can find him."

Valerian stopped his pacing and arched one eyebrow in plain contempt. "The *police*? What would you say to them, Kristina? That you changed a man into a doorstop in a moment of pique and now it's all come undone and he's on the streets, looking to commit mayhem and maybe murder?"

She shrank against the back of the chaise, properly chagrined. "Can't you find him?" she asked after a long, difficult silence and at a very heavy cost to her pride. "My powers are dwindling, but yours—"

He shook his head. "I have already tried. Something is veiling him from me—probably a warlock. And he may have powers of his own, this brass monkey of yours."

"He was an ordinary mortal!" Kristina protested. It was too horrible to think of that ghoul using magic.

"I have summoned Dathan," Valerian said, taking an exquisite pocket watch from his vest and flipping open the case. The soft, tinkling notes of a Mozart composition sprinkled the room, light as the evening snowfall. "If there are warlocks involved in this muddle, he'll know about it."

In virtually the next instant Dathan materialized, clad in kidskin breeches, a ruffled shirt, and a waistcoat. The rather dashing outfit was completed by a pair of high, gleaming black boots.

"Did we interrupt a costume party?" Valerian inquired archly.

Dathan was not amused. He dismissed the vampire with a sniff and turned to Kristina. "Have you come to your senses, my beloved?" he asked, taking one of her hands and brushing the knuckles with the lightest pass of his lips. "What a splendid pair we should make."

Valerian made a sound that rather resembled a snort. Another affectation, of course, for his lungs had not drawn breath since the Middle Ages. "How I hate to dash your hopes," he said with a complete lack of conviction, "but you're too late. Alas, our Kristina loves a mortal. I fear it's one of those eternal things, rather like my alliance with Daisy."

Dathan turned at last and leveled a look at his old adversary. Barabbas, who had been watching the warlock intently ever since his appearance, lifted his magnificent head and growled, making it abundantly clear whose side he would take if hostilities escalated.

"I hardly think you invited me here to tell me about Max Kilcarragh," Dathan told Valerian coldly, ignoring the wolf. "I know all about him, as it happens." Here the warlock paused and looked down at Kristina. "He's buried his heart with his dead wife, your Max. He might want very much to love you, but he is incapable of it. Contrary to the stage magician's assessment of the matter, Mr. Kilcarragh's soul mate was—and is—the mother of his children."

Kristina couldn't help remembering that she'd told Max that she loved him that very afternoon, in a most intimate moment, and that he hadn't answered in kind. Max was too honest to offer false vows. "Maybe you're right," she conceded. "In any case, I have other business with you. And it has nothing whatsoever to do with our bargain."

Dathan ran his gaze over her slender form. She was wearing a simple silk caftan of the palest ivory. "Why are you lying there like an invalid? Are you still ill?"

Kristina sighed. She'd tried several of the spells she'd found in her mother's books over the course of the afternoon, hoping one of them would work on the escaped doorstop, and the effort had weakened her. The worst part, of course, was not knowing whether or not she'd succeeded.

"No," she said. "I'm just tired, that's all."

A charged silence ensued. Valerian was clearly holding his tongue, though his eyes glittered with malicious amusement, and Dathan actually flushed. No one needed to explain to Kristina that both of them knew what had happened between her and Max.

Kristina gathered the parchment pages of the ancient volume and set them carefully aside. Her relationship with Max was her own damned business, and she resented both the vampire and the warlock for daring to have any opinion at all on the matter. Quietly, evenly, she explained about the intruder to her shop, telling Dathan how she'd transformed the miscreant into an inanimate object, intending to deal with him later. When the tale ended, Valerian spoke.

"Tell the truth," he said to the warlock, "if that's possible for you. Is any of this your doing?"

Dathan flung out his hands in a gesture of supreme exasperation. Again the wolf growled. "What would I have to gain by such a stunt?"

Valerian had a reply at the ready, as usual. "You could 'save' Kristina, thus painting yourself as a hero, perhaps hoping to win her heart. Brave warlock rescues fair damsel, et cetera, et cetera."

"You forget yourself, vampire," Dathan accused, glowering at Valerian. He was not afraid of Barabbas, probably because he could have broken the beast's neck with a simple motion of his hands. "You are the one who delights in high drama, not I."

"Do not provoke me," Valerian warned in a quiet voice that would have spawned abject fear in almost any other creature. "Kristina is in danger. Were it not for the possibility that you can be of assistance, I would just as soon see you bound in barbed wire and thrown into hell as look at you."

Kristina closed her eyes again. The room fairly crackled with animosity, and the tension was smothering.

"This is not helping," she said.

Valerian turned his back to Dathan and leaned against the fireplace mantel. The mirror above it did not show his reflection. The warlock drew a deep breath and let it out slowly, in an obvious bid for patience.

"I'm sorry, Kristina," Dathan said, putting just the mildest emphasis on her name, so that there would be no mistake, no suggestion that he was apologizing to the vampire. "Naturally, I will do whatever I can to help. And let me assure you—I've had nothing to do with any of this."

Kristina believed him; Dathan, though he could be devious when he chose, was also arrogant. He seldom questioned his own intentions and thus felt no need to disguise them. He was used to power; among warlocks, his word was law. "Can you find him?" she asked.

"I shall certainly try," he promised.

Valerian spoke again, in a more moderate tone than before, but with no greater affection. "Look among your own ranks," he said.

"I would offer you the same advice," Dathan replied. "Beginning with Benecia and Canaan Havermail."

Kristina felt a chill and exchanged glances with Valerian. Dathan had struck upon a possibility she had not considered. Perhaps the doorstop had not come back to life at all. Perhaps, instead, the little fiends had found out about the spell somehow and taken the brass monkey to use against Kristina, or simply to spite her. Benecia, after all, had been furious at Kristina's refusal to consider her as a bride for Dathan.

"I must feed," Valerian said. His magnificent face was utterly impassive; he would not allow the warlock the satisfaction of being right. "Then I shall find the demon babies and make them tell me what they know."

He crossed the room, ignoring Dathan as thoroughly as though the warlock had not been there at all, and bent to kiss Kristina's forehead. "Stay here," he commanded, and then he vanished.

Barabbas merely blinked; he was used to his master's comings and goings. But his fierce eyes followed Dathan closely as the visitor sank into a chair near Kristina's chaise.

"I am calling off our bargain," Dathan announced. "I want only one bride—you, Kristina."

"I don't love you."

The warlock closed his beautiful eyes for a moment, as though she'd struck him a physical blow. "I shall teach you to care for me, and make you queen of all my kind, male and female."

"I do not think witches would take kindly to a queen," Kristina said with a soft smile. "You yourself have told me that they are independent creatures. Besides, I have no wish to reign over anyone."

Dathan leaned forward, sitting now on the edge of his chair, his hands clasped together, his expression so earnest that it caused Kristina pain to look upon his face. "If I swore to keep your Max and his children safe, every moment of every day, until the natural end of their lives, would you agree?"

Kristina started to refuse, but as the implications of Dathan's words sank in, she held her tongue. This was no idle promise; Dathan surely had the power to do exactly that. As matters stood, *she* could offer them nothing but danger.

"It would be a sacrifice," Dathan said very softly. "I know that. But think of it, Kristina. Consider what it means."

She did not need to think, she knew. Just by coming into Max and the girls' lives, she had put them in mortal peril. By leaving them forever, and taking Dathan for a mate, she could undo that.

"I need some time," Kristina said. Her heart was already breaking.

Dathan nodded and rose. "I will make you happy," he vowed.

Kristina didn't respond. Her eyes were brimming with tears, and when she'd blinked them away, telling herself to be strong, Dathan was gone.

*   *   *

VALERIAN found Benecia and Canaan in a forgotten cemetery, overgrown with weeds, behind the ruins of a church in a Nevada ghost town. They were conducting one of their bizarre moonlight tea parties. They had conjured an elegant table, set with fine china and a gleaming silver service, and arranged four chairs around it.

Each of them occupied one, of course, their tiny feet dangling high off the ground in patent leather Mary Janes. They wore starched dresses, rife with ruffles, and their hair, as always, was done in gleaming ringlets. Their guests were a mummified miner and a teenage hitchhiker, freshly drained of her life's blood and staring mutely into eternity.

The relationship between Benecia and Valerian was not particularly cordial, although Canaan appeared to bear him neither rancor nor affection. Canaan was a self-absorbed creature, concerned, in true vampire fashion, only with her own pleasures. No doubt the hitchhiker had been her evening's kill. Benecia had probably fed elsewhere, since the miner was nothing more than a husk, having been dead for at least seventy years.

Benecia smiled sweetly, all the more horrible for her resemblance to an exquisitely made porcelain doll. "Valerian," she said.

Canaan looked at the newcomer with indifference and returned to her one-sided conversation with the hitchhiker.

Valerian overturned the table without moving, scattering the silver coffeepot, the sugar bowl and creamer, the costly china cups and platters. The miner toppled off his chair, and what was left of his head crumbled to dust. The hitchhiker teetered, but did not fall.

Canaan vanished in an instant, clearly a vampire who believed that discretion was the better part of valor, but Benecia drew back her perfect upper lip and snarled like the vicious aberration she was. "How dare you?" she spat.

"I would dare considerably more, and you know it," Valerian replied, unruffled. Benecia was nearly as old as he, but he did not fear her. Not for himself, at least. "Do not try my patience, little beast—if there is one penance in all the universe that might keep me from the flames of hell, it is driving a stake through your brittle heart."

The demon-child's cornflower blue eyes glinted with hatred, but she did not advance upon him. "What do you want?"

"An explanation," Valerian replied. "What were you doing in Kristina Holbrook's shop last night?"

She stared at him in silence for a long time, her expression unreadable. Finally she laughed. "There was something I wanted."

"The brass doorstop," Valerian said.

Benecia smiled coyly. "Yes."

"Where is it now?"

"I shall never tell you that," she replied cheerfully, "no matter what you do to me."

Valerian knew she was telling the truth; the fact that she longed for the peace of death was at once her strength and her weakness. Driving a stake through her heart would be a favor at this juncture, and he was in no mood to be merciful.

"What do you want?" he asked, speaking as calmly as he could.

Benecia folded small, alabaster white arms. Her shell-like fingernails were tiny and pink, and she wore a frilly white pinafore over her be-ruffled dress. Valerian recalled an incident far in the past, when she and Canaan had placed all their dolls in little wooden coffins and buried them in a long-abandoned garden, like corpses.

Inwardly he shuddered, he who hunted human prey with the rise of every moon. The difference was that he rarely killed his quarry, but simply left them in a swoonlike state.

"But you know what I want," she taunted. "So why trouble to ask?"

"Answer me, damn you."

"I want to change the past," she said with a touch of defiance and— Valerian could hardly believe it—sorrow. "I want to grow up as a mortal, become a woman, marry, and have children. Give me that, vampire, and you shall have your ugly brass monkey."

Valerian did not speak. What she asked was impossible; vampires could travel no further back in time than the moment of their transformation from human to nightwalker.

"Those are my terms," Benecia said. And then she dissipated like thin fog, as her sister had done, leaving the ruins of her tea party behind her.

Valerian buried the hitchhiker and the miner and returned to Seattle, where he found Daisy seated in a rocking chair in the living room, Esteban snuggled in her arms. They were both sleeping, and he did not awaken them.

Instead he stood silently in the shadows, understanding only too well what Kristina must be feeling, now that she had fallen so thoroughly in love with her mortal, Max Kilcarragh. Centuries of wandering, in an incessant cycle of finding his beloved and then losing her again, had marked Valerian's soul with loneliness so deep that the scars would probably never heal. Now he had found her, managed to break the curse that had torn them asunder so many times before, and he was truly happy.

With that joy, however, came a vulnerability unlike any he had ever experienced. Loving took so much courage, so much sacrifice. Always the knowledge was with him that one day, being mortal, Daisy would die. He, on the other hand, would look much as he did at that moment; he had not changed significantly in nearly six hundred years.

She opened her eyes, sensing his presence. Esteban stirred but did not awaken. "Hello, handsome," she said. "What accounts for the frown?"

"I was thinking that I love you."

"Odd. Thoughts like that make most people smile."

"Most people grow old at the same pace. Daisy, I don't want to lose you—not now and not fifty years from now."

Esteban whimpered in his sleep, and Daisy began to rock the chair gently, one hand patting the boy's thin little back. "You're torturing yourself," she accused softly. "Eventually I'll die. Then I'll be born again as somebody else, and you'll find me, the way you always do. We're meant to be together."

"Suppose I *don't* find you?"

"Vampires are so neurotic," she teased. "Of course you will." Daisy's expression turned serious, and she studied her beloved mate closely. "Did you manage to track down Kristina's brass monkey?"

"Yes and no," Valerian replied, pacing, too restless to sit. He would have to go out again, for he had yet to feed, and his powers were at a low ebb. "Benecia Havermail was behind the robbery, and she's holding the thing hostage."

"Out of spite?"

"She wants to be mortal again."

"That's impossible, isn't it?" Daisy asked, frowning.

Valerian spread his hands. "Aidan Tremayne, Maeve's twin brother, was a vampire for well over two hundred years. Today he is flesh and blood again, with a wife, four children, and no memory whatsoever of his former existence."

Daisy nodded. "I remember now." She had heard the story long before; there were no secrets between the two of them. "If Aidan could be transformed, why not Benecia?"

"Aidan was basically good, and he had been made a vampire against his will. Benecia, on the other hand, begged for the privilege and has been unabashedly evil ever since she became a blood-drinker."

"And as a human being, she would still be evil?"

"Unspeakably so," Valerian agreed.

Daisy rose, carrying the little boy out into the entryway. At the base of the stairs Valerian took the child gently from her arms, and together they climbed to the second floor. Esteban's nursery was next to their own room; Valerian laid his adopted son gently in his crib. By morning, they both knew, the baby would have climbed over the rail and curled up on the rug in the center of the floor.

Daisy took her mate's hand and led him out of the nursery. The new nanny would arrive the next day; perhaps she could get through to Esteban, explain to him that he was safe now, that he need not fear being abused and neglected anymore.

"Go and feed," she said in the hallway.

Valerian nodded, resigned, and kissed her tenderly before taking his leave.

THE sun had been up no more than five minutes when Dathan made his way down the circular stone steps to the crypts beneath the desecrated chapel on the Havermail's English estate. The parents of the two beautiful demons were nowhere about—Avery and Roxanne had gone their separate ways long before—but Benecia and Canaan lay side by side upon their beds of stone, immersed in the vampire sleep.

It would be so easy to destroy them, the warlock thought, and he had no compunction about taking their lives. Despite their innocent appearance, these were *not* sweet mortal children, but fiends of the worst order. A stake, an infusion of his own blood, or simply carrying them up the stairs to lie in the sunny courtyard, any one of those methods would suffice.

Only one thing stopped Dathan from killing them both, and that was the brass monkey. As he had suspected, and Valerian had later confirmed, Benecia knew where the thing was hidden, and she had probably confided in her sister.

He drew a steel dagger with a jeweled handle from the scabbard on his belt and for a few moments enjoyed the fantasy of plunging it through those callous little hearts, first one, and then the other. Granted, the doorstop would still be at large, but at the same time, one of Kristina's greatest fears would be allayed: the Kilcarragh mortals would be safe from this pair of monsters.

No chance of Kristina becoming his mate if that happened.

Dathan wasn't prepared to be quite that noble.

He smiled. He could, however, let both Benecia and Canaan know that they were not invulnerable, despite their highly developed vampire powers.

Using the point of the dagger, Dathan pricked his finger and let a drop of blood fall first upon Benecia's barely parted lips, then upon

Canaan's. It was not enough to finish them, more's the pity, but when they awakened at nightfall, they would know they had been visited by a powerful enemy. The message could not have been clearer: *Beware, for I, the warlock, have found you.*

Reluctantly Dathan then resheathed his blade and left the tomb.

WITHIN moments of awakening that night, Calder Holbrook went out to feed. He was back in his laboratory, going over the results of Kristina's blood test for perhaps the hundredth time, before an hour had passed.

Hunting, a delightful sport to many vampires, was a troublesome task to him, to be attended to and forgotten as soon as possible. Maeve relished her powers, her adventures, her singular challenges as queen of the nightwalkers. Calder, on the other hand, got all the excitement he needed just loving Maeve and working on his experiments.

That night, however, he was deeply troubled.

Maeve appeared, looking flushed from a recent feeding, just as the small clock on his desk was chiming half past two.

Calder turned from his microscope to kiss her. As always, the old passion surged between them, undiminished by the passage of many, many years. Before the night was over, he knew, they would make love.

"Any luck finding Dimity?"

Maeve shook her head, her blue eyes probing deeply into his, exploring his heart. "What is it, Calder?" she pressed gently. "I know you're upset—I can sense it."

He looked away for a moment. It was difficult, just knowing what he knew. Telling Maeve, and finally Kristina, would be much worse. "Sit down," he said, indicating a nearby stool.

Maeve obeyed, her gaze fixed on his face. "Tell me."

"It's about Kristina," he began, standing before his mate, resting his hands on her shoulders. "I've—well, I took a blood sample from her, because she said she hadn't been feeling well. Maeve, she is undergoing some kind of genetic transformation."

"What does that mean?" Maeve demanded. She was rigid with anguish; like Calder, she cherished their child.

He hesitated a moment, but there was no gentle way to say it. "Kristina is aging. Her blood cells are virtually indistinguishable from those of a mortal."

Tears glimmered along Maeve's dark lashes. Her indigo eyes were wide with horrible understanding. "She's dying?"

Calder struggled against his own emotions. "Yes," he said finally.

*   *   *

DURING the night the snow melted away, and Sunday dawned gray and murky in Seattle. Barabbas lay curled at the foot of Kristina's bed, apparently taking his guard-dog duties very seriously.

"What do you eat, anyway?" she asked him. "Besides little girls making their way through the woods to Grandmother's house, I mean."

Barabbas made a sorrowful sound.

"You're right," Kristina admitted. "It wasn't a very good joke. Come on—maybe there's a steak in the freezer."

She put on a robe and slippers, because the house was especially cold, and led the way down the rear stairs into the kitchen. After thawing out a top sirloin for the wolf, Kristina poured herself a bowl of cereal and curled up on the family room couch to eat.

She had just finished when Max pulled into the driveway in his Blazer.

"I should have called first," he said when Kristina opened the front door to him, "but I was afraid you would tell me to stay away."

She pulled him inside, closed the door, and then threw her arms around his neck. "Not a chance," she replied.

Barabbas stood in the doorway leading to the dining room, making a low growling sound.

"Hush," Kristina scolded. "It's only Max."

Apparently satisfied, the wolf turned and padded away.

"Did you sleep last night?" Max asked, holding Kristina in a loose but tantalizing embrace.

"Did you?" Kristina countered, smiling a little.

"You know damn well I didn't," he retorted somewhat grumpily. "All I could think about was that creep, the ex-doorstop, out there somewhere, dreaming up ways to get to you." He kissed her forehead. "Let's get out of here for a while. Take a drive or something."

The idea sounded wonderful to Kristina, who was beginning to feel like a prisoner. "What about Barabbas?"

"He can stay here," Max answered, giving Kristina a little nudge toward the stairs. She needed to get dressed, of course, before they could go anywhere.

At the base of the stairway she paused and looked back at Max with a mischievous smile. "I believe you're jealous of him," she teased.

Max shoved a hand through his hair. "Maybe you're right," he answered in all seriousness. "After all, the wolf got to stay here and watch over you last night. I happen to regard that as my job, not his."

Kristina shook her head. "Males," she muttered, and hurried up the stairs to get ready for the day.

When she came back down half an hour later, clad in black corduroy jeans, a heavy gray sweater, and lightweight hiking boots, Max was sitting in the living room on a hassock. Barabbas faced him, seated on the hearth rug.

They were staring at each other, man and beast, and Kristina wondered who would have looked away first if she hadn't entered the room when she did.

14

BREE Kilcarragh took in her surroundings with wonder. Grandmother and Aunt Gweneth said the place was called a flea market, though she had yet to spot even one bug. All she could see was a lot of strange stuff, displayed on shaky tables and in booths.

She tugged at Eliette's hand, while Grandmother and Aunt Gweneth stopped to examine a pair of salt and pepper shakers made to look like little toilets. "Why would anybody want to buy a flea?" she asked in a loud whisper.

Eliette rolled her eyes. She was older and wiser, and she never missed a chance to let Bree know it, either. "That just means there's a lot of junk to buy," she whispered back.

Grandmother turned and smiled at them. It was warm in the large building, so Bree and Eliette didn't have to wear their coats. "Getting tired?" she asked.

Both girls shook their heads vigorously. Although they missed their daddy, they liked staying with their grandparents, and today was extra special because Aunt Gweneth was with them.

"It's almost Christmas," Aunt Gweneth said. "I've got to find something really ugly for Max."

Allison Kilcarragh, also known as Grandmother, smiled. She was so pretty, Bree thought, with her nice clothes and shiny gray hair. "Good heavens, Gwen," she replied, "it isn't even Thanksgiving yet."

Gwen laughed. "I know it seems crazy to you, Mom, but Max and I get a big kick out of our little gift-giving tradition. I think he'd be disappointed if I didn't give him something really awful." She gasped suddenly and strode toward a long wooden table crowded with what looked to Bree like a lot of dirty, twisted metal. "I can't believe it!" Gwen cried, homing in on the weirdest statue Bree had ever seen. "It's an exact duplicate of the doorstop at Kristina's."

Allison made a *tsk-tsk* sound and shook her head. "That is *dreadful*," she said.

Bree agreed, and wondered what Eliette thought.

"It's a valuable piece," said the man behind the table. He had hair sprouting from his ears and his nose, and Bree instinctively took a step backward.

"Strange," Gwen murmured. "The thing feels warm to the touch."

Bree looked at the monkey and wished her aunt wouldn't buy it. Gwen was already rummaging in her purse for her wallet, though.

"How much?" she asked.

"Fifty bucks, plus tax," replied the hairy man. He was dirty, too, and smelled bad. He wasn't like the other people who were selling things behind tables; they all looked pretty ordinary to Bree.

"Thirty-five," Gwen countered.

"Oh, Gweneth," Allison groaned.

But the deal had been made. Aunt Gwen paid the man, and he put the monkey in an old Nordstrom bag and handed it over.

Eliette and Bree looked at each other, imagining the doorstop under their tree on Christmas morning. Bree didn't know why, exactly, but she was scared. She wanted her daddy. And she wanted to leave the ugly monkey right there at the flea market.

Some days, though, you just can't make a wish come true, even if you've been very, very good.

"Don't you tell your father about this," Aunt Gweneth warned her nieces, her eyes dancing with happy mischief as she looked down at them. "I want it to be a surprise."

Bree had no doubt that it would be. This thing was even worse than the moosehead—she just hoped she and Eliette wouldn't have to play this stupid game when *they* grew up.

IT was dark when Kristina and Max returned from their ride—they'd gone exploring in the nearby Cascade Mountains, and had made reservations at a secluded lodge for the following weekend. At that high altitude, the snow was deep and white, perfect for shaping into powdery balls and flinging at each other. They'd built a snowman and eaten a hot meal in a roadside restaurant before making the inevitable descent back to the real world.

After a stop at a neighborhood supermarket where Kristina bought a huge bag of dog food for Barabbas, Max drove her home. The wolf met them at the door, making that mournful sound in his throat, wanting to go out. Kristina didn't try to stop him.

Max carried the kibble into the kitchen, then made the rounds of the house, in case of lurking bogeymen, as he had after the robbery. This time Kristina accompanied him.

"I wish I could stay," he said twenty minutes later, when Barabbas was back inside and munching down on the dog food. Max had built a cozy fire in the family room, and now he stood beside the kitchen door, holding Kristina's chin in his hand.

"Eliette and Bree are probably watching for you," she said.

He nodded. "I've missed them."

Kristina envied him for a moment, this man she so deeply—and so hopelessly—loved. What a glorious blessing it must be, to have children, eagerly awaiting your return, ready to fling themselves into your arms out of sheer joy. She stood on tiptoe and kissed him.

"It was a wonderful day, Max. Thank you."

He touched the tip of her nose. "Keep next weekend open for me," he said. "And if you need anything, if you're scared, either call me or come straight to my place. No matter what time it is. Understood?"

Kristina rested her head against his shoulder for a moment. The cloth was chilly and still smelled pleasantly of mountain air, fir trees, and snow. "Understood," she said softly. But she had no intention of involving Max in her problems if she could avoid it. Only sheer selfishness had kept her from breaking off their relationship already.

Soon she would have to do just that.

Max kissed her again, this time with a thoroughness that left her swaying on her feet, said goodnight, and went out. A moment later she heard his voice from the other side of the door.

"Turn the deadbolt and put the chain on, Kristina."

Dutifully Kristina complied, though she knew it was a case of whistling in the dark. With the possible exception of the brass monkey-man, all her enemies were impervious to locks.

So were her friends and relatives, for when Kristina turned around, Maeve was standing a few feet behind her. The white wolf stood at her side, as though she were his mistress.

Kristina was surprised to see her mother, given the Gideon-Dimity crisis. When her father stepped out of the shadows as well, her incredulity gave way to a stomach-fluttering fear. They had come to tell her something, and it wasn't good news.

"What?" she whispered.

Calder took Kristina's arm and guided her into the living room, where there was no fire burning. He seated her in a chair, while Maeve settled herself in its counterpart.

Calder remained standing, too agitated to sit.

"You have often told us that you wished to be human," he said.

Kristina's heartbeat quickened. She sat up a little straighter in the chair and waited, still fearful, but beginning to hope. "Yes," she answered in a shaken whisper.

Out of the corner of her eye she saw that Maeve was weeping, silently and with dignity, but weeping, just the same.

"I have examined your blood sample over and over again," Calder went on. "I have performed numerous tests, including a DNA analysis." He paused, his dark gaze fixed upon his only surviving daughter, and Kristina remembered that he had lost a child years ago, a little girl born of his first wife. "You are aging, Kristina. For all practical intents and purposes, you are mortal."

At this Maeve covered her face with both hands and sobbed softly. She, too, had lost a loved one—her brother, Aidan, had forsaken the world of vampires to become a man again.

Kristina felt several conflicting emotions—sorrow, joy, fear, exhilaration. To be mortal! "I will die someday," she said.

Calder stood beside Maeve's chair, his hand resting on his mate's trembling shoulder. "Yes," he replied. His voice, though steady, was fractured as well.

"When?"

"I don't know," Calder answered, in his forthright way. "The process has begun—there's no telling how long it will take."

Kristina was still for a while, absorbing that, considering the ramifications. Her mother's sobs subsided as Maeve gathered her composure.

"That's why my magic has been so unreliable," Kristina mused. It was something of a relief, knowing she had no reason to blame herself. She hadn't neglected her natural gifts after all, but simply lost them.

"You could, of course, be transformed into a vampire," Calder said. "But both your mother and I know that would not be your wish."

"You're right," she answered distractedly. That life, with all its privileges and powers, was not for her.

It was a strange feeling, knowing for certain that she would one day die. She would be subject to all sorts of human ailments—head colds, sore feet, weight gain. "Do you—do you think I can bear children?" She had never menstruated, but perhaps she would start. Perhaps she could be fertile after all.

Maeve and Calder exchanged a tender look, and finally, tentatively, Maeve smiled. "If I did," she reasoned, "I see no reason why you couldn't."

Kristina had been in shock ever since the startling announcement had been made; now she realized what it meant to her parents, and she was filled with love and compassion for them.

"I won't separate myself from you, the way Uncle Aidan did, if that's what you're thinking," she said gently. "I love you too much."

Calder's eyes glistened suspiciously. "We would have watched over you in any case," he said. "Ours is a selfish grief, no lighter for the fact that we share it."

"Because I will die one day," Kristina said. She rose from her chair to embrace her father, then her mother. "Be happy for me," she pleaded softly, looking from one of her parents to the other. "This is what I want, what I've dreamed of as long as I can remember. I have no wish to live forever."

Maeve laid cool hands to either side of her daughter's face. "There is much of Aidan in you," she said. "You are wiser than I, and not so greedy."

"Do you fear death, Mother?" Kristina asked quietly. She had always wondered, but never quite dared to ask.

The queen of vampires considered. "Yes," she said. "I was raised, as a mortal, in an eighteenth-century convent, and the concept of eternal damnation is as real to me as the sky overhead and the earth below."

"And what about you, Papa?" Kristina inquired, turning to Calder.

"I have seen hell," he said. "It is called war, and it exists not in some subterranean realm, but right here on earth."

Kristina went back to her chair and fell into it. She wanted to weep, and at the same time to shout for joy. She might live another fifty years, or awaken with white hair and fragile bones one morning next week.

"What am I going to do?" she whispered.

Maeve stood beside her and laid a gentle hand to her hair. "Live," she said. "Make the most of every moment."

"But I could die tomorrow!"

"Just like any other mortal," Calder put in quietly.

At that, Maeve and Calder joined hands and, without another word, disappeared.

Barabbas laid his large head in Kristina's lap and whined sympathetically. She stroked him, staring into an uncertain future, wondering whether to celebrate her newly discovered status as a woman or to mourn. After an hour or so, still undecided, she went upstairs to get ready for bed.

In the morning she awakened early, with cramps.

At the age of one hundred and thirty, Kristina Holbrook was having her first period. She rolled over onto her side, drew up her knees, and groaned. She'd never expected it to hurt.

After a few minutes wholly dedicated to wretched suffering, she groped for the telephone and punched in Daisy's home number. With any luck at all, her friend would still be there, and not out solving a case.

"Hello," chimed the voice Kristina most wanted to hear.

"Help," Kristina moaned. "I'm human."

"What?" Daisy sounded alarmed, and who could blame her. It had been a strange thing to say.

"I'll explain later," Kristina managed to gasp. "I have the worst cramps—this has never happened to me before—"

"I'll be right over," Daisy said. "Will the housekeeper from hell let me in?"

"She's off this week. Use the spare key," Kristina murmured. "It's under the ceramic frog by the back porch."

"Great security," Daisy scoffed, but with gentleness. She obviously understood what Kristina was feeling and empathized. "Listen—just give me a few minutes to get Esteban settled with the new nanny, then I'll make a quick stop at the drugstore and come right over."

Kristina choked back a whine. If this was what being mortal was all about, maybe it wasn't so terrific and fulfilling after all. "Hurry," she whispered.

"Sometimes a warm bath helps," Daisy offered, and then hung up.

She arrived within half an hour, but to Kristina it felt more like all sixteen years of the FDR Administration, complete with retrospectives. She was still lying in a fetal position in the middle of the bed, clutching her abdomen and gritting her teeth.

"This stuff usually works," Daisy said, ripping the cellophane off a blue and white package. She had a brown paper bag with her, too, but she went into the bathroom, filled a glass with water, and returned. Two pills rested on her outstretched palm. "Swallow these and try to relax. Tension only makes it worse."

Kristina sat up, took the tablets, and swallowed them.

"What's going on here?" Daisy asked, settling into Kristina's reading chair.

She received a baleful look in reply before Kristina said, "Last night my parents broke some startling news to me. I'm completely mortal. And this morning, I woke up with the proof."

Daisy interlaced her fingers and sighed. She wasn't wearing her baseball cap, but otherwise she was dressed in the usual casual-camp way. "Nobody ever said it was easy being human," she pointed out. "Especially being a *female* human." She reached for the brown bag with the pharmacy logo printed on its side and tossed it to Kristina. "Here— you'll have to figure these out for yourself."

Kristina looked inside, saw a box of tampons, and groaned again, flinging herself back onto her pillows. Twenty minutes later the pills had worked, and the tampons were in their place on a bathroom shelf. Daisy returned from downstairs where she'd prepared a pot of herbal tea and toasted a couple of English muffins.

"Feeling better?"

Kristina nodded sheepishly. This was an experience most mortal women endured month in and month out, and she'd carried on as though she were having an appendectomy with no anesthetic. She had a new respect for the female of the human species. "Thanks, Daisy."

Daisy grinned. "After you've knocked back some of the tea and wolfed down a muffin, you should get up and move around as much as you can. Get dressed and take Barabbas out for a walk or something."

"I should go down to the shop."

"Why? Isn't there a construction crew there, fixing the door and replacing the glass in the jewelry counter?"

"Yes," Kristina said. "And I want to make sure things are going okay."

"You've heard, of course, that it was Benecia who took the brass monkey?"

Kristina *hadn't* heard exactly, though Dathan had presented the theory, the night of the robbery, when both he and Valerian were squared off in her living room. They'd all but bared their fangs.

She wondered why the warlock had not come to her with the trophy, the ugly doorstop, as soon as he'd retrieved the thing. It wasn't like Dathan to miss an opportunity to score a point, especially when there was something he wanted in return. "I hadn't heard," she said softly. "Who told you?" The question was a formality, escaping her lips before she'd thought.

"Valerian, of course."

Kristina's heart, now all too mortal, was hammering against the base of her throat. "Where is it—he—the monkey, I mean?"

Daisy's gaze was solemn. "Benecia refused to tell Valerian. She means to use it against you, if she can."

Kristina set her tea tray on the bedside table and leaned back against her pillows. "How did Dathan respond to that?"

"He was enraged, of course, but he dared not destroy the little demon because the knowledge of the doorstop's whereabouts would go with her. I suspect he found their lair, Benecia and Canaan's, I mean, and gave them a sample of warlock blood. According to Valerian, everyone in the vampire world heard their wails of fury when they awakened, deathly ill. They had probably been fed just enough to serve as a warning of Dathan's vengeance. Let's hope they are wise enough to heed it."

Although she still felt a little dizzy, Kristina's pain was mostly gone. She got out of bed, somewhat shakily. She would take a shower, get dressed, and concentrate as hard as she could on summoning the warlock. Max and his children were in more danger than ever before, now that Kristina, too, was mortal and had no magical means to protect them.

Daisy touched her arm. "I'll check on you later. Right now I've got to see how Esteban is making out, then make a run downtown to the agency."

"Thanks for everything," Kristina said, mildly embarrassed that, at her age, she'd had to have the basics of menstruation explained to her.

When she'd showered and dressed, again in jeans, with sneakers and a blue cable-knit sweater to complete the outfit, Kristina hurried downstairs. The bottle of pills Daisy had brought were clasped in her right hand; if the pain came back, she wanted to be ready.

She had barely sat down at the family room table and set herself to concentrating on Dathan's arrival when he appeared. Kristina realized, with a touch of sadness, that it was his magic that had alerted him to her need, and not her own. Hers was gone, and she was going to miss it, even though she'd wished it away for as long as she could remember.

He was dressed like a gentleman who has just attended the opera, most likely one in the eighteenth or nineteenth century. He sported a short cape, a gleaming black top hat, and very elaborate shoes, with ornate buckles and square heels. Like vampires, warlocks were facile at time travel.

Dathan approached Kristina, hardly sparing a glance for Barabbas, who gave a low, throaty growl but did not rise from his resting place on the hearth rug. Taking her hand and sweeping off his top hat in the same grand gesture, Dathan placed a warlock's kiss on her knuckles. She withdrew rather abruptly.

"Why didn't you tell me, instead of Daisy, what you had found out about Benecia Havermail?"

"Because I could not present you with a fait accompli, my dear," Dathan said, looking and sounding surprised that anyone would question his judgment. "A situation is not resolved until it is—well—*resolved.*"

Kristina lowered her head, thinking of Max, of the way he laughed, the way his eyes told her so much of what was in his mind, the way he made love to her. As though she were a goddess, powerful and worthy of worship, and yet fragile, too. She must give him up and make her way alone, as she had always done.

Dathan curved a finger under her chin and raised her face to look deep into her eyes. "You are so troubled, beloved," he said with inexpressible tenderness. "Why? I will protect your Max, as I promised to do, even though it breaks my heart to know how you love him."

She was surprised again; Dathan, for all his intuitive powers, hadn't discerned that she'd changed and become as mortal as her lost uncle Aidan. When she told him the truth, he would no longer want her for his bride and queen—a fact that came as something of a relief.

"Yes," Kristina said. "I do love Max, very much."

"But someday—"

"No," she interrupted, shaking her head. "Dathan, I have no powers. I am mortal."

"Nonsense."

"It's true. It's part of the reason I've bungled so many spells lately. My magic is gone. I am a woman, and nothing more."

The warlock's face was not crestfallen at this news, as Kristina had expected, but translucent with some inner joy. "Even better! The mating of a warlock and a mortal—"

"Cannot be that unusual," Kristina said, losing patience. While she didn't relish the prospect of spending the rest of her life, whatever was left of it, alone, she wasn't about to settle for a mate she didn't love, just to have someone to call her own.

Not that any woman could ever call a warlock her own. Like vampires, they were fickle creatures—Valerian and her parents were the only nightwalkers of her acquaintance who remained faithful to their romantic companions. Though when Daisy was between lifetimes, Valerian had certainly been known to engage in a variety of affairs of the heart.

"I think," Dathan said, "that I should take my leave now, and return when you are in a better mood."

"That," Kristina responded, "would be wise. Only don't bother to come back if you're going to hound me about marrying you, because I won't."

Dathan sighed forlornly, spread his elegant cape like black wings, and was gone.

Kristina walked Barabbas around the block—there was a scent of snow in the air again—and then took him back to the house and shut him up inside. A few minutes later she was in her Mercedes, driving downtown to her shop.

The door had been replaced, and Max's friend and two of his helpers were just finishing the repairs to the jewelry counter. The floor had been swept, and as Kristina moved among the familiar antiques, she told herself she could open for business that afternoon, or in the morning at the latest.

She wondered how long it would be, though, before Benecia and her sister returned to wreak more havoc. And where was the brass doorstop? Would he turn up one night, standing over Kristina's bed, a knife in his hand?

She shivered. Barabbas was there to protect her, of course, but she couldn't depend on a wolf forever. Besides, the animal belonged to Daisy and Valerian; it's rightful home was with them.

Maybe, Kristina thought sorrowfully, it was time to close down her shop and go traveling again. She could simply wander from place to place, the way she'd done after Michael's death. The world had changed a great deal since the days of steamer trunks and great ocean liners; countries had new borders and new names.

There were other differences, too. She was deeply in love, and on this journey she would not have unlimited time. Every moment, every heartbeat and breath, was now infinitely precious.

MAX telephoned that night, and he didn't suggest getting together. That was fine with Kristina, because she wasn't ready to tell him about her mortality. He might see the change in Kristina as a reason to rejoice, but she knew it was a very mixed blessing.

"You're okay, right?" he asked. She heard cupboard doors opening and closing, pans clanking. The man was decent to the core, a wonderful lover, and he could cook in the bargain. Amazing. "No creepy stuff has been happening?"

Kristina bit her tongue. It was all in how you defined "creepy stuff," and she didn't want to enlighten him. She needed more of those anti-cramp pills, a warm bath, and a good night's sleep. "Barabbas makes a pretty good bodyguard," she said after a few moments.

"You'll call if you need me?"

"Yes," Kristina promised. She was beginning to wonder, though, if Max had decided she was too much trouble, with all her weird relatives and White Fang for a pet. It would be easier all around if he dumped her, right then, but she found herself braced against his rejection all the same. "I'll call."

He destroyed her theory in the next sentence. "Thursday is Thanksgiving," he said. "My mother is putting on her usual feast, and she's asked me to invite you. Not that I didn't want to, of course." More pan clattering, a brief aside to one of the children, something about fishing somebody named Barbie out of the aquarium. "Will you come with us, Kristina?"

"I'd be happy to," she said, then closed her eyes against a rush of tears. Why, *why* had she agreed, when she knew it was a terrible, even dangerous, mistake to draw the situation out any further? She had already let things go too far.

"It's a long weekend," Max continued, making matters worse. "The kids usually stay with my folks, and you and I do have that reservation at the lodge up in the mountains."

Kristina had completely forgotten that, with all that had happened since. "Maybe you shouldn't be away from Bree and Eliette, over the holidays, at least. I know it sounds silly, but I didn't realize Thanksgiving was coming up so soon."

No pot clanging, no muttered instructions to the kids.

"Don't say no, Kristina," he said. "My daughters aren't being neglected—they *always* spend that weekend with my parents."

Heaven help her, she didn't want to refuse. She yearned to be alone with Max, making love, talking in front of a fire, playing in the snow. The way things stood, that might be the last true joy she ever experienced.

"All right, I'll go," she promised very softly. She would give herself, and Max, that one glorious interlude together, and then she'd do what she should have done long before and put an end to the relationship. She'd tell Max she was selling the store, leaving Seattle and never coming back, and she fully intended to keep her word.

"Pick you up at noon on Thursday?" There was a smile in Max's voice; it warmed Kristina and eased the ache in her heart just a little.

"I'll be ready," she said, silently calling herself every sort of fool.

Then, after taking two more of Daisy's pills, she ate an early dinner, took a brief bath, and crawled into bed with the stack of letters she and Max had been working their way through together. She supposed she should have waited, but that night, it seemed, nothing had the power to distract Kristina from the gloomy future but the past. The days of yesteryear, while grim in their own right, had one advantage on the years to come—they were over.

. . . Michael was inconsolable after his father's death; he blamed himself for both his parents' passing, I think, though he never admitted as much to me. He would have said even less to Gilbert, who represented everything Michael himself was not and could never be—he was good, strong, steady. Even handsome, though in a less fragile way than Michael.

Late that summer Gilbert brought me a strange and magnificent gift, a little baby swaddled in rough blankets. He explained that the poor little mite was a foundling, that his mother had given birth to him beside one of the roads passing through the estate, and had perished there.

I was filled with yearning, for while I had put my own powers firmly out of mind, I was certain that I could not bear an infant of my own. Yes, of course, my mother, a vampire, had brought me forth in quite a normal fashion, but I was an oddity and I knew it. Here was a helpless, needy child that I could love, dote upon, educate.

I felt as though I had been drowning and someone had flung out a rope, that I might catch hold and be saved.

I recall that Gilbert looked at me, and at the child, with the most moving tenderness glowing in his eyes. "I wish things had been different, Kristina," he said, and that was all.

But I knew what he meant. That we might have been together, as husband and wife, and produced babes of our own. He did not know the truth about me, though Michael did, by then, and had reviled me for it often.

I might have known how my husband would react to the introduction of a foundling into the household, although it was rightfully Gilbert's estate, and not his own. He called the infant a bastard—true no doubt, but surely not the fault of the child and very probably not even the fault of its mother—and ordered me to send him away.

I refused, and Michael tormented me day and night. Then one morning, when Gilbert was away in London, my husband confronted me yet again, in a drunken rage. We were standing at the top of the main stairway leading down into the great hall of Chel-

tingham Castle—great Zeus, Phillie, why did I challenge him then? And why there?

I had named the baby Joseph and engaged a nurse for him, and I already loved him as much as if I'd given birth to him myself. And so, in a moment of temper, I told my husband I would sooner give him up than the child.

He backhanded me then, did Michael, and I went sailing down the stairs, end over end. Had I not been what I was, I would surely have perished, and even so I suffered incapacitating injury. When I awakened, Joseph had been taken from the house, and my searching, however frantic, was fruitless.

I can write no more just now. I know you understand.

15

THE next of the many letters Kristina had written to Miss Eudocia Phillips, her former governess, was dated nearly six months after the one in which Michael had engineered the disappearance of Kristina's adopted child. Even after all this time, remembering made Kristina's heart ache, for no amount of searching had turned up even a trace of the baby boy, Joseph.

Not then, at least.

. . . Your letters have brought me so much comfort, Phillie. You would tell me, wouldn't you, if you found the story too burdensome, too full of sorrow, and could not bear the telling?

When last I wrote, I told you how Michael had taken my son from me, and struck me when I confronted him for what must have been the thousandth time. The wounds I suffered when I fell down the stairs were insignificant compared to what that final treachery did to my spirit. I was destroyed and could no longer endure living under the same roof with Michael Bradford.

Still, I had cracked several ribs in my fall and could not travel, so I had no choice but to remain at Cheltingham, at least until I'd recovered. Michael, in the way I have since learned is typical of such men, was immediately contrite, as solicitous as any husband might have been in the circumstances—rushing down the stairs, shouting that a doctor must be sent for, soothing me and stroking my hand as we waited. I lay there at the base of the stairs, beyond anguish, with servants hovering about, for Michael had decreed that I must not be moved until the village physician had examined me.

How ludicrous it seems that Michael should be my caretaker, my constant companion, when he had been the one to do me hurt in the first place. I despised him and wanted him to go from my sight, not just then but forever, but he would not leave me; even after I was carried to a downstairs bedchamber, where my ribs were bound and I was given laudanum to ease my pain. In some ways, Phillie, that was the greater torture, his continued and doting presence. The drug numbed my flesh but could not reach the anguish in my soul.

Michael held my hand. He stroked my hair. He said he was sorry and swore he had never meant to do me any harm. I believe he meant what he said, as he was saying it, but I hated him as I have never hated anything or anyone before.

"Tell me where Joseph is," I said. I thought one good thing might come out of Michael's remorse, at least—that I might learn the whereabouts of my foster child. When I had sufficiently recovered, I meant to fetch the boy from wherever he was being kept, and then put Cheltingham behind me forever. I would miss no one there, except for Gilbert.

I hoped that my parents and Valerian would come to me at last, once I had truly separated myself from Michael. I felt an almost inexpressible yearning to see them again, but I confess I was embittered, too—quietly furious that they had refused to step in when I needed them so much. Knowing that they had good reasons, and that the decision was a difficult one for them, was of no consolation then.

Michael hesitated a long time before answering my question about Joseph's whereabouts. Then, the very picture of compassion, he said, "You must cease your fretting over the brat, Kristina darling. We shall make our own babies."

I turned my head upon the pillows; I could not bear to look at him. And I was wiser now; I knew better than to let him see how I despised him. "I want Joseph," I whispered.

Michael brushed my hair back from my forehead. "He is gone," he said. Such a tender motion from the very hand that had bruised me, and sent me reeling and tumbling down a long flight of stairs.

I felt a terrible chill at the words—surely even Michael, with all his sins, would not destroy an innocent child! I was not to know Joseph's fate for a long time, and when I did, it only made me hate Michael more.

It was very late that same night, when my husband had ceased his feverish ministerings at last and left me in peace, and I was half insensible from the drugs the doctor had prescribed, that Valerian appeared at the foot of my bed.

I thought at first that he was an illusion, or part of a dream, so long had it been since I had laid eyes upon this beloved creature who called himself my guardian vampire. He has always had an irreverent sense of humor, but then you knew that.

What I remember most about that visit from Valerian was the sorrow I saw in his face and in his magnificent countenance. "Have you learned your lesson, sweet Kristina?" he asked.

I moved to sit up, but I could not.

I wanted to plead with him to find Joseph, to bring my baby back to me, but something stayed my tongue. "What lesson was that?" I asked, a bit testily, I fear, for he had tarried long in coming to me, and I had suffered so much in the interim.

He feigned one of his melodramatic sighs. "Kristina," he scolded in a quiet voice.

"All right, yes—I chose the wrong man, for the wrong reasons."

"Anyone might have made that error. The worst part, my darling, is that you stayed with that monster. Why didn't you simply leave him?"

"I kept hoping he would change."

Valerian flexed his elegant white fingers. "Do you know what it is costing me, little one, not to rouse the wretch from his drunken stupor and kill him in a manner that would cause Genghis Khan himself to cringe?"

"Yes," I said. "I can imagine."

"I have come to take you away."

I closed my eyes, but tears seeped through my lashes and sneaked down my cheeks. "I hurt so much," I said with a nod.

"I know," Valerian said softly.

"As much as I long to leave Michael, it is difficult for me to go without saying good-bye to Gilbert."

Valerian's lips curved into the thinnest of smiles. "Don't worry, beloved. One day you will undoubtedly see him again, under other

circumstances." He rounded the bed, bent over me, and touched
my forehead, and instantly I was unconscious.

When I woke, it was morning, and I was back in the house in
London where I had been so happy as a child. My parents were
asleep in their lair, and Valerian, of course, was in his, wherever it
was, but I was surrounded by familiar servants, and they fussed
and fetched and tried their utmost to bring me cheer.

My heart was broken, however, and I could not be happy.

That same afternoon there was a tremendous scuffle downstairs,
and I was dreadfully afraid that Michael had come for me, perhaps bringing ruffians to assist him. Our servants were all elderly,
and the vampires of the household could not help, being in their
usual daylight trances, far below ground.

I remember that I grasped the candlestick from the table alongside my bed and summoned up what I could of my neglected
magic, prepared to defend myself as best I could. On pain of death
I would not *return to Cheltingham.*

There was more shouting, but then I heard my personal maid,
Minerva, who had often attended me at Refuge, our country home
near Cheltingham, speak in calming tones to the protesting mob.

Moments later, she entered my room with a little bob and said,
"It's all right, miss. You may put aside the candlestick, for it's Lord
Gilbert who's come to call, not his brother. Will you see him?"

Before I could reply—my smile would have given away my feelings on the matter already—Gilbert filled the doorway, tall and
handsome, his face contorted with a peculiar combination of rage
and sympathy. Minerva perched upon one of the cushioned window seats overlooking the back garden; rules of propriety were observed in our household, by the servants if not the primary
inhabitants, and I must not be left alone with a man who was not
my husband.

Gilbert was dressed for business—he had come to London to attend to matters related to assuming his late father's title and the
estates—but he was clearly a country gentleman in his tweeds and
scuffed boots. His brown hair was rumpled where he had repeat-
edly thrust his fingers through it.

"Oh, God, Kristina," he murmured. "It's true, then. He *did* in-
jure you."

"I asked again about the baby," I said. "About Joseph."

Gilbert drew a chair close to the bed and took my hand in his.

Tears rose in my eyes and in his as well. "I have had the whole of England search for that child," he said raggedly. "You know that."

"He's killed him. Michael has killed my baby."

Minerva, who had been stroking one of the house cats, a tabby called Trinket, and pretending not to listen, gasped at this.

Gilbert and I were silent for a long time, then Gilbert spoke.

"I cannot believe, even after all Michael has done, that he would stoop to murder. Especially a child."

"Then you are a fool," I replied, unkind in my grief.

Gilbert, as usual, was understanding. "You needn't worry about Michael after this," he said. "I'll make a remittance man of him, provided I don't succumb to the urge to do murder myself. In the meantime, Kristina, you must stop tormenting yourself over little Joseph." He paused. "God in heaven, I curse myself every day for ever bringing the infant to you in the first place. I thought——"

I squeezed his hand. "I know what you thought," I said gently. "That you might give me joy."

He nodded, then bent and kissed my forehead. "I will deal with Michael," he said. "And if there is a way to get the truth out of him regarding the babe, I will do it. In the meantime, you must rest and recover."

I knew, somehow, that I would not see Gilbert again, and clung to him for a long moment when he would have turned to leave the room.

"Good-bye," I whispered.

He kissed my mouth that time. It was light, brief, but in no way brotherly. "Farewell, sweet Kristina," he said. And then he strode out of the room without once looking back.

Minerva, poor dear, was sniffling and dashing away tears with the hem of her apron when I glanced in her direction. "Such a dear man," she said.

"Yes," I replied, staring at the empty chasm of the open doorway, through which Gilbert had just passed.

"I can't see the likes of him raising a hand to a woman," Minerva observed in a righteous tone, rising from the window seat with the cat squirming in her arms.

"No," I agreed, but I feared Gilbert would do violence when he returned to Cheltingham, and I was right. Word came to London, several weeks later, by way of an intricate network of grooms and footmen and others who handled horses and carriages, that Gilbert

had gone home to find Michael preparing to come to the city and fetch me.

They had argued heatedly, as the story went, and Michael had taken up a fireplace poker, in a fit of temper, and swung it at Gilbert's head. Gilbert had deflected the blow, fracturing a bone in his forearm in the process, but had managed, all the same, to administer a memorable thrashing. Our stable hands had it on good authority, and passed the word to the household servants, that Michael Bradford had been dumped, bruised, chastened, and humbled onto a ship bound for Australia. As long as he kept himself within those far shores, he would receive an adequate allowance. Should he return to England, for any reason, however, he would be utterly penniless.

I received one letter after that, from Gilbert. He wrote that he was to be wed at last, to one Ethel Grovestead of Devonshire, and that there had still been no word of Joseph. . . .

Kristina laid the letter aside. Joseph.

She seldom allowed herself to think of the little boy, but he was very much on her mind that evening. She had found him, some seven years after his disappearance, with Valerian's reluctant assistance, working with a gang of pickpockets. Once a cherubic baby, the child was now feral and ratlike, hardly even human. Michael had put him into a foundling home after taking him away from Cheltingham in secret, a terrible, cold place where he'd been beaten and half starved. At five he'd fled the institution and taken up with a gang of cutthroats, orphans, and other lost boys like himself, and Kristina had realized at last, looking into his fevered and hateful eyes, that there was no saving him.

Valerian had understood that all along, and perhaps Gilbert had, as well. They had been shielding her, the pair of them, and she did not appreciate their efforts.

She'd given the boy, once called Joseph, all the money in her bag. He'd snatched the coins into his grubby hands, spat at her, and fled. After that, she'd done her best to provide for him, again with Valerian's aid, but after only a few months the child had perished in an alleyway, a small bundle of dirty rags and brittle bones, racked with consumption.

If Kristina had hated Michael before that, it was nothing compared to what she felt afterward. Life might have been so very different for Joseph, for all of them. . . .

She pulled her thoughts forcibly away from that dreadful time. She had dwelt on the past long enough, for one night. Now she must look forward, make plans for a new life.

Kristina switched on the computer at the small desk in the family room, got out her address book, and began composing letters to other antiques dealers all over the world. Her wares were envied far and wide, and selling them would be an easy matter, once her colleagues knew she was going out of business.

She worked into the small hours of the morning, then went upstairs to shower and crawl into bed. Barabbas slept at her feet, heavy and warm, and hers was a peaceful, dreamless sleep.

The next day she went to the shop and sent off the letters she had written the night before, via her fax machine. By lunchtime she was already receiving offers. Several dealers, in fact, were flying in from other parts of the world, while others asked for a complete inventory list. Kristina kept her stock catalogued on the shop computer and updated the information once a week. It was an easy matter to print out a copy and begin responding to the requests.

All the while she waited for the brass monkey-man to show up, human again and bent on revenge. Benecia Havermail could hold a doorstop hostage as long as she wanted to, but even she wouldn't be able to reverse the spell Kristina had cast. She would, however, have a better chance of defending herself.

At home Kristina let herself in, half expecting her assailant to pounce on her. Instead she was greeted by a whimpering Barabbas, eager for a walk and supper.

Kristina let him out, trusting him to return when he was ready, although she knew he wanted to go home to Valerian, who was his true master. Because the wolf had been commanded to keep watch over Kristina, however, he would do so, no matter how lonely he was.

While Kristina was making supper—a light pasta dish—the telephone rang. She didn't need her lost magic to know the caller was Max.

"Hi," she said.

He let out a long breath, as though he'd feared she wouldn't answer. "How was your day?"

She smiled as she chopped red, yellow, and green peppers to roast and put on top of her pasta, to give it some color and pizzazz. "It was pretty good, really. Nothing jumped out at me, or anything like that. How about you?"

Max laughed. "Wish I could say the same," he said. "My players are all keyed up for the four-day weekend, and most of them were on hormone overload in the first place. I spent the day letting the smaller guys out of lockers."

"I don't know how you stand the little devils," Kristina said, cooking as she spoke. A little salad would go nicely with the pasta, she decided.

Max, too, was making dinner; she could hear the homey, accompanying sounds over the wire. "Coming from you, that's an ironic remark," he teased. "Given the sort of company you keep, I mean."

His words reminded Kristina of all she would have to tell him, in the very near future, and dampened her spirits a little. Thinking of Michael, she said, "Considering the cruelty of some human beings I've known, I marvel that Valerian or even Dathan could be called 'monsters.' "

"Did I hurt your feelings?"

That was Max for you. No beating around the proverbial bush; just get right to the point. The concern in his voice made Kristina want to weep.

"Maybe a little, but I know you didn't intend to."

"Sorry," Max said. She hadn't known anyone even remotely like him since Gilbert Bradford, Duke of Cheltingham.

"It's all right," she insisted. Her appetite was gone, though. She turned off the burner under the pasta and took the chopped peppers out of the electric grilling machine she'd ordered off an infomercial one night, a few years before, when she hadn't been able to sleep. "Vampires and warlocks aren't subject to the rules of political correctness."

"Just give them time," Max said ruefully with a grin in his voice.

There was so much she wanted to tell him—that she was human, that she was fertile, that she was closing her shop and leaving Seattle, but none of it could be said over the telephone. She had had to give up Gilbert, and now she would lose Max, but this time she would have some very sweet memories to take away with her, along with a freshly broken heart.

"How are Bree and Eliette?" she asked, holding her breath while she awaited his answer. She was still very afraid of Benecia and Canaan; they could so easily turn their envy on Max's little girls, who had everything they wanted. Innocence. Mortality. Not just one future, but many.

"Only slightly less rowdy than my football players," Max replied. "They're getting excited about Thanksgiving—not that they're all that thankful. It's just that, thanks to TV, they know it's a greased track from Turkey Day to Christmas."

Kristina smiled again, but wistfully. Although she had had plenty of beautiful toys as a child, and a great fuss was made over her birthday, even the boldest vampires did not dare to observe the holy days of any of the great religions. Nemesis and his Superiors were very touchy about such matters, and no sane fiend would invoke their ire.

"That must be fun—filling stockings, keeping secrets . . ."

"To tell you the truth," Max confessed when Kristina's voice fell away, "it's something of a hassle. And it bothers me a lot that the central idea is Getting Stuff. Whatever happened to peace on earth and goodwill toward men?"

"I think both are where they always were—in the hearts of men *and* women. It's just a matter of what you focus on."

"You're right," Max said. "First my mom and dad made Christmas happen, then Sandy took care of it. The last couple of years I've been—well—going through the motions."

Again Kristina's heart was touched with sadness. She wondered if being in love was always like riding a roller coaster, or if her mood swings were connected to her new humanity. "I bet you're not giving yourself enough credit," she said.

"Maybe," he allowed.

It was then that Barabbas scratched at the kitchen door. Kristina stretched but couldn't quite reach the knob. "Hold on a second, will you, Max?" she asked.

His voice was warm and low, sexy as a caress. "Maybe I'd better let you go. The spaghetti is about to boil over. Call you tomorrow?"

"I'll be looking forward to it," Kristina said.

She hung up the telephone and opened the door. Standing behind Barabbas, in the early darkness of late November, were Benecia and Canaan. They were dressed as ludicrous little pilgrims, complete with buckles on their shoes, Puritan bonnets, gowns, and aprons.

"Barabbas," Kristina commanded in an even voice, "bring Valerian."

The wolf darted away into the night, and while Canaan looked unsettled by this development, Benecia smiled. Her uncanny beauty made her all the more hideous, all the more vile.

"Aren't you going to ask us in?" she asked in her small, bell-like voice.

Kristina had no choice, and she knew it as well as they did. She just hoped Valerian wasn't too far away to help. The fact that Benecia didn't seem particularly worried about the other vampire was not encouraging. Stepping back, Kristina admitted them.

"Where is the doorstop?" she demanded.

"I haven't the faintest idea," Benecia replied. "I gave it to a junk dealer. It'll be interesting to see where the thing turns up, don't you think?"

Kristina might have gone for the little beast's throat if she hadn't known it would mean instant—or worse yet, *not* instant—death. She said nothing. *What* could be keeping Valerian?

"I believe he's busy elsewhere," Benecia said with acid sweetness, as if Kristina had asked the question aloud.

Kristina drew a deep breath and let it out slowly. She must stay calm, at all costs. Vampires of this ilk were like wild, vicious animals, unreasoning, provoked by the scent of fear. "What do you want from me?" she asked in what she hoped was a reasonable and even tone of voice.

"A plan has occurred to us," Benecia said.

Canaan was still keeping an uneasy eye out for Valerian.

"What sort of plan?" Kristina went for a tone of contempt, in what was probably a futile effort to distract Benecia from the terror she felt.

"One that would allow us to be human, to live out normal lives." She paused and smiled, showing her white teeth, as perfect and pearly as a doll's. "We might even be your daughters. Wouldn't that be fun?"

Kristina swayed inwardly as the full weight of Benecia's words struck her. Great Zeus, the little beasts were talking about *possession*, planning to abandon their own vampire bodies and take over those of Eliette and Bree!

"I will do anything to stop you," she whispered. *"Anything."*

"But can you?" Benecia retorted, almost simpering. "You have no magic now. You are nothing but a mortal woman."

"Nothing but what you have always wanted to be," Kristina replied.

"Let's go," Canaan said, breaking her silence at last. "I don't like it here."

"A wise child," commented a third voice, but it wasn't Valerian who spoke. Even before Kristina whirled to look, she knew it was Dathan who had materialized in her kitchen, not the fearsome vampire.

Canaan retreated a step, but Benecia advanced, snarling, her chinablue eyes demonicly bright. She held a particular grudge toward Dathan, Kristina recalled; something on the order of a woman scorned.

"You," the vampire accused. "It was *you*, warlock, who gave us your vile blood while we slept!"

Dathan was, once again, dressed for either the theater or the opera. Kristina deduced, stupidly, that he must be quite an aficionado of the arts. He dusted the impeccable sleeves of his greatcoat with white-gloved hands before replying. "Hold your tongue, you demon's whelp, or I'll give you a dose that will make arsenic seem like ambrosia."

Benecia made a primal sound, like the hiss of a jungle cat about to spring, and Dathan raised one hand and snapped his fingers.

A circle of flame danced around Benecia's feet.

Canaan shrieked and fled immediately; sensible vampires fear fire as they do sunlight and the point of a wooden stake. Benecia, though visibly frightened, glared at the warlock as the blaze grew.

Kristina clasped both hands over her mouth, horrified. "Stop," she whispered. "Please, Dathan—stop."

He sighed, and the flames died down to a black circle on Kristina's floor.

"Get out," he said.

Benecia scowled at him a moment longer, then vanished.

Kristina turned and flung herself against Dathan's chest, utterly terrified. "You must help me—they're planning to take over Max's children—can they do that?"

Dathan gave her a gentle shake, then held her close again. "We shall not allow it, you and I," he said tenderly, kissing the top of Kristina's head. "Leave the 'littlest vampire' and her more judicious sister to me."

"What will you do?"

He touched a finger to her lips. "Shhh," he said. "Do not worry yourself with such matters, Kristina. After all, you will soon be my queen. Think on that instead. Imagine what it will mean."

She could not bear to consider the full scope of her vow, not then. She had told Benecia and Canaan she would do anything to save Eliette and Bree from them, and she'd meant it. The price was high indeed, but Kristina would not stint.

"You must give me just a few more days to end things with Max."

"I cannot pretend I am not jealous," Dathan said. "But I will grant you that request or virtually any other. But you must give me your word, Kristina. You will become my bride."

She swallowed hard, blinked back tears, and then nodded. "I promise," she whispered.

With that, Dathan bent his head and kissed her gently on the mouth. She was not unmoved—he was a creature capable of great passion— but there was no spiritual connection as there was with Max. No sense of rightness, of something ordained in a time when stars, now long dead, were tumultuous and new, bursting with fire.

Then suddenly he vanished.

Valerian arrived an instant afterward, popping in in his usual spectacular fashion, bringing Barabbas with him. Or did Barabbas possess that talent in his own right? It didn't matter, for Kristina had just sold her soul, and she was as good as damned.

"Where have you been?" she demanded, and then gave a deep, wrenching sob.

Valerian put his arms around Kristina, in the way her father might have done, ignoring her outburst. He was not at her beck and call, and he had the good grace not to point that out—though he could be depended upon to raise the subject later. "I have been doing what I could to assist your mother," he said simply.

Kristina looked up into his face, full of sorrow, glad that she was human, that she would die. "I will be wed to Dathan within a fortnight," she said.

Valerian looked truly startled, an emotion she had not seen in him in all the length of her memory. *"What?"* he demanded.

She explained Benecia's threat, brokenly, trembling all the while, and the somber expression on the vampire's face told her that such a thing was indeed possible.

"They have made some unholy bargain," Valerian reflected. "They must be destroyed before they can carry out their plans, or other vampires will do the same. I do not believe I need to tell you how Nemesis would react to that."

"What can I do?" Kristina asked, desperate.

Valerian cupped her chin in his hand, wiped away some of her tears with a thumb as smooth and cool as marble. "Only wait," the vampire said. "You were very foolish to promise yourself to Dathan, however. He will not release you from the pact."

"It is worth it to me," she replied.

The vampire kissed her forehead. "I hope so," he answered. And then he, too, was gone.

Kristina took Barabbas, drove to Max's, and knocked on the front door. Maybe she couldn't protect Bree and Eliette, with her lapsed magic, but there was a chance that the wolf could. And besides, she wanted to be able to summon Dathan if Benecia and Canaan decided to put in an appearance.

Max didn't ask questions, bless him. He just led Kristina to the guest room, kissed her lightly, and left her alone.

Sometime in the middle of the night, Bree and Eliette joined Kristina in the double bed, cuddling up close, but she knew it wasn't because they were afraid. They had sensed her sorrow, somehow, and wanted to console her.

Kristina was sipping coffee the next morning in the kitchen when Max found a moment to talk to her alone. The girls were on their way to their separate schools, via the neighborhood carpool.

"Okay," he said. "What's the deal? How come you showed up in the middle of the night?"

"I got lonesome," Kristina hedged. "Besides, you invited me, didn't you? You said I could come over any time I wanted."

"And I meant it." He glanced at the clock over the kitchen sink, and his jaw tightened. "I have to get to work. We'll talk about this later."

Kristina nodded, though she had no intention of explaining, *ever*, that two vampires wanted to possess his daughters. She had all day to think up some story that would bear a resemblance to the truth.

"I'll stop by the shop after practice. Around five o'clock?"

He would find out that she was liquidating her stock and getting ready to close down the business, but that was the least of her problems. In fact, she needed to hurry home to shower and put on makeup and a power suit, because two of her European colleagues were arriving that day to take their choice of her merchandise.

"Make it six, and I'll take you out to dinner. Bring the girls."

If Bree and Eliette were along, they could avoid a lot of subjects Kristina didn't want to talk about just yet. Like why she'd showed up at their house after midnight with a wolf in tow.

Max didn't fall for it. "I think I can get Cindy from down the street to babysit," he said. "I'll see you at six."

Forget the battle, the whole war was already a lost cause. Kristina was putting herself through hell just so she could have that one special weekend in the mountains with Max before she told him it was over, and it was selfish and unfair of her to do it.

But then, she had never claimed to be perfect.

16

TWO of Kristina's European colleagues were still at the shop when Max arrived that evening, at five after six. Between them, Adrian and Enrique had purchased nearly everything in the place, and the few items they hadn't claimed had been sold via telephone and fax to still other dealers. Both men had hired shipping companies, and Kristina's treasures were being bound up in bubble wrap, taped into boxes, and put into huge wooden crates with shredded paper for padding.

Adrian and Enrique oversaw the whole process, each one jealously guarding his spoil, and many things had already been taken away in trucks. Adrian's purchases would go to a small shop in Avignon, and Enrique owned an exclusive place in Toronto.

Max, who had had no idea what to expect, in that charming way of mortals, was flabbergasted to find the shop in the process of being emptied.

Adrian and Enrique paused in their noisy supervisory duties just long enough to assess the newcomer, then ignored him. He was definitely not their type.

Max was still standing just inside the door, looking stunned, when Kristina went to him, took his hand, and gently pulled him into the back room, where they could have a modicum—though not much more—of privacy.

"What in hell is going on here?" Max demanded in a loud whisper. Kristina knew he was worried, not angry.

"There are some things I need to tell you," she said. "We established that this morning. Now, are you ready to go out for pizza and some intense conversation, or shall we stay here and make sure Adrian and Enrique don't kill each other?"

Max's large, football player's shoulders rolled under his sports jacket; he might have flung out his arms if the back room hadn't been so small and so jammed with Kristina's personal belongings—the microwave, the stash of herbal teas, the mugs, the table and chairs. There was also a small desk, which held a laptop computer, a miniature printer, and her fax machine.

"There are *definitely* some things you need to tell me. How about starting right now?"

She moved close to him, slipped her arms around his waist, laid her cheek against his chest. He smelled of a recent shower and crisp, fresh air, and she wished she could hold Max like that forever.

It was then, of all times, that she realized who he was—or more properly, who he had been, once upon a time. The knowledge nearly buckled her knees, but she wouldn't let herself fold up now. There were too many things to be done.

"I don't want to talk here," she said, blinking back tears, her forehead pressed against Max's breastbone. "Please—there's a quiet place down the street, with candlelight and soft music and tables tucked away in the shadows. Let's go there."

Max held her tightly for a moment, then took her shoulders in his hands and looked down into her eyes. "Fine," he said. "But what about those hairdresser types out there? Do you trust them?"

Kristina couldn't help smiling at Max's description of her colleagues. "They're art and antiques dealers, Max, not cat burglars. Besides, I've already put through their Gold Card numbers. Thanks to the wonders of electronics, the money for what they've bought is being transferred into my business account even as we speak."

He smiled at that, and kissed her forehead, but she knew he was still troubled. "Let's get out of here," he said. "Unlike most people, I get hungry when I'm stressed."

In the main part of the shop the circus of labeling, packing, and arguing in four languages continued. Kristina explained that she and Max were leaving, and would be back later to lock up. She didn't bother with introductions.

It was a short walk to Luigi's Ristorante, only a block or so, and the night was cold. The stars were out, but seemed somehow more distant than before, as though they had taken a step back from a doubtful Earth. Max held Kristina's hand, but neither of them spoke until they had checked Kristina's coat and taken a seat at one of the most private tables.

They chose a red wine and ordered the house specialty: a wonderful, thick-crusted pizza with an astronomical calorie count, preceded by *insalata mista*—a simple mixed salad.

Max held his peace until the greens arrived. Then he stabbed a forkful of lettuce leaves and said, "All right, Kristina. What's the deal?"

"Are you asking why I showed up at your house in the middle of the night or why I'm shutting down my business?"

Max laid his fork down again, the food untouched. "Both," he said. He looked like a man who didn't want to hear the answer he himself had demanded.

"Unfortunately it wouldn't be quite accurate to start with either of those events," Kristina said, resigned. Amazingly, she found she had an appetite and began to nibble at her salad. She hoped she wasn't going to turn out to be one of those mortals who ate when they were stressed, like Max—with her circle of friends and relations, she'd double her weight in a month. "I've discovered something very interesting about myself, Max. I'm human. I mean, fully, completely, flesh-and-blood *human*."

She had expected him to be pleased, but as Kristina watched Max's reaction, she saw something peculiar in his face. Not fear, exactly. She couldn't be sure what it was she'd glimpsed, and it wasn't the right time to ask. He began to eat.

"Maybe you were always mortal and just didn't know it."

Kristina shook her head. "I had magical powers, and they're gone now. My father has performed tests—he was—*is*—a doctor, you know. There's no doubt that I've changed."

Max let out a long sigh, polished off his salad, and started on the breadsticks. "Why didn't you tell me last night?"

"It was late, and I felt bad enough about disrupting your household that way as it was. Besides, the timing wasn't right."

"Okay. Let's move on to that. What brought you to my door in the wee small hours, with Barabbas at your heels, looking as though you'd just barely outrun the devil?"

"Maybe I had," Kristina said, reaching for her wine, a rich Chianti, and taking a thoughtful sip. She set the glass aside. "I wanted to protect you and the children, and I knew I couldn't manage without my magic. So I brought Barabbas to serve as a sort of watchdog."

Max leaned forward, his second breadstick forgotten in his hand. "Protect us from what?" he pressed quietly.

Kristina was still a little wounded that he wasn't happier about her being mortal, which didn't make sense, of course, because she was going to have to tell him, very soon, that they couldn't see each other anymore. What she would *never* tell him was that Benecia and Canaan had plans to possess his children; he could do nothing to save them and would only be tormented by the knowledge that they were in danger.

And he'd hate her for bringing that peril into their lives.

"Just—things in general," she answered after a long, painful silence, during which she indulged in several more sips of wine. "I've already explained about my unfortunate connections with the supernatural underworld, Max. Please don't force me to say more, because it would serve absolutely no purpose."

Max was quiet, indulging in his own wine, though in gulps rather than sips. Finally, pale under his year-round suntan, he said, "Let's get back to the subject of your mortality for a moment. I don't give a damn about your lost magic, and it isn't your job to protect me or my family anyway, though I appreciate the effort. Does this mean that you can die, like everybody else?"

The food arrived, with exquisitely bad timing. They both sat in silence while the waiter gave them plates and forks and red-and-white-checked napkins, then cut the succulent pizza into wide sections dripping with cheese.

Kristina watched Max the whole time, feeling as though she'd been struck. Maybe Max had never truly cared for her at all. Maybe he'd only wanted her because he thought she couldn't get sick or be killed in an accident. The way Sandy had been.

"Yes," she said when the solicitous waiter had finally left them alone. "I'm as vulnerable as anyone else." She tried to smile but didn't quite achieve it. "Guess I take after my father's side of the family—he was still a mere man when I was conceived."

Max waited until Kristina had taken a serving of the steaming, fragrant pizza for herself, then slid a double helping onto his own plate. He ate with his fingers, while Kristina used a fork.

"Why are you closing the shop?" he asked, after refilling both their wineglasses. She knew, though, that he was still mulling over what she'd just told him, that she wasn't going to live forever.

Kristina bit her lower lip. Lying had never come easily to her, and it was almost impossible with Max. She was already straining the limits of her abilities. "I guess I'm tired of working for a living," she said. "I don't have to, you know—I have more than enough money."

"I'd guessed that," Max replied. "That you weren't poor, I mean. But you've got to admit the decision might seem sudden to the casual onlooker."

"I'm impulsive," Kristina said with a little shrug. She hadn't meant to sound flippant, but there was so much she couldn't say. Not yet.

"Am I about to be dumped?" Another Max-ism. *If you want to know something, ask.* A simple concept, in theory at least, but damn hard to emulate in practice. Or so it seemed to Kristina, who felt mired in lies and omissions.

She didn't want to give up Thanksgiving dinner with a real family, or the long, delicious weekend in the snowy mountains. It was pure selfishness, and she knew it, but there it was. The rest of her life looked too long and too lonely to survive, without the comfort of these last few precious memories.

"I was wondering the same thing," Kristina said. "Whether or not you'd decided to break things off."

"I don't know," he finally replied, meeting her gaze straight on. She loved him for that, for so many things. "I love you, Kristina—I'd like nothing better than to marry you and make babies—but it scares the hell out of me, and I'm not talking about warlocks and vampires here. It's the idea that you could—that what happened with Sandy could happen all over again—"

Kristina reached out and touched his hand. "It's okay, Max," she said softly. "I understand."

He interlaced his fingers with hers and squeezed. "I'm not going to ask you what your plans are," he said hoarsely, "because I don't think

I could deal with the answer right now. So let's just take things one day, one *moment* at a time, at least until after this weekend. Agreed?"

Kristina swallowed a throatful of tears. "Agreed," she said.

They ate a good deal of the pizza, and then Max walked Kristina back to the shop, where Enrique and Adrian were still packing and giving orders and arguing. Kristina gave Adrian a spare key—she had several, because of the new door—and asked him to lock up when they were finished.

Adrian kissed her on both cheeks, which made Enrique feel compelled to do the same, though he seemed a bit put out that his competitor had been the one chosen to close the shop. Max waited patiently by the door, then drove Kristina to her car, which was parked in a lot several blocks away.

"Feel like spending the night?" he asked, getting out of the Blazer to open her door for her and see her inside and properly seatbelted.

Kristina considered, then shook her head. She'd imposed enough as it was by showing up unannounced the night before. Another appearance would probably worry Bree and Eliette, or at least confuse them. "I could send Barabbas over, though."

Max rolled his eyes. "Thanks," he said, "but no, thanks." He bent and kissed her through the open window of the driver's door. "Try not to worry so much," he said, when it was over. He'd left her dizzy, but he didn't seem to have a clue how his kisses made her feel. "There are fiends and ghouls in the world, mortal and otherwise. I wouldn't have believed the 'otherwise', if it hadn't been for you, but you reminded me of something else, Kristina. Something I'd almost completely forgotten, because I was so furious that a woman as sweet and smart and innocent as Sandy could die like that."

There were tears on Kristina's face, and she didn't try to hide them. Nor did she speak.

Max dried her cheeks, first one and then the other, with the edge of his thumb. "You made me remember how much good there is in the world. For every demon, there's an angel."

An old memory brushed Kristina's heart, like the soft, feathered wing of a passing cherubim. Once, when Kristina was very young, Benecia Havermail had told her that she was doomed, being the child of two vampires, and would surely burn in hell forever. Kristina had been terrified and had run to her governess, the unflappable Phillie, with the news that she was damned.

"Heaven bears you no ill will, child," Phillie had said, smoothing Kristina's hair with a tender motion of her hand. "While the bodies of

innocents sometimes suffer, their spirits are inviolate. Do you understand what that means?"

Kristina, being seven or eight at the time, and uncommonly bright,
had gotten the gist. Flesh was temporary, spirit was eternal.

She brought herself back to the here and now, heartened, but still
wishing for Phillie. How reassuring it would have been to tell her troubles to her old friend, the way she had as a little girl, as a young bride,
as a lonely wanderer.

"You'll be okay?" Max asked, caressing her cheek.

Kristina nodded, and as she pulled away she said a little prayer that
Eliette and Bree would be guarded, with special care.

THERE was no word from Dathan, or from Valerian, her parents, or
any of the other vampires of her acquaintance, that night. Only Barabbas greeted her, trotting over and plopping down beside the chair in her
bedroom, when she sat down to read another of the ancient volumes
she had borrowed from her mother.

She couldn't have said why she bothered, for even if she found a spell
to protect Bree and Eliette and Max, it would be of no real use, now
that her magic was gone.

She learned nothing at all in fact, and her sleep that night was
crowded with dreams, all of which stayed just out of conscious reach
when she awakened in the morning.

After showering, dressing, and feeding Barabbas, Kristina drove back
down to the shop. Adrian had locked the place, as promised, and he
and Enrique and all their little hired elves were gone.

The place was practically empty, except for those things that had still
to be boxed for shipment to other dealers. Kristina could have hired the
work done, of course, but she wanted to be busy, to keep her mind off
Benecia Havermail's aspirations to be human and well away from the
absolute necessity of breaking things off with Max. She most certainly
didn't want to consider the implications of her inevitable union with
the warlock, so she kept her brain as blank as she could and worked
furiously until the sun had gone down and she was exhausted.

Again there were no visitations from supernatural creatures, and Kristina was boundlessly grateful. She made a simple supper, attended to
Barabbas's canine needs—i.e., a walk and a bowl of kibble—and finally
settled herself in front of the family room TV. Unable to face the old
letters to Phillie that still remained to be read, or the volumes that were
yielding no solutions to her problems, she tuned in to the shopping

channel and sat sipping herbal tea. By the end of the evening, she owned two gold bracelets and a combination grill and waffle maker.

She would figure out what to do with this largess some other time.

Morning brought some good news, however minor. Her period was over.

Kristina went through the showering, dressing, and eating ritual and, clad in jeans and a sweatshirt, returned to the shop to finish packing the last of her stock. Only a few items had not been sold; she would take those home and, like the loot from the shopping channel, dispense with them later.

By noon a delivery van had arrived, and the driver was wheeling boxes out to his truck in relays. Kristina signed the necessary papers, supplied her account number, and then stood in the near-empty shop, wanting to cry but not quite able to manage it. She'd loved building the business, but she knew it was the process of doing that that she'd truly cared about, not the establishment itself.

She wondered, with wry depression, what her duties would be as queen of the warlocks. How could there even *be* a queen of the warlocks, for pity's sake, if witches, the female of the species, were an entirely separate group? Come to that, how could there be warlocks *or* witches if the two genders hated each other too much to mate?

Kristina had decided to donate the microwave, table and chair, fax machine, etc., to a charitable group. They arrived with a truck of their own and took away the contents of the back room, the place that had been her refuge during hectic work days. She threw in the unsold antiques for good measure so she wouldn't have to carry them to her car, and then went home.

She'd been in the house approximately five minutes when Daisy called. From the electronic choppiness of the transmission, Kristina guessed that her friend was using the cell phone she carried in her fanny pack.

"You might tell a person you're closing up shop," snapped Valerian's bride, "instead of just folding your tent like some sheik and stealing silently off into the night."

Kristina smiled, even though she felt more like crying. Daisy usually had a cheering effect on her, and she hoped her upcoming, lifetime alliance with Dathan wouldn't interfere with their friendship. "Sorry," she said. "It was a sudden decision."

"Like agreeing to become Dathan's bride?" Daisy demanded between crackles. "Damn, I always forget to charge this thing. Stay where you are—I'm coming right over."

Kristina sighed, put on water for tea, and waited.

Daisy arrived within twenty minutes. Barabbas greeted her with pitiful delight, squirming at her feet like a puppy.

"You've got to take him back to your place," Kristina said. "I can't bear the guilt—I feel like the villainess in a *Lassie* movie."

Daisy shrugged out of her jacket. "Okay," she said, opening the kitchen door and cocking one thumb. "Barabbas, go home."

The wolf shot through the slim gap as though he had springs in his haunches.

Daisy closed the door. "Valerian is pretty crazy over this marriage of yours," she said. There was no judgment in the remark; it was just an observation.

"It's none of his business," Kristina replied in the same tone. The tea was ready, and she carried the pot to the family room table on a tray, along with sugar cubes, a small pitcher of milk, and two cups and saucers. The irony of the phrase "family room" struck her, and she laughed, though the sound came out sounding more like a sob.

"You're right," Daisy agreed, letting the sob pass without commenting or commiserating. "But since when has that stopped Valerian from meddling?" She sat down across from Kristina. "I guess you gave up the shop because you'll be leaving here."

Kristina nodded, stirring sugar into her tea. "There is that. And I've been in the business of collecting and selling antiques for about seventy-five years."

"Because you loved it," Daisy pointed out. She could be implacably blunt, like Max. It was one of her most endearing, and most annoying, qualities.

"It's gone," Kristina said. "That's the bottom line."

"You own the building, don't you? Maybe you could start up again sometime. If you get bored with being queen of the warlocks." There was a twinkle in Daisy's eyes, along with a great deal of empathy. "What exactly will you do, anyway?"

Kristina shook her head. "I don't have a clue—beyond the obvious, of course."

Daisy, who had been a homicide cop in Las Vegas and consorted with all sorts of sleazeballs in her more recent career as a private investigator, actually blushed and averted her eyes. Although neither of them took the subject any further, Kristina was pretty sure they were both wondering what it would be like to have sex with a warlock.

She felt a new yearning for Max, deeper and more desperate than ever.

"Where will you live?" Daisy asked.

Kristina didn't know that, either. And since she no longer possessed magical powers, she wouldn't be able to transport herself from one place to another at will as she had done in the past. "Probably in Transylvania," she said, trying to make the best of a bad situation by turning it into a joke. It didn't work.

"Don't," Daisy said.

At last Kristina broke down and cried. "I'm going to have one weekend with Max," she sobbed, "just one weekend. And the memories of that will have to last for the rest of my life."

Daisy lowered her head for a moment, obviously feeling Kristina's pain, bowed by it, probably imagining what it would be like to be separated from Valerian, once and for all. She tried to offer consolation. "You're mortal now. Maybe in another lifetime . . ."

Kristina's sobs had subsided to inelegant sniffles, but her sorrow was as great as ever. "No," she said. "I knew Max once before—he was someone else then, of course—and it just wasn't meant to be."

"Don't tell me he was that Michael character who threw you down the stairs and left your foster son in a workhouse!"

Kristina didn't need to ask how Daisy had known those things, details she had confided to no one else besides Phillie and her "guardian vampire." Valerian had told her, of course. "No," she said. "Max wasn't Michael." But she didn't offer any more information than that.

"Have some more tea," Daisy said. "Have you got any brandy? If you ask me, you could use a shot of firewater."

"No, thanks," Kristina replied. She would have liked to escape the pain, but she didn't care for the idea of dulling her senses, especially now that Barabbas was no longer there to guard her. "How's the new nanny working out? Not to mention motherhood in general?"

Changing the subject proved a good tactic. Daisy's face brightened, and the uncomfortable subjects of Dathan and Max were forgotten, at least temporarily. "She's a wonder worker—now that she's told Esteban he's safe with us, that we're not going to starve or beat him, he's doing better. He still sleeps on the floor once in a while, but he's not hiding food, and he's trying to learn English. He adores Valerian."

Kristina remembered how tenderly the legendary vampire had held the little ragged boy that night in Rio, and was touched. Ah, but it was not a simple thing, this matter of good and evil. Was Valerian, who preyed upon mortals and sustained himself on their very life's blood, a monster? What of Esteban's birth mother, who would sell her own child into an unthinkable fate? Was *she* not the true fiend, though a human heart beat within her breast and her soul might still be salvaged through grace, should she repent, however unlikely that seemed?

"To know Valerian," Kristina answered at last with a slight smile, "is to love him."

Daisy laughed. "I certainly do," she said, "but you've got to admit—it's a matter of perspective."

It was a comfort just having Daisy's company for a little while, and by the time her friend left, Kristina felt better, if a bit lonely. She built a fire, took a nap on the family room sofa, and lapsed into a dream. She couldn't remember it after she woke up, and that troubled her, for she'd been left with a sense of urgency, part terror, and part hope.

The next day was Thanksgiving.

Kristina packed a small bag for the weekend in the mountains with Max and dressed carefully in a tan cashmere skirt, high brown leather boots, and a long, ivory-colored silk sweater. When Max and the girls arrived to pick her up, she saw by the warmth in Max's eyes that she'd chosen well, and that was something of a relief, for with all her sophistication, Kristina did not know exactly what one wore to a family feast. She'd never attended one before.

Max took her bag and put it in the back of the Blazer while Bree bounced around him, babbling questions. Was Kristina taking a trip? Where was she going? Was he going along, too? Could she and Eliette go?

Eliette walked more sedately, keeping close to Kristina's side. She was usually reserved, but she'd been the one to cuddle closest the other night, when Kristina had slept over in Max's guest room and his children had joined her in bed. "Bree is just a kid," she confided to Kristina. "She doesn't know about these things."

Kristina tried not to smile. She also felt bruised inside, for she guessed that Eliette had begun to let down her guard a little, to see her as a friend. Which meant the child would be hurt again, to some degree, when Kristina and Max went their distinctly separate ways.

"What things?" she asked, casually offering her hand.

Eliette took it, after a brief hesitation. "Oh, kissing and stuff. Like you do with Daddy."

"Oh." Not a very original or profound reply, but Kristina was stumped.

Mercifully they had reached the Blazer, and Eliette pulled free and scrambled into the back beside Bree, who was already buckled in. Max helped Kristina into the passenger seat and then went around to get behind the wheel.

He was whistling softly under his breath.

"Aunt Elaine moved to Arizona," Bree chimed from her booster seat. "She breaked her heart. I think she fell down."

"She didn't fall down, ninny," Eliette said. "She wanted to marry Daddy, and he said no."

Out of the corner of her eye, Kristina saw Max tense slightly, but she had to hand it to him. When he spoke, his voice was matter-of-fact. "Aunt Elaine missed your grandparents," he said. "Besides, they're getting older and they need her."

Max hadn't exactly lied; he hadn't denied that Sandy's sister, Elaine, was in love him. It was probably true that she missed her parents, and they might even need her help, if their health was poor or something like that. But he had certainly steered the conversation away from the subject of his sister-in-law.

Kristina gave him a teasing, sidelong look, to let him know she wasn't fooled.

He chuckled and shook his head.

The day was wonderful, straight out of the fantasies Kristina had cherished all her life.

Max's parents lived in a large colonial-style house, built of brick, in one of Seattle's better, though certainly not exclusive, neighborhoods. There was a small duck pond out back, and the spacious property was fringed with fir and maple trees. A few gloriously yellow, brown, and crimson leaves still clung to the wintry branches of the maples.

The people in the living room, some gathered around a piano singing, and others in front of the fire arguing politics, looked like figures from some painting celebrating Americana. The air was filled with lovely aromas—roasting turkey, spices, scented candles, and a variety of perfumes.

Mrs. Kilcarragh came immediately to greet Max with a kiss—the girls had already shed their coats and gone running to sit on either side of the piano player, whom Kristina deduced, by the resemblance, to be Max's father.

"Kristina," Mrs. Kilcarragh said warmly, taking both Kristina's hands in hers. "It is a joy to meet you at long last. I'm Allison, and that handsome devil at the piano is the girls' grandfather. Do come in and meet our other guests."

There were an overwhelming number of people in the Kilcarragh house, but that only made it better. Kristina loved the laughter, the music, the talk, and the food, and she could not remember a happier day in all of her life.

After the meal, which was unbelievable, the men retired to watch the football game, Max included, and the women cleaned up. Kristina was thrilled to help—she had not known this particular kind of female camaraderie ever, and being part of it was an experience so sweet that it swelled her heart. Oh, to be a part of this family, to share in other celebrations, to belong.

But it wasn't to be, and all the pretending in the world wouldn't change that. Nor would she squander such a precious gift by looking ahead to a bleak future, however. Kristina kept herself firmly in the present, listening to the women's chatter.

Gweneth, Max's sister, whom she remembered from her one visit to the shop when she'd wanted to buy the brass monkey, was in charge of drying water glasses as they were washed and rinsed. Since Kristina was doing sink duty, they were in close proximity.

"I've found the world's ugliest gift for Max," Gweneth announced to the room at large, with glee and an obvious sense of accomplishment. "He'll never be able to top this."

"What?" asked one of the aunts, grinning.

"Yes, what?" echoed somebody's cousin's sister-in-law.

Gweneth's eyes twinkled as she shook her head. "I want it to be a complete surprise. Trust me, though—he will *hate* this. And the best part is, I've hidden it right under his nose."

Allison shook her head, looking less than amused. "You and Max are getting too old to play such silly games," she said. She looked around the room in general, as if seeking confirmation for her statement. "Why can't they give each other regular presents like everybody else?"

"That wouldn't be any fun," Gweneth answered.

Soon the china and silver were clean and put away, and the football game was over, and practically everybody over the age of thirty was stretched out somewhere in the big, cozy house, taking a nap.

Max found Kristina standing at a window in the dining room, watching the light change on the waters of the pond behind the house. He slipped his arms around her waist, kissed her nape, and drew her back against him gently.

"Ready to go?" he asked.

Kristina turned in his arms, looked up into his face, and smiled, even though her heart was breaking.

"Ready," she said.

"Y OU have a wonderful family," Kristina said softly as she and Max drove out of the city and onto the freeway leading to Snoqualmie Pass. She had watched him say good-bye to Eliette and Bree, and had thought that Eliette clung a little at the parting, as though unwilling, even afraid, to let him go. Perhaps the child had been remembering another day, when she'd lost her mother, and very nearly her father as well.

"Thank you," Max replied, flinging her a sidelong grin. "Since I've never met your parents, I can't return the compliment, but if they made you, they have to be special."

" 'Special,' " she said, with a smile and a nod. "You missed your calling, Max Kilcarragh—you should have been a diplomat."

He laughed at that. "I wonder if my players would agree," he replied. "You might not believe it to look at me, but I'm one of those guys who paces the sidelines and shouts when things aren't going well in a game."

Kristina studied him soberly. "Do you care that much about winning?"

"I don't give a damn about it," he answered, eyes mirthful. "I just think a little yelling and an occasional dose of pressure make the kids better prepared to live in the real world. And, no, I don't use the same techniques with Bree and Eliette, if that's what you're wondering."

"I was," Kristina confessed. "It's a bit hypocritical of you, though, wouldn't you say, to shout at other people's children?"

Max smiled, flipped on his signal light, glanced into both the side and rearview mirrors, and changed lanes. "No," he replied with certainty. "The guys on my team are all at least sixteen years old. There's a big difference."

By tacit agreement, they avoided the subject of Kristina's closed shop and all it might mean. It was as if nothing existed beyond the darkest edges of the upcoming Sunday night; everything difficult, if it had a bearing on the present, would be discussed then.

"I guess you're right," Kristina conceded. "So someday when your daughters are that age, and they complain that a teacher is pressuring them—"

"I'll try to stay out of it, unless I think there's a deeper problem."

The freeway was crowded with holiday travelers, and dusk had descended before they left Max's parents' house. He concentrated on his driving and did not look away from the road when he spoke again. "What about the letters? What happened after both your in-laws died so quickly?"

Leaning back against the seat and closing her eyes, Kristina sighed. Although she had been rereading the letters, she didn't need to do that to remember. It was just that the process made her feel close to Phillie, who had been her dearest and truest mortal friend except, perhaps, for Gilbert Bradford.

In a quiet voice she brought Max up-to-date from the place where he'd left off—explaining, though it was difficult, about Joseph, and the injuries she'd suffered at Michael's hand when she finally confronted him one too many times. She made very little mention of Gilbert, however, except to say that he'd sent Michael away to Australia, never to return.

"And did he?"

Kristina shook her head. "No," she said. But there was much more to the tale, and, as they drove, she began to tell it, unconsciously lapsing into the accent of her English upbringing and the formal phraseology of the time. . . .

"After Michael had gone away, I believed I should have peace at last, but I did not. I was frantic over Joseph's passing—ironic, isn't it, that one's life can be even more horrible than so wretched a death as he suffered? But such children were common in nineteenth-century London.

"For five years I worked among the poor—I could not remarry since I was still legally Michael's wife—but in the end the hopelessness of it was simply more than I could bear. I needed a respite, but did not know what to do.

"Finally, I decided to go traveling, simply to get away. I rode elephants in Burma and climbed mountains in Peru and Africa. I was in China, perhaps eight years after I had left England, when I began having the dreams.

"They were extraordinarily vivid and always terrifying. In them I was visiting Australia—a place I would never go, as large and fascinating as it was, because I feared encountering Michael. I could not be sure I wouldn't kill him with my bare hands if I saw him again. I blamed him completely for what had happened to Joseph.

"In the nightmares I saw a debauched Michael, aged by drink and whoring and the use of opium. He was in a small courtyard, beating a woman, slapping her again and again, first with the front of his hand, then with the back. She flinched, of course, for she was smaller, but she did not cry out, nor did she attempt to defend herself. She simply glared at him with such hatred that her dark eyes glinted in the moonlight.

"At last he hurled her down into the dirt of a flower bed. She put out her hand, only to balance herself, but her fingers closed round the handle of a small gardening trowel. In that moment I became her, entered her body, took over her thoughts.

"Now I was the one clasping the trowel. And I had no compunction about striking back. I raised my hand and, with a strength born of years of hatred, drove the point of the tool straight into Michael's throat, and deep. He had not expected the attack—indeed, it had all happened very fast, in that way of dreams.

"Blood spurted from his open jugular vein, staining his shirt, his coat, the very stones of the courtyard. He put his hands to his throat, eyes bulging with horrified rage, as if to stem the flow. Of course, he could not.

"With a gurgling sound I shall remember as long as I have the capacity to recall anything at all, he slumped to the ground and perished there at my feet, and even then I felt no remorse. My hands and dress— indeed, *her* hands and dress, whoever that ill-fated woman had been— were sticky with the crimson evidence of my guilt, but I would have celebrated, rather than mourned.

"It was always the same dream, and it went on for months on end, in exactly the same manner. Each time it ended as other people rushed into the courtyard, grasping at the woman, crouching over Michael, squashing the delicate flowers under the soles of their shoes.

"About eight months had passed, I suppose, and I was in Paris, because my mother had bid me to come to that city on other business, when I happened to pick up an English newspaper left behind at a table in front of a sidewalk café. In it was a discreet report of Michael Bradford's murder, somewhere in New South Wales. He'd been stabbed with a garden trowel, by an unnamed woman who had subsequently been taken into custody. Before the alleged killer could be tried, however, she hanged herself in her cell.

"I was so stricken that I took to my flat for three days and would not come out for any reason. It wasn't that I spared any grief for Michael, but every time I thought of that poor woman, I was bludgeoned with guilt. Had she been blamed for a crime I had actually committed, while thinking I was merely dreaming? How else could I have known so much about Michael's death if I hadn't been there?

"Eventually I had to stop asking myself those questions, for it was pure torture, and there was no way to learn the answers. But sometimes it haunts me still, even now, when so much time has passed.

"I could not seem to stop moving about the world after that. I was always on board a steamer bound for somewhere, or a train, or rattling along in a coach. I still insisted on doing things the human way, you see, but if I'd really *been* human, I'm sure the pace I kept would have done me in. Even my parents, who can go anywhere they wish, provided the sun is not shining in that place, of course, simply by thinking of their destination, were hard put to keep up with me.

"I began to collect things on my journeys—a jade figure here, a painting or a sculpture there, but the idea of going into business did not occur to me until 1925, when I finally opened a shop in San Francisco. I had garnered some friends in that city, and the need to wander lessened, though it certainly hadn't abated.

"By the time air travel was prevalent, I was off again, though I kept the San Francisco shop for many years.

"My friends grew old and died, and that was nearly unbearable for me, being left behind over and over again. I became almost reclusive and then left California, because there were too many memories.

"Finally I settled in Seattle—I'm not sure why, beyond the fact that it's beautiful, with the water and the trees and the mountains all round. I know I had a sense of belonging that I had never really known before, in any other place on Earth, as if I had come home at last.

"I was dreadfully lonely, but careful not to make many friends. I confined my social life, such as it was, to the company of my parents, Valerian, and a few other diverting vampires.

"For want of something to do, I opened my store on Western Avenue under the name of Kristina Tremayne. When some years had passed, I went away for a while and came back as my "daughter," Kristina Bennington. Then, when enough time had gone by, I reinvented myself again, this time as Kristina Holbrook. As my uncle Aidan had done before me, I willed my assets to myself, as though I were my own descendent. Otherwise, obviously, a lot of difficult questions might have been asked.

"I grew set in my ways, over the years, as mortals and monsters alike will do. I ran my shop, made occasional buying trips, attended estate sales, and the like. I read extensively and I was excruciatingly bored. Sometimes, when the dreams of Michael's murder in the Australian courtyard threatened, I didn't sleep for weeks at a time.

"Finally I met you, and everything changed. . . ."

* * *

S HE had almost said "I met you *again*," but caught herself just in time. Max had enough to deal with without adding an account of one of his past lives to the tale. There were reasons, after all, why most people did not recall earlier incarnations—good ones. The past, for mortals at least, was gone, and looking back, except to learn, was a waste of the precious present.

"It sounds like a lonely life," Max said gently. They had reached the mountain lodge where they had booked reservations the week before, and there were snowflakes dancing in front of the headlights.

"It was," Kristina replied.

"Wait here," Max said, reaching out to touch her arm. "I'll register us and get the key to our cabin."

She nodded. After so many years of doing everything by herself, for herself, it was lovely to be so thoughtfully attended. She looked forward to being alone with Max, to the privacy of the cabin, and the freedom to make love as much and as long as they wanted.

True to his word, Max returned within five minutes, climbing into the warm Blazer, tossing the huge old-fashioned key into Kristina's lap with a grin, shifting the engine into reverse. A fire had been laid in their one-room cottage, but not lit, and the air was so cold that they could see their breath.

Max crouched beside the hearth, struck a match, and got a good blaze going. Then, with a light in his eyes, he turned to Kristina, who was shivering inside her cloth coat.

"I think you need a little warming up," he said, rising.

Kristina felt a thrill go through her as he came toward her, drew her into his arms, and kissed her. It was tentative at first, that kiss, but as Max put his hands inside Kristina's coat and boldly cupped her breasts, it grew deeper and more demanding.

She had made love with this man before, of course, and known true rapture, but that first contact was a portent of something still more powerful, something rooted in eternity itself.

He stripped her of the coat, then her boots. He took off her sweater and her bra, and then, after kissing each of her taut nipples, he began unhooking her skirt. She was covered in goose bumps and at the same time approaching meltdown, so great was the heat within her.

Finally Max removed her skirt and slip and pantyhose, and she stood before him utterly naked, trembling with anticipation. The fire on the hearth was just beginning to warm the room, but a thin film of perspiration glistened on Kristina's bare flesh.

"I've been wanting to do this ever since I first laid eyes on you," he said. He was still fully dressed, except for his jacket, which he had tossed aside at some point, and now he knelt in front of Kristina like a worshiper before a goddess.

"W-What?" she whispered. Though she knew, somehow.

The cabin was dark, except for the flickering light of the fireplace, but Kristina was in a fever. She didn't know whether she had turned out the single lamp or if Max had.

"To taste you," Max answered. He caressed her belly with his fingertips, then held her hips for a moment, as though aligning her for possession. Then he began to massage her most private place, making it ready, causing it to harden in the same sweetly painful way her nipples had done earlier, at the touch of his tongue.

Kristina had nothing to hold on to, but it didn't matter, because Max was supporting her. He widened her stance a little, moved his hands to clasp her buttocks, and delved through musky silk to take her full in his mouth.

She cried out throatily, letting her head fall back, not at all certain that she could bear such pleasure.

But bear it she must, for Max would show her no quarter.

He teased her mercilessly, now suckling hard, now nibbling, now laving her with his tongue. She groaned aloud, grinding her hips without shame, desperate to be vulnerable and more vulnerable still.

Finally Max eased her back into a chair, draped her trembling legs over its arms, and consumed her in earnest. Kristina bucked under his lips and tongue, hairline and body drenched in sweat, begging him in senseless, disjointed phrases for release.

In his own sweet time he granted her appeal, but it was a brief victory. As soon as her body had ceased its violent spasms of pleasure, he proceeded to make her want him all over again. By the time Max carried Kristina to the bed, which was covered with a bright, heavy quilt, she was all but delirious and could not honestly have said whether the room was cold or warm.

She herself was burning, but the fever was an ancient one.

Max undressed at his own maddening pace, the way he did everything, but when he lay beside Kristina on the bed, and she reached out to touch him, to clasp his staff in her hand, she knew how much he wanted her. He had paid a great price to make certain that Kristina's needs were accommodated.

"I love you," she said, rolling on top of him.

"I—love—you—" The words came hoarse and splintered from his throat, for she was still holding him, her knees astraddle of his hips.

"By all rights," Kristina teased, leaning forward to nibble at his lower lip, "I ought to put you through the same exhaustive paces you put me through, but I won't. Not yet, anyway."

Max groaned. He was at her mercy now, and she was enjoying the power this benign dominance gave her. To his credit, so was he.

"There are all sorts of things I could do to you, you know," Kristina said, passing a thumb back and forth over the moist tip of his erection, guiding it slowly toward its natural sheath inside her own body. She proceeded to name a few.

Max was half out of his head with need by then. Exactly what he deserved. "Kristina—"

She took him into her, but lingered infinitely at every fraction of an inch, feeling herself tighten instinctively around him, feeling him swell and grow harder still in response. Finally, with a warrior's cry, Max grasped her hips and thrust his own upward, possessing her completely.

There was a power shift in that instant, but not to one or the other. They were true equals, Max and Kristina, as they rode the tempest into a storm of spinning lights and shattering ecstasy.

Finally Max arched high off the bed, his powerful body flexing as he emptied himself into Kristina, once, twice, three times. For her, the climax lasted even longer—she was still descending, and occasionally catching on still another orgasm, each one sweet but less intense than the last, when Max kissed her temple.

"Ummm—I think we forgot something," he said.

Kristina closed her eyes, crooned low in her throat, and then snuggled against him again. "What?" she asked.

"A condom."

"I haven't slept with anyone in a hundred years, Max," Kristina reminded him. "You?"

"Just Sandy, though it hasn't been quite that long, so you're safe with me. But what if you got pregnant?"

Kristina's eyes flew open. On the one hand, the prospect of bearing Max's child delighted her. On the other, it was terrible, because she could never marry him. She had promised herself to Dathan, and it was a vow she must keep, no matter what her own feelings in the matter might be.

"You don't suppose—?"

"Could happen," Max said. "After all, this is the standard method."

Kristina held on to him very tightly and buried her face in his chest. "Would you be angry?" she asked in a small voice.

"Angry?" The word ruffled the soft hair at her temple, which was still moist from their earlier passion. "God, no. I love kids, Kristina. And I love you."

Kristina fought hard not to cry. She was afraid Max was going to ask her to marry him, and equally afraid that he wasn't. She made a circle on his bare back with the palm of her right hand, greedy for the feel of his flesh. "I thought it made a difference—my turning out to be mortal, I mean."

"What kind of difference?"

"In how you felt about me. You admitted that part of my charm might have been the fact that I couldn't die."

"Yeah," Max said with a long, deep sigh, his arms tight around her. "I've thought a lot about that. What it all comes down to, though, is that love is a risk, plain and simple. And everybody has to die someday. I mean, everybody's human."

"Even vampires can die," Kristina said, thinking of a story her mother had once told her, about the original vampires. They'd called themselves the Brotherhood and had become blood-drinkers on the island continent of Atlantis, while participating in a scientific experiment. They had grown weary, after many thousands of years, and willed their own deaths.

Max raised himself on one elbow and looked down at her. "Really? How? Do they have to be shot with a silver bullet?"

Kristina didn't laugh, though the thought was ludicrous enough to provoke a certain grim amusement. "That's werewolves, and I don't even know if it's true, because I've never encountered one. Vampires must have blood, of course, and they can be killed by fire, by sunlight, and by having a stake driven through their hearts, just like in the movies. They have one other known vulnerability as well—the blood of warlocks is poisonous to them. Given a sufficient dose, they will slip into something resembling a coma and gradually die of starvation." She stroked his cheek, where a five o'clock shadow had sprouted. "Can't we talk about something else?"

"I'm sorry," Max said. "I should have left the subject alone." He touched the tip of her nose. "Are you hungry? Believe it or not, they have room service in this place. No doubt everything comes by dogsled."

Kristina laughed. "Hungry? After that dinner your mother served today? I may never need to eat again!"

"Well," Max said, resting on his elbows, "I'm starved."

Kristina fell back with a groan and pulled the covers over her head, and Max reached for the phone on the bedside table and called the restaurant in the lodge. She was hiding in the bathroom—up to her chin in bubbles in an old claw-foot tub actually—when his late-night snack was delivered.

He joined her, after dispensing with the food, a devilish glint shimmering in his eyes. With a growl, he flung off his robe, which came with the room, and stepped into the bath, nearly causing the water to overflow.

They made love again, there in the tub, and got the floor so wet in the process that Kristina figured the bathroom would be a skating rink by morning, if they let the fire go out.

ELIETTE liked staying at her grandparents' house. She enjoyed sleeping in the room that had been her daddy's once, and still had some of his things in it. She liked floating boats on the duck pond, though she and Bree weren't allowed to go near it unless an adult was with them. She especially liked all the sounds—people talking quietly in a nearby room, soft music playing somewhere, the creaks and squeaks as the old house settled itself for a winter's night. In the morning there would still be a crowd, but just like always, Grandmother and Gramps would belong only to her and Bree, for that special Friday.

They would start by going out to breakfast, just the four of them. Even Daddy wasn't invited on those outings, or Aunt Gweneth. Bree and Eliette could order anything they wanted to eat—even a chocolate sundae or a corn dog, if they chose—but they always picked scrambled eggs and orange juice and waffles.

Then, once they were all full, they would get back into Grandmother's Volvo—Gramps didn't drive anymore because he had a disease in his eyes, and every year it was harder for him to see—and drive to a big mall called South Center. There they went into practically every store, choosing presents for their daddy, for Aunt Gweneth and Aunt Elaine and their Arizona grandparents, Molly and Jim. They even bought stuff for each other, one going off to shop with Grandmother while the other went with Gramps.

They'd have lunch then—they usually went to a Mexican place close to the mall—and in the afternoon they saw a movie.

By the time they got back to the big brick house, they always had lots of packages, and Gramps always took a long nap before dinner. Grandmother ordered out, then sat down in her favorite chair and put her feet up, sipping tea and dozing a little. Bree and Eliette were usually pretty tired, too, but they were too excited to sleep. After supper, though, and their baths, they would barely get into their pajamas before they crashed.

Eliette smiled, just to think about it. It was so much fun.

She closed her eyes, willing herself to drift off. In the twin bed across from hers, Bree was sound asleep. But she was smiling, too.

Eliette snuggled down deeper in the covers. It was a cold night, and the weather man had said it might snow. That was relatively rare in Seattle, and Eliette hoped there would be such a deluge that they wouldn't have school again until after Christmas.

Fat chance.

Thinking about Christmas made her think about the awful brass monkey Aunt Gweneth had bought for Daddy at the flea market. It was already wrapped, first in bright red paper and then in that heavy brown stuff, and tucked away on a shelf in one of the cabinets in their garage. On Christmas Eve, Aunt Gweneth said, Santa Claus would bring it inside and put it under the tree.

Eliette made a face. She didn't like the monkey any more than Bree did; it was ugly, and besides, it gave her a creepy feeling. She didn't regard herself as a sneaky sort of kid, but if that doorstop thingy had been handy just then, she might have carried it out and dumped it in the duck pond.

"Kristina can't do magic anymore," Bree said from the other bed, startling Eliette. She'd been convinced her sister was asleep.

"That's okay," Eliette answered, feeling the need to put in a good word for the ordinary. "Most people can't anyway."

"Do you like her?"

Eliette considered. "Yeah. Do you?"

Bree nodded; it was a good thing Eliette was looking. Half the time the kid just assumed you could hear her shaking her head. "She's going to go away, though, so I guess I'd better not like her too much."

Eliette felt alarmed. Ever since her mom had died, she'd been trying to make herself stop needing people, but it hadn't worked very well. "What makes you say a silly thing like that?"

"An angel told me."

Eliette made a contemptuous sound. "Angels don't go around delivering messages, like Federal Express or somebody."

"Yes, they do," Bree insisted. "Grandmother told me that's what the word *angel* means—a messenger. And I saw one."

"Okay," Eliette scoffed. "When did you see this angel? And what did it look like?"

"Not *it*—she. She was pretty, like one of those dolls nobody wants you to touch. She had yellow hair and blue eyes and a ruffly dress with lots of lace trimming. I saw her the night Kristina came to stay in our guest room, when I got up to go to the bathroom."

Eliette felt a chill. Angels were scary, as far as she was concerned. "You ate too much pumpkin pie," she said. "Either that, or you've been dreaming. Or both."

"No," Bree insisted. "She was real. She told me she had a sister, too."

Eliette sighed, but she pulled the covers up to her chin at the same time. "This angel really had a lot to say, it seems to me. On top of all this, she told you Kristina was going away?"

"To marry a king," Bree said with awe and not a little sorrow.

Eliette felt sad, too. She hadn't wanted Kristina around at first, but lately she'd been counting on her staying and marrying Daddy and being their stepmother. "I don't want her to go," she said.

"Me, neither," Bree answered. "But grown-ups do what they want to."

Eliette nodded. That was certainly true enough. Some adults didn't even seem to *see* little kids; it was as though they were invisible or something. But Kristina wasn't like that—she noticed people, whether they were big or small—and if she went away, Eliette would miss her more than she cared to admit.

She was getting really tired, because it had been a long day. Thanksgiving always was, she thought. When a person got to be seven, they started to see a pattern in things like that.

"Go to sleep," she said to Bree. "We've got to get up early."

Bree yawned loudly. "I'm going to buy Kristina something really beautiful. Then, even if she marries that king, she'll remember us."

Eliette's throat felt tight. She gulped and let her eyes drift half closed. After a few moments she thought she saw a blond angel through her thick lashes, standing at the foot of the bed and smiling. She was just as Bree had described her, but in a blink she was gone.

Eliette told herself she was dreaming and soon enough, she truly was.

IN the morning Max and Kristina ate a room-service breakfast in bed, made love, then got dressed and went outside into a fresh fall of snow. They made snow angels and flung balls of the stuff at each other and laughed like kids. They didn't go inside until they were breathless and so cold that their feet and hands were numb.

They made love again and then slept, warm and sated.

That evening, after having dinner in the lodge restaurant, they joined half a dozen other guests for a sleigh ride over perfect, moon-washed snow. It was a magical experience, and Kristina thought she would remember the singular music of the horses' harness bells for the rest of her life.

It was an idyllic weekend, but it went by very fast, as such interludes always do. On Sunday night they sat together on the rug in front of the fireplace in their cabin, the room still resonating faintly with the power of their lovemaking, like a concert hall after a great symphony has been played.

Max took Kristina's hand, and she knew the moment had arrived, that the enchantment was over, the spell broken.

He said her name, running his thumb lightly over her knuckles. Then he whispered, "Marry me."

She looked away in a useless attempt to hide the tears that burned in her eyes. She wanted nothing more than to marry Max Kilcarragh, but she dare not accept his proposal. She had already pledged her life, perhaps her very soul, to another.

Max caught her chin in his hand and made her look at him, though gently. With the pad of his thumb, he smoothed away the tears, then touched her lower lip, leaving behind the taste of salt. "Was that a 'no'?"

"I can't," Kristina whispered. It was agony to say the words, to turn down her greatest desire, her shining dream.

He let his forehead rest against hers for a moment, and his broad shoulders moved in a great sigh that broke Kristina's already fractured heart.

"Because?" Max prompted.

"Because I'm going to be Dathan's mate."

He stared at her. "The *warlock*?"

Kristina only nodded. There was no point in explaining.

Max pushed to his feet, abandoning her, ripping himself away. "You came here and slept with me, knowing that? That you were going straight from my bed to his?"

Kristina could not speak. She merely nodded again.

Max began gathering their things, his motions wild, furious, full of hurt, and Kristina offered no protest, no words of consolation. There was nothing to be said.

18

KRISTINA and Max had left their cozy cabin at the mountain lodge far behind before either of them spoke. The atmosphere in the Blazer was thick with tension, and a fresh snowfall enclosed them in white gloom.

"Why didn't you just leave me alone in the first place?" Max ground out. He didn't look at her; understandably, he was keeping his eyes on the slippery, treacherous road.

Kristina bit her lower lip for a moment before answering. She wanted to cry—no, to sob and wail—but somehow she held onto her composure. "You make it sound as though I sought you out and deliberately led you on. I was in love with you, Max—and I always will be."

The sound he made was low and contemptuous. "And all along you intended to mate with that—*thing*."

A shiver moved down Kristina's spine, and it had nothing to do with the cold that had somehow settled in the marrow of her bones, despite the Blazer's more than adequate heating system. It was dangerous to speak of creatures like Dathan in such a desultory way, especially for Max. The warlock was already jealous of him.

"It wasn't like that at all," she said evenly. There was no way to assuage Max's pain, or her own, but she owed him some kind of explanation. Even though anything she might say would probably only serve to deepen his sense of betrayal.

The snow was blinding now, and traffic slowed to a crawl, then a full stop before Max replied. "What *was* it like, then?"

A state trooper approached the driver's side, and Max rolled down the window. Kristina held her tongue.

"Sorry, folks," the policeman told them, shivering but genial. "The pass is closed. You'll have to turn back and find a place to wait out the storm." Through the weather-fogged windshield, Kristina saw other cars making U-turns and heading in the opposite direction. Soon enough, Max and Kristina were going that way, too.

"Great," Max murmured. "Couldn't you just zap us back to Seattle or something?"

Kristina folded her arms and blinked back tears. "You know I can't," she said, shrinking into the seat.

Max reached for his cell phone and punched a single button. A moment later he was talking. "Hi, Mom—it's Max. Listen, the pass is closed, so we aren't going to make it back tonight. Will you explain to the girls? And be sure they understand that everything is okay?" There was a brief pause, then Max smiled, and the expression bruised Kristina's heart somehow because it wasn't, might never be, directed at her. "Thanks, Mom. See you."

The cordiality was gone from Max's voice and manner when he glanced at Kristina, after replacing the cell phone in its little plastic bracket on the dashboard. "I guess we're stuck with each other, for tonight at least."

Kristina pretended to be looking out the passenger window and quickly dashed at her tears with the back of one hand. "We'll be lucky if we don't have to spend the night in the Blazer, with so many people turning back," she said, hoping he wouldn't hear the slight sniffle she hadn't been able to disguise.

They were lucky, as it turned out. Their room at the mountain lodge had not yet been rented, though the whole place was full.

Kristina sensed the fine hand of Valerian, or perhaps her mother, at work, but mental efforts to summon either of them met with resounding failure. With their help she and Max could have been, as he'd put it, "zapped" back to Seattle.

Max carried the bags back in and rebuilt the fire. The bed had not been made up, since they'd left the lodge well past check-out time.

"I meant it when I said I loved you," Kristina said, huddling inside her coat and staying very near the door, as if to bolt. It was a silly urge, she soon realized—after all, where could she go? Besides, this wasn't Michael she was dealing with, it was Max, her beloved, sensible, mentally healthy Max. No matter how angry he might be, or how hurt, she had nothing to fear from him.

He turned from the hearth and rose, shedding his ski jacket and tossing it aside. "Call it off, Kristina," he said, his dark gaze holding hers. "If you mean what you say, then tell the warlock there won't be a wedding."

Kristina flushed. "I can't," she said, wishing with everything inside her, everything she was and would ever be, that she could. "I promised."

"*Break* your promise."

She shook her head. She could not tell him, even now, why she had made her heinous bargain with Dathan—to save Eliette and Bree from possession. That was worth whatever she might have to suffer in consequence of the pact and, as much as she longed to be free to marry Max instead, she hoped with all her soul that the warlock would succeed.

"At least tell me why," Max said. He went to the service bar and rummaged for a beer and a diet cola.

At last Kristina removed her coat and crossed the room to accept the can of soda, which Max knew she preferred over every beverage except water and herbal tea.

"You were right," Kristina conceded miserably, "when you said I should never have let things get started between us in the first place. I can't begin to explain the kind of danger I've put you in, not to mention your children. I'm doing this to protect you, Max, all of you—and that's all I can or will say about it."

He sighed and shoved his free hand through his hair. "Doesn't it matter that we love each other?"

She sat down in one of the chairs near the hearth, still feeling chilled, and Max perched on the arm. "Of course it matters. It's the whole reason we have to say good-bye." Kristina raised her eyes to his face. There was one thing she had to tell him, even though he probably wouldn't believe her. "We were in love once before," she said very softly. "A long time ago. It was a star-crossed match, just like now."

Max's brow furrowed into a frown. The hurt was still plainly visible in his eyes, but he was calmer than before. "I think I'd remember that," he said, sounding bewildered.

Kristina smiled, though her heart was breaking, falling apart bit by fragile, splintered bit. "Not necessarily. Your name wasn't Max Kilcarragh then—it was Gilbert Bradford. You were the Duke of Cheltingham, Michael's elder brother."

Max's eyes narrowed. "Reincarnation?"

"Sort of. It's really more complicated than that. Time is not linear, so human beings actually exist in all their various incarnations at once. They're usually not aware of it, of course."

Max set the beer aside. "I was—am—Gilbert? The good guy?"

Kristina laughed. "Yes. And probably a lot of other people, too."

He frowned. "Is this what Albert Einstein was talking about with his theory of relativity?"

"In a way," she agreed.

Max was silent, absorbing it all.

Kristina took a sip of her diet cola, wishing it were something stronger, a potion capable of quelling the terrible heartbreak she felt. "It would seem," she said carefully, "that we simply aren't destined to be together." The next part was one of the most difficult things she had ever had to say. "Very likely, Sandy is your true mate, for all of time."

Max rose suddenly from his seat on the arm of the chair and went to stand on the hearth, his broad back to Kristina, his hands braced, wide apart, against the mantelpiece. "I loved her very much," he said at great length, in a voice so low and hoarse that Kristina could barely hear him. Then he turned and looked deep into her eyes. "But I love you, too. And even though I don't remember being Gilbert Bradford, I know from the letters you showed me that he felt something similar to what I'm feeling now." He paused to draw a long, ragged breath and once again pushed his fingers through his hair. "I don't understand about eternity—I'm an ordinary man, Kristina. All I know is what I want this moment, in *this* lifetime. And that's to marry you."

Kristina looked down at her hands, which were knotted painfully in her lap. She tried to relax her clenched fingers. "That's what I want, too," she admitted. "But we can't be together, Max. It's impossible, and the sooner we accept that, the better off we'll be."

Even as she spoke the words, she knew she would never be able to accept losing Max, never get over this particular farewell. She dared not think beyond the moment when they would part, once and for all.

He came to her then, drew her up out of the chair and into his embrace. He held her close, and they wept together in silence, while outside the little cabin the snow continued to fall.

IN a cabinet inside Max's garage, the package stirred. Brown paper fell away, followed by the festive Christmas wrap beneath. The thing quivered, grew hot enough to singe the paper, and toppled out onto the concrete floor with a metallic crash.

It rolled a little way, and then, in a mere flicker of time, Kristina's spell was broken. Billy Lasser, boy criminal, came back to life.

He was only eighteen years old, but in the course of his brief existence, he'd pulled off more than his share of convenience-store heists, muggings, and rapes. Once he'd even done murder, if that was what you wanted to call it, killing a whore down on the Sea-Tac strip and dumping her off out by the Green River.

Billy smiled, remembering his cleverness. No doubt about it, the cops would have chalked that one up to a certain serial killer they'd been tracking for as long as he could remember.

But his pleasure quickly faded, replaced by rage. He had another score to settle, with that weird chick who'd turned him into a goddamn monkey. Billy wasn't overly bright, and it didn't occur to him that messing with somebody who could do stuff like that might not be a good idea. He knew two things: that he was hungry and that he was pissed off.

He looked around, his eyes adjusting to the darkness, and realized more from the smells than anything that he was in somebody's garage. Maybe if he broke into the house he'd find that bitch who'd locked him up inside a hunk of metal and make her wish she'd never been born.

After he'd had a sandwich and maybe some beer, if there was any.

Billy tried the inside door and found it locked, but that hardly slowed him down. The light switch was right there handy, and he turned it on. There was a toolbox on a workbench nearby; he took a screwdriver, and in no time he was inside.

He paused, waiting, listening. The place was empty; he'd have bet on that. There was no dog and probably no alarm system.

Billy flicked on the kitchen lights and went straight to the refrigerator. There was plenty to eat—he stuffed two packages of lunch meat down his throat without bothering to find the bread, then guzzled two beers in a row before taking a third one to sip as he went through the house.

He figured out right away that the bitch didn't live here, but he found some cash in a cookie jar on top of the fridge and stuffed that into the pocket of his jeans.

Billy checked out the upstairs, reckless with relief that he was finally free, and high on the beers he'd downed so fast. Two little girls shared one room, and one was obviously reserved for company. The third belonged to a man, judging by the clothes in the closets and bureaus. No mommy in this family.

What a pity, Billy thought.

He went downstairs, feeling a little less reckless now that the food was getting into his system, and tried to figure out what to do next. It was cold outside, and all he had was his fake leather jacket, bought at a swap meet a couple of years before.

He helped himself to a beat-up down-filled coat he found in a closet by the front door and pulled it on. It didn't fit, hung clear to his knees in fact, but Billy didn't care. It would keep the chill off.

It was snowing, and Billy walked a long way before he finally managed to catch a bus headed downtown. The weather in Seattle was usually mild, and when they got a little white stuff, the whole place freaked out.

The bus driver gave him a look, and Billy barely suppressed an urge to strangle the bastard then and there. Instead, he brought out some of the money he'd lifted from the big man's cookie jar and paid the fare.

The shop on Western Avenue was closed, of course, since it was late. Billy let himself in through the back door, a little disappointed to find that it wasn't even locked. A few seconds later he knew why—the place was empty to the walls—and now he was even more pissed than before.

He paced the darkened shop restlessly, barely able to contain his agitation. Nobody—*nobody*—was going to get away with treating him the way that woman had. What was her name?

He'd been able to hear things, once in a while, since he'd sat, helpless, for weeks, maybe even months, in this prissy-assed store, though most of that time he'd just sort of drifted, as if he'd been high on top-grade stuff.

He thought hard.

Kristina, he recalled at long last. Kristina Holbrook.

Billy went out the same way he'd come in, hurried through the bone-chilling cold to the nearest phone booth, and shut himself in. Sure as hell, the stupid slut was right there in the book, big as life, along with her fancy address.

It was almost too fucking easy, Billy thought, but he was grinning as he left the booth. Feeling triumphant, he hailed a cab.

The driver bitched about the snow all the way, and that was good, as far as Billy was concerned. Kept the guy from wondering what business a hood like him would have in such a ritzy area of the city. Not that it mattered, Billy reflected smugly, what some dumb-ass cabbie thought about anything.

Her house was big and expensive-looking.

It was also dark.

Billy blessed his continued good luck as he paid the cabbie with cookie-jar money, crossed the sidewalk, opened the front gate, and walked up to the door. He was running on attitude now, and adrenaline.

The cab pulled away, it's taillights glowing red through the heavy white flakes.

Billy sprinted around the side of the house to the back, where he broke in through a basement window. The lots were big in this part of town, and the neighbors wouldn't have heard the glass breaking anyway, he figured, because the snow was still coming down thick and fast. Billy was no weatherman, but he knew from TV that snow muffled sound.

He crawled through the space and found himself in a pretty standard basement.

It was dark as hell, but he couldn't risk turning on any lights, not yet, so he just stood there, waiting and breathing hard, until his vision had adjusted again.

Then he made his way to the cellar stairs.

No big surprise: They opened onto a kitchen.

Billy found a flashlight in one of the drawers—he'd burgled a lot of houses in his time, and they'd all had a little cubbyhole where things like that were stashed, along with a lot of assorted junk.

After pausing once more to listen, Billy switched on the flashlight and, keeping the beam pointed low so there was less chance of it showing at one of the windows, he began to explore the home of the woman he meant to punish.

He went upstairs first, found her bedroom, touched the perfume bottles on her vanity table, and fingered the jewelry lying in a pricey, Chinese-looking box on one of the dressers. These rich bitches, they didn't even care enough about nice things to take care of them right. Just left them laying around, waiting to be stolen.

Billy dangled a strand of pink pearls from one index finger. They were real all right, and old. They glowed, even in the darkness, as though there was moonlight inside them. His ma would have given anything, including him, probably, to own a necklace like that.

Not that his old man woulda let her keep it very long. Thing like that you could pawn for serious change.

Billy dropped the pearls into his pocket. He'd check out the other jewelry later, after he'd made himself at home for a while, after he'd had revenge on *Ms.* Holbrook. When she got home from wherever she was, she'd find a big surprise waiting for her.

He grinned at the thought and opened drawers until he found her nightgowns and underwear. Silk, all of it. A single pair of her panties probably cost more than everything he had on, even when it was new.

His grin faded, though his fingers worked the smooth silk back and forth. It wasn't fair that some people had so much, while guys like him got squat.

He'd make her pay, he thought, and felt better. Lots better.

Billy put the panties back and scooped an armload of nightgowns out of the drawer. Then, carefully, still with only the fading beam of the flashlight to guide him, he began laying the costly garments out on the bed, one by one, tracing the lace edgings with his fingertips, running his hands over the cloth. It felt as fine as a butterfly's wing.

God, he thought, he was getting to be a regular poet.

It took a long time to pick out which gown he wanted the bitch to wear when he took her, but he finally chose a little thigh-length number the same pink color as cotton candy, with ivory trim. He draped it over the back of a chair for later.

Then, very neatly, taking his time, he refolded all the other garments and put them back in place. After that, he went back downstairs, found a roll of duct tape, scissors, and fresh batteries for the flashlight, all in the same junk drawer he'd raided before.

Finally Billy Lasser stretched out on Kristina Bitch Holbrook's satin bedspread, hands cupped behind his head, booted feet crossed at the ankles, and waited for her to come home. He drifted off to sleep with a smile on his face, dreaming of sweet, sweet revenge.

MAX and Kristina spent the whole night making love. Their couplings were poignant, frantic, even greedy, for both of them believed that this would, indeed, be their last night together.

In the morning they awakened to find that the snow had stopped. According to the weatherman on TV, the pass was clear again, and traffic was moving at a steady rate in both directions.

Resigned, Kristina and Max showered, had breakfast in the lodge's restaurant, and set out for Seattle. Max was already running late, and although he'd called the school office from the cell phone that morning to explain his absence, he was anxious to get to work.

Or did he just want to get away from Kristina?

They stopped at her house first, of course, and Max walked her to the door, waiting while she let herself in. The pain in his eyes was so intense, such a clear reflection of what she herself felt, that Kristina could barely look at him.

"Do you want me to come inside and have a look around?" he asked.

Kristina's heart might have been in agony, but her brain was numb. She shook her head. "It's okay," she murmured.

Max touched her cheek with the backs of curled fingers. "Shall I call later?"

"It would be better if you didn't," she answered.

He nodded, leaned forward to kiss her forehead briefly, then turned and walked away. Kristina watched him until he'd gotten into the Blazer and driven off, longing to run after him, convince him that somehow everything could be all right. But that was a lie, and they both knew it.

Thoroughly weary, Kristina went into the kitchen and put on a pot of coffee. It was a paradoxical thing to do, considering how badly she needed sleep, but nothing about Kristina's life made much sense at that moment. She was too soul-weary to sort things out in any reasonable fashion.

If she slept, she would dream. If she stayed awake, she would think of nothing but Max, and how she'd lost him forever.

She couldn't win.

She dialed Daisy's number at home and got the new Brazilian nanny. Ms. Chandler, the woman told her pleasantly, was on a case at the moment, but Kristina's message would be relayed.

Kristina sighed and hung up, feeling utterly alone.

It was only when she'd poured her coffee and climbed the stairs that she realized she was not alone. There was a faint, strange scent in the air, something dangerous. And things seemed disturbed, out of place, though this last was strictly a subjective matter, a fact discerned in her gut rather than her head.

She paused, almost on the threshold of her room, the hairs on her nape standing upright. Some of the coffee splashed over her hand, burning her, but she barely noticed the resultant sting.

Her visitor could not be Benecia or Canaan—they were vampires and thus asleep in their lairs. Dathan, though fully capable of being abroad in the daylight, liked to make flamboyant entrances, à la Valerian.

Who, then . . . ?

Kristina closed her eyes for a moment and swallowed hard.

Of course. It was only her housekeeper, Mrs. Prine, back at last from her vacation.

Kristina stepped into her room and stood frozen in place, staring into the grinning face of the young man she had turned into a doorstop months before. He was lying on her bed, cleaning his fingernails with the point of her antique letter opener.

He gestured toward the chair, and she saw one of her silk nightgowns there, laid out for her. A shiver went down her spine.

"Put that on, baby," he said. "Billy-boy wants to see you in it."

Kristina's response was two words long and most unladylike.

"That's kinda what I had in mind," Billy answered, sitting up. She'd have to burn her white satin bedspread after he'd lain on it, with his filthy clothes and greasy hair. "Only it ain't gonna be good for you, honey. Just me."

"No," Kristina said flatly. If her life was to end in this room, at the hands of this awful man, that was that. But she wasn't about to cooperate in any way, and she would die fighting.

"Come here," he said.

She did, but only to fling the scalding hot coffee into his face.

Billy was screaming in fury and pain when she turned, an instant after the deed, and bolted for the rear stairway.

She was halfway across the family room, headed for the side door that led out onto the deck, when he caught up to her, grasping a handful of her hair and wrenching her back against him. Bile rushed into her mouth, and the pain in her scalp was blinding.

Billy intensified it by giving her a little shake. She caught her breath; nearly fainted.

"Let me go," Kristina said, forcing herself to speak calmly, "or I'll turn you into a toad."

Billy laughed. "I figure you would have done something like that already, if you could. What's the matter, little witchy-bitch? Have you lost your magic somewhere?"

Tears of fury and frustration filled Kristina's eyes. She didn't want to become the warlock's bride, but neither did she want to die.

Dathan, she thought desperately. *Help me.*

Billy tightened his hold on her hair, nearly pulling it out by the roots. "Answer me," he said.

Kristina spat another ungracious invective and tried to stomp on his instep.

He hurled her back toward the stairway, and she landed on the steps, bumping one shoulder hard. "I've got plans for you," Billy said with a leer that made her stomach roll again. She hated being so defenseless, and yet she was glad she'd turned down Max's offer to check the house for her before he left. Max was much bigger and stronger than Billy, not to mention brighter, but the little creep might have gotten the jump on him somehow. There was no question in Kristina's mind that Billy was armed.

She gave him a look of contempt and got to her feet slowly, using the wall for support. She was breathless with fear, on the verge of vomiting, but she wasn't going to let this little weasel know it.

"I'm afraid you're just going to have to cancel your plans," she said.

He produced a .38-caliber pistol from the waistband at the back of his jeans. Kristina recognized the weapon from the night he'd tried to rob her shop and wished she'd made him eat it. The idea had occurred to her at the time, but she'd dismissed it as gauche.

"No, ma'am," Billy answered, brandishing the .38. "We've got business to attend to. It's going to hurt, it's going to take a long time, and face it, baby doll, it's going to happen." He was standing by then, with his back to the window over the kitchen sink, leaning indolently against the counter. "First, you're going to take off all your clothes, then I'm going to look at you for a while. Have a little fun, maybe. Then you're going to put on that silky thing—"

Kristina's gaze was caught by something at the window—a flash of white—and then suddenly the glass splintered in a thousand directions, and Barabbas came through the chasm, all sleek, glorious, snarling wolf. Billy shrieked as the animal landed on him from behind, catching him by the nape and shaking him as though he were no heavier than a rat.

Wide-eyed, both paralyzed and speechless with shock, Kristina simply stood there, unable to believe what she was seeing.

There was blood and glass everywhere, and, after an indeterminate length of time, Billy stopped screaming. Barabbas flung him aside and trotted over to Kristina, as docile as a lapdog, nuzzling her thigh with a bloody muzzle.

Sobbing, she dropped to her knees and flung both arms around Barabbas, burying her face in his lush fur. Billy lay still a little distance away, and Kristina knew without touching him that he was dead. She clung to the wolf, who sat patiently, and waited.

Kristina knew she should call the police, but she couldn't move, and her mind was doing peculiar things. One moment she would be cognizant, then she'd drift off into a dream. The hands of the clock over the stove had advanced significantly every time she looked at them, and finally the quality of the light began to change and soften. Gold became lavender, and then charcoal, black. A cold wind blew in through the broken window over the sink, bringing flakes of snow with it.

That was how Valerian found them when he arrived only moments after sunset, woman, wolf, and dead man.

Muttering an expletive, Valerian rushed to Kristina and drew her into his arms. "What happened?" he demanded, and Kristina felt him trembling.

"The—the brass monkey—" she managed to grind out. "He was here—Barabbas broke the window—I think he's dead."

Valerian carried Kristina into the family room as tenderly as if she were a fragile child and laid her on the sofa. After covering her with his cloak, he rummaged through the liquor cabinet until he found a bottle of Grand Marnier. After pouring her a double dose and ordering her to drink it immediately, the vampire returned to the kitchen.

She heard him speak softly to the wolf, but Valerian spared no word for the man whose blood covered the floor and cabinets.

"He's dead all right," he said flatly upon returning to the family room.

Barabbas followed, and Kristina noticed that the blood that had stained his coat and muzzle was gone. No doubt the kitchen had been Valerianized as well; the body had probably vanished already, along with all traces of the killing. This was not a matter any of them would want to explain to the police.

"Please don't say 'I told you so,' " Kristina whispered, recalling how many times Valerian had warned her to use her magic with caution.

He smiled and drew up a chair. "I won't. Not until you're over the worst of it, anyway."

"Did you—is he—?"

"Yes, darling," Valerian said gently. "He's gone. And this time it will be forever."

Kristina was almost sick with relief. She held out a hand to Barabbas, and he came to her, licking her fingers affectionately. "Thank you, my friend," she told the animal. "I don't know how you knew I needed you, but your timing couldn't have been better."

Barabbas made a whimpering sound and sank to his haunches.

"And thank you," she added, turning her gaze to Valerian.

He blew her a kiss. "Don't mention it. By the way, the Dimity–Gideon crisis has been resolved somewhat."

Sipping her Grand Marnier, Kristina was beginning to feel calmer. "Really? How?"

"I'll leave that tale for your mother to tell, since it was mostly her doing. She'll be along shortly, I should guess. By now she's probably sensed that you've had a near miss and are something the worse for wear." He glanced at his watch, another affectation, or perhaps just a habit since, like all vampires, he always knew the time. "I must feed," he said. "Unless you need me to hold your hand until Maeve arrives, I'll send Barabbas home and take my leave."

"I'll be all right," Kristina said, and she knew it was true, despite all her problems.

Valerian vanished, after planting a light kiss on the top of her head, without reclaiming his cloak. He hadn't been gone more than a moment when the telephone rang.

Kristina reached for the receiver of the cordless phone, which was lying on the lamp table at the end of the couch. "Hello?"

"Kristina?" The voice on the other end of the line was Max's, and even though he'd only spoken a single word, her name, she knew he was in a terrible state. "Oh, God, Kristina—I need your help. Bree and Eliette are missing!"

19

MAX'S children were gone.
Kristina's personal ordeal was forgotten in the face of all that might mean. "What happened?" she whispered into the receiver, one hand raised to her throat. She held her breath, waiting for the answer, and could see Max shove a hand through his hair as clearly as if she'd been standing in the same room with him.

"I picked them up from my parents' house after work," he said evenly. Kristina knew what a supreme effort it was for him to remain calm. "They were playing in their room. I phoned for a pizza, and when it was delivered, I called to the kids to come down to supper. They didn't, so I went up to look for them. They were gone—nowhere in the house."

Kristina closed her eyes, agonized. "Have you called the police?"

"Of course," Max answered. He couldn't be faulted for snapping a bit; he must have been frantic with fear. Kristina certainly was, and Bree and Eliette weren't even her children. "They're sending somebody over," he finished, less abruptly.

"What did they say on the phone—the police, I mean?"

Max let out a long sigh, and in it Kristina heard frustration as well as terror. "That the girls are probably at a neighbor's house or hiding somewhere. They asked if I was divorced—I guess the noncustodial parent is usually the culprit."

Kristina bit her lower lip. She felt a fluttering motion at her side and was relieved to see Dathan standing there, his brow furrowed as he eavesdropped.

"I'll do whatever I can to help, Max. This is my fault."

"We can argue about whose fault it is later," he replied. "Just get over here, *please*—if I don't find my kids, I don't know what I'll do."

"I'm going to find Bree and Eliette," Kristina answered, meeting the warlock's steady gaze.

"But your magic—"

"I have somebody to help me," she said gently. "We'll resolve this as soon as we can, Max—I promise. Just try not to panic."

Without speaking a word, Dathan took Kristina's free hand while she hung up the receiver with the other.

"Benecia and Canaan, I think," Kristina said, answering Dathan's unasked question. "God, I hope it's not already too late!"

Dathan tightened his hold on Kristina, and together they vanished. Kristina was breathless when, only moments later, they reassembled. She had expected a cavern far beneath the earth, like the one in the stories Valerian and Maeve had told her about the Brotherhood, the lost forefathers of all vampires. Or the inside of some elaborate tomb. Instead they were in a sunlit garden next to a cottage with a thatched roof and painted wooden shutters.

Kristina glanced nervously at her future mate, confused. "Benecia and Canaan are here? But the light—"

"An illusion, all of it," the warlock said. "And quite probably a trap."

Benecia appeared in the open doorway of the charming cottage, a beatific smile on her face. "So," she chimed, "you've come at last." She was looking at Dathan, not Kristina, who might have been invisible for all the notice the vampire gave her.

"Yes," he replied, his tone absolutely expressionless. "Where are the Kilcarragh children?"

Benecia gestured. "They're inside. We're having a tea party. Do come in and join us."

Kristina started toward the door, desperate to reach Bree and Eliette, gather them in her arms, protect and reassure them. Dathan stopped her by extending an arm, and though he said nothing, the sidelong glance he gave her was a stern one.

He bowed at the waist—this grand gesture was, of course, directed at Benecia—and then walked toward the fairy-tale house and his hideous little hostess.

"You've certainly taken your time to come courting," Benecia said, pouting prettily. "Canaan said nothing would entice you, but I knew she was wrong."

"You must allow me to serve the tea in order to make up for being remiss," Dathan said smoothly. His smile and manner were charming now; he would have made a fine actor.

Benecia's cornflower gaze found and acknowledged Kristina at last and lingered maliciously. "Why is *she* here?"

"She wants the Kilcarragh children," Dathan answered, standing close to the small vampire now, casting back a warning glance at Kristina. "That is the bargain, isn't it, my sweet? I take you to wife, and you give us the little girls, unharmed."

"How do I know you'll keep your word?"

"You don't. That is one of the perils of entering into an affair of the heart." He took her doll-like hand, bent, and kissed the knuckles. "No more arguments, my darling. We shall drink a toast to our future together." With an elegant motion of one wrist, he conjured a golden goblet, probably medieval, studded with emeralds and rubies, diamonds and amethysts. It glittered in the false sunlight.

Kristina did not want to obey Dathan's unspoken edict that she stay where she was; every instinct compelled her to storm the bastions, to collect Bree and Eliette, to see for herself that they were all right.

Max's children, the children of her own heart. But she dared not move or speak.

Benecia stepped daintily into the cottage, and Dathan followed.

Kristina waited in anguish for something, anything, to happen.

All that came from inside the cottage was an eerie silence.

Then Bree and Eliette stepped out, holding hands and seemingly unharmed, although they appeared to be sleepwalking. They looked blindly in Kristina's direction, plainly not seeing her.

All the same Kristina held her arms out, and they came to her, slowly, and with bewilderment, still entranced. She sank to her knees in the sweet, imaginary grass and gathered them close, terrified that it was too late, that Benecia and Canaan had already done irreparable damage, had begun the process of possession.

Kristina clutched the speechless children more tightly, weeping now. She would never, never forgive herself if they did not recover. If their souls had been stolen, the blame was hers to bear, for all of time and eternity.

The scene around them was chillingly idyllic, almost cartoonlike, with twittering birds, a fresh breeze, apple trees blossoming pink and white in a nearby orchard. A butterfly with kaleidoscope wings fluttered past, and the sky was china blue and cloudless.

A perfect spring day in a place that did not exist.

"Bree? Eliette?" Kristina spoke softly to the little girls, holding one in the curve of each arm. They were wearing jeans, T-shirts, and sneakers—their after-school clothes, no doubt. Their eyes were absolutely blank, and although they did not resist Kristina's embrace, they didn't cling to her, either.

Suddenly a terrible shriek pierced the air, coming from inside the cottage. It was immediately followed by another. Then, silence again, more frightening in some peculiar way than the screams had been.

Kristina stiffened, but if either Bree or Eliette had heard, they gave no sign of it, but simply stood unmoving against her sides, staring at nothing.

Dathan came outside again, pausing to close the door tidily behind him. His smile bordered on cocky as he met Kristina's gaze; he dusted his hands together, in the time-honored gesture of a job not only completed, but well done. And despite the profound relief she felt, there was also remorse.

He had destroyed Benecia and Canaan, as promised, and that had been a service to mortals and monsters alike. All the same, they had once been *children*, those horrid little beasts; it was a matter for sorrow, their perishing, though in all truth they'd died long ago.

The warlock came to stand over Kristina, gesturing with one graceful hand toward the cottage. There was no sign of the jeweled chalice he had produced at the doorstep, before stepping inside to work his cruel mercies.

"Go and see for yourself, Kristina. The vow I made to you is now kept."

Kristina did not want to see, did not want to leave Bree and Eliette for even a moment, but she knew she must go and look upon her dead enemies with her own eyes. If she did not, she would wonder, through all that might remain of her life, if they were truly gone.

Kristina nodded and got to her feet.

"Bree and Eliette—?"

Dathan looked fondly upon Max's children. "They believe they are dreaming."

"They won't remember?"

He sighed. "Subconsciously they will know that something weird happened to them. With proper love and care, however, they'll overcome any remaining trauma. The loss of their mother was far worse."

Kristina's eyes filled as she looked down at these two precious, innocent children. They'd been through so much in their short lives, and she was sick with the knowledge that they would never have encountered Benecia and Canaan, if not for her.

Once again, Dathan read Kristina's thoughts. "You saved them," he said gently. His hand rested lightly on the small of her back, urging her toward the cottage, which was even then shifting, blurring at the edges. "Bree and Eliette will be safe with me. Go inside, Kristina. Let it be over at long last."

She walked reluctantly forward, through the swinging gate, up the walk, onto the step. After drawing a deep breath and releasing it very slowly, Kristina pushed open the door and stepped inside.

The cottage was furnished like a playhouse, with everything to scale. A table had been set with miniature china dishes and a silver tea service.

Benecia and Canaan, ludicrous shapes of pulp and powdery ash, slumped in two of the four tiny chairs.

Dathan's chalice stood between them, with one drop of shimmering warlock's blood still glistening on the brim. It seemed unlikely, given their great age, that they had been tricked into drinking what was, for a vampire, the most potent hemlock. *No,* Kristina thought sadly, *they'd known what they were doing.*

Benecia had wanted, even yearned for, oblivion and peace.

Canaan had no doubt followed her sister into the darkness voluntarily, preferring death to eternal solitude.

Kristina turned and left the cottage.

Dathan, Bree, and Eliette waited in the dooryard. The great warlock held one child in each arm, their heads resting upon his shoulders, sound asleep. For a moment Kristina was reminded of Valerian and the vast tenderness he showed for his adopted son, Esteban.

"Stand very close," Dathan said, his eyes soft and somehow sad as he surveyed Kristina.

She nodded and stood with her chest pressed to his, her arms around his neck.

In an instant they were all in Max's house, in the room Bree and Eliette shared.

Dathan stood behind Kristina, holding her in a loose embrace, and she knew he had somehow rendered them both invisible.

Bree and Eliette, meanwhile, were suddenly animated again, sitting on the floor between their two beds, as if nothing had happened, putting two Barbie dolls through a spirited argument.

"Hey!" Max yelled from downstairs. "The pizza's here. And don't forget to wash your hands!"

With shrieks of pure joy, Bree and Eliette abandoned the dolls and bounded out of the room. A tear slipped down Kristina's cheek as she listened to their footsteps on the rear stairway.

"You turned the clock back an hour or so," Kristina said, turning to look up into the splendid face of the warlock. How she wished she could love him, but it was Max she cared for, and Max alone.

Dathan shrugged. "I thought it would be better this way."

She nodded. "Thank you, Dathan," she whispered.

He laid his hands to her shoulders and kissed her, ever so lightly, on the lips. Then, in the next breath, she found herself standing in the middle of her own family room in Seattle. There was no sign of the warlock.

The telephone rang again, suddenly, shrilly, startling Kristina out of her daze. Her hand trembled as she reached for the receiver.

"Hi," Max said.

Kristina held her breath, and her heart swelled like an overfilled balloon, ready to burst. "Hi," she replied.

"Look, I know you and I didn't exactly part on the best of terms this morning—"

Kristina closed her eyes, even more grateful than before for Dathan's magic. The kidnapping hadn't happened, as far as Max and the girls were concerned, and he need never know about her encounter with Billy Lasser. "It's okay," she said. They'd made love over and over the night before, at the mountain cabin, and that would sustain her. "Saying good-bye is never easy."

"No." His voice was gruff. Kristina loved him so much that she very nearly couldn't bear it. "We've got a lot of pizza over here," he said. "How about joining us for supper?"

Kristina was an emotional wreck, after all she'd been through, and as much as she loved Max and the children, she needed to eat something, take a hot bath, crawl into bed, and sleep. She simply could not spend an evening with the three people she considered to be her family, knowing she was fated to spend the rest of her life as Dathan's mate.

"I can't, Max," she said softly. "Please understand."

"I do," he replied, just as softly. There was no sarcasm in his voice.

She sighed and pushed a hand through her hair, the way she'd seen Max do a hundred times. "There are a couple of things I need to say," she told him. "I love you. And you don't have to worry anymore, because you and the girls are safe."

"Kristina—"

"That's the end of it, Max," she broke in, her eyes burning again. "Good-bye." With that, she hung up.

The phone rang again immediately, but she ignored the sound until it stopped.

IT was the middle of the night when Kristina awakened, sensing that someone was standing at the foot of her bed. She opened her eyes, mildly alarmed, to find her mother there, looking like a vision in her flowing gown and cascading ebony hair.

Maeve smiled. "Hello, darling," she said.

Kristina sat up. "Is everything all right?"

"I came to ask you the same question. Valerian told me about the incident with that brass monkey of yours."

Kristina shivered at the memory. "Fortunately that's over. Thanks to Barabbas." She remembered something else Valerian had said. "I hear Dimity and Gideon have been found."

Maeve took a seat on the edge of Kristina's bed, smoothed her hair back from her forehead with a gentle motion of one cool hand, the way she'd done when Kristina was small. "After a fashion, yes," she said. "Dimity found her way into a parallel dimension, where she can live as a woman instead of a vampire."

Kristina thought, with some unhappiness, of Benecia, who had wanted to do that, too. "And Gideon?"

"An angel is, and must always be, an angel. He tried to follow her, but he could not, and he is inconsolable."

"He loved Dimity very much," said Kristina, who had heard the stories as a child. Too, she knew what it was to care so deeply for someone forbidden.

"It is denied to angels, that sort of love," Maeve said firmly. "Don't worry. Gideon will be fine in time, and Dimity is happy where she is."

"And Nemesis? What is his state of mind?"

Maeve looked grim for a moment. "He is furious, but since all the blame cannot be laid at Dimity's feet, and thus put upon all vampires, he has withdrawn his armies."

"He had *assembled armies?*" Kristina whispered. "Are you saying that we—that all of us—were on the brink of Armageddon?"

"Yes," Maeve answered without hesitation. "But that danger— though it will inevitably come again—is past. You will become Dathan's mate, now that he has lived up to his part of the agreement?"

Kristina nodded. "I have no choice. And I *am* grateful for what he did."

"Gratitude is a poor basis for such a union," Maeve said.

"Yes," Kristina agreed. "But I don't have any alternatives."

Maeve took Kristina's hand. "No," she answered. "Neither do I, under the circumstances. Still, I have learned some things that I feel you need to know—from Nemesis, as a matter of fact. It was he who told me I would bear a mortal child, before I knew you were growing in my womb."

"What did he say?" Kristina asked, hardly able to breathe.

"You are carrying Max's babe," Maeve said.

Kristina fell back against the pillows, stunned. Full of sorrow and of exultation, in equal measure. She could not speak, though tears slipped down her cheeks.

"There is more," Maeve went on very gently, her hand tightening on

Kristina's. "On some level, you were waiting for Max to come back into your life. You've probably already guessed that he was Gilbert Bradford. In any case, that is the reason you didn't begin aging until recently. You wanted to be in step, so to speak, with Mr. Kilcarragh."

Kristina let out a long, broken sigh. She'd come so close to complete happiness, so close to living all her dreams. "Perhaps Dathan will change his mind, once he knows I'll bear another man's child."

Maeve's expression was gently skeptical. "I know this warlock. While he has certain redeeming qualities, he is not above claiming Max's babe as his own. Dathan wants you very badly, Kristina."

"Can't you help me?"

The queen's beautiful, ink-colored eyes glittered with vampire tears. "A pact was made and kept. I cannot interfere."

Kristina nodded and leaned forward to kiss her mother's cheek. "You won't abandon me, will you? Like when I married Michael?"

"I have often regretted that," Maeve confessed. "No, darling. I shall be available to help you in any way I can. Mayhap you will come to love the warlock one day—it could be, you know, that he is your destiny, after all, rather than Max."

Although Kristina did not want that to be so, she had already considered the possibility. No doubt Max would find Sandy again, in another lifetime, and anyone he married now could only be an interim love. "Yes," she said. "It could be that Dathan and I were meant to be together, at least for a while. But I shall never love him."

Maeve embraced her tenderly. "No," she said, understanding. "But there are other joys. And you will surely cherish the child."

"Do you know about this babe—whether it's a boy or a girl? Mortal or immortal?"

Maeve smoothed Kristina's tears away with palms as smooth as polished marble. "Nemesis offered no other information than the fact that you and Max had conceived. And I did not ask him to tell me more." The great queen kissed her daughter's forehead. "And now I must hunt. Dream sweet dreams, my darling."

As surely as if Maeve had cast a spell, Kristina fell immediately back into a deep sleep. When she awakened the next morning to another light snowfall, she wondered if she truly *had* been dreaming.

Until she descended into the kitchen and found Dathan standing there, dressed for a wedding, that is. Kristina felt nothing but despair, but some quirk caused her to look down at her long flannel nightie and then at her future groom, her expression rueful.

"I'm afraid my wedding gown leaves something to be desired," she said.

Dathan raised his right hand high, palm up, and as he lowered it, a wondrous dress formed itself to Kristina's body. It was made of the finest ivory silk, the skirts embroidered with hundreds of appliquéd doves, outlined in tiny pearls. The bodice was lacy and sprinkled liberally with diamonds.

"There has never been a more beautiful bride in all of time," Dathan said.

Kristina swallowed hard. Dathan conjured a small hand mirror, and she saw that her veil, a trail of gossamer white netting, tumbled from a circlet of small white orchids on the crown of her head.

"Okay," she said, resigned. "So where's the preacher?"

Dathan arched an eyebrow. "It isn't done in exactly that way," he said.

"Then how *is* it done?"

"We will simply clasp hands and make a promise to each other."

"Here?" Kristina asked. "In the kitchen?"

Dathan sighed. "Wherever you wish, my darling. Just name the place, and we'll be there in a moment."

"Beside the point," observed a third voice.

Both Dathan and Kristina turned in surprise to see Valerian standing just a few feet away. Given the fact that it was broad daylight, that was amazing.

"How—?" Kristina croaked.

"Call it astral projection," Valerian said with an impatient wave of one hand. "I'm a magician, remember?" His gaze was fixed on Dathan, and the vampire looked as solid as he ever had. "There is a point in human wedding ceremonies that I rather like," he told the warlock. "The clergy member always says, 'Is there anyone here who can give just cause why these two should not be joined in holy matrimony?'"

Dathan flushed. "I am not human," he pointed out in a dangerously even voice.

"But Kristina is," Valerian offered reasonably. "Furthermore, I can show just cause. She loves one Max Kilcarragh—has waited a hundred years to be his wife. Even now, his child is curled beneath her heart—a heart in which Max, not you, will always live."

Dathan looked down at Kristina. "Is this true? The part about the child, I mean?"

Kristina nodded. She guessed she hadn't dreamed her mother's late-night visit after all.

"Can you never learn to love me?" the warlock asked.

A great sadness welled up within Kristina. "No," she said.

"If you care for Kristina," Valerian put in, very gently and very carefully, "you will set her free."

"We had a bargain!"

"And only you have the power to break it," Valerian reasoned quietly.

"Damn you," Dathan spat, glaring at the vampire. "How dare you speak of bargains? You once promised me a bride, and instead you set Roxanne Havermail on me like a mad dog!"

Valerian tried his very best to look contrite, but there was, Kristina thought, a certain merry twinkle in his eyes. "A nasty trick, I confess. Allow me to rectify the matter."

Dathan narrowed his gaze upon the fiend, while Kristina just stood there, resplendent in her conjured wedding dress, apparently forgotten. She did not want to remind the warlock of her presence before Valerian had made his point.

"Why should I trust you?" Dathan demanded.

"Kristina's happiness is at stake," Valerian replied. "She is like my own child, and only Daisy and Esteban matter as much. I would not play you false in such a case as this."

Dathan turned and looked down into Kristina's upraised face. "So beautiful," he whispered, almost regretfully.

"But so mortal," Valerian said. "There is a female vampire—I have trained her myself—by the name of Shaleen. Meet me this night on the north entrance to All Soul's Cathedral in London, and I will prove myself truthful."

"If you lie—" Dathan murmured.

Kristina held her breath. She wasn't even sure her heart was beating.

"If I lie, you have only to come and take Kristina back."

Dathan considered, while Kristina flashed her "guardian vampire" a scathing look. She hadn't wanted that last option to be part of the deal.

"Well?" Valerian finally prompted.

Dathan gave a great sigh. "All right," he said. He kissed Kristina, first on the forehead, then on each eyelid. When she looked again, he was gone, and so was Valerian. The magical wedding dress had turned into a chenille bathrobe.

"Cinderella, eat your heart out," Kristina muttered.

She waited three full days before she called Max, just in case Dathan's blind date with the vampire, Shaleen, had gone wrong. During that time, Kristina busied herself by sorting through old papers and other things she no longer needed or wanted. She read the last of her letters to Phillie and burned all of them.

The past was truly gone.

"Hello?" Max answered when Kristina finally called him. It was 6:05 and she could tell by the background sounds that he was cooking dinner.

"Hi," Kristina said with a smile in her voice. "This is a mysterious woman from your recent past."

He laughed. "The meter maid who gave me a parking ticket this morning?"

"No," Kristina replied in a naughty undertone. "The one you spent the weekend in bed with."

"Oh, that one." There was hope in Max's voice now, as well as humor.

"I was wondering if you could come over. There are some things we need to talk about."

"Just give me half an hour to round up a babysitter," he replied.

He arrived in twenty minutes flat.

Kristina pulled him inside, wrapped both arms around his neck, and kissed him soundly. It was a greeting, that kiss, but it was an invitation, too. If she had her way, they would be upstairs, in her bed, very soon.

"Did you mean it when you said you wanted to marry me?" she asked when it was over, and Max was standing there, still in his coat, with snow in his hair. His mien was one of pure, dazed confusion.

"I did indeed," he said. "But you had other plans, if I remember correctly."

"They've changed."

"You're not going to marry the warlock?"

"I'm going to marry you, if you'll have me. But there's something you have to know first—something that might make you feel trapped. And I only want a willing husband, Max Kilcarragh."

"What?" he asked in a voice so tender that it brought a lump to Kristina's throat and tears to her eyes.

"I'm pregnant. With your baby."

For a moment Max looked as though she'd struck him with a blunt object. She was just beginning to worry when a grin flicked up one corner of his mouth and then slowly spread until it seemed to cover his whole face.

"That's the second best news I've heard all day," he said, and despite his smile, there were tears shining in his eyes.

"What's the first best?" Kristina asked, unzipping his jacket, slipping her arms inside to embrace and warm him.

"That you're going to marry me. Oh, God, Kristina—I love you."

She took his hand. "Upstairs," she said, pulling him in that direction. "If we don't start now, we may end up making love right here in the entry hall, or on the stairs—"

They made it as far as Kristina's bed, but just barely.

In the attempt to undress each other, they became entangled in each other's clothes and finally landed on the mattress in a laughing, twisted knot of flesh and fabric.

Soon enough they'd sorted that out, and Kristina lay on her back with Max poised over her, gazing down into her eyes.

"Hurry, Max," she whispered.

He smiled. "No way," he answered, and bent his head to her breast, teasing the nipple unmercifully with the tip of his tongue.

Kristina began to writhe and moan. "Max," she said with a gasp, "we don't *need* foreplay—I've been thinking of nothing but this for three days!"

He moved to the other breast, subjected a second nipple to slow, sweet torment. "Good," he said. "That ought to make it all the better."

With that, he suckled in earnest. There were long interludes where he teased her with his fingers and with his tongue. He whispered shameless, wicked things in her ear and nibbled at her lobes.

Kristina was out of her mind with need, her body drenched in perspiration, when Max finally parted her legs and gave her just the tip of his shaft. When she begged—and he made her do it prettily—he finally entered her in a slow, deep thrust.

She pleaded some more, and the thrust quickened, deepened, but only slightly.

Finally she shouted out what she wanted, not caring who might hear, and with a sound that was part chuckle and part animal need, Max took her in earnest. Placing his strong hands under her buttocks, he raised her high to receive him, and she undulated against him, her hands moving restlessly, feverishly, up and down his muscle-knotted back.

They reached a simultaneous climax, their bodies arched high off the bed and slick with sweat, and hung there, suspended, flexing spasmodically, for what seemed like forever. Finally, replete, exhausted, they tumbled to the mattress and lay entwined in each other's arms and legs, struggling to breathe, transported.

"Tell me what changed your mind," Max said sometime later, when shadows filled the room. "About marrying me, I mean."

She explained about Valerian's intercession, but left out the near-miss with Benecia and Canaan. There was no need for Max to suffer over that—the incident of Bree and Eliette's disappearance had been erased from his mind, and that was for the best.

"Did you know I've been waiting for you? That that's why I finally became completely mortal?"

He kissed the tip of her nose. "Was I worth it?"

She smiled. "So far, so good," she replied, and pulled his head down so that his mouth found hers.

Epilogue

THE question of whether or not Jaime Maxwell Kilcarragh had been blessed—or cursed—with magical powers was as yet unresolved. He was a healthy, strapping boy, however, greatly loved by his parents, two elder sisters, and a weird but devoted extended family.

Downstairs in the large family room of the house Max and Kristina had bought together shortly before their marriage, Valerian heard happy laughter. Daisy, Esteban, Maeve, and Calder were all there, along with Max and Kristina, of course, and their daughters, Eliette and Bree.

The great vampire closed his eyes for a moment, listening, nearly rapt, for the sound was like music. It courted the ear, then went deeper to swamp the soul, causing a sweet ache there.

As he watched, the babe awakened. The room was dark, except for a small night-light near the crib itself, and the flow of autumn moonlight through the window. Valerian knew this child was safe, and yet he felt compelled to look out for him, just as he had for Kristina and, once, a long time ago, for Aidan Tremayne.

He closed his eyes briefly, for the thought of Aidan was still poignant, if not actually hurtful.

When Valerian looked again, he was no longer alone in the room. Esteban stood beside him, a sturdy, solemn-eyed lad, ready for school.

"Papa?" he asked softly, taking Valerian's hand. He'd come so far, this beautiful little one, in a short time. He spoke clearly, worked his lessons, no longer slept on the floor or hid stashes of food all around the house.

Valerian lifted Esteban into his arms, sensing his uncertainty. "Shhh," he said against the boy's small temple, where dark, gossamer hair grew, fine as fairy-floss, and a warm heartbeat pulsed. "We mustn't wake the baby."

"We are going to have cake," Esteban confided in an accommodating whisper, his brown eyes very wide. Daisy seldom allowed such treats; she was into health food.

There were times when Valerian was more than grateful that he wasn't required to eat the way mortals did.

"Don't you want some?" the child prodded, glancing back once, at the babe.

"What's the real question?" Valerian prompted. They understood each other more than passing well, this father and son.

Esteban sighed. "Do you like him better than me?"

Valerian shook his head. "No."

Reassured, Esteban began to squirm. He was probably thinking of the cake, perhaps fearing that the others would consume it all before he had his share.

With a chuckle, Valerian set the boy on his feet, and Esteban ran off again.

Valerian went to the crib side and looked down at the handsome babe, who returned his gaze directly. Then, with the slightest smile, Jaime Kilcarragh shifted his gaze to the teddy bear at the foot of his small bed, and raised one tiny hand, wriggling his fingers. The toy had been summoned, and it came obediently to lie beside Jaime, who snuggled close and went back to sleep.

Smiling slightly, Valerian turned and walked out of the nursery.

The adventure wasn't over, he thought.

No, indeed—it had only begun.